ATHENS

OR, THE ATHENIANS

a novel in five books

by

GEORGE
DALPHIN

Book One
THE AGE OF BRONZE

BOOK ONE / The Age of Bronze

ATHENS

or, The Athenians

by GEORGE DALPHIN

ATHENS

And the very first words
that the Muses of Mount Helikon
graced to me, poor Hesiod, were these:
"*Shepherds of the field, pitiful things, mere hungry bellies,
we know how to say many false things as if they were real,
but we also know how, when we wish, to tell the truth.*"

Hesiod, *Origins of the Gods*

While inspired by *many*,
(and they will hopefully know)
this book is dedicated to
JOE FOSTER.

First edition
Self-published by Man-Like Machines
Midsummer 2025

ATHENS

Book One: The Age of Bronze

- 1 -
ATHENA COUNSELOR
9

- 2 -
APHRODITE WARLIKE
105

- 3 -
DIONYSOS THREE-HEADED
189

- 4 -
APOLLO FAR-SHOOTER
303

- 5 -
POSEIDON EARTH-SHAKER
407

- 6 -
HERMES PLAN-SPINNER
505

- 7 -
HERA MAN-PROTECTOR
579

- 8 -
ZEUS ASH-MAKER
679

ATHENS

PROLOGUE

The city burned to ash the night of its great victory.

For Perikles, too young to fight, the day was an eternity, sequestered with his mother, aunts, and cousins on the island of Salamis just across the narrow waters from the old Piraeus docks, while all the adult men of Athens, citizens and slaves, battled the mighty Persian Empire's navy on the waves.

Now twilight fell upon the blood-dark sea between himself and home, while nearby nannies' prayer-songs strained to drown out shouts from drowning men. Those once-immortal Persian ships, filled with fear-levied folk from eastern foreign lands, foundered across the crowded waterway while brave Athenian ships, more agile with their myriad oarsmen, darted deftly through the sinking hulks to stone survivors. The thrashing of the dying men scattered reflected stars amid the waves, while in the Sky the real stars, appearing motionless, steadfastly rose.

Before dusk's bruise faded to Night, Athens' sacred flagship *Paralos* finally clove the sandy beach on Salamis Island where fighters' families had waited in fear all day for this, victorious sons and husbands striding down the gangplanks with their spears held high.

"Xerxes' mighty armada is destroyed!" the Democrat general Themistokles bellowed, breathless and bloodied. "Persia's admirals will be leaving their bones here, beneath our waves! Athens is master of the Sea!"

A desperate cheer of relief spread through the traumatized families. Themistokles' risky gambit had worked. Few had really expected such success.

Big-bearded Themistokles led his victorious comrade-citizen-soldiers down into their wives', mothers', and children's grateful sobs of praise, and by chance, as he passed the Alkmaeonid family, that beaming city-savior caught our man's young eye.

He bent his tall body down toward teen-aged Perikles and grasped him firmly by the shoulder with his strong, bloodied hand.

"Shed your fear, Xanthippos' son," the man-shepherd commanded through his wet beard. "We are the victors here tonight! Democracy has won over autocracy! Hellas defeats Persia! And by our victory here today, may one day the whole world be unyoked!"

Fellow countrymen he couldn't see grasped young Perikles from above and behind, many hands acting like fathers, as another cheer arose.

But while Themistokles spoke, swift-eyed young Perikles' tears were dried by shock as he noticed in the distance, over the great man's shoulder, beyond everyone, past the sinking Persian fleet on the black water, across the straits and under the stars, just over the low rise between Athens' harbor and the city itself, between the hills and the night, a hateful red glow of building fires had begun to replace the twilight blue.

The Persian land army was burning the city.

Themistokles noticed the boy's pallor shift and turned to look at what he'd seen. Red fires spread fast, roof after roof, soon illuminating the temples on the city's sacred high rock, the Akropolis. The general turned back to the boy unwilling to let his own tears fall. Seeing young Perikles through them, Themistokles found strength quickly.

"Athena understands the difficult decisions we mortals must make," he said. "Sometimes we must sacrifice Athens in order to save Athens."

1
ATHENA COUNSELOR

A

A stranger arrives at Athens at Dawn

And out from ancient olive groves the stranger comes to Athens wearing just a dusty shepherd's cloak and walking with an olive staff, possessing nothing else besides his memories and dreams.

The local farm- and fisher-folk, gathering at the city for their *Assembly*, mask their suspicious glances to the stranger under smiles.

A quiet glow upon the early darkness heralds Dawn.

Around the gate the city wall is made of old gravestones, war-black. Newly carved copies of those old monuments line the path up to the gate. Two tall columns which only years ago were part of Athens' Temple of Zeus Olympian now frame huge wooden doors - the famed Dipylon Gate.

A bent old woman passing with her goat says to the stranger, "Don't go in there! They practice the stupid magic called *democracy* in there; worse than chaos!" She makes a rude gesture at the nearest *herm*, then leaves cursing. Some countryfolk visiting town salute the herm here with extra reverence for a while, as if to apologize for the woman's curses.

At nearly every crossroads across the lands of Hellas one will find an ancient *herm* - a man-tall slab of squared-off stone with some semblance of a human head carved at the top and a dick in relief halfway down. Most herms are so old that no one knows who made them, when or why, but legend says the first herms were made by the Messenger God Hermes himself, who watches over travelers and helps or harms communication. By ancient tradition, Hellenes passing any herm each pause to touch their crotch and briefly cover their eyes in a salute of gratitude to Hermes for not misleading them. Seeing every local do the same, the stranger touches his crotch and covers his eyes in salutation to the gate herm.

Before he treads into the city, the stranger feels the edge of one of the broken old gravestones which now make up the new city wall. Beside a time-worn person's name, interlocked by mortar, is a part of what was once a temple's altar. This new wall is archaeology - a story of the city's recent cataclysms written in shards.

The Athenians proudly read the stranger's tears as awe.

ATHENS

Today Athens is a tight cluster of modest modern homes built fresh upon a base of burnt rubble. The urban sprawl is bounded by this brand new patchwork city wall built hastily from shards of the old city. Ten years' ago's temple is now ten different defensive buttresses. On the city's central high rock called the *Akropolis*, the Athenians' most sacred ancient temples rest now as scorched ruins like skeletons of sacrificed gods, smoke-blackened reminders of the Persian Invasions One and Two.

To the left side of the open plaza just inside the Dipylon Gate, two bronze statues rise twice as tall as real men, stiff and upright in the old-fashioned style, symmetrical, arms and legs straight: nude teenage boys, each wielding a stylized dagger. An engraving at the base identifies them:

Harmodios and Aristogeiton
TYRANT-KILLERS
Original stolen by the Persians. Copy by Myron.

Continuing into the city, the stranger crosses a wide bridge over a stream running parallel to the city wall with an industrial lane built up on either bank. A voice amid the morning bustle calls it "Potters' Alley". Along this street the paintings on the walls are the brightest. Everywhere is artwork; each wall shows scenes of mortal heroes, and gods who look much like them.

"Today Athena collects the honey of ideas," someone among the buzzing voices says, amidst myriad simpler, cruder, finer, and quieter notions.

The stranger takes note of Athenian habits which are different from his own land east of the Sea. Here, for the most part, people dress more or less the same, in one fold or another of simple draped cloth dyed one of just a few shades, with only the most necessary accessories such as necklace, belt, or pin, but none of the ostentatious displays of wealth which one will see in any of the cities within the influence of the Empire of Persia, in the older countries of the east. There are brightly colored fabrics here, but not the elaborately embroidered finery or golden threads of Persian city fashion. Here it is difficult to discern between master and slave merely by outfit.

Past noisy Potters' Alley the path into the city leads up a slight rise to spread wide and become the broad *Agora*, where Athenians gather to trade, gossip, flirt, fight, and debate.

All the adult Athenian men seem to be headed to the western side of the city, where just outside the unfinished wall there is a hill they call the *Pnyx*. Soon the only ones inside the walls are women, children, slaves, foreigners, and those Athenian men who spurn, avoid, or cannot handle their political duty known as *idiots*. On most days the Agora is busy with merchant stalls selling every sort of thing created or gathered by humans in the world, along with the naturally accompanying chatter, rapture, arguments, and laughter of Athenians, their enslaved servants, and the international visitors to the city who have recently given it fame as a place welcoming to strangers. On Assembly days like today, however, the men's absence, like the tide going out, has made room for a brief community of those who cannot vote, and who now enjoy the rare chance to speak with each other in quieter voices while the din of the male citizens is gathered elsewhere, wrangled to a distant murmuration on the hill of the Pnyx. One can finally hear the morning birds in the Agora.

The lean-limbed visitor takes in the scene, looking past the temporary shop stalls and fluttering banners advertising goods for sale from every distant city, to see the people of myriad shapes and colors who seem to be treating the space as if it is their home, and this all makes him start to feel comfortable that he might not be unwelcome.

At this edge of the Agora, a flame's warm breeze turns the stranger's attention to an open forge just outside the tall-columned Temple of Hephaestos Smith God, one of the only standing old temples in the city. Wind-whipped itinerant folks looking much like himself huddle around the glowing forge and its master smith who seems to reject no one from his space. The stranger notes this as a place to find again when evening falls. The forge hisses and spits, and wafts warm winds.

The homes inside the city wall are far less elaborate than their country counterparts. These urban structures are mostly small, windowless boxes, not one yet nine years old, with ruins of the old burned homes scattered among and beneath the new or rebuilt ones, all stacked upon and against each other, many sharing thin walls. An Athenian epithet for thief is *wall-puncher*. But despite the hurried quality of the buildings, their surfaces all glow with the bright, recently applied colors of animals, gods, and heroes, painted by amateurs, masters, children, jurists, jokesters, and every other sort of image-maker.

Our man crosses the broad stony Agora and finds a patch of grass to sit on, near a public Fountain House just south of the Agora, beside a line of jar-carrying women and slaves waiting to collect water.

Eastward, Dawn's pink cloak has spread, although her uncle Sun has yet to summit woodsy Mount Hymettos.

A loose group of urban children gradually gather around the stranger, as he sits unknowingly where their old storyteller, who recently died, used to sit.

"Good day, little Athenians," the stranger says with a smile, dispelling the last of his morning melancholy.

"Who are you?" one little girl asks.

"It's the Lord of the Agora!" an older boy mocks in passing, though the intended meanness wafts harmlessly past the younger ones, who take the comment seriously, and the stranger rolls with it.

"Yes, you can call me Anaxagoras. I'm new to your city."

The many children ask many things all at once. The newcomer patiently listens through the noise until he finds one question which he would like to answer, "Where did you come from?"

Anaxagoras says, "I am from the east, across the Sea, from a land called *Ionia*. We are Hellenic there, too. Have any of you heard of that place?"

Some of the children nod.

"Where did Ionia come from?" asks a bright-eyed toddler.

"What is your name, little one?" Anaxagoras asks her.

"Diotima," the toddler replies without shyness.

Anaxagoras smiles at the question. "Well, Diotima, my land Ionia is part of *Ge*, the Earth. So I suppose it 'came' from her. But also, in another way of looking at the question, *Ionian people* came from here, from Attika, long ago. Ionia is an old colony sent from this land."

"Where did Ge come from?" curious little Diotima asks.

The thin and balding stranger in the dusty traveler's cloak, drawing circles and triangles in the dust with his walking stick, asks the rest of the gathering children, "What do you think, girls and boys? Where did the goddess Ge, the very world herself, 'come from'?"

Dawn's horizontal light draws long shadows as the blue sky climbs.

"The poet Hesiod says the other gods are the children of Ge the Earth and Ouranos the Sky," mumbles a sullen little eight year old boy, who wears a crown of woven thistles and sits on his heels, already vexed by his fellows' bad manners. "Euripides", he adds, remembering his own manners and introducing himself.

Beside the eight year old, a steady-footed four year old boy crouches in mimicry. Euripides fails to notice little Krito, however, as he is side-eyeing a group of young girls who were harassing him earlier. "Mother won't say where I came from," says thumb-sucking Krito to the stranger in muddled words, holding onto the edge of Euripides' tunic for balance.

From the religious cheers of the men up on the Pnyx, it becomes clear down in the Agora that the officials of the Assembly are burning the bones of a sacrificial bull as offering to the gods and passing out bowls of its cooked meat to all the men. The eating and voting part of the meeting is about to begin. Athenians always eat while they vote, while the rising smoke of the burnt bones reminds them that they are dining with the gods.

Little Diotima sees her curly-bearded father Melqartshama beckon her from across the Agora. She gets up and scampers off to him.

Beside the other children and Anaxagoras, a muscular young sculptor named Sophroniskos kisses his roundly-pregnant young wife Phaenarete goodbye as she stands in line at the Fountain House, where she waits behind other women and slaves with her big jar at her side.

"I love you," Sophroniskos says, reluctant to leave their hug. "Are you sure you'll be alright on your own? I can't be sure how long it'll take."

"Of course," Phaenarete assures him with the expected public level of feminine demurity, then adds for spice, "the Agora is easier to navigate with the men away," and they both chuckle and kiss again. "I'll listen to the foreign storytellers if I have to wait."

Sophroniskos smiles crookedly, giving his wife a half-comical look. "Well," he says, "just don't believe every yarn you hear. There's plenty of fantastical stories being told these days, when the more exciting the story is, the more listeners it gathers."

Crouched nearby, the eight-year-old Euripides continues, returning from deep thought as if he hadn't paused, "...But Hesiod also says the Sky is the son of the Earth, and the Earth and the Underworld and Love all formed out of Chaos."

"Well, young man, Hesiod was just a poet," bald-topped Anaxagoras explains as he bisects the circle he has drawn in the dirt. "Speaking real truth is actually very hard. There are many perspectives. For example, the wise men in Elea start by considering that everything comes from something else. While all things change, young man, never does something come out of nothing."

"Just a poet! There's also truth in poetry not found in the world, Euripides," pregnant Phaenarete reassures the boy sweetly as she bends in to recenter the thistle crown on his head.

Curious Krito pushes forward past Euripides. "I know when I die I go to the Underworld. So is that where I came from, out of the ground like the shoot from a buried seed?" he asks.

Young Phaenarete and the stranger Anaxagoras laugh together at Krito's question.

Anaxagoras tells the little boy, "You're asking very good questions, which I can't answer. Perhaps nature itself can, however, if you explore, and if you are very patient!"

"Patience is hard," Phaenarete remarks to the child. "Tell me, Euripides - do you remember being very small, like Krito here?"

Euripides side-eyes little Krito, who is about half his size, and shakes his head slowly.

"I don't think so. I only remember everything being larger."

"O WOE! HOW MORTAL MEN LEARN FREEDOM LATE!
THEY BLAME US GODS AND CALL THEIR FOLLY FATE."
Homeros, *The Odyssey*
first dialogue, spoken by Zeus

B

Perikles and Aoide prepare to enter the world of serious things

The morning Sun glows soft through pink clouds, across unknown flows of aether and air, to illuminate the courtyard of the Alkmaeonid family's home in Athens, where seated on a fine stone bench beneath the dappled shadows of two young apple trees are three young men - Perikles' two older friends Ephialtes and Lysimachos, and Perikles himself, who is twenty-three now.

The three have been listening to the famous singer of epics Damon, whom Perikles' mother Agariste has hired to opine on wide-famed Homeros' classic epic song about the ancient Troian War, *The Iliad*.

Hidden where she is disallowed, little Aoide listens in, unseen.

"Honestly though, why should we learn about people who may or may not have even existed, untold generations ago?" Lysimachos asks the old singer. "What relevance could their lives really have for ours today? Men and women aren't like that anymore, nor even are the gods I dare say. Things simply change."

"Things do change, but not simply," white-bearded Damon sings, wearing a rope-belted robe like the old men of his generation used to wear. "Our world is old now, older than it seems. Even when these heroes, whose names Homeros sings, themselves debated and struggled hundreds of years ago, the world was already very old, we know. Ages of Man had come and passed, their residue covering and then swept from the Earth. And before men even walked the land, aeons known only to the gods went unseen by mortal eyes, and before that even timeless expanses of unknowable nature predating and transcending old Father Time himself. And yet, however distant from our eye or mind today, the folly and courage of each of those eras ring still with meaning here and now. All times cohere. That is why we sing these songs of men and gods from ancient times. For as you age you'll see yourself that really generations past were *just here yesterday*. Ultimately, all is interwoven, as each to all is strung."

"So what makes someone wise?" lazy-eyed Lysimachos asks.

"O," the interrupted singer answers with feigned patience, "I suppose I would say that it is *doing wise things*."

Lysimachos snorts.

Damon adds, thinking as he speaks, "We must each try to be independently wise, for it is true that stories do distort the truth. The world isn't made of words. If the meaning and the symbol were the same, there'd be nothing to see. All desire wisdom, yet it is elusive even to the gods. Indeed, of what can anyone be certain? I can only be sure I heard a story from someone who sang it thus, and can assume they heard it sung similarly. Stories are like the clouds - their forms vary, and they come and go. Wisdom, it would seem, should be immobile, and accessible to all like Shining Apollo's light."

The three young men look to each other's reactions. All shrug.

"That paints wisdom with a nature quite egalitarian," notes ever-Democratic-thinking Ephialtes with a smile.

"But even the Sun does not shine all the time," Lysimachos notes.

"Nor everywhere," says Perikles, holding his hand into an invisible spray of dancing leaf shadows.

"Also, speaking Hellenic," the old singer adds.

The three men alternately grin and grimace at the funny-if-awkward old-fashionedness of the comment, with glances to the four gardeners engaged in their present work defending against a jealous, zealous mole. Like most slaves in Athens the gardeners were most likely captured into servitude when their distant foreign cities fell in battle against Hellenes, and they speak little, but not zero, Hellenic.

Kind-eyed Ephialtes offers, "I think Lysimachos meant more like - 'How does one become wise?'"

The long-bearded singer thinks for a moment, then jokes with a wry smile, "Same answers."

Lysimachos snorts again and says, "But clearly not all Hellenes are wisemen. I know some real cabbageheads."

Perikles winces at his friend's use of that word, which is often used cruelly against his own older brother Ariphron.

Lysimachos notices, remembers having been asked not to use the word, and adds, "Forgive the word, Perikles. I forgot your dislike for it."

Improvising a melody again, long-bearded old Damon sings, "Memory mimics moments, as the singer sings the song; and the things who bring you wisdom might just bring it bit by bit, or even in disguise."

"That was lovely," Lysimachos says, "but I'm not sure what to get out of it. Understand, Damon - I'm primarily listening for clever phrases which I can use against other men in real conversation."

Damon sighs, pulls at his long beard a little, and then barks at the youngest of the men - the one whose mother has hired him today - by name, "Perikles, describe the shield which Hephaestos made for Achilles as consolation for his slain friend's death."

Perikles is startled to find the discussion has become an impromptu quiz, but he enjoys mental challenges, and thinks quickly to recall the words of *The Iliad*.

"In the center are the Sun and Moon and Earth," swift-eyed Perikles answers, sitting up, "and the constellations, surrounded in concentric circles by images of the world at work - a wedding, a trial, a farm, a siege..."

"And what would you say this represents, Ephialtes?" old Damon asks Ephialtes. "What does Hephaestos' artistic choice mean in this situation?"

The always generously smiling Ephialtes studiously answers, "Hephaestos gives Achilles the spine of the universe as his guard. But also, he frames the cosmos at large *within* the activities of humanity, like a family within a house. He describes the world with the largest on the inside, contained within the small."

Wrinkled-eyed Damon smiles, appreciating Ephialtes' analysis.

Lysimachos, who has the unkempt hair and beard of Ephialtes, but the expensive clothing of Perikles, and his own irreverent face, jokes, "My father's shield was made to show a roaring lion, but war's ravages have left the thing looking more like some half-eaten fish."

Perikles sniffs out a half-laugh, to be polite.

"I am trying to engage you boys in a serious discussion on the epic legends of the past," Damon snaps at lazy Lysimachos, who rolls his eyes. "Some of you are about to step into politics for the first time. This is what will separate you from the unwashed; no offense, Ephialtes. For indeed you and your newly wealth-blessed family have achieved a natural nobility lost by some old Oligarchs, and are exactly the friend I mean to nudge young Perikles to listen better to, as he goes out to share his will at last at Assembly. The lessons of ancient artists will ennoble your soul. But Lysimachos, your parents don't pay me to pander you into the false impression that you are funny."

Ephialtes shrugs, pretending to be offended at being called unwashed just because his family are not nobles. His two noble friends smile to him over Damon's comment, but Damon is a man of a previous generation and seems to sense none of the inter-class awkwardness.

Lysimachos asks, "Damon, tell me your honest opinion - is Homeros' story true? Did the men of epic stories of ancient times really live?"

"I will tell you the hard truth, young man," the singer sighs. "I do not know."

"Forgive my interruption, Damon," says Perikles' slave Thrax, a hugely-muscled and barely-clothed Thrakian with tribal arm tattoos. He clings to the courtyard doorway where it leads into the house, pausing only momentarily from other chores. Damon blinks to indicate impatiently that he is listening, so Thrax continues, "It is time for our masters to be off to the Assembly. I was asked to remind them when Helios got speed." Thrax's Hellenic is rough, and he always gets flustered in front of the famous singer.

"The Sun God has topped eastern Mount Hymettos; Dawn's paint has dried to blue; she goes now up to high Olympos to tell Zeus what is new. But do not be fooled by the appearance that each rising day is new. Everything that is about to happen has all happened before. You are a living wave, an Echo-just-freed," Damon sings, then, when none of his listeners seem to have felt any profundity in his words, he adds dryly, "Go, boys, be citizens."

Perikles, Ephialtes, and Lysimachos all stand at once, Perikles nodding to Thrax to bring him his cloak.

As he's awaiting his cloak Perikles hears a familiar whistle used by his young female cousins, and catches an apple that is thrown to him from the bushes before he even quite consciously sees it. The apple has a big *K* cut into the side, for *kalliste* - "to the *finest*". The *K* makes Perikles smile.

He tosses the apple to Lysimachos as his two friends are leaving. "For you," Perikles jokes. Lysimachos fumbles the catch and drops the apple in the grass, but retrieves it and bites into it as he leaves.

At the same time, out from her hiding spot behind the manicured courtyard bushes sneaks the apple's tosser, starry-eyed Aoide, who at only ten years old is already clearly the brightest of Perikles' many Alkmaeonid cousins, a clever poet and his close friend. Perikles invites her into a hug as Thrax is bringing him his cloak.

"Listening in on our lessons again?"

She chirps, "When they sing *The Iliad* to us they leave out all the fighting."

Perikles chuckles. "I'm not sure anybody needs to know how one man's entrails steamed as they spilled out of his belly or the sound of a skull caving under Ajax's rock, anyway." Perikles mimes guts spilling out of his belly as he groans out the words, knowing it'll make Aoide squeal with gory delight. He jokes, "I don't know *who* likes those details."

"I do!" Aoide laughs. She touches his cloak, which he only wears when going out into public, and asks, "Are you going to the Assembly?"

Perikles nods reluctantly. "I have to."

Ephialtes leans back through the door and shouts to Perikles, "And Democracy needs you, Perikles! There may just be an *ostracism* this year; one never knows! As ever, today every hand is needed!" Perikles waves to his friend, and Ephialtes' head disappears back into the house.

Perikles sighs and sits back down on the stone bench. Aoide sits next to him. Both of their fathers, brothers-in-law, were *ostracized*, exiled from the city for ten years, in the decade before the Second Persian War, so the word bears extra weight for their family. For a few quiet moments, they sit among the soft sounds of their family's slaves quietly planting new flowers. One of the gardening slave women, a strong-armed young Berber woman named Imilke, stands and wipes sweat from her face, then quickly offers the two young cousins a sip from her cup of water, which they both politely decline with similar demure smiles.

Perikles shares, "Honestly the Assembly scares me like a lion cave. I feel like I'm about to get onto a four horse chariot and drive it through a track full of ghosts. I just - I understand dead poets better than I do living potters. That's why I haven't been to Assembly until now. But mother has assured me I'm out of excuses. Don't want people to think I'm an idiot. I guess I probably would never feel ready."

"I wish I could go and argue and vote," Aoide says. "But father is going to make me a priestess, I just know it. I heard them say they're waiting to decide until next month after Father can consult the Wine God when they open the jars at the Anthesteria festival."

"Well, there's lots of good you can do as a priestess, if that's what your father chooses for you," Perikles says sweetly, petting Aoide's long hair. "At least he's consulting Dionysos. He's about more than wine."

Aoide shrugs out of Perikles' pet and stands, stomping away from him but then turning and stomping back with her arms folded, frowning at the ground. "I'd rather be someone's wife, so I can at least play that politics game with my husband. As a priestess I'd just be a slave to some god."

"We're all essentially slaves to the gods anyway, by order of nature," the enslaved gardener Imilke coolly suggests, standing beside them sipping her water.

Aoide retorts, "Yeah but every day, not just on festival days. And just one specific god instead of all gods on their festival days. What if I don't like the god I get sent to care for? Who wants to just make meals for some statue while real people suffer real ills?"

"Poor priestess," Imilke sniffs with sweet derision, and snidely rolls her eyes as she returns to her work.

"Look," Perikles says, and takes his little cousin by the shoulders to look him in the face. "You're not a child anymore. You're already this wise woman. And eventually, the fibers of your fate get spun into one single thread. You only get one life. We don't get to bounce from flower to flower, from interest to interest, our whole lives - just as a child. It's soon going to be time for you to become some kind of person. Me too. I'm doing it today, and I don't know what to expect."

"I know you can win any argument, Perikles," she says sweetly. "You've got more books and scrolls than anyone. Just be patient."

Perikles says with a sigh, "Most of my fellow citizens don't care what I've read on some scroll."

Aoide smiles at Perikles, to cheer him up, then decides he tricked her into cheering herself for him, and playfully frowns.

"We're the lucky ones, Aoide," Perikles says with a little chuckle. "It's good that we keep that in mind."

"The other girls don't think so," Aoide growls. "The other girls talk like we Alkmaeonids are a cursed family. Why do they say that?"

"Ignore that. What I mean is that we're lucky because we were born Hellenes instead of barbarians, and we live in modern times. Imagine being a girl in Homeros' day, like Iphigenia or Briseis. The longer men have lived here, the higher our ideas-Akropolis sits atop the rubble of their ancient mistakes."

Aoide thinks about that for a moment, looking at the flowers in the courtyard around them, then says, "I've seen men try to build high buildings, but most seem to topple once they're more than a couple of stories high."

Perikles shakes his head and smiles into her eyes, struck as always by her youthful wisdom. "Like tall buildings must have wise architects, I think civilization might be kept upright by singular geniuses like you, Aoide. Just whatever happens, keep away from teenage boys, because you never know who might be a god, and you'll do more good as a person than as some tree!"

Aoide giggles with childish carefreeness.

"I should think that I could still be useful as a tree, if need be! But, you be careful too, Perikles. The barbarians in that Assembly are nothing like the people poets write. If I were you, I'd wear a helmet day and night!"

Γ

The men of Athens hold their democratic Assembly

Athenian men cluster tightly onto the grassy *Pnyx*, their many conversations intertwining. Olive trees enclosing the proceeding wave their many little leaves.

As they climb the fine stone stairs Perikles says, "You know, the age of the word *Pnyx* - an archaic word meaning 'crowded' - is a mask meant to make this civic space seem old. Its fine stone stairs and standing platform were hewn into the hillside in the days of the democratic reforms of my great-uncle only forty years ago. Since those days just before the Wars, when Kleisthenes' reforms returned power to this Assembly from the tyrannical sons of Peisistratos who had seized it, there's been a rooting civic reverence given to this new space where the Assembly now meets, as if the ritual is more ancient than it is. Before Kleisthenes, the Assembly just met in the Agora."

"Yes yes," Ephialtes sighs at last, "I know all this, of course, Perikles. You may be Kleisthenes' grand-nephew, but I'm the one who's actually been to Assembly on the Pnyx before, many times. Not my first bull-leaping."

The wealthiest old Oligarchs gather in a group next to the stone speaking platform at the higher end of the hill which functions as this civic theater's stage, the *bema*, trying to separate themselves however they can from the rest of the population in this place which otherwise so naturally minimizes and equalizes the voices and spaces of each man.war

From the perspective of someone in the crowd, facing the bema, the Akropolis looms in the distance on the left, to the east, where morning cloudlight dapples its temple ruins. At the northern base of the Akropolis hill juts the great Rock of Ares, the *Areopagos*, that sacred stone where all those who have already served as Archon rule over the gravest trials such as murder, arson, or crimes involving olive trees.

Swift-eyed Perikles and ever-smiling Ephialtes edge their way toward the front of the crowd until they find a clear spot to stand near the important elders and officials around the bema. Ephialtes makes eye contact with big-bearded Themistokles among the officials.

"Themistokles has asked to meet you after the Assembly," Ephialtes whispers to Perikles. "I'll take you by the Democrats' club house."

Perikles nods, overwhelmed trying to listen to the thousand conversations around him. He clutches his cloak against a stiff morning breeze from the east wind, but cool Zephyros quickly flees the settled warmth of so many vigorous hearts gathered so close.

Two nearby priests burn goat bones in a silver tripod.

The man who holds the annual office of herald, named Chraedo, steps up onto the bema and addresses the crowd with a strong voice that quiets the cacophonous chatter. Chraedo holds high above his head the official scepter of his office - a tall staff which splits into two intercoiling snakeheads, the *kerykeion*, the same staff which the Messenger God Hermes himself is said and shown on pottery to wield. The cooking goat meat smell helps to stir the crowd's attention. The herald bellows.

"O gods, come to hear our prayers! Come, mighty Zeus, lord of all gods, and you, virginal Athena who loves our city most of all! Unite our many voices here, and help the wisest among us make his mind understood by the masses. And if any man here means to deceive this Assembly, or to become a tyrant, please overwhelm him with your merciless wrath!"

Beside the bema, a time official readies a simple water clock made of clay jars that pour into one another through specifically sized holes.

Chraedo the herald speaks with a resonant voice, "First of all, this month we have to vote whether or not the city wants to exile anyone this year. Now who wishes to speak on the matter?"

Stiff-bearded Themistokles, already close, steps up to the bema confidently. When he raises his gaze to address the Assembly he is confronted immediately by both cheers and boos, famous enough to be thought of many ways, but he quiets both by lifting up one hand.

Themistokles says, "My brave Athenian comrades, together we have shouldered the effort of rebuilding our great city. It has been eight years now since the Persians put our homes to the torch, but together we have put stone upon stone, and not only rebuilt but expanded this fine city of Athena and Poseidon! We should be proud."

The disorganized crowd grumbles, whispers, and cheers.

"The Olympic Games come this summer, when we should be praising Zeus, who would balk at the exiling of the powerful. Let this be our tenth spring without an *ostracism*!"

Democrats in the crowd react with the cheer of agreement that he was expecting, but that cheer is joined by a loud murmur of uncertainty that the cheerers quickly notice and begin to mumble nervously about, so that the whole crowd is soon chaos again. Themistokles scans the crowd with a frown, unsure quite how to read its mood.

After the man-herd Themistokles reluctantly steps down, the finely dressed aristocrat Thukydides ascends the bema and addresses the crowd. Few among the faces respect him with total silence. Athenians are used to this man.

"It seems to me," says Thukydides, "that an ostracism would be a good thing for our city this year. After all, Kleisthenes, your beloved Democrat, did create the tradition for a reason. And it has been too long since we had one. I am of course just a farmer, so I see things only through the eyes of someone who has worked the vineyards my whole life. But I would say, Athenians, our good city is just like my vines - you must not go too long without pruning the weaker plants, or your fields will cease to be strong."

The many men mumble passionless agreements and insults as Thukydides steps down from the bema and the handsome and lion-hearted general Kimon steps up after him, his face a stone mask of military coolness.

For each new speaker, the water official unstops a new jar pouring into another to keep time.

Hawk-eyed Kimon speaks slowly, "Our fleets recently returned from subjugating the primitive pirate clans on the island of Skyros ... where some of you may already have heard ... an eagle - the bird of Zeus - led me to the burial site of our great city's ancient King Theseos, slayer of the Kretan Minotaur and founder of our temple to Aphrodite. Now, after centuries, his bones are home in Athens."

Many in the crowd cheer, loudest of all Kimon's veterans who sailed and fought the Skyran pirates with him.

"Under my leadership, alongside Aristides the Just, we've collected innumerable cities and islands into the League of Delos, and Pausanias of Sparta continues even now to free more eastern cities from Persian control." Lion-eyed Kimon looks around at the pleased crowd like a general assessing his troops. Then he carefully, strategically snarls, "Themistokles and his so-called *Democrat* cronies hold this city back."

The crowd explodes into argument, insults, and applause. The Democrats groan in offended uproar, while the Oligarchs laugh and cheer and jeer. Those who do not follow political conversations ask others to explain.

Kimon steps down from the bema into the noisy chaos, as the old aristocrat Aristides ascends carefully after him.

The time official starts a new water jar pouring.

Despite the clamor, the crowd hushes quickly as patient Aristides assesses them, considering how to begin. Many in the Assembly shush the last arguers, until the sound of one lingering talker literally being knocked out by a punch brings the Assembly finally to a silent state of listening.

Aristides says, "Athenians: Having already been Archon, I tend to feel that today's politics are for the younger and more vigorous men who still have the breath for it. But the older men here probably know what I'm about to say. Because they will recall that it was I who was last ostracized from our city. Ten years ago. Stakys, you asked me to write my own name on your potshard for you, since you can't write, and didn't know I was me."

The Assembly laughs and those around Stakys, a doddering old man, playfully pat him.

Aristides smiles as he recalls, "You said you were just sick of hearing that man called 'the Just'. And that's understandable, Stakys."

Aristides then turns to Perikles, and the attention of many of those around him in the audience fills Perikles with an uncomfortable awareness of what he looks like that makes him blush and lower his head shyly.

"Of course Xanthippos and I were recalled before ten years, for the Second Persian War, but it would have been only this year that I would have been allowed finally to return, if Xerxes had not invaded our land in his sad attempt to impress his father's ghost."

The crowd murmurs at the coincidental timing.

Perikles tries to dispel a vision of his father, Xanthippos, who conspired with the Oligarchs in his day, and who he knows would be whipping him for thinking of voting with Themistokles' Democrats.

The herald reaches up to touch Aristides' tunic and indicates that he's nearly used his time, but Aristides simply gestures him away.

Aristides takes his time saying, "From my own work with the League of Delos, alongside noble Kimon, I can assure you: Persia will not sleep forever. We can't afford to exile experienced men. Let me be the last man Athens exiled. Let the ritual wither like Thukydides' weak vines."

Many in the Assembly cheer Aristides as he steps down. One voice calls out his famous epithet, "Aristides the Just!" Some groan at that.

The herald steps back up onto the bema. "No one else wishes to speak? Then we'll vote. Who would have an ostracism in two months' time?"

The sound of more than half of the five-thousand present hands being raised is loud but brief. Perikles and Ephialtes are shocked to see that Lysimachos is among those raising their hands.

Lysimachos shrugs to his friends with a puerile grin and keeps his hand raised while the officials are still counting. "I like to hear a debate when someone's life is on the line," he admits to Ephialtes.

"That's awful," Ephialtes sighs.

Those who voted for it keep their hands raised while the herald and two other officials with triangulating views take quick official counts. Meanwhile, everyone within the crowd looks around trying to count from where they stand. The crowd is tightly packed enough that it is not obvious from Perikles' and Ephialtes' vantage what the vote might be.

"And who would have no ostracism?"

Perikles, Sophroniskos, and Ephialtes energetically raise their hands, as do many of those around them. But it is quickly clear from the faces of the officials that the vote was positive.

"Then hear this, gods: in two months, Athens will write names on potshards and whoever receives the majority will be exiled for ten years!"

The crowd goes wild with angry, excited, and fearful discussion.

Chraedo has difficulty continuing his declarations of business over the clamor. He holds aloft his double-snaked herald's staff to get the crowd's attention. "Now I must announce the Archon's choice of which writers of tragedy will be granted a chorus for the upcoming festival of Dionysos, and the producers of those plays must be selected! Those who wish to submit their names for selection by lot, bring your nameplate to the lot board!"

Lysimachos slaps Ephialtes on the shoulder as he's headed away and says casually, "Maybe you'll win next time, Ephialtes. I'll be at the gym."

Big-armed Sophroniskos shakes his head and pats Ephialtes too hard on the shoulder, saying, "He still thinks this is knucklebones. We'll just have to make sure it's the other man ostracized, eh Ephialtes? I have to get back to Phaenarete. See you men another day."

Ephialtes shakes Sophroniskos' hand firmly in parting and then grabs Perikles' attention away from the clamorous crowd around them all murmuring about Themistokles and Kimon being targets of the ostracism. Perikles is almost too shaken up by the turn of events to hear his friend.

"Four years ago - what was the city's favorite play?"

Swift-eyed Perikles thinks for a moment, noticing that actors and playwrights have begun to gather near the bema as the more interested citizens in the new business. "*The Phoenikian Women*, by Phrynichos. But wasn't he fined for that, for showing that when foreign dignitaries were visiting?"

"But it reminded the city why they love Themistokles," Ephialtes says to make his point clear. "And, of course, who produced that play?"

"Themistokles did."

Perikles eyes the actors and playwrights gathering around them - famous people whose entourages and fan bases are gathering nearby, as interested in these results as the artists. He looks back to Ephialtes with an uncertain smile, but then shrugs and steps toward the lot board - a man-sized ceramic rectangle with ten columns of slots sized to fit the citizen nameplates - small, lead identification bars stamped with one's name and father's name which all citizens have.

Ephialtes explains, "Look, man, there are ultimately two angles on each vote, right - in favor of democracy, or back toward Oligarchy. But it isn't two monolithic voting blocs who always vote either way. It depends, each time, and you need to wrangle for the votes each time. You may think - how can we try convincing every individual man to vote the way we'd prefer? We can't. But that's not what we need to do. Almost no one votes individually; they vote with their group. And what are the primary groups that most people organize themselves around?"

"You mean the cults? The gods' cults?"

Ephialtes nods. "Exactly. Most people spend most of their time with the other people who are focused on the same god they are. And what bigger cult, these days, than that of Dionysos? And how better to get everyone in the cult of Dionysos - and, really, anyone who goes to the plays, which is everyone, even foreigners - to think highly of Themistokles?"

Ever-smiling Ephialtes nudges Perikles as he watches the theater people gather.

"You were asking about ways to use your wealth for the democracy."

Perikles nervously steps up next to the elder aristocrat Thukydides, who has just placed his nameplate into one of the slots of the lot board. Perikles tries to ignore the elder man, and the herald standing behind the lot board waiting to randomize the selections, who both eye him as he is the last in line to insert his nameplate into the board.

Swift-eyed Perikles returns to Ephialtes with a nervous look of excitement as the herald sets aside his snake staff and begins to read out the randomized selections of the lot board.

Beside the lot board, the same official who had been manning the water clock now mans a long funnel which holds at the top a bunch of black and white stones and is dropping out the bottom individual ones at random. When the first three stones dropped are black, the herald removes the nameplates which had been inserted into the top three rows of the lot board, and several men leave the front of the Assembly in acknowledgment of their non-selection.

Finally a white stone drops, and the herald checks the corresponding row of nameplates in the lot board.

The herald pronounces, "For the new tragedies of Phrynichos, the producer will be ... Aniketos, son of Peridoros!"

Phrynichos, a long-bearded old playwright from that first generation of *Thespians* who were mimicking wild-haired Thespis himself, standing nearby in the crowd, throws his hands in the air melodramatically. "Thrifty Aniketos! Then expect no frills from Phrynichos!"

Phrynichos' fanbase howls.

Soon another white stone drops. "For the tragedies of Choerilos, winner of more ivy crowns than any man yet, the producer will be ... noble Thukydides, son of Theotimos!"

Thukydides the Oligarch, standing right beside Perikles, nods with a smile and turns to seek out Choerilos in the crowd.

"And finally, the producer of the newest tragedies by Aischylos, that innovator of the stage, the producer will be ... young Perikles, son of Xanthippos!"

Ephialtes grins and shakes Perikles by the shoulders. Perikles scans the crowd for Aischylos, but when his eyes finally find the beefy, balding veteran he is just finding Perikles as well, and Aischylos' expression is a mask of disappointment. The playwright has a moment of silent but evocative eye contact with Perikles, then pushes away deeper into the crowd.

Perikles looks to Ephialtes with concern. "Aischylos fought at Salamis. He was wounded that day. I'm not sure he's the best writer for our idea."

Ephialtes shakes his head in reassurance. "He just hears Alkmaeonid in your name and assumes you vote like your father did. He'll come to respect you, I know it. Trust me, Perikles. Nobody knows you yet, but once they do, everyone will love you just as much as I do!"

Ephialtes' friendly kindness quickly turns Perikles' spirit back around to the excitement of having just been selected to produce a play, and they start to head together through the crowd, toward the Agora.

Nearby, Sophokles, a handsome young actor and aspiring writer, kicks the dust. "Idiocy! Three who've already won! Where are the opportunities for new voices?"

Chraedo the herald shrugs as he helps the time keeper start to collect the time pots. "Keep trying, Sophokles. Whose work gets a chorus is the Archon's choice, not mine. Surely someone will want you as an actor again."

Sophokles looks around quickly to make sure no one respectable is watching, then moons the herald with a quick flash of his tunic as he walks away. His fans, observing, titter from afar.

"WE GLIMPSE OUR FLEETING LOT OF LIFE AND
THEN WITH LIGHTNING DOOM DISPERSE LIKE SMOKE,
EACH ONE BELIEVING ONLY WHAT WE'VE MET BY CHANCE, PROUDLY
IMAGINING THAT WE HAVE KNOWN THE WHOLE."
Empedokles, *On Nature*

Δ

The marketplace of ideas follows the Assembly in the Agora

The assembled crowd of men disperses slowly from the Pnyx, as everywhere Athenians stand enrapt together in warm debates. Those who came from country homes or coasts begin their city-visit errands or head out the gates to start the day's journey back home before the paths are dense with ox carts.

Voices of every tone commingle across the Agora as men return to their donkeys, children, wives, and slaves. On Assembly days, commerce of a financial sort is outlawed in the Agora, but the marketplace of *ideas* is always busiest right after the Assembly lets out. An old mother owl roosts to watch unseen.

In the sand at the edge of the Agora, surrounded by children, Anaxagoras is finishing his explanation of the world's origin to little Euripides.

"...for even though we each are born anew into this world which seems to be only as old as we ourselves, in fact we are living in an ancient land which has known countless lives like us," the visitor Anaxagoras finishes.

Sullen little Euripides appears more confused than ever. "I still don't understand where the gods came from originally."

Many of the children who have been listening to Anaxagoras get up to join their families as the men return from the Pnyx. Sophroniskos hurries up to pregnant Phaenarete just as she is starting to lift her jar of water, and takes it out of her arms to carry it for her as they head off together back to their home.

"Your mind has produced an excellent thought," Anaxagoras says to little Euripides with a smile. "In Ionia, we would refer to this idea as a *first principle* - what came first? Or, what is most elemental?"

Laconic-faced Kimon approaches and looms over Anaxagoras and the children. Beside him, his statuesque sister Elpinike clings to her brother's arm but addresses the other men with a fearless expression, a distinctly defiant stance relative to the norms expected of Athenian women in public. Flanking Kimon and Elpinike are two Spartan ambassadors, Hippokoön and Melanthios, both wearing bronze Spartan breastplates, the sight of which many passing Athenians react to with concern.

The toddler Krito runs away at the sight of the Spartans, which makes the two men snort little laughs to each other.

Kimon tousles little Euripides' hair. "Euripides was born on Salamis Island, that very night we fought the Persians in the straits eight short years ago, yes?" he says.

"So I'm told," Euripides replies dryly. "I don't remember it."

"Our own little Ajax. A great Athenian hero one day."

Euripides shrugs off Kimon's hand and darts away to his mother's vegetable stall.

Kimon smiles, then gazes down upon Anaxagoras. "Now what's this story you tell in an eastern accent, stranger?"

Anaxagoras stands to greet Kimon. "Not a story, just thoughts. We like to discuss this sort of thing in Ionia. I'm from the city of Klazomenai. I've been traveling. I am called Anaxagoras."

Kimon says, "I've been to Klazomenai, on the way to Smyrna. So I'm familiar with the Ionian habit of debating the absurd."

Eagle-eyed Hippokoön spits on the ground.

Anaxagoras minds the Spartans carefully, as if they might be demons. "For you are the noble and wide-traveled Kimon, son of Miltiades, if I'm not mistaken - great hero at the sea battle of the Salamis straits?"

"You honor me too much. There were many heroes that day."

"Your glory honors all Hellenes," Anaxagoras says.

They are all distracted momentarily by a loud row between two people not far away in the Agora, though it is not visible through the crowd. In a moment, the noise of scuffle seems to echo away down a street.

Bronze-eyed Elpinike, whose noble countenance doesn't flinch a moment during the noise, says to Anaxagoras, "Well, welcome to Athens, stranger. There are two games of knucklebones most days at either side of the Monument of Heroes. The game to the west is less corrupt."

"And know that if you mean to stay or work, you'll need to register as a *metic*," Kimon adds.

The man-mountain Melanthios, older of the two Spartans, asks, "What's your trade, Anaxagoras? Have you come to take part in one of the famous Athenian religious mysteries?"

"No no, I'm just a carrier of other people's wisdom, like Empedokles and Pythagoras. A lover of wisdom am I! I participate in the constant religious mystery of living amidst Nature!"

Melanthios laughs, then frowns, at that answer.

Hippokoön spits on the ground again and looks away.

"A wisdom-lover, eh? As if the rest of us are idiots?" big Melanthios asks.

Anaxagoras shrugs and shakes his head, unsure how to reply. "Not what I mean to say at all."

Meanwhile, coming down the hill from the Pnyx into the Agora, Perikles looks for Anaxagoras, whom he had made eye contact with when coming in, and sees him still sitting by the fountain house.

"This is your chance to begin to make a name for yourself, to be more than just the son of Xanthippos," Ephialtes says to Perikles.

Perikles interjects, discreetly pointing, "I wanted to talk to this stranger. He was saying something to these children that got me thinking."

"Kimon is with him now," Ephialtes notes with a nervous nod. "That's interesting to me."

Perikles and Ephialtes approach the Fountain House, where Kimon, Elpinike, and the Spartans loom around the Ionian visitor like vultures.

"What of a spark, stranger?" Perikles interjects into the active conversation as he and Ephialtes approach from the Pnyx.

Anaxagoras turns to face him, startled, but intrigued quickly. "A spark?" he asks with a smile.

"On our way up to the Assembly I overheard you telling these children that Elean wise men believe that everything has a previous form. But strike an iron, and the spark of fire can clearly be seen, new from nothing one moment and gone the next."

"Is the spark something new?" Anaxagoras asks.

"Perikles, son of Xanthippos," Kimon says politely, introducing the young nobleman. "Perikles, this is Anaxagoras of Klazomenai. And these are Hippokoön and Melanthios, on embassy from Sparta for the Assembly. They're staying with me while they visit our city, since I acted last year as our ambassador to theirs."

"So many names all at once! I'm Ephialtes. But I don't expect you to remember my name."

Anaxagoras seems charmed by Ephialtes' humor, but the Spartans do not. Ephialtes seems unmoveable by intimidation, however.

"Come now," Elpinike sings with sarcastically melodramatic tones, "who could forget the name of Ephialtes, who rowed ever so hard at the Battle of Salamis!"

Ephialtes' friendly confidence is only barely cut down by the sleight.

Melanthios turns to Perikles, and takes a step in order to block the sun and have it gleam around the edges of his Spartan helmet as he says to the young man, "How about the son of Xanthippos? Have you even fought in a real battle yet, child?"

"A singer of songs to his mother," the other Spartan adds.

Melanthios shakes his head, "No, you're thinking of his brother, Ariphron - that eighth Sage of Hellas. Perikles here is just a bookworm. How old were you when your father was exiled?"

Perikles looks to Ephialtes, less acquainted than his friend with the small offenses of public discourse. But Ephialtes seems to be watching Perikles for how he will behave, so Perikles steels himself to remain as graceful as he can, even in the face of overt disparagement.

"Eleven," he says, finally turning back to meet the Spartan in eye contact. "And don't mistake simpleness for stupidity, friend. My brother has wisdoms few share."

Kimon interjects, "Xanthippos was a good man. A skilled prosecutor of our city's laws. A noble Oligarch."

Kimon eyes Perikles for the first time with the potency of the fact that his own father Miltiades was prosecuted by Perikles' father Xanthippos in the years following the First Persian War. Miltiades died in prison during that trial; Xanthippos died naturally ten years later after a complicated career including military victories in Thrake and ostracism by Themistokles' Democrats. The two men's sons Perikles and Kimon have never met eyes until this moment, and Kimon's cold stare chills Perikles.

To redirect the tension of the moment, the electric Elpinike says, "We need all types of men in this city. Isn't that right, Ephialtes? Where would we be without your father's cups? Nothing for our soldiers to drink from. These men are the real city wall." Her sarcasm is obvious to all.

The Spartans laugh. Kimon eyes Perikles coldly.

Kimon says, "Seek glory in the theater, Perikles. And vote with your fellow noblemen, as Solon intended. Democracy only works if good men stick together."

Perikles eyes Kimon with disappointment, then looks to Anaxagoras with a spark in his eye. "Consider the spark, friend."

Behind Perikles and Ephialtes, a smugly smiling middle-aged man dressed in a fine, flowing tunic, adorned with many gold and pearl rings and necklaces approaches from the crowd and slaps the backs of the two men.

"Swift-footed Hermes has sent me to interrupt boring conversations! Greetings, strangers, I am Kallias!" Kallias eyes Elpinike with a particularly visible lust. "Kimon, I wonder if I might have a word with you and your lovely sister at your home this evening. There's a financial proposal I'd like to discuss." Kallias only then notices the Spartans at their side. "By Zeus! Hello."

Kimon speaks quickly to stop Kallias' talking, "We do our financial transactions here in the Agora, Kallias."

Kallias looks at the other people around them with hesitant discretion, then crosses the space to Kimon and puts his hand on his arm, the same arm which Elpinike has been holding. Kallias looks first at Kimon, then turns his glance to Elpinike, then back to Kimon trying to communicate silently with his eyes. Kimon coldly reads the attempt at discretion and steels his face, looks away and speaks to keep Kallias from articulating a thought.

"We'll make an hour for you while the slaves prepare the meal. We usually sit and watch the sunset. Come then."

Anaxagoras chirps, "I always make sure to watch the sunset as well. I've also begun recently to track the movement of the wandering stars." None of the others really hear Anaxagoras, caught up in each other's drama. He smiles and looks around at them. "Surely I'm not the first person to study astronomy here."

Perikles hears him, and decides to be the spirit of politeness in this awkward moment and answer Anaxagoras to help redirect the moment. "Oenopides studies the numbering of the days of the year," he says. "He's often on the Akropolis at night. Feel for him with your feet; he lies down to watch the stars."

Kimon nods to Elpinike, and they and the Spartans take the change of conversation to disappear wordlessly into the crowd.

Kallias turns to Anaxagoras, expecting to be introduced.

Ephialtes beats Perikles to the polite introduction, "Kallias, Anaxagoras of Klazomenai. Anaxagoras, this is Kallias - enriched by the ditch." Ephialtes grins shamelessly at Kallias, awaiting a reaction. Anaxagoras looks between both, confused.

Kallias scowls at Ephialtes.

"You make it hard to be a Democrat sometimes, Ephialtes. Do you even care how I vote?"

Ephialtes replies, first joking but by the end shrugging at seriousness, "By your conscience, I hope, based on the best argument."

> "JUST AS THUNDER FOLLOWS BRIGHT LIGHTNING
> AND CLOUDS BRING SNOW OR HAIL-STONES,
> SO PROUD MEN BRING RUIN TO STATES,
> WHICH FALL TO SLAVERY OR KINGS."
> Solon, *Ship of State*

E

Kimon and Elpinike host visitors in their home

Twilight cools the sky like the world slowly sinking into a pool. The gathering of families indoors for dinner quiets the public streets to a murmur peppered by the barking of a few lonely dogs.

Kimon and Elpinike relax on their roof deck with the two visiting Spartan ambassadors, drinking wine and taking in the view across the neighborhoods of Athens as the colors shift. The hills of the Peloponnese, visible on the horizon across the water in the western distance, are draped in orange clouds. Closer, two teenage Helot slave boys play footsie while they wait to serve their Spartan masters.

"Democracy is chaos," murmurs the Spartan Hippokoön. "I would not be able to sleep."

"It is true," Kimon agrees. "I've lost more sleep to fear of the potshard than the sword. That's why I brought home the bones of our ancient King Theseos from that pirate island Skyros. Against all reason, that skeleton, more than any military victory, has made the people love me. And that love is my shield against the potshard."

Melanthios asks, "You hold sway and power in the city. Isn't it the powerful who are exile's targets?"

Kimon explains, "It's more complex than that."

Elpinike says, "Simply opening our orchards to the poor for free fig picking has probably guaranteed us that at least the hungry will never seek our exile. If there's one thing the hungry have plenty of, it's votes."

They all laugh softly and drink from their cups, and those with shallow cups are served more wine by one of the young Helots.

"It also helps that Themistokles is more arrogant than Achilles," Elpinike adds, "and there's nothing the people hate more than that. Even Aristides the Just - the only man anyone knows who might actually deserve such a title - is hated by many poor wretches simply for his fame, and despite his virtue."

Melanthios knuckle-knocks on Hippokoön's knee and notes, "It would be like the Helots deciding the fate of our people." The younger Spartan grimly nods.

Turning to Kimon, Melanthios continues, "Your city may follow Theseos through this labyrinth of democracy, but Sparta follows Herakles through the Augean stables of Oligarchy. With awful stinking work, Herakles found strength. With curious wandering, Theseos found madness. But I know I'm no good at making points out of stories. You'll never meet a Spartan poet."

Another of Kimon's slaves, the hairy, middle-aged Makedonian Amyntas, peeks his bald head up out of the roof trapdoor, standing at the top of a ladder coming from the house below.

"Sir, Kallias is here to see you."

Hippokoön and Melanthios stand, and their Helot servant boys follow quickly.

"We'll take a walk," Melanthios says.

Kimon stands also and nods a laconic farewell to them.

Elpinike commands, "Amyntas, invite Kallias to join us up here."

Amyntas nods and disappears back down the ladder, and the two Spartans and their attendant Helots climb down after him.

Kimon sits back down next to bronze-eyed Elpinike and they see the sunset in each other's eyes for a long moment as Kallias climbs up the ladder to join them on the roof. They do not stand for him.

"Good evening, children of Miltiades," says Kallias.

Elpinike snaps, "You wield our father's name like you think it is some kind of yoke that can control our emotions, Kallias, but you're wrong. Neither my brother nor I are ashamed of our father. We're honored when you mention his name."

Kallias' expression belies his genuineness as he says, "I mean nothing but honor by it."

"What offer do you have for us, Kallias?" Kimon asks coldly. "I don't want to dance around the topic like poets."

Kallias looks at Kimon somewhat nervously, then takes a nearby cup and drinks from it. He eyes Elpinike shyly but slyly.

"I'm sure you've seen Eros in my eyes, Elpinike."

"This is a noble house, not a brothel, Kallias!"

Elpinike tries to calm her brother with her eyes as she says, "As I'm sure you can imagine, Kallias, I am not unfamiliar with Aphrodite. I know how she stirs men's souls. But I am not available to you, whose wealth passed from a dying fool to a lying fool in a ditch among the dead at Marathon."

Kallias carefully says, "We can each bring up lurid rumors to stain each other's character. What I want to do is solve your problems."

Kimon sits back and looks away. "My only problem is Themistokles and his unwashed Democrats scheming to exile me."

"And how does one win votes?" Kallias asks. "Not good ideas! And despite what the Democrats might like to say, it's not even making people love you. You think the poor bastards picking your figs love you?" Kallias leans closer to Kimon. "You win votes when people owe you."

Kallias reaches out with a gesture which slaves would recognize as a desire to be served a cup, but then he glances around himself and realizes there are no slaves around. Elpinike notices the moment as well, and lowers her head in embarrassment. Kimon just sniffs. But Kallias finds his eyes while his hand is still raised, then lowers it without a cup and shrugs to Kimon with his mouth.

"I know it must be hard to keep afloat, with the weight of a fifty talent debt on your deck. Neighborhood dinners, poetry presentations, sporting games - these are the things that make people feel like they don't want to lose you. My parents choose not to claim some god in our distant family, and I wasn't born with the wealth I have now, but I don't care about the rumors about how I came to have it. Because I have it. How many slaves do you have right now? Seven, eight? Enough for the house and your orchards? I'm able to rent out eight hundred slaves to the silver miners at Laurion."

Kallias looks past Kimon at Elpinike, then back to Kimon.

"Aphrodite wants me to help you both."

Kimon looks to Elpinike with anger in his eyes, but he is surprised to find her appearing more logical about it.

Z

Ephialtes introduces Perikles to Themistokles and the Democrats

Ephialtes and Perikles navigate narrow alleys, past sleeping strangers and friendly prostitutes and solicitous doorway dogs, on their way to the low-fenced compound in the wealthy Honeymouth neighborhood where Themistokles' Democrats' club house is nestled between the Temple of Herakles Protector-From-Evil and the new city wall.

The Democrats' clubhouse is not quite as sprawling a campus of buildings as Perikles' own Alkmaeonid family's compound, but it is still a larger complex than most dwellings within the city walls and more than a touch ostentatious in the fineness of its artisanal details, such as the famously ornate sculpted lion faces at each corner of the gutters. The sounds of a raucous drinking party ring from the warmly glowing little shuttered windows, while outside, at a fine stone deck with a sculpted pool, two young lovers kiss in the friscalating twilight.

Perikles and Ephialtes enter Themistokles' clubhouse, where a young slave girl whom Ephialtes greets with a familiar "Good evening, Chloe," guides them into the men's sitting room, ringed by wall couches and short tables with flower baskets and drinks in little clay cups. Themistokles, Aristides, and a few other prominent Athenians including some whose names Perikles does not yet know all recline on the many fine couches, cups of wine in their hands or midsts, while four handsome twentysomething slave boys linger near the door and serve the men when beckoned.

Themistokles and Aristides are speaking.

"Themistokles, you built the wall - that's the most important thing. We are now safe from our neighbors. Anyway, you're now an Athenian hero, like Theseos himself. You saved our world from the Empire. I think you need not worry."

"If Kimon wants to paint this as Herakles against Odysseos, we shall let him," Themistokles is saying as Perikles and Ephialtes enter the room. He sees the two young men but does not change his expression in recognition of them yet. "That might play his way if this were Sparta, and Sparta were even a Democracy to be swayed. But this is Athens. Athenians respect guile."

Aristides says, "Well I've said what I'm willing to say in vague terms. The Fates weave the rest. You know why I can't speak directly on your behalf. No one would believe it."

Themistokles nods to Aristides and finally raises his full cup of wine to Ephialtes, who takes the cue to enter the room more fully. Perikles follows.

"Hail, Ephialtes!" Themistokles shouts. "Thank your father for this new set of cups for me!"

In the middle of the room is a table engraved with a rough sculpted map of Hellas, Ionia, and the Aegean Sea between them, with blue sand smoothed flat to represent the water. Tiny modeled cities sit on the map where the actual cities more-or-less are, and tiny wooden model fleets sit in the sand at certain ports. The markers representing the cities on the Peloponnesian peninsula, such as Sparta and Olympia, are sculpted from bronze, while Athens and its League of Delos allies across Ionia and the Islands around the Aegean Sea are represented in Laurian silver. Perikles gazes at the map-table in awe as he takes in the room for the first time. The representation of the coasts, mountains, and cities of Hellas as if seen from the perspective of the Sun chariot is unlike any work of art he has seen before.

"Xanthippos' son is examining your table for errors, Themistokles!" laughs the morosely drunk Tolmides from his couch.

Perikles, still a bit shy, just nods, scanning the room.

Themistokles rises to greet him, hugging both newcomers. "Welcome, Perikles! You've waited longer than most to join the intrigue of the city. Twenty three, yes?"

Perikles hesitantly follows Ephialtes over to the couches where everyone is lying about, but they remain standing. "Just last month, yes."

Themistokles stands next to Perikles and takes his whole body in one big arm, hugging him beside himself and facing the other men in the room as if to show him off.

"Nevertheless, I consider it my final competitive win against your father that his son would show up here with Democrats, rather than conspire with his old Oligarch friends. Ephialtes' kindness and wisdom are catching, aren't they? Homeros meant this man when he said that bold decency finds many friends."

"Decency does take boldness these days. Speaking of which, my thanks to you, dear boy." Aristides bows as much as he can from his reclined position, in gratitude to the slave boy who has just refilled his cup with wine.

"Do you know, Perikles," Themistokles says, "the day you were born, your father and I were in Delphi, where they assured him Ariphron would be an even more impressive Hellene than his namesake, your grandfather."

"I remind Ariphron every day that even Hephaestos is slow of mind and lame of body. I believe the Fates have possible glory available for every man, if he can find it."

Aristides smiles broadly and raises his cup to Perikles' comment. "Indeed, there are many different sorts of glory. How is Ariphron? I know your mother, noble Agariste, is well since my wife visits with her and the other Alkmaeonid women every other day for breakfast, and I have to hear about it at lunch!"

Perikles is unable to answer Aristides' question, so fast is the pace of the discourse in the room. His attention flits back and forth between those speaking, his mind dazzled.

Themistokles says, "It was that next year I was elected Archon. Perhaps Xanthippos' boy came just to make me feel old."

Young Democrat Myronides adds, "The same year Miltiades arrived from Chersonesos with his treasure ships, fleeing Thrakian hordes."

Themistokles interjects, "With his child Kimon, who, as a man now, aims for my exile by potshard," and spills some wine with his gestures.

Ephialtes says, "You'll have at least one advantage over Kimon at the ostracism - a more difficult name to spell!" Themistokles laughs hard at that.

Aristides adds to the memory, "He was hardly a child even then. Already trying to race you, a general, in the street! That poor man will always suffer the curse of his father's hubris."

Tolmides, from the corner, suddenly realizes, "Wasn't it Xanthippos who prosecuted Miltiades at his trial, the trial during which he died?"

Perikles nods with a grave look that hides the sheltered position Perikles was kept in until his father's recent death, as he doesn't want to reveal how little he actually was aware of that recent work by his now deceased father. Perikles doesn't want to reveal here that he fears he knew his father less well than his political enemies seemed to.

Myronides groans, "So, it was your father who prosecuted Miltiades, who was levied that massive fine and died in prison, that fine which now Kimon and his sister have inherited? By Eris, Kimon must *hate* you, Perikles."

Perikles grimaces at the thought.

Brightly-smiling Themistokles says, "Kimon's won enough praise to make up for it. You'd think he was the one who connived the building of the triremes, who set and sprang the trap for Xerxes' fleet. He may be a general now, but he was a mere soldier when he won the glory people speak of. Isn't it strange how the glory of a soldier can seem to outshine to some the truly greater glory of the general?"

Perikles is startled to realize he has been directly addressed, but quickly formulates an intelligent thought. "That speaks to the question of what stirs men's souls when a story is told. Perhaps it's difficult to explain the complicated glories of a general, and rare that the listener can fully comprehend. Whereas the glory of a simple soldier is easy to understand and get excited about."

Themistokles slaps Perikles on the arm and hands him a cup of wine. "Athena loves complex thinkers, Perikles. Drink with us!"

Perikles and Ephialtes take an empty couch together and recline against either side of it. Perikles continues to look around the room, watching how the older men behave.

Ephialtes says, "Perikles and I witnessed a very interesting moment in the Agora between Kimon and Kallias, after the Assembly. Kallias seemed to covet Elpinike right there in the market. I was worried for a moment he was some satyr in disguise!"

Themistokles says, "Elpinike suffers such humiliations every time she walks in the Agora. That's why beautiful wives should stay at home.

Many of the others in the room chuckle at this.

"Kimon is far too aware of his public image; he would not be so crass in the Agora. Elpinike may strut her beauty, but she is no courtesan. She's as noble as the Minotaur," Myronides quips.

Themistokles laughs. "We don't need to use base gossip as tools for our political goals. The virtues of our goals can only shine as brightly to the people as our ability to communicate them."

Aristides nervously asks, "Who was the foreigner who witnessed this? I'm the one who has to keep the islands in the League of Delos happy. Can't have them being insulted while they visit the city, like when Phrynichos portrayed the battle of Miletos in the theater!"

Perikles says, "An Ionian thinker named Anaxagoras."

"Ah. Big deal," Tolmides shrugs.

Ephialtes adds, "And two men from the Spartan embassy."

"What's a thinker?" Myronides asks with a little laugh.

"So the Spartan embassy are here already?" Aristides asks, intrigued.

A strange thump followed by another thump just outside one of the small windows grabs everyone's attention briefly.

"What was that?"

Themistokles says, "Just those young lovers hosting Eros by the pool. Any news of Pausanias? He's expected from Ionia soon, and I have reason to believe he will not see a happy homecoming."

Themistokles stands and crosses the room to the table map.

Ephialtes says, "They didn't mention; I didn't ask."

Themistokles explains, "Pausanias has been in the East freeing the cities of Ionia from Xerxes' now-wounded grasp. However the word among the birds is that he has turned his allegiance, that a letter was sent in his name to the barbarian King of Kings, offering to help him take all of Hellas in exchange for ruling over it as satrap and taking the king's daughter as his new wife."

"Good story," Myronides nods.

"This is more than gossip?" Aristides asks.

Themistokles says, "I have a good man's word that the messenger given the letter to take to Xerxes delivered it instead to the Overseers of Sparta, and that they await his return now with treason charges to answer."

"At least the Oracle wouldn't name you the most arrogant Hellene while Pausanias still lives," Tolmides remarks and then gulps his wine. He throws the thicker dregs of his cup drunkenly across the room at Themistokles.

All laugh.

Ephialtes says, "It sounds like that superlative may be open for the claiming soon, though."

Outside the tiny windows of the Democrats' club house, the two Spartan ambassadors, Melanthios and Hippokoön, crouch in the shadows in simple garb, unarmored for stealth, eavesdropping on Themistokles' conversation.

Melanthios shakes his head 'no' to Hippokoön.

A gasp from the corner of the building pulls their attention to the two young lovers who have just noticed the skulking Spartans. The lovers grasp each other in shock.

Melanthios and Hippokoön stand quickly, and sneak back into the nearby alleys, as Hippokoön flashes a dagger from his belt, turning it back and forth quickly so it'll glint, and holds his hand over his mouth as a silent demand to the lovers before he and Melanthios hit the shadows.

The sickle moon appears briefly between parting clouds above Attika, then disappears again into the grey-black Nyx.

H

The Alkmaeonid girls and women discuss their possibilities

"Turtle-tortoise, Turtle-tortoise, what of a thing's in its name? Mother, dancer, priestess, whore - which shall I be in today's game?"

The warmth of another day finds Aoide and her younger sisters sitting in a circle with their teen-aged Alkmaeonid cousins in the warm spring grass around a picnic basket full of biscuits and wild berry branches. While their parents chat around the old well on the street just outside their front gate, the girls pretend to be titans and animals. Their older cousin Ariphron helps the slave women carefully bedding new flowers.

Watching after the young girls is the famous swimmer Hydna, a muscular twenty-something who focuses on spying the tops of the courtyard walls for peeping boys. Unsmiling, Hydna has made it clear to the girls that she is not there to socialize. When not watching their surroundings, Hydna sits plucking flower petals and glaring into her own plucked dreams.

Aoide sits between her sisters, Deinomache and Klotho, mostly ignoring the game. Her attention keeps shifting to her father, leaning against the stone well and chatting with three old men wearing expensive-looking necklaces. Her father, meek and mean Megakles, spots Aoide watching him, then tries to hide that he had looked.

Idly Aoide hums, "I wish I was a boy."

Hydna snaps, "Don't ever wish! The gods curse wishes."

From across the courtyard, where she sits working her own mother's old bench loom, the girls' grandmother, old Koesyra, calls out, "You wouldn't want to be a boy, Echo." The older women in her family have started calling Aoide *Echo* for reasons she doesn't understand.

"Consider yourselves lucky, and secretly so. It is women who hold together civilization, while men continually tear it down. We women are the guardians of everything of true value. Make no mistake, and never lose the pride of your womanhood."

Hard-faced Hydna snorts at the comment. She says again, "Don't wish. The gods wish you would make some stupid wish, just to fuck with it."

Aoide's baby sister Deinomache whines. "Not everyone wants to always be around babies like you do, Grandma. I'd be willing to carry around a stupid little penis between my legs if it meant I would be able to do all the things that boys can do."

"Boys, our most dangerous livestock," Hydna scoffs. "They think their strength is here," and she points to her tongue, "or here," and she points to her own bulging bicep, "but really the only part of a man worth a damn is this," and she flashes a big wooden dick which she had stashed in her day bag. Her wards twitter.

"The freedom to fail, to hurt yourself, to act stupid, to be evil, is no real freedom, child," Grandma Koesyra assures little Deinomache with a smile. "Your limitations keep you noble, Deinomache. You shouldn't want to do foolish things just because you are not allowed to do them. That is boy-thinking. Be grateful you are a graceful, beautiful girl, Echo."

"Why do you call Aoide *Echo*?" Periboea asks with a tinge of annoyance, as if the special moniker is an unfair extra benefit given Aoide.

"Because Aoide is so good at remembering exactly what she's heard, just like poor Echo the nymph!" Koesyra calls out with a little laugh. "Don't you, Echo?"

Aoide shrugs. She never understood why others seem to have trouble remembering accurately what they've heard and seen.

Aoide's sister Klotho sings, "Boy-thinking, boy-thinking," as she applies reddish makeup onto their little sister Deinomache's face. "This will get boys thinking about you."

Periboea, skipping a circle around the others, says, "Makeup isn't for boys. Boys don't know what we do, because they never get to see us except in fleeting glimpses. So as far as they know, we wake up wearing makeup! They hardly notice it. It's for us. It lets you pretend yourself into whatever you want to appear to be. So you don't have to let them see the real you."

Deinomache, looking at her warbled orange reflection in a bronze mirror, asks, "Why can't boys and girls grow up together?"

Everyone's grandmother, Koesyra replies flatly, "Boys rape."

"Like in stories?" Deinomache looks to Hydna, who shakes her head and nods.

"If there aren't girls around, they'll rape each other. Better that than you. Prometheos got drunk after making us, and he made their wombs inside out, and they've been mad about it ever since."

"We know what dicks are, Grandma," Aoide groans as her cousins and sisters laugh at the old wives' joke.

"Maybe if they were more accustomed to being around us more often..." Periboea starts, but she is interrupted and hushes shyly.

Grandma Koesyra explains, "Boys are rapists not because they can't stop themselves, but because the current ruler of the Universe is Zeus, a rapist, and he shows men how to maintain control through threat of rape. But men and women still need each other to create babies. So we continue weaving and sweeping and cooking and cleaning and minding the household slaves, and doing all the work of maintaining civilized life, but we keep ourselves safe and separate from them, so we at least can have peace." Koesyra patiently weaves the weft of her loom. "Have you ever been in the home of a wifeless adult man?" she asks her young grandchildren.

They shake their heads no.

"Pray that you never do," she says. "Were it not for women, men's homes would still just be stinking, blood-caked caves in the hills."

For a few moments, everyone just thinks about that and a silence develops. The sound of the slaves gardening briefly takes over.

Deinomache asks Aoide across from her, "What are your parents talking to those priests about?"

"I'm going to be made a priestess," Aoide says.

"To which goddess?" Deinomache asks, picking the eyes out of the bald head of her little wooden baby doll with her thumbnail. "Artemis?"

Aoide says, "I don't know."

"To Aphrodite?" Periboea asks playfully as she crosses behind Aoide's back.

Aoide elbows her cousin in the knee.

"Don't!"

"Not to Aphrodite," Aoide growls.

Cousin Periboea laughs. "Being worshiped, instead of worshiping, when you think about it. Some women like it, being beloved by all men! Desire is the first god, the primary force, and only Aphrodite shows you how to be desired, to be like a goddess to men."

"Those women can worship Aphrodite then," Aoide snaps. "Beloved and desired are different, I'd say. I like Athena. I want to be an intelligent warrior, like Athena, ever-virgin, born of no man, only mind." She holds her hands around her head imagining that she is miming, at once, the birth of Athena from the head of Zeus, and the wearing of a helmet made only of thought.

"You know even priestesses of Athena aren't virgins themselves, don't you?" Periboea mocks as she passes behind Aoide again, having made a circuit around the circle of cousins one more time without passing on her game-office of Eris.

"Play the game!" little Deinomache shouts. "Stop stalling! Be Eris, Goddess of Discord!"

"I am!" Periboea laughs. "You're just too young to understand what Eris really is." She smiles at Aoide playfully, trying to posture as the oldest.

Aoide looks back over at her father, still talking with the long-robed priests. He looks at her again, and this time keeps eye contact with her, smiles to her and nods. He looks uncertain, and he is trying to hide it, but that gives Aoide hope, because she knows that anything that would actually be good for her would confound him.

Little Deinomache says, "At least as a slave to a goddess, you wouldn't have to be the slave of some man. Gods aren't real."

Aoide eyes her younger sister with surprise, impressed that she would voice such an extreme notion, and wondering where she heard it. For a moment, she muses about the notion that it might have appeared in Deinomache's head as original inspiration, not something she heard from someone else - but the only explanation for such a thing happening, to Aoide's mind, would be the inspiration given by Apollo. She considers that, even if she heard it from someone else, someone must have thought it for the first time once, and then how did the first person think the first novel thought? The notion of Apollo inspiring the idea of atheism into a mortal mind fascinates and confounds Aoide.

Some of her littler cousins gasp at six-year-old Deinomache's blasphemous statement. One of them gets right up, immediately crying, and runs off toward the adults. Older Periboea laughs with shock. But Aoide just eyes her younger sister carefully, wondering what she might have read to give her the idea, knowing that they have access to the same scrolls at home.

"I know someone who's going to get a visit from the Furies," Periboea taunts, dancing with sarcastic merry around the other girls in slow motion.

"How could there be no gods?" Klotho asks her little sister. "Think about it. What causes rivers to flow, or winds to blow, or people to fall in love? Where would everything have come from?"

Deinomache shrugs and keeps her eyes on her little wooden baby doll. She bangs it idly against the ground. "Not the gods. They're just stories. Just like everything else. Fake stories."

"That's what these modern plays do," old Koesyra sighs, weaving. "Now children can't tell the difference between myths and reality, and they think that the ancient stories are just things people made up."

"I'm going to tell your mother you said that," Periboea tells Deinomache. "You know your mother's belt isn't just a story." She looks up at the little one who ran off to get an adult and sees her now returning with Aoide's mother Threate holding her hand. "You're going to feel it."

"Now who's saying silly things?" long-necked Threate - Aoide, Klotho, and Deinomache's mother - chirps sweetly as she steps within earshot of the circle of girls. "Who said that scary thing? Deinomache, you are old enough to know better than to say things that scare the little ones. You remember how scared you used to get, when we would blow out the lamp. Now apologize to your cousin. And to the gods. The gods who surely know you were kidding, of course, if they happened to be listening. But the little ones here might not realize yet."

"Sorry," Deinomache dutifully apologizes to her sister while their aunt is there, but then glares at her once oblivious Threate turns her back.

Once the older adults have wandered out of range again, Hydna leans in to the circle of cousins and speaks in a low voice, like she's revealing a very special and dangerous secret. All the little Alkmaeonid girls listen intently.

"I'll tell you all a secret, because I'm already old enough to have been allowed into the sisterhood, so I know. The truth is - there is only one god, and it's a goddess. She created everything, and still creates everything, and we, us girls, we're all like her many fingertips, stretching out into the world. Womanhood is the only god - the only one! And so what are men, then, you wonder? Why men are broken women. Cursed, lazy liars who are our birthright ever to desire and ever be disappointed by." The tall strong young woman scoffs and leans back away to regain her could-care-less composure.

The cousins all smile, afraid to laugh too loud.

"Boys just want a beautiful breast and bottom to grope," Periboea spits derisively. "The rest of the girl can fall away for all they care."

"Well that's probably because those are the parts that they themselves don't have, right?" little Deinomache considers. "Plus those are the parts of a woman that have to do with raising babies, so those are the most important parts of people of any kind!"

Grandma Koesyra chuckles from afar and speaks just loud enough to be heard, "That is what men think they want! Men are boys forever, never men. They are enchanted by the phantoms of things, by myths they want to believe are real - including what a woman is to them! They imagine loving the breast, the bottom, the supple womb, but all they really know is the apparition of the thing. The story they can tell each other. Not the form, but the outline; not the breast, but the cleavage. The phantoms of men's desires are the real nighttime ghosts to fear, my girls."

Aoide allows some poetry to form in her mind. "Beware," she sings, "of thinking too much about how you appear, for remember that when you appear, you are an apparition."

Hydna says, "There is no origin but from Woman. And if you follow all the implications back all the way, there must have been some first woman - even before Chaos. That's reason, Deinomache."

"But if there are gods," asks little Deinomache, "you need a man and a woman to make a new baby, so how could there only have been one original god? There must have been two - a father god and a mother goddess, right? I know how sex works. And two can't come from zero. There are no gods. There's no world, nothing at all. None of this is real! It's all just words!"

"Exactly," Aoide nods, recognizing the sentiment from a poem she had read her younger sister earlier in the month. "I didn't think you understood the Herakleitos I read to you. Good girl, for really listening."

"You don't know," Klotho sneers now at Deinomache. "You've just seen dirty pictures on bowls. Some gods can arise out of just one parent, or just a severed penis or something like that. It happens."

"There are those who say there *were* two first gods," says Threate as she walks back over from where the men are discussing Aoide's future. She carries another woman's baby whom she is wet-nursing while her breasts still have milk. "Chaos, and Necessity. They might not have had penises and vaginas, but I think we all know that Chaos was a man, and Necessity was a woman, don't we, girls? It isn't always about penises. Sometimes the difference between man and woman is more about one's relationship to their world. Whether they want to cultivate or conquer it."

"So if Necessity was a woman and Chaos was a man," a thoughtful cousin considers, "then why are women left with the subservient position on Earth?"

"Subservience is a mask over responsibility, to make the supposed master feel less like a child."

Their grandmother Koesyra chimes in from her loom across the courtyard. "Think about the gods, and food on Earth. Thanks to a trick by Prometheos, it is we mortals who get the meat and fat and tasty parts of the sacrifice, while the gods are only due the smoke and bones and entrails. Similarly, it is women who are superior and more noble, more original, than men, and yet through the tricks of men, we've been delegated the lesser portions of life's joys. Because men think cheating is success, and leave it to others to sew closed the holes in that misunderstanding. And we who must apologize to the gods and give them the rest of their due."

The girls and their grandmother variously smile and frown at that, and laugh together at their mutually varying expressions.

Cradling the baby against her breast, Aoide's mother Threate adds, "We may not be given to make our own destinies, but we have secreted away the power to shape the destinies of others."

Aoide looks across her female relatives to her father and the priests, in the distance, discussing her future beside the old well.

Then she sees her grandmother beckoning her with a subtle gesture, so she gets to her feet and trots over to the old woman at the loom, who takes her in a tight hug, pulling her close.

"Listen close, young one. The most important thing to remember is not to listen to other people's voices, not really. Not above the voices inside your mind. Trust your own voices. Live within your own mind, foremost. And when it comes to the real world, the most important thing to know how to do is curse."

Old Koesyra pulls a tiny strip of goatskin parchment from within her dress and shows it to Aoide. She mimes with her fingers writing on the strip.

"And this is how. You find a very small piece of parchment like this, and you write the curse you wish upon someone who has wronged you upon it in the smallest letters that you can write, and you write it eloquently and poetically so that the gods will want to read it, and then you seal the curse into a piece of metal, and you bury it, the deeper the better, so that it will go straight to Queen Persephone, who organizes the dark doers of justice from the Underworld. That is how we defeat the work of men."

Frowning and furrowing her brow, nevertheless Aoide nods.

That night, Aoide is awakened from thrilling sky-blue dreams to find herself surrounded by men who have been watching her sleep in the dark.

She sits up in bed with a start, and covers herself with the lynx-fur which she had been hugging.

"Fear not, girl," says one of the shadowy men, barely visible in the night's darkness. "We are priests of Shining Apollo. We've been witnessing your dreaming. Now tell us, what were you dreaming just now?"

Aoide scratches at her eyes to wake her vision, but it stays blurry. Eventually she closes them and keeps them closed, and once her breathing begins to calm she is able to summon back visuals from her dreams.

She had been swimming in warm waters, like she remembered imagining her babysitter Hydna doing, and she had seen a pod of dolphins jumping not far away in the waves, and wondered if she tried to swim to them if they would flee, or if they could possibly hurt her.

"I was dreaming of swimming," Aoide says to men in the darkness beyond her eyelids. "I saw dolphins."

"It is the god's dream," one of the other priests says.

"Children dream of dolphins, too," the first priest who had spoken retorts. "We'll see if the god is really with her." Then his voice turns to address Aoide again, and she opens her eyes just in time to see his hands introducing a small snake onto the fur at the edge of her bed. "Don't think, Aoide," he says. "Just do what you feel you must."

Aoide shrieks at the sight of the snake, which though it is not much longer than her forearm and thinner than a stick nevertheless seems to start toward her menacingly. With an instinctive reaction she grabs it, gives its neck two or three fast, fearful breaks, and whips its carcass across the room back into the darkness. The fear only finally flushes into her face once the moment is over, and she pulls her knees to her chin and begins to cry quietly.

"Just as the infant god killed Python," the man whispers to the other man.

Θ

Perikles talks with his family at home before heading out

Perikles reclines on a cushioned bench in the men's room of his Alkmaeonid family home, and slowly eats olives from a bowl. On the wall behind him is a vibrant fresco of the Sea God Poseidon raping the lady Tyro while masquerading as her lover - supposedly a moment from the early days of Perikles' own family's history, as Tyro is an ancestor of the famous old king Nestor, and thus an ancestor of Perikles, as the story goes. Perikles stares absent-eyed, his mind still in the dream.

Meanwhile, his servant Thrax fusses about the room, cleaning up.

Outside, the voices of Perikles' young girl cousins mixes with the birdsong.

Perikles describes his recent dream. "Athena spoke, but was hard to understand. Her voice - rang like the Assembly, like ten thousand voices all saying the same words but somehow making them indecipherable from their number and variance. But her plea was urgent, and on the crowded Akropolis at the height of day, she ignored all but me. She spoke directly to me. In her left hand, she clutched a spear. But in her right, no shield. Instead, a smaller figure, a woman. A winged goddess."

Thrax stops his fussing and looks to Perikles. He hesitantly says, "Well I am a barbarian, and was not born knowing your gods..."

Perikles smiles and says, "No one was born knowing, my man. Speak."

"...but in my land, we have a saying: the Goddess of Victory is small enough to hold in one man's hand. That sounds like the goddess Nike in Athena's hand. Athena offers you Victory."

Perikles raises an eyebrow to Thrax. "But victory in what, Thrax?" Perikles smiles at Thrax and holds up an olive in a gesture familiar between them - in answer to which Thrax holds still, opens his mouth, and receives Perikles' tossed olive into it.

Perikles says, "Perhaps I'll hear Athena's many voices in Aischylos' chorus. I wonder what he will have them say."

Thrax begins dusting again and says, as if idly, "Perhaps you should tell him what they should say, since you're the one providing the money. What a chorus sings one day, the Assembly sings the next."

Perikles recognizes wisdom, but nevertheless says, "One step at a time, Thrax."

He reclines again into thought and takes an olive himself.

Perikles sits up again a moment later as his mother, high-chinned Agariste, nobly dressed in white with expensive blue trim, and his older brother Ariphron, walk into the room trailed by a few of their family's equally well-dressed slaves.

Perikles says, "Mother - we're in the men's room! I am an adult."

"I break the sanctity of your men's room just while the gods blink," she replies. "Your brother is finished with his lyre lesson and Damon cannot walk him to the Agora as usual. Would you walk with your brother?"

Perikles says, "I can take him there, but I can't stay with him. Today I seek out Aischylos the tragedian so we can discuss his plays for the Dionysia, and what he'll need from me as his play's producer."

"Of course. I forget that my baby is a man now, and won't be lingering with me like Ariphron. You are your father's son," she reminds him.

Perikles groans, feeling like a child, "You know I loved Father, but I hope you know I intend to weave my own fate, Mother, and will not necessarily follow the path he'd have wished I would."

Quoting an old family poem, she says, "You'll walk the web-line woven for you, praying to kind Hermes at each rare and lucky crossroads."

Patient-eyed Agariste steps closer to Perikles with a mother's concern.

"You're young, Perikles. You won't remember the way Themistokles played Athens for a fool, like a corrupt gamemaster in the Agora. Yes, we destroyed the Empire's fleet, because Athenian men are the boldest in the world, but also *despite* Themistokles' wicked ruse, not thanks-to it. He has charm, no doubt, but what he does not have is what you do have - noble birth. You are not just the son of Xanthippos; you are a descendent of Nestor, who sailed on the Argo, who fought with centaurs, and whose own father was a son of Poseidon. A god. Most men don't have gods' blood, Perikles."

Agariste's passion as she discusses Nestor, and her mentions of the mythic stories, get lost-eyed Ariphron excited.

"Iason sailed with Nestor on the Argo to Kolchis with Herakles, and Orpheos, and the twins Kastor and Polydeukes, and Bellerophon who killed the Chimera," Ariphron recites in the sing-songy way he learned it.

"That's right, Ariphron," Agariste says with a smile and a calming hand on his side. "Your ancestor Nestor sailed with all those men and brought the golden fleece back to evil Pelias. But did he give up the throne he promised Iason?"

Ariphron thinks for a moment, then says shyly, "No, he kept it."

"And how did the Kolchian princess Medea fool the evil King Pelias' own daughters into killing him?" Agariste eyes Perikles in a way that tells him she is making a point.

"She showed them how she could make an old ram young again by killing it and boiling it in her magic pot," Ariphron remembers carefully.

"But trying the same thing on their father the king didn't have the same result for Pelias' daughters, did it? And why not?"

Ariphron thinks for a moment. "Because they couldn't actually do magic like Medea could."

Agariste puts a motherly hand on Perikles' bearded face. "Themistokles is just a son of sailors. You're a direct descendant of the Sea God. That is what noble means." She pats his face like she does the slaves when she is done talking to them, and adds, "Take Ariphron with you. Aischylos will like him. Two brothers have magic."

I

Perikles and Ariphron visit Aischylos on Salamis Island to talk theater

With one hand Perikles holds the prow of a ferry which has just set out from Athens' docks at Piraeus and now takes him across the water to the Island of Salamis, across a narrow strait from Athens' port, while close to his chest he holds a small spherical pot with a little removable top and the image of an octopus painted on the side.

Beside Perikles, his older brother Ariphron clings nervously to the ferry, but also smiles at the salty air and at being out with Perikles. He watches his brother scan the world with his own unique confusion and wonder.

The sea is sapphire Aegean blue and the little village buildings on the island across the water are the familiar old colors which they have been Perikles' whole life; Salamis wasn't burned by the Persians when Athens was.

He looks down into the azure water, and briefly catches a glimpse of the dark hulk of a sunken Persian trireme as they sail over it. As he looks back up, Perikles catches the spray from a wave off the front of the ship in his hand and runs the saltwater through his beard.

The strong, young ferryman lands in the sand at the village on Salamis with a view of Athens. Perikles pays the man his owl, making him think of that final ferryman Charon who supposedly ferries the dead to the kingdom of Haides.

He looks across the water at his city for a moment, remembering that night he saw his city burn across the sinking Persian armada. He wonders for a moment if somehow his childhood has died.

Perikles leads his brother Ariphron through the brightly painted houses of that same harbor town where they huddled together eight years ago, and up to a hillock of grass on the sea cliffs of Salamis, a short walk's distance from the village but giving a lovely view of it.

There, bald-topped Aischylos sits by himself at the grassy edge of the cliffs of Salamis, overlooking the glimmering water, his smooth head shining in the sun. The waterway in front of him is trafficked by a few small vessels and one huge Qarthaginian quadrireme, with the busy Athenian port Piraeus and Athens beyond. In his lap is a scroll, and beside him are a few more.

Perikles asks, partly to announce his arrival, "Why do you come here to write? Surely it would be easier at a table, indoors. You seem to be spending more time keeping your scrolls from fluttering than writing on them."

Aischylos replies, "I've found it's easier to know a place from afar than from within. Here, all of Athens fits in my hand. Hello, Ariphron."

Ariphron smiles at Aischylos shyly, but doesn't respond. He lingers a few feet behind Perikles, nervously glancing between Aischylos and the beautiful view of the sea.

"My wife betrayed my confidence, I assume?" Aischylos asks. "I told her no one should know I'm here."

Perikles says, "Not at all. I haven't seen her. Gennadas the fishmonger told me where to find you."

Broad-shouldered Aischylos sighs, "Ah, yes. I bought my lunch from him. A mistake twice now."

Perikles walks up to the cliff edge and looks out at the straits, then turns back to Aischylos and holds up the small pot in his hand. "I brought you the finest Aigyptian octopus ink, so the next plays by Aischylos will last a thousand years."

"A thousand years, eh?" Aischylos says sniffing out a little laugh. "I should be writing Aigyptian stories if I want my work to be copied down for that long." He puts a stone on his scroll and stands, receives the pot. "Thank you, Perikles. I take this as a symbol that you intend to fund all four productions to their fullest extravagance."

Perikles says, feeling suddenly very adult, "That's my plan. Have you decided yet what you want to write?"

Ariphron eventually sits down in the grass and plays with flowers and pebbles while Perikles and Aischylos chat and intermittently watch him.

"Everyone wants kings and monsters. So I've been thinking of Phineas haunted by the harpies, Glaukos eaten by his own horses, and perhaps Oedipus and the sphinx. Then for the satyr play I have an idea about Prometheus bringing fire to man and a satyr who tries to fuck it."

Perikles laughs.

Aischylos smiles and continues, "Whenever I try too hard to please my audience, I fail, whereas when I write only to please myself, I also fail, but at least tend to please my audience."

Perikles says, "It is true that the plays of the theater can have a powerful effect on the mind of the people. When you think about it, writers have a lot of control over the will of the state."

"I should've expected you'd try to make my tragedies into a political lever."

"Phrynichos, four years ago, won with *The Phoenikian Women*."

"Scorn is heavier than an ivy crown, Perikles."

"But he won love from the city for Themistokles, whose leadership was told by the story. A tragedy for Persians is a triumph for Athens."

"And Themistokles produced that. You are too eager to become your hero, young man. Take off your Themistokles mask; you're no actor."

Perikles replies hesitantly, not wanting to offend the playwright, "All I can say is that this is the kind of play I would be really excited to put a lot of money into."

Aischylos sees Perikles' implication, and turns away with silent frustration, to face the sea. "Tragedies are like bronze mirrors, but too bright a reflection can be blinding."

"Then portray the Persian who was terrified by your audience. Tell the story through the voice of the enemy."

"Set in Poseidon's throne room, with a chorus of the drowned?" Aischylos looks back at Perikles with a brief smile as he imagines the scene. "Everyone demands that Sophokles play a woman again. They'll riot if he plays a man. Queen Artemisia of Kos is the only woman I can think of who fought in that battle. She who rammed her own ships to flee the chaos. If you had fought that day, Perikles, you would not want me to revisit it in tragedy."

"Women mourned their absent husbands and sons. Sophokles could play Atossa, daughter of Kyros, Dareios' queen and Xerxes' mother. There is no stronger Persian female character."

Perikles waits for a while as Aischylos gazes off at the sea with a slight grimace. Then Aischylos smiles and laughs softly at an idea.

"Dareios returns from Haides to tell his wife the fate of their son. It would be fun to play a foreign ghost."

Perikles says, "Or a dream? I like this. I feel the Muses amongst us."

"I fear Clio and Melpomene are tugging at my script from either end. I don't know, Perikles. What do you think, Ariphron? Are the flowers putting on a play there? Which one is the hero?"

Aischylos turns to Ariphron, who has gathered several wildflowers from the grass and is making them dance.

"I would pick wildflowers for days with my own brother if it were possible to go back to Marathon and block that deadly blow."

Perikles carefully smiles. Broad-shouldered Aischylos throws an arm around him as they head over to where Ariphron sits.

"Let's save our individual ambitions for another day, young man, and give your sweet brother some attention instead. I'm glad you brought him. Aren't you glad to have a brother like Perikles?"

Ariphron looks up and blinks over a crooked smile.

"LETO'S GLORIOUS SON WENT TO STONY PYTHO,
PLUCKING ON HIS SIMPLE HOLLOW LYRE,
AND AT THE GENTLE TOUCH OF HIS FINGER
THE GOLDEN STRINGS' SWEET SONG ENTRANCED THE GODS."
Homeros, *Hymn to Apollo*

K

Aoide is taken to the Sanctuary of Apollo at Delphi

Aoide's trip to Delphi is hidden from her at first, masked as a normal trip up to the Alkmaeonid family's seaside home on the shore of the Gulf of Qorinth, north of Athens, near the quiet beach village of Aigosthena.

The morning she is told she is leaving, and her little sister Deinomache is not also going, the two sisters hug goodbye with a rare sadness. Aoide suddenly sees her tiny sister's individuality where she had only seen a symbol before. She doesn't cry, to try to dry Deinomache's tears.

"Listen, little one. If you ever need help, go to Perikles. I know of no other men who are trustworthy. But Perikles is wise and kind. I love you, Deinomache."

"Why do you have to go?"

Aoide doesn't know, so she just shakes her head.

She has been sent to the beach house for the summer before, but always with her sisters. This time she is sent alone, with only her morose babysitter Hydna and a hired donkey-cart driver to accompany her. Hydna shows more interest in flirting with the handsome donkey-cart driver than in giving Aoide any attention. Aoide watches quietly as Attika rolls away, suspecting this might be the last she'll see of home. Relieved to leave her father, she still refuses to cry.

When they get to Aigosthena, the Gulf of Qorinth is painted pink and orange as the cloud-nude Sun Chariot sinks.

Two elderly priestesses of Apollo wearing bold, impatient expressions await them outside the Alkmaeonid beach house. Seeing the priestesses in their fine white and yellow dresses, Aoide confirms silently to herself what she had suspected on the cart ride - that she is being sent to the Sanctuary of Apollo at Delphi.

The center of the world.

"Are we going to Delphi?" she asks Hydna directly.

Hydna coldly ignores the question, which tells Aoide that she knows, and that they are.

Arriving in the mid-morning from the west, the Sanctuary of Apollo glitters with colors and unpainted marble, clinging to the mountainside like a great glorious goat.

Aoide and Hydna's journey to Delphi is mixed with excitement and trepidation for ten-year-old Aoide, as she feels the freedom from her father in the salty air on the choppy boat ride across the Qorinthian Gulf but then begins to fear the dangerous adult world of unknowns before her during the hike through sprawling olive orchards up into the Phokian mountains. The valley is filled with songs.

Finally spotting the shining tops of the colorful statues over the white polygonal wall of the sanctuary feels to ten-year-old Aoide like how she can imagine seeing a god must feel.

Delphi glows with Apollo's sunlight. The people weaving the crowd have more variety of face and hair and dress and speech than Aoide has ever witnessed, even down at the Piraeus docks back home. Many are gathered in groups around singers or instrumentalists who are practicing their art, all around and outside the sanctuary, in the presence of Apollo, God of Music.

The sanctuary itself is no bigger than a single neighborhood of Athens, clinging to the steep cliffs of Parnassos in narrow, terraced levels snaked by steep stairway paths, and surrounded by a high, square wall made of old polygonal pieces. Around that wall is a loose village of simple huts for paying pilgrims and those who service the priests. But inside the cyclopean wall of the Sanctuary appears to be more of the beauty-work of civilization - statues, paintings, treasures, and exquisite architecture - than exists in all of Athens. It is like the Olympic gathering of all the best athletes of the world, but for bronze and golden statuary celebrating civic and military and athletic heroes.

"Delphi is the center of the world," the donkey-cart driver says.

"Yeah, we know," Aoide rudely snorts.

The handsome and oblivious young man continues, "When Zeus took the throne of the gods, his first act was to survey his realm, so he sent two eagles flying from either end of Ge, the Earth, to measure her. And it was here that the birds met."

Aoide says, "That doesn't necessarily mean it's the center. Two non-identical birds won't necessarily travel at the same speed."

When they get to the gate of the sanctuary, Aoide is briefly too overwhelmed to look at anything but her feet. She starts to quietly sing to herself a comforting song. "Bright-eyed, inventive, unbending-of-heart..." she sings, invoking the virtues of Athena - the goddess she prefers and feels more comfortable with. She has never given much thought to Apollo, that quintessential Boy God.

The tall, wooden gate at the lower entrance to the sanctuary is covered with relief carvings of the many adventures of Apollo - being born on Delos with his twin sister Artemis, the infant boy killing the giant Tityos with his bow, his mother's flight with the twins from the pursuing serpent Python, the infant boy's struggle with that beast and slaying of it, his invention of the lyre, his creation of the Pythian Games as penance for slaying Python. As they enter the sanctuary, Aoide's mind sings one song over another, repeatedly interrupting itself, her eyes flitting from one fabulous artwork to the next - on one side a painting twice her height, of the heroes of the Troian War battling at that city's gates - on the other side, simultaneously beckoning her gaze, a painting just as tall, of the boy hero Bellerophon upon the winged horse Pegasos, his lead lance melting into the monstrous three-bodied Chimaera's fiery lion mouth.

"Head-born dressed in gold armor, inspiring awe in all who see," Aoide whispers.

All around, the many-minded pilgrims discuss the events of distant corners of the world, and sing out songs in praise of gods both Hellenic and foreign. More than anywhere she has been, the primary language here is song.

At first, the stones of the sanctuary appear almost furry compared to the smooth marble she is used to in Athens, until upon close inspection it becomes clear that the strange texture is actually the tiny carved prayers of priests and pilgrims which cover nearly every stone surface and column.

Just a quick scan of one section of wall beside her reveals to Aoide a flurry of the random thoughts of others from who-knows-when:

"I pray to the Goddess of the Wilds that my boy returns unharmed."

"Forgive me, Apollo, for my terrible song which everyone hated."

"Never again shall the citizens of Larissa feed the cattle of the Sun."

"I promise I will go back."

"Let my love end."

"Apollo, guide my tongue."

"How did you know you were a god?"

Aoide is so overwhelmed by the artworks and engravings that she hardly even notices when Hydna tells her goodbye, and then hands her belongings to a priest and leaves her there in his care. But when she discovers that she has indeed been left alone here, her heart suddenly fills with adventurous excitement, and that unnamed, unfaced fear of her father and his slaves beholden to him, which she has always lived with, now disappears, and the world abruptly feels brighter and richer and safer. She feels freed.

"Here Apollo slew the ancient serpent monster Python," explains the handsome young priest Therophon, whose beauty and name again remind Aoide of the hero Bellerophon who rode Pegasos. The fine-faced middle-aged priest is easy to picture commanding a noble, winged horse.

He is showing the new young priestess acolytes, all the girls Aoide's age, around their new home. The other girls seem most interested in silently sizing up each other, but Aoide's attention is focused on all the magnificent works of art that fill this sacred place.

Therophon continues, "It is said that the first worship here was of the putrid scent of the decaying carcass of the monster, which gave visions of the future to some when they smelled it. Its first supplicants were mere shepherds who discovered the remains accidentally and kept it secret for many years before a temple was built here."

Aoide is distracted from the priest's orientation by a magnificent statue of her old babysitter Hydna, standing in a pose of victorious triumph. Some text at the base describes her as the Athenian champion swimmer who swam a commando mission against the anchored Persian fleet mere days before the Battle of Salamis, swimming many miles through choppy ocean waters to secretly cut the anchor lines of the whole armada before an incoming storm, a mission which greatly wounded the fleet before that important battle. Here at Delphi a fine marble statue of the girl has been dedicated, and seeing it reminds Aoide of the first time that Hydna worked for her family, when she herself had been six years old, at a swimming tournament. In the first days of her association with their family there had been more reverence given to her heroic act, but as the years went on she became less honored in reality, and grew hard-edged and mean. It is surreal to see a statue of someone who Aoide knows to be merely mundane. Delphi is littered with beautiful statues like a battleground with the dead, but this one has captured Aoide's attention in a personal way.

She lets the magical visuals which surround her overwhelm her, and looks up at the sky, and feels like she is in an epic story.

Wild forested mountain valleys stretch out around her, and mystical Mount Parnassos looms high above, but Apollo's towering, red-columned temple is more beautiful than anything earthly, like Apollo himself, bright and soaring and confident and firm. Aoide was young enough when the Persians burned her own city's temples that she has grown up thinking of temples as ruined, blackened or white-boned things - nothing like this colossal, colorful monument. And the holy vapor that the

Pythia breathes inside, which is said to bring Apollo's voice, seems to seep even all the way out here into Aoide's nose, causing her to fall back from the group of girls she has been with and linger by this column to wonder about the smell of the god's pure knowledge.

While she inhales, she notices on a stone above the entrance to the temple are inscribed the sanctuary's three famous lines of wisdom in the biggest letters around:

> KNOW THYSELF
> AVOID EXCESS
> CERTAINTY DESTROYS

"A dung beetle crawling up the thigh of the Pythia with a Sisyphean boulder, a python coiling round the neck of the sun," belches a voice disturbed by throat nodules of unknown horror, with a waltzing iambic rhythm usually used by comic insult-poets. "We see a thing of beauty and enslave ourselves at once, though really if we had wisdom we ought instead to run."

Aoide turns her gaze from the glamor of Apollo's temple to meet the crudest, most misshapen human face she has ever seen - the very opposite of her image of handsome young Apollo. She doesn't shriek or shirk, though her eyes do automatically take a wincing defense, as the misshapen man shrugs and bows his head with modesty so that a hood falls over his half-hair.

"The poet Hipponax, of Kos," he says, "at your service. Forgive my poetic outburst, but the god struck me with inspiration. I know not what it means; nevertheless I am its slave."

She has heard of Hipponax, though his reputation is mixed. An iambic insult poet of both fame and infamy.

"So it is also with the Pythia and her oracles, I'm told," Aoide says politely, falling back to her aristocratic etiquette training, and trying to treat the deformed old man as she would any other adult. "Here, Poetry rules."

Therophon, the handsome young priest of Apollo who had been showing the new girls around the sanctuary, returns from further ahead, and can't help but grimace at Hipponax's deformed and hunchbacked visage.

"Are you alright, Aoide?" handsome Therophon asks kindly. "I just now noticed you'd fallen behind."

"The smell caught me," Aoide says, inspired by the nearness of Apollo to embrace the light of innocence and complete truth by trying to describe her mental moment very accurately, "the smell of the god's vapor. When we passed the temple.

And I was just thinking about Ambrosia, and Lykorgos, for some reason. Is that inspiration?"

Therophon shrugs, unsure how to answer, and keeps his eyes returning to Hipponax, who despite his misshapen form stands gracefully, if leaning a bit, and turns between listening respectfully with eye contact and gazing off into the surrounding vista.

"Don't worry, Aoide, you're safe here," Therophon says. "Lykorgos' kind are from ages past, like the men of bronze, of old. Modern men are more like Apollo. See here how even this fine hunchback is ennobled by Apollo's grace through poetry."

"Lykorgos killed Ambrosia, a rape gave us the grape, and so mankind's sad fate brightens Apollo's grace," rhymes Hipponax off the cuff. Then he says without singing, "At least the gods still have nectar to keep them immortal. I'd give my heart for a drink of the stuff."

Hipponax snorts, then with a single fast cough fires a large hunk of mucus into his hand, and raises the hand to show it to the sky.

"Behold, nectar of man! A bit of bile, a bit of puke, a bit of dung."

Aoide can't help but laugh at Hipponax's silly crudeness, but Therophon's frown only grows.

"Now that the vilest parts of life have been addressed, let me ask you - what do you love the most, little girl?" the malformed poet asks with a sweet narrowing of his eyes.

Aoide thinks about it for a moment, notices that the priest is listening for her answer as well as the poet, and then replies with honesty, "The smell of smoke from a hearthfire, the warmth of flame, and the beauty of the sun and clouds and stars."

With the melodramatic expressions of an actor's mask, but writ strange upon his uniquely misshapen face, Hipponax reaches over to the fire in a burning brazier attached to the exterior wall of the sanctuary, which is not far to his right, and grasps his hand into the flame as if grabbing some. Then he does the same to the smoke billowing softly up out of the fire. He smiles to Aoide, acting as if his hands are full, and he slips his full hands into the folds of his tunic, then reaches out again with both and grasps up at the sky, as if taking the sun and clouds into his very hands, and the suddenness and comedy in his gesture make Aoide burst out laughing. He brings the full hands back down to his tunic again and begins then to mime the churning of something within, hidden in the folds of his tunic, as he slowly makes his way back over to Aoide and the priest.

The particular position of the mimed churning within Hipponax's cloak makes the young priest grimace with concern about what he is about to reveal.

Once he is in front of them again, the deformed-faced poet pulls his hands out from his tunic holding a tiny, smoke-grey kitten with eyes gold like the sun and a tiny tongue like the tip of a flame.

The poet carefully extends the kitten in both hands to Aoide as a gift.

"For you," he says as she takes the tiny creature into her own hands and feels for the first time its warmth and cloud-like softness. "I found her in the woods just this morning," he explains.

The kitten's sweet innocence gives Aoide a few tears to cry, causing her to remember herself when she was much younger, and her younger sisters when they were babies. Deinomache had often asked for a kitten, which Father always denied.

"The holy ones are waiting," Therophon reminds her. "I assure you, Delphi is full of poets and musicians and every sort of person. It takes a while to learn how not to be constantly distracted by it all. But we must focus on our work for the god. And you must rejoin your fellow priestesses."

Aoide prances over to Therophon to join him, but turns once there to face Hipponax again, and says to him, "I enjoy poetry of every kind, even the comic sort. If you have a book, I'd buy one. My mother has coins."

"Worry not, young lady, I only travel on the full moon, so I'll be here all month," Hipponax sings, bowing and coming up with a tiny flower from the path. "I do not have a book, but perhaps you'll hear my howls at night!" He pops the little flower into his mouth, and, chewing it, turns and begins to hobble away down the stony path.

"The poet was very kind, but you cannot keep a cat within this sanctuary, and this is your home now. Put that beast outside the walls now," the priest commands coldly. When Aoide hesitates and cuddles the kitten closer he gets a touch warmer in his tone and adds, "Its mother will be looking for it. It will be better off in the woods where it can hunt. Come."

He beckons her to follow him over to the sanctuary's main gate, where she first arrived with Hydna, and she morosely follows him, petting the kitten and holding it up to the underside of her chin. It bats up at her face with its sharp, tiny claws, hurting just enough to stop her crying and make her giggle.

Outside the gate, Aoide walks to a sunny spot by some flower bushes where she imagines the delicate creature will be safe, or that its mother might find it, and she places it gently down in the grass. It rolls over onto its tiny paws and stumble walks over to her foot, but Aoide runs back to the gate and the priest before it can touch her and decimate her heart again.

"I promise, Aoide," says the handsome priest, "most poets are not also monsters."

"Maybe the hunchback just shows that Apollo sees more colors of beauty than we can," Aoide supposes with a sniffle of tears.

The priest Therophon looks at her quietly for a long time, seeming to try to read her like a book, even scanning left and right, then finally takes her hand and says carefully but sternly, "Perhaps you should start listening more than speaking, Aoide. Follow me now and join the other girls, and I want you to keep silent the rest of the night. You will hear the gods best in silence."

Smaller and smaller, the kitten watches her go.

"TAKE PLEASURE AND HAIL DIONYSOS WINE-DARK!
NO ONE COULD SEPARATE MY MIND FROM YOURS AS I
BUILD THE BEAUTIFUL COSMIC ORDER OF MY SONG!"
Homeros, *Hymn to Dionysos*

Λ

Perikles sits in on a rehearsal of Aischylos' play

In a meadow of wind-dancing grass with a broad, bright view of the colorfully painted complex of the Sanctuary of Demeter at Eleusis and the glittering sea beyond, Aischylos and his chorus practice this year's plays. Perikles, as producer, sits in to listen.

Bald-topped Aischylos is leaning over his script scroll in the grass, reading quickly and whispering the lines to himself while the chorus, a group of twelve identically costumed singers, gathers in a row on a large flat rock which is sitting in for a stage. The chorus are dressed fabulously as Persian elders, with embroidered tunics and eastern eye makeup.

Perikles paces nearby, stretching his limbs and enjoying the beauty of nature while he waits. Eyeing Eleusis, Perikles asks, "Tell me, Aischylos - as a boy here at Eleusis, did you ever run into Dionysos in the forest?"

"A priest will tell you," Aischylos says in an annoyed tone, "Dionysos lives in the vine itself. But please, Perikles, I am trying to read."

On the stage stone, many-faced Sophokles, dressed as Atossa in full Persian makeup and balancing a tall, elaborate Persian woman's wig, walks up to the leader of the chorus, a young man named Penander, with a wry smile. He lifts Penander's skirt and smacks his butt, at which Penander laughs and starts to chase Sophokles around the stage stone trying to smack his butt in retaliation. This leads to everyone in the chorus giggling and trying to smack each other's butts, at which point Aischylos turns back to his actors.

"That's enough, everyone!" Aischylos barks. "Sophokles, are you ready?"

Sophokles says, "Unlike you, I've memorized your lines. Penander, we begin!" Sophokles jumps to the side of the rock, then steps dramatically into the space like an entering queen, hand held aloft.

Penander begins, "Hail, Queen of Persia, mother of our Lord Xerxes, consort of the Great Dareios..."

Aischylos barks, "No no no, Penander. Sophokles is neither queen nor director. It is me you listen to. We won't start at the beginning today. You chorus understand your roles already. It's Atossa we need to work on."

Sophokles gestures dramatically as if casting a spell. "Very well then. Honey, milk, wine, oil - and rise, Dareios!"

Aischylos has a moment where he weighs the value of trying to assert control again, but quickly decides against it and steps up onto the stage stone. "Okay ... I'm the Ghost of the barbarian King of Kings, Dareios. Son of Kyros the Great. Summoned from the shadows of Haides. Wearing that fantastic mask Anaxandra is working on..." He mimes putting on a mask, the gesture instinctive in his muscle memory, and steps onto the stage stone with a grimace on his face like he imagines his ghost mask will have. He is deeply into his role, and seamlessly moves in and out of it as he acts and directs.

"Atossa, my living Queen!" hisses broad-shouldered Aischylos as the ghost of the Persian King Dareios. "Since you've pulled me with your grief from realms below ... Speak!"

Many-faced Sophokles slips quickly into a melodramatic performance with just a touch of comedy mocking Persian female stereotypes and replies, as Queen Atossa, "O, Dareios, graced with all the riches and power of the world while living ... You are blessed now to be below, for ruin of every kind has befallen your beloved land of Persia!"

Dareios' ghost recoils, "Ruin - how? By Pestilence? Or faction's furious storm?"

Queen Atossa replies, "Neither. By follisome royal adventuring, our troops all perished at distant Athens!"

Aischylos waits a beat or two and whispers to himself, "Pause for applause ..." then continues as Dareios, "Which of my noble sons led the forces there?"

"Xerxes, and by depleting each of your lands of their people!"

"Was this rash attempt made by land or by sea?"

"Both, by a double front."

"A host composed of all our peoples - how could he march to Hellas, across the Sea of Aegeos?"

Sophokles cries, "Your royal son built a colossal bridge of boats across the Hellespont from shore to shore!"

Aischylos moans, "What! Can men now chain the very Bosporos?"

Sophokles says, "I am sure some god must have helped him."

Perikles jumps up excitedly, energized by the play. "That's a great line," he remarks. "Minimize the ingenuity and courage they actually showed there."

"Damn it, Perikles - you stepped on one of my best lines," Aischylos shouts, angered to be pulled out of his own mind. "Dareios next snaps, 'Some god who clouded his better judgment!' and it should resonate through the veterans in our audience who helped fight back the King of Kings."

"I won't interrupt again. Proceed!" Perikles sits back in the grass.

"Sophokles, let's jump back to when I'm the messenger arriving with news from Salamis."

Sophokles ignores Aischylos, leaning against Penander such that Penander must also lean to even out the center of gravity. Sophokles takes a wildflower from behind Penander's ear and melodramatically plucks its petals.

"What's wrong now?" Aischylos sighs.

Sophokles grunts and pulls his fake breasts out of his Persian shirt, jumping down from the stage stone into the grass, where he kicks off his Persian spats. "This isn't a tragedy, it's a bore. Why write, why perform a story, where the characters are ordinary people, people living today, when there are such magnificent stories and characters to choose from in legend! So many stories have yet to be told in tragedy - consider! Why dip the sacred ladle of creativity into the toilet of reality!? So that I can play some turd like Atossa."

"Come on, Sophokles, put your breasts back in your dress and get back on the stone with the chorus. You're getting paid well. Don't forget the real reason for the season, Dionysos!" Perikles says as he stands and gestures with a footlong wooden sculpture of a hard dick religiously wrapped in ivy.

M

Kimon seeks the wisdom of the Pythian Oracle at Delphi

Kimon rides his best horse Arion north out of Attika, traveling alone, over the low slopes of the western side of Mount Kithairon, past high Plataia where a *tropion* of bodiless armor mounted onto crossed spears still marks the site where the tide turned at the land battle where Hellenic citizen-soldiers finally pushed back the barbarian army of Xerxes. Then northwest across Boeotia and into Phokis, wearing his long cloak and tall boots, keeping the mountains of Parnassos on his right and the Gulf of Qorinth on his left. Arion's bright white coat makes those they pass bow, or sometimes spit, in recognition that the rider must be rich.

After camping for one night in an olive-filled, star-ceilinged valley, he finally arrives at the bustling temple complex of Delphi late in the morning, surrounded by bellowing merchants and curious pilgrims. The stone cliffs and grassy terraces of Mount Parnassos rise steeply behind the sanctuary, gleaming green and grey in the bright daylight.

To the old stone herm at the last turn off the road, Kimon touches his dick and gives a salute before continuing. Each man in the crowd passing the herm stops there a moment and makes that same gesture - they touch their crotch, and salute the statue with a hand to their forehead.

Kimon gives the horse-tender at the gate a fine Athenian silver coin and a long intimidating glance.

Inside the walled sanctuary Kimon pauses. He stands there in the broad entry plaza where pilgrims gather to worship around an ancient statue of the wooden horse which Odysseos used to fool the Troians centuries ago. Two men argue over whether the statue itself is actually ancient or if it was just created recently and made to appear old. Kimon stands beholding the horse and tries to focus his mind against the noise of the crowd. He takes from around his neck an amulet with phrases carved in miniature by Elpinike, and kisses it, then raises his head back to the sunshine and brightly colored treasure-houses lining the busy zig-zagging stepped road up to the Oracle.

Another pilgrim, secretly selling amulets out of his tunic, gets very close to Kimon and tells him, "That amulet is worthless, but this one has real magic!"

Kimon quickly whispers, "I'm Kimon of Athens and my beloved gave me this."

"Let all gods hear, but Zeus and Athena particularly, that I repent wholeheartedly the terrible mistaken assumption I just made," the amulet seller tremblingly mutters.

"We're good," Kimon spits, releasing the man, who hurries away to a distant corner of the sanctuary before finding someone else to harass.

Kimon steadily ascends the wide sacred steps, ignoring the small but fabulous treasure houses that line the way, in which individual city-states throughout Hellas, and noble families, each have their own space for various devotional sculptures, precious treasures and wondrous items such as sets of gleaming armor and jewel-inlaid weapons. Most of the pilgrims around him are chatting about the treasures, but Kimon's mind is elsewhere.

As he gets close to the plaza at the top of the ascent, his attention is stolen by a call from behind him, in a familiar voice that he hasn't heard since he was in Ionia - Pausanias, a fellow commander of Hellenic forces in Ionia.

"Hail, son of Miltiades, of Athens!"

Kimon turns to see the Spartan in full armor, trudging up the Delphic path behind himself, with an entourage of several armorless long-haired Spartans following around him. Kimon knows that Pausanias is the regent of one of Sparta's boy kings, being the king's cousin and nephew of the Spartan hero Leonidas, and for the past several years he has been in the east, helping the Ionian Hellenic cities to shake the bonds of Persia, an effort in which he had been allied with Kimon's own efforts of recent years.

"Pausanias," Kimon acknowledges, nodding respectfully. "You have returned home to Hellas at last."

"Summoned," Pausanias explains, approaching Kimon but then stopping just too far away to shake hands, and standing with his arms akimbo. "To give my account of the work you and I have been doing in Ionia, killing Persians."

"Indeed," Kimon nods. "Last year, at the Strymon River, my own men had a hard-fought but useful victory. Now Xerxes' finest general Artabanos has no sway west of Sardis. For men like us know it is generals, not kings, who guide the tides of civilization."

Pausanias bows at the wisdom, then says, "I have just come from conquered Byzantion, where we installed a council of Hellenic-speaking Oligarchs."

Kimon sees the attempt to debate Oligarchy against Democracy, and attempts to avoid it. He says, "We may not all run our cities the same way, but Hellenic means civilized, if you ask me. The barbarians of Byzantion will call themselves Hellenic by choice before long, I'm sure."

The two men stop at the top of the ascent, where in the center of a small stone plaza stands the colossal, spiral, bronze Serpent Column which rises to a tripod of three serpent heads balancing a huge ornate bronze cauldron of fire. Beneath the Serpent Column is an inscription, dedicating it to the success over the Persians by *"ALL-HELLENES"*.

"Do you remember when this Serpent Column was first dedicated here, Athenian?"

Kimon says, "Of course," stoically.

"This dedication was not to 'All-Hellenes', but to *me*, Pausanias of Sparta, as the leader at the true battle which turned the tide of Persia's invasion - not at Salamis, but at Plataia, on land, fighting with spears and shields like heroes, not on boats like fishermen. It was your long god-hated Athenian Alkmaeonids, who recently put so much money into rebuilding this sanctuary, who changed the dedication, from the true hero to 'All-Hellenes', as if that wretch there has anything to do with the greatness of Hellas." Pausanias points to a hunchbacked old man with a half-deformed face - the insult-poet Hipponax - who sits on a bench not far away, scribbling at a small scroll and giggling foolishly to himself.

Kimon says, eyeing the hunchbacked poet Pausanias has indicated, "I wonder sometimes whom the gods prefer - the general or the soldier. This wretched man reminds me of a soldier of mine whom we called Ajax the Late, because he often claimed to be late to a party in Haides. He would always put himself into the fray, deflecting arrows and blows with his body, and saving countless other men over the years with his insane courage."

"Where is Ajax the Late now?" Pausanias asks with a laugh.

"At the party he'd been late for, I presume."

Pausanias nods with a grim smile. "We take up the bronze knowing we will die by it."

"So they say," Kimon nods stone-faced, picturing some of the men he has led who died violently, and the men he's killed.

"The priests make me wait," Pausanias sniffs. "They say the goat I brought didn't shudder properly, so they can say the god is not ready to give me an oracle yet, while they take the time to find out what their spies have heard about me from Ionia. I'm to wait until the hour before sunset to try sprinkling the goat again. So we've been waiting by the sunshadow spike down near the merchant stalls so my men can stay fed."

"I go to find out how the goat feels, myself, now," Kimon says. "Good luck, Spartan."

Pausanias silently nods, then simply stands and watches Kimon head up to the priests of Apollo and the sacred goat that the priest already holds on a line, having received it earlier in the day from the slaves Kimon traveled with. Kimon looks back at Pausanias once after leaving him, and wonders about the strange glimmer in Pausanias' eye.

"Kimon of Athens," Kimon says, introducing himself to the priest with the goat, glancing briefly back to the Spartan regent who is watching him across the plaza of stone. "I wish to receive an oracle from the Pythia."

The priest holding the goat tightens his tether to the creature to steady it, as another priest hold out a long water-sprinkling wand with holes at one end, and shakes it a couple of times over the beast. The goat shudders as the water falls on its back, and bleats softly. The priest holding the goat nods to the other beside Kimon.

"The god is ready for you right away," the priest tells Kimon. "Enter the temple of Apollo. The Pythia awaits within."

Kimon strides with religious gravity toward the Oracle's temple, from which smoke is emanating, trying not to look back at Pausanias but wondering if he is still watching him.

On the stone above the entrance to the temple are inscribed the sanctuary's famous lines, which Kimon thinks about briefly before entering:

ATHENS

KNOW THYSELF
AVOID EXCESS
CERTAINTY DESTROYS

    Inside the Pythian Oracle's temple, even in the sunlight of day, it is shaded and hazy. Glitteringly-adorned priests and priestesses of Apollo line the path to the Pythia - a simply clad young woman in a diaphanous white dress, seated on a three-legged golden stool over a prominent crack in the stone floor, through which invisible divine vapors supposedly seep.

    Kimon sniffs, smells primarily body odor, and closes his eyes momentarily with inner blasphemous dismay.

    The Pythia sits casually with one foot under herself on the stool, her neck loose like one who has drunk wine. She appears to be more in her own mental world than partaking in her surroundings.

    Her face looks strange to Kimon for a moment, until he realizes it is because she is not wearing any make-up.

    Kimon approaches and kneels in front of the Pythia.

    One of the priestesses lights a fire in a brazier, then covers the fire with an ornate metal cage, filling the room with smoke and weird dancing shadows.

    In a deep voice the oldest priest says, "Kimon, son of Miltiades, of Athens. Is it your own fate, or your city's, that you've come for?"

    The lovely-cheeked Pythia lowers her wide eyes to find his, and Kimon sees what he imagines to be the wildness of natural divinity in them.

    Kimon lowers his head in thoughtful prayer.

    He says, "Not my city's. But nor my own."

> "I KNOW THE NUMBER OF THE SANDS,
> AND THE MEASURE OF THE SEA.
> I UNDERSTAND THE SPEECH OF THE DUMB,
> AND HEAR THE VOICELESS."
> Pythia, *Oracle for Kroisos of Lydia*

N

Elpinike and Kallias discuss an arrangement at a sanctuary of Artemis

Hidden in the forested slopes of Mount Kithairon and nestled under the cliffs of the rocky mountainside that looms above, a secret, secluded spring creates a small reed-rounded grotto where a secretive cult of teen-aged priestesses of Artemis Who-Soothes maintain a natural forest shrine. Water trickles down the rocks of the cliffside that looms behind, into an ever-rippling pool of milky, mineral-rich water. This night, torchlight illuminates the few ancient wooden sculptures which the priestesses have stood up around the pool to represent the Wild Goddess and her animal attendants.

Reclining nude in the pool's milky waters is the stolid noblewoman Elpinike. Eight young slave-girls dressed as priestesses hover around the pool tending to her bath needs. The two farthest from the water, nearest to the entrance of someone arriving to the grotto, are armed with tall hunting bows and watch the darkness of the forest around.

Slowly, heard first crunching through the moon-dark shadows, the form of a man begins to approach. The two front priestesses knock their bows at the ready. Elpinike, reclining in the pool, waves her attendants away, and they return to positions circling the pool, while Elpinike herself remains reclining mostly under the surface.

Out of the darkness, Kallias strides into the torchlight wonder-struck, unsure which priestess is more worthy of ogling until he finally notices Elpinike reclining in the natural pool. Kallias, dressed in hunter's garb and boots, stares with lusty awe at Elpinike's barely-obscured beauty.

"I've come. I sacrificed a stag, and I'm dressed as a hunter," he relays, "just as you asked."

Bronze-eyed Elpinike edges forward in the water, a solid grasp on him with her eyes. "You are Aktaion," she declares. "Ancient hunter, lost in the woods. You've stumbled upon this sacred spring, and the wild goddess Artemis, with her nymphs." She knowingly lets one nipple escape the surface of the milky water for the briefest moment.

Kallias says, "So I see."

"Do you believe the gods take human form within us, Kallias?"

Kallias eyes the enchanted surroundings, well maintained by the priestesses for instilling just such awe. "I do believe the goddess is here."

"As a man of no nobility, you cannot know what it is like to be a demigod, to be born of the gods," she says.

Kallias doesn't know what to say, and Elpinike inches forward more, maintaining her paralyzing eye contact.

Elpinike explains, "I have had the gods inside me before, as I do now. You are speaking to, you are looking at, Artemis. The wild goddess of the hunt. Who for seeing bathe, Aktaion transformed into a stag and was shredded by his own dogs."

She stands from the pool, very slowly covering herself with her hands, and only once she does so do her slave attendants finally begin to step into the pool toward her with a dress to wrap around her wet body.

Kallias stutters, "I will pay the city the debt you inherited from your father. I would pay it twice. I must have you as my wife."

Elpinike explains, "You will pay our father's debt … and I will be your wife. But not yet. I will not be purchased."

Kallias cocks his head with a moment of confusion, as Elpinike continues.

"You'll pay our debt as a gesture of friendship to Kimon, and you'll let everyone in the city know how much you respect him, and that is why you wanted to pay his debt." Elpinike walks up to Kallias, her priestesses still aiming their knocked arrows right at him. "Then in two years time, I'll become your wife. But the two are not related. And if you ever say they are, I swear with the heart of the goddess Artemis herself you will be transformed into a stag just like arrogant Aktaion, and may the gods this time send something worse than dogs to shred your flesh."

Kallias eyes the arrows pointed at him, then the fabric clinging to Elpinike's wet body, looks into her eyes and finds the seriousness of her soul, and he nods.

Ξ

Perikles marches in the Dionysian festival parade as a play producer

Amidst the rowdy pomp parade of the Dionysian festival which waits lined up to begin their march, the young Athenian men whose duty is to carry big wooden penises on the tops of tall poles are intermixed and flirting with the many young Athenian maidens carrying amphorae of water and flower baskets, while a priest of Dionysos chastises those struggling to pull a cart carrying a giant stone penis the size of two men curled up together.

    Swift-eyed Perikles, broad-shouldered Aischylos, and bright-faced Sophokles stand with their chorus, dancers, and musicians in the parade line, waiting on the organizers at the head of the parade to signal the beginning. Everyone is in a religiously raucous party mood, many drunk already, with musicians banging drums and playing double flutes and lyres all around.

    As producer of one of the plays, Perikles wears multiple layers of bright robes and ritual amulets. Ahead of them, with Choerilos' group, Thukydides is dressed the same but more comfortable with it.

    Perikles says, "Parading through the city dressed like this may be the greatest sacrifice I will ever make for a god. I hope Dionysos is happy."

    Aischylos remarks good naturedly, "How could Dionysos not be happy? Just look at all these dicks and flower baskets!"

    Phrynichos and his son Polyphrasmon and their actors leave their producer for a moment to approach Aischylos and his crew from further back in the procession.

    Sophokles dryly jokes as they approach, "Here comes another kind of parade of dicks."

    Polyphrasmon chides, "Are we going to revisit Xerxes' defeat every four years now? Or is the history presented in your play actually the writing of my father's own tragedy? Sophokles, do you play the Muse who gave Aischylos this clever idea?"

    White-bearded old Phrynichos eyeballs Perikles as he speaks, but is clearly also addressing Aischylos who stands beside him. "Phineas, his only food rotted by the harpies - this, I imagine, describes your imagination while trying to write. And

Glaukos, eaten by his own horses, is a perfect choice to follow your plagiarism. Perikles, you are Glaukos, and your ambition is your horse. You feed it Aischylos."

Phrynichos and his crew retreat back into the crowd, finding their place further back in line again behind some basket-carrying maidens.

Sophokles admits, "He has Hermes' way with words."

Aischylos grimaces at Perikles.

The head priest of Dionysos signals to start the parade, and a great shouting and banging of drums begins that does not stop, and only increases, as the great Dionysian procession with its young women carrying water jugs and baskets of flowers and young men balancing hand-carved penises on the ends of high poles slowly begins to spread forward like a mile-long inchworm just beginning to stretch its body at the front.

Garlanded men and women dance in and out of the crowd, drinking from every imaginable container, as the parade makes its way through the gate and into the city.

All around, dicks are shaken joyously, both real and effigial.

O

Aischylos, Sophokles, and their chorus put on Aischylos' plays

Men, women, and children of Athens find their seats in the makeshift wooden stands of the Dionysian theater on the slopes beneath the rocky Akropolis, which looms behind them. Everything has been festooned with colorful flags and flowers.

Perikles and Aischylos watch from from within the narrow, temporary *skene* building which serves as backdrop to the orchestra, the circular central stage where presently the yearly tribute from the League of Delos - wealth, silver, gold, statues - is being laid out by the monthly councilors to the greedy applause of the crowds.

Perikles turns back to Aischylos after peering out through a tear in the fabric skene wall. "By Dionysos, all of Hellas is here. The theater looks so much bigger from the stage!"

Aischylos, more accustomed to the moment, nods with his arms folded. "And we're forced to follow the people's true favorite - treasure!"

Vendors walk among the crowd selling wine, bowls of soup, and whole fishes.

Before the play goes on, a priest of Dionysos gets the attention of the noisy crowd. "Please, Athenians, bring your attention now to the first tragedy by Aischylos! Please, Athenians, for the health of all our penises, show respect to Dionysos! Your attention please! Thank you."

First come the drums. At that the crowd hushes quickly, some holding up and waggling little wooden phalluses in worship of Dionysos. The chorus line, dressed as Thrakian courtiers in spotted panther skins, come out dancing all in a line, as the musicians clustered around the skene play their most excitement-building sounds in spiraling melodic rhymes.

Sophokles and Penander lead the chorus in the first of Aischylos' plays, *Phineas*. Behind them, musicians provide an accompanying sonic backdrop featuring soft drums and the eerie whine of several double-flutes. Many-faced Sophokles is dressed and masked as the hero Iason, famed for sailing with his Argonauts to pursue the golden ram's skin, and Aischylos is King Phineas, cursed king whom the Argonauts have met on their journey, wearing a mask with blood caked around the eyes and acting as if vile, monstrous harpies are swooping down on him.

"As you can see, Iason, the moment I try to feed myself from this sumptuous feast the wretched harpies menace me again!"

In the stands, Ephialtes leans over to Perikles with a quizzical look. "I don't understand how you meant this to speak to the veterans of Salamis."

Perikles grins and explains, "No, not this one, it's the second play that will resonate."

The whole city-audience is hushed excitedly for the second play.

Sophokles' high-wigged Queen Atossa asks, "Indulge me, friends, where and in what climate do the towers of this city called Athens rise?"

The crowd whistles at the mention of their city. Perikles smiles.

Aischylos directs from the edge of the stage while Penander leads the chorus of Persian elders in a conversation with Sophokles as the Persian Queen Atossa.

Penander, as leader of the Persian nobles which make up the play's chorus, responds, "Far in the west, my Queen, where the imperial sun sets."

Sophokles struts about the stage in his fine costume, wig, and queen mask. "And yet my son willed the conquest of this town?"

Penander says, "May all the states of Hellas bend to his power!"

The whole audience holds a potent silence at this vocalization of worship to Xerxes' imperial authority. Perikles waits through it nervously.

Sophokles asks, "Can they send numbers of men to the field?"

Penander says, "Numbers that the Medes have recently wrought much woe."

All groan and boo at the mention of the Medes.

"What does this have to do with Dionysos?" someone shouts from the stands.

Sophokles is a consummate professional and unflustered by the crowd, though Penander gets a bit shaken, and eyes the audience nervously. Sophokles-as-Queen-Atossa continues, "And do they have sufficient treasures in their houses?"

Penander replies, "Their rich earth yields a fountain of silver."

The miners in the audience hoot. Kallias cheers his own wealth.

Sophokles asks, "From the strong bow wing they the barbed shaft?" and mimes feyly firing a bow, at which many laugh.

"Ares forbid!" a random veteran in the audience shouts, followed by some soldierly grunting from many.

Penander says, "They grasp only the stout spear and heavy shield."

The soldiers in the audience bark and stamp their feet with pride.

Sophokles' Atossa asks, "What monarch reigns there? Whose command do they follow?"

Penander says, "Slaves to no lord, Queen, they follow no kingly power."

All the Democrats whoop with pride, while the Oligarchs grumble and whisper.

Sophokles asks, "How then can they fight the invading foe?"

Penander replies, "Some way that spreads havoc through even the numerous and glittering host surrounding the King of Kings."

Everyone in the audience cheers with civic pride, surrounded still by buildings burned by the invading Persians eight years ago.

Sophokles shudders, "You speak to put fear in a mother's breast!"

"You better fear, crone!" a random angry voice barks from the audience. "Maybe next time we'll invade your lands!"

The veterans in the audience all laugh and cheer. Perikles looks over at Ephialtes with a grin.

Later in the same play, Aischylos performs as a messenger, wearing a classic sad mask, while Sophokles continues as the beautiful and terrifying Atossa, wearing her mask painted in the many colors of Persian makeup.

With the audience on the edge of their benches now and the double-flutes laying down a rhythmically evolving background melody, Aischylos' Messenger sings, "...but behind that first squadron came their whole fleet! And only then we heard from every part this voice of exhortation led by their Democratic leader Themistokles and sung with courage by every man:

Advance, sons of Hellas! Protect your land,
  your wives, your sons, your very gods, from slavery!
Protect the sacred graves of all your honored dead!
  Today the common cause of all demands your strength!

As he recants Themistokles' war paean, the veterans in the audience who were there chant along with it in a patriotic fervor, and in natural reaction to that audience joy Sophokles actually repeats the chant a second time. Aischylos is at first furious at the improvised choice, but becomes elated when the crowd joins in with the song.

Advance, O sons of Hellas! Save your land,
  your wives, your sons, your very gods, from slavery!
Protect the sacred graves of all your honored dead!
  Today the common cause of all demands your strength!

Perikles looks around himself with awe at the excited applause. Ephialtes nudges Perikles to point out, across the audience from them, Kimon among the veterans who are chanting along with the words. Kimon seems to chant the words just to join the veterans around him, but is not necessarily happy to be doing so.

Ephialtes grins and says to Perikles, nudging his elbow, "Kimon sings himself to exile."

Sophokles' Atossa wails, "O what a boundless sea of woe hath burst upon Persia and the whole barbaric race!" with his hands at the sides of his mask as if clutching at his hair.

The crowd whoops and applauds, many rising to shout at Atossa.

By the time the last of the three main plays, *Glaukos*, is performed, with Sophokles as King Glaukos and Aischylos as Herakles, the audience is far more excited by *The Persians* than by this old familiar fable, and there is much disrespectful discussion of the previous play in the stands throughout this final one.

At the center of the theater, Sophokles hisses from behind his King Glaukos mask, "It is manflesh, Herakles, that makes my horses so fierce in battle, and so successful at the races! I fear nothing now!"

Aischylos uses the opportunity of playing Herakles to flex his muscles on stage.

Those in the crowd who are still paying attention groan with horror and delight, while Aischylos' workout buddies effuse praise for the might and courage of that widely-beloved hero Herakles Protector-From-Evil.

At the end of the day, after the children have been taken home by their mothers and it is primarily only drunk men left in the audience, the final play of the day that wraps up the trilogy is called *Prometheos the Fire-Lighter*. The long-held tradition is that the final play of the day is always a bawdy erotic-comic farce focused mainly on the opportunity to flash its actors dicks, to the roaring delight of the crowd. Many wear false, hollow, wooden ones tied to their hips, but the audience always reacts most strongly to those occasional few brave enough to display the real thing.

To raise the quality at least a bit, this performance includes an elaborate contraption of flowy red and orange veils representing the Fire which Prometheos stole from Hestia on Olympos to give to his creation, Man.

Bright-cheeked Sophokles, as the satyr who is usually found in these sort of plays, tries to hump the fire, while Aischylos as Prometheos chastises him and the audience cackles with laughter.

Sophokles' satyr shouts, "Your friend is almost *too* hot, Prometheos!"

Aischylos' Prometheos chastises, "Careful, you randy satyr, or you will mourn for your beard!"

The satyr chorus meanwhile all chase each other in circles wearing false wooden erections and playing at trying to slap each other's butts, just like they rehearsed back in the field at Eleusis.

Π

Athenians celebrate the winners of the Dionysian theatrical competition

The Agora is a sprawling revelry of drunk Athenians in the aftermath of the long day of plays of the Dionysia. All across the Agora, groups are gathered, chatting and laughing, or playing street games, or dancing and singing and parading from doorway to doorway together in lines called *komoi*, all drinking or drunk, many passed out in the street, sleeping in grassy patches and doorways, as the long day of plays fades into a revelrous evening of partying.

Hipponax and Kratinos lead a komoi line of insult poets who are quickly fading into nonsense the drunker they get throughout the night.

Two veterans walk arm in arm, sipping from the same bowl of wine.

"Here's to Aischylos! Winner of the ivy for showing Dionysos how boring men and women can be!"

"He won fair and square. It wasn't just a telling of the battle. It was a profound meditation on a mother's grief."

"It wasn't about Atossa, it was about Dareios! His failure as a father, whose son repeated his own hubris at Marathon!"

Themistokles appears out of the crowd and spills wine on them both as he hugs them from behind with cup-bearing hands.

"Fools," says the big-bearded man-shepherd, "it was about us and our great wooden wall of ships! Think of the drowned tonight as you drown in wine!"

They all drink together and quickly fall from a three-way hug of joy to a three-way hug of shared moroseness.

Nearby, lion-hearted Kimon has Sophokles cornered between a large, tight group of revelers and the side of a public building and is trying to spread the charm thickly.

"You were the queen of the day," Kimon whispers. "Only a young Athenian man could bring such beauty and grace to an old Persian woman."

Many-faced Sophokles replies coyly, "Easterners call her the most beautiful woman in the world."

Kimon says, "Money can buy nearly any words. Barbarians don't know what real beauty is."

Across the Agora, Aischylos, wearing the winner's crown of ivy, nudges Perikles and points out the intimate moment happening between Sophokles and Kimon.

Aischylos remarks, "Kimon cannot know what he's getting into."

Perikles adds, "The last thing we need is Sophokles using his gift as an actor in propaganda for the Oligarchs. Kimon saw our move. He'll try to match it."

Aischylos looks to Perikles to gauge how drunk he is. "You mistake me for Ephialtes. He's over there."

Proving himself drunk, Perikles happily slurs as he gazes into space, remembering the glory of the theater he just witnessed, "We did it, Ephialtes. Did you see Kimon himself singing along to the song of the soldiers, in honor of Themistokles? He could not but sing along - whether through a veteran's noble memory of War or through knowing those with such honor were watching him, it doesn't matter."

Aischylos looks away. "We should propose to the Assembly a monument to the genius of Aischylos."

Perikles says, "That's a funny idea. We'll see if our win pays off at the Assembly next month."

"I'll celebrate your win, then, with my chorus."

Aischylos leaves Perikles and heads over to Penander and the chorus, who are surrounded by a big group of fans.

One angry man is badgering Penander at the edge of the group. "You want to bring all of Hellas under Persian control, huh?"

Penander protests uncomfortably, looking around for help from his fellow actors, "Not me, sir! The words belong to the mask! Writer, save me!"

Sitting on a rise of grass nearby, Anaxagoras sits with old Oenopides, the only sober one, as the two men watch the drunken crowd with a smiles, chatting about the names of the stars and their constellations.

P

Athenians hold one last debate at the Pnyx before voting on whom to exile

A crowded constellation of Attikans is gathered on the hill of the Pnyx, murmuring with nervous energy as they prepare to vote for an ostracism.

This year's herald, with one hand on his tall, double-snake-headed staff and one foot on the bema, looks around with a grimace that reflects the tension of the moment. "Start the water clock once someone takes the platform. Who'll speak? Line up!"

Themistokles pushes to the front of the loose line that has begun to form, and steps up onto the bema. Beside the bema, the time official pulls a stopper which starts one jar pouring into another.

The big-bearded man-shepherd boldly declares, "I can read this city like a mother her clan. I know what you fear. But do not confuse the ostrakon for the sword! All you can cut with an ostrakon is your own collective wrists. Kleisthenes intended the ostracism to be a tool to use against men who gather too much power! No one in this city is so powerful that they should be exiled for their hubris."

Themistokles looks over at Kimon, who waits to speak at the bema next, and Elpinike who stands beside him, gracefully ignoring the ogles and whispers that her presence creates.

"Eight years ago, the free men of Athens defeated the greatest empire that the Earth has ever known…"

The whole Athenian Assembly cheers.

"…and that day, the ancient world ended! These past eight years we have seen the childhood of the modern world, perhaps even of a new kind of humanity! The future is Athenian - the future is Delian - the future is democracy! And now every city across the sea knows it.

"Miltiades, the last man we might have feared become a tyrant, is dead. We should build a shrine to Nemesis in his name and be done with ostracism for good. But since the city has already decided to hold this vote, know that those of us who wish to keep power in the hands of the whole Assembly plan to write the letters K-I-M-O-N."

Friends of Kimon, soldiers, and conservatives all grumble.

Elpinike, who legally shouldn't be there but is rich and beautiful enough that no one is willing to chastise her to her face, pushes past the stoically growling Kimon and speaks the words he won't. She does not ascend the bema, but puts a hand on it and stands beside it, and projects her voice louder than any man yet. "In fact you prove the fears of the democracy, Themistokles," Elpinike says, eyeing the crowd with a wry smile like a poet expecting a laugh, "by having accumulated so much power from so little nobility." She tries to act like she was just passing by, and had to speak.

The Assembly roars with murmurs, cheers and laughter.

Themistokles eyes the crowd, at once trying to read it and intimidate it with the particular mad genius he has gotten good at projecting.

Graceful Elpinike, knowing the expectations on her as a woman, does not linger long at the bema, but steps back behind Kimon with a noblewoman's conspicuous demurity. The official at the water jars replaces the pouring jar with a full one.

Someone in the back of the crowd shouts, "Let's ostracize Kimon, and Elpinike too!"

Themistokles continues speaking. "We emerge from the two Persian Wars as the strongest city in the Hellenic world. Sparta, who feel they previously held that position, are jealous of our rise, and aim to bring us down. Kimon, our ambassador to that war-loving city, would have us be like them, and would turn our democracy back into an Oligarchy. But under *my* leadership, we have built up our navy, defeated the world's expansionist superpower, and ended up in control of the very Sea itself! And thanks to my clever gambits, where Sparta would have us tear down our fine walls that keep us safe, I managed to trick them into delaying while we finished building! And now, we are strong *and* safe. Do not turn to Sparta, but look to Athena."

Themistokles steps down from the bema as the voice of the crowd rises.

"Vote! Vote! Vote!" the assembled crowd begins to chant.

The herald nods and ascends the bema, waving down the shouting with his snake staff. Kimon, however, steps up and takes the bema from him. The official at the water clock starts it pouring.

"I have only been general to some of you, so perhaps many of you think of me only as the son of Miltiades."

From the crowd, the broad-mouthed Democrat Tolmides shouts, "Miltiades eats ass in the house of Haides!"

Toothy Tolmides just looks at Kimon, waiting to see his reaction. Quickly seeing the remark as the attempt to bait him that it is, Kimon ignores it with two blinks of a lion's patience.

Sunken-eyed Myronides, standing beside Tolmides, slaps him in the back of the head for being so crude about the dead.

Kimon continues, "I'm no politician or philosopher. But as a general, I know that we must never look back, but always keep our eyes aimed forward. Themistokles has his anchor laid firmly at his now eight-year-old glory, and in order to keep your memory on that night, he slows the process or even directly fights the reconstruction of the Akropolis. So that now, the bones of our great and ancient King Theseos have no appropriate sacred home to rest in, but instead sit like scrolls on a shelf. And yes, I am a friend to Sparta, and I do admire their military and social self-control. We need not fear friendship with Sparta! Are not two strong men stronger when they are friends, than when they must fear each other's attacks?"

Kimon sees the water clock slowing and finishes while there's still flow, to seem succinct.

Themistokles ascends the bema again as Kimon descends. The official at the water clock struggles to switch jars quickly.

"Fools may believe you brought the bones of Theseos home, Kimon, but the wiser are the majority here. I will not deny the great military victories you've brought this city, but don't keep claiming some kind of religious authority from some poor giant's skeleton."

Themistokles addresses the Assembly, turning from Kimon.

"When I was a boy, my father showed me the hulks of two triremes on the shore. Warriors of the city, in wood. They had not wrecked, or been burned, but had been decommissioned and neglected, despite the great strength they represented for the people who had invested so much in building them. This, he warned me, was also the fate of those who try to lead men."

"Vote! Vote! Vote! Vote!"

"Have you so quickly forgotten the days before Salamis? The days after? This is why we haven't rebuilt our temples on the Akropolis - to remember!"

Kimon puts a foot on a step to the bema and addresses the Assembly, though his words are to Themistokles, who keeps the bema.

"Do you really think any will ever forget those nights our city burned? It's time we rebuilt these temples. The League of Delos protects us from Persia and brings us wealth beyond measure. Meanwhile Themistokles worships rubble and ash - these, he feels, represent his glory. You would have us live in a city of burned bones."

Kimon points to the burned-black ruins of the temples on the Akropolis, visible in the distance.

"But the gods want meat and blood!"

Kimon slaps the red-painted edge of the bema and comes up with some flecks of red on his palm.

The crowd can't hear over itself. "Vote! Vote! Enough talk! Vote!"

Σ

Names are written on potshards and the ostracism is decided

For the ostracism vote, the broad Agora has been sectioned off with wooden planks into ten different areas for voting. Athenians shuffle past ten voting jars one by one in ten quick lines, while magistrates are already counting the shards. Citizens who can write scratch names into the pottery shards which they are handed, and then toss them into various jars, while those who cannot write are in a separate line to dictate their votes to volunteer scribes who write for them.

Perikles, standing in the quickly moving line for his tribe, scratches Kimon's name onto his shard, then drops it into the jar when he gets there.

As he is returning to Ephialtes, who waits across the crowd from him, Perikles bumps into a very nervous-looking man carrying a large jar, which rattles strangely when they collide. Perikles glances into it quickly and sees the jar full of pre-made Themistokles ostraka.

Perikles shouts, "Athena! Look at this corruption! If any man wishes to vote for Themistokles, let him write it here and now!"

He takes the full jar from the man and hurls it into a nearby well, then turns back to the man and asks gravely, "Whose agent are you?"

People around begin to take note, and turn and gather. The man snorts in silent defiance, then does a fake-out look over Perikles' shoulder causing Perikles to glance away just long enough for the man to dash off into the shadows of nearby alleys.

Perikles considers following the man, but the crowd all around is too tight and raucous to easily do so, and he soon loses the thought. Ephialtes finally approaches through the crowd.

Ephialtes asks, "What was that?"

Perikles says, "A stranger, a man I'd never seen before. Carrying an amphora full of ostraka with Themistokles' name already inscribed. I wasn't able to stop him from fleeing. But I did throw his jar in the well." Perikles sighs and shrugs with frustration.

Ephialtes hands him a piece of the bread he just bought. "One volley of arrows deflected, then. Hard to know if it was the only one fired, though."

The ostracism vote is taken, and counted. It is not long in the counting before rumblings emerge into the crowd from the counters that it is clearly Themistokles who will be ostracized. He hears it before it is officially called.

Standing in the middle of a gaggle of Democrat allies, Themistokles snorts, "Athenians, it is true: you may each singly be a crafty soul, but together you make one empty fool," as the vote is being finalized.

His toothy Democrat ally Tolmides turns to Themistokles with surprise and says, "And I thought you were a Democrat, a man of the people!"

Kimon, who stands not far away, watching the counters count their piles, says, "He quotes Solon, fool. Solon, who gave us democracy."

"Go and look upon his grave for the words," says Aristides from nearby. "If you can't tell me the words beneath them when I ask tomorrow, Tolmides, wear armor."

Tolmides eyes Aristides and quickly goes through the stages of grief in his expression, then finally heads off through the crowd, toward the Dipylon gate and the graves of noble Hellenes outside it.

Themistokles declares loudly, "Athenians, you've voted for your downfall. You will learn to taste Pan's furry goat-dick."

The majority of the Assembly boos in reply, peppered with crass laughter.

Kimon stands forward in front of the shuddering herald, who is too nervous to speak. He puts a hand over the herald's hand on the *kerykeion* staff just for a moment as he says, "I'm sorry, Themistokles. But by our democratic laws devised by wise Kleisthenes, you are exiled by the ostrakon. What you leave here - your home, family, and belongings, will be kept safe, of course. You have one week to organize your concerns and leave the city. After that, if you return before ten years' time, you will be killed by the state."

Themistokles storms through the crowd, ignoring the faces of those who love and hate and are indifferent to him as he passes them close enough to kiss. His entourage uncertainly follows behind him, spreading a larger path than he did.

Lion-eyed Kimon gives a stern look of victory to Elpinike, then to his compatriots among the Oligarchs, Thukydides and Alkibiades, who step up with smug confidence beside Kimon.

The whole population roars with emotion as it closes again around the path Themistokles made.

T

Kimon and Elpinike return home from the ostracism vote

Kimon and Elpinike arrive in their home and their feet are quickly washed by their slave Amyntas. They smile victoriously at each other while Amyntas stares into his own mind, aware of their complex situation but silent about it while he works.

Once their feet are clean they head inside and Elpinike glides straight to their bedroom and falls onto the bed. Kimon follows her but then stands looking out a small window, up at the sky.

Doelike Elpinike says, "My faith in our sacrifices has borne true. I told you it would. The gods love their own children best, like any parents."

Kimon says, "You have such remarkable faith in unseen things."

"I know they exist, since Zeus himself has so often visited me in the form of my own beautiful brother."

Kimon smiles, turns to her, and begins to unstrap his armor.

"I think I feel him taking my place yet again."

Elpinike rises on the bed and begins helping Kimon remove his armor, staring into his eyes with sexy confidence.

"Nothing changes, Kimon, my father's son," Elpinike purrs as she finds his bare skin beneath his clothes. "We are the gods. As Kronos and Rhea begat all the rest. All changes made since the golden first men are nullified by our purity."

And then she begins to consume his flesh as he fills his eyes with the distant stars and holds fast onto the world by her medusal curls.

> "ALL NATURE FOLLOWS BY YOUR TEMPERAMENT,
> YOUR HEART IS PILOT OF THE FIRMAMENT!
> MAY THE SCREAMING WINDS, THE POUNDING SEA
> AND NOBLE RIVERS ALL MOVE AS YOU PLEASE!"
> Homeros, *Hymn to Hera*

Y

Aoide gets accustomed to her new home at Delphi

"Now some of you may think of Apollo on Delos, just a baby beside his sister Artemis. But your new lord is Pythian Apollo - the god as a full-sized young man, eternally a youth but nevertheless, a man, a serpent-killer and knower of the future. If you love him without also fearing him, you do not understand him. His beauty is the burning sun which illuminates everything knowable, but you will find soon that some knowledge burns your whole life like poison. Listen now for Apollo in your hearts as you sleep these first nights. But do not make any noise. If I hear girls tittering, I will get my long scourge and indiscriminately whip into the darkness. So sleep quietly." As the girls are supposed to be going to sleep on their first night at the temple, just after blowing out the lamp in their group dormitory, the nasally old priestess Kliko clicks her tongue, which is a reminder of the thorns on her whip which click against the floor.

Aoide closes her eyes as she lies still on her hay-stuffed bed, staring upward, but it is no darker than it was with them open. She experiments with closing and opening her eyes for a while there, until it almost seems to her as if she can see slightly more light on the backs of her eyelids with her eyes closed, and she begins to wonder if that might indicate that there is at least a small amount of light that she creates inside her eyes, which travels outward.

In the depths of that thought, she's startled by being grabbed around the arms, and she opens her eyes but tries hard not to gasp too loudly, for fear of being whipped.

"We're called by Apollo to dance for Auntie Moon," whispers an older girl very close to Aoide's ear as shadows run past Aoide one after the other and bare feet slap nearly-silently against stone. "Come or you're cursed dumb!"

Aoide only hesitates a moment in her bed, then gets up and follows the scampering shadows out into the sky-ceilinged sanctuary where the words carved into every wall are long-shadowed under the light of the moon.

As they pad down the path of ancient paving stones, Aoide notes their feel against her feet, and wonders if the smoother stones might be thousands of years older than the others, and could have been trod by Apollo or Artemis themselves.

"What's your name?" asks the older girl who woke her.

Aoide says, "Aoide."

"I'm Dikasto," the older girl says. "I heard you're from Athens. Is this your first time away from home?"

Aoide says, "No, but it's my first time away from Attika."

"Most of us were born in the valley," Dikasto says breathlessly, in staggering pauses between running. "Apollo prefers us to girls from Athens."

The group of young girls pass behind the buildings, scrambling down the low grassy cliffs and rocks instead of following the switchbacking sacred path between all the treasure houses which pilgrims reverently trudge up toward their destiny.

Soon they are at the Kastalian spring - a natural crevasse in the towering cliffs, down from which an ancient spring trickles and fills a large natural pool, where pilgrims wash and the Pythia bathe for inspiration from the god before each day of oracles.

"This is where Apollo killed Python," Dikasto tells Aoide as she steps down into the pool there with the other girls, who are all swimming and wading in their plain, white dresses, some singing low and wordlessly, two in the back kissing each other within a moon shadow.

"Is this okay?" Aoide asks nervously, not wanting to seem timid, but also fearing being tested and failing.

Dikasto says with a funny little smile, as she approaches Aoide and takes her hand to beckon her into the pool of spring water, "The god determines what he inspires in us, not we."

Aoide shivers as the cold water rises above her knees.

"What does he inspire in you - right now?"

Aoide's heart races in the moonlight, and she thinks of Artemis.

"Sometimes I wish I were just an animal," Aoide whispers, almost more to herself and the gods than to Dikasto. "I wish I didn't have a mind."

"Close your eyes, then, and find out if the gods will grant your wish."

Aoide smiles, then closes her eyes to begin a silent prayer, but as soon as her eyes are closed she feels the water part between herself and Dikasto and then she is dunked under the surface by a hard push on her shoulders. She comes up laughing and coughing, then begins to wrestle Dikasto in the water.

In a panting break from their wrestling, Dikasto scans Aoide's face and then asks, "You're Alkmaeonid, aren't you? You look like my friend Klarelia. She's an Alkmaeonid; she's from Athens, too."

"She's my older cousin, I think," Aoide admits.

"She's with the older girls." Dikasto's comfort level with Aoide seems to have changed since realizing she is Alkmaeonid; she seems more standoffish. Then she explains directly, "I guess your family runs this place."

"It's for the worship of Apollo," Aoide says, because that's how she's heard her parents excuse the Alkmaeonid influence at Delphi. "We love knowledge and the arts, so we want to respect their god utmost."

Dikasto then tells Aoide, "Your family is cursed. They came here to try to beg the god to save them, after getting kicked out of your own city."

Aoide just tries to keep breathing. Situations this tense always make her clam up, since at home her questions or retorts might often receive a slap from father in return.

"You know that. But do you know why?" Dikasto asks.

Something about the way she asks it seems sweet, and not hateful. Aoide has never been told the story of how her family was cursed; it is specifically avoided among her clan. Somehow she feels she can trust this new friend. She shakes her head no, she doesn't know.

"Kylon was a wrestler with many Olympic wreaths who came to the Pythia to ask her how he might take control in Athens."

Aoide lowers her head and listens low-eyed.

Dikasto continues, playing with the water, "He was told that he would succeed if he attempted to seize control during a festival to Zeus, which the Olympic victor took to mean the Olympic Games. But then when he tried to take control and become tyrant, the Archons of your city fought him, and one of them was your ancestor Megakles."

Aoide nods, having heard that an ancestor named Megakles was associated with the story, but knowing little else. Megakles is her father's name, and she has seen him mocked by other men for it, his meekness made comical by it. He would always take that public humiliation out on his daughters back at home with meanness and shouting. Aoide never understood what was behind it.

"Kylon and his men fought your city's Archons, until they took refuge in a temple on your Akropolis, where the Archons didn't want to attack them, for fear of offending Athena. But then your Archons persuaded Kylon's men to leave the temple to stand trial, if Kylon would be allowed to tie a rope to the statue of Athena which he would keep ahold of, and which would stretch all the way from the temple to the courthouse, so he would technically remain in suppliance to the goddess. But somewhere along the way the rope broke - or someone broke the rope - and it was Megakles who decided that that was a sign of the goddess' care leaving Kylon and his rebels, and he ordered their immediate deaths then and there."

Aoide wants to analyze the story, but does not know what position Dikasto might have, so she stays quiet.

"So in fear of Athena's wrath, your clan was exiled from your city for a hundred years. Your ancestors' bones were even dug up and moved up here to Phokis. That's how cursed your family is."

Dikasto seems to be trying to get a reaction out of Aoide, who lets a tear fall only out of the awkwardness of the moment, not real sadness. She has never felt filial piety to her shallow and abusive parents. Now, as she learns the true history which her family had explicitly kept from her, she feels the weight of her ancestry become spiritually heavy enough finally to slough off her body entirely, and as she imagines that molting she feels lighter, and smiles out several more tears.

"How do you know so much about me?" Aoide asks before a gulp of water from the pool; she wonders about what magic she might be swallowing.

Dikasto gets a cold, serious look and says, "This is the center of the world. All knowledge makes its way here."

Aoide scoffs and looks up at the softly swaying treetops high up on the cliff above, and the bright Moon beyond.

"Plus you're an Alkmaeonid. Your people rebuilt this place after the wars. I know how things work. I'm no child. Your people run this place. That's why you're here, even though you're an Athenian, even though Apollo said it should only be Delphian girls here. But it's just a corrupt world now, and all sacredness has become curses because men are fundamentally stupid and corruptible, and just let any old thing happen now."

"I'm not an Alkmaeonid," Aoide sighs. "I'm my own person. I'm just me."

"Well you're not Delphian, that's for sure," Dikasto snaps, and grabs Aoide by the shoulders, pushing her under the water.

Under the water Aoide opens her eyes to see Dikasto and the bright Moon above through a warbling lens. She can't decide if the best way to make friends with this girl would be to fight against her or to let herself be abused for a while, but her experience with her father at home has taught her that the latter path does not lead to happiness, so she finally finds the strength to struggle back against Dikasto's arms and pull the girl down into the water with her.

By the time both girls have gotten their breath in the air again, Dikasto is somewhere between laughing and barking to express a sort of military admiration. Some of the other girls stand behind her now, watching the drama unfold, whatever it is.

"If you're not an Alkmaeonid, then maybe you're actually a poet," Dikasto says to Aoide, their eyes locked. Aoide sees the other girls watching, and realizes it is a moment that will define her to them.

Aoide feels some energy rise in her chest, and it feels to her like a confirmation of what Dikasto has said.

Dikasto at the same time suddenly stops as she notices something behind Aoide, and nods to it so Aoide will look.

Aoide turns quickly, frightened at first by the way the thing turned Dikasto's tone.

But it is just a tiny kitten, alone in the forest, watching the girls from the edge of a bush, stepping out bravely so it is just barely visible. When Aoide spots it, it is looking at her, and it mews at her with a tiny voice - the kitten which the lump-faced insult-poet Hipponax gave to her and the handsome priest Theragon made her get rid of.

Very carefully, Aoide gets down onto her elbows and belly, and slithers like a snake very slowly toward the little creature, holding out her hands for it to smell her, patiently. It comes out before she expects it to, bravely stepping toward her and sniffing the air around her, but raising its paws like a tiny lion against her fingers when she tries to grab it. Once she clasps her phalanx around it, the kitten wraps its mouth and claws around her thumb, making her squeal while she struggles to keep ahold of it.

The other girls grin and whisper.

"Little Herakleia," Dikasto jokes from behind Aoide. "Next you'll be wearing its skin and swinging a club around. Look everyone, Aoide caught the Nemean Lion!"

The older girls laugh, but some of the other girls Aoide's age squeal at the sight of the kitten and run over to join Aoide, asking to hold it or pet it. Aoide jealously snuggles the tiny cat close to her chest, wrapping her arms around it the best she can, not responding to the other girl's requests. It looks up into her eyes with big blue ones of its own, and its fur-filled ears open up like fast flowers to listen to her, as if asking her for a name.

Aoide whispers to the kitten, turning onto her back to see it against the stars, "You'll be called Ailisto, little lion, and if you'll be my friend, I'll always be yours."

The kitten Ailisto reaches out with her tiny paws and touches Aoide's nose. All the other young girls huddled around Aoide and the kitten coo with adoration and one older girl in the back begins to compose an impromptu hymn to the kitten which, once it loops, they all start to sing as a group, among the mottled moonshadows, quiet enough not to wake anyone.

> "I SING OF ARTEMIS OF THE GOLDEN BOW,
> STRONG-VOICED AND INNOCENT ARROW-LOVER.
> OVER DARK HILLS AND WINDY PEAKS SHE LOVES TO CHASE,
> AND THROUGH THE TANGLED FOREST ECHOES BEAST VOICES!"
> Homeros, *Hymn to Artemis*

Φ

Themistokles leaves Athens

Themistokles' household slaves lead a baggage train of yoked donkeys slowly but steadily out through the Dipylon Gate. Themistokles' beloved unfinished wall is still being built on either side. The last to exit is Themistokles himself in a one-horse chariot, appearing as heroes do in stories of old on unshattered pottery. A couple of stoneworkers wave to him, still working hard on his wall.

Big-bearded Themistokles waves to his fans and followers as he pulls his chariot to a stop, steps down from it, and begins to say his individual goodbyes to the notable city figures like Aristides, Myronides, and Tolmides, who have come to see him off.

Perikles waits with Ephialtes until at last Themistokles approaches them, and grasps Ephialtes in a big hug.

Big-bearded Themistokles says, "No time to grieve, young men. The struggle against the Oligarchs is yours now. Consider whom else Athena loved - Odysseos. And wasn't he sent into exile for ten years as well, and by the gods themselves? But I know our work is in good hands with you, Ephialtes."

Ever-smiling Ephialtes says, "Stay safe in Argos. Athens' wall, which you began, will hopefully be complete and ready for your inspection when we see you again in ten years."

"I look forward to seeing it complete," Themistokles sighs, and grasps Ephialtes by the shoulder, then steps over to Perikles, looks him in the eye and takes his shoulder. "Perikles. You make sure to keep sand in the ocean." And at that he turns and mounts his chariot behind snorting horses.

Perikles' mind churns as he puzzles over what Themistokles may have meant by that. Until Ephialtes leans in and whispers, "He means his table."

Themistokles' chariot and entourage head off away from the city, along the road northwest to Eleusis which leads past all the old funerary monuments of Solon and Kleisthenes and the rest of the previous century's founding fathers of democracy.

X

The Spartan ambassadors returning to Sparta stop at a Helot farm

On a small farm consisting of just a single broad field of wheat and a tiny stone hovel roofed with straw, two teen-aged boys, Nothon and Timonos, are yoked to an old wooden plow, and drag it with great effort through the soil while their father Gylippos follows behind the plow with a long-handled spike, kicking and spiking apart the big chunks of soil that get pulled up by the plow. Surrounding the farm are the low hills of Lakedaemonia, the lands of the Eurotas River valley, controlled by Sparta.

Young Timonos sees something in the distance ahead of them, and slows his pull on the plow, points it out to his brother.

"Father! Spartans."

Gylippos raises his head quickly and first readies his spike like a weapon, then sees the Spartans in the distance and lowers it with a sigh.

In the distance, on the hill's horizon, the silhouettes of two men in Spartan armor approach at a steady pace.

"Boys, go inside. Pour some wine. Calm your mother."

The boys put the plow down in the field and head in to the hovel. They're met at the doorway by their mother Argiloë, who eyes the approaching Spartans with fear, beckoning her boys in.

Gylippos walks to the hovel and puts his spike into the ground so that it leans against the edge of the building. As the Spartans approach, it becomes clear that they are Hippokoön and Melanthios. Their armor glitters in the sun. Gylippos bathes his sweaty body briefly from a bucket.

When they are within earshot, Gylippos calls out, "Greetings, Spartan masters."

Melanthios says with a dry throat, "Prepare a meal, Helot. We've been walking all day."

Inside the tiny hovel, Hippokoön and Melanthios sit eating bread and wine at a small table clearly meant for the family of four, while the Helot family stand all around in awkward silence. Gylippos and Melanthios keep making silent eye contact with each other, but Hippokoön seems confidently unconcerned as he eats.

After they've eaten, the two Spartans in their armor step out of the house, the father following behind them hesitantly. The two sons follow behind him, the mother lingering at the doorway.

"This farm grows good grain. And your wife makes fine bread," Hippokoön says.

"We thank y--"

Hippokoön asks, "Which of your sons is stronger?"

Gylippos looks with horror at Hippokoön. His two sons look at each other nervously, and Argiloë puts her hand over her mouth. The father looks to Melanthios for support, shaking his head, but Melanthios just stares back, unemotional, still finishing a bit of bread.

Hippokoön adds, "Or are they both very strong?"

Gylippos slowly raises his gaze to his wife, in the doorway of their home. She shakes her head at him, but they have a moment of eye contact in which they both realize the gravity of the moment, and agree through silent eye contact to be honorable rather than make some grisly choice.

The father turns to his two boys, standing beside each other, one with a hand on the other's arm for comfort, though both are frightened. He looks into both their eyes, then nods to the one who was comforting his brother.

"Nothon is my strongest son."

Hippokoön walks up to the two boys, eyeing them each, and pulls the indicated, slightly taller and older one, away from his brother, who grasps at him helplessly. Hippokoön heartlessly pulls out his sword and plunges it up under the boy's ribs, into his heart from below. Bright red blood pours out as Hippokoön removes the sword and the boy crumbles lifelessly into the grass.

Argiloë screams a wordless cry to the gods and collapses in the doorway. The living brother stands shaking, not wanting to move, but unable to look away from his dead brother's body.

As Hippokoön and Melanthios walk past the teary-eyed but stoic-faced Gylippos on their way out from the farm, Melanthios stops for a moment of eye contact. "We left you a son," he says. "Keep up the hard work. It's almost time to plant. You'll need to plow faster."

The two Spartans continue off on their walk through Lakedaemonia to its capital, Sparta. At the hovel, little Timonos finally falls upon his brother Nothon's dead body while their father Gylippos crouches to comfort Argiloë and stares with hate at the forms of the men walking away.

But before long he stands shakily, and slaps his living son on the back as he passes him on his way back to the plow.

Ψ

Queen-Mother Gorgo meets with the Spartan ambassadors

The Spartan ambassadors walk across Lakedaemonian fields toward the twilight firelights of the city of Sparta.

Melanthios says to Hippokoön, "I told you, home before dark."

Sparta, in Lakedaemonia, sits on a dry river plain in a windswept valley between two mountain ranges, along the narrow Eurotas River which flows gently south along a broad, ancient furrow from the Arcadian highlands to the sea. To the west towers Mount Taygetos, named for an ancient nymph and friend of Artemis Huntress, Taygete, and to the east Mount Menelaion, named after Sparta's own famous old King Menelaos who summoned the kings of Hellas to help rescue his wife Queen Helen in days of old. Sparta is a sparse city with no wall, separated into five distinct gatherings of simple homes - loosely organized around the five ancient tribes of the Spartans - around a central cluster of hills, each of which houses its own temple and in the middle of which is an Agora-like cobblestoned empty space where most days nothing happens but on the night of no moon each month the oldest men gather to discuss laws.

On the highest of the hills the most infrastructure and the closest thing to other cities' Akropolises exists in the form of the high temple of Athena of the Bronze House, with its long, narrow stairway leading up to it from the plaza below. Before Gorgo's time, the kings used to hold court in that temple, but now old priests maintain vigil over fires in glittering bronze bowls and braziers, and the kings and Overseers meet instead in the temple of Aphrodite Warlike.

On a lower hill not far away, the temple of Aphrodite is one of the only two-story temples in the Hellenic world, with the lower story dedicated to Aphrodite Warlike, consort of Ares the War God, to which Gorgo's father had the thrones moved when she was a young girl. Within, visible behind the thrones, stands an expensive new bronze statue of Aphrodite standing in full Spartan armor which Gorgo had erected after the death of her husband Leonidas. Meanwhile the upper floor is dedicated to the older goddess Aphrodite Shapely, in a space off limits to all but those allowed entrance by the priestesses of Aphrodite, where the more ancient version of the goddess' statue sits, formed from wood, bare-breasted, head veiled, feet shackled, as the kings of old liked her. These days, Gorgo tries to make sure no one sees that version of Aphrodite except herself and the old priestesses who give the goddess her due smoke and water.

The capitals of the columns of Sparta's temples are plain, flat, and rectangular, in the old Doric style, rather than curled like the Ionians do in modern Attika and east.

Within the temple of Aphrodite Warlike, King Pleistarchos sits upon his throne, secretly stroking a tiny turtle he has hidden in his robe, while standing behind the throne his mother Queen Gorgo pets the boy king's hair. The other throne is empty at the moment, the boy king's teenage twin-leader King Archidamos being elsewhere tonight. A few attendant priestesses of Aphrodite are gathered at a far corner of the temple, whispering to each other while they tend a small fire in a brazier.

Queen Gorgo sings quietly to her son as she pets his hair and stares toward a star on the rainbowed horizon with distance in her eyes.

Before they are even fully visible, Gorgo calls out to them, waking her son from a comfort trance. "Hippokoön! Melanthios!" Hippokoön and Melanthios approach out from the darkness of the night, into the firelight of the temple interior, their armor glittering.

"Queen Mother Gorgo," Melanthios says reverently, then turns to the young king and acknowledges him secondarily. "King Pleistarchos."

Young King Pleistarchos says, "Hello." The boy holds his robe closed tight around his turtle.

Melanthios and Hippokoön both nod to the boy.

"Your night arrival feels urgent," Gorgo notes. "Tell us what tragic theater Athens had for you this time."

Melanthios says, "More imitations of the Battle at Salamis. Plenty of evidence of Themistokles' vanity, but he does not seem to be a part of Pausanias' treason. In fact, he's on his way to Argos now, an exile from his own city."

"Perhaps Athens is more powerful than its own foolish leaders," Gorgo muses. She begins to pace the stone floor of the temple, peering into her mind and trying to fathom the Athenians. "They exile their own cleverest people like we kill the strongest Helots. They fight off Persia's fleet only to start their own empire and call it a League. It may yet become necessary to re-educate Athens in the old ways of bronze and blood, and send their wooden wall of ships to Poseidon in an envelope of fire."

Melanthios nods in agreement.

"You passed through the country. What was the humor of the Helots?"

Hippokoön pats his sheathed sword. "One fewer but more glad to be alive than yesterday. Helots mourn best at the plow."

Ω

Perikles takes a walk at night, and a new Athenian is named

Adjacent neighborhoods maintain noisy, drunken parties of various base sorts long into the night in the tightly-packed homes that cling to the slopes of the Akropolis, inside the city wall, where the din of laughter, angry shouts, and dogs barking ring in the distance, but in the richer neighborhood around Perikles' family's house just inside the western wall, all is quiet. A single hooting owl in his own courtyard is louder than the distant parties.

Perikles lies on his back in bed with his arms behind his head, listening to the distant sounds of the city. He can't sleep, so he gets up and steps out onto the balcony of his bedroom which looks over the wall and across the roofs of the rich southwestern corner of Athens. In the heat of this evening, many families are sleeping on mats up on their roofs. In other neighborhoods in the distance he can see the light from the torches of parties. Beyond them, he looks to the Akropolis, high in the center of the city, a dark titan crowned with bright stars.

Perikles returns into his bedroom, throws a cloak over his tunic, and heads down to the doorway, where he takes a torch from its lead sconce.

As the light moves with his taking of the torch, a shadow appears suddenly beside him, startling Perikles before he realizes that it is just his mother Agariste.

"Good evening, Perikles," she says with an inquisitive smile. "Where are you headed in the dark of night? Might a young lady be waiting somewhere?"

Perikles sighs, and says, "No, I'm not going to meet anyone. Maybe Athena if I'm lucky. I did hear an owl. I just can't sleep."

"O, Athena," Agariste scoff-laughs, grabbing Perikles' cloak to adjust the way it hangs around his neck. "Not every owl is Athena. Aphrodite's the one you should be looking for, young man. Instead of owls, listen for doves!"

"You know, I have more serious things to think about right now," Perikles says, trying to hide his annoyance. "I'm a politician now, or working with them at least. I need to keep my mind on serious things. Men these days aren't getting married until their thirties sometimes, mother, so they can have a political career first."

Agariste listens, nodding, and sheathes her smile. "You are a very serious man, Perikles. I see that. You want to associate with other serious men. But you will be wise not to forget about all the women out there. They may not vote, but after every speech you politicians give on the bema, all those men still go home to their wives and hear the final speech in bed."

Perikles frowns, and tries to form a thought in response, but hesitates to call his mother old-fashioned.

"Use women, Perikles," his mother tells him.

He blinks, still a bit cloud-minded from trying to sleep, and unsure in the moment quite how his mother means what she's just said.

"Do not forget that we are hidden away here, every day, with hands and eyes and minds as useful as each man's. Not to use the women of the world is to walk, work, fight, with half a body."

Perikles nods, thinking of his cousin Aoide and her always-inspiring little wisdoms. For the first time since he last saw her, he misses her.

"It's not just children who need our care. Men never leave the breast. It is why we have two - one for the child, and one for the man."

Perikles grimaces a bit. "Mother..."

Agariste laughs. "Go on. Walk the world of men. Meet someone. Perhaps a girl? You need some experience before you settle down with one of your cousins."

Perikles shrugs off his mother's grip laughing. "Stop, mother, enough." He kisses her perfunctorily, then heads out into the dark city with his torch.

He leaves the Alkmaeonid compound and strolls along the outer side of the new city wall at the edge of his own neighborhood, then into the city through the Dipylon Gate and up to the now-quiet Agora. He passes a few elderly poor men who ignore his nods while seated in silence, and a young amorous couple who are trying to kiss as they walk arm in arm.

In one shoemaking stall, Simon the shoemaker is cutting sandal soles by lamp light. As he passes, Perikles nods to the man, who nods back.

"You work too hard, Simon. Don't you sleep?"

"Avoiding nightmares of bare feet," Simon responds just loud enough to be heard across the distance.

Perikles chuckles politely.

He ascends the ancient ramp that leads up from the Agora to the Akropolis, wondering how many men before him have ascended these same stones, and when they might have been piled up here. The ramp was supposedly built in the time of Theseos, but Perikles knows enough to know that that just means that really no one knows.

At the height of the Akropolis, the whole city spans out below, and young Perikles stops for a moment to look down upon it. The gibbous moon lights the rooftops. Among the roof-sleepers, which on a warm night will be many, Perikles spies a few couples making love.

Behind him, a few priestesses are still at work in the ruins of the old Parthenon, a now roofless building surrounded by half-toppled columns, while a gang of young children plays a night game flocking from one edge of the cliffs to the other.

Perikles steps toward the ruins of an even older temple to Athena, now merely a heap of rubble and column drums. The fires of the Persian army, and the ghost of the building that stood here for centuries before that terrible war, linger in the air of the place like fog across time. Looking at them now destroyed, Perikles can't shake the feeling that everything he has been taught about holiness is somehow missing the point.

"I don't know how to make you hear me, Athena. But if guiding mortal men is still something that you do, give me some sign of what I might do to earn your favor. Your city has lost its great leader, and sails rudderless now, with men trying to oar it in each different direction. I know it's the duty of the noble to do what's necessary."

Nearby, Anaxagoras' Ionian-accented voice says, "I hear the crackle of a spark in the cool air, a spark from the very armor of Athena, writ from nothing - the voice of Perikles!"

Perikles turns, surprised, and sees Anaxagoras sitting upright on the ground beside the extremely long-bearded old star-watcher Oenopides and the little boy Euripides, who are both lying on their backs in the grass. He approaches and helps Oenopides to stand.

Perikles asks, "Are you starting a night school, Oenopides?"

Hunched old Oenopides explains, "Euripides here is interested in philosophy. He tells me he wants to take over my work when I die."

Little Euripides explains, "You won't be able to see the stars from the Underworld!"

The adults all laugh.

"The perfect tact of children," Perikles says.

Euripides continues, taking offense at the laughter as mockery, "Imagine if we lost track of the stars! What if they leave one day, or Zeus blocks our view of them?"

Anaxagoras says, "Many think the stars hold secret knowledge, or even that they're somehow the gods themselves. I'm not so sure. There definitely are a lot of them, but very few of them ever really do anything except sit there and twinkle."

"As with men, it is the strange ones that are worth watching!" Oenopides says. "I've seen enough strange behavior from stars to know that they're not, as many Ionians are saying these days, just a field of mundane fires far away, or holes in some celestial sphere. The stars have a strange life of their own. Like the frog that will sit for days in one spot before it jumps."

In the nearby ruins of the old Parthenon, that old temple to Athena built a generation ago and burned eight years ago with everything else by the Persians, a ceremony is taking place. Some priestesses have begun to chant a hymn to Athena. Perikles turns his attention.

The boy Euripides says, "A new baby is being named. I saw them bring him earlier."

Perikles leaves Anaxagoras and Oenopides, and walks over to the ruined old temple, where torchlight illuminates a humble ceremony led by the head priestess of Athena, Eteobouta, around the young couple Sophroniskos and Phaenarete, who holds her days-old baby in a simple wrap. The baby doesn't cry, but looks around with curiosity.

Perikles asks, "You name this child in the middle of the night? There should be a feast, a celebration."

Sophroniskos explains, "We're not wealthy, sir. We can't afford to throw a feast for this child. A night ceremony is all we could afford. Lysimachos, son of Aristides the Just, offered to pay for a party, but I don't want my son to begin life indebted."

"Your son will begin with true nobility, then." Then when Sophroniskos squints to recognize the speaker, he adds, "Yes, friend, it is I, Perikles - another friend of Lysimachos, son of the Just."

They both laugh, and Sophroniskos nods recognition. "Of course, forgive my eyes in the firelight."

Perikles smiles. He looks back to Anaxagoras, who is standing outside the temple, looking heavenward again, his neck stretched, a big smile on his face. He says, to himself and all present, "I feel like a child who's just been born. I must get back to learning."

Sullen-eyed Euripides hears him as he watches nearby, while four-year-old Krito sneaks up behind and clings to peer around the older boy. "Go home, Krito," Euripides whines. "Find somebody else to follow."

The old priestess Eteobouta approaches Phaenarete and Sophroniskos and anoints their baby with a touch of olive oil. The priestess asks, "Now that he has lived long enough to show that the gods want this person on Earth, what shall we call him?"

Phaenarete looks to Sophroniskos, who smiles and replies, "We've decided to name our son Sokrates."

Eteobouta spreads some olive oil onto his cheeks with a finger and then kisses his head.

"Healthy, powerful. Welcome to Athens, young Sokrates."

Eteobouta eyes Euripides at the edge of the temple and Krito hiding behind him, and she smiles at the children. "Come, boys," she says. "Meet your newest countryman, little Sokrates."

Euripides and Krito slowly approach, and Phaenarete hands the baby to Euripides, who holds him awkwardly, then hands him off with a grimace to the toddler Krito, who holds the baby much more tenderly and looks into his eyes.

"Bbbllaa-gg-ah?" baby Sokrates vocalizes with curiosity in his eyes.

Krito looks around at everyone in silent shock. The adults all laugh to each other softly at his adorable reaction.

"Well, Krito?" asks the wizened priestess. "That sounded like a question. And when someone gives you a question, you owe them an answer."

Krito holds the baby Sokrates, who looks up into his eyes.

Behind them all, in the center of the temple ruin, surrounded by the dancing fires within four bronze braziers, three elderly priestesses are at work together at a huge, ornately adorned religious loom, on which their complex and very slow and deliberate work is gradually weaving a beautiful tapestry upon which one thread has just been begun.

ATHENS

2

APHRODITE WARLIKE

A

Pausanias returns to Hellas from Ionia with a captive princess

A weathered stone column stands beside a short green sapling along the path past the gates of Qorinth. No one knows the column's age. On either side, it says in rain-eroded ancient letters:

> IONIA HERE, PELOPONNESE THERE
> PELOPONNESE HERE, IONIA THERE

Qorinth is on the narrow isthmus which separates the peninsula of Pelops - the *Peloponnese* - from the mainland of Hellas, so this spot is one that many pass wherever they're going. It is a land version of the Straits of Salamis, of a form to funnel the movement of people, an old crossroads, famous for its prostitutes from the temple of Aphrodite on the summit of Qorinth's high rock, the *Akrokorinth*. The city itself is so ancient that its name retains the old Q letter which no one but the Phoenikians use anymore in other words. Those only coming for the sacred prostitutes at Aphrodite's temple often joke that the strange and archaic looking letter Q on Qorinthian coins is just a penis and scrotum.

Passersby all casually salute the old crossroads herm.

A merchant caravan leads the way for a royal train past the ancient column. Leading the royal train are four horsemen in full Spartan armor, followed by a royal palanquin carried by four Ionian slaves. Behind the palanquin a few dozen Spartan foot soldiers march in their armor, casually chatting, followed by several laden donkeys with their attendant Helot slaves.

Inside the palanquin, the Spartan commander Pausanias, uncle and regent to Sparta's boy-king Pleistarchos, sits across from his recently captured new body slave, buried amidst comfortable, brightly colored Persian pillows.

Pausanias curls his fingers repeatedly, taking pleasure in the sensations his many rings make as they slide across each other, and he gazes at the young woman across from him through the moving fingers. Outside the litter, the bright blue world sways.

"I imagine my royal box moves enough like a ship that you haven't felt like you've even touched down on land yet, eh Nikoleta? You may speak."

"I haven't felt the ground under my feet since your soldiers took our palace," the young woman replies without looking up.

"You find the courage to bring poetry into your words even here," Pausanias says with a squint through his fingers. "You may live in servitude now, but your soul is still a noble princess of Byzantion. You will know a distinct superiority over our own Helots, who are slaves by birth. You at least retain the nobility of having been won in war. Like Briseis at the shores of Troi, fought over by kings."

"It does not give me pleasure to know that there are women less fortunate than I," the young woman replies, looking up for a moment. "But if you wish me to feel still like a princess of Byzantion, you could call me by my true name."

"No. Niome had to die, with her family. At least you have your youth again, though. You are Nikoleta now, a woman only two years old. And soon enough, you will be mistress to the King of All-Hellas."

"I thought you ruled your city alongside another king," the princess says with real confusion.

"Silly girl," Pausanias frowns, "I did not say King of Sparta. I said King of *All-Hellas*. There has never been such a king. But you will be there when I create the great singular throne for Hellas, like Herakles created Sparta's two." With wide, still eyes, Pausanias assures her silently of his seriousness. He adds, for clarity, and in his excitement more loudly than he means to, "And then I will sit upon it!"

Niome slowly grows a grimace of understanding as she realizes the implications, that Persian imperial influence would also return to Hellas.

Pausanias smiles slightly, with disgust, but as someone who likes to be disgusted. "I see your parents cursed you with enough of an education to understand the world," he says as he looks away from her.

Pausanias opens the curtain of the palanquin to see the landscape they're passing. He takes in a deep breath of the air.

"It's good to smell Peloponnesian air again," he says.

Outside, the caravan begins to pass a low ruined wall, and Pausanias' face lights up, and he points it out to Nikoleta.

"Here you see the wall we built to keep the Persians out of our land. Ten years ago. You see, Spartans build walls in other people's land, so that we don't have to build them in our own."

B

Sokrates and Krito visit the Agora

The industrial district of Athens called Potters' Alley straddles both sides of the city wall around the Dipylon Gate. Not just one street, Potters' Alley is a long labyrinth of ramshackle buildings and temporary structures piled against the city wall and all strung along the swift, narrow stream called Eridanos, which many use for cleaning and waste. It is a district populated primarily by potters, stone workers, and the painters of their work. It rings during the daylight with the clatter of hammers, the clink of pottery, murmuring, shouting, and laughter.

Situated centrally inside the Dipylon Gate is the tall pair of statues - the first public statues in Athens - of the young lovers known as the *Tyrant Killers*, Harmodios and Aristogeiton, who conspired together to assassinate the Peisistratid tyrants of the previous generation.

The sons of Peisistratos were the first tyrants who tried to wrestle back democracy from the people and reinstate the rule by few. On the day of the great Panathenaic festival, the boys hid daggers in the myrtle wreath they were to offer the new tyrant, and then stabbed the tyrant in a surprise attack. A conspirator of the Tyrant Killers, a prostitute known only as the Lioness, bit out her tongue to avoid speaking during torture. In honor, now, Athenian sculptures of Aphrodite are often accompanied by a young lioness.

The current statues of Harmodios and Aristogeiton are new replacements of the originals which were carried off to Persepolis by the Persian army ten years ago, but the originals were the first public statues in the Hellenic world.

Athenian laborers often stop on their daily routines and praise the boys' sculptures by feeding birds at their base, since Athenians half-jokingly consider bird shit lucky.

Just on the other side of the walls from Potters' Alley, the city's graveyard blooms with stone monuments clustered along the Sacred Road to Eleusis - some brightly painted, some chipped and faded, some still scorched by eastern torches ten years ago.

In the other direction, into the city, the bustling market around the Agora is just a few blocks further, and traffic between it and Potters' Alley is busy early in the morning with artisans filling orders from shops.

In a tent-covered workshop nestled among other such flimsy buildings clustered around the mellow-flowing Eridanos, the sculptor Sophroniskos works with his boss Myron on an Ionian column head, while little two-year-old Sokrates toddles nearby.

Big-armed Sophroniskos tells his little son a story as he carefully labors.

"Long ago, the king of Athens was a man named Aegeos, and he had a strong young son named Theseos. Just like I have you as my son!

"Well, back in those times, there were still monsters in the world. And on the distant island of Krete there was a king named Minos, and to make a long story short, he and his wife had problems, and she ended up being cursed by Poseidon to bear a child with a bull. So the Kretan king and queen had a prince, but the little princeling Asterion had the head of a bull!"

Little Sokrates giggles at that.

"Now this was a long time ago, when things like kings and palaces were new things. King Minos was of that ancient first generation of kings, where even though he ruled from the great Palace of Knossos, he was born and died in a cave, like his own ancestors did."

As he tells the story, Sophroniskos chisels small pieces off the stone column head in order to create the iconic Ionic whorl, while Myron pours water over his work and wipes it down with a wooly rag.

"Anyway, King Minos of Krete also had an incredibly wise and clever and industrious slave named *Daidalos*. Daidalos and his nephews Talos and Ikaros were the first men to create the metal tools used by carpenters - like the saw, and the methods of carpenters. So Minos told Daidalos - make me some kind of prison for my bull-headed son Asterion. And Daidalos said - how about I make a palace for the prince that is just so confusingly constructed, with hallways leading nowhere and turning this way and that, so that anyone who goes into the building will invariably get lost and then never be able to find their way out again!"

Sokrates laughs, as he tries to imagine that with wonder.

"But Asterion was still a prince of Krete, so Minos didn't want to just let his son die in there, but he was - he was a monster, with the head of a bull; and he ate people. Did I mention that?"

Sokrates gasps.

"Yeah, he ate people - men and women. And he found youths most delicious of all."

Sokrates shakes his head no.

"Anyway," Sophroniskos continues, "eventually our Athenian prince Theseos, the son of King Aegeos, decided to sail to Krete and pretend to be one of the youths whom King Minos has been feeding to prince Asterion."

"Why?" Sokrates asks.

"Well, it's complicated, but one of Minos' other sons came over to participate in our games during the Panathenaia, and he had an accident and died. And King Minos took that out on Athens, and demanded that we start sending ships of sacrificial youths and maidens to Krete to be fed to Prince Asterion. And Prince Theseos wanted to stop all of that, so he determined to go with the ship of youths and maidens, but kill the minotaur."

Sokrates gasps. "Why?"

Sophroniskos shakes his head. "You can't keep asking why, or I'll never get through the story. Now King Minos had a daughter as well, named Ariadne, and she wasn't cursed to have the head of a cow, she was just normal. In fact she was very beautiful, and very clever and kind. And so when Theseos arrived at the court of King Minos on Krete, he and she instantly fell in love, just like your mother and I did when we first met each other. They just instantly knew that they would never meet anyone more perfect for each other. After all, princes and princesses often have to marry each other anyway. But so when Theseos was about to head into the labyrinth to face her brother Asterion, Princess Ariadne gave Theseos a ball of string called a *clue*, so that he could gradually unravel it as he walked through the labyrinth, and then use it to find his way back along it..."

"What's that?" the toddler Sokrates asks, pointing at the column head his father is chiseling.

"Sokrates, I've asked you not to interrupt me while I'm telling you a story." Sophroniskos looks up to see what his son is looking at, then answers with a sigh and a smile, "This is going to be the head of a column for the new temple of Theseos, which is why I'm telling you this story."

"Why?"

"Why what?" Sophroniskos asks, looking at his own work. "Why do it this way? Because we do it Ionian style nowadays, so it looks modern, instead of all flat and Doric like a Spartan or a Kretan might do it."

After a moment of struggling to build a sentence, Sokrates queries, "Why temple Theseos?"

"Why build a temple for Theseos?" Sophroniskos asks him, correcting his language. "Well, to house the Ship of Theseos, for one thing. That's an important relic of our city. And to give folks a place to sacrifice to Theseos if they want to honor him. He was a great hero of our city, so people like to offer sacrifices to those who they honor, and the temple is a place to do so. So it's a particular honor for me to get to work on the head of this column for his temple."

"What's an honor?"

Sophroniskos looks to Myron who just shakes his head. "O, wow. That's a difficult question to answer, Sokrates."

"What's a question?" Sokrates asks.

Sophroniskos stops chiseling with a sigh and looks to Myron, who sighs and smiles patiently. Sokrates' father shouts into the air, "Krito!" He waits a moment, then shouts again for young Krito, who he knows is next door at his father Kritoboulos' pottery workshop. "Krito! Come take Sokrates for a walk, will you!?"

Six-year-old Krito appears around the edge of the workshop's tent-flap doorway. "Come on, Sokrates. Let's go see if there are any clowns in the Agora."

Sokrates looks to Sophroniskos with uncertainty.

"Go on. I'll still be working on this when you get back. Maybe we will have come up with a way to define honor by then."

Sokrates smiles and runs over to Krito, who picks him up and tosses him once, then puts him back down and takes his hand to walk with him to the Agora just up the hill, patiently answering all his questions along the way.

"Why, those are flowers. I don't know what kind they're called.

"That's an olive tree. O, the bird in it? That's a bee-eater.

"Those are ants, Sokrates. They're very industrious, Aisop says.

"That's the goddess Enyo, goddess of war. Don't let her scare you, she isn't real; or at least that's just a statue.

"Now this is the Agora. We have to be careful; children will get kicked. We're not supposed to be here."

In the Agora, while business of a daily variety goes on at the shops along the edge, pieces of the famous Black Ship of Theseos are being carried across town to be placed and reconstructed in the newly rebuilt Temple of Theseos. A group of listeners is gathered around a debate between the visitor Anaxagoras and two other young foreigners - Protagoras, a hulking late-twenties man in a rough tunic, and Demokritos, who is just a teenager but carries himself with a nobleman's confidence and is dressed in a fine long shirt with colorful Thrakian embroidery. As the visiting foreigners debate, a beloved local Athenian street artist named Iota is doing caricatures of the men's expressions as portraits in lines in the sand.

Krito and Sokrates approach with curiosity. Krito sits down in a patch of grass while Sokrates remains standing, teetering, agape.

"It is a delicate question, indeed!" Anaxagoras muses loudly, so the crowd can hear, since they are clearly interested. "However, I know how my teacher Herakleitos would respond."

Protagoras folds his big arms and shakes his head with a smile. "There may be two ways of looking at it, but common sense tells you which is the right one. It is the Ship of Theseos, the very one which King Theseos himself sailed in. The fact that it has been repaired is insignificant. All ships, all objects, get repaired over time, and we still give them a sense of continuity in our minds."

The gathered Athenians murmur happily at the assertion that the ship is the actual Ship of Theseos.

"We do indeed!" Anaxagoras agrees. "But we think many things which are not correct, simply because it is easy or what other people are thinking." The Athenians' murmuring stirs darker, which Anaxagoras hears, and looking around he adds, "I understand that Athens clearly wants to think of it as the very Ship of Theseos, but let me ask this -- is there any one part of the ship which has not been replaced?"

An Athenian priest of Zeus Olympian in the crowd says, "King Theseos lived hundreds of years ago. No wood would last that long."

"So no, every part has been replaced by now," Anaxagoras asserts. "So, even though it was replaced piece by piece, and the parts are in the same organization that the old parts used to be in, I would say that it is *not* the *same* ship as the one that Theseos sailed in."

The crowd starts to boo like they do to insult-poets.

"The Ship of Theseos," Protagoras suggests, "is much like Athens itself, is it not? The spirit, the life of the thing, still lives even though the actual stuff of it may have been damaged or burned or rotted and replaced."

"Yes, sure, but..." Anaxagoras tries to continue, but the sentiment shared by Protagoras has busied the Athenian crowd with cheering that Abderan and his young comrade who laughs and smiles at his friend's successful argument, and idly whips up the crowd in his favor.

Anaxagoras just shrugs and gradually becomes ignored by the crowd.

Krito says to Sokrates without looking over at first, "Looks like we missed the triangle tricks. Now they're just arguing." But when he looks over for him, the toddler has toddled off.

Sokrates is already off toward another spectacle - the great ruin of the old Temple of Zeus, whose blackened hulk, ruined a decade ago by the Persians, has since been nearly covered with brightly colored graffiti both crude and beautiful. In front of the ruined temple, a couple of elderly priests of the Thunder God sit together upon a little wooden stool beside a holy bronze tripod, where itinerants are placing small offerings to be burnt.

Sokrates waddles toward the fire, gazing at the toppled columns of the ruin, and a foreign visitor stops him as he reaches into the sacred flame.

"Be careful, little Athenian. I don't want you to get burned while it seems I was careless watching. I'm new here."

Toddling little Sokrates asks, "What happened?"

The stranger eyes the ruined temple and says, "I'm new here, so I can't tell the story well, but I would guess that this was the work of the Persians, when they burned this city years ago. But this was the house in your city for your god Zeus. But it looks like he is in need these days."

"I want to sacrifice!"

The stranger, a steady-eyed Phoenikian named Melqartshama, bends down to Sokrates and asks, "Well, what do you have?"

Sokrates looks about his person, which is thingless.

"You don't own anything yet. You're still so young! Maybe once you've earned a wage and paid some of it for a bit of food or some wooden token, you can offer a bit of that to the gods. Just don't sacrifice your soft little hands! There's no earning those back."

The Phoenikian pats Sokrates on the bum along back in the direction of the Agora's crowd. Little Sokrates begins to wander toward the edge of the cluster that is listening to Protagoras and Anaxagoras debate, and asks a steady-necked grocer lady, Kleito, who is there with her husband Mnesarchos, a question.

"What are you doing?"

After glancing around to confirm the child isn't speaking to someone else, Kleito answers hesitantly, "I'm listening, little one. You know, you really should be more polite, and say 'Hello' to someone before you go right in asking them questions. Now then, what are you playing?"

Sokrates thinks for a moment, then asks, "What is playing?"

"Well that's when you ... You know how to play. All little boys do, by their very nature."

"What's a nature?" little Sokrates asks.

Kleito just shakes her head at Sokrates, then returns her attention to the debate.

After a few seconds of looking around, Sokrates continues on, eventually coming to a teetering stop in front of Simon the shoemaker's shoe stall. Simon is sitting very still in the tailor's position, cross-legged, quietly watching the world pass by outside his square tent.

Sokrates tries, "Hello."

Simon retorts, "And what exactly is that supposed to mean?"

Sokrates is taken aback by the question, and teeters as if struck physically by the thought. He blinks at Simon, who stares back at him.

"What's your name?" Simon asks after some silence.

Shyly, Sokrates just shakes his head, then asks, "What are you doing?"

"I'm practicing thirst and hunger," Simon answers, his body still motionless. After another moment, he explains, "They can be worth more than silver to those who wish to master self-control."

Sokrates and Simon stare at each other for a long time, at first stymied and intrigued by but increasingly getting to know and becoming comfortable with each other's particular marble characters - Simon a very old man and Sokrates a two-year-old.

Simon notes, "I see you're shoeless. The Agora's stones do bite."

Sokrates shrugs, and bites his fat little hand. He starts to suck on his thumb.

Simon says, "Stay here for just a few minutes, child. I'll shoe you," and begins to extricate his legs from each other.

Behind Sokrates, the crowd which had been listening to the debate has begun to disperse, and suddenly Sokrates runs away giggling and shouting, followed soon by Krito running past shouting his name, leaving Simon alone and smiling to himself.

Γ

Kimon and Elpinike discuss their future

Stone-faced Kimon and wandering-eyed Elpinike sit on their rooftop deck a neighborhood over from the Agora but in view of it as the crowd listening to the philosophers' debate disperses. Their house slave Amyntas sits in the corner, polishing bronze basins. Just below them in the street, three flute girls stand playing a melody on double-flutes.

Elpinike says, "I thought it was distasteful to see our city burned by the Persian army while we huddled at Salamis, but it was easier than seeing up-close as it gets eaten away from within by Ionian and Thrakian termites masquerading as 'wise men'."

Kimon says, "I defeat them by ignoring them."

Elpinike says, "That one is a rich man feigning to be a beggar, and that one is a slave whose master lets him act like a prince. Both are clearly clowns who missed their true profession."

Kimon laughs, and that frees up Amyntas to do so as well.

Kimon says, "I prefer Lakedaemonian brevity."

"This city needs a festival every day, or it doesn't know what to do with itself. With your leadership, perhaps some month might have a festival to Ares, to help our boys learn to really fight like heroes."

"We've already got more festival days than not. And I myself would exile every actor before I got around to a single easily ignorable foreign fool."

Elpinike agrees, "Truly, there is no one worse than an actor. The art ought to be outlawed. What is it but lying? That's why no one respectable would ever be an actor."

Kimon says, "Unfortunately, it seems the honeyed lie of the theater is the only way into the attention of many citizens, who believe no one unmasked. So it becomes a way to fool fools into believing otherwise distasteful truth."

Elpinike says carefully, "On the topic of masks, and distasteful truth..." She collects Kimon's eye contact into the sweet, pillowy net of her own, then begins to continue, but upon uttering the words stops herself, and he grimaces to communicate that he knows what she is not saying.

Kimon shakes his head softly to negate the notion, and reaches out to touch her face. She takes his hand and presses it into her hair.

Elpinike says, "We aren't children anymore. And I want to honor you the best I can. You know what father would've done."

Kimon frowns at her, as if to remind her that his were not all good choices for them, but her noble expression in defense reasserts his own same, and then he peers close into her eyes for confirmation. "I've known you your whole life, Elpinike. You know I can see through the masks you wear for others. You can't stand Kallias. You would never be happy."

"There are more important things than living to be happy, brother. And I know Kallias well enough to know that he will never be able to affect my disposition one direction or the other. You know me - I'm a cloud bird, a raptor; my bedrock is the treetops. Kallias is a ditch-dweller. We shall know of each other, but never actually meet."

Kimon laughs, but only very briefly before he is looking into her eyes with hard concern again. "But you would meet. Nightly. You would bear his children."

Elpinike looks down, then back up to Kimon hesitantly and with a coy, wry smile. "I will tell him that I love only Zeus, and warn him to expect demigod step-children. We are down to one slave between us, Kimon. You buy me flute music with what I know is next month's fig profit. This cannot last another year. Or ... Next year we can each have fifty slaves. And we can split Amyntas down the middle."

Elpinike smiles slyly at Amyntas, who smiles and gives a comical nervous expression, knowing it is a joke.

"But more importantly, you can continue your work. As the leading man of Athens. As the host of great feasts, rather than their conspicuous absentee. Athena needs you to have the wealth to afford armor again."

Kimon can't leave her eye contact - he is heart-deep in it - and his own soul-wells overflow in laconic stillness.

> "THERE IS NOTHING WHICH ESCAPES APHRODITE,
> NEITHER GODS, NOR ANY MORTAL HUMAN;
> SHE EVEN LED ASTRAY THE MIND OF ZEUS,
> THE ONE WHO REVELS IN THUNDER!"
> Homeros, *Hymn to Aphrodite*

ATHENS

Δ

Gorgo and the Spartan kings discuss the return of Pausanias

"I'm too sleepy," King Pleistarchos whines to his mother Gorgo, struggling to cling to her hips as she tries to hold him away.

"Stop," Gorgo growls, her patience gone. "You are the king, boy. You must act like a grown man around the other leaders."

"I want to stay here at home!" Gorgo's young son cries.

"The Overseers and King Archidamos are waiting for us," she snaps, finally crouching down to his level and turning his head forcefully to look her in the eyes. He tries to turn his head but she holds him firmly, and fear quickly fills the king's young face. "You don't want to look like a baby in front of King Archidamos, do you? He was just beginning to see you as a peer."

Twelve-year-old King Pleistarchos considers his mother's point with a quivering lip for a few moments, gazing into her eyes for the mother beyond the queen, and when he does not find her he begins to cry again and claw at her dress.

At that, Gorgo stands, unwilling to let him tear her best black dress, and she slaps young Pleistarchos hard across the face. Her fingernails leave three little nicks on his cheek. She grabs him by the shoulders and lifts him bodily into a standing position. When he refuses to use his legs to stand on his own she shakes him and shouts, "Stand! Stand! Stand! Stand!" until he finally does, and she steps back away from him.

"Pleistarchos, you are the son of Leonidas, the Lion of the Hot Gates! You are the descendent of one of the twin kings chosen by Herakles himself, the strongest man who ever lived! But it is up to you to *act like it!*" He keeps whimpering, staring at her, until she says coldly, "You must be still-faced now, King Pleistarchos, or tonight will not be sweet afterward. For you or your precious little turtle."

Very quickly, looking down, he calms his whimpering face into stillness, then looks back at her with a pleading emptiness of expression, his tear tracks already fading.

Gorgo nods, and walks up to him, puts her hand on his face to dab away the blood growing from the three fingernails scratches. Then she takes him by the shoulder, leading him out of their home and into the hot sunlight falling today on Sparta.

In the soft horizontal morning light, the government of Sparta is gathered before the standing, armored Wisdom Goddess in the temple of Athena of the Bronze House. The ten Overseers, elderly noblemen, stand in Spartan robes of the previous century's style, behind the two boy kings Archidamos and Pleistarchos who sit on twin stone thrones, wearing the shorter tunics more common among the younger generation. Between the thrones, draped in mourning black, is the fire-eyed Queen Mother Gorgo.

Skinny King Pleistarchos holds the stone tablet that was taken from the Persian messenger Gongylos, and looks closely at it to read it.

"We will not wait for the King's slow reading," Gorgo sighs. "Here is what it says: Your uncle, your regent, who speaks as Sparta abroad, who holds the city's spear in Asia, now offers his service, and our whole country, to Xerxes. Read, and weep, my son."

The most vocal of this year's Overseers, who often speaks for them all, asks, "What specific offer does he make to the King of Kings?"

Gorgo explains, "Sparta as the capital of the Persian satrapy of Hellas, with him its sole ruler, in exchange for one of Xerxes' daughters for a queen."

The Overseer walks up and snatches the tablet from the still-reading young King Pleistarchos. The other Overseers all follow behind him like a murmuration and cluster close to read over his shoulder and mumble to each other. "Treason! The Agiad King's regent conspiring to sell our country to Persia! Treachery! We cannot be party to this! The rest of Hellas would never trust Spartan honor again!"

The nineteen-year-old King Archidamos stands from his own Eurypontid throne beside Pleistarchos' Agiad one, and glares at Gorgo with a confused attempt at power-projection. "Thankfully one of Sparta's twin kings is a man. The treachery of your regent while away in Ionia was not unforeseen, young Pleistarchos, and is not the first from your House of Agis. I will act for both of us until a suitable regent is found for you, to replace this traitor."

"If only my boy had the same kind of companion king that you had at his age, Archidamos, when as a boy you ruled alongside my husband Leonidas, the greatest Spartan who has ever lived," Gorgo snaps. "You should try hard to be half as good a role model for young Pleistarchos as my husband was to you."

Gorgo turns from the silenced Archidamos, who sits back down, to the ten Overseers, whom she slowly approaches, and who shrink back away from her emanating confidence.

"My eyes among the Helots have informed me that Pausanias is on his way home from campaigning in Ionia as we speak; indeed he has already passed the Isthmus. He must report to you, Overseers, at this temple to Athena. Here She and I will get him to name the Athenian Themistokles, that treacherous pirate, as a part of this conspiracy, so that both snakes can be beheaded with one foot and one blade."

E

Pausanias meets with a Helot named Korax

At a small farmstead near the the village of Oion up in the old hills known as Skiritis north of Lakedaemonia, where goats and oxen linger around little wooden shelters on the hillside amidst a few thatch-roofed hovels, a burly middle-aged Helot man with long Lakedaemonian hair - Korax - chops wood outside of the largest hovel, which glows within from a dinner being cooked.

Korax looks up from chopping wood when he sees in the distance, across his low field of wheat, coming down out from the mountain forests to the north, Pausanias' entourage and palanquin tromping toward him from the horizon. He inhales deeply and smiles grimly to himself, wiping sweat from his arms onto his rough clothing.

A few other Helot workers who were weeding in the fields stop their work and bow as the royal palanquin passes them. Korax, however, remains standing and waits as the royal guards approach him and then place the palanquin gently onto the ground.

Out from the palanquin steps Pausanias, looking back into it for a moment and gesturing to another within to remain. The Spartan approaches Korax, who lowers himself onto one knee, but keeps his head high.

Inside the tiny house, Korax's wife Hippeia frets nervously putting away cups into cupboards while Korax and Pausanias sit at the main dining table. Pausanias, in his full panoply of armor, barely fits in the shack let alone the chair, but he seems to find this fact charming as he looks around himself.

He says, "If she is going to act so nervously, your wife might serve us better with her absence, Korax."

"My love, would you leave us for now?" Korax says to Hippeia. She leaves, glad to be allowed to leave the room. The two men lean forward on the table to face each other, each with a different fire in their eyes.

Korax says, "I expected your return in the spring. The men were prepared, then. It's already almost mid-summer. I can rally them again, but it will not be as easy as it would have been. The masters have everyone working the fields this month."

Pausanias says, "I thought the woman of the house had been sent away, Korax. Yet I still hear bitching."

Korax sighs, leans back, and gives Pausanias an annoyed look.

Pausanias says, "In your letters you promised me the five hundred strongest Helot killers. How many can I expect to see three days from now, armed and ready to descend on Sparta?"

Korax does some real math in his head for a second. "Certainly, at least two hundred. I suspect I can get another fifty, but I wouldn't swear to the gods or bet on it."

Pausanias leans in. "You are betting on this, Korax. You are betting the lives of everyone you know. So be right." He leans back again in his chair, and it squeaks like it is about to break under his armor's weight, but he ignores that. "Keep the secret, but get everyone you can. You have served Spartans for too long to not know that it will take four of you Helots to take down one unarmed Spartan soldier."

Hugely-muscled Korax steels his expression at Pausanias, and his whole sweaty body slightly flexes.

Z

Aoide and Dikasto eavesdrop

"Every day after the morning meal, the acolyte priestesses of this sanctuary will go out as a group, guided and guarded by their dorm mother, to collect mountain flowers and petals on the slopes of Mount Parnassos to fill their baskets that they will carry that day. The rest of the day, they are to prance and frolic about the sanctuary of Apollo, sometimes freely, sometimes in organized groups, and cast flowers and petals about with carefree abandon, until the west turns red, when they are to return to this dormitory for supper. Is that clear, everyone?"

The tough priestess with the long whip coils it slowly, eyeing the young acolyte priestesses gathered before her.

"Yes, priestess," the girls all say together quietly.

"Come then," she says, and stands aside from their dormitory door, allowing the girls to begin to file out into the sunlight. "Gather beauty."

It is Aoide's first day as an acolyte priestess, rather than just a student of the god. And unbeknownst to anyone else, she has a scrap of fish from last night's supper hidden in a fold under the belt of her dress, so that, while out in the woods, she might try to coax the wild kitten Ailisto into appearing.

The middle-aged priestess leads the young girls out through a back gate of the sanctuary, higher up the slope near where their dormitories sit, so that they are not harassed by men visiting the sanctuary. She leads the girls on a short hike up the steep slopes, to a meadow where the trees are sparse and bushes encircle a field of low grass full of wildflowers. As the priestess sits in the grass and weaves wreathes from the stems of flowers, the girls spread out and start filling their baskets with the brightest flowers.

While she gathers her flowers, Aoide keeps a continuous eye on the bushes, which seem to be the kitten's preferred method of camouflage, the few times that Aoide has seen her out here since that first day when the poet Hipponax gave her the kitten, and the priest made her put it outside. She occasionally rubs her fingers on the bit of fish hidden under the belt of her dress, with the hope that it will waft the scent onto the wind. But she doesn't see the kitten.

After an hour in the hot sun, the priestess stands with her own basket full of little twisted stem rings and she gathers the girls to place one of her wreathes on each of their heads, then guides them back down the slope to the walled sanctuary.

"I wonder," Aoide muses aloud as she prances with her basket lightly swinging, "with all these treasures and artworks gathered here - the most profound pieces of permanent beauty anywhere in the world, which men travel from beyond the homes of the winds to come and see for themselves, how can we simple girls skipping about and casting flower petals, the most measly and ubiquitous and fleeting and worthless of things, how can any of our small actions add any noticeable amount of beauty to the wonders of the world?"

"Because the daily, renewable, small things like a little girl experiencing natural ecstasies of innocence are actually the most wondrous things. A normal kiss between simple lovers, not some rape of gods. When men arrive at a place like this, and witness the wonders they've only heard described, there is inevitably disappointment, at seeing that which you've adored made mundane by simply being over there, and no more than it is. You girls, and your fleeting flower petals, are masks over the actual mundane nature of all these great works. And notice - men come to see the wonders, but their heads always turn from those when the girls come out. Even the King of Gods will get distracted by a pretty girl with a basket of flowers."

Just after they have entered back into the walls of the sanctuary, Dikasto reaches around Aoide from behind and knocks her basket out of her hands, sending her flowers tumbling down over the wall to the terrace below. Instinctively, Aoide shoves Dikasto with her elbows, starting the two into a shuffling shoving match which the priest at the head of their line quickly has to approach them to stop.

"First of all, one of you stinks of fish," the nearby priest Amphiramos chastises, whipping them each with his long, thin switch.

"She's being naughty for no reason," Aoide whines. "She won't leave me alone."

"She won't leave me alone!" Dikasto echoes. "She dumped her flowers and then started shoving me." She has a friendly, if mischievous, grin which she is trying to hide from everyone but Aoide.

"Go up onto the mountain to collect more flowers, then, just like the ones that you wasted. Both of you go, and don't come back until you each have a full bouquet for your basket just like you had before you started fooling around!"

Aoide starts to weep quietly, and the priestess sees this and swoops in close to Aoide, hovering like a hawk, her shadow covering the girl.

"Yes, I can see who is lying and who has guilt in her heart," the priestess says with a falsely sweet tone. "You see, little one, a lie cannot last within a little girl's heart. It will burn at you from the inside, and that is why you weep, while Dikasto feels no remorse. I will be watching you, little one. What is your name?"

Aoide doesn't want to respond, but the priestess repeats her question louder, and grabs Aoide's hair when she has to ask it a third time, finally making Aoide squeak out her name.

"Go up on the mountain and fill your basket back up, then, Aoide, and pray that the wild goat-men of the mountainside don't steal you away and ruin your virginity with their awful painful goat cocks. You too, Dikasto. I know you, I know you're not guiltless. Go!"

The priestess slaps Aoide on the bottom, at which she dashes off with her basket tight in her arms, her fleet clopping on the stone street until she is out the back gate of the sanctuary and running through underbrush. Behind her, she can hear the priestess cackling even after she has run some ways from the sanctuary gate.

Aoide looks back and sees Dikasto following her, grinning, heaving to keep up. Aoide snorts annoyedly and turns back, continues tromping up the mountainside, under the old pine trees, away from Delphi.

Dikasto's crunching footsteps follow her closer and closer, though Aoide refuses to look back and see her face.

"Can I tell you a secret?" Dikasto asks Aoide once they are out of earshot of the sanctuary, up the slope of Parnassos, in the trees near the meadow with the most varied flowers.

Aoide slows her walk, until finally she stops, and Dikasto passes her, then stops ahead of her and turns around.

"I'm not sure if I want to know a secret that I might need to be dishonest about with other people," Aoide admits. "Maybe you should keep it to yourself if you don't want people to know."

"I'm going to tell you anyway," Dikasto chides half playfully, half meanly. She starts to move toward Aoide slowly as she says, slowly, "I ... sometimes ... intentionally lose flowers from my basket so that I have to go pick more. Because I prefer picking flowers alone to dancing in line."

Aoide smiles and sniffs out a little laugh, glad that the secret is small. "Well I'm sorry you couldn't be alone this time."

"Anyway, it's not anymore dishonest than pretending to be happy when I'm not, which they ask me to do every day," Dikasto grumbles, sitting to pause and absent-mindedly pluck at some grass.

For a while, Aoide tries to ignore Dikasto, and focuses on searching the grassy slope for the flowers she is familiar with back in Athens, the flowers that her aunt would tell her to gather for their magical qualities in potions.

Dikasto asks her, "Why are you picking those ugly little ones?"

"These are the ones with healing magic," Aoide reluctantly explains.

"No one cares about that," Dikasto sniffs. "Flowers only matter for how they look, not what's inside."

"Until you eat one," Aoide says.

Eventually Aoide sits down next to Dikasto and sets her basket of little flowers down. She gazes down the mountain slope, into the wide valley of olive trees below, as slaves down there work the sprawling orchards.

"At least we aren't slaves," Aoide notes. "We're sort of lucky."

Dikasto scoffs, plucking at a flower's center. "At least they can talk freely about how they really feel! They aren't forced actors! They have the freedom of nobody caring about them as long as they work. Everyone cares too much about a girl, and wants them to be some phantom for them. Slaves get to be themselves."

"I wonder," Aoide says. "The slaves who worked for my father definitely weren't able to show their real feelings around him. And it made them unable to show their feelings anywhere eventually, for fear of him. Who is someone but what they get to do? They became just like dumb oxen, dead-eyed." She gazes out over the valley, imagining the faces of the many young slave girls and boys she knew back in Athens.

"Was he cruel to them if they showed emotion?" Dikasto asks Aoide, suddenly gentle with her voice.

Aoide looks back at her with a frown in her brow. "He was always cruel, but he was violent when they would act human at all. He actually told me one time that he couldn't keep slaves unless he thought of them like cattle - mindless beasts of burden. It made him feel evil to keep humans. As if ignoring that was less evil somehow."

Dikasto shakes her head. "I'm glad I wasn't born into a rich family. It seems like you would just be trapped into being evil, whether you wanted to or not. Good thing you got out."

Aoide says, "I don't want to think about home anymore," and turns away.

She puts down her basket and crawls away from Dikasto on her hands and knees, getting just a few body lengths of distance between them, while Dikasto watches her with a quizzical look. Then she sits in the grass just that small distance from Dikasto and starts making kissing sounds onto the wind, and casting her eyes in all directions looking for movement in the bushes. She crouches, and pulls a small scrap of fish meat from a fold in her dress where she had been keeping it.

"You've been keeping a bit of fish in your dress?" Dikasto asks with a little scoff. "Are you still feeding that cat?"

"Ailisto still comes for me sometimes, if I have time to wait," Aoide says, crouching down on a mossy patch of the mountainside.

They sit together quietly among the breezes, waiting for the kitten.

After just a few minutes, a rustle in the bushes heralds the arrival of the little cat Ailisto. Her bright golden eyes are wide like a wild cat's, but when she sees Aoide they twinkle happily, and she scampers over to her friend. The cat is just starting to grab the bit of fish in her little mouth when she notices Dikasto not far behind Aoide, and she starts with surprise, her eyes wilden again, and she hesitantly darts back into the bushes, dropping half the bit of fish in her haste.

"You scared her," Aoide whispers, smiling. Even such a brief visit from her wild cat friend will keep her spirits high for days.

"She's not really your friend," Dikasto chides, sitting beside Aoide in the moss. "She just likes the fish you bring her."

Aoide thinks about that, annoyed, for a moment, then replies, "Maybe I'd prefer someone who actually does nice things for me to someone who calls themselves my friend but is never really nice."

Dikasto, taking the comment to be about her, shoves Aoide and gets up to stomp away toward the sanctuary. After a few moments, she returns hastily, not looking at Aoide, grabs her basket, and tromps off again.

"I didn't mean to be mean," Aoide whines after her, intentionally too quietly, half hoping not to be heard.

Just then, she overhears two nearby voices with Spartan accents.

"The king said that Athens' walls must come down."

"He says that Pausanias, the Agiad king's regent, is furious at Themistokles for building walls that he promised Sparta that Athens would not build! But that's not all. Apparently Pausanias is so furious with Hellenes both Spartan and Athenian, that he has allied with his own slaves the Helots to upend Hellas entirely!"

"Quiet your voice, son."

"It's happening now. Every Helot I know is talking about it. There's a secret smith in a cave on Mount Taygetos, and they're passing out blades. I've heard Leonidas' nephew Pausanias, the little Agiad king's regent, plans to unify Hellas for Persia."

Recognizing political tinder, Aoide's ears perk up, and she stops collecting flowers to focus on listening.

"Will Xerxes return? I couldn't bear another generation of war. I want my sons to ride chariots at the games, not in battle."

"First the lowest men of the world will upturn society with a hundred thousand knives and make every slave a master and put the old masters underground!"

"Zeus protect us. That's terrifying. What makes you so sure you can trust these Helots?"

"I spoke to one whose life was threatened."

Aoide looks over at Dikasto, in the distance, where she clearly has also heard the conversation, and shoots out a hand to stop Aoide from moving or saying anything.

They wait there frightened, watching each other and breathing as quietly as they can, until the sound of the two Spartans walking away through the forest underbrush has faded from their ears. Once they are alone again in the quiet of the trees, Dikasto hugs Aoide tightly.

That evening, at the long dinner table where all the young priestesses eat together out in the open air, with a view of the olive valley stretching out below and the sun setting on the water of the Korinthian Gulf in the southwest distance, Aoide is approached by a girl just slightly older than she is, whom at first she doesn't recognize, though she looks very familiar.

"Are you Aoide?" the girl asks, leaning over close while she sits beside Aoide and sets down her bowl of stew.

Aoide nods and looks over at the girl. She guesses that the girl is an Alkmaeonid, like herself.

"I'm Klarelia," the girl says. "I'm your cousin. Far back, I guess. My great uncle is your great uncle."

"Hello," Aoide says with a polite smile, but before she can get another word out, Klarelia interrupts her.

"You were above the Kastalian spring around midday, weren't you? When two Spartans were filling their waterskins there?"

Aoide nods again, curious where this is going, afraid that she is about to get into some kind of trouble.

"What were they talking about?"

"Why?" Aoide asks.

"My mother asked me to collect news about the men of other Hellenic cities who come and visit here," Klarelia explains as she begins to stir her bowl of stew. "Particularly Spartans, and they don't come here often. When the information is useful, sometimes she pays me for it with honey cookies."

Aoide leans over and whispers so that only Periboea can hear her. "They were talking about Pausanias, the king's regent, making allies of Helots."

"I thought so," Klarelia nods. "That explains what I heard one say later, to a Theban."

Aoide clarifies, "They mentioned a revolt of the Helots. They fear it. That's their slaves, right?"

Klarelia furrows her brow and nods.

"What do you intend to do with this?"

"I'll tell my mother, that's all. I'm not the one who knows what to do about it. But mother has specifically asked for anything I hear about Spartan plans. Will you be my ears again, if you hear anything?"

Klarelia hands Aoide a small, coin-shaped biscuit with a man's face printed on both sides. Aoide wonders who the man is. The biscuit smells of honey. Aoide eats it slowly over the rest of that afternoon, for the cookie is so drenched with thyme honey that each bite is sweeter than anything she has ever tasted before, and lingers for a long time on her tongue.

"So, have you heard any great new poets since you've been here?" Klarelia asks her as they sit together within the pleasant, cool breezes of the mountainside.

Aoide smiles and shrugs, chewing, and Klarelia echoes her smile.

"Wait until the Pythian Games; the best singers and musicians will all be here."

Klarelia playfully kicks at her cousin's leg.

"You're so lucky. You live in the center of the world."

Aoide tries to summon the sound of a panpipe out of her memory, but she doesn't trust that what appears in her mind is the real thing. She feels equally distant from everywhere in the world.

H

Pausanias returns home

Just before he comes within view of the crossing of the Eurotas at the bridge called Babyx which represents the northern entrance to the area of the wallless city of Sparta itself, Pausanias transitions from being carried in his palanquin to riding on his fine, black, royal horse Phlogios, in order to appear more noble to his family and house slaves.

When he arrives at his home at the sparse northern edge of the city, leading his long entourage train, his sturdy and faithful wife Sophronia is standing outside the house on their fine stone patio, surrounded by the colorful flowers of her garden and wringing her hands with tears in her eyes.

Pausanias dismounts shining-black Phlogios, ties him up at the front post, and walks slowly up to his wife, whom he hasn't seen in more than two years.

"Sophronia, my wife," he says, reaching out to take her face in both his hands. He feels her warm tears and her smile half-form under worried eyes. He kisses her long, then asks her, "How are our boys?"

"They're healthy," she answers quickly. "They're sparring with the young hero Kleandridas in the courtyard right now. You should go and see them. Kleomenes is so much bigger than when you left."

Pausanias gives her a dry, distant smile, kisses her on the mouth, and walks with her into the house.

In the courtyard in the middle of the villa, Pausanias' two young sons Pleistoanax and Kleomenes are fighting with brooms while Kleandridas, a boy only a few years older than they are, barks orders from the sidelines where he is crouched, watching.

Lean-muscled Kleandridas instructs, "Stop looking at his body, small one. He's his spearhead now!"

"Father!" Little Pleistoanax, the older boy, drops his broom and runs to hug Pausanias when he appears with Sophronia from inside.

Pausanias says, "Old man," as he hugs his oldest boy.

Littler Kleomenes shyly shambles up, still holding his broom, and hugs Pausanias as well.

Pausanias says, "Young man. Have I interrupted a war between you two?"

"I'm Athena and he's old Enkelados!" little Kleomenes says, and looks into his father's eyes with a small step of courage.

"No, son," Pausanias replies coldly, "do not play as a woman. You are a man, and should play only as men."

Kleomenes lowers his head and nods.

"We were just practicing," Pleistoanax explains. He gives a princely nod of thanks to Kleandridas, who bows and leaves, dismissed.

"Your father is home from Ionia for good this time," Sophronia says to the boys while looking at Pausanias with modest hope for confirmation.

Pausanias lifts his chin, taking in his homestead with a critical eye. "No, in fact," he says. "I may not be remaining here in Sparta long."

As he is saying it, Pausanias' elderly mother Laothoe steps out into the courtyard from her private building in the back, wearing the black which she's worn since her husband died many years ago.

"Mother," Pausanias says coldly, giving her a strange stare.

"Pausanias the Easterner, home," she replies, noting the dark around his eyes.

Behind Laothoe is his younger brother Nikomedes, whom Pausanias is surprised to see here, away from his own wife and homestead many miles away, and their young sister Nikaia, aged from a gangly child into a young woman since he's been away, squinting at him from where she has been gathering flowers behind her old mother.

"Brother," Pausanias says carefully, ready in his soul to draw his hidden dagger, so severe is the look on Nikomedes' face.

"Brother," Nikomedes says, recognizing from Pausanias' expression that he must be making a strange one of his own, and attempting to remedy that with fake emotional neutrality. "We should talk in private."

Only once inside his mother's small house at the back of their family compound, away from the young ones and Sophronia, does Nikomedes finally reveal the source of his tension.

Nikomedes says, his hands on a table, looking down into strategy, "If you go into Sparta, brother, you will be accused of crimes."

"What crimes?" Pausanias asks, trying to remain aloof in case the known crimes are few.

Nikomedes looks up into his brother's eyes. "Treason against Sparta," he says, trying to express his hesitancy to believe it. "Against Hellas."

Pausanias stands still for a long time, trying not to let his gestures or expression belie his secrets. "Hellas," he says, as if just to make the concept ring in the air. He stares at his brother coldly.

Finally Nikomedes raises his chin and looks down along his face at Pausanias. "What are your plans?" he asks.

"I've been leading these men across Persian-occupied Ionia for the past two years. These men know nothing anymore except for *taking cities*. Do you really think these Spartans will turn against me at the order of some boy king, or widowed woman?"

Nikomedes blinks, shaking his head, unable to believe what he's hearing. "You think the men who haven't been abroad with you will turn and join a mutiny? You think Archidamos will co-rule beside a usurper?"

Pausanias declares, "I think Sparta has too many kings," and then stands defiantly in the echoing silence that follows.

His brother and mother study Pausanias' face with confused fear.

Eventually Pausanias continues, "In fact ... Hellas itself has too many kings. I think she deserves just one." He turns finally to face Nikomedes with full eye contact. "I will be King of All-Hellas, and All-Hellas will be allied with Persia. Sister empires."

Nikomedes sighs. "You've been away from Sparta a long time. Gorgo is not like Persian or Lydian women. She is a Spartan woman, and as much a lioness as Leonidas was a lion. You enter the city in peril."

Pausanias shakes his head, unwilling to believe that. "I am already the only man ruling Sparta. We have not become a nation of women and children in the past two years, have we?"

"Even if we did," Nikomedes says, "you well know that one should fear Spartan women and children more than the men of any other society."

Θ

First Assembly of the new year, new Archons are voted in

The first Assembly of the new year, at the height of midsummer when everyone is enjoying being outside and amongst each other, is always the busiest and most socially complex Assembly of the year. It is when the councilors, generals, and Archons of the coming year are selected. The few days leading up to the midsummer Assembly are always riven with controversies, debates, pleas, and gossip about whom the gods might choose - for even though the initial set of contenders for each office is selected by vote, the final choice is given through randomness to the gods.

As the meat of the sacrificed goats is being passed around in little clay bowls, many of which are stamped "provided for the people by the family of Ephialtes", the counselors from the previous year's council gather around the bema, preparing to host the vote for this next year's Archons and council.

Ephialtes and Perikles stand near the front of the crowded field of the Pnyx, eager to place their nameplates into the lot board.

This previous year's councilors stand around the bema, and the prominent speakers among them address the crowd with the usual yearly celebration of their own year's work.

"...And so, as the Year of Praxiergos comes to its end," declares loquacious Praxiergos, the outgoing Eponymous Archon, "we now welcome those chosen by each tribe to bring up their nameplates so that the random-lot board can allow the gods to select their preference from among those selected by men. Then, we shall vote for the generals, and then the civic accountants, and then the Archons."

Many of the assembled men of Athens cheer. The rest grumble and stand impatiently on the crowded hill.

Perikles whispers to Ephialtes, "Hopefully this will be your day."

"I sacrificed to Athena this morning," Ephialtes whispers back. "I got a good feeling from the smoke."

The herald holds up his snake staff and shouts, "Every man who wants to be considered by the gods for a place on the Council, bring your nameplates forward to the lot-board!"

While Perikles hangs back in the crowd watching, Ephialtes goes up with the Oligarch candidates from his tribe who decided to try to run against him, and the other candidates from the other tribes, as they each approach their tribe's tall rectangular ceramic lot board and put their nameplate into one of its slots.

After he has entered his nameplate into the random lot board, he waits at the edge of the crowd of other entrants, who linger around the lot boards to see which names the gods cast aside and which they select. He intermittently smiles back to Perikles as names are called out and others removed from the board.

Finally, though Perikles cannot hear it being called out over the many voices nearer to him, he sees Ephialtes turn to him and raise a fist high in the air with a big, open-mouthed grin to support it.

Ephialtes disappears into the crowd of potential councilors for a moment, then returns out from it again holding his nameplate in the air as he skips joyously back to Perikles in the crowd. On the way, many of those he passes congratulate Ephialtes for being selected.

"The gods see the same virtues I see," Perikles says to his friend as they embrace.

"I'm on the council!" Ephialtes shouts excitedly. "One of these months this year, I'll be in charge of the discussion!"

Perikles nods, smiling, his hand on his friend's arm.

"Now it is time to vote for the Archons and the generals!" the herald shouts over the many conversations of what to expect in the new year with this new crop of councilors.

"Congratulations, Ephialtes," the sculptor Sophroniskos says as he passes the two young men. "You're a brave man to take on the work of the council. I wouldn't wish the politicians life on a bad dog."

"One day you'll be Archon," Perikles says idly to Ephialtes as they walk closer to the bema where those who wish to make their case for being voted in as Archon are gathered.

"Don't you see, Perikles?" Ephialtes retorts, stopping him and starting into a whisper as if what he is saying is a secret. "Archon has become a meaningless office. All three of them. The War Archon doesn't command the Athenian armies anymore; the generals do! The King Archon doesn't command the state or foreign policy; the council and the Assembly do! And the Eponymous Archon just gets the year named after him."

"You know, I never thought of it that way. They used to be the leaders of the city, but I guess you're right - the current laws keep them from really having any actual power! The role is literally *nominal*!"

"Many men still think they're positions of power, but really they're just positions of notoriety. Best to get fools in the roles, so that they don't try too hard to leverage some power back to those offices," Ephialtes sniffs.

Rich men and nobles who vote with the Oligarchs get up onto the bema and make their claims for why they have earned the glory of being Archon and promise that they would never in a thousand years dream of trying to become a tyrant, but when it comes time to vote, the hands are raised for one who did not even get up and speak - a largely unknown actor's son named Demotion. Even Perikles is surprised when the man's name is mentioned and every Democrat hand goes up, and it makes him look over at Ephialtes to see the wry smile of pride that his friend maintains in that moment, and only then does he realize that Ephialtes must have organized this plan throughout the spring, and kept it from him.

"I wanted to surprise you," Ephialtes says through his smiling teeth. "You never get out and talk to regular people - but I do! And this year, the Archon is a solid Democrat."

The herald declares with a touch of confusion, "And so it is, our Eponymous Archon is fine Demotion, son of ... I'm sorry, who is Demotion the son of? Ah, son of Rhaegos the actor! Well, Demotion, would you like to say something to inaugurate your year as Archon?"

Young Demotion steps up on to the bema hesitantly; it is his first time at Assembly, and he appears not have expected this honor.

"Enjoy the year of Demotion!" he shouts after a brief stutter, and the whole crowd cheers. Demotion finds Ephialtes among the crowd, then, and points to him excitedly, waves.

Perikles declares, "Ephialtes, my friend, you are the god of politics."

"O hush," Ephialtes laughs softly, brushing off the notion. "The more regular people put themselves up for offices, the fewer offices the Oligarchs are guaranteed to get."

"I only gradually realized, as the Assembly progressed, how the entire production had in one way or another been part of your plan."

"There's only so much that men can do, with the random selection of lots left for the gods. But the gods let the knucklebones fall in our favor, so we would seem to be on the proper path. It always takes both effort and the gods' help - never just one." Ephialtes grins.

"So, now that you and yours are in office, only the fun part remains - spreading your ideas in the requisite drinking parties!" Perikles half-jokes, slapping his friend on the back as they start to walk into the crowd of the Agora.

"I can admit to you, Perikles," Ephialtes says, "I'm less worried about debating in the council than I am about leading the necessary drinking parties in the evenings. Myronides convinced me it's necessary, so I invited all the Democrats to Themistokles' Democrats club house mid-month. But I do fear it."

"Don't worry, I can be there with you for that, and block the blows," Perikles jokes, and he and Ephialtes horseplay-box for just a few moments before they pass a couple of young men who actually are wearing boxing wraps on their forearms, and stop out of embarrassment.

"What I really need from you, though," Ephialtes says, composing himself, "is to speak to the young men from your deme who are about to come of age, and make sure they understand how the government works."

"Teenagers are beasts," Perikles groans.

"Domesticating those beasts is one of our most important jobs. With the wrong sort of generation, this whole thing could collapse."

Perikles admits, "That's why I worry about doing it myself."

"I have faith in you, Perikles," Ephialtes says with a flat, serious smile. "You're the grandson of gods. You can do anything."

I

Anaxagoras makes friends while in line to register as a metic

"This is the office where you will all be able to register with our city as *metics*, meaning that you are foreigners and cannot vote or participate in the democratic offices, but you may stay in the city and work, and own property which our city will recognize. All you need is a name, and a land of origin." The tall, beardless painter

Polygnotos addresses the workers he has organized with a loud voice, so that all of them can hear him.

Anaxagoras stands in line with about thirty other foreign men, so that he can work with Polygnotos' painting crew that Kallias has hired to paint a wall in his house.

At the front of the line, where the young painter Polygnotos and his patron Kallias are arguing with the official in charge of metic registration about how long it will take to register this many foreigners and whether everyone here speaks Hellenic, the line of men starts to shift backward, forcing each man in line to bump the man behind him to move a step back, and this ends with the man just in front of Anaxagoras who wasn't paying attention being knocked to the ground with a fleeting Aigyptian "Sorry" from the shaven-headed Aigyptian who bumped him.

Anaxagoras helps the man to stand again, and in doing so ends up also somewhat awkwardly shaking his hand and introducing himself.

"O good day, friend-stranger. I am Anaxagoras, of Klazomenai."

"Melqartshama is my name," the man replies, brushing off his dusty pants, "but I'm not sure where to say I'm from. I haven't lived in any one city for more than five years since I was too young to remember. Phoenikia most recently, but before that Lykia, Phrygia, Lydia, Ionia, Kypros..."

"Say that you are Ionian," Anaxagoras replies with a smile. "Then you and I will be compatriots!"

Melqartshama laughs and shakes Anaxagoras' hand again. "So be it!" he laughs. "I am Melqartshama of..."

"...of Miletos," Anaxagoras says. "It is big enough, just in case no one from that city knows you."

"I will just have to pretend to know more than I do about Thales!" Melqartshama jokes.

"You know of Thales?" Anaxagoras asks excitedly. "I am a student of Thales' wisdom myself! Before I came to Athens, I was traveling Ionia, trying to learn what I could from the living philosophers who we have left."

Melqartshama shakes his head, saying, "Not many left these days. Unfortunately, it's looking like that was our grandfather's generation's thing. But I too love to study what scrolls I can find on the topic."

"I tell you, Melqartshama, philosophy is not dead as long as men like us keep the interest in it alive!"

"If you say so, friend," Melqartshama replies with a smile and a little laugh. "I personally find it lasts in the ways that are useful. Take the sage Anaximander's concept of *'the unlimited'* - *apieron* - for example. He suggests that the heart of everything real is something by its very definition unnatural, this *unlimited*?"

Anaxagoras grins excitedly and says, "O, we are friends, Melqartshama. Just as Anacharsis of Skythia said to Solon."

"I haven't heard that," Melqartshama says with a smile, thirsty for a story, "what did Anacharsis say to Solon?"

"Well Anacharsis was a Skythian, but he heard about Solon's wisdom so he traveled all the way from Skythia to Athens just to meet him. And when he showed up at Solon's door, Anacharsis said 'Hi, I'm Anacharsis, of Skythia, and I've traveled all that way to be your friend,' and Solon said 'It's better to make friends at home.'" Melqartshama only has long enough to frown in dismay at that response before Anaxagoras laughs, "So Anacharsis told Solon 'Well then you should be my friend, because you are at home!'"

Melqartshama laughs, relieved that the men in the story became friends after all.

Just then Perikles is approaching in a slow stroll, not looking for anyone in particular but simply walking for pleasure. He raises his chin in recognition when he sees Kallias, but does not at first veer over to talk to him. However, once he notices Anaxagoras lingering in the line, his expression brightens and he stops and approaches the line of foreigners.

"Fine morning, Perikles," Kallias calls out from the front of the line of foreigners. "Come, join me, talk a moment!" He gestures for Perikles to come over, so Perikles makes his way through the coming and going people to join Kallias further ahead in the line, gesturing to Anaxagoras to wait.

"Good day to you, Kallias," Perikles says. "How many workers does Polygnotos need to paint a wall? It looks like you have a whole Argo full of men here."

Kallias begins to explain, but the handsome painter Polygnotos leans into their conversation from aside and interjects before Kallias is able to speak more than part of a word, "Four walls, Perikles, not one. And he wants them finished in less than a month. Which isn't a problem - but it means I need this many men so that I can be a hundred-handed painter."

"Artists," Kallias says to Perikles with disdain, trying to commiserate.

"Anaxagoras of Klazomenai!" Perikles shouts with a smile when he is finally able to make eye contact with the man. "Working for this low-wage employer, are you?"

"Hey now, I pay the standard wage," Kallias protests with a friendly laugh. "You two know each other?"

"Hail, Perikles," Anaxagoras says, coming forward so the two men can clasp forearms. "How was the Assembly today?"

"Confusing as always," Perikles replies. "I didn't know you were a painter," Perikles says to Anaxagoras.

Anaxagoras explains, "I have convinced your friend Kallias that my skill with geometry can be applied to any trade to improve it, so I will be applying mathematics to improve the process how I can."

Polygnotos, the painter, rolls his eyes and walks away from the conversation.

"Interesting," Perikles says with a frown, uncertain how mathematics can improve a paint job, but intrigued to find out.

"Perikles, meet my new friend Melqartshama! He's from Miletos, just down the coast from Klazomenae, in Ionia!"

"We've been reminiscing about the wine of our homeland," Melqartshama says with a smile and a slight bow to Perikles.

"And arguing about Thales and Anaximander," Anaxagoras laughs.

"I've been to Aigypt," Melqartshama remarks with a raised eyebrow. "So I know that all is not water - for all is not wet! Aigypt is the best place to see that. But I'm willing to acknowledge that maybe there isn't anything at all."

"Careful what the priests here hear you say," Anaxagoras laughs with a slightly paranoid glance around himself. "I have already been chastised."

Thinking his city an open-minded place and not one known for religious extremism, Perikles asks, "What were you chastised for?"

"For trying to explain to a curious old man what Anaximander meant by 'unlimited'. He turned out to be a priest of Poseidon, and proceeded to define for me very sternly his own views on the limits of things."

Melqartshama laughs, "Were you chastised for failing to explain your own views, or for succeeding?"

Perikles, trying to keep up and failing, asks, "Who are these men you speak of - Anaximander and Thales?"

"Natural philosophers from Ionia. Men of our grandfathers' generation used to explore ideas by attempting to prove them in nature. But our fathers' generation unfortunately got caught up fighting back the Persians, so now that tradition is mostly gone. The young men of Ionia today are hardly interested in writing of any kind, let alone the esoteric and new. Which is why men like Melqartshama and myself have decided to travel."

"Indeed," Perikles nods, "and Athens is lucky to have you. I find I learn the most from the men who are most different from me. I wonder, though - what has brought you to Athens, of all cities?"

"Don't you know?" Melqartshama says with a snort of surprise. "Athens is the most famous city in the world! Everyone wants to come to Athens."

"I hadn't realized that," Perikles replies with a smile. "We're still half a ruin."

"Well, for one thing, here you can't be beaten in the street," Melqartshama adds with all seriousness. "Try living in Sidon on a worker's salary without getting caned ten times a day by absent-minded Overseers. That'll make you wear your best shirt, alright, just so you're not mistaken for a slave!"

"Wow," Perikles says, speechless imagining such poverty. He hasn't had a poorer friend than Ephialtes, and Ephialtes is just in a family new to money, hardly poor.

"Don't worry, friend," Kallias interjects. "You'll be treated in Athens as well as any citizen, no matter how lowly your quality or what country your origin. Here we recognize that Athena sees all men equally pathetic and absurd and unsuitable as suitors. Now tell this man your name and the city of your origin, so you can get your identification bar."

K

Oligarchs chat at the gym

The Athenian gymnasion called the White Dog, just outside the city wall, was supposedly set up by Herakles himself, and the building is constructed around an ancient stone platform which has functioned as an altar to Herakles since ancient times. On this ancient rock sculpted by the adoration of centuries now the boys wanting to prove their might break and bleed their knuckles as offerings to Herakles.

The gym is busy in the afternoon, full of men of every sort all nude and glistening with olive oil, but the wealthy and influential Oligarchs have one whole quarter of the place freed up just for their sons to box. Kimon, Alkibiades, and

Thukydides stand together around the entrance at that side of the gymnasion, where boxing lessons are in session. Oloros son of Phaidros, who is sixteen, and Alkibiades' sons Axiochos, twenty, and Kleinias, twelve, are being trained by the famous Olympian victor Diagoras of Rhodes. Oloros squares up against Axiochos as Diagoras circles them, shadowboxing. Kleinias, the younger brother, waits for his turn at the wall while nursing a split lip.

Clustered in the doorframe while they watch their sons, Alkibiades and Thukydides have summoned over the passing Kimon to talk politics.

Alkibiades growls, "I'd like to bring that mouse Ephialtes in here some day and have a round or two with him. I'd like to make him choke back those smug smiles with blood just once."

Kimon says, "The only way to beat someone like Ephialtes is by lowering yourself to his level, and playing the game of politics. I'm beginning to understand it, I think. It isn't knucklebones. It definitely isn't boxing. It's something more like playing the Persian game of pawns on a crossboard. Subtle moves and countermoves, no one of which can seem decisive, lest you appear too manipulative. Were the stakes not so great, I would worry the work was below my nobility."

"It's a new world, Kimon," Alkibiades says. "The old ways of our grandfather namesakes are like the skin of an old man. At first, as he slows but still lives, it merely wrinkles and sags, but once he stops dead, it'll rot away within weeks. The strength of our old ways, our old laws, is the skin of a dying man, and Ephialtes means to put coins on its eyes."

Kimon says, "That is a weird, disgusting metaphor."

Thukydides barks angrily, "Something needs to be done! Look at Xanthippos' son Perikles - a Democrat! We can't even count on our own children following us. Perhaps there's a revolution among the gods on the docket. You know how the air smells before a storm? Perhaps this is a version of that, where men's souls are the air and the gods are gathering a war."

Kimon says, "You're being melodramatic, Thukydides. I suspect men of our age have always felt this way about the young who don't have the luck of our perspective, yet. We're just farther up the hill of life than Ephialtes and Perikles and those poor uneducated masses they muster to their vote. We know what's necessary and what's been shown not to work."

Thukydides punches his palm as he barks to his friend's son Oloros. "Oloros, until your mother gets the chance to dip you in the Styx by your heel, you have to keep your guard up! How many punches to the gut do you want to take?

Axiochos is bigger than you. That means you need to be quicker! You're supposed to marry my daughter when you're older, but only if you get strong!"

Oloros turns to listen and gets punched in the face.

"You know what I heard the other day at the Piraeus docks," Alkibiades begins, making Thukydides laugh.

Thukydides says, "A thousand idiotic stories begin that way."

"I heard merchants discussing the cities of Italy. It's not the old world to the east where the real money is, but the new world, to the west. The indigenous people there can't get enough Hellenic products. And the Hellenic colonies out there, I've heard it said, are bigger and richer even than the home cities here."

"I would have to see it to believe it. I've heard Syrakousans say that their island of Trinakria is an entire world, beyond simply an island. But then everyone says that about their island. They also claim it's the island where the Sun God kept his cattle, mentioned in Homeros, but of course that's silly."

"The West, where the giants are buried under the mountains and hurl flaming rocks out," Thukydides adds.

"Not often," Alkibiades retorts. "These days the priests do their duty and keep the gods and giants appeased."

"Still," Thukydides responds, shaking his head as he imagines it, "it doesn't seem worth risking a business venture upon. If you can avoid the region where Zeus buried the giants of old, why not avoid it, you know? I've lived through a quaking of the Earth from below, and never want to again. All praise due to Poseidon." Thukydides spits in his hand and holds it against the wind to give some to the god, then runs the rest through his hair. "I'll keep my business here at home."

Λ

Sophroniskos and Phaenarete sing stories to Sokrates

At Sophroniskos and Phaenarete's tiny one-room house that evening, as Nyx lowers her blanket of darkness upon the Earth, Sophroniskos sings the toddler Sokrates a Homeric prayer to his favorite god as the little boy is falling asleep in a pile of furs beside the hearthfire.

"Sing, clear-voiced Muse," Sophroniskos sings in his low and resonant voice, "of Hephaestos famous for skill..."

Beside them, Phaenarete smiles warmly as she patiently weaves an ornate little blanket at a small loom beside her stool.

"...With bright-eyed Athena he taught men trades all across the world," Sophroniskos sings. "Men who before dwelt in mountain caves like beasts..."

Sophroniskos kneels down near little Sokrates and pets his soft-haired head. Sokrates just stares up, sucking his thumb, eyes wide.

"...But now with skills they learned from famed Hephaestos, men live easily and peacefully in furnished homes year-round..."

As he finishes the song, Sophroniskos cuddles little Sokrates from behind and wraps his big sculptor's arms around the little boy as he falls asleep among the dancing fire shadows.

Phaenarete puts away her loom work and stokes the hearthfire, which is the goddess Hestia, and should never be allowed to die.

"O wife," Sophroniskos says with a sudden moroseness, "do you ever wonder if it's fair to a baby to bring them into this misery-filled world?"

"I think about the tale of Solon answering King Kroisos of Lydia's question about who he thought was happiest in the world," Phaenarete replies after a moment of thought looking into the fire. "King Kroisos, as rich a man as there ever was, assumed that Solon, as wise a man as ever was, would see that he, Kroisos, must be happiest. But Solon answered that the happiest among men was an Athenian peasant who worked hard, raised a happy family, and had no desire for greater wealth as a king might recognize it."

"But how does one know how best to raise a happy family?" Sophroniskos asks her. "Are you happy, my beautiful friend?"

"I'm happy when I'm with you and our little Dew-drop," she answers, meaning little Sokrates. "I worry when I hear other men speak, but I'm happy when it's just us."

Phaenarete leaves her stool and crouches close to Sophroniskos and Sokrates, laying her cheek down close to Sokrates' on the fur and looking into his little eyes.

"Dew-drop, have I told you yet about *The Battle of Frogs and Mice*?"

Sokrates, nearly asleep in his father's arms, barely opens his eyes, to show that he is still listening.

"This is an old, old story, older than most," Phaenarete says smiling. "My grandmother sang me this song when I was about your age. It's by the greatest epic poet, blind old Homeros, who also sang the *Iliad* and *Odyssey*! It is best understood by young children, because as adults get larger and taller, they stop being able to find eye contact with the smaller animals of the world, and forget they're there living lives as dramatic as our own.

"So to begin my story, I pray the Muses will help me find the words, as I attempt to describe the day that the Mice of the meadow won a great victory over the Frogs of the pond, and showed valor equal to Men's.

"One day a thirsty mouse whom I'll call Crumb-Snatcher had just escaped a nasty ferret in the field and was setting his soft muzzle at last to the water's edge for a drink, when a big-eyed frog arose from the muck and said, 'Welcome friend! King Puff-Jaw am I, son of Mudman and Waterlady; and who may I ask are you, so that I might call my new friend by name?'"

Little Sokrates chuckles at the frog voice his mother puts on. Sophroniskos provides additional input to the story via thick fingers playing against his back, as the family giggles on buck fur rugs together in the firelit night.

M

Pausanias arrives at Sparta and confronts the kings

Pausanias and his entourage and guards approach the Temple of Aphrodite Warlike, where the Overseers and kings and Gorgo hold court.

Pausanias walks up with his guard of fifty armored men behind him. He himself is in the ornately carved armor which he wore in victory at the Battle of Plataia, with two big bulls clashing their horns in the center of his breastplate. He puts down his geometrically patterned shield and presents himself to the Overseers.

Pausanias says, "Overseers of Sparta; King Archidamos. I, Pausanias, regent to young King Pleistarchos, have returned from my mission to Ionia."

The Overseers stand together silently. King Archidamos and King Pleistarchos each sit in their thrones, while Gorgo steps forward from between them.

"And how fares Ionia against the lingering Persian threat, cousin?" the Queen-Mother asks.

Young King Archidamos adds, "The Athenians Kimon and Aristides seem to have collected the entire Aegean as allies in their own effort. Do you return with similar alliances for Sparta?"

Dark-eyed Pausanias says, "Not allies, but subjected cities. Most importantly, Byzantion, the great barbarian city at the mouth of the Black Sea, successor to Troi in its command over the Bosporos."

The vocal Overseer interjects, "The word is that Kimon and Aristides are only able to gain so many ally cities because of your arrogance and tyranny."

King Archidamos says, "As the regent to my fellow king, you are my equal in power, Pausanias. So you know that any foreign agreements Sparta undertakes we must agree to together."

"You are a boy yet yourself, Archidamos," Pausanias says fearlessly, evoking gasps from some of the Overseers. "You kings are not raised like the rest of us Spartans, in the toughest conditions. You are spared that hardship. And you have not yet fought in a battle, have you?"

Archidamos stutters to start to respond, but his moments of hesitation are interrupted quickly.

"And though this gorgon who still claims an old queenship may think she is the true power in Sparta, all real Spartan men know that in truth it is only I, Pausanias, commander of the armies of All-Hellas at Plataia - the savior of All-Hellas - who now commands the men of Sparta."

Pausanias glares with derision at black-veiled Gorgo.

"The twin kingships which Herakles himself put in place here do not die today!" Pausanias shouts, turning to face the Spartans of the city who have begun to gather at the smell of drama. "They do not die today," he repeats as he turns back to face Gorgo and the Overseers and boy kings, "because they died long ago, and Sparta has not had a true king for years now.

"Herakles was subservient to no Overseers, no council of elders.

"All around us, cities of Hellas wither under the disease of foolish leaders who let swineherds take their reigns of control. Under King Pausanias, there will be no question as to who commands. It will be me."

"And you yourself will be commanded by vile Xerxes," Gorgo says, then throws the tablet of his missive onto the dust and adds, "or will it be by your Persian wife?"

Behind Gorgo, a soldier drags into the firelight the still-breathing but broken body of Gongylos, the Persian messenger whom Pausanias gave the missive to. His recognition of the man appears on his face instantly.

"Yes, he is familiar to you, isn't he?" Gorgo says. She turns to the Spartan Overseers and shouts simply, "You see? The conspirators recognize each other."

Pausanias raises his hand, and his personal guard form a half-circle spreading out on either side of him, facing Gorgo and the kings and Overseers. They stomp the butts of their spears in unison, and Pausanias' heart races at the sound.

"I can't know how much your loyal guardsmen might know about the extent of your treachery," Gorgo says, holding up the stone on which his missive to Xerxes is inscribed, "but let those who recognize your writing see the words upon this stone, the words with which you offer up your homeland into Persian hands for the price of one Persian princess as your whore!"

Pausanias looks to his left and right quickly, trying to confirm that his men are remaining stalwart without giving up that he has glanced thusly, for fear it will show his uncertainty.

"I hear you traveled to the Temple of Haides to have the priestess speak to a ghost," Gorgo says. She watches Pausanias' expression, which he steels to avoid giving away any reaction. She shakes her head when he gives nothing away. "One can only wonder which ghost of many might be the one you feel you have reason to fear. But I know whoever it is must haunt you still, here." Gorgo keeps her eye contact on Pausanias, but raises her own hand into the air, and shouts, "Bring out the children!"

From around the other side of the temple, where they had not been visible, a gaggle of about twenty children all barely of walking age are herded together into view by a couple of sword-wielding elderly Spartan women. One of the women holds her sword out with its point in the middle of the group of kids.

Each of Pausanias' guardsmen recognize their children in the group. A few remove their helmets, revealing faces that have become ashen and despairful. One drops his spear clattering onto the cobblestones.

"Strength, men," Pausanias growls.

"Brasidas!" the man who dropped his spear shouts, unable to control his fear. "Don't hurt my boy, crone!"

The woman with the sword pointed into the group grabs one of the children and puts the blade up to his throat. The boy does not scream, but stares steadfastly at his father among Pausanias' guard.

"Will you be Spartans today," Gorgo asks Pausanias' guardsmen, "or will you be traitors who forfeit their entire family lines to the blades of justice? These young ones of yours are merely the first that will die, before your eyes, from among the families of any of you men who turn against the rightful kings of Sparta today."

Again Pausanias keeps his eyes on Gorgo, trying not to show his concern by looking to the side to confirm whether his men are remaining loyal to him or not. But once the man right beside him also drops his spear, Pausanias exhales long and loud through his nose, then turns on his heel and begins a fast walk away from the proceeding.

The crowd of Spartan men and women part before him, all eyes on Gorgo, waiting for some sign of what is to be done. Pausanias pushes those who do not move quickly enough, still not running but walking as quickly as his clattering armor allows, in the direction of the neighboring Temple of Athena of the Bronze House, a low, pillared building gleaming from the many bronze treasures inside.

Once it becomes clear that he is headed to the other temple, Gorgo shouts, "Spartan soldiers! Do not let this traitor reach the Temple of Athena! Seize him now, while you can!"

At that, Pausanias begins to run, his armor barely slowing him, and the men who had this morning been loyal to him start to move through the crowd to stop him. But none of them move quickly, and before any of them are near him, Pausanias clatters up the steps of the Temple of Athena and finally slows his run, stoops a moment to catch his breath in his heavy armor, then ascends the last few steps into the brightly-shining temple.

"Do not pursue him into the temple," Gorgo commands the soldiers who moments ago were Pausanias' loyal guard. "You men stand watch here, and when he emerges for food or water, take him into custody. Let no one care for him but the goddess that he flees to."

Pausanias' men reluctantly take guard positions outside the entrance to the temple, as Gorgo and the Overseers and citizens all gather in a tight crowd outside, looking in.

Inside the temple, Pausanias stands in his armor before the ancient bronze statue of Athena, also armored, and kneels before her.

"O Athena," he says loud enough to be heard by the crowd outside, "grant me sanctuary from this traitorous woman, this non-Queen."

Many of the Spartan women in the crowd outside the temple, loyal to Gorgo, groan and boo at his insult to her.

"My son the King's regent, his uncle Pausanias, has forfeited his life by betraying us all!" Gorgo shouts to the crowd around her. "He is safe in the goddess' care for now. But the moment that man leaves her grace, he will be under arrest, and I promise he will be tried at a court of All Hellenes, beside his co-conspirator, the Athenian Themistokles, recently exiled by his own city and now taking a similar refuge in neutral Argos. But be assured, Hellenes - these traitors to civilization will not go unpunished!"

The Spartan citizenry cheer laconically.

Gorgo turns to the slave girl Nikoleta who had been with Pausanias.

"You, girl," Gorgo says as she turns to face the girl and then slowly approaches her with careful, investigating eyes. "You have the countenance of a princess. No doubt Pausanias took you from one of the cities of Byzantion. Perhaps you are a princess of Byzantion itself? Yes, of course. What is your name, girl?"

The girl says, "He has named me Nikoleta. I'm a slave now."

Gorgo walks up to Nikoleta slowly. "A name for a trophy. But you are mine now. And before I decide if you will be my slave, or if the gods would prefer that a woman of your nobility ought to be free, I must know who you really are."

The girl quietly drips tears into the dust and repeats, "Nikoleta, a trophy of war."

N

New Athenian councilors are inspected by members of last year's council

The newly elected councilors for this year are gathered into their ten urban tribes at the governmental side of the Agora between the old square Council House where the city councilors meet and debate and a new, under-construction circular building called the Tholos, which is intended to be a new space for the councilors to eat and sleep. The previous office-holders are giving the newly elected councilors an official inspection and interview before being inducted into their offices and introduced to their duties. Ever-smiling Ephialtes and never-smiling Alkibiades stand beside each other, part of the same urban tribe despite their differences in lifestyle.

One of last year's councilors explains, "Now keep in mind that at least a third of you must be in the Tholos or the Council House at all times, so you will need to set up among yourselves some kind of shifts for sleeping here nights. The beds are quite comfortable, and only the western corner gets the morning sunlight before it is palatable. But you will want to bring your own blankets and any other bedding comforts you may prefer.

"And so as you may or may not know - the council works like this: each of the ten tribes is Prytany for one tenth of the year, and that just means that you will be the ones who are in charge of calling and facilitating the work of this council. And each day, one member of the Prytany will be Caretaker of the keys to the treasuries and archives and all of that, and is essentially the chief executor of the duties of this council.

"Now let me just tell you - I know you all probably put your names in, like I did, with the idea that you were going to get to be king of the city for a day. But let me tell you - it's more of a hassle than an honor, and you'd best be ready to do a lot of walking and lifting when it's your day to be Caretaker."

The newly elected officers of the council laugh good naturedly, then one of them shouts, "Now, which of us shit-shovelers shall be king first?"

"Hold on, have patience, men," last month's Prytany leader cautions with a chuckle, gesturing not to move. "We still need to finish inspecting you all to confirm no foreigners or women or cabbageheads have weaseled their way into public office somehow."

Ephialtes watches as the short, beardless councilor from last year, a pig-nosed old man named Xanthos, walks up to handsome, expensively dressed Alkibiades, who towers over the old man. Xanthos looks Alkibiades in the eyes from below and snorts. With a sweep of his hand Alkibiades moves the bottom of his cloak and kneels before the smaller man to bring their eyes closer.

"You are Alkibiades, son of Kleinias, yes? Your family is well known in Skambonidae Square."

Alkibiades smiles coyly and nods. "That's where I live, yes. You're just down the street from me, Xanthos. Surely you can account for my not being a cabbagehead. And I know we frequent different gyms, so you might not have seen my dick yet, but I assure you I am no woman."

Xanthos just grunts. "I deem you worthy of the council of Athens," he says, and waves his hand.

Alkibiades chuckles, trying hard to express comical shock to his friends at the gall of the poorer man to judge the richer man worthy.

Xanthos then steps over to Ephialtes, who is not as tall as Alkibiades and is closer to the ugly man's bad breath. "Who are you, then?" he asks.

Ephialtes winces. "Ephialtes, son of Sophonides."

Xanthos looks up at Ephialtes with an expression of disbelief. "Your father named you after the Giant of Nightmares, Ephialtes? Do you also mean to storm the home of the gods on Mount Olympos?"

Ephialtes shrugs. After a moment of Xanthos staring at him, Ephialtes says, "Father wanted me to be bold."

Finally Xanthos grins, squinting, and says, "I like your name. Where are you from, friend?" The ugly man belches, then waves away the smell of it.

"We live in the Skambonidae neighborhood, like you two. My father and mother make pottery in Potters' Alley. So we are only home at night."

"O you're the Ephialtes from the bowls! I've seen your name, but I thought it was talking about the nightmare giant. Okay. Those make more sense now. Well, congratulations on the gods selecting you for the council, friend. And thanks for the bowls! I deem you worthy of the council of Athens." He waves his hand and continues on to the man beside Ephialtes.

Tall Alkibiades leans down to whisper to the shorter Ephialtes, "We are both leaders of our city now, noble Ephialtes. And we are sons of the same tribe. So I ask you - why should we continue to be at odds?"

Ephialtes takes a long, slow breath, keeping his eyes on the men who are setting up the lot boards.

"Will you ignore me, friend?" Alkibiades snaps, already bringing out his usual tone of superiority.

"I was taking a moment to think about what to say," Ephialtes explains. He looks up at the handsome, short grey beard on the Oligarch and then into his eyes, and says, "You call me noble to placate me. I do not need to feel like I was born into privilege in order to see value in myself. I find my own value in the value of the ideals for which I struggle. And it is those to whom I will be true - not to any man, of my own or another tribe. Though through being true to my values I end up being true to all men, as that is my value. Because I know that it is only through fidelity to my values that I am best able to help the most of my fellow men, with all of whom I feel equal."

Alkibiades snorts and looks away early in Ephialtes' response, and he coughs twice toward the end to communicate clearly to Ephialtes that no one is listening anymore.

The men from last year's council who had been inspecting their tribe's incoming councilors all gather in the center of the crowd of five hundred, once all the inspections have been completed, and while one particularly old man pulls the bones out of a hare and places them into a sacrificial bronze tripod, the loudest among them shouts to the whole group, "Excellent! Strong, wise Athenians all around! So now, the last step before you all are officially members of the council before the eyes of the gods is the Councilors' Oath! So while Hermon burns this rabbit's bones here, you all should come up to this tablet and read its words as an oath! So come up here and file past. If you do not read letters, don't worry - I will help you to understand the words."

The five hundred men of the new council all cluster around the tall stone tablet which two teenage Skythian assistants are now leaning against a low column while shaky old Hermon gets some hare bones burning. Ephialtes is pushed and leaned against by the crowd for several uncomfortable minutes before he is able to make his way up to the front of the group where the tablet is readable. He stands on his toes and puts his hands on another man's back to keep upright as he reads his oath aloud from the weather-worn, decades-old tablet.

"I, Ephialtes, son of Sophonides, hereby take this oath to Athena and Poseidon and all the kings who formed this land, as I begin my office on the council of Athens: I swear that my father and mother are Athenian born; I swear that I am not less than thirty years old; I swear that I take on this office in good faith; I swear that I will advise this council only to the benefit of the city of Athens; I swear that I will advise according to the laws set down by our ancestors."

Ephialtes thinks about what he has just sworn for a moment, then adds to it, "And I, Ephialtes, though I need not do so, swear that I will advise according to what is best for the most people of Athens."

A man beside Ephialtes squints at the tablet when he hears Ephialtes add that final language, and he asks Ephialtes, "Where does it say that last part?"

"It doesn't yet," Ephialtes replies, "but it should. If you like it too, maybe we can get it added." He slaps the man on the shoulder as he begins making his way back from the oath-chanting crowd around the tablet.

Ephialtes finds Alkibiades hanging back away from the tightly packed crowd of councilors around the oath tablet. Alkibiades nods to him.

"I learned the oath by heart yesterday, so that I wouldn't have to deal with such an ant hill," Alkibiades says with a nod to the mass of men. "I've seen this happen before, and want nothing to do with sailors' sweat. Thanks to you Democrats, that swarm of wasps is all oarsmen, now - too smelly a lot to get close in with."

"Hey, I was an oarsman at the Battle of the Straits," Ephialtes replies, leaning against the same low stone wall as Alkibiades. "I know exactly what you think about oarsmen, and how only you rich men are actually able to put out the money to *build* something as complicated as a trireme, but you simply can't ignore the fact that no trireme would be able to function were it not for the row after row of those oarsmen you hate so much - those skilled naval warriors! And the ship of state of Athens is just like a trireme, impossible to run without the effort of row after row of men who need no riches to be able to do what they must - work together for the savior of all!"

As other councilors who have completed their oaths start to gather around the two men's discussion, Alkibiades holds up a hand to indicate that he would like to add something, but Ephialtes takes the accruing audience as fuel for his idealism, as he realizes for the first time that he is essentially giving a speech before the council.

"It is now our duty, we whom the gods chose, to use that same skill of working together, to bring Athens into a new era of glory and happiness - through equity between men! We here are all kings! Each dirty, calloused, one-eyed, toothless one of us!"

"O Ephialtes," Alkibiades snorts, "I want to laugh, but you go too far, and I feel it more appropriate to vomit! You really think that there is equal wisdom between a horse-owning nobleman suckled on the stories of only the best bards and taught to wrestle by Olympic victors, and some trireme oarsman whose sole education is watching his parents find cheaper and cheaper ways to make pots?"

Another Oligarch, the piss-smelling leathersmith Kleanetos, takes Alkibiades' place as he becomes too flustered to continue - this man a much calmer, more temperate man with his hands folded placidly in front of himself. This man eschews the garb of an aristocrat and wears just as rough a tunic as Ephialtes, this man a tanner of hides, but his measured manner and confidence belie his family's noble status.

"Master bowl-maker's son," Kleanetos the master tanner says slowly, "what the master horse-tender might mean to imply, though he cannot find the right words for it, is that we Oligarchs are the ones who have the knowledge necessary, the vantage from above, the generational experience of aristocracy, of being the best people, which you Democrats who cannot see above each other's heads might not know about."

"The same idea, spoken by men of different wealth or ancestry, contains the same amount of wisdom," Ephialtes replies. "It is the ideas themselves that have value, not the men."

Without clear arguments against, the nobility among the council grumble to each other at the general notion, but the men in poorer garb with dirty faces smile and nod, and grasp each other with optimism.

Old Xanthos, no longer a councilor himself, steps up beside Ephialtes with a shallow bowl full of wild berries and offers it to him, saying, "Fuel for the fire of the fight, friend, since it's yours now."

"Come, comrades," Ephialtes calls out with a broad smile, "share these berries of the field, courtesy of democracy itself, and Xanthos here! We are city councilors now, lords of ourselves and shepherds of our city!"

"Lords of the bleating sheep," Alkibiades scoffs, leaving.

Ξ

Perikles educates young citizens on their upcoming responsibilities

The Monument of Heroes centers one edge of the Agora - a wide stone podium on which stand ten tall bronze statues of the ancient heroes after whom the ten Athenian democratic tribes are named. The statues all stand stiff and expressionless in the archaic form. In front of the statue of the hero of his own tribe, old King Erechtheos, sharp-bearded Perikles stands facing a group of teenage boys from his own Erechtheos tribe.

"Now listen, boys, for you'll be voting men soon, and it is important to know how our city's government works, since gods may choose you to be a part of it. So first, let me make sure you understand the basic structure of democracy."

"In the beginning, there was only Chaos," jokes colorfully-dressed Oloros, son of the aristocrat Phaidros. His friends, Kallias' son Hipponikos and Alkibiades' son Axiochos, all teen-agers, stifle their laughter.

Perikles tries to ignore the boy, and merely gives him a stern look.

"As you may know, only ten Olympiads ago the great Athenian Kleisthenes reorganized our ancient tribes into new political tribes which each include populations of all wealth levels, from the city, from the midlands, and from the coasts. This way, each of our tribes remain essentially equal in power, and diverse in interest and voices. It also keeps politics from being just a question of who your family is, and each man is allowed to set his vote toward his own preferred agenda.

"So now while most cities have a king who inherits his power from his father, or an Oligarchy where a few rich men conspire together to rule all the rest, our city was lucky enough to give birth to the sage Solon, the wisest man who has ever lived, who invented our unique system of self-rule which we call *democracy*, so-named after the villages full of everyday people who rule, instead of a single monarch at the top of society.

"Now, as you all will very soon be passing from your teenage years into the responsibilities of adulthood, let me prepare you for what you will need to do. You probably don't remember, for you were just babies at the time, but when you were first named, your parents enrolled you in the records of our city. Once you enter your eighteenth year, you will need to come back to that same registrar, right here in the Agora, to be enrolled as a voting male citizen of Athens.

"Then, once you've registered, you'll receive one of these, with your own name and your father's name imprinted on it." Perikles hold up his own bronze identification bar for them to all see.

Young Oloros raises his hand and after being pointed to by Perikles asks, "Does yours say your father was a sea-onion?" The boys close to him laugh, while most of the rest simply listen awkwardly, waiting to see if Perikles will get angry or try to punish Oloros for being disrespectful.

"My father was Xanthippos," Perikles says, trying to remain professional and patient, thinking about how he is representing Democrats.

"So was *he* the son of a sea-onion, then?" Oloros asks. "Is that why your head looks like that?"

"He was a descendent of Poseidon, quite distantly, as a matter of fact, through Nestor, but no," Perikles says with an exasperated sigh, vainly trying to wield his aristocratic background against the boy. "Now allow me to continue."

"It must get tiring holding up a head shaped like that," the boy Oloros nods, as if in understanding agreement.

Perikles sighs with frustration. "My head is normally shaped," he finally says very quickly after struggling with whether or not to address it.

Oloros nods to his friends. "It's our heads that are strangely shaped. Sea-onion is the correct shape of a man's head."

"My head is not sea-onion shaped," Perikles grumbles.

Now all the boys are laughing, not just Oloros' friends.

"You know," Perikles says with a sigh, finally feeling overwhelmed enough to fully lean on his nobility for confidence, "my father Xanthippos commanded the Athenian contingent at the Battle of Mykale, which is basically one of three reasons you all aren't Persian slaves right now - Mykale, Salamis, and Plataia. But for those three battles, you would each have big, hairy Persian cocks in your mouths right now. So think about those sea-onion heads, why don't you."

Oloros' laughter has only multiplied, though some of the other boys are shocked back into submission by Perikles' tone.

"Do you want me to tell your father about this, Oloros?" Perikles threatens.

Teen-aged Oloros scoffs at Perikles with a mocking grin. "O, I am definitely going to tell father about this."

O

Pausanias is visited by his family at the temple of Athena of the Bronze House

"Father?"
    Pausanias wakes on the cold stone floor of the Temple of Athena of the Bronze House. He finds his knees again, but they ache from kneeling before the statue of the goddess, so he turns and sits on the floor in exasperation, uncomfortable in any position. Only after some long moments of adjusting himself does he notice what woke him - his young son Pleistoanax, standing small in the street outside the entrance to the temple, the golden afternoon light making his soft young skin gleam.
    Pausanias starts to rise, but slumps back down, weighed down more than ever by his armor.
    Little Pleistoanax stays far back, in the dust of the street, seemingly afraid to set foot even on the stone of the steps of the temple. His scared, child's voice is difficult to hear over the wind. "Father?"
    "Who sent you to see me, Old Man?" Pausanias croaks to him.
    "Why don't you come home?" his son asks.
    Pausanias says, "I am with our goddess Athena."
    "I thought you had come home."
    "I've been in the east, fighting our enemies," Pausanias says with almost no energy. He wonders if his son can even hear him.
    "I wish you had just come home," his young son whines.
    "I will, my son. But right now I must pray to Athena for guidance. So I am supplicating myself to her."
    "You dare lie in front of the goddess," Pausanias' mother's old voice chastises in a tone he remembers from his childhood.
    Pausanias only then notices his mother Laothoe standing tall at the side of the door of the temple, her face veiled in the old way of widows. She is cradling something in her hands, but being silhouetted against the sunlight it is impossible to tell what it is. Only that she is holding something with weight to it.
    "Mother," Pausanias says, raising his chin. He stands, with some difficulty in his armor.

"Son," the tall, stalwart old Laothoe says gravely. He can tell instantly that she is not going to tell him anything he wants to hear. Then finally she says, "You defile yourself with your attempts at deceit. Have you even deceived yourself?"

"You brought Pleistoanax just to taunt me, didn't you?" he asks rhetorically. "You want me to leave the goddess. But I won't. I won't give myself to that woman."

Crag-eyed Laothoe says, "You mean Queen Gorgo."

"A dead king's wife, a weak boy's mother ..."

"A woman who has beaten you. You would prefer that Sparta have no king, but merely a Persian governor. And in exchange for this lowly office all you request is a Persian princess for your new wife. Are your slave girls not enough?"

"I want to unify Hellas! King Pausanias of All-Hellas. *I* am the general who led All-Hellas to victory at Plataia - the true turning point in the Persian War - and yet somehow everyone is still talking about Leonidas' *loss* as if *that* is where Sparta's heart is buried. All I asked to match my glory was for the Serpent Column at Delphi to be dedicated there to the god, by *me*."

"You claim the glories of victory against Persia to explain your suppliance now to them?"

"You'll never understand!" Pausanias bellows, finally standing and turning to face his mother fully. "The weight of rule, of ambition against other men, washes past your veil like water across a duck's wing."

Laothoe reaches up to her veil and pulls it aside to show her full expression, which is desperate disappointment. She then shows him the brick that she has had in her hand this whole time, and she places it in the center of the entrance of the temple. She rises and looks to him again, and now, though her hard face contains traces of pity, his face is only hate.

"Gods damn you, mother," he shouts. "You have never loved a thing on Earth!"

"I have loved others," Laothoe says to her son. "But a parent can always tell when a child ought to have been reabsorbed. I should have eaten you when you were smallest, like Kronos. I knew it already then. I foolishly doubted the Fates. But I too am just a dead king's wife, and a weak boy's mother..."

Despite himself, Pausanias lets loose some tears, and looks away.

Laothoe turns away, and behind her are the other noble women of Sparta, the wives of the Overseers, and the widows of the wars, followed by the Overseers themselves, and finally simple citizens, who one after the other each place another brick in the threshold of the doorway of the inner sanctum of the Temple of Athena of the Bronze House, leaving them loose so that some light shines through, but symbolically heavy enough to be immovable.

Slowly, Pausanias is closed into darkness as the gleams of bronze fold into shadow.

Π

Kimon and Elpinike meet at the temple of Aphrodite Heavenly

Aphrodite Heavenly's temple in Athens is north of the Agora, beside the even older temple to her husband, Hephaestos. Both temples were burned by the Persians ten years ago, and the old Hephaestion is still mostly a ruin, but the temple of Aphrodite has already had its cedar roof restored, and its scorched columns repainted in bright reds and dark yellows.

Kimon and Elpinike go to the temple at night, and not together but from different directions, so that they see each other through it, in torchlight and starlight, when they each arrive on this night that they are to divorce.

No one will know. Their marriage is not on any record of the city, and no official needs to undo it. There was no dowry paid between them. But they both have agreed that the goddess needs to witness their parting. And not Hera, goddess of domestic partnership, but Aphrodite - she who brought them together in the first place.

The two walk into the flowered temple and up to the beautiful young priestess who is on duty. She rises from her pillowed bench to greet them.

"Welcome, noble siblings, children of Miltiades," the priestess says.

"We would have a prayer to Aphrodite," Elpinike tells the priestess, then bows her head.

Kimon takes a fine, ceremonial knife from his belt and reaches with it up to his sister's neck, then takes a handful of her hair and saws off a lock. He does the same to his own shoulder-length hair with a quick, careless swipe, and hands the two mingled locks to the priestess.

The priestess holds the lovers' locks above a brazier beside her couch, in which embers are lightly glowing. "Great goddess of love and beauty, Aphrodite of the Heavens, whose chariot is drawn by a dozen doves, please hear these lovers' wish." She drops the hair into the fire.

At that, the priestess raises her hand above her head and closes her eyes, and from the colored veils behind her, a flutter releases a flapping flock of doves into the room, who all fill the space for a moment with their winging until they have each found their way out the open entrance. The priestess opens her eyes calmly again and gazes between Kimon and Elpinike with a smile, her hand still raised.

"The goddess has heard you," she says.

Surprising her brother, Elpinike slaps Kimon on the cheek hard enough to make him flush, then she grabs his tunic and pulls his face close to hers, into the petrifying bath of her eye contact.

"If you ever forget your own glory, may Eros slap you again," she growls against his face. "And never believe the mask I will have to wear." She can't help but bite at a tiny kiss before pulling away, but she turns fast once out of his gravity, and does not look at him that way again.

He touches his lips to feel her kiss again in his mind, and finally first feels the pain and blood released there by his sister's bite.

The city is preparing for its yearly celebration of Athena in all her forms, the Panathenaia, the biggest and most important religious festival of the year. Young priestesses of the Wisdom Goddess are busy garlanding every corner of even the most humble and barely-standing structures with lines of braided flowers of every wild sort, whispering and laughing quietly to each other down every street.

Kimon stands upon a rock near the base of the Rock of Ares, and listens to the city, trying to appear unapproachable in this shadow as he quietly cries upon his own face.

Down in the Agora, Kimon can see Kallias standing and chatting with some of the councilors near the Council House, his jewelry standing out from the crowd of drab tunics.

Kimon waits in the shadows until he feels his face doesn't show that he'd been crying, before he finally descends into the Agora and approaches Kallias, pulling him away from the men he'd been laughing with.

"Elpinike is ready to be your wife," Kimon tells him, unafraid now whether anyone else around them hears, which a few do, and turn to listen, some more discreetly than others. "She is excited to be the wife of such a fine man. But as the brother of my fatherless sister, and the one who is responsible for her well-being, I promise you, I will not end my watch on that purpose. I will always be there for my sister Elpinike, and ... brother-in-law ... the fine and noble Kallias, son of ..." Kimon grimaces as he realizes that he does not know the name of Kallias' non-noble father.

Kallias says, "Kallias, son of Hipponikos, the great horseman," mostly to the crowd.

Kimon nods, and repeats, "Kallias, son of Hipponikos. Will you be my brother-in-law?" He holds out his hand to be grasped like warriors do.

Kallias shakes his hand like a merchant and grins broadly. "Yes, Kimon. Yes! A thousand times, yes."

As Kimon swallows his contempt, the crowd around the two men applauds, and a group of slave women sing a brief song of praise to Hera, goddess of marriage.

Kallias leans in to Kimon, touches the side of his neck with a concerned look, and brings his fingers up to show that they are bloodied. "You've injured yourself," he says.

Kimon touches his head where he roughly cut his hair and feels the soft warmth of blood. "I'll live," he says with a failed attempt at a smile.

P

Ephialtes hosts his first drinking party as a city councilor

Two double-flute playing slave girls give a brief performance to the small crowd of old hands and young new Democrats waiting outside Ephialtes' father Sophonides' house before their host Ephialtes finally, with somewhat awkward formality, opens the front door to his guests. Perikles, standing near the head of the small group of waiting party guests, leads a modest applause for the flutists before heading inside. Ephialtes nods to each man as they enter, but most deeply to Perikles, who lingers to enter last.

"If I bite my lip, you must save me, Perikles," Ephialtes whispers playfully to his friend as he enters the house past him.

"How?" Perikles whisper-laughs.

"Think of something," Ephialtes whispers back as the two men move hesitantly away from the door and join the mingling group of standing men who are all slowly making their way through the entry room and into the mens' sitting room, the andron.

Before passing through the entry room, old Aristides the Just closely inspects a painting on a board hanging on the wall, of the family who lives in the house - Sophonides, his wife, and his son and three daughters, all painted in the archaic style of the previous century.

"How old are you, Ephialtes?" Aristides asks with a smile.

"I turned thirty this year," Ephialtes replies. "Which is why I finally tried for the council. Now, would you like to..." he tries to guide the older man along with the others, into the sitting room.

"I thought you were Perikles' age. I didn't know you had sisters," Aristides says, as he moves slowly to respond to Ephialtes' gestures of direction. "Tell your father I like his choice of painter for that image - it reminds me of the old days. Charming."

By the time Aristides and Ephialtes are finding their seats beside each other on a couch in the men's sitting room, the other men are all loudly arguing about which goddess they themselves would have chosen in the Judgment of Paris, and handing a carafe of wine around to serve themselves from.

"No female companions for this party, Ephialtes?" Myronides asks from his couch across the room.

"I am wading into hosting slowly," Ephialtes admits, raising his hands in the air. "There is plenty of wine. But no, no women. And don't even joke about the flute girls - they're friends of my family, even though they're Skythian slaves."

"Too young is too young," sunken-eyed Myronides spits contemptuously, as he grabs the carafe of wine from a new, rough-edged Democrat named Antiphon. "I like mountains and grasses to have grown on the land before exploration."

"So tell us about the council," Antiphon shouts across the room. "Do you know yet when your tribe will hold the Prytany for the month?"

"Not until winter," Ephialtes replies. "And of course, with fifty men in my tribe, it isn't a certainty that the gods will select me to be one of those who get to lead the discussion. There are only so many days in each month. But you can be certain I will be sacrificing and praying loudly."

The Democrats all laugh. Another young man asks, "When will you propose enfranchising the poorest citizens, who still can't be on the council or juries or..."

Ephialtes shakes his head, already overwhelmed, and holds up a defensive hand as he stutters, "I'm only there a week so far. I do everything I can, I say everything I can think of, but there are five hundred men on that council. There's only so fast one rower can turn a trireme, you know?"

"Sure, sure," the young Democrats all nod, understanding that metaphor, most of them having oared in the triremes themselves, if not at Salamis at least in the more peaceful navy of today, where turning a trireme is still a laborious effort which requires all oarsmen working together.

Aristides comments, "Well let me tell you - be glad that we old men of the Areopagos still take on the most challenging cases, because I would not want five hundred uneducated saplings deciding on the fate of Athena's olive trees or something that could pollute the whole city like a murder or that sort of thing. It isn't even easy for us - and the Areopagos is all the best, most experienced men in one place at the same time."

"The Areopagos is a flock of mean old crows on a rock," someone whispers so that everyone can hear it.

Aristides sniffs out a little laugh and only half-heartedly looks around to see who said it. When it isn't obvious, he stops looking. "You would not want to be an oarsman in the belly of some ship with no admiral guiding your larger plans, would you? I understand that not all the old Archons are the wisest of individual men, nor the kindest, but when we are all together up there on Ares' rock, I don't know how to describe it other than to say that something magical happens. Nowhere else can I imagine Ares tamed by men, but I have seen it happen on the Areopagos."

"Aristides, you must stop aging now, so that you never leave us an Athens without your wisdom," Ephialtes says with a big smile. Then he raises his cup of wine and shouts, "Hail, Aristides the Just, model of Athenian foresight and temperance!"

All drink to that.

Aristides remarks, after drinking, "Every tradition was built for a reason, Ephialtes. I understand you desire to perfect this system of ours, as Kleisthenes improved upon Solon's inspiration, but do not equate traditional with corrupt. The nobility may lose sight of what unites them with those who are nearer to their own needs, but it is also only nobility that can provide things like education, experience, etiquette, et cetera. Imagine the Panathenaia, the greatest celebration of the gods that we Athenians put on, without the benefits of the luxuries provided by the rich."

"Do you know who's going to be singing the *Iliad* and the *Odyssey* this year?" tough young Antiphon the horseman asks.

"You see, Perikles," Ephialtes jokes, "you're right to go into producing theater. Who sings which song is all young people care about."

"I thought we were the young people," Perikles jokes back.

"So did I until I realized that now we're the ones in charge," Ephialtes remarks with a comically overwhelmed expression.

"Do you know who's singing Homeros' songs or not?" Antiphon asks again, annoyed this time. "You Democrats only know how to digress - you can't answer a question directly! Everything makes you think of something else! This is why I never come to your parties!"

Ephialtes gestures to one of his father's slaves for her to pour more wine for Antiphon, who only accepts it begrudgingly. "My apologies, Antiphon," Ephialtes assures him as the man impatiently holds out his cup to be refilled. "Don't let my social awkwardness paint Democrat ideals poorly for you - I assure you, these are only my own faults!"

"A toast to democracy!" Myronides shouts, raising his glass, and all in the room raise their own. "Invented by an Athenian, perfected by the Athenians, and spread in its less than one hundred years of life all throughout the Hellenic world because it is virtuous, and it works!"

"To democracy," everyone agrees, and drinks.

"May it uproot every tyrant across the world," Ephialtes says.

"Careful what Zeus hears you saying," Antiphon jokes. "He's a tyrant himself, so he can't hate them too much."

"No," Aristides corrects, "Zeus is a despot - he seized control and simply maintains it through threat. A tyrant is someone who has been voted into power democratically, but then seizes power for himself. Tyrants are the worst kind of people, much worse than despots."

Sunken-eyed Myronides turns the wine carafe upside down and shouts, "Is there more wine, Ephialtes?"

"O wow, we're already there," Ephialtes remarks with surprise as he stands and crosses the room to a set of jars and grabs a new carafe to dip into one of them. "Well, I had been hoping to wait until I was drunk to bring this out, but since I'm already up and refilling the wine, and I see it, I might as well pull this out now."

Hesitantly, Ephialtes pulls a scroll out from inside one of the tall jars on the floor in the corner of the room. He puts it on the table beside himself as he fills the wine carafe and then hands it to one of the young men nearby, who starts to pour and pass.

"A missive," Ephialtes says, "from Themistokles in Argos."

"What does it say?" Perikles asks eagerly.

Ephialtes looks over the scroll for a moment, shooting Perikles nervous glances, before he finally starts to summarize, "He expects to be prosecuted by a congress of All Hellenes, alongside the Spartan regent Pausanias, who apparently is back from Ionia, for whatever reason, and is wanted for treason by the Overseers of Sparta."

"Why would Pausanias return to Sparta unless he plans to take control there?"

"That's a good question. But perhaps Pausanias is innocent of the purported crimes, since Themistokles is also suspected, and we know that *he* isn't guilty of selling out Hellas to Persia," Ephialtes proposes with a shrug.

"Do we?" Antiphon asks.

Ephialtes and Perikles both shoot the kid glances to reckon how serious he is, and when he appears not to be joking, they both at once speak over each other in responding.

"Themistokles would not sell out Hellas to Persia!"

"As if Xerxes would take his mortal enemy Themistokles!"

"You young ones have a lot to learn about foreign affairs," Myronides barks at Antiphon.

"And history!" Perikles adds. "It was only ten years ago Xerxes watched from the shore as Themistokles led our ships to victory against his own in the straits."

Myronides, who fought that day, shouts, "Where do you think those ochre-colored masts stacked at the edge of the Agora came from? Those were from ships we sank, son!"

Antiphon shrinks into himself at the onslaught of barks from his drunken Democrat comrades, and starts nodding silently to show that he understands.

"And how is Themistokles' family faring after his exodus?"

"The man's long-suffering wife still weeps daily, I'm told, but when I've seen her she was smiling. Of course, few women when tested truly have the patience of Penelope. His oldest, Archtepolis, continues to race horses with my boys at the racetrack. Perikles should know - the family of exiles are not themselves disgraced."

"Not officially," Perikles adds.

"Well, you're Alkmaeonid too," Myronides notes, "so it's probably hard to tell which direction your neighbors' derision is coming from." He laughs and takes a long gulp to finish his drink, then he whips his cup to throw the dregs of his wine across the room at Perikles. The wine does not make it across the room, but Perikles dodges with his body nevertheless.

"Hey!" he shouts.

"Myronides, behave like a Hellene, not a barbarian!" old Aristides barks from across the room.

"It's called *kottabos*, Aristides; it's a game," Myronides slurs back. "You toss the chunky dregs of your wine across the room and try to get it into one of the jars."

"I know about kottabos, and it is not played upon your friend's face," Aristides admonishes, sitting up to threaten standing and crossing the room.

"Don't stand, old man, I hear you fine," Myronides replies, waving his drunken hand. "Can you forgive me, Perikles, for mistaking your noble Alkmaeonid face for the face of some god or king on a wine jar?" He laughs raucously, his eyes closing intermittently.

Perikles eyes Aristides, who shrugs to him silently.

"I forgive you if you promise to keep voting Democrat," Perikles jokes dryly. Myronides rolls his sunken eyes.

"Good man, Perikles," Aristides laughs and leans back again onto his elbow. "If I can teach you young men anything," he adds as he pours more wine from the carafe into his empty cup, "it would be to be patient with other men, and kind to them. I have found that even the angriest wretch can be brought back to reason with enough patient kindness. If you do not fear for your life, stay patient and kind. You don't keep an international alliance like the League of Delos together by acting like harpies."

While Aristides is speaking the last words of his sentence, Myronides suddenly lurches forward from his couch and vomits onto the floor, making all the men groan loudly with disgust.

Σ

Pausanias is haunted

Sparta's Temple of Athena of the Bronze House becomes a blinding oven for a few hours each afternoon. Athena's bronze shields and panoplies of armor arc Apollo's sunlight into the center of the temple, in front of the statue of the goddess, and in the fast-motion that the day begins to pass in when Pausanias has been sitting in the same position for more than one full day, the shafts of light swing like swords and seem to pierce like spears once they are aimed upon Pausanias' supplicant, motionless face. He turns from the light only to find other shafts of light, and there is a period of indeterminate time in the late afternoon where he feels there is no escape from the blinding, burning sunlight coming from every angle, multiplied by every bronze surface surrounding him, and in those moments he feels certain that he will either burn alive or become a bronze man like those of old.

Pausanias raises his eyes to the phantoms of reflection in bronze, the metal of his swords and armor. Athena is everywhere to him, except in one dark shadow, where the ghost of a girl he killed stares at him with cold eyes.

"I didn't mean to kill you," Pausanias cries to the ghost. "I heard a noise in the night, and my military instincts killed the killer they thought was there. But it was you - you who had given herself to me willingly. Or was it to spare your family? One can never know what is behind the will of others."

Shapes in the bronze reflections that surround Pausanias pierce his mind and stir its fears.

"Why do you still haunt me, even here? For two years now you've pursued me in my dreams, repeating to me your hideous poetry, but why now do you offend the light of day with your ghostly shade? At the Temple of the Dead, you told me to return to Sparta, that this was the only way to sate your hateful vengeance for my mindless murder of you. So home I've come, where no doubt you knew I'd meet this fate. Then why, among all this, why must you still visit me here to haunt me further? Will your hatred follow me even into the Underworld?"

Pausanias hangs his head and mashes at his weeping face with his futile hands.

T

Gorgo attempts to influence Niome in the temple of Aphrodite Warlike

The Temple of Aphrodite in Sparta is the only two-story Hellenic temple, with two different epithets of the Love Goddess worshiped on its two different levels. On the ground floor is the Temple of Aphrodite Warlike, that version of the goddess who beds down with the War God Ares outside of her marriage to the Lame God Hephaestos. On this floor also, years ago Gorgo installed the dual Spartan thrones, bringing the room to function as the center of Spartan government. Behind the thrones, a life-sized, modern stone sculpture of Aphrodite looks out at the throne room, fed and watered by priestesses chosen by Gorgo for their beauty and wiliness.

On the floor above, where only a few priestesses are allowed, is the Temple of Aphrodite Shapely. Up there, framed within an alcove on a large stone pedestal, surrounded by little olive oil lamps, is an ancient, barely human-looking wooden semblance of a female form, worn smooth by adoration over untold centuries.

Nikoleta kneels before the wood goddess and beholds its soft beauty.

Gorgo explains, "This is our ancient Aphrodite. This form of the goddess has been worshipped here since before there was a temple. Before there was even a city. The elders say this was the form of Aphrodite that the War God fell in love with, in the age of gold."

She approaches Nikoleta and crouches behind her, putting her arms under Nikoleta's arms and around the sides of her torso slowly, whispering ever closer to her ear.

"Only the women of Sparta truly know Aphrodite. Her full spirit. Love, elsewhere in Hellas, is a man's sport, even when it involves a woman - a game for Eros. Only when two women seek the pleasures of love does Aphrodite hide none of herself."

A couple of olive oil lamps blow out from Nikoleta's gasp at Gorgo's soft erotic grasp. She shudders in the dark before the most-ancient goddess.

"Niome!" she gasps.

Gorgo takes the girl roughly in both hands and turns her bodily to face her, the force of which shakes her hair down over her face. She takes just enough strength to pull one arm free of Gorgo's tight grasp and brush the hair out of her face before saying, "I am Niome, daughter of King ... Harpalykos ... a princess of Thrakian Byzantion." On saying her dead father's name, she briefly chokes down a tear.

Gorgo turns the girl's head to face her in the darkness. "Of course you are. I could sense your nobility instantly. We nobles always struggle to lie. Now tell me what you know about the Athenian named Themistokles."

Niome looks confused for a moment, reacting to Gorgo's erotic touches and incisive, opaque expression.

Gorgo asks with deadly seriousness in her eyes, "The Athenian Themistokles - has he met with Pausanias? Or sent him letters?"

"I haven't heard that name," Niome admits quietly, not understanding the context. "The only Athenian Pausanias spoke of was one named Kimon, but he hated him, and they were opponents in their plans."

Gorgo looks into her eyes for a moment, considering, continuing to touch her. "Tomorrow you'll be free. You'll be Niome again. But tonight, you are still Nikoleta; you are still my slave." She runs her fingers through Niome's hair, gazing at her beauty in the firelight, the shadows in the smooth curves of the ancient wooden Aphrodite behind the girl dancing with the flame.

Y

Athens celebrates the Panathenaia festival

Athens sings, the city one sprawling chorus, dressed as brightly as an actor with jars full of flower petals and colorful tapestries woven all winter and spring just for this celebration now at the height of summer - the *Panathenaia* - when every neighborhood tries to out-do each other with organized dancing and street-long sing-alongs throughout the late evenings.

The Panathenaia celebrations begin with a series of musical concerts, which always draw the most famous and gifted musicians from all across Hellas and beyond.

Each street corner is fought over by musicians, making the city ring with multiple songs and arguments.

The man currently playing in the center of the Agora, the most prestigious location where the most quiet respect is given the performer, is a kitharist named Eumene, who seems to have a supernatural ability to create sounds no one would expect from the instrument in a beautiful and haunting way. When he finishes he lets his instrument ring on its final note for a long time while everyone listens in silence, and then he raises his hand as a final gesture, and to everyone's wonder, a small bird flies in low and lights onto Eumene's graceful hand. As he turns to behold it, the Panathenaic audience all gasp, and the bird flits away just as quickly.

Applause explodes through the listeners.

"The gods love Eumene!" they begin to chant.

Ephialtes leans over to Perikles and says, "I've heard Eumene has several such trained birds for that trick."

"Whether trained or wild, it's a good trick," Perikles laughs, clapping, very impressed.

In other corners of the Agora, where usually there are shop stalls, these have been taken down to make room for rhapsodists reciting poetry and flutists playing double flutes and other kitharists plucking or bowing their stringed instruments in competition for the Panathenaic jars of olive oil which sit lined up where the voting jars are placed during ostracisms. On these trophy jars the finest scene painters have painted glorious images of the ancient stories of Athena, Poseidon, and the old Kings of Athens - Kekrops, Erechtheos, Aegeos, Theseus - and these victory jars are more sought-after than silver.

In a corner of the Agora near Simon's shoe shop, Perikles' old teacher Damon is singing the *Odyssey* to a crowd of women and children, competing for the prize for epic poetry - that prize being a jar painted with a beautiful image of Odysseos tied to the mast of his ship as the sirens sing their deadly songs in the air around him.

Damon sings, "Then Odysseos and his son attacked the leaders, smiting them with their sword and spear, and would have killed them all, preventing them from ever going home, had not Athena, Zeus' mind-daughter, shouted resoundingly and restrained the fighters, crying, 'Men of Ithaka, stop your fighting, and part without shedding each other's blood!'"

The crowd of assembled listeners react with various breaths of excitement at the powerful voice of Athena that the singer bellows. Some mouth along silently or even sing along themselves, knowing this singer's version already by heart.

The old singer continues, "They grew pale with fear at Athena's voice, the weapons fell from their hands in terror, and all turned towards the town, eager to save their lives and flee the voice of the goddess. But noble, long-suffering Odysseos gave a chilling cry, and gathering himself he swooped down on them like an eagle from the heights, just as Zeus, son of Kronos, let fly a gleaming lightning bolt that landed at the feet of the bright-eyed daughter of that mighty father's brain. Bright-eyed Athena said to Odysseos, 'Odysseos of the many thoughts, descendent of Zeus, son of Laertes, hold your hand and stop this warring among your men, lest you anger the father of gods!'"

Again, at the utterance of the voice of Athena, the long-bearded old singer bellows a powerful voice of his own, and many of the listeners can't help but call out in excitement.

"And Odysseos obeyed wise Athena's words, delight filling his heart, and Athena, head-born daughter of Zeus, in the form and voice of Mentor, confirmed a noble truce between the warring sides!"

The Athenians listening largely cheer.

"Hail Damon, the finest living singer of epic poetry!" shouts the boisterous old playwright Phrynichos, as he and his middle-aged son Polyphrasmon walk past the singer. "And hail my son Polyphrasmon, who would probably be the best epic poetry singer if he wanted to sing in that format, but instead he wears a different crown - the ivy crown of Dionysos!"

Some of those listening to Damon pause to cheer the father and son playwrights as they strut past.

"Easy to say in passing," Damon grumbles, "and rude to interject, frankly!" He then glares at those who had been listening to him until he has the attention of everyone again.

Aischylos and Sophokles, standing with a large group of dancers over by the Monument of Heroes, both call Phrynichos' name and beckon him over to them. "Phrynichos! Son of Phrynichos! Here! Come here a moment!"

Instantly donning a comic mask of disdain when he recognizes his fellow tradesmen, Phrynichos looks around the rest of the Agora's crowds as to confirm there isn't someone more interesting to deserve his attention, then finally nods to Polyphrasmon to follow him and saunters over to Aischylos and Sophokles' troupe of dancers who are all dressed as bright green leaves.

"Who are these bushes?" Phrynichos jokes, shaking his fingers at the dancers behind the two playwrights.

A couple of the dancers give Phrynichos a spiteful example of some of their moves as Aischylos responds. "We're the first shoots of spring. We've already done our show."

"Indeed, as it is summer!" Polyphrasmon laughs.

"Congratulations again on your win at the Dionysia this spring, Polyphrasmon," Aischylos says with a humble nod. "It is always a pleasure to see what the new generation thinks is worth writing about. And clearly these thirty-year-old Archons we have these days are big fans of heroes killing monsters. I'm not sure what's learned, but it sure is exciting."

Phrynichos says, "Maybe the lesson is that people don't actually want to be confused by the words of the characters in plays. They want to understand their motivations. Most sane people have simple motivations, Aischylos. Not every story has to be a labyrinth of hidden meanings."

Aischylos just shrugs with his eyes.

"Thank you, Phrynichos," Sophokles interjects from beside Aischylos, where he has been focused on shushing the boisterous dancers behind them. "I've been trying to tell him that for years."

Aischylos shoots Sophokles a confused glare.

Sophokles adds, "That the people don't want to be taught a lesson. Especially those deciding who wins the ivy crown - the Archons! These are adult men, who already know who they are - not teenagers who you can still convince to let you put your finger in their butt. People want to see and hear what they already know they like, not what you wish they wanted."

Phrynichos and Polyphrasmon both give Sophokles slanted glances. "You've been looking at too many whorehouse carafes," Polyphrasmon laughs.

"How do you know what's on the carafes in whorehouses, son?" Phrynichos asks Polyphrasmon with a playful punch. Then he grabs his son bodily and shakes him, laughing, "I'm kidding, of course! Just remember this wisdom: no bastard sons if they swallow your cum!"

Aischylos, dismayed, sighs, "This conversation found the gutter quickly. As usual, it is because of you, Sophokles."

From another part of the crowd, iron-jawed Kimon strides across the cobblestone space with his eyes on Sophokles. As he gets closer to the conversation and the playwrights all nod to him in welcome, Kimon appears to briefly regret his decision and rethink what he'd come for, but he shakes it off and seems to ignore the others as he directly addresses Sophokles.

"Sophokles," he says. "May I pull you away for a moment?"

"I didn't know you were for sale as a companion, Sophokles," Phrynichos chides. "I'm kidding, of course. I knew he was a whore. I'm kidding! Take him, he's just a dancer. We writers have art to discuss. Bye, Sophokles!"

Sophokles keeps a look of surprised disgust aimed at Phynichos for a while as Kimon leads him away into the noisy crowd of Panathenaic revelers.

Young girls throwing flower petals out of baskets start to dance into the Agora from another direction, and soon both earth and sky are filled with pink petals.

Kimon pulls Sophokles close, as if being flirty, but then whispers with political seriousness. "I have an admission which I need to make to you, Sophokles, and which I have already made to the gods, and made my restitution for. But your forgiveness I still need. So I must admit - I have stolen something from you."

Sophokles scoffs a little laugh. "Is this a joke?"

"It isn't," Kimon says, looking around to make sure they aren't being listened to. The crowd moves around them, ignoring them. "Last year, do you remember working on a scroll, for months, and then losing it?"

Sophokles' eyes narrow at Kimon. "Why would you have stolen my scroll?"

"I had one of my slaves steal it, because I wanted to read what you were writing. I wanted to know if you were any good."

"O." Sophokles' demeanor quickly changes. "What did you think?"

"I think you're one of the greats."

Sophokles grins immediately. He looks around, hoping that some in the crowd might be hearing their whispers.

"I think you should be getting choruses every year. And I could help you with that. As I'm sure you can imagine, a man like me knows people. I know how to get favors from Archons."

"Why would you help me? You're not a fan of the arts."

"First of all, you don't know me. Don't tell me what I am or am not a fan of. But you're right to guess that I am not a fan of the arts. Nevertheless, despite their low nature, what I do recognize about them is their power to give opinions to those who don't fashion their own. And surely you must also see that - you who played Atossa in Aischylos' *Persians*!"

Sophokles waggles his head in an indeterminate response. "We did win, but I didn't like that role. It's strange to portray someone who you know is out there still living somewhere. And anyway, you're right - that play was all about just reminding people of Themistokles at Salamis. It was practically Perikles' idea; he sat in on several of the rehearsals."

"I knew it!" Kimon sputters, then quickly calms himself. "Sophokles, I need that same weapon in my own war chest. I know that you've been trying to get the Archons to give you a chorus for years now. I think maybe we could help each other."

"Are you going to suggest to me subjects of plays to write, or themes to try to aim for, or what exactly?"

Kimon sighs in frustration. "You're not an idiot, man. Surely you can imagine which stories might make people remember more the virtues of noblemen and kings, and the incompetence of the desperate rabble. You're not some sailor's son - you get it. You're better than those other dancers, and any nobleman can immediately tell. It's because of how you carry yourself, your very countenance and elocution. You are from a noble family, no matter how wretched a career path you happen to have chosen. I'm just asking you to work with me to remind people of that great tradition that made you so much better than most others of your age."

Sophokles tries to frown, but can't stop smiling through his furrowed brow, enjoying the compliments.

The distant snorting of a hundred oxen down at the other end of the Agora signals that the Panathenaic parade is about to begin. Everyone turns at once to watch, and many call out or begin to sing to themselves in religious praise of Athena.

"Glorious goddess, bright-eyed, unbending of heart, inventive, pure virgin!"

"Glorious goddess, savior of cities, courageous!"

"From his awful head Zeus himself bore her arrayed in warlike arms of flashing gold! Glorious goddess Athena, who can bring awe to gods!"

In yoked rows of four, each row guided by a priest on one side and an ox-handler on the other, the long line of one hundred strong oxen, their bones to be sacrificed to the goddess and their meat fed to the drooling throngs of worshippers, are led through the cleared-out Agora toward the wide ramp which leads up to the Akropolis.

The Panathenaic parade - noble, measured, and orderly compared to the raucous Dionysia, but still full of vim and joy - follows the hundred oxen through the center of the Agora and up the wide stone ramp to the scorched temple ruins on the Akropolis. First in line are the beautiful young women who walk with confident demurity and the most beautiful of whom carry the image of the goddess Athena herself painted on a large framed board, followed by chariots pulled by the finest horses and piloted by shiningly armored young men who smile and wave to their neighbors, followed by the old men of the city, and finally by colorful rows of dancers and gymnasts of both sexes.

Perikles walks near the back of the procession of old men, talking with Metrophanes, an old man who currently holds the office of city planner.

"This ramp feels archaic," Perikles remarks as they ascend to the Akropolis. "Imagine if instead we had some kind of beautiful marble infrastructure, something modern and impressive, instead of this old barbarian-looking ramp. We might as well be Pelasgians or Thrakians."

"Infrastructure takes workers and resources, which take money," Metrophanes replies, "and while the Delian League may be rich, Athens is still getting back on its feet financially. It's only been ten years since the whole city was burned! I'd say we've done pretty well building it back up in that time, but there are still many buildings that need to take priority over cosmetic new infrastructure. This old ramp still works, young man."

Down in the cleared-out Agora, Perikles sees Kimon and Sophokles standing together. He taps Metrophanes on the shoulder to indicate to him that he'll catch up with him later, then winds his way back past dancing girls to step out of the parade and join the standing audience down in the Agora.

"Hello Perikles," Kimon says politely. "We were just discussing theater. I wonder - since your time as producer for Aischylos, have you had any thought of trying to write something for the stage yourself?"

Perikles nods and shrugs. "I'd be lying if I said I hadn't thought about it, but ultimately I don't think it's where I'll end up putting my effort. I do write some poetry, but I mostly just share it with Apollo."

Turning all heads with the excited roar of the crowd, the final climax of the Panathenaic parade appears at the far end of the street, headed up toward the Agora, held aloft by and passed along by the hands of hundreds of men whose many points of contact make the weight bearable for each, appearing to float, with its base at about head height, gracefully down the way, dwarfing all around it - the Ship of Athena, an old-style twelve-man sailing ship with the *Peplos* upon its mast - that fabulous robe of Athena, sewn anew each year by the most skilled women of the city, covered with embroidered images of the goddess' many victories, most prominently her battle with the ancient giant Enkelados. Like a colossal bird of prey the Ship of Athena with its Peplos sail glides above the heads of the people of Athens as they stare in wonder, helping it along its way with their many hands, many weeping with civic-religious joy at the experience. Over the heads of all the ship is guided slowly across the Agora, up the long ramp to the Akropolis, and finally to the old, ruined Parthenon and its fallen columns, where the ship is set to rest.

"When Athena, glorious goddess, sprang from the skull of the king of gods, all the other gods stood silent in awe," bellows Eteobouta, the oldest priestess of Athena, standing on the ruined steps of her old temple. "Great Olympos reeled at her armored might, and the whole of the Earth cried out fearfully, and the Sea roiled with dark waves and foam burst forth suddenly, and the Sun, bright son of Hyperion, stopped his swift-footed horses for a long while, until the maiden Pallas Athena stripped the heavenly armor from her immortal shoulders to assure all the other gods that all was well."

Athens cheers joyfully, and musicians across the city all begin to play at once, in a sweeping wave of magnificent human *euphoria*.

Φ

The regency of King Pleistarchos ends

"Spartan!" young King Pleistarchos shouts from outside the bricked-shut temple with as hard a voice as a thirteen-year-old can summon.

That king's cousin and regent's son, little Pleistoanax, watches and clings to his stalwart grandmother Laothoe' black dress.

"Will you starve to death in there and defile the goddess' altar, cursing your family for generations? Or will you come out here and face justice like a man?"

His mother Gorgo, beside him, pats his back for delivering the line.

Pausanias can barely raise his head. Before he has had time to think, the bricks that his family placed at the entrances are kicked in, blasting light again into the bronze prison.

He feels his body breathe deeper than it has in days as he drags his desiccated and starving body blindly over the pile of bricks out into the hot light and dust.

But the light is not the sun - it is the moon. So weak is he, the moonlight burns his eyes like sunlight. He can feel, more than anything else, the pull downward to the Earth, the push against the Sky, toward the Underworld. Only his skin keeps him from going.

Pausanias dryly begs for water with a silent moan.

Gorgo motions to the young Byzantian slave princess, who steps out from the gathered crowd.

"Now take your righteous revenge, Niome. Avenge enslaved Byzantion! Avenge your father the king, avenge your mother the queen, your murdered brothers and sisters! Take back your stolen name, Niome."

Niome steps up to Gorgo and receives the knife in her hands. She then walks up to the prostrate Pausanias.

Moonlit Niome says, "Rise to your knees, Spartan."

When he cannot rise, Niome takes him by the hair and pushes the knife into his neck, releasing a torrent of hot blood which startles and makes her drop him again, her arm gloved suddenly with dripping red.

Shuddering on the street, Pausanias' life flees out his eyes, leaving them blank.

Sturdy, black Phlogios, Pausanias' royal horse, dashes off through the city streets, across the Fields of Artemis Willow-bound and away toward the wild hills of Mount Menelaion to the east.

Gorgo turns to King Pleistarchos, whose uncle and regent now lies bleeding to death on the cobblestones. "You did well, son." She speaks loud enough to be heard by the crowd that has gathered. "You are man enough to be king now, Pleistarchos. You need no new regent."

Black-clad Gorgo turns to the assembled crowd of onlookers and shouts, holding up her son's hand, "All hail King Pleistarchos of Sparta!"

The boy king grasps his mother's waist in a childish hug, burying his face in her breast, though she keeps holding his little hand high in the air. She uses her other arm to push him away from her body, to be forced to stand on his own, which eventually he does, though still quietly weeping.

Neither Niome nor the new king's cousin Pleistoanax can remove their eyes from the dying Pausanias. Old Laothoe averts her gaze from her son's death, pulling at her hair in silence.

Tall, twenty-year-old King Archidamos eyes them all as the surrounding crowd murmurs a curdled hail to their young king whose old regent, the general who led All Hellenes to victory in the decisive land battle at Plataia which turned back the Persian land army ten years ago in the Second Persian War, slowly gives up his blood into the Lakedaemonian earth, while his oldest boy Pleistoanax watches through the gauze of his grandmother's black widow's dress.

X

Korax watches from the mountain

On the mountain slopes to the west, under cover of night and shadow, two hundred Helot warriors crouch among the shrubs - some with knives, some with clubs, none with true military weapons, all dressed in loose, dark clothing.

Korax, the uprising's leader, watches the intrigue occurring distantly in the city in the valley below, the sounds of the drama echoing around the valley as if happening much closer, while Korax's second-in-command, Chrysaor, chomps at the bit to run down and kill.

Chrysaor barks eagerly, "Discord reigns in Sparta tonight. We can still strike!"

"Ares, hold my friend," Korax whispers. "We've survived too many years of misery to run headlong into death tonight. Keep that anger, though, Chrysaor. Make it magic and put it into your sword."

Korax and his Helot warriors watch as Pausanias' armor is stripped from his corpse in the city center of Sparta, far below.

Korax raises his whisper only slightly, as he tells his fighters, and himself, "Hear me now: One of these nights the Moon will be right. I will know it, then - I'll see it on Her face. And we won't need Pausanias or any like him. But for now, we must slip back into waiting, until another opportunity arises for us to cut the throat of Sparta. And then I will wear the armor of Menelaos, and babies yet unborn will still sing when they are grandfathers about how King Korax the First was once a slave."

Ψ

Anaxagoras shares his memories of Herakleitos; Sokrates sacrifices

Anaxagoras and Melqartshama are sitting at the sandy edge of the Agora, by the Fountain House, where the cobblestones are separated from the grass by a strip of packed earth in which a stick can easily write. A group of kids and young men surround them as the two work together to assemble a device out of sticks and twine, beside a map of the plan drawn in the sand. Many among the onlookers debate what it is that the two wisemen might be constructing.

As they work, Anaxagoras tells Melqartshama, and the gathering crowd, the story of a famous wiseman whom he visited back in Ionia.

Ever drawing and bisecting circles in the sand with a long stick, Anaxagoras relates, "This was four years ago now. I traveled to Ephesos, north of my hometown, to try to meet the wiseman Herakleitos. I'd read the works of Thales and Anaximander and Solon, but I had only *heard about* the ideas of this elusive thinker from Ephesos who supposedly didn't want to write anything down - this man Herakleitos.

"Of course, he had in his last years decided that he hated mankind, and had retreated into hermithood in the hills, eating grass and avoiding all seekers of his wisdom. Nevertheless, I, a younger man at the time than I am now, obviously, hoped that I might be able to get the great man to write down *something* for me on a goatskin I'd gotten cleaned and blessed for the purpose. Some small parcel of wisdom, I hoped."

Melqartshama looks up occasionally from his efforts at tying long, parallel, straight sticks to each other at a couple of different joints, listening eagerly to Anaxagoras' story. The crowd around them listens and watches his work.

"Now for those of you listening who might not know of the great sage Herakleitos - please do not let my tale of his final days overshadow the great life that he did lead, and the great ideas that he developed!

"Herakleitos took the wisdom of Thales and Anaximander and developed a philosophy around the ever-presence of *change*. It is common among the Ionians to debate about *first-principles* - the idea that one form or process is at the heart of all things in this world. For example Thales saw the ultimate principle of the world as being *water*, that all things come from water in some form. Herakleitos held as the first principle of his philosophy - *fire*. For in fire do things change the most. I would be happy to tell you more later about his broader body of ideas. But I will tell you now of my encounter with the man at his end.

"So, unfortunately, by the time I got to Ephesos, wise old man-hater Herakleitos was deathly ill, his body inflated with a sickly moisture that gave him constant pain. I didn't dare approach him, as much for fear of being beaten by the angry old man as from disgust at his morbid state, and knowing that some such diseases can be communicable. But it only got worse, I am sorry to say, respectful of that man's ideas as I am. For it was Herakleitos who best explored the concept of flux - of change's constant presence in all things - perhaps most succinctly in his statement that one can never step into the same river twice - you see, because the river is constantly moving, and it is never the same water in any spot in the river at separate moments.

"But in his last days, in an attempt to cure his dropsy..."

Anaxagoras shakes his head and pauses his story, sad to have to tell it, but eventually continues.

"...he mixed up some big vat of 'medicine' that he was sure would suck the moisture from his body, mostly composed of ox manure and a few herbs, and he bathed in it, then laid his racked old body out upon a stone in the bright sunlight, all caked in shit mixture, sure that the Sun would activate his potion. But, sadly, there he died, never waking after falling asleep in the sun all covered in shit.

"And because of his sorry state and scent, none of the Ephesians whose job was to manage such things would approach the great man's dead body, and that night it was, sadly, torn apart by wild dogs. He was given a monument in the Agora at Ephesos, but they never did recover his actual bones."

Melqartshama finishes tying a joint on the interlocking-parallelogram device they have been constructing, and affixes one end to the earth with a sharp stick pressed through it into the ground, and slips a thin bronze writing tool into the "hand" of the arm.

"All due respect to your man Herakleitos," Melqartshama begins, but then frowns as he says, "but that is a great example of why I find wisdom is only as useful as it proves out to be experimentally. What works is reality. Function is wisdom."

Anaxagoras adds, "Luckily, he had given his great book *On Nature* to the Temple of Artemis there at Ephesos, as an offering to the goddess, so I was able to visit that text and read it, after he had died. So writing works!"

Melqartshama moves the center of the pantograph arm and the end of the device with the bronze tool in it moves in the same way, writing into the sand with the same motion that Melqartshama makes with his hand.

"There, see?" he says. "With care taken, now, I could write or draw two of the same thing at once. Or copy an existing thing by tracing its line!.."

The crowd watching coos in admiration and politely applauds.

"How did you make that?" asks a familiar voice from the crowd, and then big-shouldered Protagoras pushes forward between two older men, eating a hunk of bread with half a fish pressed into it.

Melqartshama looks over at Anaxagoras, who answers for him, snidely, "Math; learning."

"Geometry," Melqartshama adds, adjusting the twine on one joint of the device. "It always proves out. Since they're parallel, when you move this, this will always move the same."

"Number-magic," Protagoras scoffs, and takes a bite of his sandwich. "Geometry is for tricks and magic. Man is the measure of all things, am I right?"

"The thing is," Melqartshama casually adds, standing and brushing himself of dust, "too many people think that numbers are only useful for counting, or measuring. But there are hidden numbers in the *relationships* between things. Like a length of string, and half that same length. And half of each of those will be one fourth of the original. It's when you take numbers out of the counting paradigm and into the realm of relationships and proportions that their magic really starts to unfold."

"Would you teach us about geometry?" two noble boys who have been watching the whole time ask eagerly at the same time, then laugh.

Anaxagoras says, "I will see if I can explain a few basic concepts to let you begin with, sure, but then it's all about experimenting with it and finding out what the result is. Because math isn't like some poem someone wrote. It's real, and it's everywhere. It's discoverable by each person. It's sort of the foam the world is made of."

"So is math your first principle in your philosophy, then?" a bright young barber's son named Archelaos asks Anaxagoras.

Anaxagoras nods with a big smile. "Not quite, but almost. For where does all math occur? In the mind! It is the mind, the thoughts, I'd say, that is the basis of all things in this world. Mind!"

The crowd is more interested in Melqartshama's device than Anaxagoras' abstract notions. "You should make a book of drawings for things like this!" someone shouts to Melqartshama, and Protagoras raises his fish sandwich in the air in agreement. Most others simply watch and listen, uncertain.

"Yes, write a book, friend of Anaxagoras the Number-lover," Protagoras barely is able to enunciate through his mouth full of bread. "What is your name, by the way?"

"We don't use names where I'm from," Melqartshama replies. Anaxagoras laughs. Protagoras just frowns at him and shrugs as he turns away.

"You know, you won't make friends here that way," Anaxagoras warns Melqartshama with a friendly laugh, "nor will you become well known."

"I learned living in Phoenikia that it can be dangerous to become well-known," Melqartshama replies.

"Where's your young noble friend, Demokritos?" Anaxagoras asks Protagoras.

"He had to go to Aigypt for some family affair," Protagoras replies. "I'm minding his business here while he's away."

"Is he your master?" Melqartshama asks.

"He was, but he freed me. So I think I may remain here a while. Good sandwiches. Maybe I'll offer lessons in my own wisdom, for a price."

Anaxagoras frowns slightly at that thought. "You don't think it would benefit you to teach your wisdom for free? Wisdom for pay, it seems to me, would quickly corrode the quality of the wisdom being proffered."

As the crowd surrounding them begins to disperse, Anaxagoras notices two young boys crouched near where the noble boys had been standing, as if they had been watching from between the other boys' legs. It is Krito and little two-year-old Sokrates, wearing matching shy, intrigued looks.

"Can we learn number magic, too?" Krito asks. "We can't pay."

Anaxagoras nods with a smile. "Like our Thrakian friend here, young man, wisdom is free."

"I'm from Abdera; I'm a Hellene, not Thrakian," Protagoras scoffs and turns to leave with the dispersing crowd. "You can get Ionian wisdom for free, young men, but Hellenic wisdom will cost you."

Krito smiles at Anaxagoras and hugs Sokrates close to him for a moment, but Sokrates is already pulling away, reaching out with his arms to head toward another part of the Agora, so eventually Krito releases him. He keeps an eye on the toddler from a distance for a while, but soon forgets him and sits down in the grass beside Melqartshama to watch him write in the sand with his two-pen device.

Melqartshama's little toddler daughter crouches nearby, watching Krito and the other little boys playing with pieces of string that Anaxagoras hands out to them to use for measurement games. She notices Krito repeatedly looking back at little Sokrates as he wanders away into the Agora.

"Would he want some?" Diotima gets up the courage to ask the friendly-seeming new boy, Krito.

Krito, smiling at her friendliness, shrugs.

Diotima grabs one of the pieces of string and trots off after the little boy her own size.

Little Sokrates toddles across the Agora, over to Simon's shoe stall, where Simon is working in the corner, sitting tailor-style.

When Sokrates walks up to his open tent, Simon without looking up points out a tiny pair of sandals at the edge of the entrance.

Simon says, "You know, it is actually harder to make a smaller shoe? That's because I have such large hands. In my case, my hand is the measure of all things. So perhaps the big Abderan fellow was right. There, little Sokrates. Try them on."

Sokrates picks up the little sandals and looks them over. "Mine?"

"Yes, they're yours," Simon smiles, finally looking up.

Sokrates runs off into the crowd, heading directly to the public sacrificial fire, and carefully, thoughtfully puts his new little sandals into the fire. As he is about to release them, he briefly gets entranced by the beauty of the flame, and holds the sacrificial sandals a moment too long, until his little fingers feel the heat and spastically lurch back with his arm. Sokrates screeches and drops the sandals into the ashy tripod, causing a little spray of sparks. Some of the people around him gasp, and their reactions frighten the little boy further. He stands frozen for a moment, then begins to weep while he runs back in the direction of Simon's shop as fast as his fat little toddler legs can take him.

Outside Simon's shop, the shoemaker is standing watching all this occur, so he is waiting on one knee when little Sokrates finally makes it back to him, sniffing and sobbing.

"Now why did you do that?" the smiling shoemaker asks the weeping baby.

Sokrates sniffles and snorts, and tries to grasp at his face to stop it from crying, but he cannot speak through his startled tears. He gasps for air amidst his body's emotional distress. The swish and hiss of bright orange sparks replays in his mind.

Simon gets down on the ground and nestles up close to little Sokrates, so their heads are near the same level, and he commiserates, "It's okay, little one. Your tears explain. Anyway, what is speech, but perfected crying?"

Sokrates shrugs. Then he shyly says, through sniffles, "Zeus' house burned down. He needs my help."

Simon the shoemaker smiles, and sheds a little tear. "I am sure you are right," Simon says, rubbing the boy's little head like a friendly goat's.

While Simon calms little Sokrates by rubbing his curly-haired head and sitting on the ground with him, another person emerges from the legs of the passing adults - the little girl Diotima, daughter of the foreign engineer Melqartshama.

Diotima comes over with a long section of string in her hand for Sokrates.

He takes the length of string from her.

"So you can play numbers, too," she says. She shyly glances at Simon, and then dashes away again into the crowded Agora.

Simon smiles and watches Sokrates ponder the string in his little hand.

"You know," Simon tells Sokrates, "a long time ago there was a king of this city, named Theseos. And he was given a piece of string by a friendly young girl, also. It did him a lot of good. So I recommend that you keep that."

Little Sokrates smiles and grips the simple clue with love.

> "TIME IS A CHILD'S GAME OF KNUCKLEBONES.
> MAY THE CHILD BE KING."
> Herakleitos, *On Nature*

Ω

The Athenian Assembly votes on new laws proposed by the Oligarchs

Kimon stands upon the stone bema at the head of the Assembly gathered at the Pnyx and awaits something close enough to quiet for him to be heard over the crowd.

Zephyros, the Western Wind, whips over the hill and makes all beards dance. Voices are encouraged to ascend the wind.

Eventually Kimon stops waiting for this year's absent-minded herald and shouts over the din, "I will now read from this scroll we have prepared, to be certain that I am speaking accurately." At his voice, the other voices finally begin to dwindle.

Finely-dressed Alkibiades hands a scroll up to Kimon, who opens it carefully and slowly, handling it like someone who is not as familiar as Perikles is with reading scrolls. Perikles feels a small surge of superiority upon seeing Kimon's delicate handling of the parchment, and half-smiles to himself for a moment at what he reads as Kimon's incompetence, but his smile fades once Kimon speaks.

"Today we, the noble men, we few, we Oligarchs, sons of the great families of Attika, put forward a call for a vote to return our laws to their old greatness - to what we will call the 'Areopagite Constitution'."

Aischylos stands among the men of his neighborhood, listening to the color of the language used.

Kimon continues, "This is new legislation, but it is to return to an old and well-measured system - power of new laws returned to the hands of the Areopagos, those elders among us who have been Archon and have the experience necessary to understand all the complexities involved in running our city, as well as the money to do what the city needs to have done."

Sophroniskos stands among the stoneworkers who all arrived together, thinking of his wife and son back at home, hardly listening.

"Rule by random lot from among the entire citizenry was an experiment which should be discontinued. We can all see that rule by the rabble belittles the greatness of our best people."

The Assembly roars with controversy which Kimon stays cold-faced against, though he does scan the crowd to gauge the faces. For a moment, his gaze falls upon that of Ephialtes, and he looks away quickly.

"This Areopagite Constitution will return the power of lawmaking to the elders, where the power resided back in the old days. The elders of the Areopagos - those experienced men who have held the office of Archon - would be given a veto power over any new laws passed by this Assembly, and would take jury responsibility from the citizen courts in some more egregious cases, such as those involving land and property, and other large-scale matters that are best left to those of us who know what it is even about. The everyday matters, and of course the power to suggest new legislation, will remain here with this Assembly, where all men can have a voice in the matters of state, and a vote in the judgment of their peers. But the complicated business will be given *back* to the men of experience."

A middle aged sailor shouts, "And kept out of the hands of the wind-willed juries of this city, who can deliver guilty verdicts to any of you as easily as they did my brother, who was guilty of no crime, and yet judged as if he were, by a group of random farmers who didn't even know him!"

The assembly murmurs loudly all at once.

Kimon says, "When, ten years ago, the Persian army bore down on our city, who provided money to all citizens out of their own well-won coffers? The elders of the Areopagos - those men who know what it means to rule."

From the crowd, Ephialtes declares loudly, "It is exactly the fact that the men of the Areopagos have the power to sway the city with their wealth that is the reason they should not be accorded full power over the democracy. The power of money needs to be moderated, not doubled!" Ephialtes shouts. "The men of the Areopagos already have power, through their wealth! Now you want to give them more power, because of their wealth?"

Kimon says, "The Democrats would have the least experienced, greenest men among us run this ancient city of Theseos straight off a cliff."

"O stop bringing up King Theseos already," Ephialtes scoffs. "We are beyond kings. I say the wisdom of a man has little to do with his age. Behold the idiot Stakys, perhaps the oldest among us, if anyone knew for a certainty his age. And behold my good friend, young Perikles, whose wisdom eclipses even my own, with only twenty-five summers behind him!"

All eyes turn to Perikles, who instantly feels the warmth of blush.

Kimon looks at Perikles in the crowd, and takes a moment to think about how to respond to the invocation of the young man's wisdom, but once he speaks, he speaks with confidence. "The gods remember, even if you don't, just why we should never let an Alkmaeonid run this city ever again."

Continuing over Kimon's disparagement, and increasing his volume to try to drown his opponent out, Ephialtes adds, "And what has even less to do with wisdom than age, but wealth! There are too many examples to give, of foolhardy sons who have inherited wealth from wise fathers, and wise men who have chosen not to focus their lives on gathering wealth. Wealth does not imply wisdom!"

To take the mantle from Ephialtes, the Democrat Tolmides rises and speaks.

Toothy Tolmides says, "Let us not be mistaken - this is a debate not about history, precedent, or norms, but about what is best. Athena knows that it is wisdom, not men, that must rule. Now we question - what is wisdom, and who has it? Does any man here think that wisdom comes from wealth? Or perhaps, like the anthill proves the ant, you think that wealth can only be created by the wise?"

As the debate continues with lesser speakers of both sides of the debate, Kallias pushes through the crowd around Perikles and Ephialtes to stand next to them, bowing slightly to each of them once there. Lysimachos notices him nearby and waves.

"Kallias! How is your new wife?" Lysimachos asks him shamelessly.

"She fares well, thank you," Kallias replies, ignoring any intended offense. "She is taking to her new home gradually, and making the place more beautiful not only by her presence but by her design choices! She has an eye for good painters that I do not. Though I fear she does not have much skill in dealing with my slaves."

"At least she is lovely to look at," Perikles remarks. "There is no finer face in Athens, surely."

"Yes, well," Kallias mutters, lifting a foot to tap at his fancy new sandals, "these shoes are also new, and lovely, and expensive, just like my wife, but also like her, you boys can't see where they bite."

Lysimachos and Sophroniskos both chuckle. Ephialtes just nods.

Perikles asks Kallias directly, "And so now that you're brother-in-law to Kimon, the top Oligarch, obviously we're all wondering where your vote will fall today."

"My wife does not make my political decisions for me, unlike some men I know," Kallias says, eyeing Sophroniskos specifically. "Regardless who her brother is, I am a Democrat! Because I vote by my conscience, right Ephialtes?"

"Good man," Ephialtes nods, biting a small stick.

"But with Kimon flush again with income, you having paid off his great debt for him, his power to influence many is renewed," Perikles makes explicit. "So even though your vote is Democrat, it would seem your money's vote remains Oligarch."

The other Democrats nod and grumble as Kallias frowns.

"My money has no more vote than my wife," Kallias grumbles. "The gods still recognize the difference between a man and his money."

"But I am not sure if all men can," Lysimachos notes.

"Quiet now - it's time to vote."

They all hush as the herald begins to shout over Lysimachos' words.

"Now, men of Athens, we shall vote upon the proposal brought forward by the council, known as Kimon son of Miltiades' 'Areopagite Constitution'. Who would have the Areopagos return to power over the laws?"

Too many hands rise for Perikles' comfort. He frowns at Ephialtes with concern. Ephialtes shakes his head, his meaning unclear.

"And who would keep power with this Assembly?"

Perikles and his Democrat friends all raise their hands vigorously, as if the strength they use in that gesture could add power to each singular vote.

"Then the law is passed," the herald declares, and instantly the crowd is in uproar. "The Areopagite Constitution is law!" He holds up his snake-headed *kerykeion*.

The sound of hundreds of happy rich men rises among the crowd, unraveling the uncertain and disorganized grumblings of the poor.

Ephialtes says, "If he wants to, Kimon will convince these people to vote away their own power."

With rare seriousness Lysimachos grumbles, "I think he just has."

The herald shouts over the crowd, "That was the final vote for this Assembly this month!" and the crowd immediately all begin chattering and moving such that the additional words of the herald can be heard by none.

"I fear our democracy may prove to have been but a bubble on a pond," Ephialtes suddenly weeps, seeming to become truly distraught only once he vocalizes the thought.

"We're not beaten," Perikles says to Ephialtes. "We're simply at war now, and on our back foot. We were born into it, so it's easy to forget how young and fragile the very notion of democracy actually is."

A passing veteran with an old, scarred-over wound that takes up the top-left quadrant of his face pauses his walk to slap Perikles on the back of his helmet and say, "Don't you summon Ares with your war metaphors, boy!"

Perikles adjusts his helmet up on his head and self-consciously scans the many faces around himself as the Assembly disperses.

To Ephialtes, shyly, Perikles asks, "Does this helm look stupid?"

"No," Ephialtes replies confidently, wiping away his own tears with strength renewed by seeing the vulnerability of another. "You look like Zeus." He puffs his own chest up and gives Perikles a friendly pat on the arm.

A group of passing older men laugh overhearing the conversation, and one of them mutters, "Sea-onion head," to make his friends laugh again. But another among them says, also mockingly, "Zeus," and that also makes the group laugh.

As they are walking back down the hill of the Pnyx, Ephialtes nudges Perikles with an expression of reluctant optimism, as if to indicate that at least people are talking about him.

ATHENS

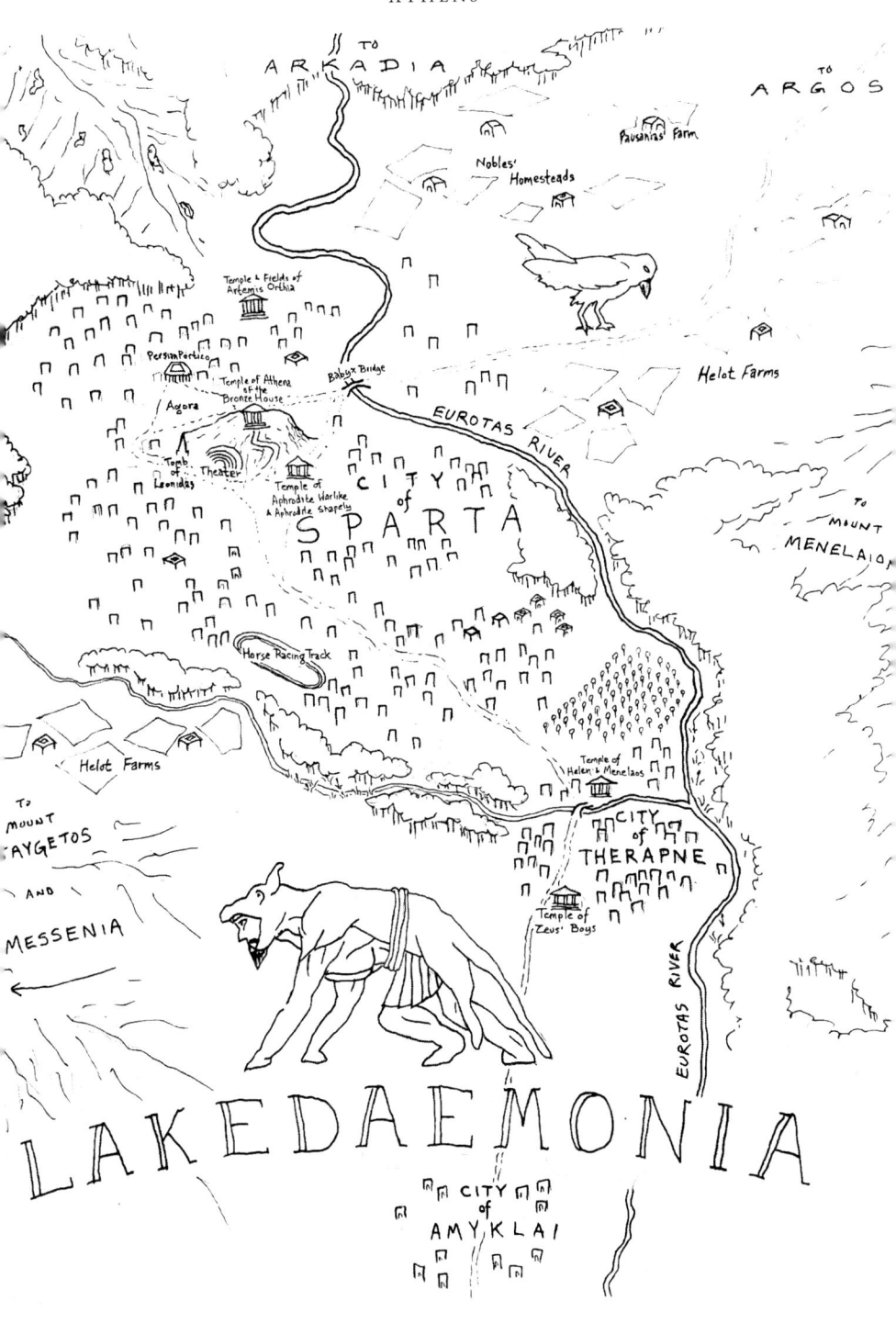

ATHENS

To Arkadia
To Argos

Pausanias' Farm
Nobles' Homesteads
Temple & Fields of Artemis Orthia
Persian Portico
Agora
Temple of Athena of the Bronze House
Babyx Bridge
Tomb of Leonidas
Theater
Temple of Aphrodite Warlike & Aphrodite Shapely
Helot Farms
EUROTAS RIVER
CITY of SPARTA
To Mount Menelaion
Horse Racing Track
Helot Farms
Temple of Helen & Menelaos
CITY of THERAPNE
Temple of Zeus' Boys
To Mount Taygetos and Messenia
EUROTAS RIVER

LAKEDAEMONIA

CITY of AMYKLAI

188

3

DIONYSOS THREE-HEADED

A

Grief as Aristides lies dying

Two cuckoo birds pull at the wings of a beetle on an ivy vine running along the doorframe of the Council House in the dark at the end of the night.

Sandalled footfalls echo through the otherwise silent Agora, until Perikles appears out from the moonshadows of an alley and trots breathless to the open doorway of the Council House, where a few of this month's councilors are asleep beneath Oligarch-funded lion skins. Ephialtes is in there snoring when Perikles arrives at the open doorway and calls his name.

Ephialtes wakes annoyed, assuming at first that his disturber is some ornery ordinary citizen, but when he sees that it is Perikles he sits up quickly.

"How fares Aristides?" Ephialtes asks, rubbing his face.

Perikles shakes his head grimly. "I fear he'll see dawn from below."

At Aristides' modest house outside the city walls, his son Lysimachos and daughters Myrto and Agnaxia are all crouched around his bed, weeping quietly. Around them, Aristides' noble old friends from that long-bearded generation stand behind his family with quiet respect, looking like the Seven Sages of Hellas.

When Perikles arrives with Ephialtes, Lysimachos sees them and reaches out a hand with tears in his eyes.

"Why must the slow death of the bed be so much more difficult than the quick death of war?" Lysimachos cries. "Where is Persephone's mercy?"

Aristides, ashen, moans.

"Try to sleep, father," Myrto whispers, petting the old man's soft hair.

"O gods, if you could only somehow let me know what to expect after death," Aristides says with difficulty. "I can face anything if I simply know what to expect. It is the uncertainty that is the only thing that troubles me now. But, I suppose I shall see. Whatever it will be - I go now to the crowded place, home of many."

Agnaxia calls out to another room, "Come Lysithes, summon that Orphic singer to give us his death song."

"No Orphics, no Pythagoreans, none of that modern death-cheating! Let me die as my ancestors did ... before the open eyes of the gods," Aristides coughs, leaning up to wave away any singer brought into the room. His daughters all scramble to help him back down comfortably.

"Quiet, father," Myrto whispers, tears falling. "Keep your strength."

"This is the last of my strength, Myrto," Aristides groans, his words breaking. "I might ... might as well use it up. I do not want you to think that wisdom is just the most cunning cheat. Sometimes ... it is steadfastness."

Myrto begins to weep loudly, and her sister Agnaxia begins to sing a mournful death song. "O let us place his bones into a golden jar, and a double fold of fat, until I myself can once again enfold him when I join him in the house of Haides..."

"Please, daughters," Aristides whispers, "don't start tearing ... tearing out your hair ... until I'm actually gone. And none of that Orphic shit, like I said - the last person who I would want to try to cheat is Haides."

Standing at the back of the grief-groaning cluster of mourners filling Aristides' death room, Perikles puts an arm around Ephialtes' shoulders, as he notices his friend has started to shed a tear.

"He lived a laudable life," Perikles whispers. "He has nothing but glory. For all we know, there will be a new constellation in the sky tomorrow."

Ephialtes nods. "That would be so beautiful. He deserves to be with the gods, eating that undying food forever. If ever a man did. I can't imagine why the gods would have made him suffer like this for so long."

Perikles hugs his friend. "I've seen mysterious disease degrade the body like this before. It's how my father went. But his was faster. And with him, it was less unclear why the gods might deign to visit such misery upon a person."

Another old friend their age, a man named Hippokreon, whom Ephialtes and Perikles used to race with when they were all boys, is standing beside them now, wearing the priest robe of the profession he has taken as an adult. He nudges Ephialtes with a slight smile. "We live in the same cosmos, don't we?" he jokes.

"O, hello Hippokreon," Ephialtes sniffs.

"Hippokreon! I haven't seen you in years," Perikles laughs quietly, shaking his old friend's hand. "Sad that these are the circumstances that should bring us together again."

"Well, I'm with the temple of Zeus now, so..." Hippokreon explains with a shrug. "And I couldn't help but overhear, and thought, 'They both remember this is Zeus' universe now, right?' I mean, I understand everyone loved Aristides, but that's because he struggled for the interests of mankind. In that way you could say he was like Prometheos."

"Is," Ephialtes corrects. "The man still lives."

"I'm just trying to point out that, while we may not know exactly why Aristides was cursed with this illness, it shouldn't be a total mystery why the gods might find some hubris in his heart. Prometheos was a friend of Man, too, and Zeus chained him to a mountain in Skythia for it. Consider Ganymede, whom Zeus kidnapped to be his cupbearer on Mount Olympos because of the boy's beauty. I'm just saying, clearly democratic virtues are not what Zeus is looking for in men. Perhaps they're even something he hates. We can't be sure. This activity is new enough, we don't have a great sense yet of how the gods will feel about it over time."

Inside the room, Aristides begins to cough without inhaling, and his daughters all grasp his shuddering body. "I go!" he wheezes. "I go!"

"That's enough," Perikles snaps at the men on either side of him. "Let's not have a debate over the best man in Athens' deathbed."

"What final wisdom do you have for us, before you're gone?" asks Lysimachos tenderly, holding his father's hand.

Aristides grimaces against some internal pains, and just shakes his head, squeezing his eyes open and shut until finally they don't shut again, and his shallow breath escapes in a long, disturbing groan, accompanied by other death sounds from within his body.

The dying man's daughters Agnaxia and Myrto begin weeping again, and pulling their hair, as the older women move in to calm them. Lysimachos, his son, has already left with his lover, unable to watch this moment.

Distant, someone sings that Dawn has appeared, and voices singing an ancient hymn to that goddess rise on the lightening darkness.

"HE DOES NOT WANT TO SEEM, BUT REALLY TO BE,
AND TO REAP THE HARVEST OF HIS WELL-PLOWED MIND
FROM WHICH THE MOST HONORABLE IDEAS SPROUT!"
Aischylos, *Penelope*, a line which made
many Athenians look to Aristides the Just

B

The funeral of Aristides the Just

Surrounded by olive trees on his family's land within view of the city walls, Aristides' family cremates his body on a pyre, while hundreds of mourners from all over Attika, and visitors from every island in the Delian League, are there to pay their respects and witness the world-famous man burn to ash.

Funeral flame consumes Aristides' body as his son Lysimachos speaks to the broad crowd of mourners assembled on the hillside. He chokes back tears and struggles to speak, while his teen-age lover Cheronidas hangs bodily onto him consolingly.

Lysimachos says, "Many have said that my father was the only man alive who might actually deserve to be called 'The Just'. Now if there was anything he taught me, it was first humility before the gods, but he also taught me humility before our neighbors, above none of whom he felt superior. And so, in the spirit of my father, Aristides the Just, I tell you, Athenians, that I do not believe that the world now lacks another man who can also be called this. If we all remember Aristides the Just, how he lived, and model ourselves upon that, then perhaps we can all come to deserve the title of 'the Just', until it is so obvious of men that they would be just, that no one need the epithet."

Ephialtes and Perikles stand together amidst the other men their age, and as the priests of Haides help weeping Lysimachos down from the stand in front of the pyre, Ephialtes leans to Perikles to whisper.

"Without Aristides, I fear for the League of Delos. It was he and Kimon who kept our allies confident. Now Kimon alone holds that rein. That positions him to appear quite powerful."

They both turn to look for Kimon among the crowd, and when they find him, he has his arm around a beautiful young woman named Isodike, a flutist of recent fame, but he is looking right at them, and he turns away when they spot him.

"While we think of him, he is thinking about us," Ephialtes notes.

Perikles grimaces to Ephialtes. "We must fulfill Lysimachos' prayer. We must tack our sail toward justice. Let the Oligarchs blow. We know how to sail upwind."

The priest of Haides and Lysimachos share the knife as they begin to serve meat off a recently sacrificed and cooked cow carcass, and the crowd begins to shift into a line for receiving food. In this movement, Kallias emerges from the crowd, finds Ephialtes and Perikles, and greets them.

"Beautiful day, friends! Sad, but sunny," Kallias says brightly.

For the moment, Perikles cannot look away from the surreal visual of Aristides' old skin becoming ash within a haze of flame under the backdrop of blue sky. He acknowledges Kallias with just a nod.

A general movement of mourners goes past the pyre to the meat being served, and when those around them begin to move that direction, Perikles, Ephialtes, and Kallias shuffle with the crowd until they are within the heat of the massive flames. The flames' bright tongues disappear invisibly against the blue sky, while a ghost of smoke forms a few feet above and whips about there before dissipating.

Up close, Perikles beholds the burning form of the man he knew. Aristides' skin shrinks blackly against his skeleton inside the fire. Perikles has to look away quickly before fainting at the sight of it.

Beside the burning pyre, a traditional Hellene funeral display has been set up by Aristides' children, with the battle-marked armor he wore in the Persian Wars balanced upright upon a fine, thick spear, and a large etched stone tablet beside it lists Aristides' many war glories.

The movement of the crowd shuffles Perikles and his friends past the pyre quickly, and soon they are back down among the olive trees where people are eating meat, as others view the corpse and tropion.

"A noble display," Kallias notes as the young Democrats reconvene into a conversational circle within the crowd of mourners.

"I found it inappropriate, frankly," Ephialtes admits reluctantly, his face showing the dismay he feels at having to say so.

Kallias reacts with surprise. "How so?"

Ephialtes whispers loudly, "Aristides was an old man, yes, but he was also a modern man. In his final years, he had grown beyond the victories he won in war. I say he won his greatest victories in peace! There is no mention of the League of Delos, no mention of his efforts to find common ground between Democrats and Oligarchs. He was a peacemaker! And nobler for it! But all anyone wants to revere is glory won in combat. Well, I feel it belittles Aristides to act like he was merely a great general of soldiers."

"But he was that," Kallias notes.

"It's traditional," Perikles considers. "A funeral is not the time to be modern."

"But it would be powerful, wouldn't it?" Ephialtes proposes. "If a man actually stood by his true ideals, even against the weight of the strongest traditions? Imagine what people would think."

"It might make them hate democracy and modernity," Kallias scoffs. "You need to learn how far people can bend before they break, Ephialtes. You push too hard too fast, and this city will snap back on you and reject all modernity and shrink back into the shadows of caves just to spite your ideals."

The rugged, fiery-minded young Democrat Antiphon, a horse-tender, starts voicing the opinions of many as he rants beside Ephialtes, "One can't help but wonder if, once that old generation of greybeards finally all die out, if there might finally be the votes to institute *full* democracy - true rule by *all* the people."

A narrow-limbed younger man named Axiochos, oldest son of the Oligarch Alkibiades, shouts past some others to be heard. "O, Antiphon, *all* the people? You mean all the male Athenians, right? You mean Athenian men of every stripe, but not just *anybody* - not *foreigners*, and obviously not *girls*."

Axiochos' mother, not far from him, slaps him on the head. "Don't go getting Democrat ideas, son. They only seem wise to a young man because they are for poor men, and young noblemen are still poor men before they inherit. But have faith in the God of Wealth - you'll inherit, boy!"

"Frankly I agree with Stakys - I'm sick of hearing Aristides called 'the Just'. He was friendly and worked with Democrats to find compromise, but he was still an Oligarch just like the rest of them. Just because he was recalled during the war for his money and men doesn't mean we should forget that we exiled him by potshard vote not ten years earlier, because he was one of the lead Oligarchs standing in the way of Democratic change!"

"Calm your fire, Antiphon," Perikles recommends with a heavy pat on the back. "It is the man's funeral." He shakes his head in recognition of those around them who are frowning at the outburst. "Think of how we represent Democrats. You too, Ephialtes."

Ephialtes frowns at Perikles and folds his arms.

"Which island do you think will try to leave the league first?" Kallias asks Ephialtes in a whisper.

Ephialtes shoves him softly with his side. "It's too soon to think strategically about this. Leave time for mourning. But my wager would be on Mytilene."

Kallias says, "I was thinking of Samos. They've got their forests, their own navy…"

Ephialtes shakes his head and sighs through his nose. "Don't say Samos. That's where the Delian fleet is."

Kallias nods. "That gives them power, and I can see them using that position to vie against Athens for leadership of the League."

"They have a strategic position for our fleet, but no real economic power of their own," Ephialtes notes. "Samos would be foolish to test Athens."

Sophroniskos, the sculptor and close friend of Lysimachos, who has been silent this whole time, says, with tears in his throat, "While you Democrats collude on how to rule the world, you miss the tragedy before your eyes - that the family of Aristides was made destitute by the Persian Wars, and poor Lysimachos had to borrow money for this memorial stone."

Kallias gives Perikles and Ephialtes a look of total shock. "Aristides, of all men," he remarks. "I thought he had the utmost acumen. I'll give Lysimachos some money, my sculptor friend; worry not."

"Aristides gave his best self, and asked for nothing." Sophroniskos fingers a tear out of his eye as he sniffs, "If the Democrats wanted to pursue real justice, you would give this family a stipend from the state, rather than watch the daughters and son of Aristides the Just degenerate into beggars … or become beholden to the whims of patrons."

Ephialtes, Perikles, and Antiphon all look at each other with dismay. Ephialtes says, humbly, "I didn't know. Aristides made no sign he was moneyless."

"Because he had true nobility," Sophroniskos sniffles. "Not the kind coins can buy." He briefly glances at Perikles with sad, glistening eyes. The muscular sculptor retracts his chin and hides his frown within his beard.

The famous poet Timokreon of Rhodos steps up beside Lysimachos and takes his hand, kisses his fingers and puts them to his own face with a soft smile. Then he turns to the assembled mourners. Some young ones in the crowd shout the famous man's name, but their parents chastise them for impiety toward the man whose funeral this is.

"Yes, I am Timokreon, of the island of Rhodos, and I have come to honor your great man Aristides with this new poem:

"While some may love Pausanias, or Xanthippos..."

Perikles perks up at the mention of his father's name, and his friends look for his reaction when they hear it.

"...instead I hold my love for a man like Aristides, as the one best man to come from Athens, since Themistokles has forfeited the favor of Delian Leto. That criminal traitor and liar, who, bribed by barbarian silver, refused to help Timokreon his friend back to his home on Rhodos, but took three silver talents and sailed off into the sunset. Damn him."

Ephialtes leans close to Perikles' and asks, "What did Themistokles do to this guy?"

Timokreon the poet continues, "Restoring some wrongly, killing or exiling others, and at the watery isthmus, loaded up to his nose with coins, he made a joke of us all and served us meat cold. We ate, and prayed for Zeus to ruin Themistokles."

Timokreon nods to Lysimachos and steps back down into the crowd.

Wiping tears from his cheeks, Lysimachos, son of Aristides, politely shrugs that away and addresses the crowd, calling out for all to hear. "And now, friends, please join us in the flower fields for funerary foot races and wrestling games!"

Γ

Elpinike settles into life married to Kallias

The bright yellow house of the richest man in Athens is only slightly larger than the other houses, but the stonework on its roof, where Kallias and Elpinike most often spend their time, is some of the finest in the city. Colorfully-painted lions with golden fur and azure eyes are mounted upon each corner, looking down onto passersby and belching water from their mouths when it rains.

Kallias sits upon an ornately woven reed chair, and Elpinike stands at the ledge, leaning on a lion's mane, near a bronze tripod burning expensive Aithiopian incense. The brown smoke wafts about her.

Kallias says, "As you know, part of undergoing the Mysteries is that you can't afterward speak about it to those who have not yet undergone the Mysteries. So I can't really tell you much about it. Let it suffice for me to say that I hold the position of torch-bearer in the ceremony."

"I see," Elpinike nods boredly.

"Yes, it's a family office, which my father and grandfather both held. So it will be Hipponikos' when I'm gone, if he wants it, if he doesn't decide to become some mercenary or actor or other such degenerate."

"Ares forbid," Elpinike murmurs, picturing the annoying teen-aged Hipponikos, her new husband's son from an earlier marriage, imagining the boy being killed in battle as a feckless mercenary.

"If you were to participate in this year's Mysteries, of course, then we would be able to talk freely about it. It really is worth it. A beautiful ... well, like I said, I can't talk too much about it without breaking my oath. But there are two times a year that we do it - in the Spring and in the Autumn - and they're like two plays which affect and proceed into each other, so you are supposed to do the Spring one before the Autumn one."

Elpinike coughs as the incense wafts about her face. She waves it away.

"You're going to reek of that stuff if you stand there inhaling it all day," Kallias remarks.

Elpinike, whose mind had been elsewhere, shoots her husband a narrow glance and then rolls her body along the balcony edge, away from the smoke. She looks away again, back into her thoughts, across the rooftops of Athens, until the wind turns and the smoke is wafting into her face again.

Kallias laughs. "Come here, my wife," he says, patting his thighs. "Sit here with me for a moment. The West Wind, Zephyros, is notoriously playful, and I'm sure he'll put that smoke into your eyes no matter where you stand. I promise no more talking about my work. Sit."

Elpinike turns to face Kallias and keeps her eyes on him, begins to stride in his direction but surprises him by merely pacing slowly back and forth across the rugs on their roof, instead of approaching him.

"Would you believe," Kallias begins, hesitating to watch whether his wife appears to be listening at all, and only continuing once she finally looks at him, "Aristides died destitute. He had no coins hidden anywhere, apparently, and owed much to many. His children are in a very difficult position."

"Lysimachos will be fine," Elpinike says. "He has two sisters."

Kallias shakes his head with confusion. "Why? Having dependents makes him even more vulnerable and needy."

Elpinike sighs through her nose and cocks her head at Kallias. "What does a farmer do when he needs money and can't feed the cattle he has?"

Kallias frowns, thinking, but then shakes his head. "I have never been a farmer."

"He sells a cow," she says, barely wanting to have to say it.

"Ah," Kallias nods, then understands her implication and adds, "O! O, I see. You think he should sell one of his sisters. What, as a slave? O, no - you think he should simply give his sisters to rich men, and collect large dowries. I - oh."

Elpinike stares at Kallias as he goes through the process of realizing how awkward his failure to grasp her implications has been.

Then Kallias turns his demeanor instantly, as he is uniquely capable of doing, and smiles, "At least Aristides went through the Eleusinian Mysteries, so he will know what to do in the Underworld to have a good…"

A shout rings from the house below, the high-pitched whining voice of Kallias' son, fourteen-year-old Hipponikos. "Father, the painter is here!"

"What have I told you about shouting through walls?" Kallias shouts back down at his son. "Show your face if you mean to speak to someone, you graceless weasel!" Kallias looks to Elpinike and says, "Surely as a woman, you must know some way to get through to that teenage fool, no?"

"I will never act like your son's mother," Elpinike says coldly, looking into Kallias' eyes to make sure he understands she's serious. Then, to avoid seeming too inappropriately impious of her new family, she adds, "He already has a mother. Anyway, it's the father who should be teaching a young man how to behave."

"You're right of course," Kallias sighs, getting up from his wicker seat and opening the trapdoor down into the house. "Well, anyway, like I said, I really shouldn't talk about the Mysteries until you've gone through them. But now, I must deal with this. Excuse me, wife." He climbs down the ladder, already greeting the painter Polygnotos before he's even down.

Elpinike remains on the roof, and leans again against the sculpted lion at the corner. The incense smoke begins to waft about her, and she enjoys the smell, at least partially because she knows that Kallias hates it.

On a neighboring rooftop of another rich man's finely detailed house across the street, a trapdoor opens and two men dressed as slaves precede a well-dressed woman Elpinike's age, who sees her immediately and waves with a smile.

Elpinike just nods.

"Hello! You're Elpinike, right? I'm Eupraxia; I'm Nikanor's wife. He wouldn't let me out to see your wedding, but let me welcome you to the neighborhood now!"

"Thank you, Eupraxia," Elpinike calls back. "You have a beautiful home. I love all of your flowers."

"Yes, that's the work of Ardys, here," Eupraxia shouts back, pointing to one of her slaves who has already started watering all the flower pots on the roof from a large jar. "He speaks no Hellenic, but he's the best florist I've found! We can loan him to you from time to time, if you like."

"Thank you," Elpinike nods with a polite smile. "You're very generous. I know my husband's slaves are supposed to be my responsibility now, but I must admit I have yet to learn any of their names."

Eupraxia smiles and shrugs. "You should give them new names that you prefer. Maybe that will help you feel at home quicker."

Elpinike nods.

"You know, several of the neighborhood women come over here on festival days and weave together - just noblewomen, all wonderful girls. I do hope you'll feel comfortable joining us anytime. You'll see them all over here, I'm sure. Just jump over whenever you hear us chatting."

"Thank you, I may." Elpinike glances down through the open trapdoor into her house, where a work crew of painters under the master Polygnotos have started filing through her entryway with many colored jars. She looks back across the street to her neighbor and says, "I must see about the slaves while we have painters working. Let's talk later. It was good to meet you, Eupraxia."

"Have a good night, Elpinike!"

Elpinike climbs down the ladder down into the house, the painters stopping in the doorway and waiting with the heavy paint jars in their arms, to give her space while descending. Once she's fully down, she nods to them thanks, and they continue filing past, into the men's sitting room where the mural is to be done.

Last to enter the house is the famous painter Polygnotos himself - a tall, long-haired, beardless man with eyes that immediately see Elpinike's beauty. He stops in the doorway and stares at her, struggling to keep a smile from forming.

The painting crew carry the last jars into the men's room, as Elpinike stands against the wall of the entryway, beside a large fern, strung in taut eye contact with smoldering Polygnotos.

Behind Polygnotos, Kallias arrives, and cannot enter the doorway past the larger man. He taps Polygnotos on the shoulder from behind, and the man turns and laughs, lets him through.

"O hello, dear," Kallias says to his wife. "This is Polygnotos the painter. Please make sure the slaves stay out of the men's room during the day, while they're doing the new mural of Aphrodite." He passes her on his way into the men's room with the painters.

Elpinike avoids looking at Polygnotos again, and walks away from the door to the men's room, into the kitchen where two female slaves - Elpinike's age but weathered to appear older - are plucking a goose on the table.

"Is this for supper?" Elpinike asks, just to give her entrance meaning.

"Yes, mistress," the slave woman with a cleaver in her hand says.

Elpinike nods curtly. She passes the two women and takes one sprig of grapes from a bowl, then turns back to the door to the entryway and leans against it for a moment, enjoying a few grapes.

She slowly saunters back toward the women's room, where she is expected to spend most of her time with the spinning wheel and loom. She tries not to look when she passes the door to the men's room.

"We must not forget to include extraordinary beauty," the painter Polygnotos remarks to his assistants as Elpinike passes the doorway to the men's room where they're working. "For it has become clearer to me than ever that the beauty she can put in even just a woman's eyes is beyond what I had ever dreamed."

Elpinike's eyes flit, as she avoids smiling.

At the door to the men's room, within which Kallias sits chatting with the painters, Elpinike hangs on the doorframe and says to her husband, "O Husband, torchbearer of Demeter, I think that I should like to partake in the Mysteries of Eleusis after all."

"The introductory Mysteries of Spring are just next month!" Kallias says, lighting up like a happy torch. "How wonderful, my wife! Now you'll get to see what I do! And the Mysteries have their own benefits, of course, as well! I couldn't be more proud that you would like to share in my secret knowledge of the mysteries of the world! You've made me a very happy husband, my dear!"

Elpinike smiles at him, side-eyes Polygnotos, then swings back out of the men's room doorway while Kallias is still speaking. He stops with a curious frown when she leaves, and smiles with a shrug to Polygnotos, who shrugs the same in response.

> "O GREAT GODDESS OF FUCKING,
> WHO LOVES THE EVENING RENDEZVOUS
> AND THE COUPLING OF LOVERS,
> TRULY EVERYTHING COMES FROM YOU!"
> Orpheos, *Hymn to Aphrodite*

Δ

The Athenian Council sends off a colony, and hears an ambassador from Naxos

Each day's agenda in the Council House is organized by the *Caretaker* - one man selected by random lot from the *Prytany*, which is the one tribe among the city's ten whose turn it is to be in charge for the month.

Each tribe gets one of the ten thirty-six-day-long months of the governmental calendar year - which is different than the religious calendar year, which has twelve months of thirty days each. Especially later in the year, after winter, there is often much confusion among the country folk who serve as councilors, as to which month it is and which day within that. The festival calendar, at least, follows the Moon, but the governmental calendar only follows governmental tables.

On this sunny day in late summer, still near the beginning of the new year, this day's Caretaker is a hunchbacked old Oligarch named Kritias, famous for his persuasive abilities. Kritias stands in the center of the floor, leaning on an old crooked cane, while the rest of the council sits in the ten-leveled seating built up against the three square walls around him. Behind Kritias the main door is open and gawkers from the Agora loiter to watch from there.

"Men of Athens," Kritias declares, "I hereby call our council to action! Let us begin with a list of the concerns of the day. We have with us, as I understand, the noble ambassador from the island of Naxos, a young man named Hegelion, with a report on Naxos' tribute to the League of Delos. We also have with us the great Olympic victor Maxon..."

Before he can continue, applause fills the small building, and the enormously-muscled wrestler Maxon, sitting at the edge of one of the rows of seating, shyly waves to his fans.

Once the applause dies down, Kritias stomps his iron-toed cane and shouts, "Order, fishermen, order! This is not the theater, though I know many of you have never sat in stands like this in any other situation. Please, control yourselves. Now, Maxon, why don't you come up here and join me as we discuss your colony's plans."

Maxon rises and joins Kritias in the center of the council house floor.

Kritias explains, "Maxon has agreed to be the founding hero of a new Athenian colony at the edge of Thrake, not far from Abdera. What is the river god there known as?"

"Strymon," Maxon replies in his famous lisp, with *R*'s weakly mispronounced. "A broad, old river from what I hear. Good land. We're excited." Maxon holds up one of his muscular arms to the crowd in thanks as he stoops to sit down again at the edge of the seating.

Kritias explains, "We have heard nine different recommendations for possible constitutions for this colony. Ultimately, you will need to come to some final decision, though. As your colony's founding hero, in your first year it will be you who will have to make the final decision if you continue to fail to come to agreements. Maxon, it appears, would like to say something. Maxon, please speak."

The famous wrestler Maxon stands again, receiving a brief applause which causes Kritias to stomp his cane.

Maxon shyly addresses the council, "I have shown to Zeus and all men at Olympia that I have arms that can grapple five men at once, and so it is with those same huge arms that I will embrace the *ideas* of all men of my colony, no matter how many ideas that is. As a representation of the many initial suggestions for constitutions for our colony, I first propose that we name ourselves *Nine Ways*, to represent the nine differing political ideas that will coexist there." A few councilors who disdain wrestling snicker mockingly at his wandering *R*'s.

The council hesitantly applaud the famous wrestler, many of them barking out his signature wrestling grunt in an effort to get him to make the noise, which he happily does, pointing to his fans with a friendly smile.

"You want to name your colony Nine Ways?" Kritias asks, unable to mask his disdain for the name.

Maxon turns to him and simply nods, smiling, still cloaked in the applause and grunts of his fans.

The ambassador Hegelion from the island of Naxos shuffles behind standing councilors to position himself near the wrestler, on whom all the attention currently falls. The Naxian ambassador loudly clears his throat and raises his hand to be noticed by Kritias.

Kritias sees him and nods. "Very well, then, Maxon, if your settlers feel they are prepared, then we ask for you the blessing of your home city's gods in your adventure out to the shores of Thrake to start an Athenian colony, which we will put on the list of colonies as being called 'Nine Ways'. If you're sure about that name. You are, okay. So now, the ambassador from the beautiful island of Naxos desires to be heard." Kritias stomps his cane to get the attention of the rowdy councilmen.

Young Hegelion of Naxos steps before the council as Maxon sits back down and just as the light of the Sun God emerges from the clouds outside, sending a shaft of orange light through the open doorway, and causing the shadows of the gawkers there to play upon the seated councilors. Everyone notices this change of atmosphere, including Hegelion, who hesitates just long enough to get nervous.

Carefully the ambassador says, "Noble Athenian leaders: please hear this important decision from the leaders of the island of Naxos. The oath our city's council took to Apollo on Delos was shared with Aristides the Just. While we grieve the death of that great man with you, we must also take full haste now in pursuing our best interests, and that is now to leave the League of Delos and go back to our own independent course."

Before the ambassador is finished speaking, half the council explodes in argument, but he finishes as if he had not been interrupted, as if he had expected such a reaction.

"Deserters!" many of the councilors of the council begin to shout.

Hegelion stammers, "Together, All Hellenes have succeeded in fighting Persia back into her homeland, and for three Olympiads now that threat has not returned. As a democratic city, surely you can respect the desire of an individual to pursue their own fate."

"This is exactly the kind of cowardice that will invite Persia to return!" one sailor councilor shouts.

The ambassador Hegelion does his best to stay stone-faced against all of the backlash, but his legs begin to visibly shake as he stands beside Kritias in the center of the shouting Athenian councilors.

Kritias sees the young man's difficulty standing, and offers him his cane, causing the Athenian councilors to shift from shouting to laughing.

Maxon, feeling the laughter, stands and jokes, "If Xerxes comes back, I'll just put him in my Hypnos Hold!" Maxon flexes his arms, mimicking that signature "sleeper" hold for which he is famous.

At the doorway open to the Agora, news is already quickly spreading of the Delian League's potentially shakier new footing.

E

Anaxagoras and Protagoras discuss wisdom with Athenians

Clowns spread news fastest in the Agora, through mocking mimes and jokes, while the actual information spreads more gradually and accurately by word of mouth.

The two clowns with the most eyes upon them, and whose antics get reenacted elsewhere the most, are two men who stand on opposite ends of the Monument of Heroes - the street clowns Magnes and Chionides. Many other young clowns compete for attention in the busy Agora, but Magnes and Chionides are the ones whom most look to for a quick and comical sense of what is important to know right now.

Magnes the Aithiopian Clown is memorable for usually involving an animal mask in his silent puns about the day's events. Today, Magnes is an owl nobody wants in their house anymore - an Athenian coin.

On the opposite side of the monument is Chionides the Other Clown, whose act is a similar silent mime to Magnes', but focused on broad human stereotypes. Today, Chionides is portraying a combination of two classic tropes - the coward-at-war, and the carefree islander.

"Owls, cheap!" shout the less-scrupulous coin-changers in the Agora as the more scrupulous ones rush to figure an appropriate new exchange rate. Coin-changers are rapidly changing their minds about the previously expected rise in value of the Athenian owl relative to other cities' coins as news spreads about the exodus of Naxos from the League of Delos. News of this value shift spreads through town more quickly than the news about Naxos, and there are soon crowds around the Agora coin-changers' tables.

Standing at the stall of a sausage-seller near the edge of the Agora, Anaxagoras is in the midst of a conversation with a group of young men visiting from Qorinth. He bites occasionally from his sausage on a stick, taking tiny bites and chewing them very slowly, and moving his attention between the Qorinthians and the coin-changers across the Agora.

"So you're telling me you think there is mind moving *everything* in the cosmos?" the oldest of the Qorinthian boys exclaims, trying to extrapolate from what Anaxagoras has been saying. "And then where did this 'mind' come from? Is it not a child of Chaos also?"

Anaxagoras tries to explain, "No, see, this is why my theory is that *Mind* is at the heart of the cosmos, rather than water or fire or air or the 'unlimited' or what have you. Because think about what *Mind* is - it is the thinker, the self! It is both you *and* me! It is really the only thing that you *are*, which *one is*. A person can lose an arm, or a leg, and still be themselves, still maintain the same mind. Mind is the experiencer, it is the only way that there could be any evidence of anything at all. Imagine a cosmos - of any complexity, from Chaos to this diverse world we see before us - but with no *Mind*? It is meaningless even to imagine such a world, because it would not be experienced. As soon as you imagine such a world in any way, that experience of it is what really makes it take any kind of shape, as the world is held *within* your Mind. And so I would say that Mind must have come first, or must somehow be the keystone of the cosmos, and I hypothesize that it was the action of Mind upon Chaos that started to separate out distinguishable stuff from the previously homogenous primordium."

The Qorinthian boys shake their heads and chuckle with frustrated confusion. "So what was the non-Mind stuff before Mind started to stir it?"

Anaxagoras shrugs. "Elemental non-Mind-ness? It is hard to imagine, and hard to talk about. Our words begin to fail our purposes. Maybe it was literally Nothing, and what we experience as Everything is just mixed up Nothing!" He then recognizes Protagoras across the Agora and smiles at the sight of the man. "There's a fellow sage; let's ask him what he thinks. Hail, Protagoras!"

"O Hermes, I don't know if I can take two of them going at it," one of the Qorinthian boys says to another, already starting to edge away. "Let's go swimming, eh?"

Two of the other boys vocally agree, and as soon as they all start to trot away toward the Piraeus docks, the one boy who had initially struck up the conversation and had been most attentive to Anaxagoras now gives him an apologetic smile before he turns to follow his friends.

Anaxagoras sighs and finishes his sausage, then begins to whittle the stick just as Protagoras walks up and blocks the Sun with his hulking shadow.

"Did I frighten away your pupils?" Protagoras jokes.

"No, I fear I did," Anaxagoras replies, standing to greet Protagoras with a grasp of the forearms. "How has today's morning treated you so far?"

"I'm wondering if we chose the wrong city to set up in, today," Protagoras notes, looking around at the bustling marketplace where so many merchants seem uneasy. "Everything I hear indicates that faltering faith in the future of the League of Delos has coin-changers doubting the owl. I may need to follow Demokritos to Aigypt after all, if this city turns."

"Turns what, turns back into an Oligarchy?"

"Or worse, who knows!" Protagoras moans. "The city invented democracy, maybe they could turn against it and invent something even worse than Oligarchy or monarchy!"

"Anarchy," Anaxagoras proposes coolly.

"We should be so lucky," Protagoras jokes.

"So what *do* you hope to do with yourself in Athens?" Anaxagoras asks directly. "Your master Demokritos brought you here and left you?"

"He's not my master; I'm free," Protagoras retorts sharply. "Noble young Demokritos freed me years ago. We're just good friends, now, and fellow travelers. He had to go to Aigypt for some kind of family business. His father is an important trader in Aigyptian paper up in Abdera. Which is what got him interested in philosophy, and led him to seek out Leukippos, whom he and I both studied under for a year before leaving Abdera."

"Leukippos, I've heard of him," Anaxagoras nod. "I wasn't sure whether he was real or not, though. I've heard some absurd claims."

Protagoras grins and nods. "He likes to spread wild stories about himself. But he's actually very serious, as well as being very funny. His major effort is an incredibly long scroll that he's been working on for years, which he just keeps adding to, which he calls *Big World System*. He has this idea that it should be possible to have one explanation, however complex, that explains not just all individual aspects of the cosmos, but also the whole thing as one."

Anaxagoras nods slowly, his chin held high and his eyes squinting, as he considers the idea. "That makes sense. An epic effort, no doubt. It's work like that which makes *students* useful - for continuing your work after you die! I used to think it was a waste of time and just a desire of vanity to gather disciples around oneself as a wiseman, but I am gradually beginning to understand how it is actually useful to have many minds working as one!"

Protagoras doesn't listen closely, but is more focused on nodding and waiting to continue his thought. "He'll never finish," Protagoras says. "But Abdera is a backward town, surrounded by barbarian hill people. You get new people with new ideas maybe once a season. And someone told us about Athens - that hundreds of ships passed in and out every day, with new people, new voices, new ideas, new stories - and that's what we wanted. So we bought passage. What about you, friend, what brought you here?"

Anaxagoras looks around carefully to make sure no one is eavesdropping in the busy Agora, then he whispers to Protagoras, "If I can be honest with another foreigner here - I came with Xerxes." He shrugs.

Protagoras belts out a single loud laugh, then gets close to Anaxagoras with a big grin and asks, quietly, "Is that a joke?"

Anaxagoras shakes his head. "No joke. Xerxes came to Ionia and mustered every young man of age, under threat to our families. The Oligarchs of Klazomenai didn't even put up a fight. They gave their sons to the King of Kings to march wherever he ordered. My people do not have the bravery that democracy ennobles men with. And so I found myself wearing a Persian breastplate and one of those stupid hats, and we marched all the way north through Phrygia, over the Hellespont on an incredible road across the sea built out of a hundred ships chained together, and then across Thrake and down the east coast of Hellas, all the way here to Attika eventually."

Protagoras slips a smile as he says, "So you've been near Abdera, my home town!"

Anaxagoras nods slightly, but says, "We marched north of it."

Protagoras' face gets serious as he asks, "Did you fight?"

Anaxagoras grimaces. "I saw war. But no, I never fought. And I never will. I find all violence idiotic, I abhor it, and I refuse to participate. But I'll be an actor for a season, and wear some king's armor and paint my eyes and march in line, to avoid being murdered by a Persian officer. Perhaps I took the cowardly path. But it brought me here, so I am glad."

"Cowardly to join an army marching to war?"

"War is always the cowardly choice. I dare propose that what took courage was to avoid fighting for that long, as a conscripted soldier."

"So were you at Thermopylae? Did you ... were you here when they burned this city?"

"No, I was with a group of spearmen who were not at the battle at Thermopylae, though I saw its aftermath. I watched the Spartans burying their dead in the now-famous mound there."

Protagoras shakes his head, struck dumb by the information.

"And then when the navy was defeated in the battle of Salamis, most of the army went west to meet their fate at Plataia, but many of the Persian commanders had already died on the march down the coast, and control of those who'd been conscripted was pretty loose by then, so I was among many who simply deserted and disappeared into the Attikan wilds. I left my Persian armor on some poor dead Thessalian I found, and became merely a traveler, a refugee like so many others."

"Wow," Protagoras says.

"I actually stayed in the countryside for six years before I finally got up the courage to enter Athens," Anaxagoras admits.

"Well I'm glad we're both here," Protagoras says with a rare friendly glimmer in his eye, and he shakes Anaxagoras' hand again.

"Will you keep my secret from Athenians?" Anaxagoras asks.

Protagoras just looks at the flowing crowd around them, then winks at the Ionian.

"Either of you two men interested in a haircut?" asks a passing youth who has been offering the same to everyone. "You could each use one."

"No thank you, friend, but, if I may - let us ask you a question," Anaxagoras replies to the man, taking him by the shoulder to bring him into a circle with himself and Protagoras as others move past behind them all, the Agora busy at midday.

The young man smiles at them both. "Are you two visitors from away? You don't look Athenian."

"I'm Anaxagoras of Klazomenai. This is my friend Protagoras of Abdera."

"Archelaos of Athens," the fellow replies, shaking their hands. "Son of Apollodoros the barber. Good to meet you both. So what is it you wanted to know? The Temple of Aphrodite is that way if you're looking for girls." Archelaos starts laughing at his own ribaldry, but stops quickly when he sees that the others are not laughing.

"We were both wondering how fertile the population of Athens might be for the cultivation of a school of sagacity here," Anaxagoras explains. "Wondering whether the people of your city might be amenable to such a notion."

"Well, I don't really know what you're talking about," Archelaos admits with a chuckle, "but I'll be happy to hear more about it if you two want to sit for a very cheap, very fine haircut by my father in that booth right over there. I will listen to as much 'sagacity' as you want to talk about."

Once Anaxagoras is seated in Archelos' father Apollodoros' barber chair, Protagoras and young Archelaos seated on upturned jars nearby, Archelaos says, "Alright, so what exactly is *philosophy*, then?"

"You want to keep that beard?" Archelaos' stone-faced father asks with a comb and knife in front of Anaxagoras' face.

"Yes, please. We are both philosophers, Archelaos. Philosophy is like a way of thinking about the world, and using the natural reasoning power of your mind to try to answer certain particularly challenging questions about the nature of our cosmos. I'm a student of Thales and Herakleitos, from the Ionian school of philosophy. Protagoras here is a student of Leukippos and Demokritos, of the Abderan school."

"What is a *school*, exactly?" asks the barber Apollodoros as he leans directly in front of Anaxagoras' face and pulls on his beard hairs to test their length.

"By school we just mean - the particular method that a group of people uses to try to mine any particular vein of wisdom. For example the Eleatic school in Elea always explores the notion that everything comes from something else, and tries to look at the natural world that way; and the Krotonic school started by Pythagoras in Kroton tries to consider everything through the language of numbers and geometry; and the Ionian school I am from tries to look to nature for evidence of its mechanics, and to find the primary principle that ultimately runs this cosmos."

"O, is wisdom a mineral, have you philosophers determined that? I thought it was just composed of words."

"It's certainly more than words, but no, I didn't mean to indicate that wisdom is literally a mineral. I was speaking figuratively."

"I still don't understand what philosophy is," the barber's son admits.

"When you speak of looking for 'primary principles' that run the cosmos, it almost sounds like you're implying that there aren't really gods controlling the various aspects of nature, but ... some mundane laws which are just like some kind of spinning wheels somewhere or something like that? But what keeps the wind following some law, other than the power of a god?"

"This a good beard length?" the barber asks after just a few snips.

Anaxagoras nods with a curt smile. "You've more or less got that right," he says to Archelaos the barber's son. "I just ... consider the water in the river. You surely don't think that the god directs the movement of each droplet of water as they move down along the course of the river."

"Is a river composed of various droplets?" Apollodoros the barber asks as he works. "Seems to me a water droplet is one thing, and a river is another thing entirely, like the difference between some little sea creature and Keto, mistress of sea monsters, herself. Like the child from its ultimate mother, droplets do certainly *emerge from* the river, but the river is not the same as the droplet, and does not behave the same."

"Well, they are different scales of water," Anaxagoras tries to explain, "but they are both water, and both seem to behave more or less the same - like water."

"But rivers flow," the barber retorts. "Water droplets just sit there. You can even touch one, and it might just sit there and wiggle against your finger. And water in the Sea behaves even differently!"

"Father, you're embarrassing me," Archelaos bemoans, sitting down heavily on a nearby tripod stool. "Please don't try to talk philosophy. Stick to barbering."

"Hey now," Apollodoros snaps, stopping his haircutting to look up and fix his eyes upon his son for a reprimand. "Philosophy becomes poison if it makes sons disrespect their fathers. You be careful how you speak to me in public; you hear me? No one can see what I'll do to you in private."

Archelaos nods. "I just don't think you understand what he's trying to talk about."

Apollodoros returns to his focus upon Anaxagoras' face, and asks him again, this time right up next to his face, "Are you sure you want to keep this beard?"

Anaxagoras smiles awkwardly and nods.

"Fine. I'll leave the beard then." He continues snipping the hair around Anaxagoras' ears with his scissors as he adds, "See, hair is composed of individuals. But water not so much. Water is stuff. Hairs are things."

Anaxagoras nods, "That is an interesting distinction - things or stuff."

A rowdy group of young men runs past, all slapping and hanging onto each other to stay close as they move among the already boisterous Agora crowds, with an adolescent combination of laughter and aggression. They swarm one of the coin-changer's tables, bunching around it together so quickly that those in the back push those in the front up onto the table, and one of them jumps up onto the table to avoid being crushed, bouncing many rows of coins into the air in the process. All the other coin-changers in view bellow in commiseration.

"The Delian League is no more!" one of the young men shouts.

Anaxagoras, Protagoras, and the barber Apollodoros all look to each other to see the other men's reactions to the news. Protagoras immediately begins to shake his head.

"No," Protagoras shouts, projecting confidence. "The league will hold! Just as one loosened string won't unravel the Great Knot of Gordion."

"Perhaps you might want to find out the news which they are basing their shouts upon, before you guess their veracity?" Anaxagoras suggests carefully with a crack of a smile. "What makes you so sure the Delian League's ties are *Gordian*?"

"The Delian League is necessary," Protagoras replies. "Therefore the politicians will not allow it to fall, for they know that it must not. People do not release the tools which give them power."

Anaxagoras smiles. "What was that saying of yours that you liked to repeat? 'Man is the measure of all things'?"

Protagoras nods, then turns as some sudden commotion from the nearby group of young men all arm-in-arm interrupts his thoughts. They are stumbling away from the coin-changers' tables, through the annoyed crowd and in the general direction of the barber's shop. Anaxagoras regrets immediately watching long enough to be caught in eye contact by the one shouting to strangers, which turns the group to gather around the little barbershop discussion.

Rudely, a round-bellied man in front named Euathlos shouts, "I'll tell you one truth, stranger - *this* is power! *This* is freedom! A coin! And the number of them that you have is a measure of your power and your freedom, nothing else."

"That's absurd," Anaxagoras retorts, turning away from another conversation. "I know you must know rich idiots, and wise beggars."

Euathlos scoffs, "I can't say I know any wise beggars."

"Wisemen who are destitute, whether or not they beg. Take Aristides the Just! Did you not think that he was among the best of men, and the wisest?"

"He was definitely a good man," one of Euathlos' friends agrees. Euathlos briefly glares at him like a traitor.

"Good, wise. Okay. But did you know that when he died, he was destitute? He had no money even for his funeral. His children had to borrow money from friends for his funeral."

"I had no inkling of that, and would not have guessed it," the men around Euathlos say to each other. "Yeah, he always carried himself with such dignity." "But I guess that's modern times, with the theater of democracy and everything - you can't tell who's really themselves and who's some masked figure anymore."

Anaxagoras explains, "No, my point was that Aristides was still the wise man that you thought he was, even though he became destitute economically. The two are not connected."

"But why would a wise man let himself become destitute? Doesn't that show that he wasn't really all that wise? I don't want to be rude..."

Anaxagoras sighs, "He was happy, and he was good, wasn't he? I'm just saying this - maybe those coins you put so much value in are really more like the masks you bemoan, just a portrayal of parody of wealth when *real wealth* is what you hope desperately that your coins might procure for you!"

Euathlos just retracts his neck in confusion, and his friends start to move away, bored, indicating their interest in leaving town.

"My point is that what someone truly needs is not able to be bought with your wealth - wisdom!"

"I'll sell you some wisdom," Protagoras chimes. "An owl a wisdom. Going fast. Owls seem to be nesting in Athens today, rather than flying."

"How does that work?" Euathlos asks. "What, do you have some kind of eastern potion or something?" He turns to his friends and mockingly says, "Ionians," making them laugh.

"I'm Abderan," Protagoras corrects, "not Ionian."

"It isn't possible to pass on wisdom," Apollodoros the barber chimes in, as he is leaning close to Anaxagoras' face to take the final snips at his beard. "One is either born with it, or they aren't. I certainly didn't pass on any wisdom of my own to Archelaos here, and he is already far smarter than I! And if I had, wouldn't he be as great a barber as I am?"

"I told you, I'm just not *interested* in barbering, father."

"I disagree about wisdom not being able to be passed on," Protagoras replies. "I've several times seen conversations turn dullards into wisemen. I will say it isn't necessarily possible with *everyone*, but perhaps even it *is* possible with everyone with the right methodology."

"Perhaps there's some tool that could be developed for the purpose," Archelaos proposes. "After all, consider how poor a job of barbering you would be able to do without scissors, father!"

"True enough," Apollodoros agrees. "You remember when all my scissors got stolen, how miserable I was."

"I do."

"What tool could help pass on wisdom?" Anaxagoras wonders aloud. "It's an interesting proposal."

"Words," Protagoras notes. "Words. And who are the keepers of the best words? Wisemen."

Anaxagoras simultaneously says, "Scrolls," and then laughs when he hears Protagoras' answer. Protagoras shakes his head, not laughing.

"Maybe some kind of special megaphone made out of some kind of magical beast's horn?" Archelaos suggests.

Anaxagoras just nods slowly, also shrugging.

"Literally anything can happen," Archelaos' father remarks, then he blows on Anaxagoras' face to remove the last of the hair clippings, and stands back, holding out his arms to indicate that he is finished.

Anaxagoras nods gratitude and puts an owl in the barber's bowl.

"Come on, guys. The barber can keep these fools' supposed wisdom." Impatient Euathlos dismisses them all with a wave of his hand and turns back to leave town through the Dipylon Gate with his friends. "City folk," they all mockingly say to each other, mimicking the subtle differences of accent between men of the city and men of the countryside.

"Come and find me if you ever want to learn how to stop being an idiot," Protagoras calls out after Euathlos.

There is an Aigyptian sailor with bright, charming eyes behind dark eyeliner waiting in line for a head shaving, and he says something in Aigyptian, with an indicative glance at the raucous young boys leaving with Euathlos.

"What did he say?" Archelaos asks his father, who speaks Aigyptian.

Apollodoros shrugs, mentally translating. "He basically said, 'You can't fix stupid.'"

Z

Aischylos and Sophokles argue about writing theater

Sharing a hot pool in the bath house known as the Nereid's Pond, in the rich Honeymouth neighborhood, marble-cheeked Sophokles and big-shouldered Aischylos lounge with a few older playwrights. More water heats in a big bronze vessel suspended over a tripod of flame in the corner of the room. In one of the other four square baths in the room, tight-bearded Perikles bathes alone, idly eavesdropping on the actors' conversation.

Sun-drunk from wrestling in the field all morning, Aischylos lays his head back and closes his eyes as he sighs, "Actors who aren't writers are just dancers. Singing someone else's composition is one thing, but writing your own work is entirely another. Sophokles, can you even make all the letters?"

"I will ignore that insulting question by simply reminding you that I have been rejected for choruses five times, and it was not simply air, nor blank scrolls, that I submitted," Sophokles replies with the careful elocution of a great actor. "Were the selection of plays not a political decision - were it, perhaps, given to the gods on the lot board, for example, instead of left to the will of the Archon - I suspect we would already have seen not only a play by Sophokles, but a wreath win as well!"

"What have you written about?" Aischylos asks him, genuinely interested. A rare smile crosses the bald veteran's face, and its rarity brings one out of Perikles as well. "They don't make me submit scripts anymore," Aischylos then says as an arrogant aside to Perikles. "I just have to want to make something. Men who are wise enough to become Archon are likely also erudite enough to trust my artistic voice."

"That is just the sort of corruption that tradition creates!" Sophokles shouts, splashing water out of the bath.

"No," Aischylos disagrees, "it is simply the benefit of fame won by consistent quality."

Sophokles grumbles, "Imagine how many potentially powerful new voices have been ignored in order to hear from those whose ideas we already have plenty of evidence of?"

Perikles perks up at that comment, and notes, unheard by either playwright, "That reminds me of the democracy itself, and how it can enfranchise the voices of those unheard."

Sophokles sighs good-naturedly. "Perikles, you are a political animal. Everything is politics to you. It comes out of your skin like sweat."

"I just don't believe that you could write an entire play," Aischylos chides Sophokles. "It isn't something just anyone can do. You know you can't just reproduce the stories you like most. You have to give stories your own twist, your own voice, some reason to be new."

"Consider bold Theseos, as tragedy," Sophokles proposes. "Boy, prince, human sacrifice, monster slayer..." He splashes more in the bathwater with each new epithet, until Aischylos interrupts him from the other side of the bath.

"We do not need to hear another word about King Theseos," Aischylos barks to stop Sophokles. "I'm finished with political material!"

"Forget those absurd bones," Perikles adds from the next bath over, where he is leaning over and listening in on their conversation. "No one really thinks those are the bones of King Theseos. No one respectable."

"Your aristocratic tendencies continue to slip out, Perikles," Aischylos chides. "You don't respect the common man, and will never become Archon because of it. You should write plays, I'm telling you. Politics is for the potters and sailors now. You don't know anyone who believes those bones are Theseos, and yet almost everyone I speak to does believe it. Because men prefer whatever makes the better story, not what's most likely true."

Sophokles continues, "Theseos need not be political material. Imagine a piece that is nothing but his adventure with the Minotaur. Just a romance that begins with his arrival on Krete, and ends with him and Ariadne sailing away from that island together happily!"

Aischylos laughs.

Perikles says, "That would be an absurdly misleading portrayal of King Theseos. It's just a small section of his story."

"But it's a good story!" Sophokles shouts, frustrated.

"It's the middle of a sentence!" Aischylos laughs. "Sophokles, I'm telling you, the opposite of what I just told Perikles - never write plays. You have a beautiful voice and can inhabit a woman like no man I've ever known, but..."

"You want to bet I couldn't win an ivy crown like yours?" Sophokles asks Aischylos with all seriousness.

"I'm not afraid of you winning an ivy," Aischylos scoffs. "I'm afraid of you souring the people on poetry altogether with your attempts."

Perikles and Sophokles both laugh.

One of the older playwrights, old Dionolochos of the tall hats, opens his eyes just long enough to look at both Aischylos and Sophokles and then grunt, "Let the actor try his hand at writing if he has the ink."

Aischylos nudges the other sleeping playwright Speudon under the water with his foot and asks him, "What do you think of the idea of seeing a play that Sophokles here wrote, Speudon? Speudon?"

Sagging-necked Speudon snores, unwakeable.

"Speudon is writing his next play as we speak," Sophokles taunts. "It will be called," and then he makes a loud snoring sound.

As Sophokles is mocking his old friend, the door to the room creaks open and three nude teenagers - two girls and a boy - sneak hesitantly into the bath room.

"Any of you interested in a companion?" the careful-eyed boy asks, rubbing his fingers together to subtly indicate payment.

Aischylos stirs the bath with his body a bit, clearly uncomfortable. "I am married," he says to the boy. Aischylos looks to Sophokles and Perikles to confirm the dismissal.

Perikles just waves his hand politely as a negative, not even turning to look at them, thoughtlessly falling back to an aristocratic habit of attempting to make the lower-class feel unwelcome among nobles.

Sophokles, however, also stirs in his bath at the sight of the beautiful young bodies, but not with discomfort. His interest rears its head.

Sophokles looks over the three young people in a quick scan and then laughs, "Are you their pimp, or a third option?"

Aischylos and Perikles stand at the same time, mumbling over each other excuses for their need to be elsewhere.

The boy sniffs out a derisive laugh and says, "I'm not for sale. You'd have Antiphon the horsemaster to answer to if you try to touch me that way, chorus leader," as he watches Aischylos and Perikles nudely walk to the door. "I'm Antiphon's for now. I'm just here protecting these girls."

"Protecting their virginity?" Sophokles asks, half joking.

"Protecting their purses. They're not Athenians; they're foreigners; you don't have to worry about their honor. We have *silphion* for that."

Sophokles shrugs to the boy pimp as his smile and nod beckon one of the girls toward him. While Perikles and Aischylos are still collecting their belongings, the thin-legged girl slips her tunic off and steps into the water beside Sophokles, ignoring the elderly playwrights sleeping gnarly feet away.

H

The Athenian Council debates how to deal with Naxos

The city council meets now in a newly completed circular building named the *Tholos*, recently designed and funded by the Builders Club, which is composed of Kimon and a few other Oligarchs who have the level of wealth that can be put to large projects without the need for public funds. The colorfully painted new building has more comfortable, tiered seating in an arc around the central speaking floor, as well as a back room with a table and some couches for eating dinner and napping. For the few months since it was completed and the Council started actually using it, complimenting its comforts to each other has become the new pastime of councilors.

The Caretaker of the council on this day is a neighbor and close associate of the Oligarch Kritias, and at his suggestion has wasted time so that the discussion on Naxos should occur closer to the end of the day, just before supper time, so that all the councilors will be hungry and spiteful when considering the fate of that island.

"First of all," the Caretaker declares, "let us all thank again the fine and noble Kimon, who arranged the funding for this splendid new council house. Remember, in your mind, if you would, for a moment, how your butts felt on that old wooden seating." He pauses for such reflection only a moment, then continues, "So, before we all go and have dinner now, we must first decide how to respond to the desertion of Naxos from the ranks of our defensive league."

"How are deserters treated in the *phalanx*?" one veteran barks, bringing to every veteran's mind the rigorous order needed in battle.

"Exactly," Kritias nods, standing beside his friend the Caretaker. "This is the Delian League's first attempted deserter, so we must here set the example for others of how we will behave in the future. Those among this wise council who have raised children, like I have, will understand the need to use the rod often early, so that you have to use it rarely in later years."

Ephialtes, always standing, says, "This sets a dangerous precedent. Is this how Athens will treat its allies? Democracy, and particularly international democracy, is still young as a concept; we have the opportunity with our actions to stand as a role model for how it might seem to be able to behave, as a system ... Let us stay on the gods' good side and make good choices."

"You still have yet to fight a battle, Ephialtes," cold-eyed Kritias retorts. "Defectors must have an example made of them, just like with soldiers, or before long we will have no allies left. Like the good man said - think of what makes a phalanx strong, the group."

"We need not fight them, unless they fight us," adds an uncouth but wealthy tanner named Kleanetos. "We need only bring our wooden wall to their harbor, and block the merchant vessels from their island. Starve them and they'll come around. It's how I deal with my boys when they're insolent."

Many of those with children laugh.

A more moderate voice from a group of fishermen on the council speaks hesitantly, "Good gentlemen of the council, shouldn't we consider what the rest of our allies in the League of Delos would think if we threaten to starve a friend? We should not want to be seen across the seas as a heartless, vicious city, should we?"

"Perhaps that is one of the many differences between you fishermen and us merchants," says Thukydides, "for I do definitely see the value in being feared by my comrades. You see, poor men - you might learn from this, not to think that affairs of state have the same stakes as waiting for a fish!"

The Oligarchs all huff their agreement smarmily, while the more numerous non-nobles bark their offense.

Thukydides adds, "Our leatherworking friend was right. They'll give up before any good men starve."

Ephialtes directs his words to the councilors he knows to be on the poorer end of the economic spectrum, "You know Prometheos made all men from the same clay, not just the rich ones, Thukydides. I don't know what it will take to convince you that keeping bread out of a man's belly is as much murdering him as putting a sword into his belly."

"Actually Prometheos created just a few men. The best of their sons stand here. As do some of the worst, thanks to your democracy."

Now many Democrats in the council start to shout Thukydides down and stand for their turn speaking.

Thukydides adds above the clamor, "But really, whores created most men!" and the whole council becomes an uproar of laughter and outrage.

"NO MORE GOOD SHOULD BE DONE
THAN THE COUNTRY CAN BEAR."
Solon, *Ship of State*

Θ

Sokrates meets a new friend on the Athenian streets at night

His parents sleeping entwined, three-year old Sokrates lies awake in his little straw-filled nook in the wall where he is supposed to be sleeping.

He watches the hearthfire, watches his parents stir against each other on their own straw pile across the room, and watches the drizzling rain through the tiny window high on the wall where the little wooden shutter has fallen open and the bright crescent Moon hangs perfectly in view against the eerie blueish glow above the imminent Sun. The combination of the drizzling rain and bright moon fills young Sokrates with a magical feeling, like it is both day and night, both raining and clear, and Sokrates starts to imagine what it might be like if the cosmos were to quit its patterns, unravel, and return to chaos.

A little owl flaps suddenly onto the open shutter, blocking the moonlight. It turns its head both directions inside the dark house, and when it sees Sokrates who is watching it silently, its eyes glow. He gasps as quietly as he can, shutting his mouth with his thumb.

Off back into the night the owl flits, unocculting the Moon.

Quietly, so as not to wake his sleeping parents, little Sokrates climbs down out of his nook in the wall and walks on the balls of his feet to the front door. He watches his parents as he opens it slowly, creaking on its old hinges with each movement, but neither of them wakes, and once it is open wide enough for his thin body to slip through, he is out amongst the moonshadows.

Sokrates looks about himself, searching for the little owl that had seen him. Few people are out in the darkness. Though the Moon provides shadows, it is shadow within shadow.

Sokrates wonders whether he ought to go back inside, but before he can complete the thought process he hears a whisper of a young boy's voice from down the street.

"Hey - you! Little boy! Come here!"

A glance in that direction reveals a gaunt, big-eared boy not much older than Sokrates, sitting on the street with his back to the wall of a house, whittling a stick with a stone.

For just a moment when Sokrates first sees him, the boy's eyes seem to flash a bit of light, perhaps a reflection off the Moon at a certain fleeting angle of his head, but it fills Sokrates with the wondrous feeling that this little boy might just be the little owl he saw moments earlier, and if someone can transform like that then they must be a god.

Remembering the stories his mother has told him, little Sokrates bravely declares, "Sokrates am I, son of Sophroniskos and Phaenarete. And who may I ask are you, so that I may greet my new friend by name!"

The boy just stares at him, seemingly confused, then pats the ground in font of himself and says again, "Come here!"

Sokrates runs over to the boy and kneels down in front of him. He watches him whittle for a moment, then asks him directly, "Are you a god? Would you tell me? Do you know?"

The boy frowns at Sokrates with confusion, but then nods and says, "I'm Chaerephon the god of this stick," and he starts whittling with even more vigor.

Sokrates smiles at the joke, but realizes quickly that joking off the notion does not necessarily mean that this person is not a god. He watches him whittle a little while longer.

Eventually, big-eared Chaerephon stands up, and with a gesture of his chin gets Sokrates to join him standing.

"What are you doing out at night?" Chaerephon asks him, noticing their different heights. "You're too little to be out this late. Do your parents know where you are?"

Sokrates shakes his head no.

"Good. Then come on!" Chaerephon takes little Sokrates' hand and starts trotting off up the street, in the direction of the high central hill of the Akropolis.

"What are we doing?" Sokrates asks Chaerephon as they scamper through the dark, moonshadowed streets of Athens, between rough, new straw and plaster walls of recently rebuilt homes and the remnants of ancient, cyclopean-stone walls of ages past with blocks larger than any man could lift.

"When I'm alone, I like to chase mice down the street," Chaerephon says, slowing to walk beside Sokrates, whose legs are shorter than his. "But I haven't seen any yet tonight."

Chaerephon contorts his neck spastically and lets out a strange, shrill chirp, followed by a couple of grunts as he shakes off the involuntary action of his body.

Sokrates watches him, never having met anyone like this before.

"My father kills mice, but my mother feeds them," Sokrates tells Chaerephon.

Chaerephon shoots a quizzical look at Sokrates, but doesn't respond. Then he takes Sokrates' little hand and dashes off again, letting go before long but continuing to look back to make sure Sokrates is still following close behind him in the darkness.

At the base of the hill of the Akropolis, where the neighborhood streets give way to a small olive forest as the slope steepens on its way up to the bare rock. Chaerephon crouches at the base of one of the olive trees and starts to dig at its roots.

Sokrates stops and watches him from a slight distance, nervous about interacting with the olive trees, which he vaguely understands to be sacred to Athena, whom he vaguely understands to be a goddess.

"Stop," he whisper-shouts at Chaerephon, but the other boy doesn't seem to hear him, so he slowly closes the space between them until he is right beside his new friend under the twisted old tree. "Stop," he says again, too loud this time. Chaerephon turns and shooshes him.

After digging in a few different places around the olive tree roots, finally Chaerephon squeaks with delight as he comes up with a tiny shape in his hands, and Sokrates finally gathers the courage to dash over to squat beside him. Once near, he can see that Chaerephon has dug up a little wooden horse shape.

"It's a knight toy," big-eared Chaerephon whispers. "I stole it from an older kid. Can you keep that a secret?"

Sokrates shakes his head no, gazing at the little horse and his friend's worried face.

"Well then forget what I just told you. I should have asked about secrets first. Pretend the words I said were just sounds. I do make sounds that aren't words." Chaerephon makes several such sounds amidst his intentional words.

Sokrates nods and shrugs.

Chaerephon reburies the little knight-shaped hunk of wood, then stands again. With a glance back toward Sokrates to get him to follow, he strolls down the alleys back toward their neighborhood. Sokrates follows, emboldened by his new friend's casualness to walk through the city at night without adults. He begins to feel like an animal whose natural environment is composed of the walls of buildings and cobblestone stairways and the piss-smell of alleyways, a city animal.

A rat stands briefly and waves at the two passing boys, unnoticed.

As they skip from doorway stone to street stone, Sokrates asks his new friend, "What does your father do?"

"I don't know what shades do below the Earth," Chaerephon answers matter-of-factly. "But my mother is a *maenad*."

"What's that?" little Sokrates asks.

"She worships Dionysos above all other gods. So she's never home, and when she is, she's drunk, or sleeping. And she goes mad with rage sometimes. But it's the god in her."

"That sounds hard," Sokrates whispers shyly. Sokrates wonders if his parents are still sleeping back in their home.

When he notices that Chaerephon is trying to hide the welling of tears in his eyes, Sokrates turns his gait to crash into and hug his new friend. Chaerephon at first accepts the hug for several long seconds, but then shakes it off with a half-smile, and wipes his eyes dry with the back of his hand.

Two bats flit overhead.

"It's okay," Chaerephon sighs.

"Would you like to be friends?" Sokrates asks Chaerephon.

"Okay," Chaerephon smiles.

They walk on together for a while down the street, Chaerephon hopping in order to maintain little Sokrates' slow pace.

"My father is a sculptor," Sokrates says to him.

Chaerephon's smile twists. "Lucky," he weeps. "You must be rich."

Sokrates first shakes his head. But then he thinks about it a little more, remembering the warmth and love in his home, and begins to nod.

Watching Sokrates' face through the whole thought process, Chaerephon smiles once Sokrates starts nodding, and asks excitedly, "You are? Is your father famous?"

At that Sokrates shakes his head no, with certainty. "No, he makes columns."

"Well, those hold up the houses of the gods!" Chaerephon notes. "I bet people give you a lot of praise for being the son of a useful man."

Then appears the very voice being discussed - that of Sophroniskos, Sokrates' father. "There you are! Sokrates, come here!"

Sokrates turns at the sound of his father's voice. Chaerephon scrambles and dashes away down the dark alleys of Athens. Sophroniskos trots up to his little son just in time to see the neighbor boy running off.

"What are you doing out here?" Sokrates' father asks him.

"I met a new friend named Chaerephon," Sokrates answers. "That's him running away. His mother is a maenad, and he doesn't have a father."

"O? Is that right? Poor boy." Sophroniskos spies the distant shadow of Chaerephon down the street as he runs over a rise and out of view. "Well luckily you do have a father, and it's me!"

Sophroniskos scoops his little son up in one arm and throws him up onto his shoulders, where Sokrates grabs hold around his father's big neck and squeals.

"Now listen to me, Sokrates," Sophroniskos says windedly as he carries his little son down the narrow streets of Athens. "You can't just wander off and go wherever you want. You need to understand that you could hurt yourself, get lost, even die, out here by yourself."

"I thought if I just kept sucking my thumb, I would at least always be able to create water in my mouth," Sokrates says from Sophroniskos' arm, his thumb in and out of his mouth.

"You need to stop that," Sophroniskos replies. "It doesn't create water, it just makes your mouth fill with some of the water you've already drunk that's been absorbed into your body. You're actually *wasting* the water that's already in your body when you do that, and that will make you *more* thirsty."

"But it fills my mouth with water that wasn't there."

Sophroniskos sighs. "Look, I can't explain everything to you in a way that's going to make sense, but that doesn't change the way things are. You need to just trust me, Sokrates, and listen to what I say and just take it to heart. I've been around a lot longer than you have, and I just know better how things really work."

He carries his son in silence for a little while, until they start to see neighborhoods near the little Eridanos River and Potter's Alley that are more familiar to little Sokrates.

"Sorry, Father," he finally says, feeling his father's care.

"It's alright, Sokrates. I don't know why I keep forgetting that you don't know anything yet! But that's why we tell stories, and talk to each other about what we know. So that all can learn. You'll learn; you'll see. It just takes time. And sometimes it takes several times. But the most valuable possession a man can hold with him are the wisdoms, the stories, the good habits and skills that he collects through watching and talking to other men. That's the only possession of any true value - knowledge! Not coins or land or horses or fancy armor - experience! Just don't go out alone at night again."

"I was with my new friend Chaerephon."

"Now Sokrates, listen to me," Sophroniskos says sharply, stopping to lower his son off his shoulders and placing him onto the street, then crouching down onto one knee to get at his level. "Whom you consort with not only affects who you'll become, but who people will think you are. You have to choose your friends very well. There are innumerable desperate, malformed people out there who will happily cling to you for safety, but who will drag you down into a world of muck and hardship with them if you let them. That's the kind of people *my* father allowed to hang around him, and they brought about his ruin. You'll notice I myself am very careful with my friends, whom I call a friend, and whom I spend my time with. It's because when two people are together, they become more like each other the longer they speak. That's why I chose your mother to be my wife - because she is such a fine person whom I'd like to be more like! And it's why I only count among my friends fine people like Lysimachos and Ephialtes, though other, cruder men have often tried to become my friend. You must not weigh yourself down with the cares of someone like Chaerephon. I would prefer instead that you find friends among the finer, nobler-minded boys of your own generation - boys like Nikeratos' son, or Kleanetos' son, I forget their names. Okay? Artisans' sons, like you are. Caring about an ill-fated boy like Chaerephon will only bring you grief. Do you understand?"

"How do you know he's ill-fated?"

"His poor parents."

Little three-year-old Sokrates shrugs, trying to understand what clearly means a lot to his father and drawn like a moth to the flame in his eyes, but only vaguely understanding. Chaerephon seemed nice.

"Folks don't pay attention as much to *things* as they do to the *relationships between things*," Sophroniskos suggests, as he thinks about it. "And whether rightly or wrongly, you'll be judged, Sokrates, for the relationships you have with others, not for who you are inside yourself independent of those relationships."

Sophroniskos nods curtly, then stands again and takes his little son by the hand, walking him slowly back through the tight, dark streets of Athens to their little home in the Alopeke neighborhood, not far from the Temple of Herakles.

As they walk, Sokrates asks his father, "What causes the dawn?"

"Well, the Dawn is a goddess, Eos. Just like the Sun, and the Sky, and the Earth. They're all very ancient gods, who each rule over their various natural arenas. And like you and me, some of them are related to each other, siblings or sons or mothers, but they are also jealous of each other's arenas of control, and protective of their own. And those are some of the biggest, most powerful, and most ancient gods, but there are all sorts of smaller and younger gods who rule over their own smaller areas, like specific rivers, or our cities, or each home, like our little hearth god over the fire."

"Am I a god?" Sokrates asks.

"You're a boy, one day a man," his father replies. "But maybe there's a singular tiny god who just rules over this right here," Sophroniskos says with a grin, indicating with both hands the volume of space that is little Sokrates' body. Then he adds, "And maybe that's you. No one really quite knows for sure how that sort of thing works. Some people think they do, but not like smiths know smithing or sculptors know stone. You won't find a soul-smith's alley in Athens."

Sokrates looks at the space around himself, and himself, with awe.

"Look there, Sokrates, do you see that point of light in the sky, directly above the highest tree on Mount Lykabettos there? That's Phosphoros, the Light-Bearer. He's a brother of the Four Winds, and a son of Eos the Dawn and Astreos the Dusk, and in this season he always wakes before his mother, the Dawn, to clean up the space in which she and her brother the Sun will have their morning meal. That's what good little boys do for their mother when they really care about her. They wake up early and prepare the home for their parents' morning chores. That's the kind of lesson we can learn from the stars, as people. Even just a little slobber-bearer like you."

Sokrates laughs as he sucks his thumb, gazing up at the single star in the east's dark-blue glow.

"Krito and I got some string so that we can do geometry ourselves!" Sokrates says. "Krito kept it, but he lets me use it to make circles and measure things."

ATHENS

"Were these those friends of old Oenopides?"

"Yeah! Foreign number-wizards and earth-measurers."

"I don't know how good that sort of thing is going to be for you, Sokrates. I've found numbers to be of little value. Looking at things, and comparing them to other things, that's what's really useful. Take the cycle of days and stars, for example. I've heard Oenopides talk about his numerical calendar of days, but something like that is just going to trip you up, when the gods show you the movement of time right there in the Sky. You only have to look. Want to know what day it is? Look at the Sky. You dilute the reality of a thing when you start thinking about it just through numbers. Want to know when it will be Spring? Wait until you see the Spring stars. After all, even the gods sometimes have other business, and might be a few days late, or early, and if you think everything is going to happen based on some table of numbers some wiseman put together, you might miss reality."

Sokrates listens intently to his father.

"I'm not saying don't listen to them. Think about it all; I'm sure it's fun to think about. I like puzzles just like the number-clowns. Just don't forget to keep looking at the real world, and don't pay so much attention to numbers and symbols. In fact, I'm gonna give you a limit on that sort of activity, Sokrates. From now on, only for the time it takes the Sun to move one hand span across the Sky are you allowed to look at or think about letters and symbols and numbers. The rest of the day, you have to live in the real world of stars and grass and girls and fish and real non-symbols. Okay?"

"But I like reading!" Sokrates complains.

"And you can keep doing it. But you have to live in this world, too, not just the world of words. You're a boy, Sokrates, not a word."

"Isn't my name a word?"

Sophroniskos sighs. "You're not your name, son. You're this boy, this skin, this hair, these incessant questions. That's Sokrates. That's my point! No name, no word, can contain any amount of the real world. That's all caricatures, even worse than those cartoons you find on cups. Don't mistake it for accurate, that's all I'm saying. Better to look at paintings than words."

Karpokles the baker and his apprentice walk past Sokrates and his father, headed to their oven for the morning, having their own quiet conversation, and the two older men nod to each other with silent cordiality.

"Who thought of the city?" Sokrates asks, slipping his thumb into his mouth without thought.

227

Sophroniskos pulls his thumb away from his mouth, saying, "Stop it, Sokrates, stop sucking your thumb. You must find a way to do this yourself, to keep this in your own mind, and keep thinking about it so that you don't lose track of yourself, like just now, and slip back into the habit. You need to be able to control your own mind, so you can control your body."

Sokrates stares at his thumb, nodding, understanding. "I won't suck my thumb anymore," he says. Then he asks, "Who started the city?"

Sophroniskos laughs at first, and shakes his head at the apparent randomness of the question.

"Well, they say the first king of Athens was a man born of the very earth, King Kekrops," Sokrates' father explains in a low and patient voice. He tickles Sokrates on his shoulders and chest. "They say he was a man up here, but instead of legs his lower parts were like two big slimy serpents!"

Sokrates gives that a suspicious expression.

"But King Kekrops showed the people how to write, and read, the letters of the world, and he showed us how and why women and men ought to marry, and how and why to bury the dead. And during his reign, he forbade the killing of any living creature in sacrifice for the gods, and showed our people how we could instead make cakes in the shapes of goats or oxen, and instead sacrifice those to the gods just as well, and how you can use little sesame seeds to make it look like the animal cake has fur. Some people still prefer to sacrifice in this way, symbolically."

"Are there really people in distant lands with snake legs, or only one eye, or the head of a wolf, or the body of a horse ..?" Sokrates asks, starting a long list of questions while chewing on the tip of his thumb.

"There are absolutely all kinds of strange monsters in the world, and men and women of every variety," the father interrupts his son. Then he smacks the boy's chubby little arm away from his mouth. "And you'll *become* a one-armed boy if you don't stop sucking your thumb!"

Sokrates' eyes light up, his smile opens wide, and he points, then, when he sees the glowing ember of the top of the Sun just beginning to climb over the eastern mountains. "Look," he whispers excitedly.

"Yes, there he is, bright and noble Helios," Sophroniskos smiles, hugging his boy. "Wrapped in the loving glow of his sister Eos, the Dawn. Sleep well, Nyx. And now, Sokrates, let's get you home to your mother."

Sophroniskos stands, but Sokrates tugs on his tunic and makes himself heavy when his father tries to lift him, and he whines just enough to make his father finally laugh and sit back down.

"Alright, we can watch the whole circle rise. But then home."

Sokrates asks, "What happens to the Sun at night?"

Sophroniskos breathes slowly, thinking, then says, "I'll be honest, Sokrates - no one really knows. But I know this - it still exists in your mind, when it's gone. Just like my own father, who sat to watch Dawn rise with me when I was a boy. Gone, but not forgotten. And here it is, another day, despite him being gone."

> "ALREADY HAVE I BEEN A BOY, A GIRL,
> A FLOWER, A BIRD, AND A SILENT FISH IN THE SEA.
> IN MIND, ALL THINGS CAN BE."
> Empedokles, *Purifications*

I

Athenian ships arrive to blockade the harbor at Naxos

Waves lap at stonework around the sky-blue harbor of the village of Naxos, on the island of the same name.

Across from the village harbor, the many-decades unfinished bottom half of a Temple of Apollo gleams whitely in unpainted marble on the little harbor island known as Palatia - long ago the island where Theseos abandoned Ariadne, where she then met and married Dionysos, and where they say the first Dionysian festivals were held; now an abandoned work site since the Persian Wars killed its architect. But the harbor is alive with activity, boats of every nation sailing in and out.

Among those sailing in to harbor is the official Athenian trireme of the Delian League, all bedecked with shining armor-clad wooden statues of Athena and garlanded with sacred olive branches, and captained by a young upstart sailor on his first command, the yellow-haired and serious-eyed Charitimides.

When the official Athenian trireme arrives within view of the men chatting in the harbor market, they immediately begin to organize the clearing of other boats to make a path for it, and summon trumpeters with their hollowed horns to herald the ship's arrival.

The Athenian vessel creaks up to the harbor stonework, ropes are thrown and tied and gangplanks lowered, and as the young Athenian captain Charitimides strides down to where the Naxian merchant leaders await him with courteous smiles, local trumpeters blow hollow ram horns from up on the roofs of the warehouses. Charitimides waves up to the trumpeters after greeting the merchant leaders.

"Your smile tells me Athens took our news well," the oldest of the merchant leaders says carefully to Charitimides, watching his expression. "Is young Hegelion, our ambassador, with you?"

Charitimides keeps a convincing mask of cheerful countenance as he replies, "Athens has heard and understood the will of Naxos. But wise young Hegelion has chosen to remain in Athens for now, as Naxos is about to deal with a fate which he was not eager to share in."

The pallors of the merchant leaders pale, and their smiles shrivel.

"I am here to tell you like a man, face to face, instead of simply letting you find out," Charitimides says.

"They've come to kill us all," one merchant groans, readying to run.

"No no, old man," Charitimides replies, "we aren't barbarians. But if you do not intend to aid in the defense of the Sea that surrounds you, then you may no longer partake in it. He who does not give aid to a union's effort has no right participating in its benefits. No more vessels will be entering or leaving Naxos. You are hereby forbidden from the Sea."

"But we're an island!"

Charitimides nods. "Perhaps you ought to have considered that when deciding to desert your comrades at war."

"The war is over," another merchant snaps. "Persia retreated!"

Another nearby merchant shouts, "This is evil work, yours, young man! Women and children will die from it!"

The Naxians all start clamoring, and Charitimides sees his position become dangerous. He shoots a silent command up to the soldiers up on the ship's bow.

"The gods are not fools! They'll see your work as murder if you starve us!"

"Is Athens now the new empire to be feared? Is that what you meant when you donned Persian masks in Aischylos' Athenian propaganda?"

Charitimides catches the thick rope thrown from a soldier up on the trireme, and he clings to it as he jumps from the dock and swings out to the wooden wall of the ship, which he catches deftly with his sea-boots and climbs right up, joining his soldiers on the deck of the ship with one final helping-hoist from the shipwright.

"I gave them the honor of telling them directly," Charitimides says to the Winds. "Tell the gods what you saw here today, Winds. Among the gods I know at least that *you* were here."

Bare-faced Charitimides snaps his fingers to his herald high up in the ropes, and that man blows his deep-voiced ram horn.

Charitimides tosses a hard hunk of bread up to the herald. The men of Naxos gather into a crowd at their docks, pointing at Charitimides occasionally but keeping quiet enough among themselves to not be heard, though water carries voices easily. "Let's get the first fleet into position," Charitimides commands. The sailors begin turning the great vessel and then rowing it over to the entrance of the harbor.

"Listen, Naxians!" the Athenian herald with the horn bellows. "If you are not to be part of the League of Delos, then you shall have no trade with the other islands of the sea! We have orders from the Assembly at Athens to block all vessels coming in or out of this harbor! Let this be an example of the fate that any ship testing our blockade can expect!"

One Miletian merchant vessel, smaller than the triremes and not made for any kind of clash, has made the mistake of trying to make it past the closing middle two triremes. The merchant captain is on deck, grasping his mast in fear, as his little boat sails into imminent collision with the speartip that is the bow of Charitimides's ship, its menacing painted eye looming above as the merchant dances upon the splintering wood of his collapsing vessel and its toppling mast.

Once the thunder of the other vessel's splintering has ebbed, Charitimides declares loudly, but without shouting, knowing that the water will carry his voice like a winged horse. "If Naxos will not be with the League of Delos, then she is henceforth forbidden from Apollo's road - the Sea!"

Charitimides eyes the unfinished Temple of Apollo on the tidal island which cradles Naxos' harbor, and worries about invoking the god so near his house, but remembers how Athens' own gods have seemed absent since the temples were burned. He doffs his fear casually when he is reminded on sight that the temple is incomplete, and so, to his mind, the god does not live there.

K

Aischylos discusses innovation in theater with Melqartshama and Anaxagoras

Brawny Aischylos has Perikles in a hold, with his face pressed against the ground. Though Aischylos is much older than Perikles, he is also much more muscular. However much Perikles attempts to wriggle out of the playwright's grasp, all he can do is spasm with his legs like a fish out of water. It doesn't help Perikles' courage that all those men grouped around, watching and cheering, are Aischylos' acting students, most of whom are strong and beautiful-bodied specimens themselves.

The Temple of Herakles Protector-From-Evil functions on most days as a wrestling and workout gym, situated at a crossroads within the Honeymouth neighborhood not far from the Democrats' clubhouse. Being avoided by Oligarchs and their sons for its proximity to the homes of famous Democrats, it is the one gym inside the city walls where actors are welcome. Due to this welcoming environment, a worship of Herakles has developed within the acting community, which has also led to a post-war generation of actors who compete for the size of their muscles to impress the older generation who fought.

"This is acting?" Perikles gasps.

Aischylos releases him roughly and stands. Perikles rolls onto his back, rubbing his sore neck.

"Acting is not acting," Aischylos responds. "Acting must be living, it must be real. As real as the world is to the gods."

"So when you're playing Dareios's ghost, do you fear the horrors of being dead?" Perikles asks snidely, laughing.

"I do!" Aischylos laughs back, seeing the question for a joke but responding with clear reverence. "I actually do."

Bald-topped Aischylos grabs Perikles again and begins wrestling him back to the ground.

As they struggle Aischylos melodramatically grunts, "I really do, though, I do, son of Xanthippos. That's why it isn't just something anyone can do, or learn how to do. It is a special relationship you must develop personally with the god, where you truly allow Dionysos to merge your own mind and that of the character. It is impossible to describe until your piety has taken you there. So when I am playing Darieos, you had better bet I am truly fearing the end of the scene, when I know that I shall return to the throng of shades beneath the Earth!"

Aischylos abuses Perikles' much-less-muscled body upon the temple sand, letting him in and out of various holds and pins.

"You see, in any drama, essentially, there are two men in *agon* - in conflict - grappling against one another for control of whatever the particular situation of that story is. After all, two characters who are in agreement, and simply friends living happily in peace, gives no opportunity for what is most important about even presenting a narrative in the first place - and that is that it should function as a lesson, or an exploration, of how to deal with scenarios that challenge the soul. See, being a playwright is really like being a sort of teacher! Only babies need narratives about simple, peaceful things."

"I..." Perikles struggles to speak against Aischylos' bicep, "I actually like...a peaceful peasant poem...with no drama. Just funny...farcical fantasies."

"No. Even Satyr plays need some kind of conflict, some kind of *agon*, or no one will have any reason to talk about it. See, that's why the old plays were so boring, with only one character on stage at a time. The old playwrights - Thespis, and those who were merely mimicking him - for some reason they just could never take that leap to introducing a second person onstage at once, who can interact and debate. Until my courageous innovation, of course."

His actors, gathered around, applaud Aischylos' mention of his innovation.

"Two voices..." Perikles grunts, "are more interesting."

"Now look, Perikles - you're not even using the left half of your body!" Aischylos grabs a nearby walking stick and hits Perikles on the left leg with it. "You lean, and compensate! You're using half of your body as a crutch, and your whole body is weaker for it! What's that - what are you pointing at?"

Perikles points breathlessly at the forms of two approaching adults and a bouncing child. Aischylos releases him at the sight of them, and stands, allowing Perikles finally to roll onto his side and stretch his tortured arms and legs.

Tall, thin Anaxagoras, walking with a tall staff, and his sturdier friend Melqartshama, sporting the scuffed leather of a busy artisan and the ornately braided beard of a Phoenikian who likes to spend money, are each holding one hand of Melqartshama's young daughter Diotima, who prances and swings between them as the three walk. The two men wave with their free arms as they approach the gathering of actors in the grass.

"Good day to you all," Anaxagoras shouts to all the actors chatting together further off. They wave, only briefly curious about the newcomers.

"My friend!" Perikles shouts to Anaxagoras, standing. "I had been meaning to introduce you to Aischylos, my other good friend, the great hero of Marathon and Salamis."

Anaxagoras smiles to Aischylos and bows, saying, "I have heard, of course, that you are also a great poet of the stage."

"But your wording implies you haven't had the pleasure of actually witnessing any of my work?" Aischylos asks.

Anaxagoras shrugs. "I'm not sure," he says. "I don't think so."

Melqartshama, beside him, extends his hand to shake. "I am called Melqartshama," he says, "and this is my young one Diotima."

"A charming girl," Perikles says politely. "How are you, dear?"

"I'm here to become an actor!" little Diotima shouts.

"Yes, well," Melqartshama begins to explain.

"Girls can't be actors," Aischylos interrupts, petting her hair sweetly. "Sorry. It's just not an appropriate thing for a girl to be seen doing. It wouldn't be right. I mean it wouldn't be right *to you*, to *let you* demean yourself like we do." The other actors laugh.

Diotima growls like a lion, startling Aischylos and bringing him to laughter. His laughing starts her cackling also, and soon all those surrounding - Aischylos' actors and Diotima's father and his friend - are laughing. Perikles laughs as he can, headlocked.

"Were you born in the summer?" Aischylos asks little Diotima, rubbing his face to stop the last of his laughter. Diotima shrugs and looks to her father, who just smiles softly and shakes his head 'no'. "Well I thought you might have been, because in the East they say that little girls born in the summer are born under the stars of the Lion. I thought maybe that was why you growled at me like a lion."

Diotima just shakes her head, and makes another subvocal growl, grinning at the old playwright.

From the doorway, a familiar feminine voice says, "And anyway, men do make the best women." Gradually the voice falls to a masculine tone as it adds, "Now tell me, Aischylos - would you prefer to hear bad news from myself, or discover it as it occurs, like the rest of the audience?"

It is Sophokles, standing over Aischylos and Perikles with so smug a look on his face that it could be mistaken for a theater mask.

"What?" Aischylos asks dryly, keeping Perikles in a headlock.

Sophokles struts slowly forward as he declares, "I have just set it up with the handsome Archon whose name I still forget - I am to have a chorus this year, for whatever I choose to write."

Aischylos nods with a wry grin. "And so you have come to the great master for advice, of course. I'll tell you this first, my friend - include nothing irrelevant! Meters and rhyming may be challenging in a work as long as a play, but don't include a lot of fa-la-la ox-shit just because it's easy or because it pleases your wife. Every part of a work of art informs its other parts. Think of how one bad dancer can ruin a chorus line. Include nothing irrelevant. Your audience may not all recognize the imperfection, but the gods will. Look to what the gods themselves make and love - it has symmetry, and elegance, and universal necessity..."

"I did not come here for your silly advice," Sophokles interrupts with a sigh. "I came to offer you a fair warning. You have won enough, my friend. It is a new generation's time - time for a new sort of plays."

"What? What could you possibly mean to imply?"

"Only that the days of Aischylos being the unquestioned king of the theater are over. Because he will no longer have Sophokles to lean upon cane-like."

Aischylos scoffs, and at the sight of that Sophokles begins gesturing dramatically, like one of his characters.

"Do you somehow think that you alone are recipient of the inspirations for great plays and beautiful language? Why, I am probably not even the only actor here who has secretly been writing their own words!"

A squirming, shrugging combination of denial and acknowledgement inches down along Aischylos' actors in a line like the gait of a caterpillar. The event pulls a near-laughing smile out of Aischylos.

"Playwriting is so much more than writing words," Aischylos haughtily begins to explain. "Everything about the incarnation of the story rests on your shoulders like Atlas holds his mother Ge. Composing, singing, embodying, the world you wish to evoke into the minds of your audience..."

"What am I, some newborn baby?" Sophokles snaps irritatedly. "Aischylos, you're not the only one who grasps what it takes to create a powerful theater experience. In fact, perhaps you might have even become so infatuated with your own particular voice and methods that you have forgotten what real creative courage is."

"If you are your own writer, now, Sophokles," Aischylos snorts disdainfully, "then you had better find your own actors, and your own places to dance and rehearse. But you should understand why you can't be welcome anymore where my own plays are being workshopped."

Sophokles creates a hybrid smile-frown and says, "I had wanted this to be a happy conversation."

"Congratulations," Aischylos sniffs, "on making it to the Olympics. Now you'll feel the eyes of the gods upon you as you grapple with actually-skilled competitors. Begone, antagonist."

Sophokles chuckles slightly, if just to show a lack of real enmity to the assembled actors, who have all watched the conversation like playwatchers, memorizing the lines for later tellings.

As he turns to leave, the priest of Herakles stops him with a hand to the chest and says, "Wait. You know you can't leave through this doorway without offering several pushups to the spirit of the doorway. Not without your muscles being cursed."

Sophokles sighs, gets down and does four quick pushups, courtesy to the spirit of the doorway, then leaves with a huff and a laugh.

The priest of Herakles shrugs his muscled arms to Aischylos.

"He's not a weight-lifter," Aischylos tells the muscle-priest. "He stays fit by fucking people over."

The gathered actors all laugh.

One of the younger, bolder actors asks Aischylos, "Are you worried?"

"Worried? About Sophokles winning the ivy crown?" He laughs theatrically.

"Archons aren't always well-read men anymore," suggests Perikles. "But it's they who are the ones who choose the winner of the ivy, not Dionysos. And it is true that simple-minded men are prone to prefer that which is novel to that which is great."

Aischylos scoffs, but also frowns as he considers the thought. "Another reason why your Democrat plan to put simple folks into the office of Archon is an offense against better men - including better writers!"

"You're the great innovator! Surely you can beat the novelty of Sophokles being writer and lead actor instead of heading a chorus. Use some great new innovation of the stage which simply outshines his entire piece!"

"Plus you've got me," adds the actor Kratinos, flexing his muscular chest and then taking a swig of wine.

Aischylos throws his hands in the air dramatically. "So my words are nothing, but it is only gimmicks and handsome actors which I ever really brought to the stage?"

"You take me wrong," Perikles retorts. "You're the one who brought the second actor to the stage, opening up the form to what it is now. Theater itself is something entirely new thanks to your innovation in the form. This is not gimmickry! When was the last time anyone presented a play with only one actor on stage? You changed everything!"

Aischylos shrugs and says, "You show that you never get out of the city, Perikles. Village Dionysian festivals are usually mostly single-actor plays, still. It isn't just a simple thing anyone can do - gathering that many capable performers to put on a full City Dionysia play."

"If it occurs outside the city walls, it may as well not be happening, as far as I'd know," Perikles jokes, nodding.

Actors who grew up on farms outside the city grumble and shake their heads, silently disdaining the wealthy urbanite together.

"What you need is something memorable," Anaxagoras proposes, "and if I may offer, I think I may have just the idea! Something my friend Melqartshama has been working on for the dock-master at Piraeus, might work just as well for you."

"How could some dock device help my play?"

"It is a swiveling wooden arm, used for unloading nets full of fish."

"My play includes no movement of loads of fish," Aischylos dryly jokes. The actors behind him all laugh.

"What works for fish," Anaxagoras says with a wry smile, "works just as well for a god."

Aischylos laughs and gives Anaxagoras a comically overwrought expression of shock. "You Ionians are the boldest men I know; so quick to test the wrath of the gods!"

Anaxagoras smiles and shrugs minutely. "When I see a god, I'll get concerned."

The actors all murmur, and Perikles and Aischylos eye each other with raised eyebrows.

Perikles then asks him directly, "Are you one of those men who do not believe the gods exist?"

"It isn't exactly that I disbelieve in the gods," Anaxagoras tries to explain, "it's more like I think that we misunderstand them by thinking of them as being like people. Winds are *something*. They're the movement of something physical - air - perhaps because of being pushed by some other dynamic thing, or changing in some way - who knows! Air is something that behaves in a consistent way. Many ways, but a consistent set. Water is something, and it too behaves consistently in certain ways. Put it on a slope and it will flow to the bottom. This is how we started to discover the nature of change over time, at Miletos. There the city sits at the mouth of a river, but Thales, the great sage, realized that every year silt from high up in the mountains was gradually being carried and deposited by the flowing waters of the river. He went up into the mountains to test and confirm what he supposed, and over many years finally he was able to effectively demonstrate to the elders of our city that he had been right, as the ancient harbor had to be rebuilt further downstream, to where the new mouth of the Meander was. The river is not being moved by some god - but by many days of consistent, mundane, observable change. And ultimately I suspect all things in the cosmos are consistent in this way - are mundane in the same way. Whereas *gods*...I am not aware of anyone actually revealing evidence of the presence or work of gods, aside from nature itself."

Perikles considers all this as he hears it, and feels the wind anew. He spends a while in his thoughts, reconsidering the possible nature of the movement of the leaves upon the trees. Where before he had always seen a single tree with its leaves shaking, somehow now he can imagine each leaf as like individuals in the population of a city, each reacting to the wind the way they do, the whole being merely a circumstantial emergent result of the interaction of each part with the others.

Fleet-footed little Diotima suddenly races into the gymnasion courtyard with a laughing theater mask held against her face. She takes it off just briefly enough to show her own grinning face, wail a mad lion's wail, and then run off laughing again.

Braided-bearded Melqartshama simply grins.

"Where did she get that?" Aischylos asks his actors. "She must have run all the way to the Temple of Dionysos to grab that."

Laughing, the old veteran-turned-playwright scrambles off to chase the little girl, suddenly a child again himself.

Λ

Elpinike participates in the autumn rites of the Mysteries of Eleusis

The Spring Mysteries of Eleusis begin as a gathering at dusk at the base of the hill where the temple of Artemis Huntress resides, just a short walk from the south-eastern gate of Athens. Out from a crag in the hillside, spilling down a little series of reed-filled rocky pools into the marsh called Frog Island, flows the cold-water spring called the Springs of Cultivation. A dusk fog wraps Frog Island in wandering webs. Clutches of gathered participants whisper wonder to each other amid the mists.

From far enough away to be respectful while still eavesdropping, non-participants who have been curious about the ceremony sit on distant hills or the heights of the city wall to catch a glimpse of the torchlit dusk event and hear the rare mystical performance by the disguised kithar player who, despite being masked, can clearly be recognized as the famous kitharist Chronomagos, as no one else's fingers play quite like his.

"And now, all you supplicants to the great Grain Goddess," the high priestess of Demeter calls out to the crowd assembled, "please disrobe and cleanse your bodies in the Springs of Cultivation." The masked kitharist behind the priestess bends his plucked notes with mystical whimsy.

This year's few dozen admittents to these introductory rites chat nervously with their neighbors as they disrobe and step into the cold pools to cleanse themselves before the upcoming rituals. Men and women moan against the cold water's chill, but mostly make an effort not to sexualize the sacred process despite their cogendered nudity. Dicks shrivel in the dusk.

Elpinike stands with her husband Kallias, official torchbearer of this event, beneath a tall, old olive tree at the edge of the group, feeling the eyes of all the other participants upon her as she hesitates to remove her clothing. Her nearness to the ritual torch which Kallias is holding helps warm her.

"This is why I told you to dress light," Kallias says with a slight smile. "I'm sorry I couldn't have prepared you better, but as you know, these are secret rites. We can't speak of it with those who haven't yet gone through it."

"I know," Elpinike sighs. "I'm just trying to avoid beseeching the gods to blind all these beggars who have never held as much wealth even in their minds as the honest description of my naked body will be to their friends who were not here."

Kallias can only shake and nod his head in general agreement, eyeing his wife's body. She senses his awareness shifting between her body, and the eyes of others upon it, and she suddenly realizes that showing her off to his neighbors may have been part of her husband's plan.

"I suppose you might think, however, that there is little point in owning something of great beauty, if no one else knows its beauty."

At that, Elpinike plucks a single gold brooch from the center of her bosom and then unwraps herself from the fine yellow cloth of her garment, handing it to her stunned husband, who has still only seen her nude a handful of times. Elpinike then strides cool-skinned toward the swampy reeds and joins the crowd already bathing in the waters of the sacred spring.

Kallias watches from the bank, remaining dressed in priestly garb, being one of the organizers of this event in his hereditary role as Torch-bearer.

In an effort to pretend that the other people don't exist, Elpinike keeps her eyes on Kallias. She sits on a flat stone between two other, younger women, and dips her face and hair into the water, whipping it back out so that her hair splashes all those around her. She stands confidently, knowing all eyes are upon her, as she splashes the sacred water onto each part of her skin and rubs and scratches away the old layers of herself with her fingernails.

The high priestess of Demeter - whose name was written on a lead tablet which was dropped deep into the Sea when she took the office, so that none might speak her name until she dies - narrates to the ritual washers as they scrub their bodies with stones and sand and fingernails.

"Tonight, we celebrate the return of Persephone to the world, thanks to ever-wise Zeus, who made peace between the grieving mother Demeter and that god of the Underworld who stole her, cold-hearted Haides, conceiving the arrangement that will once again return the rosy cheek of life to our lands! So bathe, friends, and cleanse yourself of who you were before the knowledge you are about to receive! It is for tonight that you have fasted, for tonight that you have gone without sex, for tonight is the night that you will begin *your* journey, to the secret wisdom which only the initiated may know, about how to receive life again after you die."

By the time the group is being guided out of the spring pools and toward the next steps of the ritual, Elpinike's naked body is webbed with red fingernail scratches. She receives a white ritual robe from the officiant, and gets in line with the others.

Kallias, with his torch, walks up beside her in the line, on his way to join the other officiants at the head of it, and asks her in passing, "Did you catch that, what the hierophant said? Life after death?"

Elpinike nods, annoyed. "Don't you have a torch to bear?"

Kallias frowns, confused by her demeanor, but then hurries along to the front of the line.

Elpinike takes this rare moment among many Athenians of varied backgrounds, to inspect their varied faces. When she finds eye contact, she moves on, not wanting to instill unwanted lust.

The priestess continues, as religious performers dressed as minor gods spread out an opaque fabric screen behind her, held up by tall sticks.

"Today all those things that grow from green, all those things beloved by the Grain Goddess, return to the Earth, waking from their annual depression, as the daughter returns from her throne in the kingdom of shadows to the sunlit world. Behold, now, what happened thousands of years ago right here where you stand.

"For you will hear from many foreign mystics, these days, about ways to achieve a better death experience, but this is the oldest great mystery known to men, and make no mistake - men need no other. This is the way to meet that final ferryman with confidence in your eye. Now behold, the origins..."

A man, masked as if in the theater, and dressed in shining armor studded with colorful jewels, emerges from behind the screen. His stone scepter signifies that this is meant to be Haides, God of the Underworld.

Kallias whispers to his wife, "Don't worry - it is only Apsephion, the Archon. It is one of the honors that Archons get - this moment of allowance, as Haides, to grope the loveliest girl, as Persephone."

Elpinike glowers and tries to withhold her groan, hiding her own body yet further in the small ways that she is able to just by stance.

"Good morning, Girl," the Archon Apsephion, a portly, deep-voiced man, portraying Haides, sings out, "and what flower have you found there?"

The girl portraying Persephone is one of a special group of young priestesses of Demeter known as the Bees, who keep themselves cloistered away from men at all times but these. With her dress wrapped like they do in images of women from ancient times, she looks up at the round-bodied, brightly-armored man.

"O, stranger, one like I have never seen before. And I thought I knew all the flowers!"

Apsephion-as-Haides bends down and plucks the flower, and rises and smells it. "This is the bee-bed named Narkissos," he says. "It is the child of a very ancient flower which was once a man. Have you ever heard the story of Narkissos, dear?" His voice shakes a bit; as Archon for only this one year, he is not a man accustomed to performance.

The Bee-as-Persephone slowly shakes her head with innocent, curious eyes. She is clearly much more experienced in the subtleties of performance than her partner in this scene. "How can a man also be a flower?" she asks the armored, bearded loomer.

"Narkissos, grandfather of flowers, resides now in my house, so I know him well. Take this flower, and I will take you to meet the man who became a flower."

"Is your house very far from here?" the Bee-as-Persephone asks.

"My home is not far from anywhere," Apsephion-as-Haides replies coolly.

Kallias, in his official role as torchbearer, dramatically brings his torch away then from the actors, leaving them in darkness, and another younger man throws a wet rag over the torch to quickly snuff its flame into dark smoke.

The shadowy forms of Haides and Persephone slink away, low.

Gasps of concern for the divine girl jump through the darkened audience, peppering the silence otherwise only broken by frogsong.

Then, a torch previously kept as only embers and hidden is now blown upon and revealed slowly, lighting the moment while the middle-aged high-priestess of Demeter, a woman traditionally selected for having the most beautiful and bountiful breasts, against which she now carries a tall sheaf of wheat stalks, emerges into the light with a look of worldly worry. This is the Grain Goddess herself, Persephone's mother, Demeter, whom the high-priestess has the honor of portraying.

"Tell me, strangers, have you seen a girl here gathering flowers?"

One woman among the initiates begins to weep, knowing the story already.

"O, stranger, won't you help me find my daughter?" beautiful Persinöe-as-Demeter asks each participant from a distance, but directly into their eyes.

"I will," each acknowledges, some rotely, some moved to emotion.

"I will," Elpinike says when the high-priestess, a woman whom she knows personally from noble women's social circles, asks her the repeated question. The two women smile to each other knowingly.

Elpinike stops paying attention, looking away to the silhouettes of the crowds watching the ceremony from atop Athens' wall, in the dark distance.

Eventually Kallias approaches her with her dress to wrap around her body, as the ceremony has come to a close without her noticing.

"Now do you see, my love?" Kallias asks her. He wipes tears from his face with a little laugh. "I'm sorry; it always makes me cry, to remember, to be reminded. To un-forget."

Elpinike nods and smiles warmly, touching her husband with tenderness. "It was beautiful," Elpinike tells him. "I understand why you would be proud to be a part of this."

He notices the rare warmth, and looks into her eyes with suddenly dried tears. "Flesh is fleeting," Kallias sighs. "We will all see Haides' kingdom some day. But that doesn't mean we need to stay there. Just wait till the end of summer, when we can complete the story in the Final Mysteries. It all comes together, it all comes back around, at Eleusis. You'll see. But for now, you'll have to remain in suspense. Frankly, I miss that magical suspense of not yet knowing, or of knowing the beginning but not the end. I envy you - the not-yet-knowing."

Elpinike tries to wear the mask she sees other women appear to wear to assuage their husbands, though in fact she feels the same hollowness she does after watching any mediocre play in the theater. She feels she has heard more profoundly told versions of this story, in secret gatherings of women around a loom, where the best versions of stories are told, and is dismayed to discover that this public, famous telling is so simplistic and trite.

"PERSEPHONE WHO MAKES MORTAL MEN FORGET!
NO ONE ELSE HAD THOUGHT OF IT BEFORE, TO THWART THE
BLACK GATES WHICH HOLD BACK THE DEAD IN SHADOWS."
Theognis, Megaran Poet

M

Gorgo meets with Pausanias' mother and leaves Niome with Pleistoanax

Over the Babyx Bridge and out along the brown lanes between green bean fields, the Spartan Queen-Mother Gorgo rides with her escort of four mounted knights toward her cousin Pausanias' noble family farm, now owned again by that dead regent's mother Laothoe. The Λ's on her guardsmen's shields, for Lakedaemonia, gleam in the sunlight.

Helot workers bend in the outer fields, sewing seeds by hand.

Behind the Queen Mother, but ahead of her knights, rides her young slave Niome, that princess of conquered Byzantion, confident now in her position within the Queen's shadow.

As Gorgo rides into view of the noble homestead, she first sees Pausanias' widow Sophronia in a black wrap, as Gorgo herself is, pulling weeds in the vegetable garden near the main house with her two young sons, Pleistoanax and Kleomenes. When they notice her approaching, all three stand. Sophronia bows to Gorgo at a distance before disappearing with her boys into the house. Sophronia's mother-in-law, Pausanias' mother Laothoe, black-veiled but wearing a sea-blue royal dress, steps out the farmstead's front door and walks out to meet Gorgo on the field, out aways from the house.

"Queen-Mother Gorgo," says blue-wrapped old Laothoe with a reverent but brief bow of her wrinkle-written face. She adjusts her black veil to defend against the sunlight. "What brings royalty to this house?"

"Your grandson," Gorgo tells her aunt, "Pleistoanax. We are all royalty, Laothoe."

Laothoe nods. "You, Queen, have been the daughter, wife, and now mother of kings. A Hellenic Atossa. There can be no one more royal than you are, until your son has a son, making you also a king's grandmother."

Gorgo looks away for a moment. Laothoe notices the reaction.

"How old is the son of Leonidas this year?" bold old Laothoe asks.

"King Pleistarchos is thirteen now."

Sea-and-crag-eyed Laothoe nods. "I see."

Gorgo sighs and her horse begins to uneasily pace the dry grass. She says, "I know he is not a true king. Not a lion."

Laothoe' eyes darkly alight.

"Don't take my meaning wrong. He's the product of his father's seed," Gorgo explains. "But not his heart. Not his tutelage. It does not matter who fucked a boy's mother - but who taught him, raised him, who lived with him every day. And I don't know who raised Pleistarchos. Not Leonidas, of course, who died when he was just a baby." Gorgo glares at the ground, and adds, "And not I. Helots. Slaves. Poor-souled people."

Laothoe stands perfectly still, her hands folded behind her, listening, her eyes fixed on Gorgo like a predator's on prey.

"He wets his bed," Gorgo sighs. "Still, each night. He cries at the slightest fear. He cares more for some turtle he found years ago than any human he's ever met. He's a cursed madman in the making. He will be a terrible king."

"Curses do creep down family lines, like vines down a trellis," Laothoe agrees.

Gorgo just breathes to confirm she remembers the cruelty of her own father, King Kleomenes. "It is not because of curses," Gorgo says, "but rather because of the dark days Pleistarchos was born into, and how they affected his mind. I might have been cruel to him when he was young. His father had just died. I, honestly, do not remember, but I feel it. And now, he is simply a teen-ager who wants no part of this world."

"And who is this high-cheeked creature who rides with you?" Laothoe asks, eyeing Niome sitting high on her horse.

"Laothoe, meet Niome, princess of Byzantion, and one of my closest handmaidens," Gorgo says with a sweep of her black-veiled arm.

Niome nods properly to Laothoe. "It's my honor," she says to the older woman.

Laothoe is already nodding, understanding. "And is she to be your spy here, then, left with my grandson as a supposed caretaker for his betterment though she really only means to maintain your will, and watch, within my house? Even though she cannot speak Doric Hellenic without sounding like an eastern barbarian."

Gorgo takes her time responding, as she reasserts her will over her shuffle-footed horse. Finally, she just says, with stalwart eye contact, "Yes."

Laothoe snorts and scans Niome again. She looks to Pleistoanax, hoeing with his brother in the distance.

Niome blinks, otherwise still.

Laothoe nods slowly. "He could use the tutelage of one raised at the court of a king. Nobility is a skill which the men of our Agiad line have long-since lost, and could certainly use again."

Gorgo glares. "You speak as if your grandson is destined for that throne himself?"

Laothoe turns back to Gorgo and looks boldly in her eyes. The women speak silently, through their eyes, for several seconds. By the end, they understand each other in silence, and at that psychic sense of resolution Gorgo's horse eases her shuffling hooves at last.

Gorgo says aloud, "King Pleistarchos will have a long reign. Longer than my own life, at least. He will need advisors, and that will be what your grandsons must prepare for. Your second son, as well - Nikomedes. I expect him at court. He will be a warrior."

Gorgo dismounts her horse and gestures for Niome to do the same. Then she begins walking past Laothoe, toward the two boys in the distance.

"My eldest son was also royalty," Laothoe says, following as Gorgo is walking toward the house. "Pausanias ruled as regent for your son after your husband was slain at war. It was my Pausanias who led All Hellenes at the turn of the tide, at the Battle of Plataia, and survived. You know he cannot be forgotten like some usurper. He made a mistake. But he also performed unforgettable glories that cannot go unworshipped. I think you know that his ghost would be more difficult to defeat than his living form was. And I think you can imagine that he, of all people, would not shy from his ghostly duties. Best to avoid such possibilities altogether, by simply giving the man's spirit its due."

"And what do you suggest would assuage your son's ghost's anger?" Gorgo asks with a sigh and a glare.

Old Laothoe shrugs with a cold immovability. "A statue in the city? Beside your husband's."

Gorgo tries to express her surprise at the suggestion without appearing too rude. "Beside Leonidas?"

"In a few generations," Laothoe says, stepping away from Gorgo and then dramatically turning to eye her, "when my grandchildren are my own age and their children's friends have no memory of my son's traitorous final choices, the people of that age will trust the statues more than whatever stories might remain."

Pleistoanax runs out from behind the house, but stops in the garden when he sees the look on Gorgo's face. She and he make a brief moment of eye contact, and he freezes there.

Laothoe notices the moment, and snidely comments to Gorgo, "I did try to prepare young Perseos for your gaze, but it seems he has failed to remember to avoid to meet it, and has already turned to stone." Laothoe walks back to the house, away from Gorgo and past Pleistoanax, beckoning for Niome to follow. As she walks, she mutters, "My Queen, it seems, knows only how to create statues rather than men."

The comment cuts; Gorgo pictures Leonidas when he was strong and alive, and she boxes with a tear before it is able to escape her eye, until a rush of the wind whips the tear back in.

Gorgo clears her throat, to make Niome turn and look at her. She lowers her chin, but keeps her eyes on the younger woman, and Niome nods, then turns back and follows Laothoe into the house.

N

Themistokles flees east across the sea in disguise

An Aigyptian merchant ship skips over the leaping blue waves, sailing toward the rising morning sun. Its shorn-bald captain squints his ink-darkened eyelids against the bright orange sun disc.

"Aten, Sun Disc," the Aigyptian captain prays, "another fine day you bring. I promise you, I will make it a good one here within my domain."

A Hellenic merchant from Argos steps up beside the captain, finishing his morning swig of fortified wine. The two men nod, and take in the beauty of the breeze for a quiet moment.

Beneath them, unseen, dolphins race and sing. One rises to skim the surface.

"Won't be long before you start seeing herms on the dolphins out here," the Aigyptian captain muses in near-perfect Hellenic to the Argive merchant beside him, just to make idle conversation.

The two men stand side by side at the bow of the Aigyptian's boat, matching each other's level of costume finery, as they spy the horizon hills of distant islands. Behind them, further back on the deck, the Aigyptian's diverse crew of seaport emigrants loiter amidst the spooled ropes and await next orders.

The captain adds, "This sea is already Athens' road, after all. Did you hear? They've claimed it officially, and closed it to Naxians!"

"O Poseidon's mercy," the merchant replies bemusedly. "Not a good time to be Naxian, then, I suppose. Makes me glad I am not from an island."

Costumed in the tunic of a lowly fisherman, the exiled Athenian Themistokles sits upon a coil of thick naval rope at the side of this Aigyptian merchant vessel upon which he has bought passage across the Sea. Acting like he is scanning the waters for fish-sign, he listens silently to the conversation between the ship's captain and the Argive merchant. He is hoping not to be recognized, and if anyone on the ship were to recognize the famous Athenian, it might be these two aristocratic men.

The sky-blue waves stretch out toward softer blue in all directions, as little white clouds watch from the other blue above.

While Themistokles huddles near the fishermen and sailors on the ship, several of them have begun to share stories of the strangest things they have ever seen at sea.

One says, "I've seen Keto, oldest monster of the deep, rise right up out of the ocean!"

"Every sailor's seen Keto. She may look odd, but she's no monster - in fact, she's a good augury! Keto never visits those who are fated to sink in storms."

"You just saw a really big fish."

Themistokles tries to listen past the nearer fishermen, to the conversation happening at the ship's bow, between the Aigyptian captain and the extravagantly-dressed merchant from Argos.

"Athens is the new Queen of the Sea, I hear," says the ship's captain in his Aigyptian-accented Hellenic. "Must have some kind of pact with your Poseidon. Even my own sailors are sacrificing to him these days, even though they're Aigyptian!"

"You give the Athenians too much credit," says the Argive merchant to the Aigyptian captain. "Sparta will keep that city from getting too powerful, just you wait and see. The word in Argos is that our city needs only to let those two cities stay concerned with each other, and then you'll see *our* fate rise again across these islands. Peace is the true benefactor of Man, not war! But keep sacrificing to Poseidon, even if you are Aigyptian. Can't hurt to have a Sea God on your side, eh?"

The Aigyptian captain shakes his head. "Athens' supremacy is one none of the rest of you Hellenic cities have grasped yet. It's her navy, her ships! Nothing is as powerful as a ship. Athens knows where to invest. As do I. And it's not in gods. There is only one god, the Sun, and he is far too powerful to require our offerings. I make offerings to no one except my crew, who aid me."

Themistokles cannot help but smile at these sentiments, but he turns his head and covers his mouth lest it somehow give him away.

"I don't want to argue with a ship's captain on the value of his own livelihood, but I assure you, as a merchant with scores of such sea voyages behind me, to all the ports of Poseidon's sea, it is *pottery* that has the most consistent value. Even more than the grain or oil that it might store."

"I have a way of proving that boats are the best investment," the Aigyptian says with a sly smile and a look over at the merchant, at which point Themistokles begins to get a dangerous vibe, and becomes more aware of his surroundings in case things advance as he fears they might.

Seeming to sense the same vague tone change, the merchant turns to the captain and asks, "What do you mean?"

The Aigyptian eyes the beardless boy, barely an adult, whom the Argive has been traveling with. "Just you and him, no?" the Aigyptian asks. "He your muscle?"

"What's your implication?"

"Well it's me and my three men who run the ship, as you've seen," the Aigyptian notes with casual threat. He stretches his arms up on a taut line of thick rope that runs up to the mast, and his big biceps present themselves at face level. The Argive merchant stands back against the railing of the ship, between the edge and the Aigyptian.

Slowly, just to signal the possibility, the captain raises his sandalled foot up to the Argive's chest, and holds it there, his long, muscular leg extended while the rest of his body remains hanging onto the rope. The Argive clings nervously to the railing at hip height behind himself. Further up the deck, Themistokles sees the merchant's companion stand, noticing the situation.

The Aigyptian captain casually threatens, "We have you hostage as long as you're beholden to our service. I could extort any amount from you, because your life is in my hands."

"I see your point," the Argive stutters, trying to maintain the sense that this has all been a playful hypothetical.

"I could just kick you right overboard and take your boy as a slave and just sell all your junk as if it were mine," the Aigyptian suggests.

"My city knows of my journey," the Argive says. "They made notes of your ship, and your men. My city is just like the giant it's named for - you know Argos, right? The giant of a thousand eyes! You wouldn't be able to flee far enough to be safe from the sight of Argos, you donkey's daughter. Now get your foot off me."

The Aigyptian squints at the Argive, then laughs and lowers his foot back onto the deck. Just as he does, the ship begins to lurch between two chaotic waves, nearly knocking the merchant off balance. The Aigyptian captain thrusts out a hand for him to grab onto, with a haughty laugh.

The captain sneers, "You Hellenes, you're the second best at everything - second best at sailing, after the Aigyptians, second best gods after the Phoenikians - but you're the best at one thing: *lies*. The cartoons on your pottery that everybody loves, your crude poetry, your sacrilegious plays, your mathematical games ... your tricks and ploys. Everything pointless, childish, unrealistic, meaningless, and unnecessary, you all are great at."

The Argive brushes off the marks left on his tunic by the Aigyptian's sandal, as he says, "With cowardly liars for our leaders, it's no wonder you think that. With Hellenes like Themistokles and Pausanias leading us into Tartaros while secretly working for Persia. But real Hellenes like Argos' King Pheidon are good and clever people, and famous for our oath-keeping, if perhaps also for our crafty trickery"

"At least there you have nothing to fear," the captain scoffs. "You have heard wrong about Pausanias and Persia."

The merchant reluctantly shakes his head and reasserts, "I'm telling you, Themistokles of Athens and Pausanias of Sparta are both already working for Persia. You'll see. I have it from good sources. Hellas is going to be a Persian territory one way or another, if the sons of Kyros continue to breathe air. That's why I head east. Whether I will return is yet to be seen."

"Pausanias was killed in Sparta, after being tried by the Overseers there," the Aigyptian laughs derisively. "You know seamen get news faster than anyone. I've heard this for sure. Pausanias was working for Persia, and Sparta found out, and summoned him home to stand trial, and now he's dead. I'd bet you your fare the same fate befalls Themistokles. And anyway, I don't think Xerxes would ever let Themistokles, who tricked him so embarrassingly and destroyed his entire armada, survive a single day in Persia let alone work for him. Themistokles dies by Hellene hand, you wait and see."

The Argive folds his arms. "Themistokles is as corruptible as any man, as is Xerxes. They are two rats. There are too few men who actually follow ideals - only money, only power and leverage."

The Aigyptian captain turns and walks away miming a chattering mouth with his hand, walking effortlessly across the tilting deck while most others onboard grab something for safety.

Themistokles pulls his fisherman's cloak up around his neck and clings to the big coil of rope he is sitting against as the ship rocks upon the crest of another tall wave. Foamy spray comes up over the side, and a small fish with it onto the deck.

One of the sailors in the group that had been sharing stories barks over in Themistokles' direction the question, "So, fisherman, how about you? What's the strangest thing you've ever seen with your own two eyes?"

The wily Athenian man-shepherd in disguise pictures being on board the flagship trireme at the Battle of Salamis, seeing his enemy the King of Kings Xerxes, sitting upon a high golden traveling throne on the beach of Munichya just outside Athens, staring at him. He wants to describe it, but cannot chance revealing his true identity. The story must hide.

"A huge turtle," Themistokles replies. He holds his hands apart and says, "This big!"

All the sailors laugh at Themistokles, but since it is a ruse of his design, he is able to grin confidently to himself beneath his performance.

"The Rivers had an Assembly to prosecute the Sea
for making their sweet, drinkable waters brine.
In her own defense Thalassa Sea Goddess simply said, 'Look, I
am just salty, and it's you who come to me!'"
Aisop, *The Rivers and the Sea*

Ξ

Melqartshama and Anaxagoras show Aischylos their device

The playwright Aischylos and his circled group of actors stop their idle singing exercises and fall into a hush when they first see the device unveiled.

"The god-device is what we're calling it," Melqartshama says.

"And it is mobile; you have brought it here!" Aischylos marvels.

Anaxagoras follows him while Aischylos circles the tall, wooden crane, inspecting its mechanics. The device stands upon a heavy tripod base and swings its tall arm at a joint, using some similar mechanisms to the ones Melqartshama developed for his writing device in the Agora, and others borrowed from the fish-net cranes at the Piraeus docks, except this machine has a narrow shelf at the end of the arm where a person can sit or stand, to then be lifted high into the air by a heavier person on the other end.

"Behold," says Anaxagoras, as he sits on the platform and gestures to Melqartshama.

Melqartshama leans upon his end and begins manipulating a lever there, as the end with Anaxagoras is swung up into the air, so that his dangling feet are at Aischylos' head level.

Aischylos laughs loudly when the tall, thin philosopher rises so suddenly into the air. "I say! With this machine, we can make a god fly! Theater shall never be the same again! Truly the gods must love me, for now, in my old age, innovation simply falls into my lap!" Aischylos laughs, reaching out to Melqartshama for a quick hug. "My producer will pay whatever is necessary. But, like the device itself is made to hide behind veils on the actor, so that the effect is most profound upon the audience, similarly your work, my friend, must be hidden behind my name, so that the work does not become so clunkily full of names that the viewer looks away annoyed."

"Just so long as you pay for it," Melqartshama reiterates.

"You there, Penander," Aischylos barks, pointing to the actors who are seated together playing a low stakes game of knucklebones. "Come and help us test this device."

Lithe-limbed Penander rises and steps over to the mechanism, eyeing it with distrust. "I am not eager to test your trap, gentlemen."

"I've tested it with my daughter," Melqartshama says, taking the arm of the device and causing it to swing side to side. "And she is not as small as she used to be! She flew through the air, to incredible heights, with ease. All you need is two or three people with a total weight more than the person who shall fly, to maneuver this end."

"Whoever wants to be the first man to truly know the freedom of the birds on wing," Aischylos says with an actor's gravity and a writer's subtle melody, "should hurry to beat Penander to that glory."

Penander gets his butt onto the device before his fellow actors are able to finish the scramble to stand. He takes a few of the transparent colored veils that were draped upon the stand, and spreads them out to better hide the area where the device will raise him.

"Hold on, friend!"

As Penander is still fussing with the veils, Melqartshama and Anaxagoras lean together against the other end of the device, and fair Penander rises swift as smoke above a fire, the veils fluttering beneath him.

"Great rowdy Dionysos, behold!" Aischylos shouts with excitement, laughing. "It looks incredible!"

All the other actors cheer and sing out. Some of the musicians rumble their drums and whistle into their double-flutes.

"I soar!" Pernander exclaims. "I'm a bird above the clouds!"

"Now this will be something that audiences will never forget," Aischylos laughs, beckoning for Melqartshama to let his actor back down. "Come, Penander, and be careful upon your veils there."

"A spy!" Penander shouts, before he is brought down from the device, pointing at something which he sees while aloft. "One of Sophokles' boys! There, Aischylos, look!" Then he looks around himself again, while aloft, and muses, "O how far the gods must see!"

Aischylos spins on his heel, scanning fast. "There! Grab that boy!" He points the same direction as Penander.

Several of his actors stand and scramble to grapple the little boy who had gasped at the sight of the machine, giving away his hiding spot beside a pile of costumes. The boy, caught, is still draped in bits of costumes.

"Now, who goes there?" Aischylos growls playfully. "Isn't that Ariston's youngest son? Spying for Sophokles, are you?"

The actors hold the wriggling boy, who is no older than five, until Aischylos has time to saunter up to him with mock menace. He pulls a long seabird feather from the belt of his tunic and takes a hold of the little one's foot while two actors hold him by the shoulders.

"Who sent you?"

"My name is Nobody!" the little boy squeals.

"We've all heard the Odyssey," Aischylos laughs with his gang of actors, "we weren't born yesterday! We know you are Ariston's boy. But who sent you? Was it Sophokles? Are you a spy for Sophokles?"

He tickles the boy's feet with his stiff feather. All around cackle.

"Yes! Yes! Stop!" Ariston's boy laughs.

"And what play are they practicing over there?"

"I was told not to tell!"

"O you'll tell," Aischylos laughs, "you'll tell the vengeful spirits of retribution why you thought it would be clever to hide and spy where you weren't welcome!"

"No!"

"Now you tell Sophokles that I will meet him at the Ram's Stomach tomorrow at dusk, if he wants to have a truce and discuss all this. But if he keeps sending little spies like you, be sure that the next ones will come back just bones! Now are you sure you won't tell what Sophokles is planning?"

Aischylos keeps ahold of the little boy, and keeps tickling him briefly every few seconds to elicit frantic laughter again and again, but the boy, gasping, will not relent, and squeaks out between gasps, "I'll die of tickling before I give it up!" like he means it, and fears death by tickles. At that tinge of real fear in the boy's voice, Aischylos relents and releases him.

"No one has ever died of laughing, boy," the beefy old playwright sighs to reassure him at least a little. "Now get out of here and don't come back." He slaps the boy on the bottom, which sets him racing back home.

O

Sophokles and Aischylos meet at a tavern to talk about their plays

The Sacred Path leads out of Athens through the Sacred Gate in the north section of the city wall, just west of the Dipylon Gate. From there the Sacred Path flows out past those rows of colorfully painted gravestones of famous dead Athenians, between the hills west of the city and then along the coast northwest for a day's walk to the Sanctuary of Demeter at Eleusis.

Alongside the sometimes cobbled sometimes wild Sacred Path, just past the home of the first fig-trees, is a trendy new cottage with a dried old ram's stomach hanging from its roadside shingle to indicate that this is the Ram's Stomach Drinking House. The actual stomach hanging from the sign, tanned into the toughest leather, is daily filled with seeds and worms so that its few old holes might summon the presence of many birds to bring extra attention to the sign.

Aischylos shoos the birds that crowd the sign, where they only momentarily hop away to pause their shoving and positioning for the seeds on the ground. Unaccountably-many birds flap away, briefly forming a tunnel around Aischylos as he passes through their assembly.

The tavern door is built from planks and iron so carelessly thick that it is barely moveable even just to slip past.

Inside, the Ram's Stomach is a large single room with the kitchen included, in the old way that Hellenes used to build their houses and Pelasgians of the hills still do. The oven and cooking surfaces take up the whole back third of the place, separated from the clientele only by a curtain of hanging herbs, but there is still enough room for six square tables, each with seed sacks on the floor to seat four.

When Aischylos wrenches his body in past the heavy door, all four groups already seated turn and face him and greet him with a hearty welcome; some indicate with their eyes that they recognize the famous playwright, but none acknowledges it openly.

"You might consider that your sign brings troublesome amounts of birds," Aischylos offers to the proprietress of the place in the back kitchen, who merely nods and gestures from behind the herb curtain to find a seat.

Seated in the back, barely visible through the hazy smoke from the barbarian kitchen, Sophokles raises his cup to Aischylos. He rises as if to stand, but coughs at the smoke in the upper air and refrains from fully rising. Aischylos makes his way past the curious eyes of the other customers to Sophokles, who upon closer inspection is wearing a fake mustache which Aischylos immediately admonishes with a snort.

"I am in disguise, as you ought to be," Sophokles explains without having to be asked about the mustache.

"As what, some Kelt? A mask is representational; a disguise is supposed to be convincing. Convincing, your costume is *not*."

Sophokles unties the fake mustache behind his head and flops it onto the table, taking a relieved sip from his drink. "It was impossible to drink past anyway."

"Have you brought me here to test your clown routine?" Aischylos chides, waving to the proprietress for a drink.

"The rumor that my boy spies bring me is that you've found some way to make your actors fly," Sophokles says, only finally looking up at the end. "Of course I don't believe them, but I can't help but wonder what they might have seen that would give them such an impression. Or have you just somehow convinced them to make me wonder if I'm insane?"

"I'm not a sorcerer," Aischylos says, not avoiding a slight air of flamboyant mystery. "I am a writer and an actor."

A few of the men at the tables around them indiscreetly pause their conversations and one knocks on the table to celebrate confirmation that it is indeed the famous man they'd thought it was.

Sophokles pretends to ignore their audience. "But you're working with those Ionian mechanical wizards. The one who made the double-writing device in the Agora, and the mathematics painter. Your own Daedaloi. But wings that work are a diversion, I think - too right on the nose with a Daedalos metaphor. And we both know that nothing flies without wings of one sort or another. But I know that it must be a story involving Daedalos that you write. Unless all that is a diversion, to make me think that."

Aischylos just nods, brushing his fingers repeatedly through his long beard. "Yes, yes," he says as Sophokles speaks. "I am focused primarily on fooling you, yes. I am like your Odyssean mustache there."

Sophokles chuckles. "Perhaps I am trying on a new character."

"Character is king," Aischylos says, nodding. "Whatever you write, your characters must be written both believable and fantastic; it is a narrow weft. No one remembers the ideas you hide within a piece; they only remember the characters."

"Look, don't act like I'm some brand-new student of the art of playwriting. I've been working with more writers than just you, for years and years. I know how plays are written. I know what makes one good. Don't you realize that every bookseller in the Agora can find a copy of one of your plays among their stacks? People hear the plays performed. There's no way to keep them from remembering the words."

"Copies get words wrong," Aischylos says playfully. "None of the booksellers have *official* copies of any of my plays."

"As someone who has memorized most of your plays, I can assure you, I know the few mistakes in the common copies. I tell people when I see them reading them. I make corrections on people's copies. So most people in Athens do have the correct words. At least of *Persians*. It's not like anyone is reading your play *Glaukos*."

"You should be an insult-poet, not a playwright," Aischylos sighs. "Pick a trade. The theater is not a space for clowning."

Sophokles shakes his head dramatically, and takes a long sip from his drink. Then he slyly smiles.

"Let us tell each other the names of our primary plays, and only that. Not all of them, just the main one; as you said, the one they'll remember."

Aischylos stares silently at Sophokles for a few moments, then says, "Alright." He raises a closed fist between them. "On the final finger."

Sophokles nods, and watches as Aischylos unfolds first his thumb, then each finger to the last, and on the small final finger they say their names simultaneously.

Aischylos says, "The Phrygian," as Sophokles says, "Triptolemos."

Aischylos slams the table.

"You mean to speak of Demeter?" Aischylos shouts with disdain. "I know for a fact that you haven't even taken part in the Mysteries of Eleusis yet! What do you think you even know about Triptolemos?"

At the same time, Sophokles scoffs, "Meanwhile your title could not be more vague. You think it will intrigue audiences to wonder 'What Phrygian?', but really it will only bore them as they imagine napping shepherds in floppy caps."

"You forget - I already have fame! Audiences know my work will be beautiful, and so the title becomes a wonderful mystery when it is vague. Whereas you whose work the audience cannot yet imagine must lean on a title that hints at religious controversy. Have you somehow been initiated into the Eleusinian Mysteries without my hearing about it, or are you simply going to write the story of Triptolemos from a perspective of total ignorance?"

Sophokles lowers his head but keeps his eyes on Aischylos and then after a dramatic pause says, "Wouldn't you like to know…"

"Dionysos forgive this idiotic actor," Aischylos grunts, looking away. "He is undirected, and loose without a writer. Someone write for him!"

"I write, direct, and act my spirit, just like you, Aischylos! You will eat these words when our grandchildren repeat the great works of Sophokles at the Panathenaia alongside Hesiod and Homeros, and ask who is meant by the strange name Aischylos! Now go and dream of sheep with your Phrygians!"

Aischylos says with comical disdain, "I did not give you my true title."

Sophokles keeps a straight face to say, "Well neither did I, then."

Aischylos frowns, taking up his cup and sipping at it. "I'm not finished with my wine."

"Neither am I," Sophokles says, drinking from his cup as well, and repositioning his butt on his stool.

"Then we shall sit together a while longer," Aischylos says as if it is a threat.

The two men sit in silence, looking past each other as they finish their cups of wine. The other men in the drinking house wait, still eavesdropping on the two famous actors. The whole place is quiet until Aischylos finally finishes his cup and stands, tosses an owl coin onto the table and side-steps out the narrow space past the heavy door.

Π

News from abroad arrives at the Piraeus docks

While incoming ships row up along the coast, their sailors sing to signal to their friends and families that they'll be docking soon at Piraeus harbor. One such incoming ship is on its way now, its song echoing.

Deep ocean stream of salty waves
by brazen trident's will behaves,
carrying home us sailors brave
to land, to home, to future grave

Ever-smiling Ephialtes and lion-eyed Kimon stand together at the new stone Piraeus docks, overseeing the addition of new planking to the city triremes so they might be able to hold more soldiers.

Ephialtes shades his eyes from the afternoon sun as he spies the distant incoming ship from which the sailors' song rises like a rainbow from the horizon. "You think that's Charitimides back from Naxos?"

Kimon nods curtly. "You can tell it is by the shape of the figurehead. Don't you know the different sacred ships? That's *Paralos*."

Ephialtes ignores the question and asks, "What do you think will be the news?"

"Naxos needs the sea. She won't be able to last long disconnected from the rest of the world. Her leaders will see their options are limited, and come back to their senses and rejoin the League of Delos. But not yet."

"And how do you feel, as a general, about this tactic, I wonder?" Ephialtes asks Kimon.

Kimon breathes slowly through his nose and gauges Ephialtes' expression, to see what sort of answer he is expecting. "Siege is a common tactic. It's not one I enjoy, but it is sometimes necessary."

"This wasn't a siege, but just a blockade."

"A siege is a blockade. And a blockade at sea is a sort of siege. The tactic is the same - to separate the enemy from supplies."

"So Naxos is our enemy."

Kimon waggles his head in annoyed recognition of the need for a better term. "Our antagonist in this endeavor."

Ephialtes sniffs with frustration as he looks away for a moment, then in a fit of confidence he turns back to Kimon and snaps, "You know, Kimon, you're not the only one who can be a general of men. Democracy is a tide which raises boats of every size."

Kimon looks at Ephialtes with surprise for a moment, realizes he is seriously suggesting he himself could be a general, and laughs genuinely.

"What?" Ephialtes protests. "To be a general is just to figure out what would be most prudent for our army to do, and go and advise them there on the spot as they act."

"Just," Kimon laconically mocks.

"It's not something you need to be an athlete to do, is my point," Ephialtes says. "Athena is a general, too - not just Ares. Wisdom, forethought, prudence - these win wars. And also prevent them."

Kimon sighs as the trireme pulls up to the stone harbor edge and he prepares to catch its thrown ropes. He says to Ephialtes, "We do our best here on Earth, and the gods choose what and whom they prefer. It is the gods, not men, who choose the results of democracy. If the gods choose you to be a general one day, I will assume they know something I don't."

Ephialtes sniffs away the insult with a smile-of-spite.

Ephialtes thinks a moment and then adds, "The gods have been swayed by the words of men before."

Interrupting that thought by Ephialtes, Charitimides calls from the prow of the trireme, "The blockade continues, and trade with Naxos has ceased! It can't be long before their stores are emptied and they have no choice but to relent!" He holds both hands above his head in a gesture of victory.

"Then those cowards will be our allies again!" the pessimistic Oligarch Alkibiades spits mockingly from a group nearby.

Ephialtes turns to Kimon with a resigned look. "Hopefully your strategy of starving the poorest people of a democratic friend-city, if not ally-city anymore, will prove successful before that island becomes a graveyard, forsaken not by the gods, but by men."

"Your mistake is in thinking that the Persian Wars are over, Ephialtes," Kimon declares. "War is never over. War is the constant threat of the stronger over the weaker. If those who are presently powerless rose up and took power from those who have it now, they would not set up some kind of unprecedented reign of peace. They would take power for themselves in recognizable, familiar ways, like their overlords did over them. The imbalances that lead to strife will never end, like eddies in the ocean. Ares will never be sated of his bloodlust. And though Athena will always temper my hand and keep me from it, Ares will never stop filling the hearts of warrior-men like myself with the desire to crush the throats of timid, useless rabbit-men."

Preceded by a series of other people less and less distantly through the crowd each shouting "Here comes Kleinias!", the handsome young Kleinias, youngest son of

Alkibiades, runs up through the crow from the direction of Athens and comes to a stop near his father, bent and panting from running.

"If you have news, son, tell me first," Kleinias' father Alkibiades barks. He bends close to his son's mouth and takes in his panted whispers, then stands erect again with a wry smile to his fellows.

"What is it?" Kimon snaps, annoyed.

Alkibiades gives Kimon a brief look of disdain, but then reluctantly says, "An army from Argos has razed ancient Mykenai."

Some around him gasp.

Kleinias nods, acting like he was the one who delivered the news to all.

"Taken all the women there as slaves and leveled those ancient walls of Agamemnon," Alkibiades adds. "No doubt taken as souvenirs and sacred additions to their own city walls at Argos."

"They've been threatening to tear down those walls for decades," Kimon notes. "The ruins of Mykenai were little more than a bandit haven."

"Mykenai provided troops in the Persian War," one of the other Oligarchs notes.

Kimon turns to him and dryly asks, "And did you meet any of them? Scoundrels, all. But even scoundrels have to soldier up when civilization itself is threatened."

"And Tiryns," Kleinias adds excitedly, with a finger in the air. "They razed Tiryns as well!"

"So Argos has decided in one fell swoop to clear out the ruins of the old world to make room for the new," a nearby boat-seller analyzes. "At last. Good for them."

"The two most ancient city walls in the Hellenic world!" Ephialtes cries out. "How can they have excused such an action? They may have been decrepit, but they are ancient and revered spaces!"

"Argos is a democracy," Kimon notes. "Are you sure you want to question the process behind their decisions, Ephialtes? See, this rule by the uneducated is foolish, but you can't properly judge it. None of you have ever passed through the highlands of Argolis where the ancient walls of Mykenai and Tiryns rise - rose - because those old ruins are just bandit strongholds, home only to brigands and fugitive Helot slaves escaped from Lakedaemonia. If Argos wants to fill their workhouses with slaves of the lowest kind, let them. That's the kind of slave who will revolt and kill their master in the night. A real slave, one with some honor of his own - is the kind won in war. That's the only good kind of slave. Right, Amyntas?"

Kimon's hirsute slave Amyntas nods with a careful smile.

"Now this man has honor," Kimon says, slapping his slave on the shoulder. "Argos just chooses to take in vermin and try to yoke them. They should have slaughtered the whole populations of those wretched dens."

Kimon turns to Ephialtes, who looks appalled by what Kimon is saying.

"Don't look so shocked, Ephialtes. There's no Palace of Agamemnon at Mykenai anymore. Perhaps there never was. All we know is that a ruin sits upon a hill, with two primitive old lions on a gate leading into rubble. These ancient stories sung by poets, each giving their own manipulative version of events that maybe never even happened. Who knows anyone who was really there, hundreds of years ago, before even words? Nobody can know that."

The sailors on the incoming sacred ship begin shouting across the water the names of their friends and family waiting at the dock, as they become close enough to discern faces.

"Naxos starves!" one shouts, raising some half-hearted cheers among a lot of unsettled murmuring from the crowd on the dock.

Ephialtes' usual smile curls with concern.

P

Aischylos reveals his innovation at the Dionysian festival

A pregnant silence spreads as Aischylos' first play begins with a single actor on the stage, draped in a plain white sheet, merely a motionless human form.

Most in the audience can tell that the form is clearly the playwright Aischylos himself, just from the muscular shape of his body and the single sandal sticking out. The solitary actor on the stage is a reference and throwback to the old plays a generation ago, from before Aischylos himself changed the tradition to having two characters instead of only one.

"Aischylos himself," someone rudely whispers the obvious, only momentarily breaking the magical hush. They are quickly shushed by many.

Aischylos lets the moment hang in taut silence for several more seconds.

Just as a bird begins to sing upon the wind, finally breaking the simple quiet of the rustling trees, the chorus of the play begin to march out from inside the skene building, which has been painted with large brown triangles vaguely reminiscent of distant mountains, while also in the style of the old geometric patterns which older generations used to paint on their pottery, giving the space an abstract but ancient quality, quite opposite to the modern norm of painting increasingly realistic backdrops onto the skene. After Aischylos' silence, the chorus' footsteps play like very subtle percussion.

The instrumentalists who are circled around the edge of the stage - the famous visiting kitharist Chronomagos accompanied by numerous young women blowing double-flutes and others drumming - begin to introduce the standard accompanying music, Chronomagos making his strings sing uniquely to match each character's mood.

In the stands, Ephialtes and Perikles sit together with several other younger Democrats.

Ephialtes leans in close to Perikles and asks, "So this is the one which is supposed to have the new innovation?"

Perikles shushes him, nodding and shrugging at the same time. "One of them, yes. I don't know which he'll save that revelation for."

"I like that he begins so sparely," Ephialtes whispers.

As the chorus finally all turn to face the audience and give them a straight-on view of their masks, it becomes clear that the twelve chorus members, six on each side of white-draped Aischylos, are playing the parts of six youths and six maidens.

"The Labyrinth and the Minotaur?" Ephialtes whispers to Perikles, guessing the plot of the story. Perikles pats his knee again and does not respond, rather than continue a vocal back-and-forth. Ephialtes frowns at the reaction and somewhat annoyedly folds his arms and returns his attention to the stage.

Penander steps out from the skene wearing the mask of a Lydian king. "Show me, good ladies of Thebes, where my noble daughter Niobe is bathing in her tears and bedding on her torn hair, as I have heard."

The chorus sing together, "Her wailing has gone quiet, good King Tantalos. Niobe grieves in silence now."

The Athenian audience all listen with reverent patience. Over the years, a trust has grown for whatever Aischylos presents to the city, and less and less does one hear thoughtless shouts or voiced disdain during the performance, at least during Aischylos' plays.

This presentation of Niobe's story proves loquacious and actionless, with Penander's King Tantalos diving deep into soliloquies on grief and hubris full of many layers of rhyme and irony.

Throughout the whole first section of the play, Aischylos-as-Niobe sits nearly motionless and veiled, silent, the tension building steadily for any move or word.

It isn't until the second scene, after a change of backdrop and a shifting of masks, that Aischylos-as-Niobe finally speaks, alone on the stage but for the grieving chorus who mime what he describes. By the time Aischylos' character finally speaks, the energy he has built up around its expectation fills the audience with excitement which only increases when Penander appears high on the skene in the middle of the speech.

Aischylos-as-Niobe sings, "I beg the gods to recognize what they certainly know, that my heart is not stone, and my intent was not cold, when I spoke of my children with the pride and joy of a fruitful mother! I can only lament my unlucky marriage to a man who would attack Apollo's temple rather than face the terrible reality we must accept, our seven sons and seven daughters lying dead before our eyes, gone before their grandfather!"

Penander dressed in the short tunic of a huntress with one side of his chest bared, a quiver of fake arrows slung across one shoulder, his long hair up in a bun, the very image of Artemis Huntress, appears seated upon a wooden depiction of the bright white Moon, and as she draws her bow and aims its long arrow at Aischylos-as-Niobe, Penander very slowly begins to descend, his legs curled up beneath him as if he is swimming the clouds, white veils meant to represent moonlight dangling beneath and fluttering in the breeze.

The moment he begins to gradually float downward without appearing to hold anything but the great bow of Artemis, gasps spread through the audience, followed by a few prayers to the goddess as if the assumption is that it must really be her. Penander cannot help but crack a smile at the sound of the prayers, and at his smile, a few friends of his in the audience begin to laugh, but that noise is overwhelmed by the shouts of praise and loud applause as the audience continue to witness Penander-as-Artemis float gracefully down toward Aischylos' Niobe.

"Poor Niobe," Penander says as Artemis, amidst the sounds of the audience's awe, "your tears will never cease, and your heart will become more like stone than you can realize."

Aischylos can barely hear his own voice over the applause as he delivers his next several lines, but he cannot let it worry him while basking in the warmth of the breeze of praise.

Σ

Sophokles performs his first set of plays at the Dionysian festival

On the next day of the Dionysian festival, it is time for Sophokles' set of plays. General excitement is high among aficionados of theater to hear the new writing-voice of such a familiar singing and acting personality.

Aischylos sits in the highest part of the audience stands, and keeps a female mask at hand as if he might wear it while he heckles. Occasional pulls from a jar of wine at his feet keep him moist of mind.

The chorus enters the stage from behind the skene, all masked in the faces of pretty young girls with flowers in their hair. They line up, half on one side and half on the other, as the musicians begin a pastoral Arkadian melody.

Behind the chorus, two characters step forward - two well-known actors, but neither of them Sophokles himself.

Aischylos smiles with confusion. "He deigns not to act in his own play?" the playwright scoffs to one of his friends down the stands from him. "I knew that rascal couldn't juggle all that goes into directing his own play. It seems writing, directing, and starring all at once were too much for him."

Voices lower down in the stands shoosh Aischylos.

Many-faced Kratinos and a younger actor named Brason step forward from either end of the chorus, who are all dressed in tunics with a distinctly Eleusinian edging embroidery.

Kratinos, wearing the mask of a handsome prince of olden times, sings out, "O daughters of Eleusis of the golden fields, you have become too practiced in your grief! If it wouldn't seem impious, I would beg you to sing instead of weep, and dance instead of weaving wreaths of woe! But as you know, my sister, sweet Kallidike, I am just as chained to the fear for our sweet lady as you are. I can forget our pains no better than you."

Brason, masked to be a beautiful ancient princess, sings back, "As long as our sweet lady's noble daughter stays encaged by that great King of Death Haides Hearth-Snuffer, how can any mortal heart live for joy?"

Brason-as-Kallidike and Kratinos-as-Triptolemos embrace in melancholy for a moment as the instrumentalists surrounding the stage swell up a big dramatic sound of imminence.

Surprising all, the chorus separates in the center and onto the stage walks a *third character*. It is Sophokles himself, behind a mask made from finely-woven wheat strands, wigged with golden curling hair, and holding sheaves of wheat against his false bosom, the Grain Goddess Demeter.

Sophokles-as-Demeter declares, "The scent of *kykeon* has been my guide back to golden Eleusis!"

The introduction of this third character is such a novel change from tradition that the audience all gasp and go silent as she begins to speak to the other two characters, the actors of the chorus all listening in a row behind.

One rude young man whispers too loud, "What's going on?"

"That's Sophokles!" another replies. "A third character on the stage!"

Kratinos-as-Triptolemos bows to the new character and sings, "Lady Demeter First-Shoots, the truest blossom of the field!"

Brason-as-Kallidike also bows and sings, "The goddess has returned! All dressed in wheat, as if she has good news!"

The chorus sing and dance a circle round the three.

> O hear us, you mortals who eat the grain,
> who plow black earth for Demeter's sweet gifts,
> remember now when our Lady of Seeds
> walked veiled among Men in search of her child!

Sophokles-as-Grain-Goddess then gracefully removes the large wheat-woven mask, revealing a gleaming bronze woman mask below.

I who gave Men the secrets of the seeds,
who taught mortals to turn the dark soil,
who made wilderness bloom into fields,
it is I, Demeter-Who-Feeds!
For when Men see a true goddess arrive,
all frills are blown away, leaving but truth,
and only by removal of disguise
can the full visage of wonder be seen!

Many in the audience cheer, and some laugh at the brazen boldness.

Aischylos, grumbling, kicks the wooden seating in front of him, which is filled by actors from his own chorus, who pat patient compassion back onto his legs. He angrily toe-swats their hands, making them giggle.

The giggling, however, fails to fluster the ever-professional Sophokles, who merely raises his voice to overwhelm other noises.

Sophokles-as-Demeter steps confidently to the front of the stage and says, "Six months ago, I came to you here at Eleusis lost, and looking for my daughter. That night, you took me in, and gave me soup and comfort. Your servant made me laugh when I thought I would never laugh again! And you helped me in my search, as fruitless as it was fated to be. But today, at last, I come to you with better news, and gifts of gratitude for your taking me in."

Aischylos grumbles quietly to himself as long as he can, but finally can hold it in no longer and stands up to shout at Sophokles.

"This isn't even how this story goes!"

For a moment, the play freezes on the stage as the actors look to Aischylos up in the stands.

Many near him in the stands turn fully to look at Aischylos.

He continues to shout, "As expected, this fool who hasn't even been through the Eleusinian Mysteries has no idea how Demeter would speak, or what the real story of Triptolemos is! This is just ignorant prattle! I mean some stories you can play around with, but this story is important!"

Half an apple hits Aischylos in the head from behind, startling him. He looks back and to his surprise sees Kallias standing up and glaring at him.

"Um, maybe don't speak of the Mysteries in public, Aischylos?!" Kallias, in his role as a priest of Demeter, shouts.

Aischylos stutters, gesturing to the play, which has stalled for the moment and which now waits for the shouting match to end while all eyes are turned to Aischylos.

"But, but he's the one who's misrepresenting Demeter and Triptolemos and how they..."

"He made no oath to keep the Mysteries secret, let alone know them at all. He can present whatever he likes. But you, who know the Mysteries of Eleusis, have taken an oath to keep them secret! Yet here you are blurting about them!"

A finely-robed priestess of Demeter sitting elsewhere in the stands, with her children, snatches an apple right out of the biting mouth of her young son and hurls it at Aischylos, though this time Aischylos has the awareness to dodge the throw, and it instead hits a woman further down in the stands, who shrieks with surprise. From both left and right, more semi-soft objects such as mixed nuts and scraps of food get thrown in Aischylos' direction, and the crowd begins to boo as one big chorus. The priestess of Demeter gestures broadly for the crowd to ramp up its booing.

Golden curls bouncing, Sophokles gleefully signals to his actors to continue their play, even though he knows much of the audience isn't paying attention as they pelt Aischylos with their theater snacks.

Under the rain of hurled food and garbage, Aischylos finds himself overcome, causing him to stumble and slip down a few of the steps leading down between the stands to the stage. He scrambles on the ground toward the low, rectangular stone altar of Dionysos at the front of the stage, knocking some of the grapes and dicks off of it. As soon as he throws his body upon Dionysos' altar, the food throwing dwindles.

"Dionysos, protect me!" Aischylos shouts. "And Demeter forgive me! This play is so bad it caused me to accidentally forget my oath to you! Forgive me, gods! Dionysos speak to lady Demeter for me, please!"

The audience groans and boos, but the priests who care for the altar of Dionysos run up beside Aischylos and hold their hands up to the angered crowd, indicating that this suppliant is now protected by the Mirth God Dionysos, and so all pelting ought to cease.

One of the priests cannot help but laugh at the situation, while the other beside frowns at him disapprovingly.

That night, Sophokles wears the ivy crown as the city celebrates his win.

The running joke among the drunken, chattering groups is for a third person to interrupt a group of two and introduce themselves as the Bane-of-Aischylos, at which all laugh.

Aischylos' actors linger together near the Fountain House, murmuring to each other as a spiteful group, but Aischylos himself is nowhere to be found.

"A new king of the theater has been crowned in Athens!" a young prostitute shouts into the air, meeting cheers of agreement. "Hail Sophokles!"

"The king is dead," murmurs one of Sophokles' actors, grizzled-bearded Kratinos. "Long live the new king." He drunkenly leans on Sophokles. "So it always has been, and always shall be. The pupil dominates the teacher, the son dominates the father, so the chorus boy dominates the director."

"Perhaps you mean one director dominates another director," Sophokles corrects, pushing Kratinos away patiently. "Once a chorus boy, not always a chorus boy. And once a great playwright, not always a great playwright, in Aischylos' case."

"Or perhaps it's just that the people prefer what is novel," Kratinos slurs, pointing prominent eyes at Sophokles, clearly trying to instigate some emotion from the handsome playwright. "One cannot rightly say that Aischylos' plays were not great. Only that yours were selected by today's Archons, for whatever their reasons."

Sophokles shrugs, and agrees, "True enough. But I do think the ivy crown looks good on me, so I think I'll keep it, regardless of its emptiness."

"You don't mind, then, that your win is marred by issues external to the actual quality of the two plays? That it first became more about competing innovations in gimmickry, and then simply about one man's public embarrassment?"

Sophokles smiles, already shaking his head and folding his arms. "I do not care," he says. Then he throws his arms above his head and shouts and laughs to his actors, "Drama! Tragedy! They are many-layered. Let the audience's reaction decide what greatness is."

Watching with the rest of Aischylos' actors from across the Agora, Penander glowers, attempting to mask it with nonchalance.

Broad-bearded Kratinos, after offering swigs from his belt-pouch wineskin to Sophokles and some others in the chorus, addresses the whole group. "Also, Sophokles," says Kratinos, "you have shown for all of us actors that the path to being a playwright ourselves exists within our own wherewithal. Perhaps I myself might try my hand at writing, as well!"

Sophokles sniffs, "Not you, Kratinos. Of all people, not you. I know the sort of stories you would try to hoist upon the people. If you thought Aischylos had it hard tonight, I can hardly imagine the treatment you'd get if you tried to subject the Athenian audience to one of your absurd, nonsensical wordplays. For all our sakes, Kratinos - do not write! You are too important for my chorus. You add that dissonant part which mimics the chaos of reality."

Kratinos laughs, but when some in the chorus laugh with him, he barks at them and throws up a hand. "No! I am not one in a chorus."

"You're drunk, Kratinos," Sophokles. "Don't quit my chorus drunk."

"You have a place in Aischylos' chorus if you prefer, Kratinos," Penander suggests, ambling up to Sophokles' actors with faux nonchalance. He looks back to the rest of the actors from Aischylos' chorus and beckons them with a head nod to come join him. "I have his trust, so I am sure he would agree."

"Where is Aischylos, by the way?"

"Probably still under a pile of rotten fruit on the altar of Dionysos."

Sophokles and all his actors laugh quietly, while Aischylos' actors loudly frown, gathering behind Penander.

Kratinos steps between the two groups and holds up his wineskin. "O great Grape God, jokester of Olympos, teller of twisted tales, lover of donkey's bottoms, suck out our hatred for each other and spit back mirth into its place!"

The two groups of actors face off to act out the dance of a drunken brawl.

T

A new ambassador from Naxos speaks to the Athenian Council

In the bright new council house, within a broad shaft of bright Athenian morning sunlight from the doorway, the old Naxian ambassador carefully gets down on his knees and prostrates his torso forward until his head touches the ground, as if the council is the King of Kings.

He raises his head and says, "Masters of the sea, Athenian councilors, my people have sent me to beg of you … Please allow our humble island to rejoin your mighty League of Delos, lest your blockade starve our simple city to bones. We can only beg."

An Oligarch seated in the stands laughs, "At last, the League is 'ours'!" His friends and employees make sure their agreement is seen.

"Stand, Naxian," says fine-garbed Alkibiades as he approaches the man and puts his hand on the the man's bent back. "We never wanted to hurt your island. We need Naxos. So of course, rejoin us once again, and be our friend."

The Athenian councilor helps the old Naxian to stand again.

The Naxian says, "Athenian council, you have proved your point. Naxos has sacrificed extensively to Apollo and Artemis, those twin gods born on Delos, in hopes that they will make you see our true regret and welcome us back into your noble league of defense against the Eastern Empire."

The council murmurs and grumbles.

"You see, poor men of the council," Alkibiades says coldly, "that is how you get things done civilly. You lean on someone just enough to remind them that unpleasantness is possible, so that you can avoid the violence that would otherwise be necessary. And this way those with power can maintain it without living in a world drenched with blood! Threats! Wise reminders of power's flow, these are the civilized spears."

No one cheers. Someone farts, but the tension levels allows few to laugh.

"Speaking of threats," the ambassador from the distant eastern island of Rhodos says, stepping forward to take the place of the humbled ambassador of Naxos.

"We hear the ambassador from Rhodos."

"Persia..." he says, looking around and letting the word linger its menace in the silence. "Persia returns to loom its shadow over western Asia. We have heard in Rhodos that they intend to conquer Pamphylia, just to our east, as a doorway to recapture all the ports of Ionia, and from there they will be able to assault all of Hellas. Xerxes gathers together his army built of every barbarian nation once again."

"It's too soon," someone replies. "There's no way he has any real power regained yet."

Another yells, "He has no navy!" and the first agrees.

"The Phoenikians who provide the Persian navy are the finest shipbuilders in the world," Ephialtes reminds the council. "If they focused their efforts, it is not insane to think that Persia could have rebuilt their navy by now. It has been more than ten years since we sank Xerxes' armada."

Many of the veterans in the council bark with pride at the reminder.

"Let Ephialtes be a general," the old Oligarch who laughed at the Naxian shouts, "if he thinks he knows how to outsmart Xerxes!"

He clearly meant it as a cruel joke, but the Democrats around Ephialtes start to chant in response, "General Ephialtes! General Ephialtes!" and Ephialtes the city councilor and cupmaker's son cannot help but smile and shrug an audience-assuring gesture of possibility.

Y

Perikles has some friends over for supper

"First, stand steady," the fighting teacher says through his own helmet with a sigh.

Perikles stands in his home courtyard, sweat-drenched in the full suit of his father Xanthippos' fine old armor which he wore in both Persian Wars. Sharp-bearded Perikles has never been fully armored before, and he can barely stand under the weight. But he likes how he looks in it.

In front of Perikles, the famous swordsman Grylla stands waiting to be sparred with. Calm-eyed Grylla says, as he demonstrates with his own legs, "A strong stance is the most basic defense that any man, regardless of armor, can take for himself. You look like a wind would blow you over."

Perikles pushes his helmet back on his head, gasping for breath.

"Your helmet does no good sitting back there," Grylla sighs, shaking his head. "Put it back on."

"It is impossible to breathe with my face trapped in this bronze prison," Perikles snaps with frustration. "I don't want to do this today."

"Too bad," Grylla snaps back. "You have to. You don't have a father to slap you into doing it, but your mother's hired me to play that role." Grylla gives Perikles a half-joking, half-threatening look. "If I were a Persian, or a Spartan, or some bandit with no respect for your nobility, I would do a lot worse. And it's *that* which you have to learn to protect yourself from. Now brace yourself, because I'm about to toss you something, and you're going to have to catch it. And in the future, I want you always to stand as if prepared to catch anything. You need rougher friends, Perikles."

Grylla crosses the courtyard to a rack of tall spears beside the garden shed, and grabs two of them out of it. Then, giving Perikles plenty of time to prepare, he tosses one of the spears. Perikles catches the long, heavy spear, but is not able to keep his body from swaying back and forth and nearly toppling over in doing so.

"This is your spear. If nothing else, you need to know how to hold a shield, and wield a spear in one hand. Okay, now this end, this is obviously the end you want to point at your enemy."

"Why is there this hook back here where I hold it?" Perikles asks, shifting the six foot long wooden shaft in his arms so that he can inspect the hooked iron spike on the far end from the main blade.

"Well first of all, you're going to need to get used to holding this in just one arm. But that - look here."

Grylla takes the spear from Perikles deftly and grasps it in one arm, leaning it partially against his bicep to control its side-to-side movement. He lifts the spear fully upright, then looks down at the ground and seems to hunt through the grass with his eyes for a moment. Perikles looks down as well, as Grylla explains, "This, this is mostly a counterweight for the main spear blade up there, but this is also - this is your lizard killer!" and then he jabs the bottom spike down into the dirt, and lifts it back up with a little mole impaled upon the iron.

"O dear," Perikles groans at the sight of the speared mole.

"You can't be disgusted by this level of gore, man. A man has a lot more guts to lose in real combat, and you can't let blood scare you."

"No no, I'm just annoyed to learn that we have moles in the courtyard." Perikles sniffs out a little laugh to Grylla, but Grylla is not at all amused.

"You need to keep your mind in a martial mode, man."

Perikles puts his martial equipment on the ground. "You know, Grylla, I am grateful for your tutelage, but I just have other things to think about. I've seen battle occur, and it is something I mean to avoid. But if I happen to find myself forced to fight, I am sure that instinct will take over."

"Look here, man," Grylla says calmly, sitting down upon the stone bench in the center of the courtyard and giving Perikles an empathetic expression. "This isn't easy. Believe me, I understand. Maybe I forget sometimes just how hard it is when you're first starting out, but trust me - that's evidence that it gets easier, the longer you do this kind of training. And it will make the difference one day between your seeing old age or not. Because here is the sad truth of battle Perikles - or maybe it is a happy truth. Men of every nation will scream courage at each other from afar, but when they actually march up face to face and are within swinging distance of each other, most men will not fight. Because men are social animals - we care about each other, we need each other, we look to each other for how to behave. We know and mean nothing by ourselves. And so it seems to be written into our souls by the gods to abhor seeing the human body damaged. O we'll hit and slap and wrestle each other to the ground, we'll break each other's bones unknown hidden behind bruised skin, but tearing open that skin, revealing the inner workings - that men know is only for the gods. And so most men will do everything in their power, even on the battlefield, to avoid having to push a weapon into the body of another man - they will even let themselves be killed, to avoid that horror. And so, when battle happens, there is a reason that some men are able to appear to be so lionine, so courageous, so much better at combat than others. It is because they are the only ones really willing to kill. And kill they will. I've seen one man kill hundreds upon one battlefield. Hundreds, Perikles, of other men - one. And so, when you find yourself on the field of some battle somewhere - and you will, one day - if you are not one of those men willing to break the flesh of your comrades, then you will die there that day."

Perikles grimaces at the horror he is imagining.

"O and Perikles, that one man who killed hundreds on the field of battle - he was a Spartan."

"I hear you, spear-master, I do," Perikles nods, putting his helmet down on the ground. "I just, honestly, I think that you who fought in the Persian Wars are so haunted by that experience that you think that all life must be about preparation for war. But it is not that time anymore. The whole world has changed. Persia has changed; Hellas has changed; the international situation has changed. There is the Delian League. I really don't think that I need to be prepared to fight other men in battle."

Perikles sees, behind Grylla, his body slave Thrax gently waving from the corner of the main house.

"Well, thank you Grylla," Perikles sighs, wiping sweat off his head with the back of his arm and then offering his hand to be shaken. "I have friends arriving now, so - if you don't mind…"

The fighter nods and says, "Yes, that eastern 'wiseman' friend of yours, right? I saw him walking slowly, staring up at the clouds, on my way here. It's amazing that he took this long to get here."

"You were riding your horse, I presume?" Perikles asks.

Grylla nods. "I was. But still. Perikles. Beware of eastern folk. I know you're probably excited to share with him some scrolls or maps you have, or buy some of the like from him, but let me show you a map of the world that an easterner sold to me, ten years ago, when his people bent their knees before Persia and marched into our city to enslave us."

Grylla lifts the flaps of his military skirt, revealing both his big, swinging dick, and a scar just as long down the inner part of his right thigh, slightly misshaping the muscle there. He lowers the flap slowly so as not to slap his dick with it.

"That's where some Lydian or Ionian or Phrygian or who-cares-whence *easterner* put his spear into my thigh. That's *my* map of the world. So I say again - beware what easterners might want to bring into your home. Remember how the wise hide their assault within Troian horses."

Perikles finally rolls his eyes and looks back at Grylla with a certain noble derision as if his time is being wasted.

Grylla understands the unspoken request that he leave, and he nods and obliges.

Perikles shouts so Thrax can hear him, "See them in, Thrax!"

The ox-shouldered Thrakian politely leads into the Alkmaeonid family courtyard two guests - Ephialtes, who is familiar with the place and walks right up to Perikles for a friendly hug, and Anaxagoras, who steps slowly into the space taking in its beauty gradually.

"Your home is exquisite!" Anaxagoras exclaims. "Like the gardens of Kyros!"

"Why, thank you," says Agariste, Perikles' mother, from the doorway to the women's side of the house. A couple of her personal slaves linger just behind her. "But I know you are being kind. I have seen paintings of eastern splendor. We make no attempt at such ostentation."

"Mother!" Perikles calls out, still hugging his two friends. "This is Anaxagoras, of Klazomenai in Ionia. He's the sage I've been telling you about. And, of course, you know Ephialtes."

"Ah, your Pythagorean," Agariste nods. "Welcome, friend-stranger. Already I can tell that your family is noble, at least where you are from."

"Well, I am not actually a Pythagorean," Anaxagoras notes with a polite nod of greeting, "but I am a student of numbers, so I consider the company of the Pythagoreans welcome. But you are correct, madam, about my family's wealth, back home. I'm sure that horse-breaking into civility which we noble children all receive is still readily visible beneath my attempts to subdue it."

Perikles and Agariste both smile at that good-naturedly.

"And I am Ephialtes," Ephialtes jokes, knowing that Perikles' mother disdains his lower-class origins, "though I do not expect you to remember my name, utterly lacking said nobility as I do." He laughs, to make it a joke.

"Come, Anaxagoras!" Perikles says, leading the way into the men's side of his family's house. "I've been eager to show you my library!"

That evening, after the sun has sunk, Perikles and his friends and family all sit down to supper together at a long table in the courtyard, under a violet twilight. Joining his mother and brother, Perikles' two aunts and a few young female cousins have come over from their house to join the supper, but they remain politely quiet while the head of their family speaks with his friends. The Alkmaeonid family's many slaves lay out a diverse spread of polished, finely-carved bowls filled with fishes, figs, and other fruits from all across the ports of the sea.

"I wish to thank you for this most welcoming supper, Agariste," Anaxagoras says as he seats himself. "I have been made to feel nothing but welcome here in Athens since I've been visiting."

"O, it is our own good fortune to have visitors, to be able to show the gods our best *xenia* - kindness to strangers. You offer us a chance to show the heights of civilization." She nods to the slaves, giving silent instructions with her eyes, as she speaks.

Perikles' aunt Threate asks, "And how long have you been in Attika, Anaxagoras?"

Anaxagoras hesitates a moment, before he says, "Just a few years."

"I'm sure your people miss you back in Ionia," Ephialtes says kindly, with his ubiquitous smile.

Slaves of myriad distant origins - men and women from Skythia, Persia, Babylon, Aithiopia, and Qarthago - serve artfully arranged plates of octopus and greens under finely engraved, thin-hammered silver dome covers.

Anaxagoras leans in closely to examine the tiny winged horse which has been sculpted onto the handle of the silver dome which covers his dinner.

"You remove that," Threate condescendingly instructs him, with a glance to Perikles as if she wonders where he found such people. "Your meal is beneath the silver cover. That keeps it warm."

Anaxagoras laughs. "O, I know! I was just inspecting this wondrous, miniscule Pegasos," Anaxagoras explains with a smile to his noble hostess. "It is some truly impressive craftsmanship. So fine, such detail."

"A local boy does them," Agariste says. "Small fingers can do fine work. And the silver is local as well."

"Your family has some of the finest objects I have ever seen," Ephialtes agrees politely to Agariste. "You have excellent taste, and clearly you've been collecting beautiful works for a long time."

"That is the benefit of having an old family," Agariste nods. "Thank you, Ephialtes, it's kind of you to say. Yes, we still have some figurines from many generations ago. I feel it is they that continue to give us the luck we maintain even today, even despite curses called upon us from strangers. It's why I tell no one where they really are. Not even Perikles." Agariste winks at Perikles with a little smile.

"You mean the old geometric ones?" Perikles asks, and his mother nods. "You'd be surprised, mother - no thief these days would want those."

"I assure you, Perikles," his mother replies, "there are men, even thieves, who would know well which of our old pots are truly most valuable, even if you wouldn't - and it is 'the old geometric ones', as you call them!"

Perikles shrugs.

"What it must be like to grow up surrounded by such fine things and beautiful artwork," Ephialtes remarks to his friend Perikles across the table, shaking his head in wonder. "It has filled your son with a spirit as beautiful as the works that surrounded his childhood, Agariste."

"And such a library!" Anaxagoras adds. "You have not only raised a son ennobled by the beauty that surrounds him, but also wisened at an early age by the minds that live within the scrolls in his library! I have never met one man who keeps the text of so many scrolls in his own head like a traveling library himself."

"Yes, well," Agariste says, looking at Perikles, "we are proud of him. Even if you boys now work against his father's old friends."

Perikles adjusts himself in his seat, and gives his mother a somewhat frustrated look. "We mean to strengthen our city, by strengthening the most men within it. And strength, as you know well, Anaxagoras, strength comes from health. And health comes from being treated well. The Battle of Salamis proved to the world the power of Democracy - of an entire city of enfranchised kings. We mean only to further strengthen Democracy herself, and if Father's friends find themselves on the opposite side of that debate, well then…"

"Perikles has become one of our best communicators," Ephialtes remarks with pride.

"So where are you living, Anaxagoras?" Perikles asks. "I see you in the Agora so early, it almost seems that you sleep there."

"I have been," Anaxagoras admits, somewhat reluctantly. "Many of us without permanent homes in the area take our evening refuge gathered around the blacksmith's forge, where there is always warmth even on a windy night."

"You sleep with the homeless at the blacksmith's forge?" Perikles repeats with surprise. His mother flutters her eyes closed for a moment like she does when she smells something rotten. Anaxagoras just nods. "My friend, I will find you good lodging. A man of your mind mustn't be relegated to sleeping on the street, and getting fleeting warmth from a smoldering forge."

"I really don't know what to say," Anaxagoras stutters, embarrassed.

"I don't mean to embarrass you," Perikles assures him. "But please, allow me to help. I am certain that I can find someone who has a room which can be yours. I want to make sure that I have access to your wisdom, and I can already not afford to have someone like you waste away in my own city."

Periboea, one of Perikles' young cousins, says, with a voice so shy it comes out as a hoarse whisper, "Living downtown has its benefits."

Her mother Hipparete smacks Periboea beneath the table and shoots her a glare. "You speak when you're spoken to."

Anaxagoras offers the now-embarrassed young woman a kind smile and says, "I have found that to be true in most cities. Would you like to hear about some of the other cities I have been to in my travels, young lady?"

"She isn't available to forcigners," Hipparete tells Anaxagoras as if he has just asked to marry Periboea.

Anaxagoras just nods and gestures his regret at pressing any unknown boundaries.

Hipparete quickly glares her daughter into neutralizing her pained expression.

Agariste throws on a quick mask of pleasantry as if no awkwardness has occurred, and says, "O slaves - do bring us more wine, won't you? Of course, my fine son Perikles grew up with his brother Ariphron, and an absent father, so he has become something of a bookworm and a collector instead of a horseman or athlete like other boys his age want to be."

"Collector?" Anaxagoras asks eagerly. "What, beyond your books, have you collected, Perikles? I am most interested in collections of things which are similar."

Perikles eagerly says, "I have jars fulls of different stones which I can show you."

"He collects clever street people, as well," Threate chuckles, leaning in close to her sister.

Agariste shakes her head with soft negation and whispers, "Be nice."

Threate then recomposes her polite demeanor and asks Anaxagoras, "So what is your specialty, or school of thought, as a philosopher?"

Anaxagoras says, "Well, I am from Ionia, so I have primarily studied the writings of the Ionian thinkers - Thales, Anaximander, Herakleitos."

Threate shrugs to indicate the names are unfamiliar.

Anaxagoras simplifies, "Our school of thought is based on exploring the notion that *change over time* can be studied, *similar things* can be compared, and from this some truths about Nature can be mapped out."

"Nature? Are you one of those atheists?"

Anaxagoras takes a long moment of silence to look around at each set of eyes at the table before he carefully answers. "I only know that I have never encountered evidence of a god."

Agariste cocks her head to indicate her derisive confusion. "You walk upon a god. You live beneath a god. You breathe in and out the Winds, who are gods. Don't you?"

Anaxagoras gestures and grimaces at the challenge of explaining himself. "I don't deny the Earth and the Sky, and the Winds. I just think that evidence has shown that they may behave in consistent ways on their own, not necessarily at the will of immortal, invisible entities."

Hipparete asks, "What's the difference?"

Agariste adds, "Your linguistic distinctions are like ... poetic wordplay. Is that what this is, are you a poet, a singer?"

Anaxagoras looks to Perikles.

Perikles says, "I think Anaxagoras is just talking about things like the movement of water, the rolling down a hill of a stone, the melting of metal - that sort of thing, which happens the same way all the time. He's not necessarily saying there aren't any gods, but just that the gods don't do *everything*, and some things happen by their own nature."

Anaxagoras nods. "With the world free of war for the moment, there is able to be a movement of people and a free exchange of ideas which cannot exist when armies are marching and killing. And with that movement of people and exchange of ideas, we've been able to see a ... a buildup, an accretion, of disparate wisdoms which all cohere into one wisdom-weave which all interrelates. And I suspect that, if we are able to continue to avoid war, this interweaving wisdom of the different and yet overlapping experiences of the many different people around the world will continue to reveal new and emergent greater wisdoms, perhaps of the sort that we cannot even fathom yet. This is why I feel the work of the mind is of the utmost importance. Ultimately, all is Mind."

"All these good ideas will be worthless, though," Perikles says with hesitance, "if the Empire were to return to our shores, and we were unable to defeat them."

Swift-eyed Perikles reaches down and grabs his helmet from the grass, places it on his head, then shifts it back a bit so he can see his friends. The Alkmaeonid young people laugh carefully, but their parents do not smile, and Anaxagoras blinks away some rough wartime memories, unnoticed.

Anaxagoras lifts his cup. "To peace." He drinks.

"ALL THINGS, INDEED, ARE THREE, NOT ONE –
THE PAST, THE LIVING MOMENT, AND THE FUTURE –
POWER, POSSESSION, AND ENERGY –
THE KNOWN, THE FORGOTTEN,
AND THE UNKNOWABLE."
Pythagoras, *Semicircle*

Φ

Aischylos and Podarge sail west; and a colony leaves for the Strymon River

Hugging her husband Aischylos, colorfully-veiled Podarge says, "Tell me again about Syrakous."

Bright-eyed Podarge clings to her husband Aischylos, standing at the stern of the Qarthaginian merchant ship that is preparing to take off for that far-Western Hellenic colony on the island of Trinakria. An ex-dancer from the theater, she never quite stops dancing, even with the subtle movement of her head to catch the wind within her veils.

"Remind me how unlike Athens it is," she says.

Sad-eyed Aischylos sighs, but provides the semblance of a dramatic description despite his malaise, with gestures of half heart. "Its walls are said to be the greatest in the world - greater than Babylon's, if not as old. So we will be perfectly safe from any western barbarians or monsters. And the Syrakousans haven't seen any of the Athenian plays yet, so everything will be new to them there! At least there's that."

"Don't tell me about the theater scene; tell me about the restaurant scene. Tell me about the food." Podarge clings close to Aischylos' muscular arm and lays her fluttering-veiled head upon his shoulder.

"Squid, I hear, is good there," Aischylos remarks with uncertainty. "And the wheat there will be fresh instead of imported. The best bread. In the west the best bread is from Syrakous. In the east, it's from Chersonesos."

"Mmm, bread," Podarge smiles as she closes her eyes.

As the season when the Sea is safest has finally arrived, numerous ships visiting from distant ports are now lined up at the Piraeus docks, loading and otherwise preparing for their next journeys.

On the next vessel over beside Podarge and Aischylos', families are packing whole houses worth of belongings in great strapped-down piles. A little girl too young to help waits against the prow of the ship, gazing at the glistening water, playing idly with a wooden dolphin. She notices Podarge looking at her, and they both smile.

"Good morning," the little girl says politely.

"Good morning!" Podarge calls out across the span between the boats. "You look like you're getting ready to sail off somewhere - how exciting!"

The girl nods. "We're going to start a new colony in the north. Are you sailing away today, too?"

"We are! This is my fine husband, the playwright Aischylos. Aischylos, say hello to my new friend."

Aischylos grumpily and tersely waves.

"We sail west, for Syrakous. But we, I hope, are just visiting. We aren't taking all of our things, because we will be back."

"That is yet to be revealed," Aischylos grumbles.

"Where do you sail to?" Podarge calls out to the little girl on the next boat.

"To build a new home, a new colony!" the girl replies in a loud shout. "We sail north!"

"Well, may Poseidon bless your journey, and may Hestia give you a fine new home in distant lands!"

As children do, the little girl has already looked away, her attention drawn elsewhere.

Podarge waves with a big smile, trying to regain the girl's attention, but then side-eyes Aischylos and asks him, "There aren't really cyclopes on the way to Trinakria, are there?"

Aischylos just shrugs to her with honest uncertainty. "I've heard differing accounts. But most say the cyclopes live further north, past the strait of the Skylla and Charybdis, both of whom I'm told sleep these days, and anyway, we aren't going that direction."

Podarge groans. "We're passing Skylla and Charybdis? Whom Odyssseos couldn't even pass without losing his ship?"

"Passing them. Not crossing through them. Don't worry, dear. We won't even see them."

Podarge groans.

Aischylos continues, "Travel to and from Syrakous happens all the time. We should be perfectly safe. This merchant doesn't want to lose all this cargo! I spoke to the captain, who just came here *from* Syrakous, and guess whom he brought with him from that city, to attend the Olympic Games in Elis? The king! King Hieron of Syrakous himself. So the captain will surely do his best to avoid monsters on his way back."

> "WHEN THE THISTLE BLOOMS, AND THE NOISY CICADA
> HIDDEN IN LEAVES WING-SINGS ITS POEM,
> THOSE LAZY DAYS OF SUMMER, WHEN GOATS
> ARE MEAT-PLUMP AND WINE IS THE TASTIEST."
> Hesiod, *Works and Days*

X

Hellenes from all across the world gather for the Olympic Games

Every fourth summer, all across the Hellenic world, from the islands of Rhodos and Kypros in the east where Dawn heralds the Sun, to the colony cities of Trinakria and Massalia in the distant west where the Daughters of the Evening sing that same Sun to sleep, all Hellenic cities send their best athletes to compete in a set of holy athletic games at Olympia, to show the reigning gods who on Earth is best.

These are the Olympic Games.

Four such famous holy games are celebrated across Hellas - the Olympic Games at Olympia, the Panathenaic Games at Athens, the Pythian Games at Delphi, and the Isthmian Games near Qorinth - each taking place in staggered four-year intervals so that every year has one set of games or another. But the Olympic Games are the oldest, supposedly originated by the ancient King Pelops himself, and are held in honor of the King of the Gods, the Lightning-Bearer, Zeus.

Most citizens of the Hellenic world count their years in *Olympiads* - sets of four years - starting from the origination of these games, as if civilization has only existed as long as the Games have.

As the season of the Games approaches, Hellene athletes who wish to test themselves make their way across seas and mountains to Olympia, in the hilly northwestern corner of the Peloponnese known as Elis, to train with their competitors and take part in the famous procession that begins the festivities. It has been the tradition since the first Games that during the month of their celebration all warring between Hellenes is ceased, and enmities between cities are temporarily quashed. Nevertheless, Athenians and Spartans at the games mostly keep their distance from each other these days.

This year, the foundation stones have been laid for what will one day be a grand new Temple of Zeus, and many of those who traveled across the seas to be here cluster around that broad stone base and talk about it as if the temple already exists. Worshippers burn the bones and fat of animals there as offerings to Zeus, while their friends and families feast on the meat of the same animals in the flowering fields around the temples of old Olympia.

One of the Olympic officials, called *Judges-of-Hellenes*, dressed in long white robes to wield the apparent authority that comes with appearing archaic, steps up onto a large, wooden speaking platform at the center of the race track, surrounded by bright green garlands and symbols of Zeus Olympian, King of the Gods - eagles, bulls, and thunderbolts.

"Hellenic brothers from every corner of the watery road," he speaks in a voice that carries across the densely peopled stands, "welcome one and all to the seventy-eighth Olympic Games!"

Seated all around the large altar of Zeus, the eldest Judges sit with the local high priestess of Demeter, a beautiful and bountifully-bosomed middle-aged woman named Kallirhoe whose lively conversation often steals the Judges' attention away from the games.

The men filling the stands applaud with religious and tribal excitement, each city's people eager to see their own champions wreathed as greatest in the eyes of the King of Gods for the next four years.

Down on the fields and tracks, the most muscular and beautiful Hellenes prepare their naked bodies with a layer of olive oil.

"Let it be known, that while it is only Hellenic men who may partake in this holy contest, recently it has been shown by the noble King Alexander, first of his name of Makedon, that his people are in fact the descendents of sons of Herakles who journeyed from Argos, and not barbarians after all! And so, as fellow Hellenes, the Makedonians will henceforth be included in these games!"

"Welcome, barbarians!" a friendly Argive Hellene shouts from the stands.

Lion-skin caped but otherwise fully nude, in an attempt to resemble famed Herakles Protector-From-Evil, King Alexander of Makedon takes the moment to step up onto the platform with the herald and address the booing crowd, the shriveled lion head of his cape draped beside his own.

"Hellenic kinsmen! Are we not all brothers? Like many of you, we Makedonians are the sons of the monster-killer Herakles, and your beloved poet Pindar would like to deliver a new poem he has written about that very topic. Pindar, get up here and read your poem."

King Alexander brusquely gestures for the famous poet Pindar, standing nearby, to ascend onto the platform with him. Pindar is a well-known poet in the Hellenic world, and not afraid of public performance, but the way Alexander manhandles him clearly makes him uncomfortable as he begins to read his ode to the Hellenic ancestry of the Makedonian people.

Pindar, whose odes to victors at the Olympic Games are highly prized by those who can afford them, sings resignedly, "O mother of these golden-crowned games, Olympia, mistress of truth, where seers examine burnt offerings and test Zeus of the bright thunderbolt, to see if he has any word concerning mortal things, please remind us now of the many sons of Herakles, including those he left in ancient Argos, who then went north and founded that hilly country which we now call Makedon..."

The Hellenes in the audience variously boo the Makedonian or cheer with a polite sense of *xenia* - welcomeness to strangers. The two sentiments are about equal in the crowd of spectators after the vouchsafing of Pindar's poem.

Makedonians elsewhere within the crowds are showing off their wealth by paying with gold coins for items and services for which only a silver coin is expected. Word has spread quickly among the merchants, and many of the wandering ones have begun swarming the few competing Makedonians, groveling to serve them for their golden coins.

Meanwhile, at the footrace track, Kimon has stepped down from the stands and onto the grassy field with the other runners preparing to compete. He removes his tunic and hands it to one of his body slaves as another one pours a little bottle of olive oil onto his shoulders and spreads it down with her hands over his hard, curvaceous body.

All across the field, the oiling of the naked bodies of the strongest and most beautiful men of the Hellenic world serves the double purpose of preparing the athletes for their contest and showing off the forms of their bodies to each other and the crowd. Lusty men relish this part of the performance, and some shout out to Apollo about the beauty of the human form, while others whisper to each other about what the athlete's lovers must feel.

Beside Kimon, the Makedonian King Alexander walks up, his naked muscles already glistening with oil. The long-maned Makedonian pulls his hair back and ties it into a bun, showing off his biceps.

"Greetings, fellow Hellene," says Kimon with a nod to his competitor. "We welcome all those who worship Hellenic gods, and live a Hellenic life."

"I will feel at home once I've won a few of these contests," the king boasts, stretching his calves. He then smiles charmingly, forcing a reflective smile back from Kimon. "With whom am I competing, fellow Hellene?"

"Kimon of Athens."

"King Alexander of Makedonia."

The two nude men shake hands, then get back into stance to run.

"May the man Zeus loves most win," the king says.

"Where is Makedonia again?" Kimon asks, stonefacedly staring forward.

The king frowns, then says, "North."

"Do you have a city up there, or do you just live in the trees?"

King Alexander is just beginning to stutter his offense when the Judge-of-Hellenes drops his arm to start the race, and Kimon and the other runners dash away. The Makedonian king stumbles off after them in frustration.

Many fast footfalls but few actual moments later, Kimon reaches the finish line second behind another Athenian, a non-famous man, the other runners right behind them, King Alexander of Makedon amidst the middle of the pack.

The northern king approaches Kimon as he is accepting a cup of water from a nearby fan. "You Athenians certainly earn your reputation for cleverness," King Alexander says to Kimon, winded. "I won't be distracted the same way again, I assure you."

"Smart," Kimon says, nodding.

The two men shake hands again.

A white robed Judge-of-Hellenes walks up to the sturdy Athenian who won the race, with a woven olive circle for his head, many cheering Athenians amassing behind him.

"Ephesiax of Athens, winner of the stadion footrace!"

Kimon slaps his compatriot on his panting back and turns to Alexander. "I feel it's worth it at least to try, to test myself against other men before the gods. Anyway, when Athens wins, all Athenians win." Then he addresses Ephesiax and shouts, "All hail Ephesiax! Here, brother, let me buy you an ode from Pindar."

"My thanks, Kimon!" winded Ephesiax gasps, leaning on his knee. "I voted for you for General!"

"Then you helped defeat Persia."

Kimon offers the man a hand, and he and Ephesiax walk arm in arm off the field, toward the crowd gathered around the poet Pindar, their slaves following behind, carrying their clothing and oils.

In the stands, Perikles and Ephialtes sit together with their old teacher Damon and his friend the poet Simonides.

Damon says, "Kimon is wise not to win. He displays as much honor as the winner, yet does not have to carry the apparent hubris of glory. He is a formidable opponent for you, boys."

Perikles nods. "His courage and manliness are enough to sway the minds of most simple-hearted men who don't want to hear about the complexities of virtuous government."

Ephialtes sighs. "I would want to be his friend, or more, if it weren't for his politics. He is a likable and beautiful man."

Simonides leans across his friend Damon to address the younger men. "When a man is too strong to confront directly, that is when you go after his friends."

Ephialtes' near-constant smile wavers as he says, "I don't love how we are sounding here. Are we the heroes or the monsters?"

Damon says, "Strategizing your life is not monstrous, Ephialtes. Nor is using war metaphors. We are not talking about actually attacking the man, simply beating him in the battle of wits."

Perikles nods, "Battle of wits, I like the phrasing. You are too clever, Damon."

Damon admits, "I'm not the first to say it."

To Perikles and Ephialtes, he asks, "Have you heard about the Spartan Pausanias, and his ignoble end?"

Ephialtes nods grimly. "I've heard things I wouldn't want to repeat without having seen them myself."

Perikles says, "I heard of his end, yes."

"A dark one," Damon notes.

"Well I can tell you one thing I was there for, myself," Simonides says, leaning in close to the Athenian men so they can hear his rickety old voice. "Some years ago, before he left for Ionia, before the Second Persian War, I was in Sparta for one reason or another. I forget exactly why I was there. But I was invited by the kings, who at that time were old Zeuxidamos, and Leonidas' son's regent, Pasuanias. I was in their tent after a hunt, and we were all eating and drinking in peaceful silence for a while, after some earlier discussion about the habits of hares. And Pausanias just says to me, 'Ho, Wiseman, say something wise.'"

Ephialtes smiles and shakes his head with commiseration.

Simonides rolls his eyes. "So, I thought for a moment, and then I said, 'Remember that you are only human.'"

As Perikles and Ephialtes consider the brief bit of wisdom and nod approvingly, Simonides nods with them, gesturing as if to underscore the phrase's obvious wisdom.

"Hard for some to hear," Perikles notes slyly.

"Well," Simonides says, "the Spartan laughed at it, at the time, and cast it aside." As the three men return their attention to the footrace on the track below which is about to begin, Simonides casually adds, "He should have listened better."

The middle-aged Athenians' casual eyes are drawn by some commotion across the field.

Down beyond the race track, a crowd has gathered around a fight between wrestlers preparing for the no-holds-barred *pankration*. A single Spartan, who has just arrived in Olympia, has begun shouting to the athletes to test themselves in one-on-one unarmed combat against him. Already, very quickly, he has incapacitated two young takers. As the wounded drag themselves away from him, the raging man continues to bellow at all those in sight, "I am just one Spartan! I am just one Spartan!"

The whitest-haired of the Judges-of-Hellenes who run the Olympic Games arrives through the watching crowd, flanked by several rod-bearers and whip-holders, who point out the offending man to the trainers of the Spartan competitors who are not far behind them.

The Spartan trainers move in to contain their man before he gets them all kicked out of the holy games. The mad Spartan's compatriots grapple him to the grass as the games' official whip-bearers lash them all.

> "FIFTY DAYS AFTER THE SUMMER SOLSTICE
> IS THE RIGHT TIME FOR MEN TO GO SAILING,
> WHEN THE SEASON OF DREADFUL HEAT IS DONE.
> WHEN WINDS ARE STEADY, THE SEA IS HARMLESS."
> Hesiod, *Works and Days*

Ψ

Elpinike participates in the culminating autumn rites of the Mysteries of Eleusis

"Come all you whose souls are unpolluted by evil, all you who live a righteous life, whose hands and hearts are pure, and whose voice can be understood! Welcome to the Mysteries! Anyone whose hands are soiled by crime, or mind spoiled by evil, or whose voice is unintelligible, begone now! Polluted people must not participate here!"

"Remember - *mystic* means you shut up about it. You must be silent throughout the revelation of the Mysteries, and you must never speak to the uninitiated about what you have seen or heard here."

White-robed mystic initiates of the Mystery of Eleusis begin their march in a long line one by one slowly out through the Sacred Gate of Athens and along the Sacred Path along the river Eridanos to the coast and northward along it to Eleusis. Musicians and dancers line the path, performing dances sacred to Demeter Goddess of Furrows and Shoots.

"Iacche! Iacche!" That single shout rises everywhere like a cloud.

Elpinike, hidden within the diaphanous white robe and veil which each mystic must wear, walks in anonymity near the middle of the line.

Her husband Kallias, torchbearer of this famous ceremony, smiles to her when she passes him. He wears his purple robe and a myrtle crown, signifiers of his important role. All those servicing the ritual wear circlets of myrtle tonight.

At the far back of the procession is the ritual cart pulled by two huge oxen, carrying in it the thickly veiled form of the mystery god Iacchos, while dancers along the side of the procession who have already been initiated in years past shout "Iacche!" to the passing covered god.

The dusk breeze is warm; summer is ending. Over the Gulf of Saron and the Peloponnese to the west, the setting Sun reddens the sky.

Not far down the Sacred Path, the line of mystics file past a famous house surrounded by flourishing fig trees.

A priestess stationed there explains to those passing, "At this house, Phytalos gave our lady Demeter sanctuary during her search for her lost daughter. And in gratitude for his care and kindness, Demeter gave to Phytalos the secret of the cultivation of the fig! And here were grown the world's first figs!"

The initiates bow to the priestess and the fig tree house as they pass. Musicians following alongside the march play flourishes about figs and fig-wasps on their flutes and lyres.

"Hail, Demeter, and this, the first fig tree, planted by the very hand of Phytalos!"

The priestess of Demeter grabs one thick branch of the wide-trunked fig tree and shakes it, so that its figs rustle within its leaves.

The elderly man and woman who live now in Phytalos' famous old house proudly stand in their doorway and bow and wave to the passing initiates, pointing to figs on the ground as available for those who want them and pointing out to avoid the one which has been claimed already by a wasp, gesturing broadly instead of speaking since there are often strangers from far corners of the world participating, as even those who have become enslaved are allowed to participate in this ritual.

Since he is an official of the ceremony as torchbearer, no one bothers Kallias when he lingers to walk beside his wife instead of keeping the careful distance between the torchbearers behind and ahead of him as he ought to.

Ahead, the leaders of the procession shout, "Hail Demeter!" The prayer spreads back along the line, with the implication that all are to join in.

Elpinike speaks only loud enough for herself to hear her own voice, and for others to see her lips moving. "Hail, Demeter."

"Isn't this beautiful?" Kallias says to his wife, looking left, out over the nighttime sea. "I think this is my favorite part. It's always so beautiful at dusk this time of year, and to get the opportunity to walk this path, with all these people, and the warmth of the fire, just like Demeter did, it always just fills me with such a wonderful feeling. Don't you feel that, my darling?"

Elpinike ignores Kallias.

A passing priestess garlanded in wheat sheafs hands Elpinike a circular seed cake shaped to resemble a bull with little horns. "Ox cake," the woman says as she is handing them out. "Eat slow; there's poppy in it."

A younger woman, playing the part of Demeter's light-hearted maid Iambe, flits past, flashing her breasts and laughing.

"People are complaining that it's dark ahead," someone whispers loud enough that Kallias can hear it, and it reminds him of his duties.

"I should rush ahead," he tells Elpinike, with an apologetic smile. He blows her the tiniest of kisses and then takes his torch further ahead in line, where they are immediately thankful for his presence.

Patiently, Elpinike follows the line, the lapping black waves of the Gulf of Saron to her left, until the lights of Eleusis grow into the city surrounding her.

The walled sanctuary of Eleusis is built around the huge Initiation Hall called the Telesterion. A set of stone tablets laid out around the entrance to the temple list the foods which initiates entering must not have in their bodies: crab, mullet, whistlefish, chicken, pigeon, beans, wheat, pomegranate.

"Those mystics who are to be initiated tonight, come and cover your eyes to begin your course."

The high priest of Demeter and Kallias the torchbearer stand together at the entrance of the Telesterion, while several young mystagogues, guides who have already been initiated and now wear myrtle crowns as part of the ceremony, approach each initiate and wrap a heavy white blindfold around their eyes beneath their white veil.

Elpinike approaches and receives the wrap, her world goes dark, and she begins to be guided by a small female hand in her hand.

First, she is led into the cool interior of the Telesterion. She feels and hears the presence of numerous quiet fellow initiates all breathing nervously and shuffling their shoes, but otherwise remaining silent as commanded. After a while of waiting, she is approached, and crowned gently with a ring of myrtle.

An elderly voice creaks, "We banish you, profane ones! Away from here, all you atheists! Stay far, any who is yet unfreed from evil thought! Any of you found to have lingered here unwelcome welcome death."

Elpinike feels her white mystic robe grabbed and pulled up and away from her. Only momentarily she instinctively grasps back to keep it on, but she thinks quickly and refrains, allowing her garment and veil to be removed. Only her blindfold remains. The sounds surrounding her assure that the same is happening to all the initiates. In a few moments, the same hands return to dress her again in a light fur wrap which barely covers her shoulders and torso.

Carefully Elpinike looks downward past her blindfold, and sees that her naked body has been wrapped in a soft spotted doe skin.

Theatrical wailings rise in the air from multiple voices all performing together, in a way that at once mimics natural cries while also pushing them into strange and unsettling directions with little flourishes of wildness.

She is pushed forward by several hands. She can feel that she is close to many other bodies. Hands push and slap and grasp at her. She is slapped across the face, her hair is pulled. The slap loosens the blindfold.

All around her, the dark and light seem preternaturally mixed, with shadows flitting in and out of flame and ebbing far and near with eerie speed. Right beside her, between herself and another woman's body, a transparent screen suddenly bursts up from the floor, pulled upward from above by a line, painted with an unearthly image of some monster from Tartaros the likes of which Elpinike has never imagined. Another darts up further ahead, between two other mystics. Men and women all around her groan and scream with fear and delight.

"This is the realm of Tartaros!" a voice booms, as more sounds of thunder emanate beyond it. "These are the souls of the dead, of those who are condemned to a dusty world of darkness and regret! This is the anguish of those who have lost the path to gardens of delight!"

Far ahead, lit from behind by a fire, the form of a nude man is strapped arms and legs wide to a slowly spinning wheel, while women beside and before him whip at his body with branches. Presumably this is meant to be Ixion, whose punishment in Tartaros is described this way.

Elpinike is hardly in one spot long enough to take in any one sight. Those putting on this performance push and throw her body this way and that, to the ground and back up, and on through the crowd of other mystics so that each one can see each corner of the room-wide performance.

Three black snarling dogs gnash just out of reach out from the shadows of one corner, held fast by their black-robed trainer so that nearly all that is visible is three sets of flashing white teeth and eyes in the darkness. "Kerberos, three-headed guard dog of the kingdom of Haides! Here to tear apart any who tries to leave the land of death!"

There, shoulder deep in a pool with grape vines draped just out of reach of his stretching neck, would seem to be Tantalos. And there, struggling under the mimed weight of a huge crag of stone which the temple would seem to have been built around, must be Sisyphos. And here, frustratedly weaving a rope of straw while a donkey behind him gnaws at what he has made, is old Oknos. The theater of the famously tortured.

Just as Elpinike has made one round of the presentations barely visible amid the fire-dancing shadows and thrashing of guiding, dancing bodies around her, suddenly the light changes, shadow-makers are moved and bronze mirrors are shifted to reflect extra light from the fires, and a door opens at the far end of the room with even more bright firelight flashing out from within, as the clear figure of Demeter, sheafed in wheat, carrying a tall wide-mouthed torch, appears and slowly, regally enters the room. All the scurrying dancers-as-the-tormented dip out of sight and hasten an exit, leaving the mystics suddenly at ease and alone with the priestess-as-Demeter.

"It is I, Demeter," she declares in sonorous voice, "who lightens and pleases the hearts of mortal men and women. Listen now, and hear my guidance, mortal souls. The land of life, where all of us are now, for all but a lucky few it is a great succession of errors and loss, painful wanderings, and confused disappointments."

Elpinike hears this and wonders what other people's lives must be like. She feels lucky.

"But when you leave this life, however that might be, you will be able to pass into green meadows with the sweetest breezes, where beautiful concerts and brilliant discourses can be heard, and heavenly visions unlike any on Earth. It is there that men and women, with this initiation, will finally have true freedom, restored to being masters of themselves, beholden to no other mortal, crowned in august myrtle. You will be able to hold conversations with the most just and wise men and women who have lived before you, and in future days those who lived after you. Or..."

And on her utterance of "or" the person making the thunder sound with the sheet of bronze slightly rumbles it, and shadow-makers shift the firelight.

"Or, you can be among the multitude of uninitiated, massed with profane barbarians, ever plunged and sinking in the mire of purest darkness."

A man dressed in ancient-looking garb, presumably Triptolemos, who was first taught agriculture here at Eleusis by Demeter herself, steps forward pushing a wooden cart with a large inscribed stone on it.

"These are the answers you must give to Persephone when you meet her after death, to be welcomed among the initiated souls," Demeter declares, gesturing to the stone with her wheat bundle. "Read them here, and remember. For it is I, Demeter, who gave to men the magic of the plow, and fruit, and law."

All around, the previously tormented dancers are now dressed in ancient tunics of Eleusis just like the man playing Triptolemos, as they carry in the body of a mountain ibex with long horns and place it onto a stone altar opposite the doors. The ibex trails blood all the way to the altar, still in its last breaths and heartbeats, until it is placed into one of the fires which had been used for light earlier in the performance. The creature jerks one last time, then slumps just as its body begins to burn.

The man playing Triptolemos here steps forward only long enough to invoke his three famous maxims, "Respect your parents. Produce fruits for the gods. Spare the animals."

The priestess-as-Demeter stands before the stone altar where the ibex's body smolders and burns. This is a rare ritual called a *holokaust* - meaning that the entirety of the sacrifice will go to the gods, burned in whole.

Demeter raises her hands high as she begins to sing, and the chorus of priests behind her joins in. "O Haides, King of the Dead, please open your arms for this mortal creature which we are sending your way, through the Underworld doorway of flickering fire."

Flames tenderly unweave the body into charcoal and smoke.

Ω

Themistokles arrives at Persepolis

The Persian Royal Road flows unbroken like a river of stone, all the way from Sardis in Lydia on its western end, through the cliff cities of Kappadokia, and the ruins of old Urartu, past the many road towns of broad Media, finally into the distant interior of Persia, past Darieos' old summer capital at Susa and along its secret easternmost track to the winter capital of Xerxes - that legend of imperial luxury on Hellenic lips, the City of the Persians - *Persepolis*.

During the long days along the way, Themistokles' Persian escorts try to point out various buildings and monuments of significance to them, but being unable to read his escorts' wedge language *Cuneiform*, Themistokles finds they all blend in his mind - a famously complicated knot between two pillars in Gordion, a huge three-headed stone bird in Urartu, a man-sized obsidian finger in Susa. The days of his month on the road run together, not least due to his remorse at leaving his homeland.

Where the Royal Road finally ends, the palaces of Persepolis are built atop a stone terrace beneath a backdrop of high brown cliffs.

Before one ascends the symmetrical double stairway leading up to the terrace, the buildings up there loom like cloud castles. Ascending the stairs, the wall beside Themistokles is carved in relief with images of powerful men of all different sorts carrying what appear to be the fruits of their lands. At the top of the stairway and blocking entrance to the plateau of palaces is the Gate of All Nations, a tall, three-walled structure held up by four huge columns and guarded by two colossal bull statues flanked by two equally large *lamassus* - winged lion bodies with human heads. The stone beasts wait atop the stairs in silent steadfastness. The huge statues at first startle Themistokles, as he has heard stories of monsters of many sorts but has never seen ones quite like these.

The Persian escorts mock his reaction and reassure him, "You only need fear the lamassu if you mean evil to the King. Keep moving." They are treating him as a dignitary, but barely. Disdain seethes beneath each polite word, for all here also know the name Themistokles as the admiral who sank their great armada.

As big-bearded Themistokles is gawking at the lammasu, a sturdy Persian man in padded armor, ornately embroidered with the images of two lammasu on either side of his chest, approaches from the shadows with the cold look of master written upon his face.

"Artabanos," the head of the escort says to Themistokles, gesturing to the man. "Commander of Xerxes' armies; Prince of Hyrkania. General, this is Themistokles, the Hellene who led their navy at Athens."

"They call you the King of the Democrats," Artabanos says, standing very close to Themistokles. "Welcome to the City of the Persians."

Themistokles nods, looking around. "Your architecture is beautiful, and very impressive. I saw walking up these stairs the images of all the different sorts of men whom Persia no doubt yoked into building it all."

"You mistake the images for what they might mean in your own society, Hellene," Artabanos corrects. "It is you who keep men yoked. The King of Kings of Persia is no master of slave-kings. Other kings rule their own lands, and their people come to Persia willingly, gratefully, thankful that such a worldwide organizational power exists to maintain international peace. All those men you saw on the walls of the stairs were bringing tribute to the King of Kings, not supplication. You saw love, not fear."

Themistokles nods, shrugging. He is trying to be patient, and open to the world he is about to join.

Artabanos asks, "On your way here you surely stopped at Susa, our old capital. There, I wonder, did your escort show you the great Pillar of Hammurabi?"

Themistokles nods, glancing back at his escorts. "We saw many strange and impressive things," he says. "Remind me which pillar that was."

"The finger," his lead escort sighs.

"O yes, the big stone finger!" Themistokles nods, turning back to Artabanos and holding up his index finger. "Most impressive, taller than a man. It was a large, well sculpted finger."

Artabanos begins to pace the small, shaded space between the giant lamassu, the shafts of light from the doorways rising and falling across his body as he moves through their bent beams.

"They may not have explained to you that pillar's full significance. That was the original pillar of the Law Codes of the ancient Babylonian king Hammurabi. The first king to write down in stone the laws which would rule his people. An eye for an eye, and a tooth for a tooth."

"A finger for a finger," Themistokles adds as a joke, straight-faced.

Artabanos continues, "It stood in Babylon for a thousand years before the Elamites sacked the city and took the Finger of Hammurabi into the hills. But of course when King Kyros the Persian swept through all lands, he united Babylon and Susa under one ruler, and now all those across Persia may travel freely to see that most ancient monument of the rule of Law, as peaceful visitors."

Themistokles nods. "We write down our laws on stones, too."

"Your laws which might change one year to the next?" Artabanos scoffs. "The gods can see you will run out of stone before long."

"We have good quarries, lots of stone," Themistokles disagrees. "Also, we've learned to write very, very small."

"I only mentioned Hammurabi's laws to underscore our own modern version which you see here." Artabanos walks to the central wall of the Gate of All Nations, and holds his ram-skull lamp up under a big iron slab full of inscribed Cuneiform script.

"Here you see our own Persian Law Tablet - inscribed for eternity in iron instead of stone. Can you read Cuneiform?"

Themistokles shakes his head 'no'.

"Of course I shouldn't expect a barbarian from the hinterlands of civilization to understand the oldest script of man. If you could read you would have known that the Finger of Hammurabi was more than a mere finger. But now I know what to expect you *not* to know. What this inscription tells you is that this is the law which was written by Kyros. It tells you that men of every land, of every sort of lifestyle, of any preference for worship, are all protected equally in the lands ruled by the King of Kings, and not even a King beneath him may take these protections from their people. This is the power of the King of Kings."

Artabanos glares at Themistokles as if waiting for him to fall to his knees in realization of the glory of the Persian laws. But Themistokles just smirks at him defensively, as if unimpressed.

"I see it," Themistokles says.

"Even though our actual religion's original texts are written in gold ink upon the leathered skin of the first men," Artabanos says, unrolling a scroll for Themistokles to see, which by all visual cues could believably be exactly what he has just described, its gold words on dark leather glinting in the torchlight, "nevertheless we do not threaten the lifestyles of citizens who choose to worship lesser gods."

"My own land's gods are too clever to chain themselves to eternal oaths in golden words," Themistokles says, admiring the beauty of the cuneiform marks in literal gold. He then looks up to Artabanos' glare and says, "My own land's gods are agile and wise, and can dodge even golden traps. They thus keep themselves from being tied down to metal words by not making promises they can't hold up. Even Prometheos got freed."

"Yes, I've heard your sanctuary at Delphi has three sacred sayings, and one is something about an oath being madness. Seems like the ethos of a culture of liars and cheaters, to me," Artabanos growls.

"You're not lying if you don't lie," Themistokles says with an impish half-grin, knowing that Artabanos knows that Themistokles tricked Xerxes into the infamous sea battle at Salamis. "Words can be slippery things, with the oil of wisdom and logic."

"Yes, I've also heard how you use your oils to get slippery, too. In war as in love, eh, Hellene? Perhaps slippery is another good word to describe the Hellenic ethos. You don't have religious texts which lay out your morals and ethics with clarity?" Artabanos asks.

"Not permanent ones," Themistokles replies lightly. "We have songs, stories, but I don't think any of us really think one mortal man's choice of words could truly limit let alone even describe the will of any god."

Artabanos seethes, "What every barbarian, for their ignorance, can never understand - and I have seen it hundreds of times from people of every land we conquer - all barbarians make the same claims of virtue for their lawlessness, referencing some half-thought notion of their 'freedom'. Ignorance can never understand how boringly consistent it is. If you had access to all the knowledge of the ages, at the very least by first simply reading and writing Cuneiform script, you might begin to have some inkling of what I'm even talking about. But your ignorance blinds you. Let's move along."

As soon as the great door of the Gate of All Nations begins to open, Themistokles glimpses behind it the colossal *Apadana* across a wide plaza. Its colors are bright, but foreign to Themistokles' eye; the blues are paler, and the reds darker, than the dyes they use most commonly for painting buildings in Hellas, just like the tastes of familiar things have been strange to his tongue the deeper into Persia he has traveled.

Artabanos leads the way, Themistokles following, with a Ψ of scimitar-wielding Persian guards spread out behind him like geese, as they cross the wide plaza between the many Persian palaces, toward the biggest building of them all, perhaps the biggest in the world from what Themistokles has heard - the Apadana.

As he and Artabanos begin to cross the plaza, it becomes clear that the building is even farther away than it had at first appeared, the plaza even wider, and the Apadana's scale larger. This illusion makes the building seem to grow as they walk toward it, and the distance to it seems continually to increase.

The columns supporting its entryway are at least four times as tall as any Themistokles has seen before, and he would absolutely have believed that they had been built by gods, or giants at least, if the Persians all around the world were not so proud to assert that only their artisans could have built the Apadana. As he beholds it, on the approach, its foreign colors occasionally obscured by dissipating dust devils riding down the side of the mountain cliffs behind it, Themistokles almost doesn't notice the gathering crowd of courtiers, men born from earth of every shade, women side by side who to Themistokles' narrow eye could not look more different, who all gawk at him and whisper to each other as the Hellenic hero is led past.

Walking up the wide front steps of the Apadana, its columns become colossal, looming down upon Themistokles like he has always imagined the ancient titan Atlas might appear while holding up the Sky.

The fineness of garb and adornments of the courtiers rapidly increases in splendor with proximity to the Apadana, such that those standing on its porch and just inside its enormous gold front doors actually appear to be having difficulty standing under the weight of so much metal and jewel; even the cloth in these people's tunics is woven through with threads of gold.

The chatter of the twenty to thirty top-tier courtiers inside the Apadana all stops and echoes reverberating for several seconds when Themistokles and Artabanos first enter the space.

Across a room broader than the whole Athenian Agora, on a throne of solid gold edged with bright blue lapis, small at first across the expansive space, sits the man who has haunted Themistokles' mind for decades - the Persian King of Kings, Xerxes. Themistokles last saw the King of Kings perched atop a similarly ornate but traveling-sized golden throne on his own Attikan shore, from a ship, as their armadas clashed in that snake-wide waterway between Athens and Salamis. He has not seen him since winning that battle; Xerxes escaped and was not in Hellas for the final land battles.

Artabanos leads Themistokles slowly across the wide Apadana, toward the throne of Xerxes. The Persian courtiers make no sound as he passes, but watch him from between inked eyelids.

Though he wears a robe embroidered with some of the most beautiful red and purple fire and birds Themistokles has ever seen, up close Xerxes becomes just a man. Themistokles looks for the lines on his face, and reminds himself that each of those lines is a mortal concern.

Beside him, Artabanos kicks at one of Themistokles' feet, trying to get him to kneel, and Themistokles takes the cue to do so, ignoring the insulting manner in which it was communicated.

Kneeling, Themistokles smiles at Xerxes.

Xerxes eyes Themistokles with obscure seriousness, clutching an iron sphere in one hand.

"You've traveled far, Hellene," Xerxes says, in strongly-accented Hellenic. "From enemy to friend is a long and arduous path with many steps and many stops. You have only one more step, before I call you ally. Come here and kiss my royal ring, then prostrate yourself before your lord."

Themistokles stares silently, stone faced, for what feels like far too long, but it turns out to have only been a second or two, before he stands, crosses the space between them, kneels at Xerxes' feet and kisses the outstretched fingers of his old mortal enemy. Then he moves back and puts his arms and face to the floor for what feels like too brief a moment, but it is as long as he can stand to do so. He rises to his feet, takes another step back, and looks back up at Xerxes with the same confidence as before, if no smile.

The big-bearded Hellene clears his throat then, and carefully says, "I have traveled far, along your impressive Royal Road all the way from Lydia, and seen many beautiful Persian buildings, but nothing in the world is as beautiful and impressive as your Apadana here."

Xerxes smiles, and the courtiers all around him titter about the deference this famous Hellenic general, destroyer of the Persian fleet, seems to be giving to their great leader.

Bold-faced Themistokles continues, "Our temples at Athens were not quite as impressive, but they were beautiful also, truly beloved by the gods. And all I can think as I stand in this structure is - I hope that if a Hellenic army were to find their way along that long road to these temples, these magnificent works of men and gods - and we Hellenes have found that the gods do love symmetry, both in objects and animals *and in events* - but I think in such an event those hypothetical Hellenes wouldn't just burn these beautiful buildings impiously to the ground."

Stern-faced Artabanos snaps a hard glare in his direction, shocked by what seems like insolence.

Distant-eyed Xerxes raps his iron ball against a sparking stone on the arm of his throne to quiet the murmuring of the courtiers, and barks haughtily, "That I would like to see!"

The lamps flicker and the shadows lurch as Xerxes' Persian courtiers filling the Apadana's many-columned space all laugh, and it echoes.

ATHENS

ATHENS

4

APOLLO FAR-SHOOTER

> "SHE, LIKE THAT *FINEST* APPLE,
> RIPENED HIGHEST ON THE TREE,
> WHERE MEN'S HANDS COULDN'T REACH
> SO THEY PRETENDED TO FORGET."
> Sappho, Mytilenean Poet

A

Aoide learns, and wonders

Cloud shadows dance across the olive trees down in the valley of Delphi.
    Summers come and go alike, and merge in the simplicity of idyll.
    "What should you think when you encounter an unknown word?"
    Aoide, now sixteen years old, sits at the edge of the group, watching the workers in the olive rows below, as the poetry teacher gives a lesson primarily intended for the younger girls. She is here to help with the younger girls' guidance, but mostly ignores the lesson, bored by everything lately. While others talk she builds and dismisses little songs in her mind, never to be heard, only intermittently listening to the words of the others.
    The young women, gathered on a grassy slope just downhill from the village, overlooking unending rows of olive trees in the valley below, all look to each other, unsure quite what the old priestess might be wanting as an answer. Sunlight warmly falls, invisibly making all things visible.
    "What I mean," creaky old Kliko explains, "is - how do you go about unpacking an unknown word to best determine what it might mean?"
    "Well," one girl proposes, "whether or not it rhymes with words you know?"
    The priestess sways her head, and says, "Do its rhymes affect the meaning of a word, really?"
    "It affects what other words you might use it around," the girl suggests.
    Wrinkled old Kliko shakes her head.

"Words have parts," Aoide interjects, "like anything - like people, and animals, and flowers. When you see a new animal, you look at its parts. Does it have paws, or hooves, or feet? Does it have wings, or hands, or four legs? So, words have parts as well, which indicate parts of the meaning."

The younger girls all give Aoide quizzical looks, confused.

"Aoide is right, of course," the older priestess says. "Words are not magical things, but natural things, like plants and animals. Now there are two different types of words, and there are two different forms that each can take. Who can name the two types?"

"Hellenic and Barbarian?" one girl guesses.

"Very good! And what are the two forms?"

"Spoken and written," another girl sighs, finding it obvious.

"Exactly. These spoken words dissipate, as you can hear, for once I finish speaking them, they ring only in your mind, and no longer in the air. But *these words*," the priestess says emphatically, pointing to the Hellenic letters inscribed upon the stone wall beside her, covered by writing, "*these words* last *forever*, such that even after men have all died and the gods have chosen some other sort of game to play with the cosmos, these words written by men will remain on this stone, as temples to today's thoughts. It has been said, of old, that a picture is worth a thousand words; but the true meaning hidden within those words is that a glyph - a *written* word - is worth a thousand utterances, *spoken* words. So that, my dears, is why we have you copy old works."

Aoide speaks up, "It certainly *is* true, though, that rhyme and melody affect your words. Even written words, for if there is a melody or rhyme to the words themselves it will be captured in the glyphs just as much as the meaning, and when the reader hears the words in their mind their rhyme or rhythm will retain just as much power as it was born with. Rhyme, rhythm, and melodiousness can be used like magic, to empower words in a wide variety of ways - to make them unignorable, or more welcome to the mind, or immediately distasteful to the mind."

Kliko frowns at Aoide. "Yes, well..."

Aoide says, turning to the smaller girls and away from the priestess, "You know, there's a story I was told when I was young, and being taught my first letters. It was a warning! Do you know where the first letters came from?"

The little girls shake their heads, entranced by Aoide's young boldness and ability to command the moment better than the priestess.

"Letters were first invented by an Aigyptian. I don't remember his name, but he was an advisor to the ancient Aigyptian king Thaumos, long ago. And he came to the king with his new invention - letters! Glyphs which each represented an idea or a sound. And which could glow with information for any who learned the secret magical formulas of the glyphs. At first King Thaumos was overjoyed at the power of the invention! But the more he thought about it, he became dismayed, and he warned his clever advisor that this new magic might have a secret curse hidden in it, as the king described imagining a future in which men and women no longer held ideas in their minds and memories, but stored them all in glyphs which they had to access in order to know anything, and he could see people counting on these glyphs more and more and using their own minds less and less, until no one was able to commit anything to memory anymore, or just the habit had died out. So he warned the advisor only to share his secret with those who he felt could withstand the curse of the letters!"

The girls listen enrapt, as if being told a horror story.

"But of course, the secret of writing was too powerful, and it escaped its bounds and spread across the world, to be adapted to all the languages of the world. Now even Skythians use letters. And no one keeps the whole *Iliad* in their mind anymore, because they can read it."

Kliko clears hear throat in an attempt to regain the moment.

Then, unconnected, Aoide says, "I was just thinking this, though: what if Helios is an arrow, not a chariot?" while looking up at its white circle behind the grey clouds of an overcast summer day.

"It is Helios' fiery chariot," retorts dry old Kliko. "What would make you think otherwise?"

"Well, we *call it* Helios. And so we imagine it is this god, or his chariot. But I was just remembering the chariots I've actually seen, and how rarely they travel in a continuously straight line, even with the best drivers. The sun, however, seems to never waver in its path, but travels more like something falling or fired. And it appears to be a circle, not the shape of a chariot."

"No one can really see the Sun Chariot, for it burns the eyes to look upon," Kliko retorts. "To think you have gauged it properly with your eye is folly. What you are seeing is the mask of imperceivability which keeps the gods from being really seen like mortal things."

"But right now, I can see it as through a veil, with the cloud cover," Aoide replies, looking up. "You see, it appears to be a perfect circle."

"That's enough, Aoide," old craggy-faced Kliko snaps. She wields her whip while looking away, but sending her meanness toward Aoide. "There is a reason I have named my whip *Hubris*."

For a few quiet moments, as the cicadas sing of the summer heat, the other girls quietly continue copying ancient texts onto newer, less-rotten goatskins, ignoring the awkward vibe which developed between the teacher and her assistant.

Aoide keeps thinking about the Sun, looking up at it with one squinted eye, and the priestess notices her.

"It is much higher up in the sky than it seems, I imagine," creaky old Kliko adds after several moments of silence. "That is why it appears to move so slowly. No doubt the sky is even broader than the Earth, which is unbelievably broad. After all, the Earth is flat, while the Sky is a curved dome. A man can travel for a year and not reach the edge of the Earth. And yet Helios' chariot crosses that space in the span of a day, every day. Now have you ever seen an earthly chariot travel at that kind of speed?"

"No, I haven't," Aoide admits. "It is hard to imagine."

"Yes, well, godly things are not exactly like mortal things. We use mortal terms in an attempt to describe godly things."

Aoide and the younger girls sit quietly for just a short while longer, as a welcome breeze rustles the grass around them, but after some quiet thought she speaks up again.

Then another girl says, "But Apollo *is* an archer, isn't he? So it would make a certain sense. Perhaps an arrow would be a better metaphor."

One of the younger priestesses, a girl of ten or eleven, smiles at the thought, and holds her hand in front of her eyes to look up at the Sun.

"Aoide, you must supplicate yourself," Kliko the elder priestess snaps, turning to face Aoide in eye contact. "You must ask for Apollo's forgiveness. Shining Apollo is an archer, yes, but he is also the god of knowledge, and it is known to us that the sun is not simply some arrow. It is the brilliant golden chariot of Helios, son of Hyperion. In front of the young ones, Aoide, really."

As if on cue, the great Sun Helios emerges warmly from cloud cover for a minute, with all his bright heat.

Aoide closes her eyes, dwells within the sunlight's warmth upon her skin, and begins reciting the Homeric hymn to Apollo that she has known since she was small.

> *O Apollo far-shooter, how shall I now sing of you,*
> * you who are in all ways worthy of song?*
> *For everywhere, O Artemis' brightly shining twin,*
> * every song sung by lips falls upon you...*

As she sings, Aoide looks up at the Sun, trying hard to push through the fire its circle creates within her eyes, wanting in a fleeting fit of teen-aged hubris to see whether it really was a chariot or a circle as she has heard. For a few moments of startling, blinding awe, she keeps her eyes on the hot Sun and sees a pure circle.

Quickly, she sees nothing more. Blackness and a circle.

Aoide shouts out and looks away, holding her eyes shut with her fingers, but all she can see is the blackness and the circle.

She feels Kliko's big form grab her as she is falling, suddenly overcome with dizziness and a throbbing behind her eyes. The other girls start to squeal with concern when Aoide falls.

"Foolish girl, did you stare at the Sun?" old Kliko chides as she holds her cool hand over Aoide's eyes and cradles her body in her lap, sitting on the grass. "You know Apollo doesn't let us mortals see the forms of the gods. Haven't you been told not to look directly at them?"

Ever so gradually, her sight slowly returns out of the shadows.

But the circle, now black, never leaves.

Even when she closes her eyes, even when she sleeps, everything else Aoide sees is occluded and centered around the perfect black circle.

ATHENS

B

Ephialtes prepares to head east with the fleet, with Kimon, both generals

Perikles and Ephialtes embrace, waiting together at the Piraeus docks as Ephialtes is preparing to board with the outgoing fleet headed east.

Perikles says with a mask of middle-aged seriousness, "General," making Ephialtes blush.

It is Ephialtes' first year in that highest military office, voted in by his tribe and the gods this summer. He and nine other men will be this year's Generals, including Kimon, who has held the office many times before.

On the boat already, rugged Kimon is ordering rowers into their correct positions while simultaneously overseeing the addition of extended planking to the decks to allow for more hoplite marines to board each ship.

Like it felt in the days before the Battle of Salamis, the docks are loud with the rowdy voices and metal clatter of men preparing for war.

"By Zeus, I feel like I'm headed off to besiege Troi," Ephialtes groans, looking down along the row of triremes readying to embark.

"You'll be home before ten years, I'm sure of it," Perikles says with a little laugh.

"Or, if Hera finds some reason to hate me as she did Odysseos, it could be twenty," Ephialtes snorts. He adds, half-jokingly, to the wind, "Praise be to Hera, kindest of the women!"

Perikles tells Ephialtes, "Be brave, my friend, but also be safe."

"At least I won't be rowing this hulk. You may have the harder task, moving minds here in the city. I think we've got the votes for our plan, but these things constantly fluctuate. You must keep the people in favor of the new temples."

Perikles nods, picturing the chaotic Assembly packed with men all looking at him impatiently. Even going to the Pnyx for Assembly is difficult enough for Perikles, but he dreads the idea of speaking there.

"One more thing, Perikles. While I'm away, I want you to decide upon the artist for Athena. These sorts of tasks should go to men who know what they're talking about, and when it comes to art, I simply don't. But you clearly do. You have great taste, and you know great people. Have a few people do some miniature mock-ups for you or whatever it takes to make a decision. But we should know who we'll be using before the vote."

Perikles nods again, this time catching Ephialtes' eyes. "Okay. I know just whom to ask, to begin."

"Lysimachos' sculptor friend?"

Perikles nods, smiling. "He knows all the other sculptors, and he has the language to talk about sophisticated ideas, which is not true of all stoneworkers."

"You know what you're doing," Ephialtes nods, slapping his friend on the arm and lifting his bag of belongings over his shoulder. "I will burn some creature's bones for your success. Be well, Perikles. You are my most trusted ally."

Perikles smiles to his friend, then notices just past him Kimon looking in their direction as he organizes the adding of seating planks to the trireme. When Perikles sees him watching them, Kimon looks away.

"Be careful around Kimon," Perikles remarks cautiously. "You never know what men of war will be capable of. Or, perhaps better said - you *do* know what men of war are capable of."

Ephialtes just looks over his shoulder at the soldiers, then nods grimly. "I have a shield of eyes upon me," Ephialtes sighs.

"And the shield of your office, yes," Perikles nods. "I'm sure you'll be fine. Sea-legs soon."

Two long-bearded old fishermen walking past behind Perikles bump into him as he is stepping backward, and one of them gruffly shouts, "Mind your steps, sea-onion's son!"

As Ephialtes steps onto the military trireme's deck, Kimon turns to him and shakes his hand, the eyes of all the soldiers watching for the energy that occurs between the two leaders. Ephialtes smiles and shakes Kimon's hand long enough to pull a rare forced smile from the usually stalwart Oligarch.

Meanwhile, Perikles spots a Qarthaginian vessel just pulling in further down the row of docks, and onboard, standing at the prow like a figurehead, is a familiar face which brings a smile to Perikles' own face.

Behind that figure on the distant prow, the Qarthaginian captain of that ship steps up and heralds to the crowds at Piraeus, "Returning from distant Syrakous, Athens' most famous son, Aischylos!"

Some among the dockside crowds cheer like an audience at the theater.

Γ

Aischylos returns to Athens

"Aischylos is back! Sophokles, Sophokles, Sophokles, Sophokles!"

One of the young acolyte actors, a little boy of barely ten, runs out from the crowd shouting Sophokles' name.

"What is it, boy?" Sophokles barks as the boy crashes into him.

"Aischylos is back from the west!" the boy bellows. "He was on a boat at the harbor that's docking just now!"

"Are you sure it was Aischylos the playwright? Not some nobody of the same name, or someone being called 'Aischylos' in mockery?"

"He was heralded by the boat's captain!" the boy shouts.

"Keep practicing your voice; now go on," Sophokles says, pushing the boy off him and sending him running. He looks to his handsome new chorus leader, Teleklon, with a suspicious side-eye. "If Aischylos has returned, then he thinks he has something great to show."

Teleklon shrugs. "As a fan of all poetry, I'm excited by the notion."

Sophokles throws a braided flower stem at Teleklon, saying, "You must hate Aischylos, if you love me."

Teleklon laughs at Sophokles and stands from the thick tree root he was sitting on. "O, I'm going to go see Aischylos!" he blurts, then trots off in the direction of Piraeus, laughing.

"Don't make me beat you in a foot race, you turtle!" Sophokles shouts after him, sighing and shaking his head at the other members of his chorus who are all still sitting around watching him. Teleklon starts to run, but returns to his modest trot after looking back and seeing that Sophokles has not stood.

"Bet you can't," one of the younger men chides him.

Sophokles raises his eyebrows at the man, then gets up and dashes after Teleklon. Teleklon doesn't notice until Sophokles is crashing into him in a running attempt to slap his back which causes both men to tumble into the grass beside the path.

After some laughter and rolling in the grass together, the two men walk arm in arm, sharing the memories of obscure poems, on the long walk down the road to the port of Piraeus, holding their hands over each others' eyes to block the glittering off the sea just beyond their destination.

A crowd has gathered at Piraeus as the news has spread of Aischylos' return from the West.

The man himself, draped dramatically in a long sailor's rain cloak which covers all but his head, has waited to speak until all of his belongings have been brought down from the ship and his wife and her things comfortably set off toward their Athens house, and a portable platform positioned for him to step up on. Once he is standing on the little stage, rows of merchants' ship masts arrayed behind him like a skene, the excited crowd finally notes that he is waiting for their silence, and they gradually quieten and hush each other. Eventually, over that barely contained anticipation, he begins to speak.

"Athenians, foreign friends, all those with ears! I, Aischylos, have returned to Athens for this hundredth anniversary of the Panathenaic Games!"

The crowd of assembled people cheer, most of all the worshippers of Dionysos who follow the plays and playwrights religiously.

"We love you, Aischylos!"

"Athens has missed you, greatest of the playwrights! Never leave us again! The Dionysian festival wasn't the same without you!"

"Go back to Syrakous!"

"Welcome home!"

Sophokles gives doubtful looks to his friends in response to the comments from the crowd.

Aischylos is silent again until the crowd quiets down.

"In honor of the twenty-fifth Panathenaic Games, I have written an epic set of plays to pale all others."

The crowd of theater fans cheers at the sentiment. Some of the less-experienced actors gaze at the playwright with awe, imagining their own adjacent glory if his claims prove true.

"Tell us about Syrakous!" someone from the crowd shouts. "Were its walls truly on par with those of Babylon?"

"Well," Aischylos replies, "I haven't been to Babylon, so I cannot say for sure, but I've seen paintings of the great Walls of Babylon, and I saw the fine Walls of Syrakous up close, and I would be very surprised if Babylon's ancient blue walls are anywhere near as impressive as those in Syrakous. But such is the benefit of modernity. For one thing - the Skyrakousan Walls are built directly upon the edge of the Sea! And they were only built a few Olympiads ago, unlike Babylon's which were built by ancestors long forgotten, before men knew what they know now. I seem to recall that Babylon's walls have been breached, at various points in their long history, but I suspect it will be many generations before men develop methods clever enough to breach the Walls of Syrakous!"

Athenians excited about modern technology and stories of distant wonders cheer.

"And how about the *garos* there?"

"Worry not, garos-seller. Athenian fish-sauce will forever be superior worldwide."

Fine-faced Penander emerges dramatically from the crowd with a warm smile. Aischylos comes down from his platform and meets Penander in a hug for a long moment.

"I was genuinely afraid you might stay away," Penander says.

Aischylos shakes his head, looking around at the Piraeus port town. "This is my home," he says. "It is wild how much it has changed in only a year! Was that building there when I left?"

"Thrown up within one month, that was. Some Ionian brothel, I think. Some thief punched a hole right through the wall to steal the feel of a breast, the other day, though, so I don't think it's sturdy enough to be here next year. I wouldn't get on the roof."

"You sound like you know the place well?" Aischylos laughs.

"I'll introduce you to the current girls."

Patient Podarge, wife of Aischylos, walks up behind her husband, having just returned, and gives Penander a look like she heard him. Penander just laughs uncomfortably for a moment, then shuts up and slowly disappears into the crowd as Podarge and Aischylos embrace and kiss, then continue guiding their slaves with the unloading of their belongings.

Mildly-sober Kratinos steadily stumbles out from the crowd with some street food in his hand. He watches Aischylos' slaves making the subtlest comedy of his reactions to their endeavors, bringing them all to start laughing more and more until Podarge comes to the edge of the boat to see what the commotion is. On seeing Kratinos, she rolls her eyes.

"Is that some breakfast rat from the prison food cart?" she chides the actor below.

Kratinos smiles, and takes a bite of his meat pocket. He gestures up to her with it. "Welcome back to Athens! You are a sad city's medicine!" He uses the word which used to also be used to refer to poor ancient folks who would be selected to be exiled from their city to appease the gods, a *pharmakon*, specifically to insinuate the reason for their having left.

Podarge eyes him scornfully, but uses the comment's mask of innocuity to take the opportunity to ignore it.

"Kratinos!" Aischylos shouts before he is seen, as he signals to Podarge to switch places with him at the edge of the boat. "You are in the costume of a sober man, why?"

"Without you, all has changed," Kratinos dryly jokes. "You will find the trees fly now and the birds are rooted to the ground."

"I have new plays to perform," Aischylos says, ignoring the actor's nonsense. "Tell me."

"Not yet. I must prepare the earth for these seeds, I must plow this city." Kratinos nods with a big smile, appreciating the comment as crass humor.

"You see," Aischylos says to Kratinos, "the story *actually* begins before it is shown, with the build-up *toward* the story - like the Sacred Path to Eleusis is the lead-up to that story. The whispers, the proclamations, of what to expect - they do half, at least, of the work of forming the story in the viewer's mind. They plow the field. Viewers have often already formed their opinions on the piece before sitting in their seats in the theater, based on what has been said *about* it in the days before. That is why we must control that narrative, as early as possible, and tell the audience exactly what to expect, and exactly what they ought to think, so that they can know how to position their minds in preparation for it. So I shall reveal my story only gradually, like a sprout."

Δ

Ephialtes and Kimon sail east, potentially to war

Kimon and Ephialtes, both Generals now, sail east to distant Pamphylia, on one of Athens' sacred state triremes, the *Paralos*, with a fleet of military triremes behind them all packed with Athenian young men wearing their fathers' armor, ready to fight. Some compare marks on their armor and tell the war stories behind them.

A colorfully painted nereid, one of the half-fish daughters of that primordial titan of the sea Nereus, points the way with her confidently upturned chin as the figurehead of the Paralos. Behind her, Kimon and Ephialtes stand together, watching the waves crash against the keel.

Ephialtes nervously runs his hand over the figurehead's colorful sculpted scales, letting the sea spray wet his fingers. "So where are we sailing to first, again?" he asks, grimacing against the bracing wind.

"Knidos, in Karia," Kimon replies with a stern look of derision at Ephialtes' failure to remember. "There should be two hundred ships gathered there from the Ionian island states, and a contingent of Ionian troops whom we had stationed in Karia expecting Xerxes to march his army back via Sardis along the Persian Royal Road. But since their fleet and army are both gathered at the Eurymedon River, we know that their intent is instead to sail along the southern coast of Asia, no doubt taking each port to advance forward their base of operations. Our mission is to either take or ally with Phaselis in Pamphylia, and make sure that Xerxes can't pass that place."

"I do wish I had focused more on my geography studies," Ephialtes sighs.

"Pamphylia is the easternmost Hellenic region of Asia. Past that, if you don't turn south to cross to Kypros, then you're in rugged Kilikia, the land of pirates, on your way to the cities of Phoenikia, where the Persians build their fleet," Kimon explains patiently. "Pamphylia is eastern Hellas."

"So Phaselis will be this year's Salamis," Ephialtes tries to analyze.

Kimon just shakes his head. "You must never think that one battle will be like another, or you will lose. No, it will not be like Salamis. For one thing, you will find I am a different sort of general than Themistokles, who liked to think himself

Odysseos, winning with tricks. I respect Ares too much to try to fool the War God. Diomedes is the hero I make my sacrifices for; his was a wisdom built from courage and daring, not tricks."

"Ever friends and comrades, Odysseos and Diomedes. They night-raided the Troian camp together," Ephialtes says.

Kimon puts a hand on the back of Ephialtes' neck for a brief, friendly squeeze. "As Themistokles and I fought together in the Persian Wars. I'm glad to hear you know your *Iliad*, Ephialtes. Its stories contain all the wisdom any man needs. I say skip the *Odyssey*."

Ephialtes sighs and says, "I've been trying not to think about the *Odyssey*. The last thing I want to imagine is angering some god who keeps us from getting home for ten years. I have someone back home whom I love too much to not get back to for ten years."

Kimon half-smiles and guesses, "Perikles."

Ephialtes sees a dolphin dance upon a wave in the distance and points to it excitedly with a smile. "Look there!"

"Have you not sailed out of the Gulf of Saron before, Ephialtes?"

Ephialtes shrugs a no.

"If we weren't in a hurry, we'd stop and fish here where the dolphins play," Kimon notes casually. "But we must get to Knidos by tomorrow."

The salt air rushes past. White clouds slowly romp along the horizon.

"Where do you think Themistokles is now?" Ephialtes asks.

Kimon looks back to him with a glance of guarded surprise. "I would have thought you would know. Last I heard, he disappeared from Argos. No one seems to know to where."

Ephialtes nods. "That's as much as I know, too."

Kimon shoots Ephialtes a sustained squint, to silently communicate suspicion. The two men scrutinize each other's faces for a few moments in silence, a rare opportunity for adversaries up close.

Kimon says, "Ephialtes, good man, I don't understand you. You put your name in to be chosen as a General, and yet you have no actual interest in military matters. Why put yourself up to be General, then? Just because it is one more office of government you haven't held yet? Are you trying to collect them, like animal trophies?"

Ephialtes sneers an attempt at a scornful scoff, but his generally positive demeanor keeps him from being able to make it sound too harsh, and he himself is chuckling at the attempt before it's over.

"I'm not disinterested in military matters. I'm just not interested in seeking glory in combat, myself. But I do understand the need for the activity, and the benefit to our city that it reaps. Not all military action is fighting, though, Kimon, my friend. Perhaps you and the other Generals will find it valuable to have the viewpoint of a peaceful man to consider, rather than always thinking of military matters as soldiers. As a General, I hope to minimize our need to risk the lives of Athenians."

Kimon sighs as he nods. "Well, at least there we agree. However, having a fair bit of experience in military matters, specifically the fighting part, I happen to know that one of the best ways to protect your men is to keep them both courageous and a little afraid. But yes, I hear you - peace lends time to strengthen the arms of the man at war."

Ephialtes shakes his head. "You still speak as if battle is the first principle, the primary virtue. What I'm trying to say is that *peace* should be that first principle, that purpose for any battle. And yet battle does not equivalently strengthen the arm of the man at peace. It weakens him."

Kimon retracts his neck instinctively at that comment, and gives Ephialtes a quizzical look. "Do you really think that battle weakens men?"

Ephialtes reluctantly nods, looking Kimon in the eyes to show courage. "Their hearts, their souls, I do. I've known too many men invisibly wounded by war. I think your desire to see glory may glare so brightly that you miss seeing the suffering of your comrades at home. It seems to me that blood curses all who see it."

"Peace is not just about avoiding fights," Kimon says.

"I hope you understand that I don't plan to simply watch what happens as those who have fighting experience do things in the normal military way," Ephialtes assures Kimon. "I have ideas. For example - Phaselis. You have explained that you intend to besiege that city into joining us against Persia. But would you hear my plan?"

Kimon cocks his head, doubtful but patient.

Ever-smiling Ephialtes explains, "What I do best is talk to people. I talk to everyone. So I've been talking with the men on board here."

Kimon's eyes turn suspicious again.

Smiling, Ephialtes continues, "You may not know this - I didn't know this - but the men of the island of Chios and the men of Phaselis have a long-standing friendship. It goes generations back. We have a small contingent of men from Chios onboard, you see. They're worried about their friends and family in Phaselis. They're worried they'll be asked to besiege the city, or worse, fight and kill their friends."

Kimon nods, beginning to understand.

"What I propose will not at all affect our chance of alternate fall-back plans being effective. It is just a chance I feel we ought to take before we risk anyone's lives."

"Speak it," Kimon sniffs.

"We should have the men from Chios make our case for us, that Phaselis has no chance against either Persia *or* Athens - I mean Delos - and that they ought to simply join us peacefully, and move with us against Persia before Persia moves west again and enslaves them first."

Kimon sighs. "You're new to leading military men, Ephialtes, so I will introduce you to a secret which you would normally learn by experience. Men want those in power to be the ones who enact that power. When the man who is in power leaves the actual work to other men, those men begin to feel like maybe the one with the power can't actually maintain that power. Like maybe theirs is the real source of power."

Ephialtes half-frowns, half-smiles at the notion.

"It is we, the Generals, who must enact whatever plan we have. And it is we who must speak with the leaders at Phaselis. It is not appropriate to have some random Chians making the case for the League of Delos. The people of Athens voted for *you* to be their General, not those Chians. This is not some Athenian court where a fisherman can read the words of a stonemason in order to make the case for some new law."

"It's a new world, Kimon," Ephialtes says. "Utility defines the good. I think it's worth a try."

Kimon sighs through his nose, then takes a deep breath of sea air. Finally he says, "You are a duly-elected General of Athens, Ephialtes. We may follow your advice, and give your plan a try. But if it doesn't work, then we will fall back to the previous plan, which is to besiege and starve the city into submission. Because, Ephialtes, this is not just an experiment that can fail, unlike politics at home. If we fail in our mission, Persia will return. We will have another generation of war. We must keep that from happening, whatever the cost."

"Well, at the very least, our great League of Delos will protect Athens, right? Our island allies are our phalanx astride the waters, like our own many-bodied iron Talos..."

"Don't try to get poetic, Ephialtes. Have you ever *been* to Delos?" Kimon asks Ephialtes, then sighs and adds, "No, wait, I remember, you haven't left Attika before now."

"It's the birthplace of Apollo and Artemis," Ephialtes begins. Kimon starts to shake his head, and Ephialtes stammers for a moment but then continues, "It's a cosmopolitan island, where men from every corner of the sea intermingle. I understand there is a temple for every god of every land, from the Hyperboreans to the Aithiopeans, so that no man will feel he's a stranger there."

"It's a slave market," Kimon says coldly, looking away from Ephialtes finally. "Its cosmopolitanism is only meant to summon every sort of men to purchase and sell slaves there, and to service the *slaves* of many lands."

"But it is also central in the Aegean Sea, and it's where Leto bore the gods Apollo and Artemis..."

Kimon eyes the undulating horizon and says, "Apollo and Artemis have both been absent from their home island for a long time. They dwell elsewhere now. There is little holy on Delos today, Ephialtes. It's not ancient times anymore. The gods aren't babies. But I will say, if there is anything beloved by the gods there at all, hopefully it is our Delian League. Because I fear Persia feigns sleep, and there may be a third war ahead of us yet again."

Kimon looks into the bracing sea wind as if trying to spot the future.

"It is up to us Generals to try to stop that," Ephialtes says with a nod forward into the wind.

Kimon nods, and eyes Ephialtes, then joins his horizon gaze.

E

Euripides and Sokrates get frightened

Strong-fingered Sophroniskos's new coworker is a boy near Euripides' age, who at a scrawny fourteen seems ready to grow into a full-blown teen-ager any minute. Named Phidias, the boy is a silphion seller's son who has taken up residence in a cot in the stonemasons' workshop while his father is away on a mercantile expedition to the distant desert city of Kyrene.

To the surprise of everyone, the boy has an uncanny instant talent at sculpting clay forms, so what was originally an offer of a lump of clay to stop the lonely boy's weeping has turned into a real job at the statue workshop.

And now what was supposed to be one season's arrangement is approaching a year. No one yet dares suggest that Phidias' father might not return, as sea voyages are notorious for getting held up for as long as months. The boy focuses on his work - sculpting the smallest votive statues of the gods, the kind that people carry with them in secret pockets.

The workshop's owner Myron has already become momentarily famous for Phidias' fine little figurines.

Sokrates, Krito, Chaerephon, and Euripides spend many days in the corner of this workshop where Sokrates' father Sophroniskos works, and today little Diotima is also here, having followed Sokrates. In recent days they have taken to irritating young Phidias as a way of trying to get him to join their little friend-group, though he has persistently avoided the bait thus far.

Euripides has quickly become fascinated and jealous of Phidias' preternatural precocious confidence and mastery. He watches the other boy's artfully-working face carefully, but tries not to get caught staring.

Today, tough-skinned Myron has young Phidias carving fluting into the edges of column barrels, a job he enjoys less than sculpting his miniature god-forms. Sullen Phidias wears no mask over his resentment of the task.

Sophroniskos, behind a curtain on the other side of the room, is busy chiseling out dog-headed gutter drains, and is accustomed to ignoring his son and his friends as they play in the corner of the shop. He quietly makes up silly songs based on Aisop's fables which he sings to himself.

Meanwhile, Krito and Chaerephon are drawing heroes and monsters in the sand, and Euripides is using a piece of charcoal to draw on part of the plaster wall which they've been reticently given permission to draw upon.

Euripides, fourteen now and long-limbed like a colt, has been focused in recent months on the dream of creating a career for himself as a painter of scenes from the theater onto pottery. Now, he is very carefully working on a drawing of the famous hero of the Troian War, Achilles, who has recently been the hero of plays in the theater. He takes his time getting the shapes of the armor right.

Krito, ten years old, spends most of his time these days copying whatever Euripides is doing, so he is drawing in the sand whatever Euripides draws on the wall. Chaerephon had been doing the same, but has grown bored, so now he and Sokrates, unsupervised, are left free to harass Phidias.

"What would you make if you were allowed to make anything you wanted?" Sokrates asks Phidias after a back and forth about how irritated he is at having to carve out column fluting.

Phidias shakes his head, sanding hard. "I can't afford to think about that. There is no perfect world, even in imagination! All grows out from the shit of the real. And I have to do what I have to do. If I don't finish this fluting today I'll have to whip myself. I swore an oath to the Winds."

"Why'd you do that?" Chaerephon asks incredulously.

Phidias just shakes his head, immediately feeling misunderstood.

"In order to make a true work of art you must first make the whole world," says Euripides, repeating something he heard long ago. Euripides has his face very close to the charcoal drawing of Achilles which he is making. As he works carefully on a fine line of the warrior's armor, Chaerephon leans in close to watch, causing Euripides to shout, "Back off while I'm working!"

Phidias groans, "I should say the same thing! I'm at work, guys!"

"We're at your work, too," Chaerephon jokes, then chirps in his particular way.

"Ugh, it freaks me out when you do that!" Phidias shouts. "I wish you wouldn't hang out here just because Sokrates' father works here. Isn't there somewhere you kids would rather be? That shoe shop?"

"Simon's gone this month," Krito explains, watching Euripides work carefully, as he himself carelessly recreates the same image in dust.

Euripides slips with his charcoal and makes a mistaken mark, then groans and throws his charcoal down.

Phidias cranes his neck to better see Euripides' drawing.

"See, now, look at what you're doing there," Phidias remarks, pointing with his tool to the drawing which Euripides has done on the wall. "I can tell immediately whom you're trying to depict. Achilles. You know how? Two ways. First of all, that's who everyone has been painting on their cups ever since Aischylos' plays about Achilles. And second of all, you're drawing him exactly how you've seen everyone else draw him. And then, there in the sand I wouldn't be able to tell what you're trying to do, Krito, but it's obvious you're just copying the copier, despite failing."

Krito frowns at his sand drawing.

"You're just not artists. At best you're copiers. Artists make *original work*," Phidias sneers. "It's okay, though. The world needs copiers too."

He turns back to his own work on the column, thinks about what he's just said, and then melodramatically hangs his head.

"Originality is impossible!" Sokrates shouts, throwing his charcoal into the air and causing Chaerephon to nervously chirp in response.

Sophroniskos bangs his hand on the table to startle all the kids, and says, "Shut up! Now listen, we're gonna debate a topic. We'll each give an answer to a big question, after taking some time to think about it. I'll go first. Ready? Okay. You can play too, Diotima. But everyone has to shut up when someone else is going, and if you don't I'll kick your butt out of here. Ready?" Shiny-headed Sophroniskos finally looks back around at all the kids once he's stopped snarling, and when he finds them all still silently startled and listening, he nods and continues. "So the question is - What is the best art form? I'll go first."

Sophroniskos then proceeds to furrow his brow in thought and work his big fingers in the clay he had been fashioning earlier.

Phidias murmurs, "I wish I knew other real artists."

After a few seconds Sophroniskos says, "Now here's why I would say that architecture is the best art form, to my mind. Buildings are civilization. They're where we live, they're where our gods live, they're the very stuff of modernity. Outside of buildings, you're in the wild. Architects construct our modern universe! Architects will redesign the whole of Ge the Earth, I'd say, before Time is over. Architecture."

Sophroniskos then looks to Phidias with a competitive seriousness.

"Alright little one, now you. I suppose you'd say sculpture is the best art form. What would your reasoning be, though?"

Phidias frowns at the presumption, but the shrugs and nods in agreement. "I would, you're right," he says. Then, with a tone which clearly indicates he's being comical, he says, "I suppose it would be because sculpture is what can come the closest to representing a woman."

The boys all laugh. Diotima smiles.

Phidias then says, more seriously, "Or a man. Or a god. Without sculpture, we wouldn't be able to visualize the gods. Think about that."

Euripides pipes in, "I'd say it's painting! Because both architecture and sculpture need to be painted before anyone wants to look at them. Painting is like the breath of art, it's what brings everything to life!"

"Good phrasing, Euripides, that's nice," Sophroniskos says.

Sokrates, getting confidence from seeing Euripides jump in without being asked, jumps in himself. "Well in that case, wouldn't it then really be art-criticism, the appreciation and discussion of art, be it architecture, sculptures, or painting, which is the ultimate expression of art? Without the beholder, art would just be like windy ruins somewhere unknown."

Sophroniskos smiles and slaps him on the back. "That's not *art* though, Sokrates. That's just babble. Once art has been created, any number of people will say any number of things about it, but that doesn't change what it is or what magic the artist put into it. Art criticism is not art."

Sokrates frowns.

Sophroniskos then turns to little Diotima, sitting in the narrow window to the street. "How about you little lady? What's your thought?"

"I was gonna say dancing," Diotima whispers shyly, "but now I see that's not the sort of thing you meant."

Sokrates starts to playfully dance in place. Krito laughs, and when Chaerephon sees that response he too starts dancing, but not in place, kicking and jumping around and whirling accidentally into a tent pole, which shakes the whole workshop.

"That's it!" Myron shouts from the neighboring tent. "No more children who don't work here! Either get to work fluting or get out!"

"Out, out, vermin!" Phidias shouts, kicking at the air behind the running butts of the boys as they race out the door of his shop.

Chaerephon races off toward the boys' home neighborhood and Krito instinctively follows after him. But Euripides, the oldest at fourteen, stops at an alley and lets the younger ones run on, thinking he's lost them.

Euripides wanders the dark streets edging the Agora, behind the shops, where the paths get barely wider than a donkey's shoulders, and finally takes a crouch in the shadows of some tall drygoods jars behind the raisin-cake shop, but in view of the bright crescent moon over the Akropolis. Just a few paces behind him, Sokrates gets down onto his knees on the alley cobblestones beside Euripides, which is his first indication that six-year-old Sokrates had followed him instead of the others.

An eagle above cries, lifting Sokrates' eyes. In the cloudless blue sky, the white moon is half full.

"Why do you think the light on the moon changes?" Sokrates asks his older friend.

"She changes her dress just like any other woman," Euripides jokes, and laughs softly to himself, though he stops when little Sokrates doesn't laugh with him.

"Is that a dress?"

Euripides nods. "Sort of. I mean, the gods aren't quite like you and me. They sometimes take the form of mortals, but they can look like anything. And Selene, the moon, looks like that. I don't know why the light moves across her every month. Maybe it has something to do with Apollo, and the sun chariot as it passes underneath the Earth at night."

"So that is the goddess herself?" Sokrates asks, still looking up.

"Do I hear two little boys wondering about the mystical shadows of the world?" whispers an eerie voice from the alley behind the two boys, startling them both and making them shout briefly with fright.

They turn to see an old, white-haired woman with long, crooked fingers and eyes sealed shut by some disease of the skin, dressed in black rags.

"Would you boys like to know your futures?" the old woman asks. "You need not pay me anything. The spiders want you to know."

Euripides swallows hard and looks over at little Sokrates, who doesn't look scared yet, so Euripides turns back to the old woman with borrowed courage and whispers, "Yes, ma'am."

The old woman swoops up close to the boys quickly, her tattered black cloak fluttering, and Sokrates jumps at the startling movement, but chuckles instead of appearing frightened. Euripides, however, holds back a sudden sob, and doing so makes a little tear fall from his eye. The woman looks down upon Euripides through her one almost-good eye, and breathes in a long sniff, then lifts the edge of her sleeve with the other hand, as out from beneath the raised sleeve slowly creeps a fat, black, long-legged spider. The spider walks out onto the woman's knuckles as she speaks and Euripides stares at it in disbelief.

"A thousand years ago, when the first people were born from the gods, the beautiful young woman named Arachne dared to claim she was a better weaver than Athena, and the goddess turned her into the first mother spider, so that this young lady here is one of her descendents. But what is not always told in her story is that Arachne was such a miraculous weaver that she was able to foretell the future in her weavings. And though few know it, or how to read them, her children the spiders of our world still maintain that ability. I am one of the daughters of the sisters of Arachne, and I know how to read the futures of little boys in the spider's webs."

"Will I become a wise man?" Euripides asks the woman.

The white-haired woman lifts her wrist to her ear as if to better hear the spider's whispering. Then she looks back and forth between the two boys as a look of shock rises upon her face in such a way that her eyelids finally partially open.

Before she can speak, fourteen-year-old Euripides starts running, and Sokrates quickly follows in a sprint of sympathetic fear, as the old woman cackles light-heartedly to herself in the shadows behind them.

Somewhere in the narrow alleys of Athens, dashing between chatting groups of bystanders, Euripides loses little Sokrates, but is too frightened of the old seer woman to stop.

Euripides sprints all the way back to his home, where he runs into his father

Mnesarchos standing outside the front door and whipping the fur off a stretched hide.

"Whoa, whoa, whoa," Mnesarchos growls, grabbing Euripides by the tunic so hard that he partially pulls it off. Euripides struggles to keep his clothing covering himself, and pulls away. "Where are you going so fast, son of mine?" Mnesarchos grabs Euripides again, but less roughly this time.

Euripides tries to avoid his eye contact so that his father won't see how scared he is. "Nothing," he says. His father grabs his face and turns him to face him, and sees the fear. Euripides starts to cry.

"Nothing is not an answer that makes sense in response to the question I asked you! Now what is this girly crying," Mnesarchos grunts, shaking his son's shoulders. "What's wrong with you, son of mine? No son of mine is gonna get scared by nothing. What scared you, son?"

"It was a blind, old witch," Euripides cries, his fear bringing to mind the anger of the gods, which makes him fear lying. "She offered us an oracle, but then she had this huge spider that crawled out of her sleeve, and Sokrates started running so I ran after him!"

"Sokrates? I told you to stop hanging out with younger boys. You need to start trying to befriend older boys, so you can learn how to behave next year! Teaching younger boys what you yourself have already learned is like giving away your hard-won fortune!"

"Yes, sir," Euripides says between sniffles.

As he starts to beat his hides again, Mnesarchos says, "Really, you're of the age where you should start to be thinking about trying to draw the interest of some man looking for a boy to teach the ways of life to, if you know what I mean."

"Ugh, I do know what you mean," Euripides groans, rolling his eyes. "You're disgusting."

Mnesarchos thinks again about what his son just said and laughs and hugs Euripides tightly, then releases him. "A witch, huh? So what was your oracle?"

Euripides just shakes his head, afraid to answer.

"What did she tell you?" Euripides' father asks with seriousness this time. "You have to tell me; as your father I have the right to know your future if you know it."

"I didn't wait to get the oracle. We ran away!" Euripides cries. "She scared us!"

Mnesarchos groans and grabs Euripides, pushing him to walk. "By all the titans in Tartaros, son of mine, I will show you how to respect your elders. I don't care if this old woman looks like Echidna herself, you have to be respectful of your elders, and you have to be extra respectful of those whom the gods have touched, like seers! This seems to me obvious, but apparently you need to be taught this sort of thing explicitly. Now where was this old witch?"

Euripides first just points, but Mnesarchos gives him a stern look which sets the boy walking, still pointing with the deep hope that it might at some point make his father go ahead and let him stop. But Mnesarchos just plods patiently behind his son as Euripides leads his father down the streets of Athens still pointing, while weeping noisily and wishing the scene could end.

"You are going to learn some respect, son of mine," Mnesarchos growls loudly. "I won't have you out there representing our family disgracefully. Which way now? O, her - yes, I see her."

Right where he and Sokrates left her, the old blind woman is still sitting against a low stone wall at the edge of a city street. As Euripides and his father approach, she raises her head as if noticing them despite her blindness.

"Pardon me, fine woman," Mnesarchos calls out, overselling his respect for the gnarled old woman whom he certainly would in any other moment disdain. "Was my son here just recently disrespectful to you?"

"Why yes," the woman laughs, "yes, he and his friend left me without hearing what the spiders had to say!"

"Well, what do you have to say to the witch, Euripides?"

Euripides stares forward in what feels to him like an eternity of defiant silence before finally relenting and saying, "I'm sorry if I was disrespectful, ma'am."

"And?"

"...And what do your spiders say about my fate?"

Slowly the old woman stands from the low wall and lurches up toward Euripides, as his father holds him firmly in place. She lifts her sleeve up to her ear and acts like she is listening to the implied spider inside. "Listen little boy, my sister spiders whisper what they overhear under the dining tables of Olympos. And for you? What is your name, young one?"

Euripides looks to his father with the pleading eyes of a beggar, trying to get him to let them just go home, but his father nods gruffly to continue, so he tells the woman reluctantly, despite fearing that she'll have some magic that can use his name to do him harm, "Euripides, ma'am."

"Son of Mnesarchos," his father adds.

She listens again to her sleeve. The big black spider creeps out again onto her wrist, and when it stops the woman makes a series of faces as if she is listening to spoken words.

"Ah," she says with a smile, and addresses Mnesarchos instead of the boy, "your son is granted luck by the Fates. They speak of many victory crowns in his future." She holds out her dry old hand.

As Mnesarchos searches his belt for his coin purse, he asks the woman, "And if I were coinless, would his fate be different?"

The old woman takes the coin she is handed and then spits the word, "Obviously," back at Mnesarchos, before turning to shamble away.

Crouching down beside his son, Mnesarchos smiles and says, "Now, did you learn to respect your elders, no matter how ugly and deformed they are, and even if they listen to spiders or spirits or things like that?"

"Yes," Euripides nods.

"And hey cheer up. You heard the seer - you're going to be some kind of athletic star!" Euripides' father slaps his back hard as he guides him back to their home. "I told you you ought to get out on the gymnastics fields."

Euripides' eyes narrow.

Z

Protagoras makes an agreement with Euathlos

"So you claim you can change my destiny?" round-bellied Euathlos asks with disbelief, lounging on the ground as he slowly eats a fig pastry.

"Your character determines your destiny," Protagoras retorts, "and I claim that I can change your character by changing the way you decide to respond to situations. You are not, after all…"

"I am no character!" Euathlos hiccups.

"O you're a character," Protagoras disagrees. "Like it or not, you are a character and this is a tragedy, a goat-song for sure! No man is any previously existing thing until he *pretends* to be it first, in his mind. And then he becomes it. All is false first, imaginary second, and real last. Then false again, once it is over. Let that be your first lesson."

Euathlos shakes his head, squinting at Protagoras. "I'm still not even confident that what you say is true - that one man can pass on his wisdom to another man. I have had people try, but I've never felt any wiser afterward. I've even tried magic, but that didn't seem to work either."

"What exactly is it that you want to be able to *do* better?" Protagoras asks the young man.

"I want to be able to speak so that it moves other men," Euathlos sighs. "And women, also! But only the right men and women. I do not want my words to summon irritating men, for example, or cheap women."

"I can teach you how to speak properly," Protagoras says to Euathlos' shield of suspicious eyebrows, "but it will require learning how to *think* properly."

"I just want to make sure I'm not getting into some kind of trickster's agreement, where you're going to sell me misguided pseudo-wisdom and I'm not going to know any better, or wisdom that makes people hate me, or weighs down my fate like a warp weight. I must remain free and nimble!"

Protagoras confidently says, "What I am offering you is wisdom itself - pure wisdom, like clean water. The thing held most valuable by the wisest men, by the oldest men, by women who are looking to marry, by everyone you might want to ever interact with."

Euathlos shakes his head. "I know plenty of people who find wisdom to be a hateful thing. Don't you know that men mock the gods, mock wisemen, and mock the leaders of even democratic cities where they themselves have chosen the leaders?"

"If it is not useful on people, then it is not wisdom. If you're thinking of useless so-called wisdom, that which is hated by normal men, then I say what you are referring to is not wisdom but merely wears the *mask of wisdom*. True wisdom will be useful to you, even if it is not what wisemen would call wisdom. What I would teach you is *true wisdom*, not the *mask of wisdom*. And yet, paradoxically, *true wisdom* involves wearing a sort of mask, to actually convince people of what you want based on what they expect to hear, instead of trying hard to explain some rarified truth which will come across to foolish men as foolery."

"I'm confused already," Euathlos sighs. "You truly are wise."

Protagoras sighs. "Here, write on this stone, with this piece of charcoal. Show me your letters. Can you spell your name? We'll start there."

Euathlos takes the charcoal piece and slowly begins to make lines with it, drawing them very carefully one by one, and struggling to remember which letter is formed from which lines.

"Good," Protagoras nods. "Now can you write something about yourself?"

Euathlos, in a snaking line which goes first left-to-right, then mid-word switches back the other direction, writes

EUATHLOS WILL SO
NAM ESIW A EB NO

"You can always tell a farmer from a city man," Protagoras notes, holding up the large shard that Euathlos has been writing on. "Just get them to write a few words. You write like the ox plows. It is infuriating for a cultured man to try to read."

"Why?" Euthalos asks, grabbing the shard from Protagoras and looking at it. "It's the most efficient way to move. Only an idiot would lift up his plow in order to start each row from the same side."

"Except lifting your wrist is infinitely easier than carrying a plow. And when I, a reader, come upon this piece of writing, I have no idea whether to read from left to right or from right to left, unless I start at the very beginning and follow the labyrinth."

"Well, why would you start reading in the middle?"

"Any number of possible reasons!" Protagoras scoffs. "That is the magic of the written word - you can access it again and again, and revisit different sections as often as you see fit. We live above the world of the words as if we the reader were a god, able to see each part and move between parts swiftly from one higher vantage, above the time of the moment."

"Well I think if I wrote a beginning, I wouldn't want someone just jumping forward to the middle and skipping it. So maybe I want to make it harder to access the middle of my writing without starting at the front."

"You're a fool, Euathlos," Protagoras sighs.

"Exactly!" Euathlos shouts with a pastry-mouthed laugh. "That's why I've hired you! Whatever mysteries I have to go through, I must come out as a wiseman! Anyway, isn't it a more defensive position for my writing to have, being difficult to read, so that only the smartest people will be able to access its wisdoms?"

"If you want to hide an idea," Protagoras sighs, "just don't write it. You *do* have a mind, and I have found no bottom to the storage capacity of my own. The only reason to write is because you want to share your mind."

"Well, I forget what I was doing right after I start doing it," Euathlos retorts. "In fact I have forgotten already why I thought you might be able to help me."

"Because you're a rural idiot with no experience speaking in public to city men, and you are taking that other man to court for ... for what again?"

"I'm not sure whether it would be wise to tell you or not," Euathlos admits carefully. "Your wisdom might be such that you could use it against me in ways I could never foresee. No, I think I will leave you ignorant of my friend's supposed crime."

Protagoras shrugs every so briefly as if to underscore that he cares exceedingly little anyway. "Fine," he says. "I don't think I need to know what someone claims you've done in order to simply help you understand better how to help yourself in arguments of words. I'm still sure that I can pass what wisdom I have in a way that can help you."

"Because I don't just want to be able to get through *this* court case, but any court case that might come up before me in the future. I don't want to have to hire you each time I get taken to court. What about this," Euathlos proposes. "I pay you nothing ... *until* I win my first legal case!" The look on his face says that he feels extremely clever for having thought of it. "Because I do want to be wiser, and I cannot even begin to imagine how to be. But I am, until I win this court case, coinless, as you saw."

Protagoras thinks for a while with an expression of suspicion, but after several seconds finally agrees, extending his hand to be shaken. "Very well. You will pay me the full amount, once you have won your first legal case."

"Hermes of the Marketplace, seal our deal." Euathlos smiles, and he shakes Protagoras' hand, then tosses the last bit of his fig pastry into his own mouth.

"THE GOOD AND THOUGHTFUL GET THAT WAY THROUGH THESE THREE THINGS - NATURE, REASON, AND HABIT."
Pythagoras, *Semicircle*

H

Sokrates learns his letters

A visitor from the island of Chios named Ion is teaching some of the younger children their alphabet under a tent set up on the outskirts of the Agora, while their parents busy themselves in the bustling marketplace.

Sokrates sits among a few other boys his age, and in front of a row of girls who are also their age. Sokrates has a hard time keeping his eyes from meandering back over his shoulder, since he doesn't spend much time around girls his own age.

The young, short-tempered teacher Ion barks, "Eyes front! Alright, so who knows which letter comes first?"

Sokrates looks around at his fellows after a moment of quiet, then turns back around to the teacher and raises his hand.

"Alpha," Ion says, looking right at Sokrates. "The first letter is *Alpha*. Is that what you were going to say?"

"I was going to ask if it gave birth to the other letters, like Ge did the other gods."

All the little boys and girls around him titter.

"Letters are not people, nor are they gods," Ion says curtly. "They are merely forms, patterns, glyphs. They do not go about having supper and taking baths and making love to each other and raising little baby letters together. They are simply a set of shapes, each intended to relate to a certain sound that your mouth can make. And when you get very good at recognizing these symbols, you can sing out each sound one after the other very gracefully in such a way that it sounds essentially identical to this, speaking normally. But beware - for if you spend a lot of time with these symbols, you'll find they can cause you to sing their sounds even without your intending to! So don't look at them too closely for too long. Letters are also the repositories of powerful magic that can make you lose your mind, or fall in love against your will, or be haunted by demons, or any number of things like that. So you have to beware and only read *good* words."

Sokrates, listening, ponders.

Some of the children around Sokrates start to avert their eyes from the letters within view.

"Where did the idea for letters come from?" asks one of the young girls behind Sokrates.

Ion answers, "The titan Prometheos invented them initially, and first gave them only to the centaur doctor Chiron, so he could record the words of his songs. But your Athenian King Kekrops stole the letters from him like Prometheus took fire from the gods and your king adapted them to use in all sorts of other ways, like account keeping for the home, and the bureaucracy of the state. And then, over many generations, stupid men and women have deformed them into what we write today."

"Wow," says Sokrates. "So can I use them however I want?"

"No. That was my point."

Sokrates squints with his whole face.

"You can't just put letters next to each other willy-nilly and make nonsense words!" Ion snaps. "Letters only work when they are used in useful ways, like soldiers in a phalanx. And for all you know, if you say nonsense words, you might accidentally be saying the magic words of some terrible spell, and wake up with your parents dead or something like that."

A group of older, teen-aged girls carrying baskets full of unplucked grapevines crosses past behind the children, chatting gleefully together and giggling at the glances of one of the older boys in the back of the learning group. That boy's friends start to chide him with whispers and playful pushing as the older girls flutter past.

"Listen, children! You in the back, stop your chattering or I'll tell your fathers you were worse than you were. Listening? Good. Now between you all, in the grass there, is a long scroll which I want you all to read quietly together. Whoever reads fastest can be the one to unroll it, but be careful. I have to return it to its owner."

"Is this Hesiod?" one of the older children asks, starting to carefully unroll the scroll on the grass.

"No, no, these are poems by Aisop. Better for children. But still important - just as important as Hesiod! You'll read Hesiod when you're a bit older. But Aisop is essential. Even farmers need to know these poems. Even fishermen. Even girls. So read as many times as you need to, to understand. Now I'm going to speak with these other adults, and you all must stay totally quiet, or I'll seem like a bad teacher."

The girls and boys gather in the grass around the long scroll filled with tiny letters. Some help the younger ones to read with whispers, but mostly they stay silent. Others ignore the words and play instead with ants and grasshoppers.

Soon, from across the many other voices, an excited woman shouts,

"Aischylos! Master of the Athenian stage, Aischylos has come home!"

At that Ion gains a grin and looks up excitedly.

A gathering of actors, maskless but costumed in a variety of the chorus costumes from Aischylos' past few plays, dance through the crowd of the agora casting flower petals, while several musicians perched on rooftop corners begin plucking their strings and blowing their reeds.

Broad-shouldered Aischylos, orbited by dancing girls in diaphanous dresses, walks out from the road to Piraeus into the Agora crowd, meeting a hail of cheers.

"Athenians!" Aischylos declares with his booming voice, "As you may have heard, I have recently returned from western frontiers with a new set of plays for the Dionysia!"

A crowd of worshippers of Dionysos and theater fans quickly surround the famous playwright.

"Tell us of your travels!"

"Did you present any plays in Syrakous?"

Ion stands on his toes to try to see over the other fans. The children all watch the commotion curiously.

"We presented *The Persians* to the court of King Hieron of Syrakous, who gave me this golden laurel in appreciation, in celebration of the play's depictions of Athens' great victory at Salamis!" Aischylos carefully puts onto his bald-topped head the ornately sculpted golden wreath of which he speaks, and the crowd cheers just at the sight of it, but then again and louder in celebration of their man Aischylos. "And so," he continues, "I have returned to Athens, with a new inspiration for a new set of plays - all of which tell one larger story together, as a trio of stories - a *trilogy*! Something unlike anything Athens has ever seen before!"

The crowd roars with enthusiasm. Ion makes an effort to shout louder than those around him, "We love you Aischylos! The island of Chios loves Aischylos!"

Aischylos hears the shout and looks over the crowd to find its mouth. When he sees Ion he smiles and waves, and says, "Are you from Chios, friend?"

"I am Ion of Chios!" Ion shouts, between two wordless yelps of excitement. "I own a scroll of *The Persians* and I've read it at least a hundred times! Everyone I know on Chios has heard my many thoughts on that play, and all agree it to be the finest example of a patriotic poem written in reverence to the great Hellene."

"Yes, yes, thank you," Aischylos waves, turning away from Ion's direction once he realizes that the man has a lot to say.

Ion momentarily gets dismayed by the dismissal, but quickly goes back into wordless excited whooping in Aischylos' direction for several seconds before he finally turns back to his students with a sigh.

"How do you spell *that*?" Sokrates asks snidely, as soon as he has Ion's eye contact again.

Ion slaps young Sokrates across the cheek, then points his finger firmly in the boy's face and says, "Respect those who have deigned to teach you! Treat me poorly, boy, and I'll teach you misguided ideas! And you'd never know you had faulty knowledge. Think about that!"

Holding his stinging cheek and glaring back at the teacher, Sokrates defiantly says, "I'd know."

In the back, another young boy Sokrates' age, a tanner's son named Kleon, grabs a grasshopper and pops it into his mouth, crunching on it very dramatically in the faces of some boys seated near him, who squeal disgust.

Θ

Perikles meets Phidias to discuss a project

Potters' Alley smells of clay and ink, on top of the usual sweat and piss of the rest of the city. Carts clatter down the lane and rows of pottery wheels whirl with the work of weary women over workshop masters barking orders which echo down along the little stream they all wash their tools and hands within.

Every other shop is just a tent made of little more than sheets and poles set up between the more permanent structures of clay and packed straw ribbed by beams scavenged from Persian warships, all rebuilt in those tough, cold months that followed the city's burning in the Persian Invasion Two.

Perikles wears his roughest cloak to venture down into the industrial neighborhood, so he doesn't look too out of place.

A filthy boy, smudged-faced little Chaerephon, runs down the lane past him and Perikles tries to stop him with a wide gesture like he intends to catch the boy. "You, boy, just answer me this - where is the shop of Sophonides the cupmaker?"

"Follow me!" dirty Chaerephon shouts as he dodges past Perikles, who has to jog to keep up with him.

Not far down the stream running down the middle of the street, the boy points to a certain larger but still ramshackle building as he runs past it, and Perikles stops there. It is the open back wall of a pottery factory where six Italic slave women, all hard-knuckled and middle-aged, are spinning six pot wheels amidst numerous heaps of wet clay.

Only one of the women even looks up at Perikles. "You buy them in the front, around there," she says, pointing in a swoop to indicate going around to the other side of the building.

Nervous around such a rough woman, Perikles keeps his eyes on her and tries to apologize with his expression as he calls out past her, "Sophonides?" The woman looks away from him with a shrug, slapping more clay down.

Ephialtes' father Sophonides, a big-bellied, broadly smiling man with a huge, curly beard, hobbles out from a door which leads into the front of the shop, and, leaning on an olivewood cane he calls out to Perikles across the women's noisy wheel spinning.

"You must be Perikles! I've heard all about you, son! Come, sit down! You want a cup of honey-water?"

"O, well, I would, sir, but I am actually in something of a hurry," Perikles stutters, trying not to sound ungrateful.

"No problem, good man; you're busy; I understand. He's over there, across the stream. The tent with the blue stripes."

"That's Sophroniskos' workshop?" Perikles asks, just to confirm the man is giving him the correct information. Sophonides nods with a curt smile. "Thank you, sir!"

Perikles holds the lower parts of his tunic as he crosses the wet, slippery plank bridge that crosses the stream running down the center of Potters' Alley, nodding good day to some of the worker women washing their hands in the stream.

The tent which Ephialtes' father pointed out, the one with the blue stripes, is a large one set up at the height of a two-story building over a shady area littered with column *drums* - the sections of a column which get put on top of each other to make a full column - and a couple of tall stone sculptures which are clearly gods-in-the-works for temples somewhere. Athenian sculptors provide statues for temples across the whole Hellenic world, since where the best marble is quarried is also where the best sculptors reside. Sophroniskos primarily provides column drums, so the tall statue forms must be experiments at breaking into a new artform.

"Hail, Sophroniskos!" Perikles shouts to the tent as he approaches it from the stream, shaking some wet clay clumps off his sandals.

"Good day!" shouts the sculptor's voice from the depths of his tent. "Myron, would you see who that is? I'm inextricable!"

Perikles is greeted at the edge of the tent by Sophroniskos' boss Myron, who bows slightly. "Good day, noble Perikles," he says respectfully. "My assistant has been expecting you. Sophroniskos, it is Perikles!"

"O!" There is a loud crash back behind the curtains where Sophroniskos is working, followed by laughter and playful curses. "Gods ignore my words! Everything is fine. I'll be right there!"

Perikles takes a seat on a tall tripod stool and waits for a moment.

With a start, he notices the young toddler Sokrates sitting on the ground near one of the walls of the tent, staring at Perikles with patient, expectant, curious eyes. Perikles smiles.

"Hello, little one," he says. "What's your name?"

Little Sokrates stares shyly, frozen in silence.

Finally bald-topped Sophroniskos emerges clapping clay from his hands. He sees the salutary detente, and stands Sokrates physically by lifting him under the arms.

"Perikles, this is my son Sokrates," Sophroniskos says, holding his boy forward by the shoulders. "He claims he doesn't know anything. I have my doubts."

Sokrates looks the nobleman Perikles shyly in his eyes. He examines the man's face and beard, and the fine edging on his tunic. Perikles smiles.

"Hello, Sokrates. Don't worry. Nobody is born knowing."

"Except Athena," Sophroniskos suggests. "Born right from the head of Zeus, *she* was."

Perikles nods. "Quite apropos, in fact." He looks down at Sokrates again and asks, "Do you know about Athena?"

Sokrates frowns at the question, thinking hard about it, looks up at his father for an answer, but when Sophroniskos just shrugs, Sokrates finally answers Perikles with a sullen head shake for "no".

"Come on Sokrates, you know about Athena," Sophroniskos laughs, pushing his little boy away. "He just doesn't know how to answer. He just doesn't want to say anything, rather than be wrong." Sophroniskos turns to his young son Sokrates and commands, "Summon Phidias, boy."

Little Sokrates gets up and tromps into the other room, then returns with another boy, whose body looks hardly any bigger than little six-year-old Sokrates, though the way he moves and the look in his eyes evoke an age much older even than his actual years.

"You are Phidias," Perikles says, meaning it to be a question but saying it more like a declaration. The boy does not respond, or even move his face from staring at Perikles. He is like a statue. So Perikles continues, "I hear you're quite a fine sculptor. Is that right?"

Phidias looks over at the sculptors' master Myron, then says shyly, "Hephaestos has granted me skill at his arts."

"He doesn't even need to draw before he works," Myron says with wonder in his voice, clearly impressed, his eyes glittering as he smiles at the boy. "He simply works directly from his mind, as if Hephaestos is looking through his very eyes."

Perikles asks Phidias, "It was you who made the statue of Miltiades for his son Kimon last year, yes? The full-size one which so many folks said looked alive?"

Phidias nods with a bit of a smile.

Sophroniskos sighs noisily through his nose, clearly annoyed by the boy's success.

"Your work is unlike anything else," Perikles tells himself. "Some prefer statues to look like they always have - stiff and strong like an Aigyptian. But your Miltiades captured how Hellenes really hold their bodies, really move. Even a rigid statue, it moved, it lived."

Gently, Perikles turns to Sophroniskos and nods in a way that nobles do to servants, to let them know that they are no longer needed here. Sophroniskos frowns at the gesture, but after a moment understands what is implied, and collects Sokrates and leaves Perikles and Phidias alone in the tent.

Phidias shrinks slightly and keeps a worried look just outside of Perikles' confident gaze. Perikles tries to use a soft voice.

"So I've heard you've made erotic artwork. That it was realistic forms of men and women, made for men and women's pleasure, which is what got you so famous so quickly. I have not seen any of these works, but I have heard of them. So tell me, please, boy - is this true?"

Phidias grimaces against the question. But after a moment of Perikles' consistent confident gaze, he slowly nods.

Perikles nods understanding, and smiles to try to show that it's alright. "I have no problem with this, Phidias. But some older folks might have. So all I would suggest is that you refrain from that sort of work from here on out, and do not claim authorship of any of what you have done, but rather simply let those days and those works pass from your mind, and act as if you never did them. That is, in public. Of course, the skill and experience you gained from those works will inspire your further work, but ... you know what I mean. If you are to do what I would ask of you, you will be a famous public artist, and you will need to, at least for appearances, seem to be the sort of author whom the whole city would be proud of."

Phidias sighs and nods, and says, "I understand."

Perikles smiles, continuing to watch the boy's shyness, remembering when he himself was that young, impressed with the boy's self-creation at such a young age.

Phidias shrugs and shifts his feet, holding his hands behind himself.

"So if you were to be hired to create a sculpture of Athena, I mean one colossally sized to stand upon the Akropolis and represent our city to every horizon ... can you imagine what that might look like? Do you think you could give that sort of real Hellenic life to the image of a goddess?"

Slowly, the boy looks up, but past Perikles. Looking into middle space, Phidias says, "I can picture Athena."

Perikles peers to see if somehow he can find Athena reflected in the boy's eyes, but when he does catch a form there he quickly realizes it is just himself distorted.

From his belt Perikles retrieves a heavy purse, filled with silver coins, and he holds it out to Phidias, who is hesitant to take such wealth from a nobleman. "I want you to take this, and show me what you can do in ivory and gold, Phidias. In miniature, show me what you would do if it were huge. Show me Athena First-in-Battle. Spear in hand, that ultimate goddess of courage and foresight, and single-minded leadership. Imagine her standing on the Akropolis so tall that she can be seen from the Sea, representing our city for all."

Phidias' inner eyes race. Perikles sees that visions are happening behind the boy's eyes, and smiles.

"It will require either hubris or inspiration which few men have," Perikles says, feeling he is near to glory, "but somehow I foresee you are already saddled with both."

I

Kimon and Ephialtes confront the city of Phaselis

Across the sea, beyond the eastern island of Rhodos, past even the horn of Lykia east of that, the Pamphylian coast is still Hellenic land, but to Ephialtes' eye, having never left Attika before, the imagery on the temples which he can spot from their ships looks so strange that he would have believed they were Persian, or of some other obscure eastern tribe. He has never seen such monsters in stone before - winged bulls, lion-headed snakes, fish-birds.

Marveling at the view, he says, "We really are east of the sunrise."

Stone-eyed Kimon, beside him, sniffs out a laugh, as he whittles a little mermaid from a hunk of wood. "Nowhere is east of the sunrise," he says. "However far east you go, the sun still rises east of you."

Ephialtes sniffs out his own little laugh at that, as if the idea is absurd. "It's like the world exists to trick us."

For a few salty moments the two men watch the Pamphylian coast glide past their port side.

Kimon finishes his mermaid, considers it, shows it to Ephialtes only briefly enough to glimpse, and then tosses it casually into the waves ahead.

Kimon turns to Ephialtes and says, "We are fellow Generals now, Ephialtes. We can't be adversaries."

Ephialtes' cheeks redden. "We, as men, have never been adversaries, Kimon," he says. "We might just have advocated, in debate, for differing ideas. But it is the ideas, then, which are competitors. You and I are always fellow Athenians and friends, even when our ideas compete."

Kimon narrows his eyes. "Ephialtes, I am not an idiot. And we are not simply neighbors in the perfect democracy in which each man is equal. We are representatives, even leaders, each of our separate groups of citizens. Democracy is not about individuals, but factions, and one man outside a faction is nothing. So I know that you and your so-called 'Democrats' have factional plans against my own group of traditionalists..."

"Traditionalists!" Ephialtes scoffs. "Oligarchs hate to be called what they are."

Kimon shakes his head. "No we don't. Rule by the few is always what the real dynamics of the world process out to anyway. Democracy is a theater made to appear to enfranchise those who are gullible."

Ephialtes frowns, putting his face into the wind so that the wind will seem to be the cause of his rare frown.

"Do you want stories to take home?" Kimon asks Ephialtes, reaching an arm down to help him stand.

Ephialtes dons a comical mask of thinking hard about it for a moment, but mostly to be funny, then stands with a hand from Kimon.

Kimon leads Ephialtes to the landing boat, and they both climb down the side of the trireme into it, joining the soldiers already there. The four rowers, one of whom Ephialtes knows and winks to, then begin to row them toward the little stone dock on the beach.

A high, white-topped mountain looms behind the city as they approach. Ephialtes pictures the ancient hero Bellerophon, who was from this area, flying about from cloud to cloud on his winged horse Pegasos.

Kimon's forces surround the city's walls, which are closed and defended against them.

Phaselis' Oligarch leaders soon arrive at the top of the gate wall.

"Kimon of Athens, we have heard of your great conquests throughout Asia. But you are far from Delos here. Persepolis' shadow looms longer than those out west would understand. Each rising sun brings the tip of that shadow all the way out here."

"I bring new tides," Kimon says up to the leaders of Phaselis. "Athena has put victory already in my hand."

The Phaselian Oligarchs just frown.

"Bring me the men from Chios," Kimon tells his slave Garshasp.

Two men from the island of Chios arrive from among the soldiers with Garshasp.

Kimon explains to the men, "We must speak to them in some words which you know they will trust, being close friends of theirs with a long shared history. Words that will convince them that we must be friends against Persia, rather than fight here and each weaken each other." Kimon looks to Ephialtes to confirmation.

Ephialtes nods. "In words they will recognize as being yours. Words of uniquely Chian friendship."

The men from Chios nod, and look to each other, thinking of what sort of words will sound uniquely Chian. "We can do that," one says with a confident sniff.

To the Phaselians up on the wall, the Chian man shouts, "Men of Phaselis! I am Tritonos of Chios, and this is my good friend..." He pats the other Chian man on the shoulder until he quickly tells his name. "...My good friend Evamemnon!"

"What are you traveling with the Athenian army for?"

"The Delian army!" the Chian man shouts. "The Athenians are merely part of the Delian League! As is Chios, as is Phaselis. We are all one big city, when it comes to fighting Persia, no?"

"We here at Phaselis are on the periphery of the league's reach, Chian. Just about as far to Athens, for us, as it is to Persepolis."

"Perhaps in wing-beats of the bird, but certainly not in thoughts and customs! You are Hellenes, like us! Chios and Phaselis have long been friends! Your allies have arrived!"

The men up on the wall appear unmoved.

Kimon then steps forward and calls up to them. "Men of Phaselis - I am Kimon, of Athens." He stares at them in silence long enough to see the looks of recognition cross their faces. "I see you have heard of me, and the other cities I've taken. Surely, then, you must know that I will not let *your* great city stand in the way of my goal. A goal which should also be yours - keeping the Empire out of Hellenic lands!"

"Hellenic, Persian," one of the men on the wall coldly jokes. "Just words."

"If you force us to take this city by storm, instead of joining us peacefully," Kimon says, "I will make sure to find you and take those ears off your head. No one will ever speak your name again."

The man frowns at the sound of that.

"But if you join us, and help us to defeat the Persians here at your own very doorstep, then you will be heroes for all time, and keep those ears to hold up the crowns of victory which Hellenes across the world will forever want to put upon your heads."

The Phaselian men at the top of the wall confer. Then the others leave while one remains and addresses Kimon loudly.

"We've heard that the Persian army does come. Now, as we speak. They sail along the coast with pirates from Kilikia, in Phoenikian ships. They come to take us first. We were prepared to choose peace over war."

Kimon says, "Then we will stop them before they get to the Eurymedon River. But you will need to decide now, not after that, whether it will be force or peace by which we enter your city."

The man at the top of the wall looks down behind him for a while for confirmation, then turns back and waves big and wide, so it's clear - the answer will be positive.

Kimon's troops finally relax into stances of ease again, sensing the drop in pressure.

"We leveraged them into being our ally by threatening their existence," Ephialtes summarizes boldly.

Kimon looks at him coldly. "Phaselis was already under threat. We communicated that to them. They made the right choice. Sometimes just holding a sword, just being strong, is enough of an implicit threat to avoid battle altogether, Ephialtes. And so then, isn't violence avoided by the sword?"

"A threat is its own sort of violence," Ephialtes supposes.

"Tell that to a wounded man who hurts ever after," Kimon scoffs, turning away. "Fear is better than wounds. Shame is better than pain."

After a moment's thought, Ephialtes offers, "Compassion is better than compulsion."

Kimon thinks about that, and sniffs a laugh. "And the difference might be just words." Then he turns to the assembled soldiers and shouts, "Back to the ships, men! We have a Persian fleet to catch!"

The Athenians roar and murmur.

"WE BEG OF YOU ATHENA CITY-PROTECTOR,
AS STRONG AS ARES, BUSY WITH THE WORK OF WAR,
GIVE US SWEET VICTORY AND HAPPINESS!
IT'S YOU WHO SAVES THOSE WHO COME BACK ALIVE!"
Homeros, *Hymn to Athena*

K

Aoide has a visitor from Athens

The carefully arranged innards of some poor rodent sit in the doorframe of Aoide's dormitory. She crouches over them, inspecting them closely from above. Behind Aoide, some younger girls are gathered, peering over her shoulders and groaning one after the other with disgust as each sees the organs, then makes room for the next.

"Why does she keep bringing you mouse guts?" one of the littlest girls asks Aoide.

"They're offerings, just like we give to the gods! It would seem she thinks I'm a goddess," Aoide muses with a smile. "She does this a few times each month. Even if I don't see her. She lets me know she still thinks about me by leaving me these offerings."

"Why does she only leave you the guts?"

"Well you know why we humans only burn the bones and fat and guts for the gods, right? It's thanks to Prometheos fooling Zeus on our behalf! So maybe there is a kitten-Prometheos who pulled a similar bait-and-switch on kitten-Zeus!"

The little girl laughs as she is pushed back out of the way by a bigger girl who also wants to see the gore.

"Are you a goddess to the animals?"

"Is it because you saw the circle?"

"Which festival days does she worship you on?" Aoide is asked.

"It varies month to month. Sometimes she leaves the head," Aoide says through a smile in her own head. She tries to subsume showing how much she likes the feeling of being treated like a goddess.

"What does a head mean?" another girl squeals.

"Aoide!" calls a familiar voice from Athens behind her, causing Aoide to stand at attention. It is the voice of an Alkmaeonid woman, one of her aunts or grandmothers, though she has been away from Athens long enough to not immediately remember which.

In front of the visitor stands the elderly priestess Kliko, who glares at Aoide distrustfully. "What is that you peer at on the ground, girls?"

"Another offering of rodent organs from Ailisto," Aoide replies dutifully. Finally she catches a glimpse of the visitor behind old Kliko - it is graceful Agariste, her aunt and the mother of her cousin Perikles.

"Don't call it an offering," Kliko snaps. "Beasts of the wild revere only Artemis, and you will invoke her wrath if you even *seem* to be trying to take any of her supplicants, you arrogant little creature! Did I hear you say *kitten-Zeus*?"

Kliko can't help but chuckle at the idea when she herself says it, and all of the girls titter when the priestess laughs, allowing Aoide to finally smile again. But the priestess swats at the air in her direction to get them all back in the dormitory, and laughs, "You spend too much time listening to the absurd insult-poets, Aoide. I'm serious - don't spend so much time down there near the gate, okay? That's not the kind of poetry Apollo likes. That's Dionysian stuff. Understand?"

Aoide nods because she knows she has to.

Behind old Kliko, Aoide's aunt Agariste reveals herself from behind the old woman. Agariste smiles at Aoide and beckons her over.

Kliko says, "Your aunt is here, Aoide, visiting from Athens. You may spend the day with her, but she is to be back at the dorm by suppertime, if you please, Agariste."

Agariste nods, then holds out a hand for Aoide to take. Aoide does as she appears to be commanded.

Together they walk out into the sunlight, and begin to pace the stone streets of the sanctuary together.

"How are you finding Delphi, Aoide?"

"Good, Aunt; thank you."

"Are the priests and priestesses teaching you interesting things about Apollo and apollonian things?"

"Yes, Aunt. Praise Apollo for this sunlight."

"And are you happy here? Have you found friends among the other girls?"

"Yes, Aunt."

Agariste stops and turns to face her niece. "Aoide. I want us to be friends. I want you to feel like you can tell me truly anything. Do you have anyone here whom you can tell anything to - no matter what it is?"

Aoide thinks, then shrugs. She knows that there are some things that are not supposed to be talked about.

"You don't have a close friend your age? Or a boy who dotes after you and would listen to anything you say?"

"I have a friend," she offers with a shrug. "And I had a cat friend, but they don't let me out to see her much anymore. She lives out there, on the mountain. They don't let her in the walls anymore."

Still-necked Agariste smiles. "The other girls, the local girls - they don't give you too much trouble?"

Aoide shakes her head 'no'. "Not anymore," she says. "They used to, but I think they consider me one of them now."

"Good," Agariste nods. "I wonder if you've ever wondered about why we chose to send you here, to live with these Delphian girls. Have you?"

Aoide thinks about it, remembering back to her earliest days in the sanctuary, when she felt most alone and fearful. "My father didn't want me to marry," she says. "And my mother didn't want me to escort. So they made me a priestess."

"But you could have been a priestess of Athena, or Artemis, or Demeter, or Hera, back in Athens. By the look of you, you could have been one of Artemis' Bees. But we sent you to *Delphi*, to the center of the world, instead. I understand it might be easy to think that this was some kind of exile from your home. But I want you to understand that we chose you for this because of how *brilliant* you are - because you are important.

"You see, and I'm sure you know better than I do by now, Delphi is not just the center of the world; it is the head of the world - the eyes, the mouth, the ears. All information, about the world, about distant lands, filters through this small space. All plans pass through this stone skull - these walls."

Aoide looks around at the many faces from all around the world.

Agariste says, "Did you know that our family rebuilt this place after the Sacred War? While we were out of Athens, for reasons too complex to get into. This place owes our family an unpayably serious debt. That is why you'll always be safe here, Aoide. They know who you are here. Those in charge. You have a protection which other girls don't. But don't take that to mean that you shouldn't fear the usual things, like bears or boys."

Aoide glances at a beautiful young poet boy named Bacchylides, sitting not far down the slope of the valley, just the curls of his hair and the edge of his lyre visible from their vantage but Agariste still sees her see him.

While they're looking, the poet boy starts to quietly sing a song out to the valley and strum smoothly on the strings of his instrument.

> *Will I get rich and live in peace,*
> *or dwell always in painful toil?*
> *If only I knew what to plant*

in my own fertile mental soil!
But all who live know fickle Fate
casts shadow over mortal eyes.
If only I knew whom to love
and what the gods consider wise.

"Listen," Agariste says with a smile and a suddenly distant expression, "do you hear that? I heard Echo singing back his song. It's a good sign when she comes around."

"I didn't hear it," Aoide says, "but Echo is often on the mountain."

"Nymphs prefer the wooded wilds of the world," Agariste says. "Everything that little girls feel, the nymphs feel tenfold. But they don't speak to just anyone. I have heard her voice many times, when the women I was with didn't hear a thing. That is because she and I share a distant relation, as the daughters of the gods. You have the blood of gods, too, Aoide, as part of the Alkmaeonid family. These Delphian girls, they don't."

Aoide looks away, still not sure how she feels about her family back home. She knows that girls her age are being wed in Athens, and she sees the new way that men look at her body, and it only makes her more attached to the idea of being virginally joined in service to Apollo.

"Echo is a good role model," Aoide remarks, turning to the wisdom-lined Agariste with a young woman's sharpness, "for girls who want to keep their own voices to make sure they can beat any boy in a foot race."

Agariste gives her a serious look. "Have boys been giving you trouble?"

"Not me," Aoide shakes her head, "but I hear things."

"Of course. And how about the Delphians, the Pythia and their caretakers and priests and priestesses, are they treating you well?"

"Well enough," Aoide says. "I don't want to be treated too differently than the other girls, though."

"That's wise of you to know," her aunt agrees. "It is important for those of us who happen to have been born into positions of wealth to keep in mind that, even though we may have money and means, it is not wise to live too differently or separately from your fellows. Or at least not let them see it."

Agariste winks as she leans in close to Aoide then and playfully pushes her body with her whole side, while hidden within the move she hands Aoide a small pouch.

Aoide finds the pouch in her hands as her aunt pulls away, and keeping it close to herself, gives Agariste a quizzical look.

"A small collection of jewelry and coins for you. Don't let anyone else know. But use these as you need to, sparingly, to get yourself what and where you need. You're our eyes and ears here, Aoide. And this is where everything happens. All knowledge, all ideas, pass through these walls. We are trusting your judgment about what to listen to. If it seems important, we want you to know about it. Understand? So listen, yes. But also learn."

Aoide feels around inside the small bag of wealth and nods, barely understanding, but imagining herself at the center of a speeding racetrack while she sits among the gently swaying leaf shadows.

"So what is it you want from me, exactly?" Aoide asks boldly, looking her aunt in the eyes. "Am I to be a priestess, or a spy for you?"

Agariste sees the boldness and gives a careful, confident, opaque smile. "You listen to everything, and learn as much as you can. Every story, and every rumor, and every song. It is not just truth that is important. Lies and fictions tell just as much. Songs which seem to mean nothing. It all adds up, Aoide. We want you to listen to it all."

"What about my own song?" Aoide asks, rhetorically.

Agariste sighs and looks away with the distant mask of a smile. She says, "Even when you sing alone, you are heard at least by the birds and the winds, and you just might be heard by a god. You never know. But you will find, there is no original song, Aoide. Whatever song you see as yours, it is just your part of a long, old song."

"You never know?" Aoide echoes as a question.

Λ

The Spartan kings and their courtiers have supper after a hunt

The royal entourage of the two Spartan kings are all gathered together for a candlelit supper beneath their long, red royal tent out on the grassy plain, under the dome of glittering stars, after a long day's hunt during which nothing large was killed, only a few rabbits and brush birds.

The two kings, Agiad King Pleistarchos and Eurypontid King Archidamos, and their entourages line each side of the long table. Black-clad Queen-Mother Gorgo sits at the head, her personal slaves crouched in the shadows behind her.

"Tell me, King Pleistarchos," says King Archidamos' elderly but still formidably muscled military advisor Braximmachos, "what would you say was the lesson from today's failure in the hunt?" Twenty-five year old King Archidamos turns to hear his fellow king's reply with a smug look on his face.

King Pleistarchos, seventeen years old now, has only recently begun to finally grow the musculature and facial hair of an adult Spartan man. But in an effort to put on an affect of maturity, he takes a long sip from his cup of wine before answering.

"The king thinks," one of the Eurypontid entourage jokes, making the others laugh.

"I do think," young King Pleistarchos says after swallowing, "but what I think is not for you to know."

Archidamos sniffs a derisive laugh at that and shakes his head. "I remember being your age," he sighs. "Everything is about what you think will make you *seem* tough, *seem* like an adult. Better just to try to *actually* be strong, *actually* be mature in your thinking. That way you don't have to mask anything."

Pleistarchos stares coldly at Archidamos, but keeps his thoughts.

Several official visitors to the Spartan court are also here, further down the table - ambassadors from fellow Peloponnesian cities Sikyon, Aigio, Orchomenos, and Elis, and the famous old traveling poet-sage Simonides.

"There is a lesson in everything," King Archidamos tells the younger King Pleistarchos. "Whether or not you can find those lessons determines whether or not you will become a clever king."

"Hear, hear, child!" the weathered old poet Simonides calls out in his raspy voice. "Your twin king steers you true. There truly is a lesson in everything, buried within, often invisible at first. But everything must be mined for that most precious metal, the strongest and lightest metal - wisdom! It does not free itself but as dust, like gold."

King Archidamos says, "Alright then, wiseman, tell us what wisdom you see in today's failures."

"Well to begin with, it would seem your prayers to your statues did nothing," Simonides boldly says while chewing on some bread. He swallows while everyone stares in shock. "You sacrificed and begged, and they did not come through."

"Do you claim the gods have given up on us?" asks Gorgo.

"Just that perhaps they don't have ears."

The Spartans puzzle with that response.

Old Simonides shakes his head. He sniffs a little laugh for a moment, and seems to decide to change the subject. He pulls something from a pocket inside his robe, and hands it to the Spartan beside him, to begin it being passed around - a small hunk of rock with a spiral shell embedded in it.

"Where would you guess I found this?" he asks the table as the fossil is passed around.

Gorgo asks snidely but frankly, "Do you suppose it is some god's ear?"

Simonides smiles a simple no.

Finally it gets to Archidamos, who touches it carefully. "Some island?"

"There are mussels like that on Salamis," King Pleistarchos notes.

"I found this high up on Mount Etna, in Trinakria. High on the mountain!"

"Birds do carry things from the sea and drop them," one Spartan Overseer suggests. "I've almost been hit, myself!"

"Or the mountains used to be under the sea!" Simonides suggests with a dramatic flair.

The Spartans variously give confused looks, unsure what Simonides is getting at.

"My point is that things change," the old man explains. "Sometimes quite drastically. And even if some bird carried this from the sea to the mountain, that is still evidence of the change that one being can make. Enough such birds might bring the whole sea to the mountain."

King Archidamos interrupts angrily, "This is why we have become weak! This is why we fail in a simple hunt. We listen like Athenians to rambling poets who call themselves wisemen, instead of strategizing the improvement of our position!" He turns bodily in his chair to face King Pleistarchos. "King Pleistarchos, what do you think ought to be done about the Athens problem?"

Simonides shrugs and shakes his head, returning to his drink.

King Pleitarchos stares back at King Archidamos, for a moment responding only with shuddering eye contact and powerful silence. The other Spartans begin to shift as if realizing he will not speak.

But then he does. Young King Pliestarchos says, "Athens has their Delian League, among the islands. Their strength floats. They grow strong with allies, and they bully them into submission. Perhaps they are a growing Empire themselves. I'm not blind to this; I'm not an idiot, Archidamos."

The whole table listens with silent surprise at Pleistarchos' mask of confidence.

Archidamos slowly proposes, "Sparta has found a balance of power. We enslave our neighbors, and we intimidate those just beyond, but we do not try to maintain power in distant lands. Cities who try to collect Empires always fall. This has been the lesson of the Babylonians, the Assyrians, the Persians, and it will soon be a lesson historians tell about the Athenians. They reached too far, and they lost balance. We must do what we can to topple them while they teeter."

"The islands try to back out one by one, and the Athenian fleet sails to and fro to catch them," Pleistarchos says.

Archidamos nods, "Like a little shepherd boy with no dog. See, yes! There is the lesson! Athens chases her sheep to and fro, catching one and losing another. If one were to intend to confront this shepherd, or take a sheep, it would be wise to do so while he is distracted."

Gorgo clears her throat and all look to her. She takes her time eyeing them all before carefully speaking. "You think like a dog, like a man. Of course. Because we have raised you only to think like dogs. You cannot begin to fathom the complexities which you are not considering. Your worldviews are inherently *male*, seeing the world only through the narrow view of helm, thinking only dog thoughts."

The men all increasingly furrow their brows at her, but listen, and look to each other's reactions silently. Some make their discomfort known by breathing loudly.

"Even you kings!" Gorgo nearly shouts, looking right at King Archidamos, and then turning her eyes to her son King Pleistarchos. "To be a Spartan *man* is to be the best of dogs - loyal, single-minded, tireless, fearsome. Spartan women must be like eagles - harsh, wise, quick-acting, ever-thinking, seeing-all, knowing-better. You dogs cannot begin to actually circumspect the real situation of the world, the danger of Athens and democracy, the danger of 'wisemen' and 'poets', let alone the actual efforts that might defeat these enemies. You think only in terms of the tooth and claw, the spear and shield. You would wrestle fruitlessly against each other forever, to no gain."

Queen Gorgo gestures with her head for one of her slaves to refill her cup with wine, after which the slave slinks back into the shadows behind her. Gorgo drinks.

"Paradoxically, it was by the wisdom of a man, wise Lykourgos, when long ago we decided to channel the inheritance of wealth to the one running the house, the widow, the one who needs the wealth, and to focus our men on what they do best - struggle, whether with a plow or a wolf or each other. That's why our law flows wealth to the widows, so that we can actually use our wisdom to keep our strength in the right place, instead of destroy ourselves by giving all the decision making power to grunting men who know no better than whatever keeps their belly full and their dicks cumming."

The men in the tent shift uncomfortably under the implications, looking at each other laconically.

"You Spartan women are unique among women I have met in All Hellas," admits the beautiful Byzantine princess Niome. "You alone seem born with the certainty of the gods that it is your right to rule men."

Gorgo looks up at Niome and snarls a pleased smile in her direction, thinking about what was said long enough to retort cleverly, "That is because Spartans, alone among Hellene women, are actually able to birth *men*."

King Archidamos, trying hard to remain appearing cool and unphased, raises a cup toward Gorgo and says, "To the mothers of Sparta."

Gorgo drinks, then says, "To Princess Sparta."

M

Sophokles and friends celebrate the naming of his first son

Sophokles' brightly painted house rings with chatter and laughter on this rainy day, as all of his friends and family have gathered to celebrate the recent birth of his first son, who is to be named today.

Broad-shouldered Aischylos arrives with his bright-eyed wife Podarge, and a couple of the young children of another playwright take their cloaks to hang, having been given that duty by their parents. Podarge immediately scans the room for the other wives, sees them and waves and laughs, already expecting jocularity.

"Stay with me, this time, please, my dear," Aischylos begs his wife in a whisper with a hand to the small of her back. "I dread a competition of wits against the new father. You must be my shield from it."

Podarge rolls her eyes and snorts. "As you wish," she says, waving apologies to her friends and pointing to her husband as blame.

Gravelly-voiced actor Kratinos, a wineskin slung over his shoulder, swaggers up to Aischylos before they have a chance to enter the fray.

"Aischylos!" Kratinos shouts, already smelling of wine. "Famed genius of the stage! And his beautiful wife Podarge! How are you two on this beautiful day?"

"Doing well, Kratinos, thank you," Podarge replies charmingly. "You smell like you are doing well also. Tell us, where is the wine jar? We will surely want to pour ourselves some."

"Drink from my skin, here!" Kratinos offers, slinging the full sack around his shoulder and splashing a bit from its mouth in the process. Aischylos and Podarge both back away from the graceless drunk with their hands up to block splashes. "O dear, my apologies! You are the cup-drinking types aren't you? The jar and cups are on the other side of the room, with the fancier foods."

Aischylos then asks, "Did you have any trouble getting here from Eleusis? How was the road?" Knowing each other from Eleusis, a common topic of smalltalk is the state of the road to and from that city.

Kratinos replies, "Flooded, actually, just before Milenos' turn by the fig orchards. So I left the path there, went up to the hill and walked its ridge until just past the house of Pelon."

"Hermes always provides a way, even if he blocks another," Aischylos nods. "Praise to Hermes you got here okay."

"To Hermes Way-Shower!" Kratinos shouts, and takes a swig from his swinging wineskin.

Sophokles approaches with the wide grin of a new father, and he laughs, "Now here are two old men just talking about the paths they took to get here. Classic!"

"Hermes ignore this distracted fellow's impiety," Aischylos says and he greets his comrade with a grasp of the arm. "He does not want to get lost any more than anyone else, despite what it might seem."

"I don't know," Sophokles laughs, "I rather like getting lost a little bit, sometimes. Hermes is a playful god, if you remain playful in your heart."

Podarge hands Sophokles a folded cloth stuffed with small carved toys for the baby - an ox, a horse, a sphinx, and a lion. Sophokles receives the gifts with a smile and kisses Podarge on the cheek. Aischylos looks bored but nods politely to everyone around.

"Have you decided upon a name?" asks Podarge politely.

"Granting the gods are kind enough to let him live, we plan to name the boy Iophon," Sophokles replies with a tired smile. "Perhaps you might try this one day yourselves," he then jokes to Aischylos, who struggles to avoid glaring at him.

Podarge explains, with a glance at her older husband, "Aischylos is more concerned about his *poetic* progeny for the time being. However, I do remind him that while my love will last longer than his fine quill pen, my usefulness for child-bearing will not last forever."

"We will generate eventually," Aischylos assures them both with a sigh and a calm-down gesture. "Now that I know I can create masterpieces, I would like to have created at least a few more before I focus on rearing a son. I wouldn't want to resent my child for getting in the way of my creating art."

Podarge rolls her eyes secretly to Sophokles, who gives her a smile.

"Although, my friend Aischylos," Sophokles remarks slyly, "surely any glory of theatrical success would pale to the military glory that you achieved defeating Persians in *both* Persian Wars. Surely the many lives your war work saved has already multiplied and even given grandsons by now!" He slaps Aischylos on the back, and Aischylos can't help but smile and bow at the kind reminder of his service as an Athenian veteran.

"That's kind of you to say," says Aischylos. "My fine brothers were the real war heroes in our family, though."

Sophokles morosely nods, unable to think of anything reverent enough to say. He then nods politely to each and retires back toward the room where his newborn son is crying.

N

Perikles discusses the Athena First-in-Battle with Phidias

Potters' Alley bustles behind Perikles and young Phidias as they huddle together inside the sculptor Myron's workshop tent. A large new marble statue of the Minotaur Asterion whom King Theseos fought in ancient tales is on its slow way to the Temple of Theseos and everyone with nothing better to do is watching the pull and debating better ways to do it.

"Think about it this way," Phidias says, struggling to ignore the outside voices. "There are two different images - first the image that seeks to mimic *reality*, what things *really* look like; and then the image that seeks to show people what they *expect* things to be *depicted* as looking like, the traditional *symbol* which is understood to represent a thing. The image of a woman, for example. Picture a woman in your mind. Any real, actual woman."

Perikles first pictures his cousin Periboea, with whom he knows his mother has been trying to set him up for future marriage. His mind cycles between his many Alkmaeonid cousins and aunts.

"Now picture an image of a woman, from a pot. Or a statue of a woman. Now try to notice the differences. Why do we portray women as we do?"

"Because it's what we want to see a woman look like?"

"Because it is what people are *expecting* to see! Because it is only possible to make so many marks on a pot - marks have a certain *minimum size*. In fact, when they are shown something that looks like reality, people first think - how bizarre!"

"This sounds like a question for philosophers, not artists," Perikles half-jokes good naturedly. "I'll have to remember to pose this to my friend Anaxagoras of Klazomenai. Have you met him?" Phidias indicates no. "I'll introduce you, if you like. He's a great thinker, and a skilled geometrician - a measurer of the Earth! I suspect I do know what his answer to this question would be, as he has strong opinions about preferring that which nature proves true over that which men have long held to be true in their minds."

"And so his answer would be..." Phidias asks hesitantly.

"His answer would be to mimic reality, not expectation."

"And this is a man whose thinking you admire?"

Perikles nods easily.

"Then, if you please, I would like to show you a miniature I've already produced with just that goal in mind."

Phidias goes to a table full of small objects which are all covered by a dark brown sheet. He feels under it until he retrieves something which he brings back to Perikles hidden in his two hands like a secret. When he hands it to Perikles, it almost comes alive in his first sight, and being so small in his hands, the object momentarily makes him feel like a colossal god.

The statuette is barely taller than the length of a finger, but in its details and artistry there is more life, more vivid subtle realism, than Perikles has ever seen at any scale in statue, and insomuch even this small figurine has the overwhelming quality of a life-sized person.

"Pygmalion!" Perikles whispers excitedly, thinking of the ancient story of a sculptor so skilled that he fell in love with his own statue.

Phidias sniffs out a sigh and retorts, "Please. Pygmalion only loved his creation like a woman, like a mortal romance. My adoration of *my own* work is the divine love you have of a god, and like Homeros says - the two are not at all the same."

Perikles chuckles, "So a comparison of you to legendary Pygmalion is inappropriate because it is not hubristic *enough*! I am impressed, son, with your confidence; I will definitely give you that."

Phidias pulls his hair like a grieving daughter and comically groans, "You're the one paying me to visualize and manifest the gods! The job demands confidence which I must summon or manifest one way or another!"

Perikles just nods, turning the little Athena around in his hands. He tries to imagine it scaled up to a massive size, looming from the Akropolis over the entire city, visible from the Sea as ships sail in to Attika.

Perikles puts Athena carefully back down on the table.

"I'm sorry," Phidias sighs, and begins to loose tears.

Perikles takes the boy by the shoulders and asks, worried, "Why do you cry?"

"Why do you?" Phidias asks back with wet and worried eyes.

It's only then that Perikles realizes that his awe at the image of the goddess has made tears gather in his eyes. He feels their warmth, smiles, and wipes them away.

"I didn't know that I was," Perikles says. "Your artwork's beauty struck me numb to my own awe. This is beautiful, Phidias. I sense the soft feel of the fibers of the Fates in the air weaving us together. But now then tell me this - can you create this, but ten men tall?"

Phidias gasps silently, then frowns in thought, and looks again at the statuette of Athena, already a sizable piece of ivory and gold despite being only about a hand high.

"In marble?" Phidias asks.

Perikles shakes his head and holds the statuette up again, into a shaft of light where the gold glows and the ivory shines. "Just like this, gold and ivory - *cryselephantine.*"

Phidias sniffs and minutely shakes his head, then asks, "Is there so much wealth in the world to pay for it?"

Perikles hands Athena back to Phidias and says, "You let me worry about that. Themistokles got the Oligarchs to pay for a fleet to vanquish Xerxes, didn't he? Well, I mean to get the Oligarchs to pay for artwork to vanquish the *hearts* of all men, to awe-strike their minds before they can even think of war!"

"How does one build something so large?" Phidias asks the air.

"I imagine: in parts," Perikles suggests. "Like the Delian League itself."

Phidias nods at this, as if it is actually profoundly useful wisdom. Then he asks the real question which has been haunting him, "Why me, though? What made you select me?"

Perikles tells him, "I know you can do it. No one else is this skilled, young man. The gods have put some great spark into you. You are the future. You make art like a wiseman, not like a salesman."

Perikles rubs Phidias' shoulders and then takes his leave.

Phidias shrinks, already inspecting his small Athena and trying to visualize what it will take to construct its parts colossal, and in the finest materials known. Imagining the little sculpture gigantic makes him suddenly feel even bigger himself, titanic. He imagines what it must feel like to be one of the gods. Phidias' confidence engorges, and he lingers upon that engorgement for a while there by himself, while no one is looking.

Ξ

An Alkmaeonid family dinner with guests

As the eastern stars are appearing opposite the sunset, Perikles and his mother and brother Ariphron are joined for an outdoor supper by his aunt and cousins, Agariste's sister Hipparete and her daughters. Klotho, the oldest, and Periboea, her younger sister, sit to Perikles' right, his brother and mother to his left. Perikles, as male head of the household, sits at the head of the table. Though he hates the conspicuousness of that symbolism, and would prefer to appear more egalitarian by sitting on one of the long sides like the others, he knows his traditional mother will not let it go unless he sits in the symbolic seat of power. Crickets creak from the bushes. Neighborhood dogs whine.

    Perikles explains, feeling very proud of himself, "And so, with the public wealth we have accrued from the League of Delos, I'm hoping to convince the people to finance a great statue of Athena. Something excellent and inspiring which all can own in commonwealth. I've found an incredible young artist whose work is unlike any before."

    "Art unlike anything before usually looks bizarre," Hipparete says carefully. "Are you sure that's the best choice? Wouldn't a classical style be better? Not everyone shares your modern tastes, Perikles."

    Perikles' mother Agariste nods and adds, "Also, it will matter to the people, surely, *which* version of Athena you are going to represent. Beautiful young Athena Girly? Or mannish, unlikable, inscrutable Athena Battlewoman?" She and her fine-featured sister chuckle to each other.

    "I was thinking the many veterans of the Pnyx would appreciate Athena First-in-Battle," Perikles suggests. "I don't think men are able to appreciate the wisdom and virtues of Athena Girly as well as you noble women who understand the dangers and magic of having-been-girls."

    Big-shouldered Thrax brings their crab-meat bouquets in bowls, serving Perikles first. Perikles notices his kindly cousins smile coyly to each other after catching one another glancing at Thrax's muscular arms.

    Addressing the moment indirectly, Agariste says, "Don't underestimate the importance of beauty. It is what the gods created the world *for*. If not for pleasure, beauty, love, and joy, there would be no reason to bear the ills and wars of the world. Women would stop bearing children."

"And grace," Hipparete adds as she knocks the table with her knee to get her daughters to behave more appropriately. They twist their smiles shut.

"Well," Perikles says hesitantly, "I must admit, mother, that one thing I've learned from working with Democrats is that some of the things which we noble families think make life 'worth it' can never even be hoped to be attained by other people, people without property. It is a different world for the poor. Yet still honorable, respectable, and worthy."

"You think the poor don't value beauty?" Agariste asks. "I would think that they value it even more highly even than we do, since they do not also need to consider the values of economic things like horses and orchards. Freedom from nobility seems to me to be the freedom to live any kind of life, the freedom to get up and move to a new land, that sort of thing. Beauty has value to everyone, Perikles!"

"Less, though, perhaps, to the hungry, or the fearful," Perikles suggests. "That's what I mean."

Agariste shakes her head with a coy smile. "Those dying of thirst will still appreciate a beautiful painting. Or a beautiful woman."

Agariste eyes her nieces around the table. "Hasn't Klotho become beautiful as she blossoms into a woman?" Agariste asks her son Perikles as she dips her cup into the krater of wine. Ariphron ogles Klotho and nods with a twinkling gaze.

Perikles and his young cousin Klotho meet in a shy moment of eye contact as she is avoiding his brother's gaze. She hangs for a moment in his eye contact, then smiles away from it. He hasn't seen her since she was a much younger girl. At the same time, he sees Klotho look at him, and he wonders what he looks like to a girl's eye.

Perikles nods to his mother's question.

Beside her sister, Periboea sits silently and listens, staring, feeling invisible.

"I don't want you looking at girls from other families, Perikles," his mother tells him matter-of-factly. "No one wants to marry into the - well, anyway, we need to keep our money in the family. Look to girls like Klotho, or one of your other cousins, when you start to think about setting up a family of your own."

Perikles glares a forced smile into his plate of food.

"You've become a fine, respected man the last few years," Klotho says with demurely restrained confidence, looking up from her own lowered face. "Any one of us would be lucky to be married to a man of your magnanimous mind."

"And your lovely alliteration alludes to your own erudition, dear cousin," Perikles replies with a respectful nod under a worried brow, "but, mother," he says, turning his eyes to his mother if not his neck, "I must admit that, as with politics, in love I hope to follow my own heart, and not necessarily do what you and father would have wanted me to."

"This is not about your father anymore, son," Agariste snaps, icing up. "You, Perikles, have the reigns of us all, not because you're the most prepared to hold those reigns with mastery, but merely because you are the oldest man, and the laws of our city are that *men* hold all the power, and you have your little dick."

Everyone sits in awkward silence for a moment, which Agariste lets hang there willfully for all to experience. Perikles thinks of the theater, and imagines Aischylos under the mask of his mother's face.

She continues, "You know, Klotho, in other lands it is not always the same. In Sparta, it is the widow who inherits all, leaving the men yoked by their crone landlords. But not in Athens. Despite not knowing why or what we ought to do, or having any experience in the ways of men outside your fables and poetry, nevertheless it falls to a *boy* to steer our family's ship of home within the stormy sea of state..."

"I fear if I let you, you will go on like this without end," Perikles interrupts. "Mother, this is not about other economics. I believe in Aphrodite's wild will in love, and I simply do not wish to be married without the arrow of Eros in my heart. And since I am the lord of our house I know that you have to respect that. I love your mother, Klotho, and you, and your sisters, O Klotho - I see your little tear and hate that I have made you cry - but this is a misunderstanding between my own mother and me, and should never have involved you so intimately."

Klotho raises her tear-dripping chin. "I'll stay or leave as you prefer, cousin."

"Klotho," Hipparete coos empathetically.

Perikles says, "Stay, dear, stay. Finish your fish. Mother, I am sorry that it is not a fair world for women. And I do recognize your wisdom. I know you grew up with some of the finest minds that Hellas has weaned. I wish I could have known your Uncle Kleisthenes. But it isn't that time anymore. It is now, today, the modern era, not the past."

"You are half-right," Agariste snaps, leaning in close to Perikles. "What we are experiencing is *postmodern*. This is not even modern anymore. This is some strange new form of men like when the golden men of old ate flowers and couldn't die. This is a time of cosmic empires overwhelmed by the power of organized fishermen. Literally anything could happen. Keep that in mind. Anything can be done. If it seems like it could happen, it can happen."

Just then muscle-laden Thrax appears in the doorframe with his hands primly folded, awaiting being noticed.

"Yes, Thrax?" Agariste asks him.

Thrax looks to Perikles and steps aside to gesture to the two men waiting behind him, Ephialtes and Anaxagoras.

"Ah, there they are," Perikles says with a smile, standing and striding over to hug his friends in welcome.

"Perikles," his mother snorts, "I wish you had told me you had invited friends. If I had known your Ionian friend was coming by, I would have gotten out the fancy Hurrian silver. Or that big bowl your father got from Ephesos - the one with their lady Kybele of the many breasts on it."

Anaxagoras bows slightly in appreciation of her knowledge of his homeland. "Your worldliness knows no bounds, dear lady," he says to his hostess as he approaches her and bows again beside her.

Agariste grins at his uppercrust charms. "Your friend may masquerade as a beggar, my son, but he still cannot hide his nobility," she says. Anaxagoras, closer to Perikles' mother's age than to Perikles', chooses the chair beside Agariste.

"Indeed," Perikles agrees as he seats Ephialtes near himself. Klotho and Ariphron shift their seats to make room.

Agariste gives Ephialtes a familiar nod and half-smile, notably failing to note any nobility of his. Ephialtes smiles through the transparent diss.

"Well, whatever state our home is in, your friends are welcome," Agariste reasserts, and snaps up in the air to get the attention of her slaves in the distance. She gestures to the two new visitors, to indicate to the household staff that new meals are needed at the table, and those people quickly move into action.

"Forgive me Anaxagoras, but remind me again what it is that you do?" Hipparete asks gracefully.

"To be honest, there has been some phrasing debate of late, among the olive rows, as to what we ought to call that which we do."

"Among the olive rows?"

"Ah, that's where this thinking and talking and listening goes on. Just north of the city, in the orchards, when it's nice out."

"Phrasing debate?"

"Well, you see, the old-fashioned term *wiseman*, or *sage*, just feels so ... I don't know, presumptuous, pretentious. I like to call us *thinkers*, however many have pointed out that even the stupidest folks are still thinkers. And so there have developed two schools, you might say - one who likes to call us friends of wisdom, or *philosophers*, and one who prefers to call us wisdomists, or *sophists*, as if wisdom is something that one does."

"So what would you call what you do, exactly, then, Anaxagoras?" keen-eyed Agariste asks, interlacing her fingers.

"I myself shy away from controversy, when I can." Anaxagoras smiles with polite awkwardness as he considers how to put it. "I suppose you could say, noble lady, that I investigate. However, instead of investigating salacious things like cheaters and thieves and lost loves, I investigate the mysteries of nature! Wisdom isn't something that I would claim to *do*, but it is something that I like and try to pursue."

"Like the *erinyes* pursue wicked souls," Perikles nods. "You pursue wisdom. I like that."

"The mysteries of nature?" she asks. "Which god's cult is that?"

Anaxagoras smiles. "Well, you could say it's sort of a new cult, though most of its adherents I think would prefer not to think of themselves in the same way that they think of religious cults. You see..."

Perikles interjects, "Careful," fearing that his friend is about to espouse atheism, and the sort of reaction that might receive.

Anaxagoras hears him, and nods with a sigh. "By the mysteries of nature, I merely mean - whatever can be gleaned from merely watching the flows and features of the evident world."

"Give me an example," Agariste suggests, eyeing Perikles' discomfort.

Patient Anaxagoras thinks a moment, chewing, then has a thought, swallows, and says, "Take this delicious meal, for example. See, anything, really, can be an arena for the investigation of nature. Why do we eat food?"

The Alkmaeonid family all look to each other to watch each other's thought processes as they engage their own.

Periboea speaks up first, suggesting, "Because we're hungry."

Anaxagoras says, "Ah yes, that is one reason. And what makes us hungry?"

They think again, until Periboea jokes, "Wanting food." The table all laughs.

"Yes, it is fun to play with words, isn't it?" Agariste says with a smile to her sister Hipparete. "They are like birds, some beautiful, some loud..."

Anaxagoras, excited by his thought process, doesn't hear Agariste and speaks over her, continuing his own conversation with the younger folks. Eventually Agariste trails off annoyedly and listens to them.

"But so what makes us hungry, really? Why do we eat? It is because our bodies need food, to grow and to work, especially as young ones when we are growing so much so quickly! Where could the material for our bodies come from, if not from within the food and drink that we consume, right? But how would human blood and muscle and bone be made out of fish and bread and wine? Are these things transformed? Or are they perhaps simply *rearranged*?"

The Alkmaeonids make a variety of faces, to and among each other, as they consider the eastern thinker's notions.

"It would seem to me, the more you think about it, that there must be a little bit of everything in everything, but just in different amounts or arrangements in different things. And so, in order to build the blood and bone and flesh and hair which your body needs more of, you desire that which has particles of that material in it, which is the food you eat."

Hipparete puts down her fork with a face of distaste.

Agariste sees the discomfort on the faces of her family and says, "What if we save the, as you call it, *wisdoming*, for the boys' room after everyone is finished eating and having this nice meal in peace?"

Anaxagoras smiles a polite apology and quietly takes a bite of squid.

O

Protagoras tries to teach Euathlos how to be wise

Protagoras paces between the olive trees as Euathlos repeatedly draws and aims his bow into the distance and then relaxes without firing. They have walked out to this shady place north of town in order to talk away from rumor-spreading eyes. Euathlos is afraid of appearing to be ignorant while learning how to be wise.

"Now imagine that you have been accused of murder," Protagoras proposes.

"What fun! Whom have I murdered?" Euathlos asks with jollity contrasting the hypothetical. He aims his arrow at a tree without pulling the string tight.

"In court, of course, you can admit to having murdered no one! Murder is only *criminal* homicide, so if you happen to find yourself having killed someone you must immediately begin to conceive a number of sets of circumstances you might be able to claim which would give your killing a non-murderous context. Perhaps the man was robbing you, for example."

Euathlos says, "So it was a man!"

"Perhaps it was just an accident, even," Protagoras supposes.

"A clumsy thief - I know a few just like that! Are you telling me that you are going to teach me how to get away with murdering any one of them without consequence?"

"Gods ignore him; no, you fool. I am proposing what is called a *hypothetical* - a potential situation intended only as a sort of theater or game with which to hone your mental skills. Let us say, for example, that some man has fucked your wife."

"I'm not married," Euathlos replies, but when he sees Protagoras starting to fume again, he adds, "but I understand that this is a hypothetical situation so, okay - let us say that someone has fucked my wife. First of all - describe my wife. She must be beautiful if other men want to fuck her. But is she kind? Is she demure? Or does she talk back to me a lot?"

Protagoras shakes his head for a moment, then returns to the conversation. "She is a normal woman."

Euathlos asks, "And who is it that has fucked her? Did he rape her violently, or did Eros convince her to enter into a willful affair with him?"

"These details are irrelevant," Protagoras sighs, "if all you are considering is whether or not our laws allow you to kill this man. If you are wed to a woman, and he fucks her, you can kill him, and it would be a legal homicide. So long as he wasn't, for example, at the altar of a god or the like. You are considering only issues within your own mind, but considering the laws - they are only thus. Do you see what I'm getting at? The law is not the same as ethics. You may recognize that it would not be the same ethical choice to kill a man who had merely convinced a woman to fall in love with him as it would be to kill a man who had violently raped a woman. But nevertheless, they are the same before our current set of laws. Some philosophers may teach you how to arrive at ethics which do not function in actual society, but I, myself, find that it is not useful to learn to row a boat on dry land."

"So I ought to learn the laws of the land, in order best to cheat them to my advantage."

"To whatever end - you ought to know the laws, and expect to be governed only by the law. Unfortunately I cannot teach you any tricks to defend against psychic attack from natural spirits of vengeance and remorse which might harry those who have done actual wrong. The point I am trying to make is this, Euathlos - the situation determines the argument you must try to take. There is no right and wrong on their own - those are things that depend upon the context, and which you must find in each unique situation. And our current context is this society, these people and their expectable reactions, among which are - Athenian laws."

"But how can one ever expect to move a court of five hundred random men, when every two men have such different minds and must be spoken to individually in such different manners? How does one speak to five hundred at once, and expect them all to understand the same words?"

Protagoras shakes his head. "The magic of democracy is that you don't have to convince *each* person, you only have to convince a *majority* of the people. Most people won't even listen to you, really. Only the wisest men will really be listening to you. But they are also the men whose opinions idiots take as their own, to avoid the mental price of building their own thoughts."

"Like I am doing here with you now!" Euathlos notes.

Protagoras nods reluctantly. "But what that means in the court house is that you are not really speaking to all five hundred men, but only to the ten or twenty whose minds are even prepared to think about what you're really saying, and whose decisions are strategically relevant to you. This is where you need to aim your argument. And then, it is a question of whatever works, as no two people are going to communicate in quite the same way."

"Are you saying it would be necessary to *know* all of the men I'm trying to convince?"

"No; that would be impossible. This is when it becomes necessary to build *stereotypes* of people in your mind, based on cues recognizable at a distance. Things like their gait if you see them walking, or their posture if they are still. Their hair - is it mussed, or kempt, or even pinned and colored? How recently was their clothing cleaned? That sort of thing. These can give you cues as to how to speak to different sorts of people, based on the different sort of manner you know each is expecting."

"Look here, wise man," Euathlos snaps. "I'm paying you for wisdom, not boredom!"

"You have not yet paid me anything," Protagoras reminds him. "And you only will if you're able to eventually win a legal case. So you had best listen to me and actually think about what I'm saying!"

Euathlos puts down his bow and sits heavily, plopping his chin onto his hand and giving Protagoras wide eyes in a mockery of rapt attention.

Protagoras frowns at the performance, but begins propounding anyway.

"Wisdom, of course, is always contextual. What is the issue at hand? You have asked me to help you win cases in the juried courts of Athens. This means swaying the minds of your fellow men, and *appearing* to be the one who is correct. Now a lot of that has to do with words, but it also has to do with your demeanor. And many times, a battle is won off the battlefield, beforehand. The same is true in law as in war.

"Allow me to play both roles for a moment. So now I, the defendant, have just explained my case as you heard. So now imagine that I am changing masks, and am now representing the accuser. For, as you see, the wise man should be able to make any case, from any angle! And, in fact, considering your opponent's best possible case is the best way to consider your own defense against it, or path around it!

"Alright - sit down there and pay attention, as I will now play both parts in a hypothetical dialogue. Now the first speaker, myself, is meant to be *you*, and the second speaker, myself, will represent your accuser."

Protagoras puts his hand over his mouth for a moment, readying his mind for the exercise, then begins pacing between the olive trees and holding a one-man mock debate.

"Good morning, citizen! I am Euathlos, ex-fool, and I have a concern I wish to speak to you about.

"Ah well, good morning, friend! How kind of you to begin with a cordial nicety. I, as a very normal person, do appreciate that and, though I might not always admit it, I am genuinely disarmed by such rituals of the marketplace. And without them, I might be predisposed *against* you. But I am not! So what can we discuss here today?

"I am here to accuse you of theft, sir, and I mean to have it judged in the court of law.

"O my, okay, well let us discuss it here, if you would, on the street, that we might come to some kind of mutual agreement and not have to bother five hundred other men with the matter!

"You see, Euathlos, it might often be easier to win your desired result from a would-be court adjudication by preempting the whole endeavor on the street yourself and convincing the other fellow that court would not benefit him! Euathlos?"

Protagoras sighs through his nose as he notices that Euathlos has fallen asleep leaning on his bow. Protagoras tickles the man's nose with a leaf of olive, but it does not wake him, though it does make some passing girls laugh.

Π

Perikles delivers his first speech to the Assembly

The five thousand faced Athenian Assembly all stand behind Perikles' shoulders as he waits beside the bema at the height of the Pnyx, trying to pretend he is not about to give his first speech to thousands. He is trying instead to imagine that he is about to look into that same bronze mirror in his mother's room to which he has been practicing this speech all month. The Assembly's familiar drone of voices, even quietly chattering as they are now, has never hung so heavily over his psyche before this moment. With all those people behind him, and his sense of their eyes falling upon his back, Perikles pictures himself as the titanic god Atlas, holding up not the world itself, but all the people on it.

Finally the herald motions with his double-snake staff to Perikles, while descending the carved steps of the bema and shooting a little "good luck" glance his way. Perikles picks up his soul like a shield and uses his legs to carry himself up onto the stone platform.

When at last he lets his mind see what his eyes behold, he is facing a sea of faces, each subtly rising and falling like wind-whipped waves as they lower and raise their heads, idly scratch their ears, lean to the side to whisper to each other, and stretch their backs, but also by and large keep their eyes fixed upon him, waiting for his words. Perikles breathes in slowly, then unrolls the scroll he brought for accuracy beneath his view, though he never looks down at it, for he has memorized his own words and has taught himself to look beyond all the people, to the horizon, in order to keep from being tripped up by any one man's reaction.

"Let us all give ear to Zeus!" someone shouts mockingly from the crowd, and many laugh, though the crowd does quickly quiet again.

Perikles declares, "I come before you today, Athens, to explain a proposal by my good friend Ephialtes, who is currently serving as our general in the east, putting a stop to Persia's naval adventurism. While he's gone, he asked me to describe his idea, which is this:

"We propose the creation of a beautiful, colossal statue of our great patron goddess Athena, to stand on our Akropolis, so high that her spear should be seen by ships at Sea."

Immediately, Perikles is interrupted by shouting, but it is only a few heart-stopping moments before he realizes that it is in agreement with his words. The shouting is brief religious applause in praise of Athena and her founding of the city and guidance in war. Perikles catches his racing heart with a swallow and smiles.

"We believe that our sacred height has lain in ruin for too long! As our fighting men push back Persia yet again, it is time for us to show the world the majesty of our great goddess, with a tall, courageous, powerful vision of Athena First-in-Battle towering above us all each day. With our collective will, and collective wealth, and the skill of Athenian artisans, each of us can be wealthier than the Persian King of Kings, by owning as our commonwealth a work of art greater than any other wonder on Earth."

The majority of the crowd is uncertain through much of the speech, but rises into a roar of applause by the end.

"Straight from the head of Zeus, may Athena shock the gods, and men!" someone shouts, making Perikles smile broadly despite his preference for a sober, serious appearance.

Athens roars, imagining their towering goddess of war and wisdom.

Perikles stumbles slightly where he stands, realizing only then that he has been entranced by the shock of realizing that his plan appears to be beloved by all - Democrat and Oligarch.

He has never seen the whole Assembly agree before.

Democrats gradually get a chant going among the whole crowd, "Athena First-in-Battle! Athena First-in-Battle! Athena First-in-Battle!"

The sound intoxicates Perikles, and he knows immediately that he wants nothing more than to make this feeling happen again.

P

Aischylos performs his first new plays since returning from the west

Sunlight warms the theater of Dionysos on the grassy slope of the Akropolis as citizens and visiting foreigners find their seats before the presentation of Aischylos' new plays. Many sit and then stand again, discussing various ways to fan or shade their seats before sitting, and some choose to sit in the cool grass instead of the hot wooden stands.

There is a palpable religious excitement, both at the notion of new plays from the award-winning playwright, and in anticipation of the new statue of Athena that has recently been voted into production. The Akropolis where it will stand looms rocky behind the stands, and many people turn in their seats to gaze up there, pointing and chatting about where exactly it might stand and from where it might be visible, as if a ghost of Athena First-in-Battle already exists before she is built, dashing headlong into people's minds.

Aischylos' actors file onto the stage for the first of the three plays, which he has been spreading market rumors about all month, describing it as a trilogy of interlocking tales making one larger story - something previously thought too complex for the majority of attention spans.

Sophokles sits low in the stands, just behind the front rows set aside for foreign dignitaries, so that he will be very visible to the actors if he chooses to make any particularly emotive reactionary faces.

The actors, down on the stage, line up behind masks. For this play they are costumed as ancient Thebans, and Aischylos stands in their center dressed the same as the rest.

A single flutist on her double-flute blows a melody which signals the beginning of the play, and beckoning silence from the crowd.

"Citizens, fellow children of Kadmos and his warriors who rose from dragon's teeth like seeds," sings Aischylos in a mask with the face of an arrogant but confused old man, "I, Laios, have returned to my home city from the court of King Pelops, who had received and raised me as an exiled boy! I see now those usurpers who had my poor regent killed, Zeuthos and Amphion, are dead, so I am home to claim my rightful throne!"

Later in the day, when the high sun has had time to build up some heat in the heavy air, the second play of Aischylos' trilogy - *Oedipos* - is at hand. Hand fans flutter under sun umbrellas.

Aischylos wears a wide-eyed mask as the king of Thebes, Oedipos, foreshadowing to the audience who know his story the eyes which are later to be gouged. The mask looks hard at its two fellow actors on the stage - Penander and Malakios as the sons of Oedipos, Eteokles and Polynikes.

Aischylos' wide-eyed Oedipos bellows, "Why must Thebes be ever-stricken by sons of kings cursed to unknowingly crush their father? Eteokles and Polynikes, you have done exactly as I commanded you must never do, and served me on the silver smithed by city-founder Kadmos himself. Of all things, this! And not even the shoulder of this hare, as is my due, but just a haunch, the best meat kept over there on your end. These cannot be but simple mistakes; you cannot be that inept; and thus I cannot but determine you are trying to pile on your disrespect. Well, sons of mine, not to be out-done, I curse you both, for all these slights, and in no casual way! Not unspecific is my curse, either, but that you each should die by each other's hand. How's *that* for cursing, sons? May Hekate see it done."

As Eteokles son of Oedipos, Penander declares, "Thebans: The Fates' foretold hour has come." The third play is an exciting success from its very beginning.

The western clouds over Attika are already reddening by the time this third play - called *The Seven Against Thebes* - is beginning on the stage. Capes and shawls have been thrown over cold shoulders in the audience. The earliest lamps redden blue shadows.

"Mine is the hand that steers our ship of state," Penander-as-Eteokles says, raising his hand dramatically, "and as a sailor knows the pilot must not ever close his eyes."

The chorus, dressed as the women of Thebes with sorrowful masks and wild, grief-torn hair, begin creeping out of the shadows of the skene and onto the stage around Penander-as-Eteokles. The course of the narrative has been planned to make perfect use of the longer shadows of twilight during this most dramatic third part of the trilogy.

"If things go well, all thanks will go to the gods. But if things go badly for us - and, gods, please forbid that they do - then all know that there is only one name which would be muttered with distaste throughout the street - mine, Eteokles. Zeus

Protector, earn your epithet and protect Thebes now!"

A soldier's mother can take no more, and starts to weep beneath the memory of her dead son.

Whispers and tears roll through the stands as the actors hush briefly out of sympathy, then continue.

Two dogs a few streets away start barking over each other across a puddle, gradually adding unexpected tension into the war play.

> *O hear, dear gods, our just request!*
> *Save our city! Save our city!*
> *Repulse the spear, to every ear,*
> *send fear against the enemy!*

Σ

Ephialtes and Kimon meet the Persian fleet at the Eurymedon River

The Eurymedon River's wide mouth is dense with Phoenikian ships - too many to count. Each one has embroidered onto its sail the image of a different ancient monster.

The Athenian fleet, with generals Ephialtes, Kimon, and Myronides onboard the lead ship, slows their approach now that they are within view, while they decide exactly how to proceed.

The soldiers, already armored up as soon as the enemy ships were spotted, are variously exciting the group with assertions of imminent glory, reassuring each other that they will see their loved ones again in Athens or below the Earth, and doing little war dances with their accompanying songs of praise to the War God Ares Man-killer.

O shield-holder, flame-commander, King of Manliness,
drive cowardice out from my head, with your rattling armor!
O horrifying one, who lusts to drink man-slaying blood,
strengthen my arms, that I might kill to live, to kill once more!

"I'll tell you what one of the nice parts of being a rower below decks is, Kimon," Ephialtes remarks nervously to Kimon, who stands beside him blocking the sun from his eyes as he spies the fleet ahead.

"What's that, Ephialtes?" Kimon asks, barely paying attention.

"You can't see anything. So you don't know when to be afraid. All you can do is lean into that oar when they tell you to. Context is what's frightening."

"You will be able to write a great treatise after this, Ephialtes," Kimon says dryly.

"Hmm, you think so?"

"*'On Being Frightened'*."

Kimon leaves Ephialtes and begins barking to the soldiers stationed on the deck below. Ephialtes stands stunned for a moment by the insult.

"It is nearly time for us to begin killing barbarians!" Kimon shouts, to a roar in response from his rows of armored men. "Behold, on their sails, the monstrous lords each band of eastern makeup-wearers worships! Do you want to be their slaves, or their masters?"

The soldiers beat their chests with bestial virility.

"Now imagine for a moment the hearts of the Persian soldiers," Kimon proposes to his men. "The last they saw of us, we were destroying their entire armada in the straits of Salamis!"

The soldiers roar with pride.

"*We* are the immortals, now, in their minds!" Kimon bellows with a charismatic grin. "To them *we* are the monsters, indestructible! I have bet Ares Man-Killer this fine ring, worn by my father Miltiades at the victorious battle of Plataia, that these barbarians will turn and flee from our very voices!"

The men roar like never before.

"Look at their fleet!" Kimon shouts above the wind. "Look, see for yourselves!" He points, so that the soldiers will actually turn and look. "You see, Athenians, how few ships they have, compared to our mighty triremes? Their generals know just as we do, that they're no match for these arms. Let's see how much fear we can fill their hearts with, before they even see our eyes!"

The soldiers laugh and cheer as their fleet sails toward the Persians.

Kimon shouts to his men, "Let the enemy hear your lion roar!"

All the men on the flagship roar like lions as loud as they can, and the roar quickly spreads across their whole fleet as the other ships hear it.

Within a minute, the Persian fleet ahead all begin to turn around, to head back up the river.

"They flee!" someone shouts, and the men all roar with pride.

Kimon laughs, and Ephialtes wonders if it is the first time he has seen that happen.

"They must have an encampment close by," Kimon says to some men standing nearby.

Kimon smiles like never before, and looks at Ephialtes, who cannot help but smile back just as brightly. His eyes go wide as he asks Kimon with disbelief, "Have we turned the Persians with our roaring?"

"Did you roar with us?" Kimon asks him, charisma twinkling.

Ephialtes nods, though he knows he only roared quietly.

"Then maybe so, Ephialtes." Kimon slaps him on the shoulder. "Maybe that was enough." He watches the Persian vessels complete their turn and start to head up the river instead of engaging the Athenians for a short while before adding, "After all, Persians are no less fools than any other kind of men. No one wants to get killed."

He leaves Ephialtes at the prow and strides back off toward his soldiers, where he begins connecting with each one in a close, quick conversation.

The ship's captain walks up behind Ephialtes and starts to rub his shoulders with thick, powerful rope-pulling fingers.

"Don't worry, cup-maker," the captain says. "You'll see the men fight yet. Only now you'll get to see blood, on land, instead of drowning men and shattered planking. It'll be more exciting, you'll see! The gods prefer it."

Ephialtes nearly crumbles under the ship captain's too-rough backrub. His fear reawakens. "If you don't mind," he says, shirking away from the captain's hands.

"You're tense, son," the captain laughs.

Up ahead, the whole fleet of Persian vessels has turned and begun to head up into the Eurymedon's wide mouth.

"Xerxes moves," Kimon says to himself, as he watches the uncertain moment unfold.

"Do you think Xerxes is there, on the ships?" Ephialtes asks.

Kimon sniffs a little laugh and shakes his head. "Xerxes' greedy will is in this whole endeavor, and that is all I meant. But no, the man, his body, I do not suspect is actually here this time. And if he is, we know already from last time, that he is too smart to get on board a fighting ship."

Ephialtes frowns with concern, feeling this ship beneath him. It lurches against a wave, and he grabs the rail with renewed fear.

"There we go," Kimon says to himself once he sees the confirming sign that the ships ahead are actually turning fully around, to head up into the river. He turns to the soldiers, to shout, "They mean to land!"

The soldiers all cheer. "At Eurymedon, the Persians flee!"

"They only land for one reason," Kimon proposes, grasping at the air eagerly as if literally seeing an opportunity there. "They land to meet up with more of their army. But we will land, as well, and stop them first. And just you watch, Ares, as the Persian commander turns his army right around! Ha!"

Myronides glances with suspicion to Ephialtes, then looks to Kimon and asks, "They have decided to withdraw and leave their ships. Wouldn't it be wiser to stay and secure them, and take that win, and their ships, rather than risk ourselves yet further by pursuing them inland?"

Kimon says, "No, Myronides. That would be to act exactly as they hope, to let them reconnect with the rest of their army. Their choice to leave the ships is a trap, to keep us here, where they will then fall upon us with their merged and prepared army. We should pursue them now, catch them in the woods before they meet their friends up-land, and if they come, we'll kill them too."

By the time the Athenian fleet is beaching beside the Phoenikian ships on the wooded shore of the Eurymedon estuary, the Persian army who had been on the boats has already left their ships and retreated deeper into the surrounding forest.

Myronides looks to Kimon, who takes being looked to as confirmation that he is in charge. Kimon turns to the soldiers and raises his spear.

"We find and conquer the Persian army here! Forward, men!"

Into the forest they go. Myronides follows Kimon's lead, acting like a general and raising his shield as high as he can as they march.

Ephialtes stands by the ships, frozen with fear. He watches the other men march into the woods until it is only their voices that he can hear.

His gaze slowly lowers to the ground, and his own feet, as he wonders what it would take to make them march into the woods toward the fray. A bronze sword on the ground beside him gives him visions of battle.

Just then, the dissipating sound of his compatriots marching through the woods transforms with a shout into the furious noises of pitch battle. Metal deflects metal and man defeats man in a hypnotic and terrifying burst of anger and fear. Shouts of terror and glory and strategy echo.

Reticently, Ephialtes takes up the bronze sword.

Its weight instantly frightens him, as if the blade begs to be dropped, or it is being pulled from below by Haides himself, but Ephialtes clings to it angrily and lifts it again, and on that second swing it is suddenly lighter to him. He feels himself vibrate with fatal energy, a scissor of the Fates now in his arm.

Ephialtes' mind races with visions of himself trudging forward into the forest, toward the battle, toward future assertions of his glory in battle, toward questions of what it is like to cut down a man, but the struggle in his mind keeps his actual body shudderingly motionless.

His eyes are pulled away from his internal mind's view to the forest just ahead, as the sight of men and arms and flashes of light from moving metal edge into his vision through the obscuring trees. The line of fighting shifts closer, ebbs back, like a creeping wave of tide.

Violent lines of poetry from Homeros sing their bloody scene into Ephialtes' mind. Limbs cleave longways, skulls are pushed from their heads, and guts are strewn steaming upon the grass in metered lyrical lines of horror.

Ephialtes hides behind the Persian donkey baggage train and watches over the back of a sniffling donkey as the line of fighting moves like a long wave variously shifting farther and closer to him. His fear keeps him motionless though he knows he ought to race in there and join the other Hellenic heroes, that perhaps just like Kimon said with the roaring, perhaps the addition of Ephialtes' extra effort to the collective might be just enough to push it over the horizon to victory, perhaps just like his own individual effort in the deep sea of men that is his city's democracy has begun to actually show results, perhaps, Ephialtes wonders, his courage or lack of it in this moment could be the difference between a Persian future for the whole world, or a Hellenic one.

Before he can choose, though, the Fates break off a Persian warrior from the line, backing away from the fighting and accidentally moving gradually toward Ephialtes with his back turned.

For several excruciatingly long moments of soul-weighing, Ephialtes stands with the War God Ares Man-killer right beside him shouting at him that the moment is now, the sacred kairos, the hole of the shuttle, the time to kill. But then the man turns around, startled to see Ephialtes, raises his spear, and the War God is gone from Ephialtes' mind, leaving just two men.

"I could have killed you!" Ephialtes shouts at the helmeted Persian. "I could

ATHENS

have killed you, but I held my hand. I'm a man like you are, and I don't want to kill any man. I beg you, as the king of yourself, to grant me the same mercy!"

"Drop your sword, then, and be my captive," the Persian demands, speaking Hellenic. "Persia treats its captives well; you must have heard."

"I have heard that, but I won't, I won't," Ephialtes stutters back, barely able to push the words through his fear. "I'm a man, like you. I won't submit to you. I beg of your humanity, let me be!"

"No one is free," the Persian coldly retorts.

"Athenians are," Ephialtes replies confidently, raising his chin.

The Persian stands ready to engage Ephialtes in combat for several moments, even begins to circle him, but his thoughts seem to churn, and then suddenly he is distracted by something behind Ephialtes which pulls away his attention, and that moment is enough to cause the Persian to return to Ephialtes' face with a fresh moment's mind, and this time instead of deciding to fight, he decides to leave. The Persian lowers his spear with a flash of disgust across his face and backs away for several steps, then turns and trots into the trees, away from both Ephialtes and the battle, a third direction, toward his own future.

Ephialtes turns to see what changed the Persian's mind, but all he sees is the softly bouncing tree limb that the thing must have just flitted from.

For a time, Ephialtes remains crouched there, wondering if the man will return from some other direction, listening to the distant sounds of clashing metal and cries of death and glory.

For a while, Ephialtes worries that he is nothing but a coward. He punches the donkey cart's hard wood corner to try to feel a semblance of the pain that he knows his comrades are reaping in the battle. He cries and grunts with each wound-groan the wind brings him.

Until suddenly he is grasped from behind, and he fears for a moment that he is about to be killed, or taken as prisoner into Persia. A life of servitude in some desert stable flashes through his mind.

But the hands pulling him around are wounded ones, and the face behind them is Hellenic, and grateful to see him. "General!" the wounded man cries gratefully.

Ephialtes helps the injured man to the ground, and retrieves some nearby rags to wrap the man's slashed thigh and hands.

"I begged the gods that there would be someone here to help me," the wounded man tells Ephialtes as he winces in pain while being wrapped.

Ephialtes takes a long breath at hearing that. He looks into the sky at the clouds hovering above and wonders.

    More men stagger out from the forest with injuries, or dragging their dead beloved friends. At the sight of these bloodied warriors, as their number rises in the first moments of his seeing them, Ephialtes' heart falls. He fears his people are losing the fight.

    But one of the fighters, clutching a right hand severed of some of its fingers, runs right up to Ephialtes and the wounded man he's wrapping with a big smile, and shouts as he's kneeling, "Persia turns! They will be our captives here, just like their ships! Never a greater victory for Athens in all of history! We are the warriors who won the furthest victory from home that a Hellene has ever won! Athena has given civilization victory again!"

    The wounded man being wrapped pulls at Ephialtes arm to get his attention, a smile growing amid his twisted grimace of pain. "The gods love us, General!" he shouts. "And bigger than that, you know what that means? You know what that means?"

    "What?" Ephialtes asks, sniffing out a laugh of relief.

    "It means that the world will improve! The gods love civilization! We made the right choice with democracy! The empowered people defeat the slaves of the autocrat over and over! The world is *good*!"

    Ephialtes' grin grows, unable to feel the same way all those around him are feeling. However the memory of his recent flood of fear ebbs back around it, and his smile twists.

    Before long the clashes of armor and spear fade and are replaced by the shouts of the victorious, and more and more men return from the forest, now largely unwounded, though far from unbloodied.

    "Hey Lysias, who am I?" one soldier shouts to his friend, then lifts his war skirt and bends over and sticks his ass out.

    "Looks like the Persian army to me!" his friend Lysias shouts, and their company laughs heartily. "They just bent right over to get fucked!"

    In among the trees and sticking shrubs the dead and dying lie upon rippling paintings of blood.

    Kimon trudges out from the calming fray, toward Ephialtes and the other Generals, clean of blood but for a single splash up along his shoulder. But the blood is not his own.

    "Again you grace me with victory, Ares, lord of war. As I promised, take my father's ring, worn on his spear-hand at Plataia."

    Kimon buries his ring deep in the soil with his finger, then kicks at the place where he did so, covering it with dirt and leaves to hide the hole. Kimon then removes the armor, helmet, and shield from one of the dead Persians and places it upon the lower limbs of a sturdy, man-high sapling so that it seems to float above the field like an armored ghost - the classic *tropaion*, symbol of ancient victorious warriors, to show where the tide of the battle turned.

When he has completed it, he finds the soldiers all gathered round him, reverently respecting his work.

"Who fell?" he asks the group. There is a brief silence, and then he looks around, making myriad eye contacts, asking again, "Did any of us fall?"

One after another, for several seconds, men say other men's names. Throughout the five thousand soldiers who fought, names of those who won't return.

"O Haides, dreaded king of the lands of the dead," Kimon says, "hear these names, and kindly make room for the incoming souls of our enemies, and heroes' houses for those fine Athenians who fell here today."

Myronides slaps Ephialtes on the back as he turns to the old red-robed entrails-sage and says, "Now read the guts."

Kimon then takes Ephialtes by the shoulder and looks into his eyes. Ephialtes looks back into the warrior's slightly spasming irises.

"General," Kimon says resolutely after a brief assessment, and turns back to the fighters gathering behind him.

Ephialtes wonders what Kimon saw. He feels stronger than ever that men cannot actually see into each other's minds, and that we are all masks to each other. He feels opaque and alone in the midst of the men's roars of glory.

T

Niome is summoned to the kings of Sparta

Careful-eyed Niome hurries across the hard-packed dust of the Spartan Agora, past the low depression where she remembers the blood of Pausanias pooled a few feet from his dying body after she plunged this dagger into his neck. In her hands today, glinting with sunlight when she looks at it, is that same dagger. She rushes under the day's bright heat, holding her veils close, hoping to be ignored by the Spartan citizens who stop their daily routines to watch her step hurriedly past.

Her padded slippers are muffled like mouse feet as she ascends the broad stone steps to the Temple of Aphrodite Warlike, where her mistress Queen-Mother Gorgo awaits her, wrapped in black as always, in permanent mourning.

Once there upon that height that looks across the Eurotas River valley and the sprawling tribal clusters of the houses of Sparta, Gorgo takes the dagger from Niome.

"You sent for me, Queen-Mother?" Niome asks respectfully.

Fire-eyed Gorgo looks at the knife she has taken.

"You've been in Sparta now for three years. You have been tasked with the care of Pleistoanax, son of Pausanias." Gorgo raises her eyes to Niome's. "Your captor's son."

Niome nods curtly. She quickly masks any feelings about the subject that might have otherwise escaped her eyes, but she sees in Gorgo's eyes that she has seen her do this.

"I would not be surprised if this was a boy whom you might want to take some form of revenge upon, to balance accounts in some way with his father's crimes," Gorgo says. She eyes Niome for a reply.

"No," Niome says, letting free her honesty. "I took more from Pausanias than he did from me. But the goddesses I look to have shown me peaceful omens and peace of mind since then, so I feel Pausanias and I have nothing more to do with each other. The boy does not deserve to pay for his father's crimes. He scarcely knows of them, or could understand them."

Gorgo shrugs, understanding and moving on. She begins to pace around

Niome, who stands unturning.

"And how do you find the spirit of young Pleistoanax? He turns thirteen this year."

"He is like any thirteen-year-old, confused. He goes hunting with his uncle Nikomedes now. He sometimes seems happy." Niome looks carefully for Gorgo's eyes, attempting to find the fellow caretaker that might exist there. "How is Pleistarchos?" she asks.

Gorgo's eyes freeze and her face hardens.

"Forgive me," Niome whispers, regretting the risk.

"Pleistarchos, the Agiad King?" Gorgo asks rhetorically. "The son of mighty Leonidas? How is his *spirit*? Or how is his health? Or how is his fate? What do you ask about, exactly?"

From her hung head Niome says, "His happiness."

"His father came home from the First Persian War broken, silent, and shaking," Gorgo glowers. "Because eastern cowards like your people bent the knee to the King of Kings and marched into our lands to subjugate us."

Niome closes her eyes, fearing that Gorgo might murder her with suddenness, considering which way she ought to run.

"But I understand, princess," black-veiled Gorgo continues, easing Niome's fear gradually, "because I too am from a cursed family. The gods provide kingship to families along with a curse. Never will we know peace. Never can we value happiness, for it will never be ours. All of the suffering across all the land finds its way, like rivers to the sea, into our nightmares, into our spirit itself. So I know that there are no people of rich and generous spirit in my family. Pleistoanax and Pleistarchos are both destined to be miserable people just like us. Like me, and like you. There is no escape from that fate. The only way to bear it is to stop expecting, to stop wanting, the sort of pleasures and happiness that regular people live for."

Niome opens her eyes gently, fixed on Gorgo.

Gorgo sees a hard-fought serenity in Niome's eyes. For a moment, their eyes wrestle in motionless emotional agon.

Niome says, "I am not miserable, my queen. I live in a beautiful place."

Gorgo corrects, "Lakedaemonia is a windswept plain."

Niome says, "I live with sweet and loving people."

Gorgo, with increasing frustration and confusion, corrects, "Theano's family are wretched, hard-hearted Agiads, just like me."

Niome says, "Sophronia is kind and graceful, and her royal boys are boisterous but learn quickly. Grandmother Theano is indeed hard-hearted, but I know what she has seen. She has shared with me her stories of her youth. Even Nikomedes likes to laugh."

Gorgo hides her glare beneath something like a smile. "Niome, what are you?"

Niome squints with confusion at the question briefly, but then quickly understands the Queen-Mother's implication. Still, she lists her initial thoughts first, before the answer she knows is wanted. "I'm a woman, a mortal, a Thrakian, a noblewoman, a slave."

Gorgo adds, "And a spy. And what are you embedded with this family to watch for? Their emotional health? No, child. You are there to watch out for the interests of King Pleistarchos, Agiad King of Sparta. I know that you are too smart to be mistaken about this. So do not tell me, ever again, about the family's *spirit*. Tell me about their *plans*."

Niome lowers her head. "They have not shared with me, or in my earshot, any conspiracies to thwart your power, Queen-Mother, or the power of your son. Nikomedes is a loyal Spartan dog, eager to be more useful, active with the practicing soldiers. Sophronia, the widow of the man I killed, lives within a silent peace I wish I understood, where it seems that she alone exists in her mind. Her boys are old enough to fend for themselves, yet I follow and watch over them to make sure they don't get into mischief. And Theano, elder matriarch, might like to make some machinations, but finds herself older every day, and though she shows a strong face, in reality she is depressed and listless most days. It would seem wealth has wounded her."

"They do not disdain you for the murder of their son, their husband, their father?" Gorgo asks directly. "His blood was on your hands."

Niome looks right into Gorgo's eyes. "We all killed Pausanias. Theano knows that. The boys blame her. But even they hold some guilt over it in their hearts. His name is spoken once a month, in honor, on Noumenia, but it lingers in all our minds most nights, I know. You cannot kill someone and then ignore their ghost."

Gorgo replies, "I have killed men I've never met, by the thousands. Barbarians and Helots and Hellenes alike. Names I'll never know. Believe me when I tell you, you are imagining any ghosts you see. There are no ghosts. I would know."

Niome says, "We experience different worlds. Mine has ghosts."

Y

Aoide meets a Pythia

Dikasto has Aoide's head in her lap as they laze together on a sloped meadow just up the mountainside from Delphi while below them the sanctuary and the valley are falling into dusk shadows. The stars are just waking.

Dikasto pets Aoide's hair sweetly, as she sings, "Silly Athenian girls who dare Apollo to share his highest knowledge end up with big black holes in their minds."

"Just my vision," Aoide replies softly, "just my eye. Not my mind. Maybe the hole in my sight was to make room for all the wisdom he put in my mind. Maybe what I saw was the hole created by Apollo's arrow fired directly into my eye?"

Dikasto laughs, impressed. "I love that thought! Are you sure it wasn't an arrow of Eros? No love suddenly filling your heart?"

"No, just wild wisdom. I'm sure it was Apollo. He must have been riding with Helios on the Sun Chariot. I feel like that's part of the wisdom he gave me, a knowledge of where the wisdom came from."

"How do you know?" asks one of the other girls sitting with them.

Aoide thinks about it for a while, looking up at a star, then says, "I don't. I don't know. I sense. But who knows? Isn't that one of the maxims of Delphi - 'Certainty destroys'?"

Dikasto retorts, "But isn't the primary maxim 'Know yourself'?"

"Is it possible to know without certainty?" the other girl asks.

Aoide starts to nod. "Isn't that what we do all the time, when we touch the unseen, and see the untouchable, and hear the unknown ... and know the unheard?"

"Know the unheard, what could that mean, though?"

"Think about it. Don't say anything, but think about it," Aoide replies, thinking about it while she says it.

Dikasto suggests, "I think it's like Herakleitos says, knowledge is inherently knowledge of a moving river. Certainty is the mistake of thinking the river is a constant thing, unchanging."

Aoide says, "It's actually possible to *nearly know* an incredible amount. The whole world is, you know, *true*, after all. If truth and knowledge mean anything at all, if the question is useful at all, then surely what is true and knowable is *the cosmos itself*, reality. And it *does happen*, and we *do perceive* it. And it *is* possible to learn about other people's experiences, when they talk or write about them, and to add all of that up into one truly colossal eagle's-view vantage on the cosmos, on, like the world beyond the horizon, and time beyond the moment. Perhaps not exactly accurate, evading the danger of certainty, but far from as wrong as nothing."

"What?"

"As wrong as nothing - that is to say: if I said that there was nothing, that would be wrong. And describing all this non-nothing as *anything*, any set of words, is more accurate than not describing it."

A deeper female voice, adult but young, swoops in to hover over the lighter girls' voices, saying, "Apollo must be happy today, for he is stirring the minds of girls everywhere."

It is one of the women called Pythia, standing not far away, wearing her long blue dress with elaborately embroidered edging, walking with an olive staff and clutching a large cup to her chest.

"Pythia," the girls around Aoide and Dikasto all whisper reverently, bowing their heads to honor her.

Dikasto, though, grips Aoide tight at the sight of the young woman. Aoide looks up to her friend's face to find it glaring at the Pythia. The Pythia cocks her head at Dikasto and gives a strange masked look which Aoide can't quite read. Then the revered young woman find Aoide's eyes.

"Is this Aoide, the Athenian?" she asks in her resonant voice. Her eyes look right at Aoide's, unfaltering and confident in a way she has never seen before, even in actors or political leaders.

Dikasto holds Aoide close. She pets her hair again to make an appearance of coolness. "She's mine," Dikasto says.

Aoide scoots forward from her friend and stands to match the other girls, giving a confused look to Dikasto. Dikasto reluctantly follows along and stands as well.

"I'm Aoide, yes," Aoide says.

"I've heard about you. Saying you saw the perfect circle. Knowing everything about the world which you've heard, like a human book. You are something to talk about, Aoide." As she speaks, the Pythia slowly walks past the other girls and approaches Aoide. Dikasto positions herself right beside her friend defensively. The Pythia turns to Dikasto when she sees this and says, "O Dikasto, why do you choose to be so difficult?"

"Because this girl is good," Dikasto says hushedly, barely to be heard. "She's not for you."

The Pythia continues pacing past and around Dikasto and Aoide as she ignores Dikasto's whispers and says, "A spy for the Alkmaeonids? But of course, she knows that we know already what her true purpose is. For she knows that we are the ones to whom Apollo grants utmost knowledge. Apropos of all your musings here this afternoon, no? How old are you?"

Aoide says, "Sixteen."

"You've been here how long, now?"

"Six years."

"Almost as long as you lived at your home."

Aoide shakes her head when she is reminded of Athens and her family. "I barely remember home," she admits. "I feel like I woke up when I came here, and the child who I was before that I don't know."

The Pythia nods. "It's said some bodies are the hosts to many souls. Most only just have one, and ever feel alone. Some lucky few are born with two, who help each other whispering within one mind, and often mistake themselves for one. I've heard of sages gifted with a soothing mental trio. Too many more will lead to madness, though."

Dikasto gets Aoide's attention with her eyes and shakes her head with serious gravity, seeming to indicate that Aoide shouldn't listen to this woman. Aoide squints a silent query, Why? Dikasto just looks at the ground.

The Pythia walks past them and turns. "Everyone but Aoide, please head back to the Sanctuary. Hands are needed. Run on now."

Aoide looks into the grass nervously while the other girls all leave, until she and the Pythia stand together amid the insects.

"Now tell me, Aoide, where you think your thoughts come from."

Aoide squints, and thinks about the question. "I mean, it varies, I suppose," she says as she considers it. "Some thoughts I formulate myself, quite carefully and intentionally. And some are thrust on me by the events of the day. Other people's words. But some, certainly, seem to bubble up from unknown depths, or waft in on a wind like some strange scent."

"Do you ever hear voices in your mind?"

Aoide thinks about that. Then she slowly nods. "I suppose that I do. I hear my own voice, but I can also hear others. I can summon them, to say words. But then sometimes also they do speak. I always kind of assumed that that was something like what they are referring to when they speak of Apollo."

"Aoide," the young Pythia says in her strange voice, "you seem like you hear the voice of the Mother of Monsters, even if you don't know what that voice is. Do you want to know a secret?"

Aoide immediately thinks about her youthful conversation with Dikasto amongst the flowers of the hillside, and what she thought about honesty and secrets back then when her mind and the world it wove were simpler. She takes a short while to respond, dwelling in that thought.

The Pythia cocks her head like a bird at Aoide during the silence.

"I'm not sure if I want to know something if it needs to be a secret," Aoide eventually replies, trusting the mysterious reasons that Memory brought that moment to her mind. "If what I'm hearing in my mind is this Mother of Monsters you mention, I'm not sure she'd want me keeping secrets. I feel like what I'm given in mind is to be shared."

The Pythia grins, and grasps at the air as if casting a spell. "Aoide, you're excellent. I am going to tell you about the Mother of Monsters. This is an ancient and important secret, and one you must decide whether you wish to keep to yourself, or not. But it doesn't matter that much if you share, because people probably wouldn't believe you. The draw of the standard story is just too strong, told by men, and money, and stone, as it is."

Aoide listens, unhidden.

"You see, we Pythia are not really priestesses of Apollo. That is a performance. We work in concert with the priests and priestesses of Apollo here at his sanctuary, but this oracle was given to Ge, Mother Earth, to beg forgiveness for Apollo's murder of Python, who was the grandson of Mother Earth, after all. And who in fact was Python's mother? Why, of course, Mother Earth's first daughter, that long-forgotten, darkness-shrouded mistress of mysteries - Echidna, the Mother of Monsters. See, we Pythia, we are not priestesses of Apollo, but of the slain son's mother, she who is first to comfort all mistreated women - Echidna, Earth's first daughter. You know that Apollo leaves this sanctuary every year, for months on end, to live in the north with the Hyperboreans. But who never leaves? Echidna, and her Mother Earth. They host Dionysos for parlor games and good sex throughout the winter!"

Aoide realizes that she is expressing disbelief. She tries to get her face under control, but then laughs at the difficulty of doing so. The young Pythia grins, pleased with the way the knowledge is affecting her listener.

"All true," she says. "So we Pythia maintain a centuries-old secret knowledge, you see, passed down from woman to woman, from old Echidna herself long ago in Skythia. And so, though we have been maintaining this ground in Hellas for so long, we are still at heart a Skythian cult, Aoide, and so you will need to learn some Skythian secret words in order to continue. For Skythia is where Echidna was born. Where she gave birth to Herakles, Python's brother."

Aoide listens, shocked and confused, and cannot avoid showing on her face her disbelief. "Herakles was a monster?" she asks.

The Pythia sees it and narrows her eyes, but then smiles. "You don't believe me?" she asks Aoide.

Aoide can only shrug with a half-smile in response.

The Pythia nods. "Siblings can be very different. Herakles was technically a monster, but he was also a man. Python was a monster, and a dragon. Aren't your sisters a bit different from you?"

Aoide smiles and chuckles slightly, which suddenly eases her tension drastically. The Pythia smiles back.

"These are the songs which make our minds. Echidna, the Mother of Monsters, married lawless Typhon, who taught men how to flout laws and destroy systems, and she took in all his ancient evil, all those dark thoughts long hidden from the world, and gestated them into real children - the vilest ancient beasts of our world, such as the dragon Ladon, the giant lion of Nemea, the horrible three-bodied Chimaera, the inscrutable Sphinx, and that guardian of the Underworld, the triple-dog Kerberos. Without these mythic monsters, the Earth would be wild! Against all expectation, in fact it is the monsters of Chaos and their maintenance of madness which allows the rest of the cosmos to dwell in semblances of peace and order. We madness-keepers are medicine for a world sick with stultifying norms. For little bits of weirdness and madness are what allow the Good to break free, to be born a monster and become a hero."

Aoide looks out over the valley, these words painting each person anew in her mind.

The Pythia touches Aoide's face as she says, with wide-eyed intensity, "You see, Aoide - in Tartaros, the titans are imprisoned; and in the Underworld, the dead are imprisoned; just as in Olympos, the gods are imprisoned. But all of these exist as *inner worlds, inside* living people's souls. What seems to be outside is inside. We each are the shell of the whole cosmos, not a cell of it. But that means that inside *each* of us are *all* these gods, and all these monsters, and that we are actually each other. But what you disbelieve in *does not cease to exist*. That is why the sanctuary's motto is 'Know thyself'. For each mind and the whole cosmos are one and the same, as all of each is contained entirely within the other!"

Aoide furrows her face, trying to understand, and tears begin to fall when she must admit to herself that she doesn't. It sounds like madness.

"I'm afraid I don't understand," she sadly admits.

"Good," the Pythia replies. "If you said you did, I would know you were a liar. But don't be afraid of your lack of understanding. Listen. Just keep listening."

The Pythia puts her hand inside the cloth of her dress and makes a shape beneath it that resembles a person, with a lump for a head, and two arms. She delicately mimes with her fingers such that the bit of cloth moves just like a real woman.

"Like this, does the Muse inspire the dancer," the old Pythia says. "She does not enter you, like a lover or a worm, but like a lyre or a word, she inspires you invisibly to turn your mind this way or that."

Aoide smiles, feeling she understands. Then, as she thinks it, she asks, "Who is puppeting me when I'm myself?"

The Pythia smiles slightly, then frowns and whispers, "You are never yourself. We are always the gods. They're a sort of false-real; being immortal means they're just ideas, who find fruition through us, through the wind and the world. They're not real, and yet there is nothing but them."

Φ

Athens celebrates the victors of the Dionysian theater competition

"Eyes dropping tears, but not a cry, their steeled spirits glowing with courage, as lions pant with dreadful battle in their eyes!"

Two teenage boys clash sticks as they recreate a fight scene from the exciting third part of Aischylos' recent ivy-winning series of plays about the kings of Thebes.

Most folks having forgotten all about the other plays in the trilogy makes it clear that the action-packed final part - *The Seven Against Thebes* - was the most popular by far. However, one part of the last play in Aischylos' set, the satyr play *Sphinx*, has inspired a few people to create little straw wings and wigs with straw straps and they have managed to get them onto a couple of Athenian street cats in a drunken attempt to make them look like that mythical Sphinx.

One of these so-sphinxed stray cats has curled in the lap of a sleeping stranger - the old, deformed poet Hipponax, who nods in and out of drunken consciousness with a hand-written sign hung around his neck:

POEMS FOR WINE

The straw-wigged cat sits nobly on the old poet's lap, cleaning its own face, ignoring the indignity which has been placed on it.

"There's always a cat with you," Kratinos says to Hipponax as he kicks him awake. "But it's never the same one."

"Cats get me," Hipponax grunts. "And I get cats. Insomuch, I nap." He curls back up against the stone wall and waves Kratinos away. "I have no more poems and want no more wine."

A string of dancing girls and actors arm in arm parading jauntily across the Agora catches Kratinos' eye, and he pats Hipponax's cat, singing his own twist on an old wartime hearth song.

Wait for me, wife, here at Hestia's fire
As citizen, I'm called to fight in War!
So oil me and strap my mask on tight,
For I might just fight for my life tonight!

Kratinos stands and takes the arm of one of the girls as the dancing group passes him, asserting the demeanor of a soldier serious about partying as he is pulled along with the dancers.

Aischylos takes this opportunity to let go of the group, and slow his own pace to a halt in a group of pleasantly laughing onlookers who greet him quite merrily. Among them are the young sculptor and father Sophroniskos and his quietly-alert-eyed wife Phaenarete.

"What a marvelous delight Dionysos must take in your plays, Aischylos!"

"It is interesting that you chose to write about Thebes and Argos, instead of about Athenian history, this time."

"Well, a mirror is not always the best way to examine the world. Sometimes one must look around," Aischylos calmly replies.

Phaenarete says, "I like that it was a war story, but it didn't actually show the killing - that all happened by implication, off-stage. I thought that was clever and tactful. Not like some of these plays that aim directly for the basest interests of their audience."

"Thank you, dear lady," Aischylos says with a bow.

An elderly visiting dignitary from Phoenikia interjects, "I liked *The Seven Against Thebes* better when I read it in Akkadian and it was called *The Epic of Erra*. But you made it Hellenic in your own very Hellenic way, so - here's to you, Aischylos! Interpreter of the classics for a Hellene audience."

Aischylos frowns at the comment and stops looking at the Phoenikian man, turning to address his other fans instead.

"I've never heard of any such Akkadian story, and neither has anyone in my audience, so I am not concerned with my story's similarity to any such thing. Didn't the Ionian wiseman Herakleitos say that one cannot set foot in the same river twice? Well similarly, I'd say no play can be performed twice, so different is each performance. Even the same actors on two different days will perform two different plays."

"You should find better actors, then," says young Polyphrasmon, fellow playwright. "Or direct better, so that they know what they are supposed to be doing. A good director doesn't have any loose performances, just like a good ship captain doesn't have any lazy oarsmen."

Some nearby listeners applaud the clever analogies being passed back and forth, as if the public dialogue itself is theater.

"I myself would love to see some theater about *ideas*," remarks ever-haughtier Protagoras in passing, a couple of curious young men following behind him agreeing just because he said it.

"Do they practice theater up in Abdera?" a proud Athenian actor asks the Thrakian thinker. "Maybe you should write something and see what the Archons of your city think of it."

"Writing is for listeners," Protagoras replies. "Thinkers speak."

"That's one of your best thoughts yet! I'm going to write that down," says one of his young followers.

Sitting nearby with some of his rowdy friends, big-bellied Euathlos laughs at Protagoras. "Whirlpools of nonsense feeding themselves," he says. "Thinkers, that is. Real men don't think, they do. Am I right, friends?" His friends all laugh and salute him like he's herm.

ATHENS

Protagoras hears the jeer and turns to the man he schooled earlier, seated among some filthy fellows fresh from the gym. One throws an apple core in general disparagement.

"Euathlos!" Protagoras shouts. "How fares your legal case?"

"O, that," Euathlos snickers, giving a sideways glance to one of his friends. "I have decided to avoid all those who hold public offices after all. A woman told me real women do not like such men. So you will not be seeing me before any jury. And, since we agreed that I would pay you once I win a case, looks like I won't have to be paying you!"

"Wait," Protagoras starts to protest, but is interrupted by Euathlos and his friends all laughing at him.

One of Euathlos' friends shouts, "O, the wiseman just got schooled!"

"Did you perhaps always intend to avoid legal cases in an effort to avoid ever having to pay me for my services?" Protagoras asks Euathlos, to be clear.

Euathlos doesn't respond, but just stands from his seat and starts to walk away, giving Protagoras the most arrogant look of victory imaginable, while his friends follow suit, some even playfully shoving Protagoras' hulking form with their shoulders as they pass him.

"Well then I'll see you in court!" Protagoras shouts after Euathlos.

X

Sokrates and friends hang out at Simon's shoe shop

A hazy rain leaves the Agora cool and quiet on this overcast day. Two owlets roost beneath a stone lion-shaped corner spout, reaching to drink from its steady drop.

Simon sits waiting for customers. In the corner where they often are, Sokrates, Krito, and Chaerephon sit drawing in the dirt, while lanky Euripides scratches whitely onto a piece of broken pottery with chalk.

"Explain to me the problem you have with this young man Phidias," Simon says. "Surely any problem can be solved, at least a problem between two sane people."

"What if he's insane?" Chaerephon squeaks excited at the notion.

"He's not insane," Sokrates says. "He's just an artist."

Euripides explains, "He doesn't like us."

Simon says, "O I'm sure that's not the case."

Sokrates admits, "It's probably because we made him break one of the pieces he was working on one time."

"Well, Phidias is an artist, like Euripides. Artists can be touchy about their art," Simon says.

Euripides shyly replies, "I'm not a real artist yet, not like Phidias."

Chaerephon then asks, "But what makes one a *real* artist anyway?"

Simon the shoemaker kindly smiles. "Wanting and pretending leads to being. Think about it - everyone is born anew, no one has experience until they try to do things. Every artist had to decide at some point to start doing their art. I think it's more about a dedication to the effort to be an artist, which makes one an artist, rather than already having made a lot of art. There are plenty of men out there who claim to be artists because they show work decades old, yet they are never making art anymore. It is always the future which makes someone what they are, not the past. What you are trying to be, not what you have already been." But as he thinks about his own words, they seem to make him melancholy.

"He's said we can't hang out at the sculptors' tent anymore."

"Well," Simon says, "it sounds like you ought to do something nice for him in order to make up for it. If it isn't something you can fix, or restitute, then you should think of something else which is equivalent. Like, maybe, make him one of your drawings."

"He doesn't like our drawings," Chaerephon whines.

Simon laughs good-naturedly and shakes his head. "Well, good conversation can be an underappreciated artform. Perhaps he just needs more of that."

Krito says, "Phidias is a great sculptor, but less great at conversation."

Simon smiles. "You, however, Krito, are a true artist in the form."

Krito bows slightly, like an actor might.

"Simon, do you ever fear death?" Euripides asks out of nowhere.

Simon looks up with warm eyes and the ghost of a smile, or the smile of a ghost.

"I'm not worried about myself; I just wonder if someone as old as you worries about it," Euripides explains carefully, and immediately punches the dirty ground when he realizes how rude it came out.

Patient-eyed Simon chuckles goodnaturedly. "Don't worry so much, Euripides. There's nothing wrong with stating the obvious. Not very many people live without dying. So it is something the living are bound to think about. Though perhaps anyone who is able to avoid such thoughts is the better off for it. But no - to answer your question - I don't fear death anymore. I used to. When I was your age, and even more so when I got a little older. But not anymore. The older you get, the more you get used to what it's like to be alive. But you also ... you forget about things that aren't right around you. And most people aren't dying every day. In fact - almost everyone who dies, only ever does so once. Few get a second chance to do it better the second time. Much like weddings."

"You just compared weddings to dying," the businessman being shod comments dryly.

"Intentionally," Simon adds with a wink to that adult, then returns his attention to the boys and continues, "though my ultimate point was this - I like to think of the time after I have died, or before I was born, kind of like the space in this world which isn't me. You know? I don't worry about the fact that I am here instead of over there. That I am me but not also you, and not the tent flap or the grass clod. I am not your hair; does that disturb me? No. Nor does the fact that I will not be alive for every day of the world."

Sullen-eyed sixteen-year-old Euripides stares forward as he says, "I feel like I'm just beginning to understand the world around me, and that I really exist within it. And, like, I'm me, and I'm the only one who knows what's going on inside my mind. All these thoughts, all these ideas, all these fantastic imaginings - nobody else can see them. Unless I paint them."

"Or you can create them in people's minds with stories, with words," Simon adds. "Or even, these days, depict them before people's very eyes in the actual performances of people, with the great modern development called theater! When I was a boy, it was all just poems. Nobody was *acting*. These days, now, they're practically recreating the events! I'll tell you - hearing them sing those war songs in *The Persians*, when I was there that night, gave me chills! It made me imagine what it might have seemed like from the perspective of Dionysos himself! Fascinating, isn't it?"

Euripides sighs. "You can't do as much fantastic stuff in theater as you can in a painting. In painting, you can depict *anything*."

Chaerephon prods Euripides playfully and mockingly asks, "*Anything*? What do you want to *depict*, Euripides?"

He and Sokrates laugh, and Euripides grimace.

"I don't know why I hang out with babies." He gets up from the ground as Sokrates and Krito reach out moaning about how he shouldn't leave, but Euripides bats their hands away and stomps out into the busy Agora.

"Euripides is an artist," Simon says. "Sometimes he needs to do his own thing. Just like Phidias. It is the difficulty of knowing artists. But they're worth being patient with, boys."

"Are we not artists?" Chaerephon asks.

Simon shrugs. "I don't know. Are you?"

"What does it mean to be one? How would we know?" Sokrates asks.

Simon says, "I suppose you would be making artwork of some sort or another. Or thinking a lot about artworks, at least. Are you?"

Sokrates, Krito, and Chaerephon all look to each other questioningly, wondering to see if the others do, and as they all shrug away the notion, seeing nothing from each other, they all turn back to Simon with shrugs and the shaking of heads, which in their simultaneousness make Simon laugh heartily.

"But what are we, then?" Krito asks. "Everyone I know who's interesting is an artist. Everyone else is just their audience."

Simon chuckles at that.

"Are you an artist, Simon?" Sokrates asks.

Simon raises an eyebrow at that. "I make shoes," he says. "Boots, sandals, slippers, socks. I shoe."

Krito says, "I think I want to be a wiseman. It seems like that would be the best sort of profession, by its very name!"

"Being an aristocrat sounds better," Chaerephon adds.

They all chuckle a bit. Simon says, "That requires a different past, not a different future."

"Yeah you can't just become an aristocrat, but it seems like maybe anyone can become a wiseman. There are even slave wisemen!"

Simon nods. "True."

Sokrates says, "I want to be a singer!" And he chortles out an irritatingly loud melody until all the others groan for him to stop.

Simon sighs. "Sokrates, please. Think of other people."

"You didn't like my song?"

"You are being a troll for no reason," Simon says with a direct stare into the boy's eyes. "Don't waste the tool of trolling, so that people start to ignore you. You want to maintain that tool for when it's really useful. And if you really want to be a good singer - be quiet, and listen to women."

"What about you, Chaerephon?" Krito asks.

Chaerephon stares at Simon with a fearful look for a while, looks to his friends, then answers sheepishly, "I don't know. I guess I ought to visit the Oracle at Delphi and find out what my fate should be."

"So yes, Chaerephon," Simon says, "if you want to go and have the Pythia at Delphi tell you your fate, you will need to first get some money to travel there, and bring a goat for them to sacrifice."

"The money is just to travel?"

"Well yes."

Chaerephon nods, doing some mental planning. "Travel to the mountains with a goat, okay. In one lifetime - that sounds doable. I've heard people say it's just a few days walk."

"You might want to bring a friend," Simon suggests with a smile.

Chaerephon frowns. "Simon, I hate to say this to you, but I think you might be a little too fragile to come with me into the mountains."

Simon and Sokrates chuckle. Sokrates laughing says, "He meant me, Chaerephon! Not him! He's already been to the Oracle. That's how he knew to be a shoemaker here in Athens, right?"

Simon laughs very briefly, then shakes his head and says, "No, Sokrates. Actually I decided that for myself. I have never visited the Oracle."

Sokrates and Chaerephon both look at Simon with surprise.

"How do you know if you're doing the right things with your life, though?" Sokrates asks. "I mean, wouldn't you like to *know*? Like, *for sure*?"

Simon raises an eyebrow. "The very Oracle herself makes as her main maxim the following phrase: *Certainty destroys*. People usually read it wrong, top to bottom, and read that last. But it is first when you look at it from below."

"I thought you said you hadn't been to Delphi," Sokrates slyly notices, raising an eyebrow like he saw Simon do.

Simon smiles at that. "I said I haven't visited the Oracle. I went to Delphi, once. I turned around. I decided that I didn't want the ... the magnetism of knowing."

"What is magnetism?"

"It's hard to explain what I mean," Simon says.

"You all should have maxims like Delphi," the customer suggests half-mockingly. "You've got the oracle of youth here in the minds of these talkative urchins, shoe-maker!" He laughs and pats Sokrates on the head dismissively.

"We should!" Chaerephon agrees, misunderstanding the tone and reading none of the customer's sarcasm.

Sokrates asks, "Where did Delphi come up with their maxims?"

Simon shrugs, but then answers, "The only ones I've heard of coming up with lines of clever thought formed into words, are people. So those maxims must have just been the clever thoughts of people from the past."

"Maxims are so reductive," Euripides dryly interjects, still looking closely into the little drawing he is making on his piece of paper, carefully making only small marks for fear of messing it up. "Anything described in words is going to be hollow compared to something people can actually *see*, like a painting or a performance."

"And maybe words aren't the best way to describe wisdom," Chaerephon proposes. "What if, for example, melodies of music are the best way to depict wisdom? Our maxim would need to be a melody. Or, like, a repeated beat on some drums." Sokrates starts slapping the ground to start a beat, and Chaerephon begins clucking with his tongue in time along with it.

Simon chuckles and says, "That is an interesting idea. But is there any meaning passed on in melodies?"

"The call to dance!" Sokrates shouts, shaking his butt while he slaps the ground and grinning broadly at the adults.

The customer eyes Simon with dwindling patience. "You have these boys here for what purpose, again, friend?"

Simon apologizes with his eyes and says, "They are here to learn."

"Shoemaking?"

Simon shakes his head slowly, eyeing the boys. "No, somehow they have never seemed interested in learning to make shoes."

Chaerephon excitedly shouts, "Euripides! Sing for us! Make up some words."

Euripides just rolls his eyes so the adults can see it, and remains at his delicate work drawing a scene on his piece of parchment.

"To answer your question, though," says a sudden female voice, surprising all the boys, who look up to see the customer's young wife bending in to the tent to kiss her husband sweetly between words, "it was the sages of old, some of the Seven Hellenic Sages, who gave Delphi their maxims. There are many more than the famous three! But the three are the main ones."

The customer stands, feeling the fit of his new boot. "Seems good," he says to Simon. Then he touches his wife's face condescendingly and says, "You can't just repeat whatever you hear, dear one. These boys know no better than to believe you! It was the Pythia, ancient Pythia in days of old, but not the male Seven Sages, who first spoke the maxims of Delphi. I don't think they, who are themselves purveyors of wisdom, would want to display some visitors' fare on their facade! Even wisdom-brokers must be salesmen!"

The customer's wife rolls her eyes so the boys can see it.

"How can we know any of that, though, even?" Chaerephon is bold enough to ask the adults, who smile to each other at the question.

"I spoke to folks who *work at* Delphi, while I was there," says the customer.

"I heard from literally every other person I've ever spoken to about Delphi," says the customer's wife.

"Yes, well," the customer shrugs.

Simon says, "The first great maxim of Delphi, *Certainty destroys*, speaks to the very slippery nature of cosmos itself, let alone wisdom or truth. For is not everything changing? For doesn't the whim of the gods constantly hold the world's apparent norms hostage? At any moment, the gods have it in their power to change everything."

"Also," the customer adds, "you have to keep the story going."

The boys and Simon all look to him questioningly.

He explains, "The perceived story that everyone else around you thinks is going on, the way they word it, the way they expect you to see it. If you start wording things differently and describing a different situation than they think they see, they'll start to call you mad rather than question themselves and their own ways of wording the world."

Simon nods and smiles slowly to the customer. "I am glad you came by today, friend."

Sokrates looks to Simon with seriousness. Simon questions him with a glance. Sokrates asks, "So are any of the stories true?"

Simon shrugs. "They are the best we can do. Many people make a real effort to at least seek the truth with their words. But every story fails at being totally true, for it is only ever one person's perspective. Even a painted image full of figures can only show it all from one vantage."

"The theater shows many people's perspectives," Euripides counters.

"In a way," the customer's wife agrees, and her husband nods when she looks to him.

"And what are the other Delphi maxims - Know thyself?" Sokrates shouts. "How am I supposed to do that? What does that even mean?"

"A reasonable question," Simon agrees, "since we are all constantly in a state of change, of becoming. And yet Anaxagoras would remind us that Herakleitos would say something about how underneath the constancy of change is a different sort of permanence, the rationality of *physics*, of *nature*. Thing change, yet retain their nature. So the question is not 'What are you?', Sokrates, but more like, 'What is your nature?'"

"Suddenly I realize I know nothing at all!" Sokrates shouts, throwing his hands in the air dramatically from where he sits on the bare earth. "I'm just this pair of eyes that has heard a lot of stories and dreams about other people's memories, all of which I *know* are *not* accurate! I float in a fog of unknowableness!"

Sokrates looks to Simon with more real angst than the old man has ever seen on the usually-lighthearted boy before. Simon gives him a hesitant look of calm confirmation, and the semblance of a smile.

"That's not un-wrong," Simon says with intentional crypticism.

Sokrates looks to his friend Krito, whom he has known all his life, with wide eyes like what he sees is baffling him.

Krito smiles under a mask of comedic worried eyes and, to be playful, says, "It's me, Krito; you know me!"

Chaerephon and the adults all laugh. Euripides eyes Sokrates with tension, waiting to see how he'll respond.

Sokrates shakes his head melodramatically.

"Knowledge is a deep ocean if it's even possible at all, and all I can do is look down into it from a boat floating on the surface," Sokrates says.

The customer and his wife briefly applaud, as if it was poetry. Simon silently smiles with pride.

Krito scoffs.

Little Sokrates retorts confidently, "One thing I know for sure is what I don't know. It's what I think the most about. And I feel like now I understand it. Not knowing, I mean."

Simon laughs, and that makes the boys laugh.

"That's my kind of wisdom, Sokrates," Simon laughs. "The kind we can all agree is true, onto which so much more can be built, with steadiness!"

Simon grabs one of the strips of waste leather from the boot-cutting process, and takes a few quick seconds to etch words into it with the point of his booting tool, then finds a nail and hammer and nails the strip of leather up onto the narrow crossbeam opposite where the customers sit.

"There," Simon says as he returns to his customer, whose boot is still far from finished, "what do you think of that?"

Above all of Simon's shoes, scratched into a shred of dark leather, hang the words:

I KNOW WHAT I DON'T KNOW

"It's great!" Chaerephon shouts excitedly. "Sokrates, you're a published poet!"

"A perfect summation of classic Athenian absurdity!" the customer chuckles as he is departing. "That's what we really come to Athens for - the comedy!" He takes his young wife's arm and disappears back into the crowd, adding his laughter to the bustle.

Simon shrugs off the customer's comment and says, "I think it is a good first maxim. Know what you don't know. Which, of course, we understand to mean: be aware of what you do and don't really know. Not some paradoxical nonsense which any set of words might be twisted to mean if one assumes the speaker was a madman."

"I know what I don't know," Chaerephon reads aloud.

"Except that's not what he actually said," Krito notes.

Simon says with a smile, "It summarizes the general idea. Write your own letters if you want them exact."

Chaerephon jokes, "And who knows what really happened anyway? It's in the past."

Sokrates looks up at the little leather letters and smiles.

Ψ

Euripides witnesses a secret ceremony

"I know you're hiding! Euripides, come out! You're going to the horse track to learn to ride! Euripides!" His father's voice makes Euripides cringe.

Into a short cliff not far from Euripides' family's house just outside the city wall, fourteen-year-old Euripides has dug out a cave sized just right for him to fit, as a place to do things which he does not want to be seen doing. He crouches there now, hoping not to be found by his father.

The cave is mostly hidden by a row of tall green reeds, but has a view between them westward to the sea. In the afternoon the ocean water glitters between the reeds. When he does not want to be found, when he does not want to have to answer to anyone, Euripides comes here, and the more often he has come here recently, the more he has started to decorate it with little flowers and garlands and shells lined up on the nooks in the walls, to make it a pleasant place to sit and read scrolls when he has them.

Euripides crouches in his hand-dug cave-fortress waiting for his father to give up on looking for him. A worm in the soil near his face threatens to encroach, but then turns around and heads back into the earth.

"Euripides, if I find you, and discover that you've been hiding from me, I swear you will have earned a beating that you won't soon forget! Hiding is as bad as lying, when you know you're being looked for! Euripides!"

As he huddles, Euripides begins to look around himself in the crevasse of earth. He examines the crumbly brown soil, flecked with pebbles, threaded by thin roots. Touching a clump of grass roots startles Euripides when he discovers a thick netting of spiderweb with a big white spider sitting in the center. Euripides' fear lurches in his chest as the spider, too close for his comfort, moves a foot the moment the boy sees it.

Euripides becomes even more still. He waits through several long moments, during which he can also hear distant shuffling which he suspect is his father putting tools away over by their house.

But then he sees a moth fly in and get a little stuck on the web. The spider clearly also notices. With fearful thoughts of the spider's wrath, Euripides decides to touch away the little bits of web sticking the moth's wing just barely to the web, and after just the briefest effort at that the moth suddenly flits away, back out of the cave and into the sky.

Euripides looks at the spider, and wonders whether the spider is looking at him.

Carefully, he inches sideways out of the crevasse, and then gets up and rushes through the brush of the gulch, away from town, fearing also his father still potentially spying for him from some distance. He keeps himself low until he is out of sight of his house.

Once he is on his own, Euripides begins to wander the paths just outside the city wall, walking fast and pretending that he is busy with some household errand in order to avoid any curious neighbors who might otherwise say hello or ask him where he's off to.

He watches the way other people behave, in particular the other teen-aged boys he sees who are mostly older than his fourteen years.

There are those groups of boys who wrestle and fight each other in the grass, shouting with simultaneous anger and joy. And there are those boys who all follow the one boy who is minding his parents' horse, all debating about its upbringing and care as if they are all experts on horses. And there are those boys who stand around swapping rhymes from each other's poetry and practicing theatrical dance moves. As a boy who spends most of his time inside his own mind, Euripides feels remarkably alone and unsure what if any group of boys he might one day fit into.

His attention flits to a girl about his age, just on the cusp of puberty, when she runs past him and away toward a copse of trees on the horizon, clutching something close to her chest - a little sculpture of a person made of sticks.

Intrigued, Euripides waits until he feels unseen by passersby and then slips off in the direction of the trees where the girl went. As he crosses the grass between himself and that secluded clutch of woods just outside earshot of the bustle of the city walls, he begins to hear many voices, all girls.

Euripides crouches where the bushes part, so that he can see but still feels hidden by shadows. In a small clearing inside the copse, circled by little white mushrooms, he can finally see the origin of the voices - a big gathering of little girls who all appear to be around the same age, perhaps just a few years younger than himself, and are all crowded around what seems to be some kind of ritual involving a two little dolls made of sticks sitting on a large dead stump. One of the stick people has flowers stuck all over it.

"The Queen isn't ready yet!" one girl squeals. "Don't start the proceedings until the Queen has given her command!"

"We have to pour the ambrosia!"

"Who's going to be cupbearer to the Queen?"

"I'm carrying all her many children, the leaves!"

Then, whipping Euripides' heart like a horse, one of the girls shouts, "Wait, look! There's a boy! Look, a boy is spying on us!"

The girl leading the ceremony, her face illuminated from below by the flickering flame of a fat wax candle she's holding, starts darting her gaze among the shadows all around Euripides, where another girl below her is pointing while looking right at him.

"There, he's there, look!"

"It's *Euripides*!" As she says his name, the lead girl's eyes find his, and Euripides' heart shrivels at once like a raisin. He feels the shadows encroach all around him. He thinks of when he told that spider witch his name, and worries that his name has somehow since become a curse.

One by one, very quickly in succession, the girls all shout at him, "Artemis curse Euripides!"

"Artemis the Bear, curse Euripides!"

"Artemis Protector-of-Girls, and beasts who play among the heather, hear our prayer chanted together, and curse Euripides *forever*!"

Euripides scrambles to turn and run back into the narrow streets between houses, hearing the whole crowd of girls' voices behind him all rise in shaming chastisement, then shouting his name and curses upon it until he can't hear them anymore among the nearer voices of the city.

As he runs, Euripides truly fears the Wild Goddess Artemis Protector-of-Girls might hear human voices today and turn him into some meadow beast, and he keeps glancing at his hands and legs while he awkwardly runs home, to confirm he's still a human boy.

Ω

The Athenian fleet returns from victory in the east

With painted eyes scarred from mortal wounds delivered upon other ships, the fleet of Athenian triremes are finally home from the east and bringing down their sails as they tie up at their port moorings at Piraeus.

Agile-eyed Perikles arrives there at the docks as the rowdy soldiers begin to come down the gangplanks.

He has flashes of memory from that night on Salamis, awaiting the return of the heroes of the fight. He is grateful he no longer has the fear and uncertainty of a child, but finally feels he understands world politics and has confidence in the events which he is now part of arranging.

Beside him ever-graceful Elpinike clings to the arm of her husband Kallias, who smiles politely when Perikles arrives to join the crowd of those awaiting their men.

"Surely Helios is still behind those clouds, eh, Perikles?" Kallias jokes good-naturedly.

"One hopes so," Perikles nods politely, not smiling, trying not to worry about the state he might find Ephialtes in, if he has even survived the mission. He scans the men on the ships, looking for his friend among them.

"I've heard positive shouts from the soldiers," Kallias assures him optimistically. "Apparently we make up for our own lost men fivefold in captives!" Elpinike glares at Kallias and claws into his arm, as he reacts to her grasp with a wince and confused look. "What, darling?"

"That is a rotten way to talk about our dead heroes."

"You're right, of course. I measure everything in terms of its equivalent number of slaves, these days. Such is a businessman's mind."

Perikles can only grimace. Finally he sees his friend Ephialtes helping some other men haul rope on one of the closest triremes, and his mood turns back around.

"There he is," Kallias says positively, seeing what Perikles has seen. "Ephialtes looks strong! He's become a man, at last, perhaps."

Seen only by Perikles, Elpinike shakes her head to negate the notion.

From the boat's crowd of soldiers Kimon appears, with two of his strongest lieutenants at his sides, and all three hold their Athenian shields high, confidently, like the gesture is not new to them.

The cheer is epic, heart-felt, and spirit-lifting to all. It draws tears of civic pride even to Perikles' eyes, particularly to see that same pride among his countrymen.

"Again!" Kimon shouts, about to continue, but seeing from the reaction that it is all that needs to be said. The cheer resounds again, and it is several beats before he can be heard again shouting, "Again! Again we have pushed back the Empire of the sons of Kyros! We, Athenians! With our Delian League allies, and the blessings of Poseidon Horse-tamer and Athena First-in-Battle, we have sent them back where they came from! And behold, we return with more ships than we left with!"

The dockworkers and sailors all laugh and cheer, and the shipwrights begin chattering with excitement at the prospect of incoming new captured Phoenikian vessels, which are always rich with innovations to be copied or developed upon.

Elpinike goes right up to her brother and kisses him warmly on the lips, too excited to notice her surroundings for a moment.

Her husband Kallias, coming up right behind her, watches the kiss with a frustrated eye, but then disarms it by copying it, taking surprised Kimon by the face and kissing him perfunctorily on the lips, then stepping back and putting his arm in Elpinike's.

"Welcome home, brother-in-law," Kallias says.

Kimon winces a bit, but keeps his cool, and waits until Kallias has glanced away before he shakes his head to himself in frustration.

"I hear we've won a fabulous victory," Kallias says excitedly. "I say we prepare immediately the production by artists of some great symbol of that victory - some sculpture worthy of display at Delphi itself!"

"I've already made some!" shouts the potter Euphronios, holding up a pot painted with an image of a barbarian dressed in animal skins, standing bent forward with his butt sticking out, and a nude soldier with a fine-cut Hellenic beard and his hard dick in his hand, with letters between the two:

BUTT-FUCKED
AT EURYMEDON

The crowd cheers the crude cartoon.

Kimon and Ephialtes shrug to each other with a shared grin as all the soldiers coming down the gangplanks behind them start to get rowdy at the sight of the pottery celebrating them. One soldier pulls up his skirt and starts swinging his fattening cock around like a sword, to the laughter of a few.

"Fuck the Empire!"

"We've sure fucked Persia!"

Celebrations spread throughout the population of Athens faster than the wall of rain of a storm crossing through.

"Praise to Athena, First-in-Battle!"

"Praise to Poseidon, Master of Ships!"

So as not to choose one of them, Perikles calls past Kimon and Ephialtes to one of the other generals, though it is a bit awkward.

"General! I've gathered twenty idle citizens, patriotic Democrats all, from the Agora; where do you need them? Shall we help you unload these triremes here?"

The distant general on the trireme indicates with a gesture to his ears that he can't hear Perikles.

"This other boat needs help first," Kimon orders, pointing to the non-military ship which accompanied the Athenian fleet into the harbor, and is just now finally getting docked among the large triremes. "It's full of refugees who have been wandering far too long. Get them all help and lodge them in some of the abandoned buildings here at Piraeus."

"Yes, sir," Kimon's lieutenant nods, before walking over to the other docking vessel to help its bedraggled captain get the gangplank situated safely.

With an appreciative nod to Kimon, Perikles signals to the foreman of his gathered group of idle men to follow Kimon's lieutenant and help him unload the incoming ship. As the lieutenant catches a thrown rope and helps guide the ship to the docks, Perikles notices the clusters of refugees huddled under blankets upon its sea-lashed decks.

"Where are these people from?" Perikles asks Kimon, watching as several women and children are helped onto the gangplank by an enormously muscled man who spies their Piraeus surroundings with paranoia.

"Refugees from all across the Aegean," Kimon replies. "An Aigyptian family, stranded on an island for months after a shipwreck. A young girl on her own, we know not yet from where. And also an extended family of secretive mystics from Greater Hellas, in the southern Italy area."

"Mystics, you say? From which city?"

"Kroton," Kimon says. "The city of the Pythagoreans."

Swift-eyed Perikles raises an intrigued eyebrow.

"From what I gathered speaking between ships," Kimon says hesitantly, "their city was taken over by influence from Oligarchs in nearby Sybaris. And once the Sybarites had power in Kroton, they burned their Temple of Mathematics, murdered Pythagoras, and exiled all of his followers from the city. I'm told that, though they keep it secret, this very boat carries Pythagoras' own wife and daughter, in disguise. That big man - that's Milo, the famous wrestler, and I hear he is husband to Pythagoras' daughter."

"They keep it secret, though?" Perikles asks. "So what makes you think it is really them?"

"I hear it's part of why other communities rejected them as refugees, but you're right," Kimon grunts, already turning away, "rumor is below me. It's the lone girl who probably needs the most help. She's an orphan, and has clearly experienced terrible sorrow and fear."

The ship of refugees is a smaller vessel, not an official ship of any city but just the construction of one man's own mind. Its captain is a craggy-faced African man whom Perikles has seen before named Memnon who has taken on the personal quest of sailing all around the Aegean Sea and rescuing castaways and other refugees. In his work, he has brought many such saved souls back to Athens, since it is known to be a city welcoming to strangers. Grizzled, quiet old Memnon and Perikles give each other respectful grimaces as Perikles steps onto the older man's ship.

Knowing that Memnon does not like to speak much Hellenic, Perikles simply gestures around the deck of the ship to ask if he can look around, and Memnon nods and looks away, returning to his rope work.

Perikles goes up to the little girl and crouches beside her.

"Hello," he says with quiet care. "Where are you from?"

"From Athens," she says with a whimper.

Perikles cocks his head, suddenly recognizing the little girl.

Upon seeing his recognition, she finally summons the courage to speak, and in one long series of outbursts that ends in a sob, she says, "My parents sailed with the founders of Nine Ways. My brothers and I sailed with them from Athens with the wrestler Makon, to start a new city. We tried for peace but the barbarians of the hills wouldn't accept our terms. So one night they came and killed everyone! ... I'm the only survivor of Nine Ways!"

Perikles grabs the little orphaned girl in a tight hug, shedding tears sympathetically with her as he gradually fathoms her trauma, while trying also to measure in his mind the loss to Athens of her colony at Nine Ways.

"Where did you find this girl?" Perikles asks the captain of the vessel.

Old Memnon steps over and tries to comfort the girl with a big heavy hand on her back, and clearly she has come to trust this man, as she eases somewhat at his touch. "Coast of Makedonia," the old Aigyptian captain says.

Perikles weeps, unable to form words, picturing all those eager and optimistic adventuring Athenian colonists who set sail for that coast. He stands and embraces the captain, with one hand still in the hair of the orphaned girl.

Men and women all around, seeing Perikles' emotion, begin to weep and wail in a spreading symphony of sympathy.

Unaware of the dichotomy, some of the victorious soldiers fresh from war, lead by Myronides, start singing a song thanking the Sea God Poseidon for their own safe return.

Dark-haired lord, Earth-Shaker, god of the great treeless Sea,
Master from Mount Helikon to the Aegean's deep,
You of the double lot, Horse-Tamer and Ship-Master,
Carry home safe all who sail upon your waves!

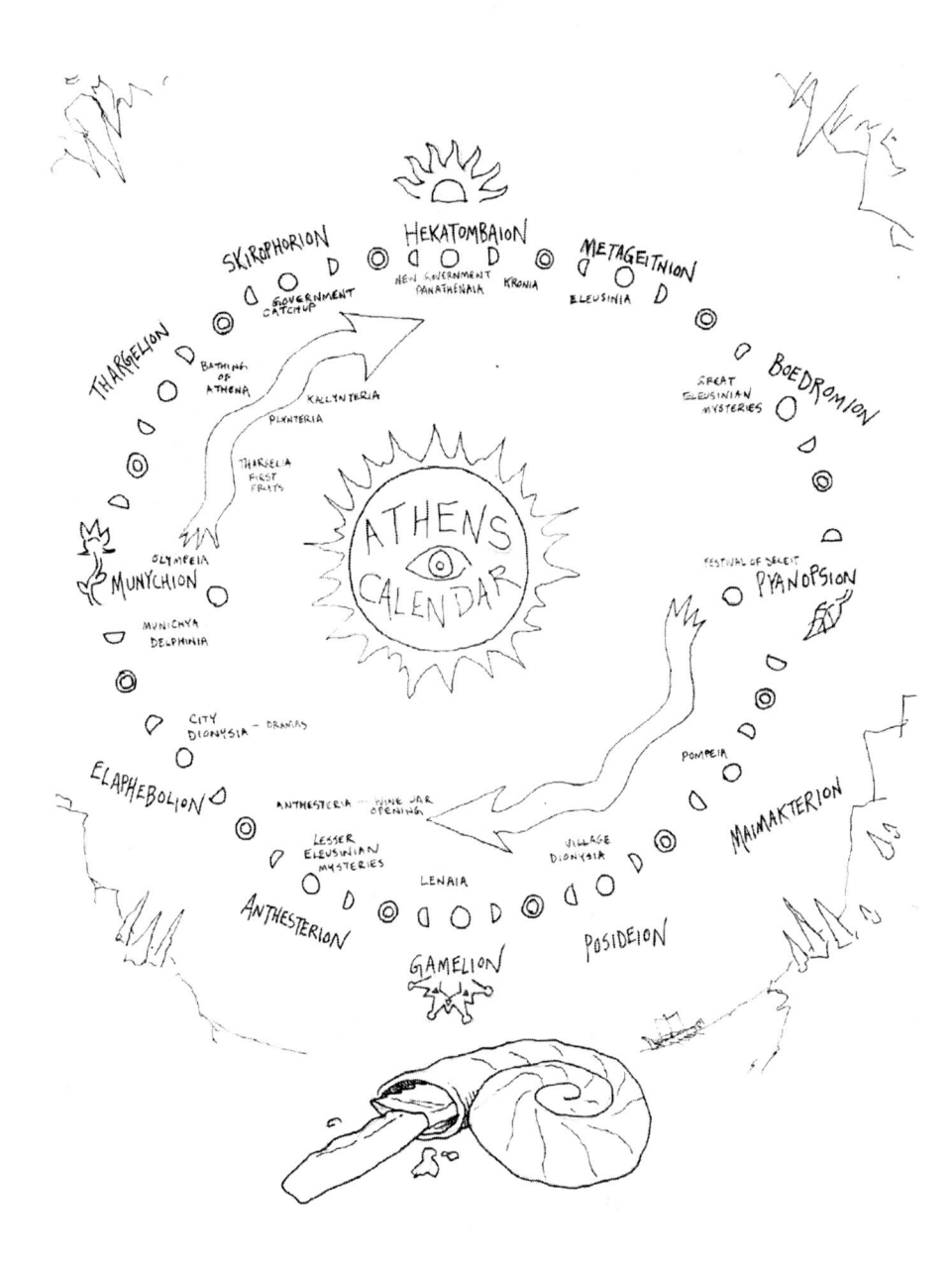

ATHENS

5

POSEIDON EARTH-SHAKER

A

A new day rises over Lakedaemonia

Crows rise from the Lakedaemonian fields and ride the wind for a while.

Rows of teen-aged Spartan boys are gathered in an open portico on the northern edge of town near the Temple of Artemis Willow-bound, following along in the exercises of their brawny calisthenics leader, all naked and oiled. Among them is young King Pleistarchos, nearly nineteen now. He struggles to maintain the patience to continue the exercises, which the other boys have done every day of their lives, but which are new to him.

"Be brave," Queen-Mother Gorgo mouths sweetly to her son when he looks over to her for sympathy.

Gorgo's Helot servant Qorina stands beside her with a wax tablet, noting what the Queen-Mother is saying. Gorgo sees her note down her comment to Pleistarchos, and smiles at it.

"I didn't mean for you to write that down, Qorina, but I like that you did. Now where was I?"

"You were listing the families who had paid their dues in wild game, to determine who was deficient."

A sudden excitement among the boys draws both women's attention. A tiny juvenile rabbit - almost too small to see but old enough to be spry - has made its way inside the portico and is hopping between the feet of the exercising boys, some of whom have stopped their routine to scramble after the creature.

"Boys!" the exercise leader bellows, reaching for his whip on the wall.

"No," shouts Gorgo, who sees a natural lesson from the gods in the rabbit, "let them chase! Whoever brings me that baby hare alive will be on the fast track to being one of my son's personal royal guards!"

As she is speaking, the rabbit dashes out the other side of the portico and off into the high grass of the surrounding fields.

A few of the most ambitious of the bare-bodied boys immediately chase after it like a pack of clumsy puppies, barking orders to each other and laughing.

Young King Pleistarchos runs out with them, but seems more interested in giving orders to the others than himself chasing the rabbit.

"If you catch it without hurting it, you can be my right-hand man!" the young king calls out, following the fastest boys.

Gorgo smiles and follows the fray out into the field. She looks east, toward the morning star, to gauge how soon Dawn might appear over Mount Menelaion.

But just then, with sudden fury, Poseidon Sea God starts to violently shake the very land of Lakedaemonia from beneath!

Ever more fiercely, the ground lurches. Legs buckle beneath strong men and women. Chasms rumble open in the Earth herself. Walls are pushed away from each other, collapsing roofs.

On western Mount Taygetos, visible from the whole Eurotas river valley, ancient landmark spires of rock crack and fall.

Right behind Gorgo, knocking her to her hands and knees, the portico in which the remaining few children and their trainer and Qorina had remained now collapses upon itself in a shroud of stone, crushing all within. Blood flies amidst the eruption of rubble. Qorina's shrieking gasp is cut short within the thunder of the building's fall. Stone dust billows across the grass.

Cracks creep along the columns of the tallest temples in the square, and the drums which compose them begin to shake apart. The Temple of Artemis Willow-bound, the oldest stone building in Sparta, crumbles with an explosion of stone dust which blooms across the whole city.

All the old and roughly constructed buildings, most homes, quickly follow one by one and collapse in sprawling heaps beside each other, blossoming a secondary cloud of browner debris upon the Eurotas plain like a fog of rock eating the land.

Many Spartans die in their beds in these first moments of the earthquake, victims of their falling houses.

"Poseidon!" Gorgo bellows to the heavens as she is shaken off her feet. "Great god of the Sea, Master of Horses, Earth-shaker, dark-haired lord please, have mercy!" The cloud of temple debris enshrouds her and fills her lungs with each word, causing her to cough and cover her face with her black widow's veil.

The Earth-shaking ceases just a few infinitely long moments after Gorgo's begged prayer, as if the god had to think about it.

"Thank you, Sea God," she gasps aloud, weeping in bursts with relief at having been able to stop the god's wrath. "However we've angered you, we will repent fivefold, I swear!" Gorgo grabs a fist-sized stone from the ground near her feet and quickly cuts her palm with it, then flings some of the blood from the wound down onto the ground, to make any watching gods know that she meant her vow.

Out from the fallen Temple of Artemis Willow-bound, lifting a broken ceiling beam to stand, and covered in marble dust such that his entire form is pale white like a ghost, rises the strong, young King Archidamos.

"I will never understand these gods," King Archidamos groans. "We gave Poseidon how many bulls last month? I want the number."

At the edge of the sparring fields, the old doric-columned dormitory, where the teen-aged soldiers bunk and communally eat during the years of their training, has crumbled only on one side, and now half of its young occupants are shouting through a desperate struggle to save the other half of their comrades from the rubble and fallen support beams where those still alive are trapped among the bodies of those who have already been crushed to death. The still-standing side of the building shifts unsteadily above, as if it could collapse completely at any moment.

Seeing this, with whip speed King Archidamos signals to the commander of his personal guard and runs over to the building, with those few of his armored men who luckily remain racing behind his heels.

The king's guard command the young soldiers away from the dangerous building and get to work more carefully at the job of freeing the trapped children, but it is only a few more short minutes before the rest of the building collapses quite suddenly all at once, taking everyone by surprise and sending several of the trapped teenagers with four of the king's guard swiftly to the care of Haides Many-host, God of Death.

"O gods," King Archidamos utters, frozen by shock, as the cloud of dust settles, "spare Sparta. Have mercy, I beg you." He darts his eyes all around, looking for what to do next, then barks to his guards who remain, "Spread out and save who you can!"

Gorgo runs to the children on the field of Ares Man-killer, the boys who had chased after the rabbit and now stand dumbstruck, unsure what to do. She looks among them for her son the king. Naked and covered in stone dust which has clung to the oil on their bodies, all the boys look like identical ghosts, and Gorgo genuinely wonders for a heart-stopping second if she is transitioning into the Underworld.

Before she spots him among the dust-paled young ones, Pleistarchos calls to her, running into her arms. "Mama!"

"O Pleistarchos," Gorgo cries, hugging him and lifting him in the air. "You are alive! Now you see how the gods reward those who get up early to exercise!"

"Yes Mother!" Pleistarchos sobs.

"Now you know." The Queen Mother then releases her son and looks around for the other noble boys of her house, her nephews. "Where are Pleistoanax and Kleomenes?"

"They're not here," Pleistarchos sobs. "Did Ares kill them as well? O how much I regret not exercising earlier!"

"We'll see," Gorgo sighs. "We'll go to the house of your aunt Laothoe and find out if any of the buildings there killed their inhabitants. And it isn't Ares who shakes the earth, Pleistarchos, it's the Sea God Poseidon Earth-shaker!"

"I know, but it's Ares who hates me for not exercising," Pleistarchos says, struggling to understand. "So are they friends?"

Gorgo eyes the city around her, and the other king and his living men struggling to help injured Spartans out of the rubble of their homes.

"Honestly, Pleistarchos, this isn't necessarily about you," she explains. "Don't question the Sea God. If he gets Zeus' help, they can raise the sea up to the clouds and submerge every mountain. They've done it before. Powers that great, you just have to bend before them, give them whatever they want."

Pleistarchos sobs, struggling to hide it while the other boys stare at him, silent and stone-dust-masked.

All around the city, those citizens who survived the destruction of the buildings have begun to sift through the treacherous rubble to pull their belongings and loved ones out of their ruined homes. Sobs soar everywhere.

King Archidamos approaches Gorgo with a desperate face. "This is bad," he says. "We must not linger like injured beasts, licking our wounds. We must rally immediately! Send the alarm across all of Lakedaemonia, and to our allies, to armor up!"

Gorgo thinks about it for a moment, then nods, but adds, "We do not have to trumpet to our allies that we're wounded."

"Spartans!" Archidamos shouts, turning away from Gorgo and addressing all within earshot.

Many of those who have been excavating their homes stop and lift their heads to listen.

"Raise the alarm, all! Sparta must immediately rally here around your kings! Our enemies will use this moment if we're not wise! So first don't waste your time looking for anything but your armor and your weapons, and then bring yourself here!"

As the king speaks, a rumble precedes the arrival of four large, frightened bulls, racing at full speed between buildings and right through the center of Sparta, then off again across the fields on the other side of town, the eyes painted on their hindquarters to ward off lion attacks lurching as the beasts run.

Wails rise throughout the stone fog as the dead are found. Wounded house dogs raise a harmonizing howl.

Two crows which had risen before the quake land safely again upon the two sides of Qorina's broken tablet which read:

BE BRAVE

B

Korax sees a future

Korax's guerillas gather quickly at a ledge high on Mount Taygetos, just outside the cave which has been their summer lair.

Their leader has mentioned often in their meetings that a sign from the gods would be clear, and all of them have recognized this to be exactly that. Many are hoppingly excited, as if the shaking of the earth gave their shoes invisible wings.

"Poseidon is our patron in this fight," says Chrysaor, Korax's second-in-command, as the men all watch the commotion in the Eurotas river valley far below. Buildings all across the valley have collapsed, and shrieks of fear ring distantly from everywhere. "Everyone start focusing your sacrifices on Poseidon."

Korax looks up and sees the white half-moon lingering high in the dark blue morning sky. It reminds him like an ax blade hanging over the city.

He whispers to himself, "They say King Korax was once a slave."

"O King Poseidon, hidden in the depths from sight,
when calm, you wander through the dolphins' deep,
and sweet waves lash the shore with endless flow.
Be kind to us, now, please, with gentle winds."
Orpheos, *Hymn to Poseidon*

Γ

Athenians feel the effects of the earthquake

The little River Eridanos runs right past Sokrates' house on its way down to Potters' Alley. Growing up bathing in it and watching his father wash his stonework in it, Sokrates has come to feel like the little river is a member of his family, or at the very least, a neighbor.

Sitting down at the edge of the flowing waters of Eridanos now, Sokrates and Krito dip their bare feet into the wet grass.

"Do you think Eridanos likes it when we dip our feet?" eleven-year-old Krito asks his littler friend.

Seven-year-old Sokrates nods. He watches a leaf in the flow as it goes past their feet and on downriver, toward Potters' Alley.

Just then, on the other side of the stream, a few young teen-aged boys and girls, including their occasional friend Euripides, come along following the leaf and chattering to each other about it.

"I bet an owl it will stop before Potters' Alley!" one girl shouts.

"I bet a kiss it won't flow all the way to the Sea!"

Jogging along with the mostly older kids, Euripides notices Sokrates and Krito sitting on the other side of the stream and minutely nods to them, indicating with his minimal greeting that he doesn't particularly want to be acknowledged by them.

Sokrates stands and looks to Krito to gauge if he wants to follow the gang of teen-agers. Krito makes a reluctant face, but follows when Sokrates begins to trot after them.

The leaf sails along, pausing momentarily in this eddy or that, but always regaining the main flow of the stream and continuing along through town, into the industrial street called Potters' Alley.

The shops and manufactory tents are quiet today, as it is the Sixth of the Month - Artemis' birthday, one of the many monthly days when public work and commerce are on hold in favor of festivity and worship. Few are out in the streets except for children and foreign slaves at work on buildings and gardens. Hellenes are all home baking circular Moon-cakes for Artemis which will be illuminated like the Moon this evening with wax candles and shared in the dark moonlit outdoors in celebration of the Wild Goddess.

Sokrates and Krito follow the teenagers all the way through town, along the flow of the little Eridanos River, past the piles of stone slabs and rows of silent potters' wheels, to the Sacred Gate where the river flows out to the west, through wild meadows and reedy gulleys to the Sea.

Once they are outside of the city walls and in the land of birds and bees, Sokrates and Krito keep a bit further back from the older kids, so as not to draw their attention. As so often is their mode, Krito follows the curious Sokrates partially out of concern and partially out of admiration of his courage.

The older kids lose interest in the leaf once it gets stuck in a reed bed, and instead race onward down the path to the seaside, where they quickly strip their clothes and get into the water to float and flaunt and fight playfully. Euripides stays toward the edge of the group, not wanting to get naked, and he ends up sitting on a large stone and drawing on it idly with a white rock.

Sokrates and Krito arrive at the seaside several minutes after the older kids, and do not see Euripides off to the side, so they begin to play together by themselves in the tidal flats where crabs and clams reside.

Euripides spots them, and watches them play, but stays silent and alone, relishing his feelings of aloneness at this time of this life.

Sokrates starts playing with a crab in the sand where the water is lapping with the waves, filling and emptying a little pool. The toe-sized crab has settled and decided to defend its position against the giant above. It hunkers down in the sand, snuggling deeper each time the water flushes its sand, and snipping at Sokrates' fat feet whenever he tries to fuss with it.

Just as Krito is arriving from the deeper water, a second little crab of the same size skitters over to defend its mate, waving its pincers at Sokrates and then hugging the other crab to show that it will protect it.

Sokrates laughs with glee at this development in the drama, and sits back on his heels, prepared to tell Krito the whole story.

"This crab is so brave!" Sokrates shouts.

Krito sees the scene as he arrives, and says, "Of course! Crabs are the bravest creatures. You know about Herakles and the crab, right?"

Sokrates shakes his head. "Mother says I'm not old enough for Herakles stories yet."

Krito says, "Well in one story, Herakles has to fight this monster called the Hydra. It's this big monster with thirty heads like snakes. And when Herakles is fighting it in its swamp at Lerna, he accidentally steps on a little crab like that one. But what's great is that the crab is so brave that it fights back, and it snips Herakles' toe. It's that bravery that's the reason that Hera put the crab in the sky as stars. Because bravery isn't always smart. The crab snipped at Herakles, but it was just a little crab like this, so Herakles just - smashed it. Bravery isn't always smart, but people always like it either way it turns out. Even the gods."

Krito stomps on the crabs in the sand with his sandal.

"Don't!" Sokrates shouts, and pushes him back into the shallow water.

The crabs skulk deeper into the sand, mostly unharmed.

"They're just crabs," Krito half laughs, half whines. "Stop hitting me, Sokrates. I'll tell your mother you did. We eat crabs all the time. Just not ones that small, because they're worthless."

"It was protecting its friend." Sokrates makes a crying face. "They were brave friends. They weren't worthless to each other. Only to you."

Krito shrugs.

Then Sokrates asks, "If the gods liked the crab's courage so much, then why didn't they help it fight Herakles? Or at least help it not get squished by him. Even these crabs here were able to avoid your foot. Hera couldn't have, like, given that crab some sand to sink into?"

"Well that crab was fighting Herakles. You haven't heard his stories, but he can kill anything. Like, *anything*. So even with sand like that, Herakles' foot is way stronger than my foot."

Sokrates makes a questioning face, then smiles.

Finally after a while of brooding by himself, Euripides' loneliness becomes the sort which desires company, and he hops down from his stone and ambles over to where Krito and Sokrates have been playing in the tidal mud. He walks over silently, and Sokrates and Krito both look up and acknowledge him silently.

Euripides crouches down where Sokrates and Krito are crouching, to see what they're looking at.

"The crabs are showing the gods their bravery," Sokrates tells Euripides.

"Wait, wait," young Krito says, touching Euripides' shin as he sits beside him on the edge of a tidal stream. "Look at the water."

Where a rock disturbs the flow of a little river from further up the beach, the water is retreating in a manner that has created a series of little repeating whirlpools, each one arcing into the other and replicating their precursors with a sort of stepped symmetry, one flowing out to one side, creating there a new whirlpool which flows back out the other side, creating another littler whirlpool further along on that side. The repeating whirlpools gradually shrink and dissipate six or seven steps down along the line of them.

"Look at how they curve into one another," Euripides notes, putting his finger on the rock that starts the little disturbance path and making the whirlpools shrink and grow as he presses down upon it. When he removes his finger the road of vortices returns to its previous form, more or less.

"Could this be a god?" Krito asks.

"It looks like the repeating pattern of waves that artists put on pottery," Sokrates notices. "Maybe this sort of thing is where those artists first saw that pattern."

"Everything is the *work of* some god," Euripides snorts at Krito. "But this isn't the god itself."

"But not everything is where the god is actually working right now," Krito huffs back. "Like some things in my house I set up earlier, and they're still that way, but some things I am currently working on. This looks like somewhere where the god is actually working right now, like that's the mark of his finger right now."

"I think it's just how the water happens to run into itself when it moves around that rock," Euripides replies, partially just to be contrary. "Haven't you ever seen waves before, Krito? Or are you too poor to have ever traveled anywhere on a ship?"

"I've been on a ship plenty of times," Krito whines, folding his arms.

"Yeah, you've been on boats," Euripides chides.

Then, as they are watching the pattern in the little beach river's flow, the water down at the ocean begins itself to shift again, retreating yet further out, and pulling the little river into a wider and fatter format which makes the whirlpool trail disappear altogether.

All the boys look down the beach at the Sea, which has retreated further down the beach than low tide would usually take it. Almost as quickly as they notice it, men in the harborside tents behind them have noticed it as well and begin to shout back and forth about Poseidon's wrath. The boys all turn around to watch the commotion.

"Poseidon's mad! Get ready, men! Get off the ships!"

"Get off the ships! Poseidon's wrath is coming!"

Up on the stonework harbor's edge in the direction of Piraeus, the priest of Poseidon who is on duty today has a staff held high above his head and he is waving in broad gestures to men unloading big jars from a line of ships down at the end of the harbor. Those men scramble to carry what they have in their arms down the gangplanks and safely onto the docks before any potential incoming wave arrives.

An old fish merchant standing near the boys explains to one of his teenage employees, within earshot of the boys, "This is what happened at Poteidaia, up in Thrake, during the Second Persian War. First Poseidon shakes the earth, then the water recesses, and then it comes back with a rage, like Poseidon pulling back his fist. I need to get to high ground, quickly. You stay here and cover the stall, secure it to the ground. Then get yourself home." The merchant rushes off toward the road back to Athens, leaving his young employee frightened and busy.

"What does this mean? What's happening?" Krito, tall already at eleven years old, takes short and stocky seven-year old Sokrates in his arms in an instinctual protective gesture. "Is it Poseidon, really?"

Aischylos, who happens to be standing in the nearby crowd of fish shoppers, narrows his eyes, breathing fast, but thinking carefully, then he nods curtly to Krito. "I think so," he says, clarifying, "Poseidon, moving both the Earth and the Sea. Or perhaps using one to move the other. But yes, for sure, Poseidon - master of the Sea, shaker of the Earth, tamer of Horses. O Poseidon!"

Cloud shadows cause soft darkness to ebb and flow, writing slowly across the land with sunlight.

Just a few moments of waiting gives way to a sudden return of the sea to a quick high tide which rocks all the boats noisily against the piers, and the crowds practically roar with the mass of their murmuring throughout Piraeus about what Poseidon might be so upset about with no war happening.

Urban sea-birds chatter and follow each other in flocks from perch to perch, nervously shitting everywhere.

ATHENS

△

The Spartan kings assess the damage, weakened, vulnerable

The western mountains drape Sparta within the sunset's shadow before the evening sky fully reddens - in that west where the Helot homeland of Messenia rests in generational ruin. Twilight starts early and lingers long.
    Bees zip home from the field flowers to their warm hives.
    The Temple of Aphrodite Warlike is abuzz like a wartime camp.
    Helot slaves dash in and out, taking orders and information from the Kings and Overseers inside to the soldiers waiting outside and the leaders of distant settlements.
    King Archidamos has set up a long table like the ones they put up in his regal hunting tents, and on it are innumerable parchment skins and potshards inked and scratched with village lists and resource numbers and tribe names from every corner of Lakedaemonia. King Pleistarchos stands at the other end of the table, watching the flurry of conversations between elderly Overseers in an overwhelmed daze. Both kings are dressed in their fullest regalia, as if to show that their power is not diminished. Behind them, Queen-Mother Gorgo sits cross legged on a tall tripod, carefully embroidering a scarf with the image of two intertwined lions, her mind floating above the din.
    "We must get organized with information," King Archidamos says mostly to himself. "Our understanding of the true numbers in play function like the eyes of eagles soaring above the situation."
    "Folly," chides the lead Overseer. "Numbers never tell a story, King. You must interrogate Helots, torture them to get the truth, and find out what they know." The other Overseers all debate at once.
    "All the villages of the Eurotas valley are as ruined as Sparta," sputters a breathless Helot runner representing his village. "The villages in the hills don't appear to have lost as many buildings, though. And I can't speak for the coasts. We haven't had a runner arrive yet from Helos in the south. But the great spire of Mount Taygetos fell! I saw it fall!"
    "Yes yes, we all saw it fall," the lead Overseer snaps curtly. "Get this Helot

out of here if he doesn't have any new information. What we need are accurate numbers! Not more personal anecdotes!"

While weaving, Gorgo says, "If you were to look to the stories of our ancient heroes - Prince Lakedaemonios would seek first to protect Queen Sparta."

King Archidamos nods to one of his own Helot slaves to guide the boy away, and turns to address Gorgo past her son the King. "So, Agiad house, how best can Lakedaemonios, our land, protect Queen Sparta, our city, when the very land itself is what destroyed the city?" He turns away from her and looks to one of the nearby priests as he grunts, "I wonder sometimes if these gods aren't due to be overthrown, as little as they seem to care what we give them in due and noble sacrifice!"

"We *must* have done *something* wrong," the priest shrugs. "The gods reveal what pleases and angers them with their reactions."

"What if Poseidon just got angry for no reason?" Archidamos shouts. "What if the Sea God is just getting old and is lashing out at his loved ones for no good reason? I'll tell you, if the gods are like us men are, then that is definitely something that could happen. That is exactly how my own grandfather treated my father when he became very old."

"Do not denigrate the very old," growls the oldest of the Overseers. "We have earned your respect."

"Have you?" Archidamos snaps. "I thought we had earned Poseidon's respect, and yet he pushes us down for no reason! I thought you priests and elders had figured out what the gods like and dislike, and what the signs of birds and clouds and all that mean, but evidently no one knows anything!"

King Archidamos shoves the elderly Overseer to the floor.

The Overseer bellows a high groan, and curls in on himself. King Archidamos turns away from the old man shaking his head at Gorgo.

The other Overseers rush in like a flock to check on the elder man. "You have injured him!" one of them shouts back at the strong, young king.

"We are fools to wrestle among ourselves like teen-agers!" another Overseer shouts at young King Archidamos.

The lead Overseer replies, "My King, you may think--" and then belches blood as he is suddenly stabbed in the back with rushing speed from behind.

Several other men and women in the room release shrieks of horror all as a chorus one after another, followed by the guttural sounds of their simultaneous murders in a terrible moment of explosive percussion.

A squad of scores of Helot killers has all begun their assault in unison, with stealth attacks upon the most dangerous men on the periphery of the gathering surrounding Aphrodite's temple.

As quickly as they killed their first targets, the many killers cast the dying aside and move in upon their next victims, who, though still startled by the horror of the moment, at least now are able to raise a hand or move a foot in defense of themselves.

Gorgo shouts, "The Helots are uprising!"

King Archidamos bellows, "Men!" That is all he needs to say. All those with weapons draw them. Sparta takes a fighting stance.

One of the Helots shouts in a high-pitched voice, nearly breathless, "We are not your Helots, we are Messenians!"

Archidamos is momentarily surrounded by four Messenian killers, each armed with the long hatchets that he has seen them using on firewood every day of his life, and had never thought of as weapons, always being surrounded by finer military tools. The four attackers circle him. He swings both ends of his spear, trying to threaten at least two of them at all times. Before six moments of this pass, the bravest of the four attackers chirps to the others and then darts in toward the Spartan King, first swatting the tip of his spear away with their axe, then kneeling fast and swinging it down at Archidamos' knees, but the king's training instincts see the move before his mind does and he finds himself leaping the axe swing. He falls backward on landing, and catches himself with the lizardkiller backend of his spear, but is awkwardly prone for a few long moments in which two of the attackers see an opportunity and move in on him. However, both are met from behind by the king's guardsmen who pounce on them, pull them away, and dispatch them.

The next minute is a long one full of fury and bloodletting, wreathed in screams from every participant in the mad melee. Spartans pile onto the desperate attackers despite the slashes they know they will take.

"Blood!" Archidamos bellows at the sight of it. "Steaming blood for the gods, Ares Man-Killer! Come quickly and lap it up before it congeals! Come, Ares, while the wounds still steam!"

As quickly as the moment occurred, the King's guards who are still alive surround Archidamos with their spears out, forming a sort of circular phalanx.

The attackers here are dispatched, but sounds of struggle and shrieks of murder rise like crows from the fields in all directions. Spartans look to each other, seeing each others' wounds before their own.

In the chill of the evening, the dying's bloodfalls steam visibly like breath. As the living look around at the bodies on the ground it only then becomes clear - all these attackers were teen-aged girls, their hair shorn and breasts bound.

Gorgo approaches bloody Archidamos, reverently and fearfully keeping her eyes on his heaving form. "You've done all our ancestors proud today, King Archidamos. You became a Spartan man today."

The king glares at her condescension, but also glows a little in the light of the compliment, and he struggles between the two emotions.

The old Overseer whom earlier Archidamos had shoved down, overwhelmed, pulls his hair and shrieks at Gorgo from his place on the ground, "What do we do?"

Gorgo steels herself and says, "This was not a single battle. These slaves have just begun a long-planned revolution, and they intend to utterly upend this land. In order to succeed, they must be gathering somewhere as an army. So we must go and defeat them *where they are*. Before they form."

"But ... they're everywhere. They run our households."

"Well what do you want me to say?" Gorgo shouts angrily. "We have to stop them! We've grown weak! It's time to get strong again!"

"We have to summon our allies. Send runners to every city of Hellas with an army. Summon them, to help. We are at war - it is appropriate to call on our allies."

Runners breakfoot.

"IT'S WE WHO DANCE AMONG THE SHADES,
TO THE GREAT GODDESS OF THE DEAD'S DELIGHT,
ALL DRESSED IN FINELY-WOVEN NIGHT,
BRIGHT TO THE DEAD EYE AS FORGOTTEN LIGHT!"
Sappho, Mytilenean Poet

E
Aoide follows a song

The same evening falls on Delphi behind thick clouds, no sunset. The day's light disappears before most notice the fading.

 Aoide lies in her straw bed, gazing into her mind's waking dream, where she is listening to the wordless singing of a handsome goatherd boy she saw recently from a great distance, across the valley, a boy who might look like anything up-close, and could never touch her, who might be Apollo for all she knows, but his thick wordless song can fill her.

 Suddenly the little cat Ailisto mews from the doorway of Aoide's dormitory, too urgent-minded even to fully enter the door, sticking only her little head inside quick enough to sing. Aoide laughs at her when she first sees Ailisto from her bed, but she soon notices the concern in the cat's voice and changes her own tone to match.

 "What is it, little lion?"

 Ailisto yowls again, then disappears back out the door, swishing her tail so the tip remains barely visible at the edge of the doorway, awaiting the sound of Aoide following.

 Star-eyed Aoide, eighteen now, stands and follows her cat friend's low-shouldered slinking out of the dormitory and through the north gate of the sanctuary, up the lightly forested hillside leading around to the cliffs which tower above the sanctuary and feed the Kastalian Spring below. Two times, Aoide stops, losing the sense of urgency she'd felt at first from the cat's worried mews, only to have Ailisto return from ahead and shout at her again, eyes flashing wild fear.

 "Mercy, kitten, what is so grave?" Aoide asks sweetly into the dark.

 Once she is halfway up the steep grass behind Ailisto's little prancing steps, Aoide hears a high-pitched whimpering sound which starts her heart racing. But when she gets to where Ailisto has stopped, near an overhung nook in the roots of an old tree, her heart swoons from concern to delight.

 There the little cat has made a nest of leaves for four tiny kittens, all squirming and mewing against each other and rustling the leaves.

 But on closer inspection, Aoide sees that two more kittens are there, but are motionless. Ailisto licks them and mews toward them, yowling at Aoide. She goes up to the wriggling bunch and touches their wet little paws.

Aoide thinks of how she has joked about being a goddess to Ailisto. She wishes now more than ever that she had the powers of a goddess, and could possibly do something for these two stillborn kittens.

Tearing up, she goes to pick them up, but Ailisto swats at her with claws out, and growls a sad growl.

She sits in the disappearing twilight a while, petting Ailisto and her living kittens and grieving over the dead ones, not knowing what to do with them. After a while of imagining meaner animals finding the poor dead kittens where they lie, Aoide decides to scoop them up and take them away from the kitten nest.

Ailisto sings a mourning song and jumps at Aoide's knees while she carries the kitten bodies away through the brush.

On any evening, a song is no stranger to the wind, as Delphi is a valley where poets come at all times of the year to find inspiration. But while Aoide is carrying the bodies of the poor lost kittens on this particular evening she finds a gathering of voices meet her ears, several singers all sharing a lyre, taking turns one after the other, shards of song mortared together with laughter, and she begins following the sound before realizing that she has been led astray from her initial purpose.

Carefully, but quickly, she bends down and digs a little hole into a mossy rise with her fingers, places the little death-sleeping kittens into that earthen bed, and covers them again. When Aoide leaves them, Ailisto stays there to mourn.

Continuing on toward the sound of song, Aoide comes upon a little clearing overlooking the valley below, with a nook of rock where four young men, each differently colored and just as handsome as the next, are sharing the air around a young woman with a lyre. At first she thinks she has never seen any of them before, until one turns a shoulder and she recognizes him - the poet Bacchylides.

"Aigypt now!" the finishing singer shouts, and the shorn-bald dark-skinned man beside him continues the song like a baton-racer.

> *Herakles came to Aigypt next, to do a little good,*
> *but foolish King Bousiris met him at the Nile's mouth,*
> *with just this one request of that hero-Hellene,*
> *to put a muzzle on that mouth, and nevermore know drought!*

"Does *drought* rhyme with *mouth*?"
"Muzzle the Nile's mouth! If only we could!"

"Tyrrhenia now!" The Aigyptian poet slaps the knee of the man beside him, a paler lad with a big, curly beard, who laughs and takes a few moments to silently compose his lines.

> *When Herakles passed through the land of sweet Italia,*
> *with Geryon's cattle, stolen from him fair,*
> *he took a nap in dappled sunlight, as is nice to do,*
> *but right in view of local girls' despair.*
> *The maidens washing dresses in their gentle River Po*
> *and weeping for their brother who had drowned,*
> *beheld the hero's body resting gently in the grass nearby*
> *and stopped weeping to start weaving a crown!*

Aoide only notices that the eyes of the woman with the lyre are on her when she sings out, "Delphi now!" with a sly smile.

The singers all look to her, and become her waiting audience.

Aoide imagines singing, but her body holds still, and her throat tightens. Before too much awkward time has passed, she decides to be graceful through honesty, and says, "I'm shy about my voice."

"Your voice, or coming up with words?" the Aigyptian poet asks.

"Just unleash the eagle in your heart!" a listening girl shouts.

"Your words will pass through all our ears and then with lightning doom waft up like smoke for gods to hear and then be gone from Earth entirely, never to be heard again," the Tyrrhenian poet says, impressing Aoide with his referencing of philosophical poets she has heard before.

Aoide looks around at this small group of mortal poets on this hillside, on this fleeting day. All smile to her and wait with patient ears.

Very reticently at first, but then with rising glee, Aoide sings.

> *When Herakles met Pythia, at Delphi's Oracle,*
> *she would not sing one word to him, not one sonorous rhyme,*
> *and though he tore the place apart, there is no answer for*
> *the man who demands cure for madness of his own design.*
> *So Zeus sold Herakles to slavery like an old milking cow,*
> *to work with women in the weaving room for one whole year.*
> *I tell you, as our songs echo through olive valleys now,*
> *unknown ears listening in the future can also hear.*

Zeus rumbles behind the night clouds, and the mountain winds start to rush about, shaking the trees. The singers all smile excitedly at the wildness, and sing without words into the firelit dark of the future.

Z

The Athenian Assembly discusses what to do while Sparta is weakened

Eagles circle high over Athens, unwatched from below.

Hillfolk, urbanites, and fishermen alike are crowded once again upon the Hill of the Pnyx for the Athenian Assembly. Men each eat their small portion of the sacrificed bull's meat, while braziers hold the bones and innards burning for their smoke to feed the gods.

Ephialtes stands upon the bema, facing the faces.

The time-keeper starts a jar pouring, slowly summoning quiet.

Over the last of the voices, Ephialtes shouts, more comfortable than ever before speaking with confidence, "Our entire governmental structure is built on the idea of trusting the gods. We give them authority through our lot-based decision making. The gods present us with what they would prefer in the world, and we do the best we can not to get in their way. Right?"

Ever-smiling Ephialtes waits for the crowd to begin to murmur some agreements, so that it sounds to the uncertain as if their neighbors agreed, and then he interrupts that murmuring with another shout.

"Well, the gods have spoken, and they have spoken loudly so as not to be misheard! At least Poseidon has clearly spoken, and he has decided to kick Sparta to its knees."

Rumblings flow through the Assembly, fearful of the gods but also grateful to imagine Sparta less threateningly powerful.

"And was it not Poseidon himself who contested with Athena to be our own city's patron god? What about our ancient Erechtheion, ruined by Persia too long ago now? And our once-great temple at Sounion, also destroyed by the Persians? We have no reason to cross the power of Poseidon. We should let Sparta find their own fate, and not tie ourselves to them in a matter which is clearly between them and the gods. Just as Poseidon will also take the man who swims out to save a man whom Poseidon has chosen to drown in his watery depths - we should not go down with Sparta."

The herald Androkles, a nervous old net-maker, raises up his kerykeion snake staff, shouting over the crowd's voices, "Please, please! Let us allow the Spartans themselves to make their own case. A runner, I hear, has just arrived from Lakedaemonia. Summon him to speak."

The Assembly parts to make way as a weary, nude, sweat-glistening man made entirely of muscle is guided through the crowded space. The long-haired, bare-faced Spartan emissary ascends the bema and addresses the assembled crowd of Athenians as many in the crowd compare their own bodies to his. He takes a few moments to breathe before he speaks.

"Hellenic brothers - this is our call for aid! It was not long ago that we all came together, like the noble kings of old lining up to sail to Troi, but instead to fight back the villainous sons of Kyros and their infinite barbarian hordes! Well, barbarian hordes threaten again, but this time from within! Our own slaves, this time, rise up against a wounded Sparta. And you know that Sparta would not ask for help if we didn't need it."

Myronides shouts, "If the Messenians are barbaric, it's because you have made them so through torture and enslavement. They're Hellenes. You're not!"

"Spartans are the sons of Herakles!" the Spartan retorts angrily.

"Fake history! You're Dorian invaders," Myronides retorts. "We know our history, unlike you who fool yourselves with false histories in order to fool others."

The Spartan takes a heavy breath, then says, "We have sent runners to all the cities of Hellas, all those whom we fought with against Persia just a few short years ago. Have you forgotten that we are allies? Do you really think you would not be under Persian rule were it not for the valor of Leonidas?"

"Sparta has been talking about invading Attika for years now. Sparta is a threat to democracies throughout Hellas. We should not help Sparta in their time of weakness, but rather join with those Messenians whose land has been in Spartan control for generations and finish Sparta off for good!"

The Assembly roars; the surrounding olive trees quake.

"The gods show what they love and don't love - and it would seem today they don't love Sparta!"

"We've heard very different suggestions here today, as to how to react to Sparta's moment of need," Androkles says, breathing patiently through his nose to stay calm as the men around him seethe with anger at each other's opinions. "Perhaps what we should do, rather than either extreme ... is nothing at all."

While full-throated disagreement maintains its grip on the men of the Assembly, the suggestion of doing nothing brings more calm to it than either previous proposal.

The Spartan shakes his head and tromps back off through the Athenian crowd, pushing some who block his way. Some in the crowd try to follow him and assure him that they would like to help, and that the democracy does not speak for them.

Before long, the Assembly disperses with less interesting matters attended to quickly by the few who remain.

Alkibiades the Oligarch approaches Ephialtes as both are walking back down the hill with the crowd.

"You know, young man," Alkibiades says, touching Ephialtes on the shoulder, "there may just be a future in politics for you yet."

Ephialtes scoffs.

Alkibiades continues, "You should consider yourself lucky that our man Kimon whose voice the people love most is off subduing another island back into the sway of the League of Delos. When Kimon returns from Thasos, your side won't have the advantage anymore."

Alkibiades slaps Ephialtes on the arm, then heads off down an alley following footsteps in the sand that say

FOLLOW

ME

H

Preisias, a Theban in exile, trains Helots for war

"Each phalanx the finger of a hand, they must act from one mind. That is why you need drums. The drum is the weighted warp for the weave of the general's plan, keeping the movements of each phalanx united. Have you gleaned *no* Hellenic military wisdom from your proximity to the Spartans? How can no one here have a real drum?"

One of the boys pounds on his sternum to show that it works as a drum.

"A real drum, I said. We're civilized Hellenes, not barbarians."

The exiled Theban war hero Preisias stands at the head of a tightly arranged unit of sixteen Helot boys and girls between ten and thirty years of age, each holding a full-size military spear, some barely able to.

"Spartans aren't Hellenes," the chest-drumming Helot boy spits. "The Dorians invaded this land. We Messenians are the real Hellenes."

The Theban nods to the boy and says, "You only meet Ares through bravery, boys, but I promise you - he will add his fist to your own if you let him into your hearts. You'll need him if you think even the sixteen of you working as a unified phalanx could bring down one Spartan soldier. But when all your Helot brothers across this land arrive from the Arkadian hills and the slopes of Taygetos and the remote peninsulas of the south, and all the phalanges of the Pelopponese are working together as a single wise general's hand - just then, just maybe, you might be able to win your freedom for ever after, and freedom for your yet-to-be-born children and grandchildren, and peace for this land which has only known enslavement since your Spartan invaders arrived twenty generations ago. And look now to the horizon, boys, east, there - your wise general Korax arrives."

Hearing the distant rattle of armor, Preisias puts sinking-red Helios behind him and spies to the northeast, where a broad army of silhouettes marches, still appearing over the near hill-horizon.

"So war has begun," the Theban sighs. "Who's ready to kill your captors, and the captors of your mothers and grandmothers?"

The youths, a moment ago wearied from exercises, regain energy quickly and all cheer.

"Keep it up," he commands them as he steps away to meet Korax and the approaching army.

Korax walks at the head of his army of former-Helot warriors, gathered from the homesteads and villages all across Lakedaemonia. Most of them wear little more than straps of thick leather, though a few have suits of Spartan armor which they've stolen and then removed or disfigured the L. They all carry spears, but few carry the usual accompanying sword. The organized fighters number under a thousand, with at least five times as many women, children, and elders unable or unprepared to do war.

Preisias walks up to meet Korax ahead of the army. The two men shake hands, and then Korax hugs the Theban mercenary tightly.

"You came," Korax says grinning.

Preisias nods, holding Korax's hand. "Love demanded I do."

Korax and Preisias kiss, and touch each other's faces, each tearing up at the sight of the other.

"Here are five thousand men and women ready to fight," Korax says, gesturing to the horde gathered behind him.

"I see *maybe* two thousand fighters," Preisias retorts, sizing up the group.

Korax says, "Everyone fights. Everyone fights, or everyone dies. These people know there is no going back."

Preisias sighs, running his hands through his hair. "Korax, I'm trying to be realistic and honest with you. I owe you that."

Korax turns to the youths whom Preisias had been organizing and commands, "Gather into our marching group, noble Messenian warriors! We follow the setting Sun to the palace of Nestor at Pylos, the old capital of our ancient homeland! We need the blessing of our ancestor heroes."

Preisias sighs and pulls his hair with frustration. "Korax, you must understand, legends are not all based on reality. There may never even have been a King Nestor. The old stories of Homeros are just that - stories. Just look at Mykenai, the supposed palace of King Agamemnon, but really just an ancient ruin peopled by brigands. And similarly, any palace that may have existed at Pylos in the past is simply not there anymore in this age. Following your plan, we would go further west than we need to, and get stuck in dangerous, ruined land, to be scattered to the wind by the Spartan army. Do not make the mistake of chasing ghosts."

Korax listens, but then replies without looking at him, "Pylos is a question of morale, Preisias. The Messenians among us in particular need this. It's our ancient homeland, back when we were one of the countries that could provide a hundred ships to the task of rescuing Helen, when our King Nestor was the most highly respected mind among all the kings of Hellas who sailed to Troi. Frankly, Preisias, I trust Homeros over you."

Preisias replies, "I agree that the men need morale, but you are thinking in terms of legends instead of reality. You say the palace of Nestor is there, but I've heard from men with no reason to lie that all of Pylos is little more than windswept ruin, without a palace in sight. But on Mount Ithome, close to the Lakedaemonian heartland, and closer to where we are now, there's a fortress I have *been to* and know how to defend. The old Messenian fort there is real, and if we can make it, if that Spartan army doesn't intercept us, then just maybe we can get a foothold and really take back this land."

"They'll intercept us," Chrysaor says morosely. "We must die fighting on Spartan land, so our ghosts can haunt them in their homeland. I don't mean to be left haunting some windswept plain the Spartans can easily leave and ignore."

"They're weak and frightened," Korax assures him. "We will make it to Pylos first, and see for ourselves whether the land of our ancestors is only a legend, because we're leaving now. Either we will become legends ourselves through magnificent acts, or the gods will strip us from the world."

Korax starts walking west, toward the distant mountains, and the troop of former-Helot warriors, including the young ones whom Preisias had been training, all start to pick up their shields and helmets and follow.

Chrysaor signals the boys being trained and points to indicate that they should join the army, then heads off after Korax loyally, prepared for any death.

Reluctantly, the Theban fighter follows his friend fateward.

"O SOUL, DEAR SOUL DEFORMED BY FATES' AGON,
HOLD FAST AND MEET YOUR RUSHING FOE HEAD-ON,
AND THEN, WHATEVER HAPPENS IN RESULT,
WAIL NEITHER IN LAMENT NOR IN EXULT."
Archilochos, Parian Poet

ATHENS

Θ

Sokrates and friends chat with philosophers at Simon's shoe shop

Simon's shoemaking tent is an oasis of shade at the edge of the busy Agora on this hot, sunny day. It is one of the rare days when there is no religious festival, so commerce rages.

Euripides, Krito, and little Sokrates sit quietly among the sandals, reading from a scroll of geometrical puzzles.

Old Simon sits cross-legged, building a traveling boot around the ankle of a Phrygian aristocrat who is visiting Athens for pleasure.

Anaxagoras, who recommended his friend the shoemaker to this aristocrat in the midst of a conversation about their homelands, now sits across from the Phrygian man, sharing tales of his own home in Ionia.

Archelaos the barber's son sits patiently beside and behind Anaxagoras, listening and absorbing.

"How long will this take?" the aristocrat asks Simon.

"I'll only need you for this one," Simon says. "Then I'll make the left by simply copying the right."

"Most clever!" the aristocrat smiles. "You work-a-day men are full of little wisdoms, aren't you?"

Simon smiles politely.

The Phrygian then turns to Anaxagoras and says, "So anyway, my Ionian friend, if Ionia is as fertile as you say, then I may just have to invest in that Meander farm the farmer-gentleman suggested after all. I knew Athens would be a great place to learn secret wisdoms! Your Eleusinian Mysteries were strange and intriguing, but I'm not sure what to actually get out of them. This kind of wisdom, however, is actually valuable!"

"Well, as I was trying to explain," Anaxagoras adds, "Ionia is a big place, and it will depend entirely on the specific valley, and the year, whether or not your orchards will be a wise investment."

"So how did your friend Thales go about making all of his money on his orchards, as you described? Which valley did he grow in?"

Anaxagoras shakes his head. "This is why I wasn't sure if I should try to tell you this story - it seems you have thoroughly misunderstood it. First of all, again, Thales was not a friend of mine; he lived a few generations ago. And it wasn't that he found a remarkably fertile valley which might still be just as fertile today, but rather that he studied over time the specific patterns playing out in the myriad valleys of Ionia, and determined that every so many years certain regions would produce a great olive crop. It was patterns that he found useful. And it was not orchards that he invested in, but oil presses! He bought all the presses in the region, knowing that when the olive harvest came in, he would be the only person they could sell to."

"So I should invest in oil presses," the aristocrat nods.

"I fear being connected to the inspiration for your choice. Those burdened with scientific notions which they do not know how best to use risk falling into a well while looking at the stars. Perhaps you should speak with someone better able to communicate with you. I fear this has been a language failure."

"Not at all! I feel it has been a success!" the Phrygian aristocrat smiles. "Worry not! I will not make the same mistake as Thales - I will look out for wells!" He looks down to Simon and asks, "Much longer?"

Anaxagoras corrects, unheard, "Thales did not fall in any well. I was being figurative."

"Not much longer," Simon says. "Just need to hold this sole here until the glue dries. It won't be long."

Anaxagoras looks to the boys in the corner with their scroll of geometrical puzzles, and says, "I see you boys are discovering the magic of patterns just like Thales did."

"So are all these your kids?" the aristocrat asks Simon and Anaxagoras.

Both men laugh.

"No no," Simon replies, "they're just friends of mine. I have many friends, of many ages."

The Phrygian nods suggestively and says, "These ones are a bit young for that, though, no?"

Simon shakes his head minutely and corrects, "Ours is not an erotic friendship, but merely a colloquial, conversational one."

"We hang out here to listen and talk," Krito offers shyly.

"It's almost like a Debate Club," Euripides suggests playfully. "We talk about weird things, weird ideas. Can I ask you a question, sir?"

"Of course!" Anaxagoras replies joyfully. "My favorite thing in life is considering what the best answer to a new question might be."

Euripides smiles at that notion, and asks, "Did you say that you knew Thales, the wiseman from Miletos?"

Anaxagoras says, "Well, I feel like I knew him, but really I've just read all of his writings. At least, all I could find. But no, I never did meet the man; he was from my grand-father's generation."

"Did your grand-father know him?" Krito asks.

"No," Anaxagoras replies with a touch of melancholy, "my grand-father wasn't interested in what you called 'weird ideas'. He was too interested in the admiration of other men, who in his day disdained the wisemen of their day whom we revere now. The movement of ideas over time flows like the sediment of the great Meander River; they accrue gradually, and not where you'd expect, and usually downstream. But where there is flow, matter is inexorably moved - or in this analogy, ideas."

"And then one day you realize that your harbor has been silted up, and you have to move your city downstream!" Archelaos chimes in, remembering a story Anaxagoras told to him earlier, of how Thales realized that rivers move sand, and, from that, that all nature is a moving fluid, by watching the silting up of the Miletos harbor over a lifetime of years.

Anaxagoras nods with a confirming smile.

"And what about you, young man," the Phrygian asks Archelaos, "are you this man's assistant, or slave?"

"I'm here to learn from the wiseman," Archelaos matter-of-factly says, gesturing to Anaxagoras. "I guess you would say I'm a student of the school of Anaxagoras. You could say I'm a slave to wisdom."

Anaxagoras humbly shrugs. "His claim, not mine. Though I appreciate the sentiment."

"O?" the Phrygian aristocrat asks playfully. "And what makes you think this is a wiseman? He doesn't have a long, white beard or any other usual signifiers of a wiseman. I mean no offense, of course - I'm just curious, what led you to trust the wisdom of some random stranger?"

"Well," Archelaos stutters, "he speaks smartly. He makes logical comments, which cohere reasonably with other logical ideas, and with what is evident. What he suggests proves out, I find. And he knows a lot! He's experienced a lot. Met a lot of people, traveled to many places. And he's read a lot. He's like a one-man library, himself! Ask him anything."

"I don't really know any books," the Phrygian man admits. "Except Homeros and Hesiod, which were read to me as a boy, but I will be the first to admit

I remember only a few lines and have no certainty at all that I remember them accurately. But I recognize them when I hear them!"

Sokrates then sings out lines from the Odyssey which he is fond of, to show off that he has them memorized.

> *The gods sometimes make foolish folks do things which appear wise and insomuch drive sensible people out of their minds*

The adults all laugh, as Sokrates has made the lines his own.

Krito smiles at the apparent wisdom of his little friend. "Did you come up with that?" he asks.

"That was *The Odyssey*!" Euripides scoffs derisively. Krito shrinks.

"Do the gods really determine what goes on within our minds?" Sokrates asks the adults with a serious look on his face.

All present look to each other for a moment.

Simon says, "I think it is a mix. Ourselves, the world around us, the gods. I know for me, sometimes I labor at thought with intention. And sometimes a bird or cloud will cause thoughts to appear in my mind. And once in a while, I think of something seemingly out of nowhere."

Anaxgoras shrugs. He hesitantly says, "If I am being honest, I have never seen the actions of a god in the world. Their presence would seem to be only in stories. Everything which I have seen occur in the world seems to behave consistently, as the mixture of its particular elements would always do." With a little sly smile, Anaxagoras adds, "If the machinations of nature are the gods, then it would appear the gods are slaves."

The Phrygian frowns with just his mouth and raises his eyebrows. "Gods, please wait until I am out of range before you show this man how wrong he is." Then he chuckles and slaps Anaxagoras jauntily on the arm, to show that he is half-kidding.

Simon shrugs and says, "The gods surely understand how ignorant we are, just as we do not begrudge oxen for not reading."

"Has anyone ever tried to teach an ox to read?" Chaerephon asks.

The adults all laugh.

"Probably," the Phrygian chuckles.

"Simon, how did you get so smart?" Krito asks.

Simon smiles gratefully. "Well, for one thing, asking questions just like that! But I also make an effort to exercise my mind just like muscular men do with their muscles! Of course, exercising your body is important too. What I do is this - I try to continually give myself little challenges. Sometimes that's just - get out of bed. Sometimes it's making my walk slightly more rigorous for my muscles. But most often it's something mental - challenging my thoughts, or my presuppositions. Giving myself little riddles or thought-experiments, or new angles from which to think about the world that day."

"That sounds frustrating," the aristocrat suggests.

"Not if I keep all those self-imposed challenges in the context of only being minutely important, and totally uncritical if they fail or don't pan out. But sometimes, sometimes, they are extremely fruitful! I see it much like planting flowers. Many of your seeds won't grow, but those that do … become flowers!"

"You know, Simon," Anaxagoras replies, considering the notion, "I think there is a great deal of wisdom to be born of that idea. I do see what you mean, and it is not a way that I had thought about thinking. But I do now, so thank you for that!"

Sokrates smiles, always pleased when adults are grateful to each other the way they teach children to be. Encouraged by the friendly feeling, he asks Anaxagoras, "What about you, friend, what would you recommend someone do in order to become wise?"

"Read," says Anaxagoras, first to Sokrates, then to Archelaos and each of the other boys one by one. "Read. Read. Read. And read. Read everything you can find made of letters. Grapple with the challenge of reading even unfamiliar letters! Read as much as you can get. Because the past is not gone, but its best moments have been captured in words like octopi in fish jars!"

"So words are sort of like webs that trap ideas?" Sokrates asks, intrigued.

"Oh I like that," Archelaos says, nodding and grinning. "That is a funny visual to think about, Sokrates. Very nice."

"Remember when that spider witch showed us her sister spiders, when we were little, Euripides?" Sokrates asks his friend excitedly, the moment just flashing back to him.

The adults give intrigued faces.

"It was just over there, some years ago, back when I was little," Sokrates relates. "And this weird old witch woman asked me and Euripides if we wanted to hear our fates, and then she said that she was told about the future by her sister spiders, and she had all these huge spiders up her sleeve that came out and did a little dance to tell the future or something. But we both got so scared that we just ran. Remember, Euripides?"

Euripides nods reluctantly. "Yeah. My father caught me running from her and made me go back to her and apologize."

The adults all laugh.

"I remember that lady," Simon nods. "I think she was only in the city for a couple, two or three, years. Then I heard she went to Argos."

Just then, Euripides' mother Kleito's voice startles Euripides from the crowd. "You should remember to thank your father for teaching you manners once we get home! It is a wise man who knows how to show other folks gratitude, even those who appear destitute, or mad. You never know who might actually be a god." Perfectly-mannered Kleito appears at the shop entrance with folded hands and a low-eyed, friendly, but forceful, smile.

Euripides nods. "Hello, mother. Do I have to go home right now? I was learning!"

"How to make shoes?"

"I was helping these boys do mind-puzzles, and then we were all talking with these foreign wise men."

Kleito looks up to Anaxagoras and the Phrygian aristocrat and says, with the mask of a demure smile, "He used to know his public manners better, when he was a boy. Somehow, with the teen-aged years, such manners seem to slip from his memory. Please forgive my otherwise fine son."

"Mother!" Euripides groans, rolling his eyes.

"That is one strike of the whip," she snaps, blinking wide eyes at her son in a way that he recognizes as serious. "Now I don't want to have to stitch you up from more than that. Do you, Euripides?"

Euripides' eyes go vacant and he puts on a blank-faced mask to cover his embarrassment. He stands, arms hanging heavy, and walks over to his mother, who is already smiling away her own embarrassment in little glances of gratitude to each of the adults in the tent.

"Thank you, Simon, for putting up with Euripides," Kleito says.

"He's got wisdom beyond his years, good lady," Simon replies. "I am the grateful one."

Kleito smiles a thank you, patting her son on both shoulders, then turns him to leave with her. Euripides eyes a quick goodbye to his young friends. Sokrates and Chaerephon pull comic faces back at him.

Kleito keeps her hand on her son's shoulder as they walk, even though he's nearly as tall as she is already. He several times tries to shrug her hand away, but each time she gently returns it.

"You're my baby, and that's that," she snaps playfully. "I want people to know it."

Thinking of the story of Arachne, Euripides asks his mother, "Mother, are you a good weaver?"

"I think I'm pretty good," Kleito says with a touch of humbly contained pride.

"But you're not *that* good, right?" Euripides asks her intently.

"There are certainly better weavers than me," she admits.

"Good," Euripides sighs. "I just wanted to hear you say it."

"And to think I was going to give you a special present today."

The snare catches Euripides easily, and he immediately presents a puppy face to his mother. "What present?"

Euripides' mother smiles patiently and steers the two of them to the edge of the street. There, after just a few moments of playful hesitance, she reveals from her satchel an arm-length tube wrapped with two blue strings which Euripides immediately recognizes as a roll of parchment. He inhales deeply at the sight of it.

"For me?" he asks. He has seen wealthier boys be given such rolls of paper by their parents, but never imagined his parents would entrust him with something so expensive.

"Now you be careful with it," she says as she hands the roll over to him.

As Euripides unties the strings and unrolls the sheet, he realizes it is a single sheet of parchment, thick and rough, with a couple of patches near the edges where there is still a bit of hair from the animal's skin. He frowns at the single piece of parchment.

"O don't frown," Kleito sighs. "When the words you write on this make you famous, then you can afford to buy your own replacements for it. But for now, you need to be grateful for what you can get."

In his mind's eye, the paper begins to fill with inky black textures, all interwoven and overlapping, and he begins to imagine how this one sheet of paper might be able to function as many, if he uses its space economically.

Euripides rolls the sheet back up and hugs his mother tight.

"I love you!"

"Just promise me you won't go drawing naughty women on it."

Euripides groans and rolls his eyes.

I

Protagoras takes Euathlos to court

Protagoras stands before the five hundred man jury of the Athenian law court, a truly diverse assortment of Athenian cityfolk, fishermen, and a few hillfolk seated near the door where they can keep eyes on their animals tied outside.

While he has spoken often in the Agora of how one ought to speak in court, this is actually Protagoras' first time speaking to an Athenian court himself. He finds the moment more intimidating than he had expected, particularly as a foreigner to this city. The Athenians eye him expectantly, ready to listen and judge, like an audience at the theater.

Across from Protagoras, against a backdrop of the theater-seated throng of men who happen to have been selected by lot for jury duty this month, sits his enemy in this agony of words, his ex-student, ugly, pot-bellied, ever-smug, and a year more street-smart, Euathlos.

"Gentlemen of the jury," Protagoras begins, and immediately a few men laugh at the pretension of his delivery. He stops with a snort, but then decides he must continue through whatever sort of interruption a barnyard might provide, and begins again. "Men of the jury…"

Some of the cannier among the men chuckle, barely audible in the large room. Protagoras waits, looking around to see who would laugh at his correction, and shakes his head when few do.

"…I am here to present to you the crime which has been done against me by that man there, Euathlos. I will attempt to be brief and concise, but for the time that I do take, I beg the gods to soothe your senses and make your seats comfortable, so that you will be as disposed toward what I say here as if you yourself were down here saying it.

"Now as you yourselves can understand, I am a man who possesses not all but certain wisdoms. I do not possess *all* wisdom, but that amount among all wisdom which I do possess is mine. And if I desire to share it with someone, it is my prerogative to be able to go into a contract of trade for it. This, my friends, is exactly what I did with Euathlos.

"I did not deign simply to share with him my wisdom because we are friends. I would not be able to distinguish this man from Deukalion across the Agora."

Jurors laugh at the mention of Deukalion, that first man whom the precocious titan Prometheos sculpted out of primordial clay.

"I have not known him for more than a month. So when he asked for my time, and my effort, and my wisdom, I told him that I would only be willing to give them to him at a price.

"Now here is where the challenging aspect comes in, but do not get confused! For this remains a simple contract, and one which has now come due.

"What Euathlos and I agreed to, which Hermes of the Marketplace bore witness to from on high, was this - that I would spend my time sharing my wisdom with Euathlos, and he would pay me for that effort only once he or someone for whom he had advocated had won their first court case. The implication, of course, was that Euathlos was planning to take my wisdom into a career of writing speeches for others headed into court. However, instead, after I completed my part of our deal, Euathlos told me he no longer had any intention of aiding cases in court."

Some of the five hundred men in the jury chuckle at that. One yells out, "Sounds like he got you!" and other men laugh at that comment.

"You might think that would be the case," Protagoras notes, holding up a finger, "except for this - we are now, he and I, engaged in a case in court. If I am to win, then that means that Euathlos must pay me what I am owed. However, if Euathlos wins, then he will have won his first case in court, triggering the circumstances of our contract, and forcing him to pay me. So, you see, my friends, there is now no way out of the payment for our friend Euathlos. I have cornered him here, in court, before all your eyes. In *either* case, I *must* be paid."

Some men of the jury go wild with laughter, while others groan and debate, as soon as Protagoras sits down.

Euathlos frowns, confused.

Startling all, a councilman in the upper stands suddenly shrieks and slaps his own face. "Ah!"

"A refutation of the logic?" one near him asks.

"I'm stung right under my eye! Run! Wasps!"

His seatmate points and shouts, "There's the nest right up there under that ceiling beam! Artemis of the Bees protect me!"

Instantly that whole corner of the building is abuzz with councilmen standing and fleeing from the southwest corner of the ceiling, where a wasp nest has begun to release its inhabitants into the air around.

"Shall I..." Protagoras trails off, wanting to continue making his case, but no one is paying attention to him anymore.

Even Euathlos on the other side of the floor is focused now with glee on the spastic swattings and group retreat from the upper stands.

"Wait wait," the day's Caretaker, Telemonion, says. He stands and grabs the nearby staff of an older man, and begins reaching the staff up toward the wasp nest.

Immediately, many in the building protest.

"Hey what are you doing? Don't!"

"You're just going to make them angry."

After just a few prods from the cane, Telemonion gets under the nest and succeeds in knocking it to the ground, where the grey-wrapped orb proceeds to roll down the steps between the stands, while infuriated wasps dizzily swarm out from it.

The wasps chase the jurors around and eventually out of the law court, spreading them into the Agora where they themselves buzz and dart and startle others with their commotion.

K

Political maneuvers are discussed in Potter's Alley

"Goddess hide from me the immensity of the task that yet lies undone ahead," Phidias groans as he stares at the barely-humanoid hulk of wax looming in front of him, the size of a person. At this phase, it could as easily become a cyclops as it could become the Wisdom Goddess, and Phidias has become overwhelmed with this month's bout of self doubt.

Carefully, he lifts his carving knife to the form and cuts away some corners of a curve. He feels the line with his fingers, wondering if the skin of a goddess would feel like the skin of a regular woman.

In just that moment, the voices of his patrons Perikles and Ephialtes leapfrog over the other voices in busy Potter's Alley as they approach, energetically discussing Phidias himself and the very project which is the source of his angst.

Phidias quickly closes the large curtain which hides the work-in-progress from all view, and crosses to the other side of his studio where he can pour himself a drink before the Democrats arrive.

Perikles says, "Hail, Phidias!" as he and Ephialtes emerge from the crowd. "Pour us a drink! We must speak!"

"I'm already quite drunk," Phidias warns.

"Well, then we should join you in that!" Perikles says good-naturedly. He says to his shoulder-heavy Thrakian slave, "Thrax, find us two cups of wine, would you? Surely someone on this street has some to sell! Thank you!"

Kind-eyed Ephialtes tells young Phidias, "Don't worry, son, we are merely here to talk with you about the image of the goddess."

Phidias breathes slowly and says to himself sarcastically, "O, only that."

Ephialtes and Perikles each pull up a sculptor's stool and sit beside each other. Only then do they notice little Sokrates sitting in the corner, watching the whole scene like a confused but intrigued audience. Ephialtes gives the little boy a smile, and Perikles gives him a serious nod.

"My boss lets his other workers just have their kids around here," Phidias explains.

Perikles says, "I've met young Sokrates before." Then he leans down a bit toward the shy boy and says, "You know, I was there when you were named, Sokrates!"

Sokrates smiles.

Phidias interjects, "I really would prefer to be left alone during this stage of the composition of the piece, gentlemen, if you don't mind. Collaboration in sculptural forms can lead to horrific, chimeric results. It truly is best to leave the composition to one person. Ask any artist."

"Well we just had a few ideas," Perikles says carefully. "I do understand, of course, and your artistic vision and skill are why we hired you for this work, so don't worry. But as we all know, Athena is a complex, multifaceted figure, and any number of versions of her could be depicted which would each present our city in very different lights."

Ephialtes sits forward to add, "For example, the gesture of her arms. Or the look on her face."

Perikles says, "Think of how the original Harmodios and Aristogeiton statues which stood before the Persians stole them had Aristogeiton's dagger raised up, as if in active threat against tyrants considering monarchical dreams. But the copies by your boss Myron has the arms at their sides. And both are beautiful, both represent the tyrant-killers, but the minutest difference of gesture makes a profound difference in the effect!"

Phidias sighs. "Of course. All of this is elementary in artistry. You are not the first to consider this."

From the street crowd, another voice hails them - that of Kallias, who has just gotten a fresh cut of his hair and beard. "Hail, Perikles and Ephialtes! And hello, friend! I am Kallias!"

Phidias holds out his hand to be shaken, but when Kallias gets near enough to do so he eyes the sculptor's dirty hand and retracts his own.

"With respect, good friend, your hands are a bit dirty," Kallias says. "But no doubt it is because you have been hard at work."

"This is Phidias," Perikles introduces. "Phidias, our friend Kallias, torchbearer of Eleusis."

"I have heard of you," shy young Phidias admits.

"I have heard of you as well," Kallias replies excitedly. "I understand you're the miraculous youth these men have chosen to be our city's great artist, to design the very form of our patron goddess herself! Congratulations, my boy! You must be quite a genius."

Phidias grimaces evermore as Kallias effuses his compliments, until finally by the end, at the word *genius*, Phidias' nerves cause him suddenly to vomit. He catches most of it in his hand, and turns away to spill out the rest.

"O gods!" Ephialtes blurts in disgust.

"Are you alright?" Perikles asks the boy, putting a hand on his back.

"It can be hard to know how to respond to compliments," Kallias politely acknowledges.

"Forgive me," Phidias sputters, already shedding tears he can't control. "I've been drinking, and I'm just so nervous about this work."

Perikles quickly takes the boy in a hug and rubs his hair, like he would a younger cousin. "Now now," is all he can think to say.

"A lot has been put upon your shoulders, for a boy of such a green age!" Kallias says. "It is understandable that you would be overwhelmed sometimes. But you have been given skill by the gods, the likes of which no other man today can match! I have seen your sculpture of Aphrodite, young man. I thought it was a real woman, painted! It is unimaginable to me how you must do what you do. But you are able to do it!"

Phidias grimaces out a thankful smile through his tears.

Perikles says, partially to break the awkwardness, "So, Kallias, what has brought you into Potters' Alley?"

"Yes! One would no doubt be surprised to see me here, where clay or paint can so easily be splashed upon one's garments! Well, Perikles, it is because I was told that you and Ephialtes would be here, speaking to your secret artist! You know, everyone has been wondering which artist you are working with for the Athena statue! Do not worry, your secret is safe! Also, anyway, the Agora is a bore today as folks debate some legal paradox."

"So what is it that you came to see us about?" Ephialtes asks with over-masked impatience.

Kallias smiles and gets comfortable with one foot up on a nearby stool before he begins his story. "Well," Kallias starts in, "it was Strepsiathes, one of his soldiers, who told me this, so I do take it as having some truth to it. Apparently, while Kimon's men were at Thasos there was some kind of threat made by the mainland barbarian chiefs, threatening Hellenic colonies in the area. And in order to avoid a fight, Kimon was paid off by that chieftain with a chest full of treasure. I imagine like his father Miltiades he no doubt stashed it on some foreign beach to be a bank from which to draw in secret."

Perikles and Ephialtes eye each other.

"That would, of course, be bribery by a barbarian. A deceitful, honorless, pathetic crime for a general of Athens," Kallias specifies.

Perikles nods, thinking, and says simply, "Indeed."

"I can understand preferring it to risking a fight, when you're on an island and they've got the mainland," Ephialtes acknowledges. "But yes, the old men of the Areopagos would certainly not approve. Or at least they wouldn't feel they could afford to appear to approve."

"You say *barbarian* as if all non-Hellenes are the same," Perikles slightly scoffs, "but what specific clan was it? Do you know?"

Kallias leans in to say, "The Makedonians, I understand. That arrogant upstart chieftain Alexander who was at the Olympic Games!"

"They are hardly barbarians," Ephialtes retorts.

"They would like us to think so!"

Perikles eyes Ephialtes. "The Makedonians are Hellenes. They are not uncivilized. They just sided with Persia like cowards when it came time for War. Paying off some roofless Pelasgians might be less concerning, but a secret deal with the Makedonian king is another thing."

"Thank you for sharing this information with us, Kallias. You remain a friend of democracy!"

"O I am just a slave to the flows of gossip, an echo of what I hear! And truly,

I value nothing higher than having a story to tell which interests my listener!"

Λ

Citizens discuss politics and jurying in the Agora

For days, the legal case of Protagoras-versus-Euthalos is the hot discussion of the moment in the Agora, as it is overextended while the law courts are closed for festivals and for an extra day to clear the wasp nests. Everyday people debate the legal case the way they usually do boxing matches. Everyone has an opinion and many different groups are enjoying its unique paradox. It mostly overshadows the political maneuverings around the rumors returning from Kimon's expeditions north to Thasos, just off-shore from the Makedonian coast where the colony of Nine Ways was lost just a few years ago.

"But if Euathlos wins his case, the verdict of that case is that he does not owe Protagoras without winning a case. But once he has won his first case, he owes Protagoras according to their contract! The moment in question is the very moment that he wins the case, immediately after which he will owe Protagoras, though he will at least have won his case! Whereas, if Protagoras wins the case, then Euathlos both owes Protagoras and has lost the only legal case he partook in!"

"It cannot be that if Euathlos wins he still must owe Protagoras. The point of him winning is so that he will not have to pay Protagoras. The law cannot prevent us from a just outcome! That's exactly why we've put the laws in human hands!"

"Euathlos *will* eventually owe Protagoras no matter what. He simply does not owe him *yet*. Human courts cannot rush future events into the present just because someone is impatient for a contract to come to fruition. The courts should next adjudicate that the olive trees bear fruit early!"

Axiochos and Kleinias, the sons of Alkibiades, stand together with some other teen-aged boys near the Monument of Heroes, carving sexual images into apples and tossing them to passers-by.

"You know, Kleinias," Axiochos muses, "I think that I might try to get on a jury every month. I've never gotten more gifts from folks I don't even know!"

"But you have to sit in that court house all day," Kleinias says. "Isn't that miserable, those seats, not being able to get up and run whenever you want?"

"It could be a lot worse. And you get to decide people's fates. It's like getting to be Paris Alexandros, except judging some stupid ox-shit like this instead of which goddess has the better butt! No matter how insignificant the issue, somebody has a lot riding on it, and that leads to the whole jury caring about it, and suddenly everyone wants to do you favors to get you to vote their way! It's great." He tosses an apple into a passing group of dancer girls, who catch it among them and then groan and throw it back after seeing what he carved into it.

One of the rich boys' friends their same age, unflappable Nikias, remarks coolly, before biting an apple, "Take a bribe for something as holy as government work, and the gods will never forgive you."

Axiochos scoffs and notes, "There are plenty of ways of being favored without taking a bribe. And we all know the gods respect those who are clever enough to slip through loop-holes and cheat with technicalities. The gods love that!"

"I don't know if they love it," Nikias retorts, "but it does seem true that they can fall for it." He shrugs and bites an apple.

Ephialtes' voice appears through the bustle of the crowd before the Oligarch boys see him, saying, "You know, boys, none of the gods are stupid. If you're going to try to fool them, you certainly ought not to say it where you can be heard. With age and experience, you'll learn - the less you try to fool people, the easier everything becomes! The most common mistake among you Oligarchs is to dismiss the commonwealth, not only economic commonwealth, but the commonwealth of ideas created by those engaging together in good-faith communication!"

"Don't pigeonhole us," Kleinias says. "You don't know how we'll vote. Isn't your best friend Perikles, the son of an Oligarch? You should be trying to get our votes, Ephialtes, if you're really such a politician."

"Thankfully I am not under the same sort of curse as Sisyphos," Ephialtes replies, readjusting his tunic in a dismissive gesture, "and I am not obliged by any god to undertake that which is obviously impossible. What you don't realize, as someone without maturity and wisdom yet, is that to those of us who do have it, it is painfully obvious who lacks it. And once you're there, you will understand, but in the meantime, you are nothing more significant to me than an obviously unready child. Good day to you, young one, and good luck on your journey toward adulthood."

Ephialtes turns from Kleinias, who is still just a teen-ager, but his older brother Axiochos, who is twenty years old and tall, steps forward with sputtering anger and kicks Ephialtes in the butt, pushing him forward onto his hands and knees in the street.

Ephialtes stands and brushes himself off quickly, but he is unable to hide the pain of his skinned knees and hands, and cradles them as the stinging ache gradually increases.

Those nearby in the crowd boo at Axiochos' cowardly kick, and one large, passing elder shoves the youth in passing, but Axiochos ignores it and quickly regains his threatening footing. Beside him, Kleinias follows his older brother's physical cues but can match little of the buoyant courage.

As the crowd is booing the meanness and a kind elderly woman is helping Ephialtes to brush himself off, a councilor steps out of the council house, and all nearby in the Agora turn at once for his news.

"Has the court come to a decision?"

The councilor nods, seeming somewhat delirious.

"And what is the answer?"

The councilor urps, "Yes!"

Everyone squints at him until one asks, "To what question was that the answer?"

The councilor shrugs, "Don't ask me for exact words. The gods remember."

As if in answer, another man just emerging from the Council House shouts, "Euathlos wins! And so he must pay Protagoras! And so, by winning, he loses!"

The crowds of the Agora variously laugh, cheer, and mock the decision.

Chionides the clown, in the manner of a herald, shouts, "Be it known, so-called wisemen are just charlatans, and wisdom is for fools! Nothing means anything, and everything means its opposite!" while his colleague Magnes, who mimics animals, buzzes about pretending to sting people with a fig branch.

M

Songs fill the valley of Delphi

A drum echoes sparsely with a patient pace. Two double-flutes make a shifting parallelogram of harmony. Three singers create a closely-harmonized bed on top of which a solo singer slowly lays the words of the poet Sappho.

Aoide sits in the grass with music all around her. Her friend Dikasto nuzzles her head on Aoide's stomach, lying perpendicular.

An injured rabbit, who will never again move from the tuft of grass where it now effortlessly breathes, listens peacefully, hidden for the moment amid sunshine, paying attention to words it doesn't understand.

> *Immortal Aphrodite, on your fine garlanded throne,*
> *daughter of Zeus, wile-weaver, hear my prayer!*
> *Although you could with ease destroy my vulnerable heart,*
> *please do not crush me with painful sorrows of Love!*

"This is Sappho?" Aoide asks.
"Quiet," Dikasto hushes her.
"It's so sad," Aoide whispers. "It doesn't rhyme."
"It's beautiful. Life is sad. It's real. Life doesn't rhyme."
"Life usually rhymes."

> *If you have ever heard my wail before, then hear me now!*
> *I am not more or less in Love than I have ever been!*
> *You drive your famous chariot of gold, drawn by sparrows,*
> *and ask me why I call again, goddess, although you know!*

Dikasto flits her eyes up toward the goatherd boy with the drum on his lap, lets the toes of one foot encroach upon some of the boy's sandalled toes and explore there. The drummer boy smiles at her shyly.

"Where'd you get that drum?" she asks him.

"I made it out of the belly of one of my goats."

Dikasto makes a briefly horrified face in Aoide's direction and snickers.

"Where'd you get that beauty?" the drummer boy asks. Two of the backing singers add long Ooooo's to their singing for a moment to chide him.

Dikasto smiles. "Right here in this valley. Same place I got everything I have."

"You've never left this valley?"

"Don't have to," Dikasto says coolly. "The world comes here. Trust me, I have the same kind of wisdom as a woman who's traveled the whole world, and I got it without having to go anywhere!"

"Do you think there is a woman anywhere who has traveled all over the world?" Aoide asks.

"There are queens with great power and freedom!" Dikasto retorts. "Queen Artemisia of Kos led troops from across the Sea to assault Hellas! Some people actually *revere* and *listen to* women! Like here at Delphi, everyone in the world comes here to ask the Pythia what she thinks."

"Is that what they do? Is it 'what she thinks' that she's being asked?" Aoide asks, clarifying. "Or is she just the conduit for Apollo's divination?"

The complexity of that question quiets the conversation for a while, and the music is able to take precedence again as everyone ponders, each alone in their unique uncertainty.

As ever in the valley of Delphi, conversational voices in languages from across the world mix upon the wind, and are heard softly with the music as if they are the intended song. Smiling as he understands the spoken Aigyptian, the young Aigyptian poet with his lyre begins to translate what is heard into song.

In Aigypt, men are worrying about the Spartan threat,
calling them dogs, and like dogs dangerous when hurt,
saying that Hellenes ought to put them down
while civilized dog-trainers have the chance!

"What do Aigyptians care about what Hellene cities do?"

"O you know, everyone just likes to know the gossip, and add to it."

"What happens in Sparta has much to do with the cares of Aigyptians in Aigypt, as what happens in Aigypt affects what happens here in Hellas, even all the way up in Makedonia! Apollo, who lives here in the summer, goes up north to the Hyperboreans in the winter, and Helios with the Sun Chariot travels the whole breadth of Ge each and every day! You ought to believe that the events of one corner of the world affect events in every other corner! Poseidon shook Lakedaemonia, and we all felt it! And not just in the shaking of the ground, but in the echoing out of the effects of that shake-up. Refugees from the Peloponnese all tell the same story - chaos in Lakedaemonia. Not all those refugees are fleeing the destruction of their houses! Some are fleeing the violence of the rebellion which has resulted!" says the drummer boy.

"And Aigyptians are watching this rebellion," adds the Aigyptian boy, "and wondering if the same great story might work with an Aigyptian accent."

"Would Aigypt dare rebel against Persia?" Aoide asks, intrigued.

The Aigyptian boy nods to her with a flourish on his lyre. "Aigypt is an ancient, proud land, with our own line of kings thousands of years back. There are many in my land who are not content to simply atrophy in the shadow of foreign rulers. There is a young Aigyptian prince who dares to suggest independence, who defies his father's supplication to Xerxes openly in the streets, and there are Aigyptians at home and abroad who are proud of him for it."

"Dikasto! What are you doing here with these goatherds?"

Surprising the group, crag-cheeked Kliko is there in the trees, wielding her whip.

"So this is where temple duties are abandoned." Her voice carries no anger, only a familiar disappointment. The young musicians fall silent, their instruments settling into their laps like guilty things. "Young women of Delphi do not consort with goatherds."

"They were singing Sappho," Dikasto says, as if this explains everything.

"Sappho." Kliko tests the word like a bitter herb. "And tell me, what does Sappho know of Apollo? What does she know about service?"

The Aigyptian boy opens his mouth to speak, but Kliko's glance silences him.

"Love poems have a lot to teach about service," Aoide attempts.

"A few love poems do not excuse you from your duties," Kliko continues, aiming herself solely at Dikasto and acting as if she is ignoring Aoide. "The temple's daughters have higher purposes than listening to shepherds sing about kisses." Her eyes hold Dikasto like a gorgon. "Or have you forgotten what privileges you were granted? What trust has been placed in you?"

Foreseeing arguments against her, Dikasto shouts, "Poetry is the most important thing in the world. And this is the center of that world! It would be blasphemous torture to disallow me to hear the poetry of the day!"

"It is not safe for girls here!" The old priestess glares around at the young poets and musicians, who smile to each other with harmless shrugs.

As she stands and crosses over to the priestess, Dikasto gives Aoide a little glare and asks, "What about Aoide?"

"Aoide is Athenian. I cannot speak for Aoide. But you are a Delphian girl, and you will behave as Delphian girls are expected to! I'm sorry if it doesn't seem fair, but life isn't always fair. Sometimes it just is what it is."

Dikasto fumes, groans, and tromps away through the bed of fallen leaves, the priestess following behind.

Aoide watches, sitting still, burning inside. "Should I go after her?" she asks the boys around her.

"Trade freedom for *nothing ever*," says the Aigyptian boy, as he lifts his instrument and starts singing again.

Aoide winces inward though, hearing the music through a hazy lens, thinking too hard about how lacking the word *freedom* is in real meaning.

N

Korax speaks to his people at Pylos

The ancient palace of King Nestor at Pylos, on the far western coast of the Peloponnese, exists now as only ruins on a dry hill overlooking the western sea. But even the thousand-year-old ruin displays from its remnants what a brightly painted and elaborately sculpted palace once rose here. Now only one roofless room remains fully intact, a storage room still bright with remnant flecks of painted dolphins cavorting among ancient blue waves. Spreading away from that one standing room, the walls of the rest of the palace sink toward the ground as they span out like a giant dying stone octopus left to dry to death just above the beach.

The weary throng arrives toward the end of a long day of hustling, so all are ready for rest and grateful for water from the ancient well here.

"Thank the gods for the work of ancient men long dead," the Theban commander laughs as he raises the first water-filled bucket. All the Messenians nearby dryly laugh and cheer.

Korax inspects the painted room from the old palace with some women who are there giving praise to the ancient artist, then walks over to connect with Preisias, who has become his right-hand-man.

"Your King Nestor seems to have lived well indeed," Preisias notes as he hands Korax a cup of water.

"It appears to have been a beautiful palace, once. That room is just a storage room, I think, and yet see how they painted it. It inspires me to paint every room of my own future palace, after we win this war."

"Will you build your own, or will you take one of Sparta's fine homes?" Preisias asks him with a half-smile.

Korax sighs long and slow. He takes in the sea breeze.

The Palace of Nestor is just at the head of the long beach at Pylos. A couple of long, narrow islands are just off-shore, and beyond their trees the sky-blue Sea lined with whitecaps.

"I think that I will build my palace here," Korax says. "I like it here. I feel a camaraderie with King Nestor as I stand here on his beach, where he himself must have stood and looked. I can see how this view might give a man the calmness of mind to cultivate wisdom. Yes, here; here is where I'll build the Palace of Korax." He turns to Preisias and says, "Come then, and let's go win this war."

Korax strides past Preisias, who follows behind him moved by the man's vision, and they approach the great mass of men, women, and children who until just a few days ago have all been working as slaves of the Spartan state.

"My brothers and sisters!" Korax shouts. "Not one of us … was ever won in war. Each and every one of us … was born to an enslaved mother, and forced from infancy into this evil, monstrous system, so that Spartans can live the most privileged life of any people under the Sky. A life utterly without worry or toil, where they can focus only on themselves. No one has ever deserved to be destroyed more than god-hated Sparta!"

The men and women assembled before him cheer wearily.

Korax continues, "Once, too many generations ago, Hellenes respected *wisdom*. And King Nestor, who ruled from this great room whose ruin we stand in now, was respected as the wisest of the Hellene kings at Troi. Then, years later, but long ago, the great King Lelex led our people out from the lands where the Sun rises from, and across this Sea, to sandy Pylos, here, and made *this* our home."

Messenian mothers hold their children tight, to indicate to them that now is particularly a time to listen.

"Lelex made peaceful trade and marriage with the local kings, and shared in the bounty of this land for two generations of peace. It was not until the mad King Eurotas, the River-cutter, crossed those mountains from Lakedaemonia, that this land tasted blood. And it is the curse of that king's murderous crimes that still haunt this land! Only by driving out the fate-cursed sons and daughters of Eurotas will this land see peace again!

"I look out here across my people - women and men, all warriors, all breathing the fresh salty air as people recently escaped from their enslavement, freed by themselves in their courage inspired by an act of the Sea God on their behalf. Smelling the sea of their ancestors' beaches. This is where we were meant to make our homes. This is where the gods led our ancestors to. And this is where I will build the new palace of Messenia, once we have returned the Spartans' hospitality trifold!"

The gathered men and women roar a voracious approval.

"Spartans are not Hellenes! They are no more Hellenes than Makedonians! They are an invading barbarian force, in power only because of their slavish devotion to their War Goddess! But, like in the days of old, any amount of power can be toppled by the well-applied leverage of *cleverness*.

"Nearly a hundred years ago, just longer ago than the oldest men alive today could recall, our great grand-fathers rose up against their Spartan masters, just as we do today. And it is *here* that they fought their decisive battle, before their final glorious end at the Battle of Boar's Grave. But here is the reason why we will not fail as they did, and why we will not return to slavery as they did. We, who share the same blood as those heroes, will never go back to enslavement!"

Korax signals to Preisias with an extended hand, and the Theban walks up to him with a long spear. Korax receives the spear from Preisias, touches its stone top tenderly, then raises it high above his head and addresses his people again.

"Behold the *Spear of Lelex*! Found, today, by Preisias, hero of Thebes, during our march to this place, when we passed Boar's Grave! Found at Boar's Grave, beside this ancient helm - clearly the helm of the same king!"

Preisias holds up a bent old artifact, a hunk of bronze inscribed with some ancient whorls - the "helm".

Holding up his spear, Korax shouts, "And so, reaffixed by Iophon, spear-maker to the kings of Sparta, to the end of this perfect young shaft of olivewood, this ancient king's blade has risen today to draw Spartan blood once again, in my hand!

"I say: Henceforth, by the power of the Spear of Lelex, I am King Korax, of Messenia! And you shall never again be known as *Helots*, but henceforth only by your rightful name - as Messenians!"

Preisias gives Korax a quick questioning look, but then steps forward and raises his own sword, shouting to the assembled crowd, "All hail King Korax of Messenia!"

Confusedly at first, but eventually as one, the gathered warriors begin to chant, "Come and take them! Come and take them!" - that same famous war chant which the Spartans shouted at the Persians back in Persian Invasion One.

Korax shouts, "Long have men been held by evil conquerors as slaves. But never again shall *we* be. This year we will bring death to all slave-holders! Let our Spartan captors be only the first to fall beneath the spear of justice!"

The Messenians roar and murmur about these bone-white glimpses into their foggy ancestral memory, still dirty from disinterment.

On a new purple dusk horizon, the old white Moon has risen.

Ξ

The Spartan kings and Overseers in their war camp

Rising moonlight illuminates the work as Sparta's people rebuild their houses from the wreckage wrought by Poseidon's fury earlier in the month. The efforts continue day and night, while for now the Spartans live and sleep under long, broad tents of deer-skin on high poles, with communal eating and sleeping areas in rows of bunks and long tables, like scouts at war.

"It's just a big *agoge* for everyone to share in," one elderly Overseer reassures the cramped and wearied citizens. "It's like the old days, when Lykorgos held the first such grand supper, for only twenty men! Now look at this table - there must be a hundred here!"

Everyone grumbles agreement, doing their best to remain fearless. The night hovers dark just outside, filled with the flow of unknowns.

The two tents nearest to the Temple of Athena of the Bronze House are finer than the rest, and inside reside the two kings and their courts.

At one end of the large Agiad royal tent where Gorgo and her son and their attendants rest upon the finest lion skins, the best ones softened by generations of use among their ancestors, the attendants chat to each other in low voices on one side of a hill of furs while Gorgo and King Pleistarchos lie together on the other side. The young king's cousin Pleistoanax lies across from them.

All are listening quietly to a traveling story-singer.

"Sparta was the daughter of King Eurotas, who created our river by cutting a path for the marshes to drain to the sea," the old white-braided story-singer sings to the children from the middle of the tent where she sits, cross-legged. "Now King Eurotas gave his kingdom and his daughter Princess Sparta to the hero Lakedaemon, son of Artemis' handmaiden Taygete - queen of Mount Taygetos - and Zeus, King God. That's why we call our land both Sparta, and Lakedaemon, our land's founding lovers' names. For King Lakedaemon adored Queen Sparta, as she was the most beautiful and honorable of women, worth defending at all costs, just like your own great Queen-Mother. It is why men still shout her name in battle, dedicating their manly effort to the defense of her ancient honor. Think of all who cry in battle, 'Sparta!'

"And so Queen Sparta and King Lakedaemon had two children - Prince Amyklas and Princess Eurydike, who went on to marry the king of Argos and was the mother of Danaë and therefore grandmother of the great hero Perseus. But Prince Amyklas, who founded the town of Amyklai just down the river where the orchards are so fruitful - for that is what honor brings to its land - Prince Amyklas became king of Sparta after his father, and their line ruled these lands until Herakles arrived and created our dual lines."

Gorgo looks over to King Pleistarchos just as he is lifting his little turtle to touch its nose to his. "Put that away," she snaps. The Queen-Mother reaches out toward the turtle, and her son shirks quickly back, protecting it from her and backing away.

"Don't hurt him. I won't let you hurt him."

She lowers her chin to gaze at him with hard eyes. "Give me the turtle."

Pleistarchos shakes his head no, and hides the little creature in his cape, under his arm.

"You would protect that thing over your very country," Gorgo says glowering.

"No, I just won't let you hurt him."

"Everything is a window into something larger, Pleistarchos. Nothing is simply a mundane moment. Everything touches the eternal, everything has meaning. And attached to this moment is every other moment where you have defied me, or prioritized your own unfathomable quirks of character over the duties of your noble office!"

"You're just cruel," King Pleistarchos cries, letting his tears flow and releasing the mask of grief which he has been holding back. "You're just angry that I love something, even if it's just a little turtle, instead of it being you, or *Sparta*, whatever that means, or my father's noble ghost! Well I don't love any of that, I don't love my people at all, or my land, or you! I only love my friend who is the only one who is always sweet to me." The king holds his little turtle close in his lap and shrinks his whole body around it.

Gorgo bends down in front of him, holds her son's shoulders in her hands and stares into his wide eyes. "Pleistarchos," she says to him, shaking her head, "why did I birth you? Why did I give my blood to the gods, sundered my heavenly furrow where young men can no longer play, in sacrifice to this world that you - *you* - might be *this man*?"

Pleistarchos stutters, wounded, but can only look down and listen.

"You are the son of the greatest Hellene! And he, the lion Leonidas, was that great man because *I* demanded it of him! It was this beauty, this love, which led Hellenic manliness to achieve its summit!" She hits her own body when she mentions it, and pulls open her dress to reveal one still-shapely breast. "This breast which was not for you. Too powerful was its greater purpose - upon men of power, to command armies, to inspire the desire which unmans great men. And yet here *you* are - *this man*."

King Pleistarchos, nineteen years old now, but half that in his heart, shakes his head at his mother, tears welling in his eyes.

"If you do not take control of your life, of *who you are*, no one will ever love you, my son," Gorgo says, swallowing the tears that her son's own beckon from her. She sputters, "If you cultivate the attention of weak spirits who feed you petty reassurances, you will never grow strong enough to survive in this world of men."

Gorgo turns to Pleistoanax.

"Pleistoanax, learn from your cousin, before you make the same mistakes which have held him back. Listen to your elders, to your uncles, to the stories of heroes. Do not fall into the madness of cowardice."

"I'm not a coward!" King Pleistarchos croaks through his tears. "I just don't think you're a good person. I don't think any of us are good. We have earned this cursed life."

In the Eurypontid king's tent nextdoor, they overheard the outburst. The Spartan men all grumble at the despair of their king. King Archidamos looks on with a mix of satisfaction at the security of his own power position and concern for a lost boy.

"Too many words," King Archidamos says laconically to the Lakedaemonian men surrounding him.

Concision soothes them.

A Helot runner is ushered panting into the tent, and all turn to listen to the message relayed by the Overseer helping the tired man to stand. "The Helots return from the west, and march back into Lakedaemonia."

"They have gathered hill people from the ruins of Messenia, surely," the eldest Overseer bemoans. "This will be a clash of civilization against a return to primitivism! They mean to conquer this land back!"

"And our own army?" King Archidamos asks the Overseers as a group. They all look to each other uncertainly. The king punches at the air like a boxer. "We must gather to meet them! Are we or are we not the Spartan men our fathers raised us to be? Go, all you men of any strength at all, and gather all who can fight to meet these rebellious slaves head-on! We will not fall into despair over brief winds of fate. We are Spartans!"

Spartans voices swirl, and men begin to move.

In the Agiad tent, Pleistoanax and King Pleistarchos' eyes briefly meet, each separately quavering and confused.

Gorgo looks beyond young Pleistoanax and notices the absence of his caretaker only then. She asks him, "Pleistoanax, where is Niome?"

Pleistoanax looks up to his black-veiled aunt with careful eyes as he whispers fearfully, "She fled, when the slaves all fled."

"But she is not a Helot," Gorgo retorts, contorting her face with frustration. "She was a noble servant. She would give up that life, one in which she is treated as the princess she was born as, for the life of a refugee, a rebel on the run like some scared rabbit?"

Pleistoanax sees the confusion in his powerful aunt's eyes, and begins to understand. Beside her anger, he also sees his cousin the young king's face, relieved, compassionate, a hint of a smile through his tears. Pleistoanax nods curtly, not wanting to engage his aunt's wrath, but wanting to do honor to his confidence.

Gorgo fumes, and lets her face fall back within the shadows of her veil. "Then let her sleep outdoors in fear forever."

O

Athenians celebrate a night festival to Selene, the Moon Goddess

The Athenian festival of Selene Moon Goddess is celebrated at night, once the Moon has the full attention of the Sky, outshining the stars around. It is more of a festival for adults and teen-aged Athenians than the usual daytime festivals criss-crossed by racing children. In the cool of the night and the light of the bright Moon, lovers find the festival of Selene a particularly romantic time, and many are locked in embraces, half hidden in moon shadows, among the olive rows and stony steps and grassy slopes of the rocky Akropolis.

"The people of this city are hungry - not for truth, or wisdom - but for poetry! For fantasy."

"For comedy!" hunch-backed Hipponax shouts. "I mean, for comity! That is to say, for cum and titties. Athenians take note: I will be sitting on this friendly dog if anyone wants to purchase more poems like that."

"For commonwealth, and camaraderie!" shouts old Eteobouta, High Priestess of Athena, in her creaky, deep old voice, holding her hands high into the air. Her younger attendant priestesses coo and sing wordless agreements.

"All-bright Moon Selene!" shouts Hippokreon, long-bearded priest of Zeus Olympian. "The finest of Zeus' lovers, the best in bed for sure!"

Eteobouta softly shoves Hippokreon with a smile.

"Now play, all lovers, like Zeus and Selene! Be seen within the light-at-night, but worry not to be perceived!"

Everywhere couples embrace and kiss, the usual taboo against public love displays briefly waved by festival tradition.

In a grassy corner of shadows, Alkmaeonid sisters Deinomache and Periboea hold hands with each other as they simultaneously have their first kisses with their rich young secret suitors, Kleinias and Hipponikos.

Striding through the amorous Agora with a group still discussing the day's business, lion-eyed Kimon touches the shoulder of one of his Oligarch compatriots and then leaves them to amble on his own. He rebuffs a few young prostitutes and a friendly noble widow's compliment before finally seeing the silhouette of the one he had been looking for, whom he aims his walk toward.

"Why Kimon," says bronze-eyed Elpinike, "you are back from Thasos. I had heard as much."

"You know there's always much to see to here in Athens when returning from missions abroad."

"Your fig orchards, your horses, your wife; I know."

"The battlefield of politics, it seems, has been busy while I was away. I've been told to worry about the intentions of the Democrats, that they may have some prosecution in mind."

"Your men," Elpinike whispers, "have been telling stories."

Kimon sighs and looks up at the stars for a moment. "No doubt. When rare occurrences happen, no one believes them. No one would believe that an Athenian general and a Makedonian king could simply like one another and come to an agreement, I suppose."

Elpinike suggests, "Most men cannot imagine virtue."

Kimon whispers, pressing Elpinike with his presence toward a shadowy corner of walls nearby. "You've been in my mind. Always."

She touches him beneath his tunic. Her fingertips are Spring.

He whispers, "The house won't lose your scent, like a ghost."

She whispers back, "I have only been able to climax alone."

Kimon blushes lust.

"I found a bird's nest half-made of your glistening hair out back where you used to brush it. I won't ask to be inside you, sister. But please, hold onto my dick."

"Not here," Elpinike whispers back, barely keeping him back with her glistening eyes. She tries to maintain a sultry face against the desire to cry, though she is unsure how well amid her simultaneous grief.

Elpinike reaches out to grip Kimon through his tunic for just a moment, but then slips past him and steps carefully from grass to grass across the stony edge of the Agora, not looking back at her half-brother as he pulls his hair in frustration and watches her walk, trying to build lasting memories of the way her dress flutters behind and against her.

Π

Perikles hosts a drinking party for Democrats

"You know, I've heard it said that the ancient Assyrians, those wise and mighty precursors to today's barbaric Persians in the East, had a saying - that anything important ought to be debated both sober *and* drunk, and both decisions given equal weight."

Many men cheer that sentiment and enjoy their drinks.

The most influential Democrats are gathered at a late-night drinking party at the Alkmaeonid family compound. Perikles has had his slave Thrax turn the male sitting room into a party room - crowded now with enough couches for the twenty-to-thirty fluctuating partiers, with the most expensive rugs removed to avoid their being ruined by wine or the results of its excesses.

Long-bearded Damon, famous singer of epics, has been opining on the concept of democracy itself. Lying back on a couch with his feet up on his new young lover's lap, a twenty-something named Aristodoros, old Damon winks to request a foot rub.

Anaxagoras offers, "The very wise man Herakleitos would say, regarding the nature of change, that you cannot step into the same river twice. And yet, conversely, I feel as if I am drinking from an ever-full cup here in Athens, so often is this same cup refilled."

"The Cup of Theseos!" Thrax cleverly shouts, referencing the continually-rebuilt *Ship of Theseos*. "The wine of Theseos in the cup of Theseos!" as he pours yet more into Anaxagoras' cup.

A young Democrat hears the positive reaction the lines receive and says to Perikles of his slave's remark, "You should make that language yours. You know, claim you said that."

Just then Perikles' mother Agariste peeks her head in from the doorway to the courtyard. "O Thrax," she calls, shooting quick, motherly smiles to some of the young men in the room, "when you have a few free moments, I'm going to need you in the kitchen." Thrax nods curtly, indicating he'll be there shortly, and long-necked Agariste swings back out.

"Perikles, you're thirty years old," long-bearded Damon chastises. "You should not still be interrupted at your drinking parties by your mother! What if one of us had his dick out?"

"You should build your own home in town," Ephialtes agrees. "You could be closer to all the conversations on the street, that way, and maybe you wouldn't seem so closed off to the 'naval rabble'." Ephialtes winks as he uses the wording which he has often been called himself.

Perikles just shrugs and nods, taking a sip from his wine. "I'll consider it. There is much to be said for living near your mother, though."

All the men speak over each other short acknowledgements of that, and assertions of how sweet their own mothers are.

"You can assure her you will visit her often with the laundry you don't want your wife to do, when you have one," Antiphon jokes.

"Why would there be laundry I didn't want my wife to do?"

The other men all laugh.

"A woman can smell another woman's blood," Myronides says. Perikles makes a horrified expression that causes sunken-eyed Myronides to laugh and add, "Menstrual blood, Perikles. For the love of Hera - get a wife! You need a woman in your life, boy."

"How do I meet a woman - that's what I want to know!" Perikles sighs in exasperation. "One I'm not related to."

"At a festival, Perikles!" Damon shouts, laughing, spilling his wine. "Just grab the ugliest dancer! She will be grateful!"

"Every other day is a festival, practically, these days!" Ephialtes says.

Perikles agrees, "True enough! And thank democracy for that! Those are the youngest girls though, the girls you see at festivals. How are we supposed to get to know the unattached women our own age, you know, twenty-somethings? The only women I've known are my cousins. And all they ever want to talk about is family gossip."

"At least you have beauty in your family," Antiphon comments to Perikles as he sips at his wine. "If I had to choose my cousin for a wife, I'd sooner choose my horse."

"You're just looking for an excuse to choose your horse!"

All the men laugh.

Ephialtes drains his cup of its wine and then peers at the bottom, sloshing the thick dregs in a circle. When the other men see that Ephialtes' cup has only dregs left, they all begin encouraging him to throw those thick bottom-bits at the lampstand across the room, chanting "Latax, latax," which is the word for both the thick dregs of wine at the bottom of the cup, and the sound that the little disc hanging under the lampstand makes when hit perfectly by a solid wad of wine-dregs thrown from a cup across the room.

Having become quite expert at this game since beginning to throw regular drinking parties, Ephialtes lines up his cup, grinning and biting his tongue, then flicks his wrist, flinging the little lump of wet redness perfectly through the air so that it hits the disc on the lampstand, knocking it down onto a lower disc and making the desired ringing sound - *latax!*

All the men cheer playfully.

"Perfect Kottabos shot, man!" shouts burly-armed Antiphon.

Long-bearded Damon takes a long sip from his cup of wine and then exhales a sound of relishment. He declares, "Perikles, it is alright for you to prosecute Kimon based on uncertain information, because it will position you and the Democrats better in the power structure of our democracy, and it will hinder Kimon and his Oligarch friends. Consider comparing it to singing a song! One or two fouled-up words are alright if they help you keep your pacing and tone in a broader way. It is the song that matters, not each note, and you are trying to get to the good parts! The good parts of your song, Perikles, are the future years when you have the power to exert justice for many. You can only achieve this if you build up your own power among the people and undermine those who do justice harm."

"Listen to the old singer!" Ephialtes cheers, raising his cup, and all in the room follow the gesture, then drink. "That is the wisdom of the vine if I've ever heard such!"

"It is time to get some women in here," Myronides snorts drunkenly, sitting up in his couch with some difficulty. "Where's the slave? Have him bring in those women you ordered. Or Perikles, you just do it. I love being a Democrat, because I get to treat Oligarch sons like I would anyone else."

Perikles sighs, then stands.

As beautiful young noblewomen and foreign slave women file through the curtained doorway, each of the Democrat men coos with admiration and call out for one or the other to sit near them. While this is happening, long-bearded old Damon ignores the entering women and continues speaking to the younger men, playing a game of trying to keep their attention away from the women's forms with his continuous lecturing.

"Democracy is far from perfect, friends. But because it is a joint venture between men and the gods, it is uniquely capable of *improving*. However, as demagogues and wannabe-tyrants have already shown in generations seemingly distant to you young men, but all too recent to old mummies like myself, democracy is equally capable of *worsening* as it is of improving.

"I am old enough to remember how the people reacted to your great uncle Kleisthenes' reforms, Perikles. Of course 'the people' is a thoroughly reductive and nearly useless term, but nevertheless you know what I mean - the masses, the majority, *hoi polloi* as it were, not to be rude about unwashed folk, of course, Ephialtes."

Ephialtes laughs, drunk enough for courage. "Why do you always say shit like that about me, Damon?"

"What?" the famed old man asks, bending his neck around on its couch arm to look at the younger man.

"You mention the 'unwashed', and then excuse yourself to me with the clear implication that you see me as such. It is really rude, but you must not realize."

"O Ephialtes," Damon sighs, "I am not interested in trying to sound like men of your generation. You know what I'm talking about."

"Yes, you're indicating that I and my unmonied fellows are of some lesser essential type than more well-appointed men. But virtue does not come with wealth, nor does villainy come from destitution."

"You are right, Ephialtes, villainy does not come directly from destitution. It comes from ignorance and fear, which come from destitution. But the water of the Eridanos which flows into the Sea is the same water which once was snow on Mount Hymettos."

"Such poetic metaphors from our wise elder," young Antiphon laughs, already deep in his cups. "Next you'll be telling us how democracy flows like wine into the vessel of the people. If only it were so simple. If only people's minds flowed like rivers."

"You mock, but the flow of power is worth understanding. Take water - it always finds its level, doesn't it? No matter how you try to dam it up, to hold it in reservoirs of privilege..." Long-bearded Damon pauses to drain his cup, spilling a bit of red down his white beard. "But that's not what I really wanted to discuss tonight."

"Here it comes," Perikles stage-whispers to Ephialtes. "Another lecture on the modes of music and their effect on civic virtue."

"No, no." Damon's eyes have taken on that particular gleam that means he's about to hold forth at length. "I want to talk about something far more important. About how the Areopagos has become like a stone in Athens' shoe - a small thing causing a great lameness."

Several of the younger men groan, but Ephialtes leans forward, suddenly intent.

"Things weren't always as they are! You young forget! Consider how a pebble in a stream changes the water's course. How it creates eddies, disturbances. How it..." He frowns, losing his metaphor in the wine-fog.

"Perhaps we should leave hydraulic philosophy for a soberer moment," suggests Myronides diplomatically.

But Damon is already pushing himself upright on his couch, swaying slightly as he assumes what they all recognize as his teaching pose. The old singer of epics sits up, taking on a drunken mask of seriousness. "Look, though, boys, it is important to understand. The young may not remember, or might not have learned ... you get used to things the way they are and assume that it must be how they've always been."

"You're rambling, long-beard," one of the younger men laughs.

"No, no, listen," Ephialtes says, leaning forward toward Damon. "He's about to tell the tale of Solon. I've heard him introduce it before, always along a path of thought like this."

Damon laughs softly and nods. "Few men have the minds anymore to tell a story the same way twice. But yes, Solon! I will not tell his entire story, but you all need to understand where our *democracy* came from."

Ephialtes eyes the younger men to make sure they see the seriousness which he is giving the moment, and he models sitting forward with patience and grace as Damon takes a drink to cool his throat before speaking, and the other men largely follow his manner.

"When Solon was a young aristocratic poet living in Athens two hundred years ago, there had never been a city ruled by its people. Rule had only ever been by the few, or the one - oligarchy or monarchy. Most living Hellenes had never known true freedom! Even an aristocrat like Solon. He may have had a relatively pleasant lifestyle, but he lived in a time of tyrants, which had coagulated economies to the point where more than half of the citizens of Attika were essentially debt-slaves, and no one saw a way out of the death spiral of power accruing upward and debt flowing downward. But Solon, being both a poet and a nobleman, was so respected for his mind and his heart by the people of his time, and the troubles with tyrants and debt-slavery were so bad, that the village elders of Athens agreed to give to Solon an unprecedented emergency power, to create laws as he saw fit, in order to rebalance and protect the city of Athens. So he did, he worked for months on his plan of laws, collaborating with his fellow sages of the time, and the Oracle of Apollo at Delphi, to come up with the best, fairest system, unlike any that had ever been tried before - the joint rule by the people and the gods, through a combination of voting and random-lots. And he eliminated all debt, because he knew that without that, the economic momentums of the past would just continue unabated, and no amount of the will of the people would stop that power stranglehold. But with each person instantly imbued with equal political power, as well as equal economic power in the form of debtlessness - suddenly, a new Sun rose on Earth, a new goddess named *Democracy*."

The wine-proud Democrats placidly applaud the telling.

"And now every city across the Sea wants to be a democracy, because they see not only the happiness and righteousness of its citizens, but the power it provides to a state. When each man is sometimes a king, each man then cultivates the ambitions of a king, the broad mind of a king."

"Or ought to, at least," Ephialtes asserts with a little sniff of a laugh.

Thrax then mimes writing as he says sarcastically, "Each man."

"Yes, well, each Athenian man of age who is not an idiot," Damon corrects himself with a little laugh.

Perikles sees Thrax's eyes roll and sits forward. "You know, what if we were to enfranchise literally *every* man in Athens?"

"What, you mean like slaves and foreigners as well?"

"And how about women!"

The men all laugh. The women sitting next to them glance at each other loudly, but say nothing in this moment.

"Yes, though, what about it?" Perikles suggests, wine-drunk enough to let a thought process flow. "Haven't we seen the empowerment of more individuals in our society bear fruit of greatness and happiness, and apparent belovedness of the gods?"

"If you empowered foreigners and slaves into the vote," Damon says with a sigh, "then you invite the democracy to become swayed in the direction of foreign interests. And women - if we enfranchise women to vote, then men would end up enslaved, and only the few Adonises among us would have any sway or ever have a family. Imagine, if women could choose their own mates! We ugly men would be out of luck entirely."

"You would certainly have to learn to play the lyre, then," laughs Antiphon as he mimes strumming at his lovely escort's bared bush. She plays along laughing softly as he begins to play her vagina like a lyre with his fingertips, and she covers his fingering back up with her dress folds.

"Keep your votes," adds one of the escorts, "if you keep giving me money. I'd rather be free *from* citizenship, rather than freed by it."

The other escorts squint uncertainty to each other about that sentiment, but at first stay quiet about it, until one gains the courage to say, "I'd be happy to be able to do everything a man does, honestly."

"I just convince my friends that they ought to vote how I would," another says while playing with a lock of hair on Myronides' head.

"You couldn't get anyone here to vote against democracy," Myronides assures her with a little laugh and a pinch of her nipple.

"Ow! Hey!"

"Well, are we trying to do what is most advantageous for us personally in the moment, or are we trying to do what is actually most *just*, most *fair*, most *logically equitable*?" Perikles asks with a drunken eagerness at the notion of pushing the logic of compassion to its extreme. "Why, after all, are women not empowered to vote, and live individual lives on their own, just as a man does? And why must a person who has been captured in war be treated like a fundamentally different sort of person than someone with better luck?"

"Because we can," Myronides explains, "and because we have been. Doing this, treating folks this way, I mean. It isn't necessarily *good*, and certainly the gods seem to show that they like it when we behave better, but this is the way things have been done for a very long time."

A slave whom Perikles has not seen before appears at the doorway and clears his throat respectfully, then says, "Perikles?"

Bright-eyed Perikles stands, spilling his drink a bit in his drunken movements, and laughs at himself. "I'm telling you," he says as he stands, "we need to think more about what is *right*, rather than what is *normal*!"

"See how Perikles runs at the behest of slaves!" shouts Myronides drunkenly. "They hear his assertions of their equality, and wish to make it so!"

Perikles sighs loudly once he and the slave are out of earshot from the men in the men's room.

"Myronides is a donkey's ass when he is sloppy drunk," the slave mutters to Perikles to help him feel better.

Perikles chuckles good-naturedly and nods in agreement. "What's your name?" he asks the slave.

"Bellerophon."

Perikles shakes the man's hand. "So what am I summoned for, and by whom?"

Bellerophon bows to someone yet-unseen the way a slave would to an aristocrat, then backs out of the door. Perikles is at first merely saddened to think that his effort to span the economic gap between himself and the man seems to have failed, until he notices the other aristocrat in the room to whom the slave was bowing.

It is noble Elpinike, wife of wealthy Kallias, sister of Kimon. As she lifts her veil, her beauty becomes like a spear which she wields willfully.

Perikles quietly gasps, "Elpinike!" Then he whispers with a forced frown, "What are you doing here?"

Bronze-eyed Elpinike says, edging closer to Perikles with slowly wiggling fingers that seem to be indicating a desire to touch him, but could also be the gestural component of some unknown spell, "I come of my own will, but on my brother's behalf." She looks Perikles in the eyes and he is momentarily disarmed by the eroticism she is able to project from them.

He raises his head upon his neck. "To what end, noble woman? Does your husband, Torchbearer of Eleusis, know you're here?"

"Nobody knows I'm here but you," Elpinike says quietly, and she touches his arm gently with her fingertips. "And nobody will ever know. So if you tell anyone, I will deny it vigorously."

She touches his chest with her full palm, pushing aside the fabric of his tunic. Both their eyes are upon where they connect.

"I assume you've fucked with whores," she says. "But I would bet coins that you have never made love with a noblewoman." She looks up from where her fingertips are touching him, to his eyes. "Would I be right?"

Perikles keeps his eyes down on where she is touching him.

When it becomes clear that he is not responding, she continues, "I am a whore tonight, myself. But I am *also* still a noblewoman, as I will not be a whore tomorrow. You see, I have made a secret oath to Aphrodite, overseen by her priestesses in the temple, to give myself to any man who pays, but only tonight. And you are the only man that I'm telling about it. But it is not coin that I will take as payment. I would have instead, from you, an oath. That you will stop your plans against my brother."

"What are you asking of me?" Perikles asks her, for clarity.

"I just said it. Refrain from your prosecution of Kimon," she says. "Or if you cannot stop the proceedings, then you can simply present a weak case. All you would have to do is make clear the hearsay that your evidence truly is. If you promise to do so, I would be happy to make it worth it to you tonight."

"One man cannot stop the flow of justice," Perikles says.

"Words," Elpinike retorts. "You know better than your words."

Elpinike gently rubs a knuckle of her other hand against her breast, until her nipple bulges stiff against the fabric of her dress.

She whispers, "The richest man in Athens gave a fortune to make me his wife. Imagine why."

Perikles takes a long moment to look upon her beauty close-up. Her dress is a complicated combination of veil and lingerie, thin enough to be transparent but wrapped around her body enough times to obscure the details of her form, lined with fresh flowers along the edging, two big pearls strung on a gold wire around her neck. He finds her eyes at first guarded, but once he meets them and they look into his own, they melt a bit, and for the age of a tongue of flame the two share a genuine smoldering moment.

"I am sorry, Elpinike," he says with a wince at his own rudeness, "but a purpose like yours would require a slightly younger woman to succeed."

She sniffs once in derision, grimaces, then turns and strides away, while saying, "Then I shall have to complete my oath to Aphrodite with one of my wooden figures."

Elpinike veils her face quickly as she strides back out through the kitchen of Perikles' house. The young servant woman stirring the cauldron of stew eyes them both only briefly, keeping her eyes primarily in her pot.

"YOUR HEALTH'S THE FINEST THING IN LIFE,
AND BEING BEAUTIFUL TAKES SECOND,
WHILE HONEST WEALTH COMES IN THIRD PLACE,
AND FOURTH PLACE IS YOUR FRIENDS!"
Popular Athenian Party Song

P

The Pythia and their attendants share Hekate's Supper on the Moonless Night

Delphi is dark. The Moon is a black circle in the black Sky, though it is agreed not to acknowledge her, and to act like she is not there.

"Each month's Moonless Night, *Noumenia*, is like a homeless night *between months*, a night unmoored from nature's norms, when spirits of the dead go unguarded and are thought to visit the mortal world," the old priestess explains to young ones.

"Two generations ago, my generation's grandparents allowed their parents' foreign slaves to invite the eastern Ghost Goddess Hekate into their lives, and now each night of Noumenia has been given a special supper - Hekate's Supper - during which it is said that the ghosts of the restless dead, who accompany Hekate and her flame-spitting underworld hounds up to the living world, can be appeased and honored in order to defend against their vengeance, by putting out plates of supper for Hekate and the dead to feast upon, lest they feel unwelcomed. It is a night that often frightens those whose minds have been lingering on death or regret."

Aoide, though, in Delphi, having lately begun to slough off her childish fears and reverences, feels now like she lives above such superstition and knows better than to fear like a child.

Sitting at the celebration of Hekate's Supper with the rest of her dorm-mates, Aoide stares at her friend Dikasto's face and thinks about the things which she knows are real, and worse than mythical monsters, since they are shielded from justice by their masks of normalcy.

Not meaning to, she bangs her fists on the table. Eyes dart her way but no one mentions it.

Outside, the destitute, passing, or poor take scraps from the meals left out on the street outside the sanctuary for the ghosts. Mean children watch and call the desperate who take food from these dinners "ghosts".

Inside, the evening's usual discussions drift like incense. The new young priestess Perialla describes the day's omens dutifully while the male priests nod, as if knowing - a dove's strange flight, an unexpected hazy rain. Two younger priests debate the proper timing of tomorrow's sacrifices over her. Kliko speaks quietly with a visiting priestess from Qorinth about grain prices in Krisa.

"And how did our young temple girls find the preparations for the feast?" Perialla asks, more from habit than interest, happening to choose Aoide to lean toward.

Aoide makes a face at Dikasto across the table, but Dikasto won't look. She seems lost in a darkness.

"Well enough," Aoide says, feeling Dikasto's distance. She looks into the flame in the nearest brazier. Just as Perialla is about to ask something else of someone else, Aoide then adds, "Though I wonder why we prepare such elaborate meals for ghosts when living people starve outside our walls."

"The gods must be fed first," says one of the younger priests. "It is their due. And anyway, we all know that the poor do end up taking most of what is there."

"Like women must be married first," Aoide says softly. "As it is men's due." Conversations pause. The visiting priestess sets down her wine cup.

"You've been thinking about your sisters again," Kliko says carefully.

"I've been thinking about justice," Aoide replies. "About how she is a woman."

Dikasto watches with a wincing intrigue as the adults react to Aoide.

"Child," Perialla begins, but Aoide cuts her off.

The high priest Goryntas coldly says, "She doesn't know about love, yet. She sees how her sisters and friends react to boys and men and doesn't understand why they would act the way they do. Isn't innocence adorable?"

"Love is just another way to make us servants," Aoide continues, her voice steady now. "We call it divine so we don't see the chains."

Old Perialla shifts on her cushion. "Where is this coming from?"

Aoide says calmly, "I hate love. Look at what it does to us. To all of us. The moment a girl first feels it, she becomes someone's property."

"We are all slaves to Eros, Aoide," Goryntas says, eyeing her as if realizing suddenly that she might be becoming a sexual object in this moment. "Men and women."

"You speak from pain," says Kliko carefully. "From what happened to you, or someone you love?" She looks to Dikasto, seeing the two girls eyes finding each other.

"I speak from seeing clearly." Aoide's voice rises. "While men write poems about love's beauty, girls disappear. While they sing about desire, we lose our names, our choices. But why? What is superior about being a man?"

The priests exchange disturbed glances. One opens his mouth to speak but Aoide starts speaking again.

"Justice is a woman, because she knows what it is to be powerless. Suffering wears a woman's face because she knows what it is to be used. Where are the goddesses of freedom? Of choosing our own fates?"

"The Fates weave the way for all mortals," Kliko says, "even men. None are free. Freedom means nothing."

"There is no freedom from desire even for the gods," says the high priest. "It moves the world, child. Creates life itself. You might as well ask the rivers not to flow."

"Then the world is built in chains."

"Yes!" Goryntas nods confirmatively, and the male priests around him start nodding just to copy him, smiling as if it is funny. "The Creator of Man was chained for his art!"

"No," says the visiting priestess, adding a fresh voice which intrigues all at the table. "The world is built on *necessity*. Who is also a woman. The first woman, Necessity. Before Love, before Earth, before Time. All else *required* Necessity. The flow of generations, the hard truth that joy and pain are inseparable twins, children of ancient *Necessity*."

"Like Artemis and Apollo?" Aoide's little laugh is bitter. "The virgin and her brother who can love as he pleases, rape any mortal and make her famous? Like the poor laurel tree."

"Like birth and death," Kliko says. "Like summer and winter. Some patterns cannot be broken, only understood and expected."

"Then understanding itself is a kind of chain."

An owl calls somewhere in the darkness. The flames in the braziers shift, and the shadows follow along.

"You think innocence is freedom?" asks Perialla gently. "You think any of us can escape desire's web? The high priest is right: even the gods are caught in it. Even the stars dance to its music. The Sky is a web in which we are caught."

"Then I reject the stars' music." Aoide's voice has gone quiet again, but there's iron in it now. "I reject the dance. I reject any power that needs our submission to exist."

Kliko hisses each time she says "reject", her face growing worried.

The oldest priest, eyes nearly hidden within the wrinkles of his age, says, "She has strength. Of mind - strength of mind. She has certainty. Like few do. Do you hear it? Her words are not just words."

When he speaks, the others all listen carefully, for his voice is soft and hoarse. And when what they've heard confounds them, they dwell there with it for a while in their minds despite resenting it, thinking, not discounting it, processing. All eyes are on Aoide.

"You cannot pull down the stars and change them around," high priest Goryntas says deep-voiced. "You are whipping up ghosts you haven't imagined yet, girl. This is the Moonless Night! Neither Apollo nor Artemis will be there to protect you between the shadows of the trees and the starlight. You cannot simply go about saying whatever you want, and calling it poetry to evade all consequence!"

The visiting priestess also stands, then, and stares down the high priest. "Apollo is with the Hyperboreans who live beyond the North Wind, and will not return for many weeks, Goryntas. It's just us men and women here on the mountain, with the Earth and all that's under it. But that does not mean that girls have no protectors in the darkness."

Old Kliko rakes her thorny whip *Hubris* against the ground, and the sound is all that's necessary. It is a long-necked hydra of lion's claws.

The conversation becomes a silent one for the rest of the night, just eyes and the sounds of eating.

Dikasto looks at Aoide like she is looking into the Sun, as if she is blinded by her, but cannot look away.

"I DO NOT EXPECT TO REACH THE SKY."
Sappho, Mytilenian Poet

Σ

Perikles prosecutes a case against Kimon before the Areopagos

A group of bored goats watches a flock of fluttering people all gathered on a big rock just down the the olived slopes of the Acropolis hill from them.

Down there, Kimon faces Perikles upon the Rock of Ares, surrounded by the old men of the Areopagos.

The Sun hangs high and hot, and the smell of sweat has just begun to fester among all these many old, seated men. Wicker hand fans wave away the flies.

The Rock of Ares is an enormous stone on the western slope of the olived hill of the Athenian Akropolis, large enough to seat about fifty old men without any of them feeling too crowded. The way up to its top requires first climbing a steep, narrow, and slippery set of stairs that hundreds of years earlier were certainly carved without the elderly in mind. Each old nobleman's ascent onto the rock is a reconfirmation that the man is still capable of wielding his body in a challenging world. This cabal of elders, called the Areopagos after the rock they meet on, is composed of each man still living who has ever held the office of Archon. On the Rock of Ares this group of elders has for centuries traditionally overseen the most important trials which are judged to be too important to leave to the varying justice of citizen juries - crimes like murder, arson, bribery, or anything involving olive trees sacred to Athena. More recently, ever since the Oligarchs' so-called 'Areopagite Constitution' was voted in just a few years ago, the men of the Areopagos have also had a final veto power over any new laws passed by the Assembly, a power which they never had in the past, though the legislation was presented as if to be a return to historical precedents poorly understood by the masses.

Today, Kimon himself stands accused before the elders of the Areopagos, and Perikles stands in prosecution of him.

Perikles' uncle Megakles, who was Archon between the Persian Wars, winks ever-so-slightly to his nephew.

"Tell us now, Perikles son of Xanthippos," says Praxiergos the Speaker of the Areopagos, "what you accuse our general Kimon son of Miltiades of having done, crime-wise."

"Bribery," Perikles declares with a frog in his throat, and then coughs several times. "Bribery both *by* barbarians, and *of* barbarians with public funds," he repeats, to underscore the lowliness of the accusation but also because he isn't sure whether his first utterance would have been heard.

"As sons, like fathers," one of the old men jokes, a reference to the fact that Perikles' father Xanthippos prosecuted Kimon's father Miltiades for similar crimes twenty-five years ago.

The old men of the Areopagos grumble amongst each other. Kimon stands and stares Perikles down with a coldness that genuinely chills Perikles' skin. Perikles wonders about stories he has heard about certain gorgon-faced shields actually maintaining Medusa's ability to petrify with a gaze, and he begins to try to avoid looking Kimon in the eyes with the subtle subconscious fear that his opponent might have some similar ability.

"How do you respond, Kimon son of Miltiades?" asks the Speaker.

Kimon says resolutely, "I have never bribed anyone, nor ever taken a bribe anywhere, from anyone, for any reason."

And at that utterance, Perikles thinks of the rumors he has heard about Kimon, Elpinike, and Kallias, and he gains some amount of confidence back as he feels that, whether Kimon is guilty of any crime now or not, it is surely a lie to say that he has never taken a bribe of any kind.

Perikles turns to face the old men of the Areopagos. "Before Kimon and the men under his command had even returned from Thasos, news had come from merchants of that island indicating that our general Kimon had given a bribe to the mountain tribes of the mainland there. And then when they returned, we learned that he had also been given a bribe from King Alexander of Makedon, for a promise not to invade his lands up north. Which, as you all know, Athens had no plans for anyway. And, of course, All-Hellas saw the two men shake hands at the Olympics, and who knows what they spoke of."

The men who have been Archon whisper amongst each other just like they do down in the Agora every other day. Perikles finds the fact that their voices are the same up here as they are in less ceremonious moments somehow disconcertingly demystifying. A hidden nearby owl looks away.

Kimon stands, letting no amount of his mask of military resoluteness slip. He stands before the old men like he knows they imagine a great old general from their own day would appear, shoulders high, arms holding an invisible spear, looking at no one in particular and insomuch seeming to stare down the whole group.

Old Praxiergos croaks, "Kimon, son of Miltiades, you may now present your defense."

"There is no proof of what this man says," Kimon declares, not looking at Perikles, but just at a few of the old men whom he knows will share his sentiment. "The gods know he is only repeating rumors whispered by lesser men who wish to ruin my name. You all surely remember how his father tried to do this very same thing to my father six Olympiads ago, when you were all young men, and he and I just boys."

Finally Kimon's eyes turn to find Perikles, and fix on him as he goes on.

"And surely you all remember how my father, great Miltiades, who brought civilization to Chersonesos and tamed the wild women of Lemnos, that noble man withered in prison in his weakened old age, and died there before he was able to clear his good name of those salacious accusations."

Perikles' face gets hot as he pictures his own old father in those days, always angry, seemingly self-hating. He has worried long that he will become like his father in all the ways that he long ago determined not to, and now fears with real dread that perhaps he already has.

Kimon finishes, "Be more careful with Lady Justice, Dike, than the men of that age were, for her sisters Eunomia and Eirene, Order and Peace, listen to her."

The old men of the Areopagos respond to everything very gradually, looking to each other a lot.

"Well," one of the oldest men says slowly, gesturing to add to the length of his pause, "his story was very *detailed*. Are you proposing that Perikles simply *invented* all of those details?"

Kimon snorts, and says, "He has many friends throughout the city. Sailors, noblemen, men of every type. And so he has just as many mouths to hear rumors from, and is able to add all of that up with his clever mind into a complete story, as if one man told him one elaborate truth, when in fact, it is like a man made of straw wearing the cloak and hat of a..." Kimon sputters, starting to stutter in his speech, and some of the old men begin laughing.

Megakles asks Kimon, "And your comment about Order and Peace - was that intended as some sort of threat of Oligarch disorder in the event of your punishment?"

Ignoring that question, Kimon says, "It was here that the first trial by jury occurred on Earth, when the gods convened here to judge their brother Ares, after he killed Poseidon's demigod son in righteous revenge for the rape of his own demigoddess daughter. And how did that first trial end?"

The old men of the Areopagos look to each other.

"Ares was acquitted, because his action was just," Kimon says.

Perikles adds, "But he *did* commit the act, and he certainly did not deny that truth. Do you, Kimon, still deny that you paid the barbarians of Thrake to keep them satisfied while you were there, or are you trying to refer to this mythic anecdote in order to indicate that your actions were just? Did you do something just, or did you do nothing at all?"

Kimon sighs. The Areopagos rumbles archaically.

"The Makedonian king Alexander and I did meet," Kimon says carefully and slowly, and the men of the Areopagos all inhale together. "But he did not bribe me, and I did not bribe him. We merely spoke as men of gravity who respect each other, and we were able to come to an understanding which led to both our armies departing without warfare. The efforts of peace are not to be so distrusted that any success is seen as surely somehow corrupt!"

Megakles speaks up. "But the Makedonian armies were previously threatening Delian presence in Thrake and Thasos, and then after your private meeting with King Alexander suddenly their interests were changed? How could this be, without some kind of change in strategic calculus, some kind of offer or exchange?"

Kimon says laconically, "It is called diplomacy."

The old men laugh at his curt confidence, and because many of them have distaste for Megakles and enjoy seeing him mocked.

Speaker Praxiergos asks, "How do we vote, Areopagos? Has the wide-respected general Kimon committed a crime in his office, or has he merely executed his office faithfully and successfully, as our city and the gods demanded of him? Show hands for innocence!"

Hands rise, and on seeing them more hands rise, until unanimity, and Kimon, with a snow-cold glance to Perikles, is acquitted of wrongdoing.

"Kimon," says the Speaker of the Areopagos, with a tiny wink, "you are free to go. See you at the party tonight."

T

Korax's army meets the Spartan army on the slopes of Mount Ithome

Korax's Messenian army of fighting men, women, and children marches slowly, no faster than their few baggage oxen can pull. Eastward, back across the plains of Messenia, they have marched for days and finally reached the base of Mount Ithome, where long ago there was a Messenian fort.

Preisias sees it first, in the distance, and points out the ruins of the fort at the top of the mountain to Korax.

"If we can get the people to the top," Preisias says, "and the spring still flows, then we should be able to defend from there for a long time."

"I am here to win a war," Korax corrects, "not to wither on some windy mountaintop, forgotten by time."

The sprawling army arrives at the western slope of Ithome where the mountainside makes an enclosing bowl shape. The ruins of an ancient town cling to the earth like the half-buried bones of some vulture-picked carcass. An ancient well's stone infrastructure from an older era must have been too much work for any of the looters of this village to destroy, and the weary throng make their camp around the old stone pool where even the War Goddess Enyo's city-destroying furors have proven unable to upend this ancient work of some unnamed nymph-worshippers who merely wanted to make collecting water easier for others in the future.

Among the many Messenians, there is a stewing mix of emotions. Some of the young are eager for battle, for their myriad overdue revenges. Many debate the merit of gathering together as a group like this, and some suggest scattering to the Four Winds, so that as many as possible might survive to live lives elsewhere. Some of those with children let their young ones act like nothing has changed, like they are in any other common day, playing amongst the rocks and flowers, while other parents tell epic tales to paint these days into the great mural of meaningful moments.

The farmer Gylippos leads his son and tiny daughter to the edge of the well once others ahead of them have had their turns and made room.

Timonos first gets water for his baby sister Eleni, then for his father, and finally sips from their family ladle himself.

"Do you think our ancestors really lived here?" Timonos asks his aging father, looking around at their surroundings and the other families.

The hard-faced farmer considers the time-smoothed stone he sits upon, slowly beginning to nod in silent affirmation.

"I think their ghosts are here with us now," eager-hearted young Timonos says. "And Nothon's ghost is with them." He keeps hard, passionate eye contact with his father when he mentions his brother, murdered by the Spartans so long ago. Tears soon break his eyelash phalanx.

Weathered-eyed Gylippos looks away and nods. "And your mother," he adds, grasping Timonos by the neck, and then slapping it softly the way his mother used to, without looking at him.

Timonos watches the back of his father's balding head, then matches his distant gaze. Little Eleni watches a distant flock of birds with simple joy.

The old farmer Gylippos says, hushed by a gust of wind, "She does possess me some nights, sweet Argiloë's ghost. Fills me up. Every Moonless Night I try to summon her, but I always understand that sometimes she must be needed elsewhere. She is so loving - I'm sure many other phantoms count on her in the Underworld. But sometimes she does come."

Both look up then to the horizon, noticing at the same time the very moment that the approaching line of Spartan shields becomes visible on the top of the hill on the other side of the valley. Their fluttering red capes back-light the shields, still just a distant line but a familiar sight.

"Okay now listen, son," Gylippos says quickly, keeping his eyes on the incoming army but taking Timonos' shoulder in his hand. "We are headed to the top of the mountain. The Spartans have to cross the valley and come up at us from below. Wherever you are, you keep the Spartans below you. Understand? You do not move downhill. And you keep the women and children whom you're protecting behind you, further uphill than you. That's the only goal right now - uphill. Even a long spear held by the longest-armed Spartan has a disadvantage coming uphill. You understand? There is one virtue today - uphill."

Timonos nods. "I get it." He looks at his father's uneven, old-legged stance. "You should start uphill now, then. Take Eleni. I'll guide the people behind me, upward, and keep guard over them. Trust me, now, Father. I love you, I've always listened to you, I understand, and I'll do my best. Take her; go!"

Gylippos begins to weep, but waves it away with a gesture as he takes his little toddling girl and starts his hobbling up the rocky hillside toward the northern ridge of the woody mountain where the slope to the summit is the most gradual.

Eleni watches her brother over her shoulder as her father holds her hand and hobbles away up the mountain with her. She calls out, "Brother!"

"Sister!" he replies loudly. "I'll always love you! I'll see you soon! Follow Father!" Timonos tries to keep a smile for her till she is out of sight.

Then Timonos takes his wooden spear and holds it in some of the ways he has been taught to, takes a few practice jabs into the air. As he does, he thinks about the ghosts of his ancestors who fought in this same space, and his heart races as he imagines one of them helping him thrust harder.

For a few moments, watching the Spartan army descend the low hills across the valley, the number spreading and becoming ever-more clearly numerous, Timonos stands alone on the windswept hillside, and wonders if he will end up facing them alone.

Then a voice calls out from behind him, "Boy! You mean to use that spear usefully? Then come join the line here and protect these folks!"

"Do you see the future?" Preisias asks Korax with a Fate-braced grimace, as the lone boy downhill from the group lopes back up toward them.

Korax doesn't think, just nods. "I see it."

Korax stands upon the sloped field, the ruins on the mountain of his ancestors behind him. His enemy must march upward to come fight him.

Beside him his fellow former-Helots, the new Messenian army, all line up and match his courage. Most are armed with weapons fashioned dangerous out of the tools of their trades yesterday - hammers, sickles, scissors, and scythes.

"No doubt our enemies have made immeasurable sacrifices to the wide-ruling gods. But they are mistaken to think that the gods value their mortal wealth - guts, bones, smoke - and that is why the gods disdain Sparta despite her piety to them. Zeus has delivered onto their ancient Heraklean thrones only kings and queens as mad as Herakles! Herakles is the one whom Zeus made a slave! Poseidon has shaken them to their knees, positioning them for a swift beheading! The third brother is Haides, who no doubt has a whole section of Tartaros being prepared for the shades of those we will kill here today - mad bastards who have well-beyond earned today's revenge!"

The Messenian boys and girls around Korax appear more afraid than encouraged by his chosen words.

"Breathe out your fear and breathe in courage, brave Messenian warriors!" Korax shouts. "Your ancestors will all hear stories of what you do today! Word moves fast among the dead."

"You're not exactly inspiring bravery," a distant-eyed young woman with a homemade wooden spear beside him tells Korax very plainly.

Korax notices her natural bravery and squints against the sunlight behind her. "What's your name?"

"Niome, princess of fallen Byzantion. Until recently, a slave to the Queen-Mother's family."

Korax nods, furrowing his brow against the winds of Fate. He turns and shouts to the line, "The gods have granted that the great heroine Niome fights with us!" He looks Niome in the eyes, making her a peer in a moment. "So the Fates have surely deigned we shall not fail!"

Preisias walks ahead of the group, shouting to them all. "The Spartans will shout insults, curses, perhaps even exhortations of goodwill and kindness, memories you share together. They will use your names as magic words. Do not listen to them! Hear only the snarls of wild beasts when they speak! For they will use your name to get into your mind, and you must not let them! Today, you must have no names. You are only furious spirits of vengeance summoned forth by your ancestors. Tomorrow, you will get your names back, wherever you find yourselves."

Preisias turns to one of the smaller children listening nearby.

"Now you children have a very important task. You must all run about behind us and gather stones, anything smaller than a grown up's fist, and you must gather them in little piles here on the ground behind us. You must never stop gathering stones, and staying behind our line, until I call out 'Rabbits!', at which point all you children will race each other to the top of the mountain. Understand?" He sees Timonos, the tallest of the children on this day, and nods to him, in that silent gesture making him their leader.

Timonos nods back, and scans the heads of his children's-phalanx, learning their forms quickly. "Hear that, everybody?" he calls out to the line of young ones.

The children all nod and shout assurance. A few cry with fear, but stand with their fellows determined to follow the order despite.

"Ready!" a woman shouts, and all eyes turn to see the Spartan lines encroaching imminently, up the slight slope from below.

Slow strides, long minutes, lifetimes. A wise few hide in chaos just long enough to flee the power of the colliding lines.

Rocks, shields, arrows, blood-hammered lungs. Fist to sword, sickle to spear, the Spartans and the brave of those who used to work their fields once called Helots, before that Messenians, now all fighting heroes, clash. Untold iliadic violence plunders unsung mothers' efforts from the Earth.

But through it all, the ally of the Earth aids most. Her vantage and position, as the very mountain, holding one line ever higher, helps throughout the fight to keep the disadvantage with the Spartans. The facts that they have been unserved, unfed, and frightened by an angry god's apparent wrath, for near a month now, do not help.

Backing slowly onto Mount Ithome, making use of cliffs and hills and rises where they can, the Messenian army of girls, boys, and other heroes green to glory rages with each casualty and sings at each success, but soon notices they are singing an ancient song merely punctuated with wails rather than overwhelmed by them. Children fall to protect their elders. Women strong from water-carrying show Spartans weary from worry what muscle and wherewithal are with weapons wrought from worktools.

All far and near, L's fall.

As the sun clears a cloud, the Messenian fighters around Korax all glow at the same moment of miraculous sunlight, and one unnamed one shouts, "We will be the ones remembered for conquering the Spartans as their slaves!"

"Yes!" Korax shouts in response. "We will be the ones remembered! Both Mother Earth and Father Sky are here to aid us heroes! Fight, friends!"

Chrysaor steps up to an approaching loose phalanx of Spartans with a fancy silver sword.

"Recognize this?" Chrysaor shouts at the Spartans. "Taken from your own royal horde! This great silver sword of Sparta, owned by one of your revered kings! Now watch as it-"

The Spartans separate and one darts forward with his spear, reaching far. Chrysaor dodges, but the Spartan guesses right.

Half of Chrysaor's face is cleft and swings off to the side like a doffed mask. The enraged Chrysaor still staggers forward blindly swinging his blade, but the Spartans spread and wait for the blinded skull-face to stumble, then all go in and spear him in the back to finish him off, skewering his body against the Earth and then pulling out to create little volcanoes of blood.

One Spartan kicks the sword out from the dying man's hands. Another picks it up, and quickly the silver sword is passed back to the leader of that phalanx, who holds the glinting blade high over his head so that all the Messenians can see that it has been taken.

In his comrade's distant death, elsewhere in the fight Korax suddenly sees the future founder, like a ship striking an unseen rock and lurching.

At the same time, the rest of that phalanx spreads out and encroaches quickly upon those Messenian fighters surrounding Korax, many of whom are frightened by this small group's particular bravery.

All around, battles are fought, just out of range of song.

King Korax turns in both directions to gauge the chances his people might have of making it to the mountain top. Though they were ruined generations ago, the fortifications up there, used properly, could still provide some aid in defending that summit for an extended period. There is a spring up there, above the ancient walls. It strikes him that if they make it there, perhaps they could last forever. He watches the assembly of freed people rushing up the mountainside as a mass, many stopping to help the slower ones or those who fall in their haste. A real strike from an arrow which wings his shoulder armor wakes him back to the real world around him.

"We cannot defeat the Spartans on the ground," Korax says. "No one ever has. No one ever will. I don't know what I was thinking. I thought I could stand against the sea--"

"What are you wasting time talking for?" Preisias shouts.

Korax shakes himself out of it. "Go!" he shouts back to his Theban comrade Preisias. "Get them all to the mountaintop!"

"Do not sacrifice yourself, Korax," Preisias begs his friend with a look of long-forgotten love. "You are a man."

Korax grasps Preisias' hand for only a moment as he says, "I am a king." And in his eyes he begs his friend to understand. "Protect my Messenian people, on the mountaintop."

Preisias nods gravely in final eye contact with Korax. He gestures wide with his sword for those around him to follow, and then he points his sword to Mount Ithome, which suddenly seems like a titan holding their back who is on their side in this battle, one of Mother Earth's ancient colossal progeny awakened today.

Preisias shouts, as loud as he can, "Rabbits!"

All up the mountain, hidden children rise and start their race to the top. Timonos runs with them, keeping them together like a valiant sheepdog.

Preisias gestures to some young parents and old wise ones who haven't been fighting, all to follow him to the top of Mount Ithome.

Korax scans those left around himself. A brave few older men, mostly, maintain the line, along with a handful of glory-drunk youngsters.

Beside him, as if replacing Chrysaor as his right hand, stands strong-stanced Niome, wind-swept princess of Byzantion, who until recently had been the caretaker of young Pleistoanax.

"Now, Niome, retreat." He looks to her and nods seriously, giving her the honor to go.

Niome says, "Of course not," unmoving.

Korax grimaces, feeling both their fates tangled and unable to save himself, but now deeply more grievous about it with Niome wrapped up in the same inevitable pain. He struggles not to weep as he mourns her imminent death in a moment as fast as a fleeting morning dream.

Then he sees the glory she has chosen, and how he is wrapped with her in it. He can no more deny her glory than himself.

The daylight on everything becomes as beautiful as new love in Korax's final moments. As he fights for his life, knowing he will die, the colorful grass and flowers and blue sky all embrace him like never before.

As others fight around them, a line of six Spartans marches up toward Korax and Niome, spears raised, panting as they ascend the long, low slope of the hill. Their spear tips wobble, weary. Korax grunts and glances, wordlessly noting this all to Niome. She nods confirmation.

Niome and Korax wait for the six Spartans to march just outside spear's length, rapidly eyeing each other in silence to confirm their combined movements, then they both step forward suddenly, parrying two tired speartips with their weapons before lunging in at the two men carrying the spears in order to knock them apart, and the inward two into the middle-most two. The courageous joint move startles and confuses all six Spartans at once, giving Korax time to very quickly plunge his blade into both nearest men's necks.

The blood splashes Korax's breastplate, and rings it like *kottabos*.

The remaining four Spartans stumble back, their spear-wall dissolving. They have trained all their lives to fight as one creature, but split apart, they move like severed limbs, graceless, uncertain.

Niome darts between two of them like a hawk between branches. Her blade finds the gap above a greave, and another Spartan falls screaming. But as he falls, his wild death-grip catches Niome's collar, and though she tears free, the motion pulls her to the cliff's edge, teetering. A Spartan shield crashes into her from the side. For a moment she seems to hang in the air, her body a dark shape against the valleys below. Her eyes meet Korax's as she falls, and then she's gone, vanished over the edge with tumbling stones into a shadowy crevasse. More Spartans coming all below, pressing upward.

The few Spartans standing nearby try to reform their line, but the slope works against them. One slips in his dying comrade's blood, and another helping to stop his fall instead gets caught in the tumble. Their comrades' spears waver uncertainly. The middle one, just a boy, stops fighting to loudly pray.

Korax can smell their fear now, sharp as iron. The same fear he carried for years while he worked their fields. Each motion feels like a sculptor's mark in stone now, as if the ancient kings of Messenia guide his sword arm. Each kill is for Niome now, each death an offering to her shade.

Death. Death. Death! The next Spartan to die sees some raw fire in Korax's eyes that makes him step backward. His sandal catches on a root. In his face, Korax sees generations of masters watching their power crumble. King Korax strides up to the Spartan, sword-swats away a swing of his spear and then halves the man's neck with a single lash of his sword. The Spartan falls like reaped wheat.

He keeps trudging up the low sloping hillside toward the mountain, following the movement of his people further up, lingering at the back to catch as many Spartans as he can before they get too near those more vulnerable above.

Two Spartans rush up the grassy slope toward him together, making a two-man phalanx with their spears crossed. Korax crab steps to the side to force them to veer, then chops the tips off both spears with one slice. He grabs onto the two spearshafts and uses them to wrestle the Spartans on the other ends away from each other, knocking one onto his butt. While the one Spartan is prone, Korax dashes close upon the other and pushes the Spear of Lelex between the man's breastplate and pauldron, only grazing his underarm, but releasing gouts of blood from the cut. That man screams and falls, grasping desperately at his wound, while Korax resteadies his spear and plants it heavily into the face of the other man who had been knocked down. The Spartan's brow spreads against the spear.

And then the man with the wounded underarm, before he dies, arrives behind Korax with the blow that kills him, unseen.

Helping his father and sister to ascend the last steep rise at the summit, to where the crowds of Messenians who made it watch the tumult below from relative safety, defended by a few brave female archers here at the top, Timonos finally feels Death's hand leave his shoulder.

Timonos looks down the mountainside, his sister's shoulders in his hands, their father panting on the grass behind them. He thinks of the Troian hero Aineas, fleeing burning Troi with his son in his arms and his father on his back. Timonos realizes that this is how heroes of old must have felt - just like normal people, fearful and uncertain.

Broken Spartan shields with their iconic L's litter the slopes of Ithome. The

Messenians, in their poverty, leave little on the field but their bodies, blood, and broken tools.

Tiny to Timonos at such a distance, a crow alights onto Korax's lifeless head, scans its surroundings, warns others away with a shriek, then peels off an eyelid to begin the work of removing the now-sightless eye.

Y

Aischylos and his chorus perform at the Dionysian festival

Wide white eyes behind their masks, Achilles and his Myrmidons stride round the Dionysian stage, Aischylos miming that wrathful ancient warrior Achilles' famous pompous strut, with his chorus as Achilles' loyal men called *Myrmidons* mimicking him.

Throughout the audience wooden dicks are waggled at the manly display onstage.

Kimon and his troop of loyal veterans watch from the stands with Athens' other several thousand citizens, the soldiers uniquely eager for this particular play. Achilles' famous ant-like Myrmidon warriors, with their prowess and orderliness, are always popular among soldiers.

Aischylos-as-Achilles asks, "Men of mine, Myrmidons, speak now, of what you would choose without me. For surely mine alone cannot be the determining factor, the single fulcrum on which the fates of this great host of Hellenes, and the entire city of Troians, alone would turn. For if, as they say, my absence alone could be the cause for the failure of our army's fight on the field, then somehow I alone would be the end-all of Hellenic might, myself All-Hellas, the all-or-nothing, and I cannot claim that to be the case without implicitly minimizing every other great Hellene warrior around me whose hearts beat just like mine. So tell me, Myrmidons, what would *you* do?"

Just as the chorus appears prepared to respond, Penander races out from between them wearing the mask of a messenger.

"Wait, great son of Peleus, Styx-dipped lord of Phthia, and hear this saddest of all possible laments - our noble comrade, your best friend, Patroklos has fallen under Hektor's evil spear!"

"What?" Aischylos shrieks as Achilles, gripping at the hair behind his warrior-mask. In his fervor, the actor bites his lip, drawing blood, which draws drama deeper into his performance.

"Wearing your own armor, nonetheless!" Penander-as-messenger wails. "He took it secretly and fought as you! Numerous Troian men fell to his spear, but shining-helmed man-killing Prince Hector--"

"Do not say it!" Aischylos-as-Achilles clutches at his breast, staggering backward as if the messenger's words are arrows. The chorus freezes mid-step, their masks showing perpetual horror, feet planted like roots in the dancing circle's dust.

"O but I must, great son of Peleus," Penander continues, his messenger's mask gleaming with painted tears, "For noble Patroklos lies dead in your armor, while Greeks and Troians clash and clatter over his stripped corpse like carrion birds fighting for feast-flesh! Great Hektor, tamer of horses, bronze-speared night-bringer, has sent your dearest friend down to the house of Haides!"

"No!" Aischylos releases a wail accompanied eerily by a warbling aulos double-flute. "O gods who dwell in houses built of golden light, why plant such bitter fruit within my breast? Why seed such savage sorrow in my heart?"

The chorus begins a low, undulating keen that builds slowly in power, "Aiai! Aiai! The spear drinks deep! The bronze blade reaps its crimson fruit! Iron-hearted Fate spins out her thread while mortals dance upon the narrow edge between glory's height and ruin's depths!"

Aischylos-as-Achilles tears at his warrior's mask but cannot remove it, trapped in Achilles' grief like a man sealed in a bronze bull. "My Patroklos! My better self! My gentler heart!" His voice drops to a loud whisper which still carries to the furthest seats. "O you who taught my rage-filled spirit peace, who cooled my fire with wisdom's healing stream! Now you lie cold upon the bloody earth, while dogs and birds fight for your lovely flesh!"

The chorus dance in intricate patterns, their synchronized sways creating waves of lamentation that ripple through the audience.

"See how the gods plant pride in mortal hearts, then harvest grief when glory's flower blooms! See how they weave both victory and doom into one cloth of gold and crimson thread!"

"O Zeus," Aischylos cries, raising his eyes up to the Sky, "You who gave me the choice of fates - long life in shadow or brief glory's blaze - is this the price of deathless fame? To watch all that I love fed to the dogs of war? Then hear my oath, sealed with these tears of rage: Before Helios' bright chariot circles thrice, great Hektor's blood shall stain these hands, and lands! Though Fate herself stands in my path, though all the gods raise storms against me, I shall send his shade to greet sweet Patroklos in the sunless lands below!"

The chorus sways like reeds in a storm wind as they sing out, "Hear his oath, you deathless ones! Mark his words, you Fates who spin! When rage and grief twine in one heart, what mortal bonds can hold them in?"

In that moment of raw anguish, even those audience members who had still been drinking and joking fall silent. The only sounds are the wind in the olive trees and the distant bleating of sheep on the slopes of the Akropolis. The gathered audience sit transfixed, as if Achilles' grief has transformed them all into stone.

Kimon stands before anyone else and begins applauding.

Everyone notices him, for a moment he becomes the stage center, until some loyal veterans he's led stand and join him in applause, and soon the stands all roar with applause and focus returns to the stage.

As Achilles, brawny Aischylos bows, smelling ivy more than blood, while behind him in celebration the chorus lose their focus and begin to simply dance.

Φ

Anaxagoras visits the home of the Pythagorean refugees

The nighttime Piraeus docks are a place of swiftly moving shadows, and seemingly more voices than people, as walking lamplight fleetingly illuminates the gathered groups of port pedestrians. The docked boats creak against a late high tide. Anaxagoras leads his young mentee Archelaos, the barber's son, down into the rowdy laughter and bawdy threats of the metics and foreigners and sea peoples of the darkened docks.

"Mind your hands, young man," Anaxagoras recommends to Archelaos as they venture through a rather tight crowd.

"I've been down here at night before," Archelaos assures the older man. "My friends come down here to drink and joke. This is where the insult-poets fight. You act like you're the native and I'm the visitor!"

"Well this is also where the Pythagoreans have taken up residence," Anaxagoras explains again, "if what my friend Perikles tells me is true."

"I've heard questionable things about these folks known as Pythagoreans," says Archelaos in a whisper. "And frankly I don't know what to believe. I've heard Pythagoras was able to be in two places at once. And that he commanded a river to stop flowing. And that they don't eat beans, because they think that when you fart you're losing your soul!" He snickers at that last one.

Anaxagoras acknowledges, "I, too, have heard many strange things about these folks. However, I have reason to know that much of that which sounds absurd is exactly that. Pythagoras believed strange things about polygons, and numbers, perhaps, but was simply a man, not a magician."

"I thought you hadn't met him."

"Well, I know the world, though. I have been around, Archelaos. I have talked to many people and seen much of what people have discovered around this wide world. There is great variety, without a doubt. But I suspect that certain things like *magic*, *ghosts*, or *superpowers* ... would be more evident in the day-to-day world if they were real. There would be more than whispered rumors."

"I don't know," Archelaos says, suspicious of his teacher's skepticism. Then he asks, "So why do you want to meet them? Especially when they clearly try so hard to make themselves hard to find?"

"They are a group who have given the discovery of accurate logic and rigorously coherent knowledge a reverent primacy for decades now," Anaxagoras explains. "They likely have a great deal of accumulated organizational wisdom, and I am sure it would benefit my mind to hear them talk about it themselves. If knowledge were not power, the Sybarite neighbors of the Pythagoreans' town of Kroton would not have invaded and burned the Temple of Learning."

Anaxagoras and Archelaos continue into ever-narrower alleys until they come to one which ends at a large double door into a tall, three-story building which looks like it could fall over at any moment. Narrow windows glow with lamplight from the upper stories. And above the door, there is a five-pointed star painted in red paint, with what would appear to be very accurate precision in the equality of the sizes of its points.

"There, see?" Anaxagoras says, pointing out the star to his pupil. "The perfect five-pointed star is the symbol of the Pythagoreans."

"How do you know?"

"I have heard."

When Anaxagoras and Archelaos arrive at the tall, leaning building with its red pentagram above the door, they find the street eerily empty of the usual dock workers and merchants. The windows above seem to watch them like dark eyes.

Anaxagoras raises his hand to knock, but before his knuckles touch the wood, the door swings inward. A man fills the doorframe - not just tall but impossibly broad, as if two wrestlers had been fused into one form. In the shadows of the doorway, his muscles all ripple with each movement.

"Lost?" The giant's voice is surprisingly soft, almost musical.

"No," Anaxagoras replies carefully. "We seek wisdom."

"Wisdom?" A hint of amusement. "There are men in the Agora who will sell you wisdom for a few coins."

"O I know them personally!" Anaxagoras chuckles. "We seek better wisdom. From Kroton, where they built a temple to learning."

The giant goes utterly still. Behind him in the darkness, something moves - the rustle of robes, and wings in wicker cages.

"What do you know of Kroton?" The question comes not from the giant but from somewhere in the shadows beyond him, a woman's voice, aged but sharp as a blade.

"I know that once there was a Temple of Learning there," Anaxagoras says. "Until the flames came."

The muscular man in the doorway grimaces. "Flames do not just *come*. Some man, or god, brings them." He breathes through his nose like he is getting angry. Anaxagoras feels Archelaos grip his tunic.

Momentarily, Anaxagoras looks into his memory, and tries to look away from the flames there.

"Many things burn," the old woman's voice says. "Knowledge. Cities. Dreams. What remains when the ashes cool?"

"Numbers remain," Anaxagoras answers. "Patterns. The eternal truths that Pythagoras discovered."

A soft laugh from the darkness.

The muscled giant says calmly, "He is telling us what he knows we want to hear."

The old woman's voice says charmingly, "Discovered? Or was he merely the first to hear what the cosmos has always been singing?"

Suddenly young Archelaos sputters, pointing in recognition, "Milo! You're Milo the wrestler!"

The giant smiles and sighs.

Archelaos instantly gets shy around fame. "I saw you at Olympia when you won."

The giant - Milo, Anaxagoras finally realizes, the famous wrestler of Kroton - steps aside. In the dimness beyond him stands an elderly woman, her silver hair bound with purple ribbons.

"Are you ... Theano, wife of Pythagoras?" he asks gently.

She sighs softly. "Widow of Pythagoras." Then she hardens her face and adds, "No, I am not." Anaxagoras briefly smiles understanding. "You are from Klazomenai," she says, not a question. "Your mind hums with theories about the nature of things. But tell me, seeker of wisdom - what do you know?"

Anaxagoras opens his mouth to begin listing his accomplishments, his insights about the natural world. But something in Theano's eyes stops him. Instead, he bends and begins to draw in the dirt before the doorway. His stick moves in an ever-tightening spiral, each turn precisely diminished from the last. Young Archelaos watches as his mentor adds a sequence of smaller and smaller squares along the curve, each fitting perfectly within the spiral's decreasing spaces.

Silvery Theano moves to the doorway. Her eyes widen almost imperceptibly as she watches the pattern emerge. Archelaos watches her watch.

"The squares shrink forever," Anaxagoras explains, "each exactly proportioned to the last by the same divine ratio. Yet they never reach the center. The spiral continues infinitely inward, like the shell of a nautilus, like the pattern of leaves on an olive branch, like..." He pauses, seeing something new in his own drawing. "Like everything that grows."

"You've seen it then," Theano says softly. "The number that cannot be spoken. The ratio that divides the finite from the infinite." She kneels beside his drawing, her fingers hovering over the dirt but not touching it. "My husband called it the Golden Number. But he would not teach it to initiates until they had studied for five years in silence. And here you draw it in the dust like a child's game."

"Is it not beautiful?" Anaxagoras asks. "Should not everyone know..."

"Beautiful?" she cuts him off. "Yes. Like the face of a god is beautiful. Like staring into the sun is beautiful." She brushes her hand across the drawing, erasing it with a single gesture. "Tell me, Klazomenian, what happens to those who look too long at the sun?"

Anaxagoras looks up, startled. Behind him, young Archelaos shifts uncomfortably.

"The infinite cannot be contained in finite minds," she continues. "My husband learned this. The ratio you've drawn so casually - it cannot be expressed in numbers. Not in fractions, not in roots, not in any language of numeracy we possess. It exists between numbers, between thoughts, between worlds. To contemplate it too deeply is to go mad. It may be something only for the minds of the gods."

She turns to face the dark interior of the house. "Milo, bring wine. And you, Klazomenian, show me what else you think you know."

But as Anaxagoras moves to follow her inside, she holds up one hand. The gesture is gentle but carries absolute authority.

"First, what do you intend to do with our wisdom?"

He pauses in the threshold.

"I am writing a book," he begins. "About the flows of nature."

"No." The word falls like a stone into still water. "You will not write of these things."

Theano brushes away his drawing with her sandal.

Anaxagoras tries to explain quickly, "I am a lover of wisdom, myself, and I am eager to share experience, to share mind-work, with those who have dedicated themselves to rigorous thought. As I'm sure you're aware, word has spread of the teachings of Pythagoras, and his wise and experienced friends and family. Anyone would be greatly honored and advantaged to be granted any amount of time to simply sit and share words with any of those who studied with or knew the man." Anaxagoras smiles and indicates his own pupil standing beside him. "I am also a teacher, myself, as this young man Archelaos, an Athenian, has deigned to spend his time with me to see what wisdom I can share. So it would be to the benefit of us both, and any future folks who might decide to do as Archelaos here has, if you would share with us any wisdom."

Silver-braided Theano listens patiently to Anaxagoras' fast-paced and somewhat stuttering assertions, glancing with a miniscule smile between the older man and the younger one behind him, but her welcoming tone has shifted, and she now clearly stands blocking the entrance with a graceful arm.

"For my own part, though my own wisdom is merely gathered, I have seen and heard enough in my time to understand that I know more than many other people, and so have tried the best I can to collect those wisdoms which I have been lucky enough to find into a collection of writings, which I am calling *The Flows*, since it is primarily about how Nature flows naturally, and without an agent, all over the world..."

Theano very slowly frowns as Anaxagoras continues, and he slows his words as her face hardens and her gaze upon him becomes distant.

"What is wrong?" he asks. "Please forgive me; I speak when I should listen."

Theano asks coolly, "You are writing a book about the secrets you have learned? Where will you keep it? Is it just for this young man?"

"No, I mean to sell copies of it, so that wisdom is available to all."

Milo looks to Theano and says, "He would never keep our secrets."

Theano shakes her head grimly and furrows her eyebrows with tense memory. "Knowledge is the ultimate wealth, stranger," she says. "And you would open up your mind orchards for all to ravage? We who loved my husband made the same mistake, and paid the ultimate price for it. And I will never make that mistake again. Knowledge, wisdom, your *mind's world* - keep these secret, stranger! Do not share your mind! Do not share your wisdom. It will *not* be safe out in the world! Do you really think that buyers of scrolls in the Agora will read your words and digest them into the wisdom which you hold so dear? No. They will invade and burn your Temple of Learning, and smear their shit on the ruins. Protect your wisdom, stranger. Burn what you have written."

Old Theano gracefully reaches past the huge wrestler Milo and shuts their door.

Archelaos looks to Anaxagoras with a tear gathering in his eye.

Anaxagoras sighs. "Don't despair," he says. "There are many schools of thought. We have just learned a new one."

X

Oenopides teaches Sokrates and friends about the natural world

"Thunderbolts create mushrooms," creaky old Oenopides explains as he leads the children along a rough path through the woods just outside Athens. "Your mothers will all be very grateful for the baskets full of them which I will send you home with - trust me!"

Through the trees to the west, down the hillside behind them, the distant city walls of Athens are still visible, dotted with lamplights. A few teen-agers including Euripides and Nikias lead the twelve-year-old Krito and eight-year-old Sokrates in a line behind the old man Oenopides, the kids all struggling to walk slow enough so as not to pass the codger's meager gait.

"I thought the Kyklopes created the thunderbolts, and Zeus Protector owns and wields them," handsome young Nikias remarks. "Are you telling us that's not how it is?"

Oenopides nods, "Well, yes, the poets will tell you that the Kyklopes created the thunderbolts, with Hephaestos' forge, and gave them to Zeus for his fight against the Titans in ancient times. But really, how would poets know that? I have found little reason to believe that thunderbolts actually come from the hand of Zeus. It seems more likely to me that they are merely created by rainstorms, naturally, physically, like the light from lamps. After all, what do poets know? Why would poets know about ancient or mystical things any more than any other man? They're really just guessing, or trying to excite children. But we're not children anymore, are we, boys? And adults prefer to know the *truth*."

Sixteen-year-old Nikias says derisively, "Sokrates is only eight. I wouldn't say we're all quite adults. But don't worry, Sokrates, he's just trying to instill independence and manliness in your mind; he's not going to make you do anything too adult."

Oenopides chuckles and sighs and confirms, "No, no, nothing your mothers won't agree with. Except for the fact that I did mislead you about my intent in bringing you out here, and we are not, in fact, here to hunt for mushrooms. I have quite another lesson for you boys tonight!"

Many of the older boys groan, having heard of Oenopides' attempts to convince others to track the stars, a proposition which Athenians broadly mock as boring and pointless.

"Yes, yes, it is the stars!" Oenopides responds to the groans. "We are here tonight to learn and talk about the stars! And why not? What is so groan-worthy about learning about the stars?"

"The stars don't do anything," one boy answers.

"The only useful thing I know of that they do, is entrance young ladies," Nikias says for a laugh. "Just point out constellations like the finger-fuck, and the mouth-work, see them?"

"Now Nikias," Oenopides groans back, "you are the one who just said there wouldn't be anything too adult. Don't go showing off as if you've had any luck with any ladies. I think if you were using the stars the way you say, you'd be a lot more grateful to them and interested in them."

"Okay, so what is so interesting, then, about the stars, grandfather?" Nikias says with a flourish of his hand, exaggerating respect like an actor playing an ancient nobleman in the days of Homeros.

"We know the world consists of loops within loops. The Aigyptians have been making records of the movement of the varied lights in the night sky for hundreds of generations, and there are many things that men have confirmed - things that happen with great regularity, every year. And every year, every loop of the course of the stars across the sky, has always had the same number of days. Every loop of the Moon has always had the same number of days.

"And yet every day does not last as long as the next. The length of the day is its own loop - the days get shorter, and the nights longer, in the months of winter, and then they slow and swing back. Like an iris within an eye within a head. Like a swinging bob moving in a circle. Loops within loops."

"Because Persephone goes down to Haides' kingdom to reign there half the year, and Demeter falls into melancholy over it," Nikias says.

Oenopides just shakes his head with a patient, bored little smile. "No. That may happen, but it cannot be coincidence that the cycle of day-length happens to coincide with the cycle of the seasons."

"Perhaps you consider the relationship backwards," Nikias suggests, "and the cycle of day length is a product of Haides' six-month contract with Persephone, like some cyclical equivalent of putting constellations in the sky."

"What do you think the stars are?" Oenopides asks, first seemingly as a question to Nikias, but then looking around to the group.

For a long pause, no one wants to answer.

"Fires?" Krito guesses. "Like lamps?"

Oenopides points at the young boy to indicate it is an interesting answer.

"Dead gods?" asks Euripides.

Oenopides shrugs a little like this answer seems less likely.

"Or like some kind of mystical tropaion of the deaths of gods?" Euripides adds.

Oenopides just raises his eyebrows at that and looks to other boys. When no one else gives guesses, he says, "All good thoughts. Let us consider what we are able to know about them. They are up there in the sky, right? What else can you know about the stars?"

"They're beautiful," Nikias suggests. "They sparkle like they're on water."

"Ah but do they? Do they all?" Oenopides chuckles excitedly. He gets very close to Nikias and points with his whole arm up into the sky, his shoulder right against the boy's face. "Look there at that one, the red one there. Is it sparkling?"

Nikias shirks at first from the old man's proximity, but once he sees the star in question he relaxes and nods, and says, "O, why no, that one isn't! How funny."

"Most do, to be sure," Oenopides says with a pat to Nikias' head, "and it was a good observation. But some don't! Just as some of us have different traits from each other, even though many other traits are the same. Do you know what is special about that star there, though? That is the one we call Ares, as if it is the War God himself there all covered in blood and fire. And unlike the fixed stars, the ones which sparkle, he is one of the moving stars, which do not sparkle."

"I don't see it moving," Euripides notes. "I've been watching it since you mentioned it. Does it just move sometimes?"

"It is constantly moving, but very slowly!" Oenopides says. "When you watch things over time, as I have the stars, you will find that some things which appear still are actually moving in slow-motion."

The old man leads the boys to a grassy rise overlooking the sleeping city. Here the wind carries fewer cooking smells and lamp-smoke, and the bright stars above shine clearer. He settles onto the ground with a grunt, his joints creaking like old wood.

"Look there," Oenopides says pointing with a trembling finger. "That's where Atlas holds up the great dome of the sky. Watch long enough and you'll see all the stars process around it like dancers in a circle. All except the five wanderers - see that red one there? That's Ares, marking his path through the celestial spheres."

"But why does Ares move differently than the other stars?" Nikias asks.

"That's one of the great mysteries," Oenopides says. "The fixed stars move together, like moles or scars on the black skin of Ouranos Sky God himself as he tosses and turns in bed. But the wanderers - Ares, Aphrodite, Hermes, Zeus, and Kronos - they dance along their own paths, sometimes even seeming to move backward! I've watched them for more than fifty years now, marking their positions, and still they surprise me."

Young Sokrates sits forward, his eyes wide. "Is that why you say everything moves slowly? Because you have to watch for so long to see the patterns?"

"Exactly!" The old man ruffles Sokrates' curly hair. "Most people think only about what they can see happening right now. But the wisest thoughts come from watching what moves too slowly for most to notice."

"Like how people grow old?" Euripides asks quietly.

"Another astute observation."

Nikias jokes, "Smart boys don't need to ask questions."

Old Oenopides chides Nikias with just a look. He continues, "We don't see ourselves aging day by day, but compare how you feel now to how you felt in last year's sandals! The stars teach us patience." He gazes up at the glittering dome above. "When I was your age, I thought the gods lit new fires in the sky each night. Now I know they dance in perfect circles, eternal and unchanging. They are not like us. There is much that we do, which the gods do not have to do."

"Are they watching us from up there?"

Oenopides shrugs. "Only sometimes. You can get their attention."

"So if we watch carefully enough, we can predict where they'll be?" Chaerephon asks eagerly.

"Who cares where a star will be?" Nikias asks.

"If you track the wandering stars carefully enough, you begin to see patterns. Some say wisdom and future events can be found therein. Cycles within cycles, like wheels turning within larger wheels. The Aigyptians have been watching them for thousands of years, such that they can predict exactly when eclipses will occur."

"But isn't that the gods' business?" Nikias objects. "Shouldn't we leave such things to the priests?"

Oenopides smiles gently. "The gods gave us minds capable of understanding their works. Surely they meant us to use them? Every pattern we discover reveals more of their divine wisdom."

The old man falls silent for a long moment, studying the eternal dance above.

Sokrates looks around at his fellow boys, up at the stars, and down the hillside toward the lamp-fires of Athens, as the quiet sounds of the night hillside surround them.

When he speaks again, Oenopides' voice has lost its excitement and holds instead a deep weariness.

"Promise me, boys, these few things," Oenopides says, looking them each in the eye one after the other. "Promise me that you will be moderate with wine, and always properly dilute it with water. And similarly with wealth, always properly dilute it with spending, for wealth is like blood, and it is meant to move, as where it coagulates it festers. And do not live your lives without *thinking about them*, for it is not simply to live that has value, but to build good memories. For you will never be able to relive your past, but you can remember it, and that is nearly as good. But also, the more you learn, you will be able to cultivate and exercise and perfect your memories, so that they can bloom into beings even greater than the real moment was! And what a life you can have lived then, as an old man, filled with fanciful memories more wonderful than any real life could have been!"

The boys giggle, some in wonder, some in mockery.

"I have a secret to tell you boys, since I'm old and likely near a natural death, and need to fear the law of men little anymore. I have an increasing suspicion in my final years, that the stories of the gods, and the nymphs, and all the invisible things, are actually not literally true, but are instead something more like theatrical masks for the sublime forces that *are* real but we do not have the words for. For example knowledge - wisdom - Athena! I suspect that the story of Athena being born from the head of Zeus after Hephaestos split his skull with an axe and the story of Alkmaeon opening the skull of the ram can be triangulated. And it makes me wonder if perhaps, inside my skull, if you split it open after I die, if you might find some kind of stuff that you can drink or eat, which will be my wisdom, or my memories - or even potentially my soul itself! Perhaps if you supped of my skull's ambrosia thusly, you could gain my wisdom, or I could join you in your body, or something like that!"

"Mm hm," Nikias muses doubtfully, eyeing the other boys with growing uncertainty.

Oenopides creakily bends down to search the grass for a flower.

Nikias playfully pokes at Euripides under his clothes.

Holding up the flower for all to see, old Oenopides says, "You see, my boys, there is little point in living a life if not to examine it and discover what it really is - to take off its mask! How beautiful and strange all the tiny corners of this life are. And even more so the unseen, and the distant - the wind, the stars! O how I miss the stars during the day."

"This senile old fool is repeating himself," Nikias whispers to Euripides.

"I think he's just trying to get across that an unexamined life is not worth living," one of the other boys retorts.

"Yeah, I heard him, kid," Nikias snaps impatiently. "But I think he was talking about turning up rocks to find bugs, or the like. You're kind to quote the most profound nugget of his nuttiness."

"The power of framing," Euripides comments.

"How do you mean?" Sokrates asks.

"I mean, the choice of what to include within the bounds of a story. Or a memory. And, inherently, also what to exclude."

"Like how I am everything except that which is excluded from me," Sokrates jokes.

"Promise me, boys," the old man says with a grunt as he sets his body gently down onto a steep slope of grass. "Promise me that you will examine me after I die, in ways that I could not while I lived."

"What do you mean?"

"Inside my head! Like the ram. I want you to find the stuff of my knowledge, and examine what my mind was made of."

The boys all look to each other nervously.

"After I die, simply collect my body in secret, take it far from the city where none will see you, and then open my skull with an axe. Just like Hephaestos did to Zeus. And draw and write about what is inside! That is, if my soul doesn't jump out armored like Athena!"

Oenopides grins at the boys, flashing his few teeth. He laps at the teeth with his old tongue, then sits back upon a rise of moss and stone. "Promise me you'll open my skull when I'm dead," Oenopides again demands, holding up a finger.

"Yes," Sokrates says.

Looking to Sokrates to share his bewilderment, Euripides takes a while to answer, but finally nods and says, "Okay."

"Hopefully much can be learned out of my head. Once I die, just find an axe and split me open, and find out what was inside. Perhaps my wisdom will be some kind of stuff you can eat or drink straight out of my head; who knows! Try everything. Be my welcome guest inside my skull."

Oenopides gets up then and hobbles again along the path, gleeful now if not any more energetic.

Out of sight of old Oenopides, Nikias tries to get all the other boys' attention as he shakes his head quietly but vigorously, as if to assert that none of them should ever do what the old man just asked of them.

"Why don't we just axe your head right now?" jokes Nikias as they continue on behind the doddering old man. Krito and Euripides snicker.

"No no," Oenopides replies calmly, "please don't. I wouldn't want to separate my eyes while I'm still using them."

Ψ

Aoide is taken to the house of the Pythia

Male voices in argument waken Aoide and all the other young girls in her dormitory. Many sit up at once in their bedding and look to each other, still groggily making sense of the muffled angry shouting and wondering if the others have been awake longer.

Aoide, the oldest among the girls in her dorm now, goes to the door and listens closely there while all the younger girls gather silently around her.

"If it were anyone else!" one male voice shouts. "If it were *anyone* else! But *she* is *heard*! Her voice does not simply dissipate! She has connections to Athens; she is Alkmaeonid!"

"Calm yourself!" the other, older male voice. "Calm, and quiet! Do you want to wake the whole sanctuary?"

As the voices are in mid-speech, the door suddenly bursts open, slamming into Aoide's listening head and knocking her bodily into the group of other girls. All the girls shriek.

Behind the door is Kliko, the elderly priestess, and she is moving faster than Aoide has ever seen her move. Her arms shake with energy as she shouts, "Where is Aoide? There you are!"

Hands seize Aoide in the darkness before she can cry out. A wool cloak is thrown over her head, smelling of laurel and myrrh, blinding her sight. "Quiet," whispers a voice she knows, one of the Pythia's serving woman.

The two sets of hands hustle her through corridors she has known for years but which now, blind and stumbling, seem twisted as a labyrinth. The women's footsteps are eerily silent, as if they have been wrapped in wool.

Somewhere ahead, a door creaks. The women guide Aoide's body through a doorframe, past a third woman who blows a nearly-silent kiss.

Cool night air touches her face through the cloak. They're outside now, moving uphill. The paths grow steeper, rougher. Stones shift under her feet and strong hands steady her before she can fall. No one speaks.

In the unique strength of one of the pairs of hands, Aoide recognizes her old babysitter Hydna, the famous swimmer, whom she hasn't seen in years. A subtle something in the breath belies her voice as well, and Aoide is sure it is her.

She begins counting her own breaths, trying to track their passage. Left at the shrine of the nymphs - she knows that corner's sharp turn. Past the ancient olive tree - she smells its silvery leaves. But then unfamiliar ground, paths she's never walked. The mountain air grows thinner and colder.

A dog barks in the distance and everyone freezes. One woman, not Hydna, makes a soft grunting sound. After a long moment, they move again.

Finally, another doorframe and then stairs beneath her feet, worn smooth by generations of secret steps. Another door opens sucking her in; she feels the change in the air more than hears it.

The cloak is pulled away.

Aoide stands in a room she has never seen, though it can't be far from the sanctuary. Ancient women sit in a circle, their faces weathered as the mountain itself. One tends a small fire. Another spins wool with practiced fingers. None look surprised to see her.

"Welcome, daughter," says the oldest, her voice like dry leaves. "The Pythia send their greetings."

"Why," Aoide begins, but the spinner cuts her off with a sharp gesture.

"No questions," she says. "Questions draw lightning. You'll stay with us until the moon changes face."

The old woman by the fire adds another branch without looking up. "We've kept many secrets safe over the years," she says into the flames. "The gods entrust their treasures to our hands when men's schemes grow too bold."

Aoide opens her mouth again but finds her words stolen by a long, unstoppable yawn, and her eyes swim in heaviness. She can barely keep them open. The wool they wrapped her in must have been drugged.

"Sleep," says the spinner, her voice growing distant. "The Pythia know what they're doing, even when we don't understand."

The last thing Aoide sees before darkness takes her is that beside her sit a couple of skeletons her same size.

Ω

The Spartan leadership discuss the situation on Mount Ithome

"Ithome is our Troi," one of this year's Overseers says to King Archidamos, who sits upon his throne inside the Temple of Aphrodite Warlike, where his courtiers and a few of the ten Overseers are gathered for discussion. "But unlike Menelaos' warriors of old, who fought on foreign soil, we can easily maintain siege in our own land. Even if the last of these rebellious slaves live ten years, they will be years imprisoned on a rocky mountaintop, cut off from cultivated lands of men until they die."

"You're not alone, old man," King Archidamos says with low, firelit eyes. "I would bet that every man besieging a city for the past thousand years has imagined themselves to be just like those Hellenes at Troi."

"Yes, it is hubristic, obvious, overblown, and wrong," King Pleistarchos sighs. "It shows how misguided and egotistical we are."

Beside King Pleistarchos, the old poet Simonides carefully keeps quiet, though his eyes react loudly to each spoken comment.

As the Spartan king is speaking, the ground quakes again for just a few moments, softer and briefer, but of the same character as that morning quake that leveled the city only days ago. All the soldiers standing at guard on the edges of the room take a war stance and look around for Helot attackers.

King Archidamos looks to the priest Triops, who steps forward to speak.

"Poseidon reminds us," says the old priest, touching the false third eye that he wears in the center of his head like an off-kilter eyepatch with a blue and white stone attached. "It does not matter how far from the sea you go, but the Sea God's wrath can always reach you."

"Then tonight we will sacrifice as many bulls as we have, to the king of the watery depths, the first trainer of horses, great Poseidon, that he might forgive us for whatever the fuck we might have done," King Archidamos snarls to King Pleistarchos.

"We do think that we have discovered the potential cause of this earthquake," the old priest Triops says, giving the Overseers a cold side-eye.

"Do tell," Archidamos says, seeing the glance and turning his gaze upon the Overseers while the priest goes on.

"There is a very ancient temple to Poseidon at Tainaron, on the southern tip of our lands. It's that temple near the cave called the Foxhole - one of the entrances to the Underworld."

"Of course, I know of it," Archidamos nods.

"Just at the beginning of this month, apparently there was an incident involving some Helots who were to be punished by their caretaker, and they took refuge from his violence in the temple of Poseidon at Tainaron. Our Overseers gave the order to kill them there. No doubt encouraged by Athena's silence when they pulled Pausanias from her temple, to kill him. But at least with him, he was killed outside the temple. I hear that these Helots were killed *inside* the temple, perhaps even upon the altar itself."

King Archidamos shakes his head slowly, sighing with frustration, glaring at the Overseers.

"We must learn from our mistakes," King Archidamos declares. "The gods show us what they love, and what they hate. We will not defile their temples with blood. I remember another time that a temple was defiled, here in our very city of Sparta." He looks at Gorgo and Pleistarchos.

Gorgo ignores the comment and asks the room, "Where are there still threats?" When all are silent in response, she continues, "We have beaten the Helots on the field, in their most organized semblance of an army, and at the very least cornered them on that mountaintop. However, even though most Helots did not officially join that organized rebellion, they are all still threats to us, if we have any sense of their desire to rise against us. We must never mistake ourselves again for being safe."

King Pleistarchos sets his little pet turtle on the table in front of himself. It begins to very slowly explore the space around itself with tiny, timid steps and sniffs. All the elder Spartans around the Agiad king watch in awkward silence until King Archidamos laughs.

A younger Overseer says carefully, "The Agiad king wishes to show the virtue of *patience*. His great wisdoms all come from Aisop's animal fables. The turtle is his favorite."

Pleistarchos looks over at Simonides with a frustrated plea to reason in his eyes.

Simonides gives the king a momentary look of pity, then says, "There is much wisdom in the work of old Aisop. Indeed, he was a slave, but one with a wise and noble mind, and clearly beloved by the gods. And his stories, if not held as high as those of Homeros, surely are retold in more homes. And that is because they are clear, and simple, and true. Like true beauty, and true wisdom, they are easy to understand."

Pleistarchos smiles and sighs for a brief moment, his eyes on his turtle. He holds out to it a bit of leaf to eat.

Old Triops then holds up his hands into the air and says, "O Muses, give me the voice and memory to relate again the wise slave Aisop's old story of the Eagle and the Fox. The two clever creatures were friends, and decided to live close to each other, so that they might each be safer. So the Eagle built a nest high up in a tree and there gave birth to her chicks, while the Fox arranged a home for herself in the brush near the base of the tree, and there had her own pups. But one day while the Fox was away hunting for a meal for her pups, the Eagle returned to her nest without anything for her hungry chicks, so she flew down into the brush and took one of the Fox's pups to split up and feed to her young. Of course, once the Fox returned home and her other pups told her what had happened, she was unable to see her own grief so blinded was she by her urge for revenge."

King Archidamos begins to nod sternly, finally seeming to understand why the priest chose this story.

Triops continues, "Now being unwinged, the Fox was unable to pursue the Eagle up to her nest. All she could do was stand far away where she could see the Eagle's nest and shout curses upon it. Until her curses brought her attention to some priests of Zeus sacrificing a goat in a tripod of fire nearby. Seeing the flesh of the goat burn, Zeus, hearing her curses, formed an idea within the Fox's mind, and she ran past the ceremony of the humans, grabbing in her mouth a small log aflame, which she carried to the base of the tree which she and the Eagle called their homes.

"The Fox, enraged, then removed her own pups from their home in the brush, and set fire to that very brush at the base of the Eagle's tree, at which the Eagle flew to safety, but her children whose feathers had not yet grown instead tumbled from the nest, through the sparking air, into the fiery brush, where the Fox retrieved them and devoured them within sight of the Eagle."

"Yes," Archidamos says. "For those who break the bonds of friendship will see the worst revenge. And what is a slave supposed to be, if not the best friend a master can have?"

King Pleistarchos spits out a scoff and then says loudly, and clearly, "You are stupid."

Everyone silences in shock and looks at both kings. Simonides puts a hand on the king's shoulder with a worried glance, but Pleistarchos shakes it off. King Archidamos starts to posture as if about to deflect the comment to another person, but Pleistarchos quickly continues.

"You, Archidamos, you utter fool. Your inhumanity, the inhumanity of Spartans altogether, has already brought the wrath of the Sea God upon us. Which god's wrath will be next? How many gods will it take to destroy our society utterly? Or will your wicked idiocy force the weakest to rise and defeat the strong? We deserve this shame!"

All the other Spartans present have begun to murmur just loud enough to nearly drown out the young king's vitriol, so he keeps ramping up his volume until he is shouting and the murmuring matches it.

"Enough," Gorgo says, trying to let her coolness ease the vibe. But no one calms.

"It is never enough!" King Pleistarchos shouts. "There is never enough misery for you! There is no escape! We are all slaves!"

Low-eyed King Pleistarchos, son of Leonidas, grimaces as he holds up an engraved iron bar.

"With this curse-poem, which I shall never let any mortal eye read, I now curse every living Spartan with all the power of my royal blood, and there is nothing you can do about it, for Lakedaemonia has banked the wrath of all the gods, and I hereby now call upon their wrath."

King Archidamos groans, pulls his hair, stands and says, "Theater. Lion's son, you bore everyone." He and his entourage start leaving in a growing group.

King Pleistarchos scowls at his mother, then darts outside the tent into the nighttime black, draws back with full effort and pitches the little iron ribbon of curse-words as far as he can hurl it.

The landing iron curse drives deep into the ground, blocking the path of some poor worm who then is forced to go around.

The PELOPONNESE

THE ISLAND OF KING PELOPS

6

HERMES PLAN-SPINNER

A

The Spartan Assembly holds their annual declaration of war against the Helots

Where a wolf died on the mountainside, flung by a goat too tough to take, black buzzards have made a crowded pnyx to feast.

On the night of each full moon, Spartan men all gather in Sparta's city center for their Assembly. Every male of more than thirty years stands where they can see and hear and smell each other, while the ten annual Overseers line up at the front like a chorus. The two kings stand at the head of the Assembly, but as citizens. All the women, children, and Helots remain elsewhere.

Since the earthquake, the gathering of this Assembly has become a stark reminder of what they struggle for, as those many men who now live in temporary shelters elsewhere throughout the valley of Lakedaemonia return to their flattened city, still darkened with blood spilled both by the Sea God and by Helot knives, to hear the next month's planning. But more than ever, tonight's low, reddish full moon has a particular power, as this is the month in which, traditionally, the Spartan state redeclares their eternal war against the Helots. This year, that declaration has a new and critical intensity.

"All the gods listen behind those clouds," one of the eldest Overseers remarks to a few younger listeners in the crowd.

The youngest of the Overseers pounds his stick on the stone beneath him to quiet the crowd, then backs away and gestures to the steadfast, stone-faced King Archidamos in his long Spartan-red cape.

King Archidamos declares, "Now again, as we have for two hundred years, we declare war for this new year upon the Helots! But this year we do so with a renewed passion, and a reminder of why we Lakedaemonians subjugate those who live around us. Because we sons of Herakles are surrounded by dishonorable peoples! So our ancestors subjugated them, and made them *Helots*, forever to be Sparta's slaves.

"Now, this year, as they have done notoriously in the past, they have once again betrayed us in our moment of weakness. They have struck at our back when we were down, and forced us into a position of total war. So if we need to destroy every single living Helot family, and find new slaves elsewhere afterward, then that must be what we will do! Ares stands with us against the cowardly slaves!"

The assembly of men around him largely roars with agreement.

"All other men are Sparta's slaves by natural right!" he shouts, and the gathering roars agreement again. "But we only need to keep the local ones. Distant barbarians can be our slaves once we get there."

Many younger Spartan men laugh. The veterans of old wars merely stare stone-faced as their scars itch.

King Archidamos looks to younger King Pleistarchos - not a boy anymore, but still a slender, hunched figure when comparably adjacent to the taller, more confident Archidamos. King Pleistarchos makes no indication of wanting to add words, so King Archidamos snaps his fingers and points to the long-beard who is heading the *Gerousia* - the Council of Old Men - this year. The head of the Gerousia steps forward and unrolls his scroll to the part which he means to read. It takes him a while to find the right place.

"O gods of Hellas, hear us now as we give our blood to this oath - that we Lakedaemonians will make glorious and relentless war upon our enemies the Helots, in order to return them to the state of wretched slavery in which they belong! Consume this holy smoke we send you, the body of these strong oxen, and join us here tonight, O gods! O three great brothers who rule the world, hear our call! Poseidon Earth-shaker, hear our call! Haides Host-of-Many, hear our call! Zeus Cloud-gatherer, hear our call! Aid us in our just control over the fruitful valleys of Lakedaemonia, and aid us in the defense of our homes against these vicious attacks from within, and put fear into the hearts of those who wish us harm!"

The fear-weary struggle-muscled Spartan men murmur mixed emotions.

While the men are away at their assembly, the women and children of Sparta who wait back in their homes are visited by the Queen-Mother Gorgo's loyal young Spartan women, and some noblewomen are even visited by the Queen-Mother herself, in secret, where they are told simply, "The meadow of Artemis Willow-bound on the eve of Hekate's Supper. Bring your children. No men."

"The meadow of Artemis Willow-bound on the eve of the Moonless Night. No men. Bring your children."

"Fear not a myriad of men, nor flinch,
but let each one hold their blade straight,
make Life the enemy and dark spirits of Death
seem sweet as the rays of the Sun!"
Tyrtaeus, Spartan Poet

B

Themistokles rides on a royal hunt with Xerxes

"The auroch is rare now, and avoids the smell of civilized horses, so we must approach the plain on foot," Artabanos explains to Xerxes as he dismounts, gesturing for those behind to do the same. "If we are lucky enough to witness one meet the great lion in wild combat, the gods will surely be smiling on us all year. It is worth the chance, to come here."

Xerxes smiles to Themistokles and the other courtiers who have joined him on this outing - an important cedar merchant from Sidon, and two young princes from the old royalty of Babylon.

"Are we to see the kill occur, General?" the merchant chides as he navigates his big body off his horse. "Or will this be one of those safaris merely built of wondrous words, describing what the guide has seen, while those guided are left with their imaginations, and some pre-arranged aftermath?"

The two Babylonian princes oblige the merchant with a smattering of polite laughter.

"This is not a safari," Artabanos retorts with an icy glance. "This is a divine augury through bearing witness to nature's agony, in a way that would not occur if we were to interfere with it. We must be reverent to what we are about to behold. And I alone will have the knowledge to grasp its meaning."

"Of course, that's what all safari guides are told to say," the older Babylonian prince says snidely. "It helps present the impression that our tour of the wild beasts of the wilderness is anything like reality instead of the staged modern theater that all of this ultimately really just is. Nothing is wild anymore. I can see lions eat bulls a hundred different ways in the city. I say man has killed his gods, and nature too. It's man's world now."

"That is a disturbing paradigm you articulate, sir," Themistokles remarks coolly. "I am impressed with the scale of your hubris. I would not be surprised to hear you next *dare* a god to strike you down tonight."

"Let one do it now if there is one anywhere," the Babylonian man says. He rolls his eyes and adds, "O look, none did."

"Quiet," Artabanos hushes, gesturing for everyone to crouch down. A movement of his guards' spears leads everyone to follow his command and lower their bodies to the sand.

In the valley below the herd of aurochs linger, to drink more, rather than leave, as it seems clear the largest wants to do. The towering bull auroch called the king, taller than a man at its shoulder, stamps its hoof and snorts, pacing, while the women and children take ease and water at the stream. In the underbrush at the base of the hill, just a long dash from the water, Artabanos' lion pair stalk, hidden only nominally, as the bull does see them, and continually looks right at them. But neither animal's eyes work like the other's, so neither knows accurately how to judge whether the other sees them, and they each must assume that the other does. It is in this detente that the predator and the prey coexist, most days, in calm, right beside each other, death on everyone's mind, normal.

"Tell me, Hellene," says the younger and bolder of the two Babylonian princes, "what made you give up your country, which you fought to save so famously, and join the court of your ultimate enemy?"

Themistokles looks into the eyes of the Babylonian prince, investigates his face, as the man waits for an answer, until he stops waiting and simply scoffs.

"None of you are traitors to your homelands, just because you chose to submit to the King of Kings," Xerxes corrects with a touch of confusion on his brow. "The righteousness of Persian authority, the morality of our ways, represent a majority of one, in me, who surpasses all your democratic or oligarchic or monarchic customs of old. Never doubt your decision to submit to me."

Themistokles and the Babylonian princes all look to each other with masked grimaces. Only the Sidonian merchant nods in solid agreement.

"After all, didn't the foolish majority in your city choose to exile you, their own hero?" Xerxes asks Themistokles directly. "Clearly rightness is foiled by the masses' enfranchisement. Your skill and cleverness will be much better used here for

Persia than for the chaos of that Assembly."

"So, I have been meaning to speak to you about..." Themistokles begins.

"About what I want from you," Xerxes interrupts, then gives him a playfully annoyed glance. "You hem and haw like a Kwarazmian, Hellene. You should assert yourself more directly and always tell me exactly what you're thinking. Let me not learn late what you were thinking, ever again."

Themistokles nods, grimacing against the feeling of submissiveness. "Well, I am now telling you - I wonder what your plans might be for Hellas."

Xerxes smiles and reaches out to lightly touch Themistokles on the side of the arm. Xerxes says, "I did not call for your help in invading Hellenic lands when we were moving our fleet on Pamphylia. You should stop worrying. I am not going to ask you to fight your own people. I am not foolish enough to think that would be a good idea. I have other plans for you, Hellene. Don't worry, though - these plans still call for your great naval mind. Just not against Hellenes, whom you might have too much compassion for."

Themistokles nods and allows a half smile to indicate his gratitude.

"But I would bet fighting Aigyptians wouldn't give you as much pause," Xerxes offers, eager to gauge Themistokles' reaction.

Carefully, trying never to let too much show on his face, Themistokles nods and sniffs what he hopes seems like a satisfied sigh, saying, "Fighting Aigyptians is like fighting any other barbarian."

"And just what makes one a barbarian?" asks the younger of the two Babylonian princes in with a wry grin to his brother.

"What else?" Themistokles half-jokes. "Not speaking Hellenic."

The Babylonian princes laugh, but no one else does. Artabanos gives Themistokles the evil eye.

"My wife learned Hellenic," the cedar merchant says coyly, "just so she could read erotic poems about love without men! I've never had much use for written characters of any language, myself. There's no life to them, too much opportunity for misunderstanding without eyes upon eyes and hearing the tone of the delivery of the words..."

"Quiet now," Xerxes says, watching Artabanos' eyes as he scans the desert ahead. "The pride stalks."

Artabanos nods, his eyes narrow.

The lions stalk patiently, murderously, upon the cluster of bulls. The lions split up slightly as they encroach, but clearly all are honed in together toward one of the weaker-looking small males toward the edge of the group. One of the lions encroaches quicker than the others, and some noise or scent awakens the interest of the quarry before the group had intended. Soon, all the bulls and cows have risen and begun to tromp away, up the hillside in a cloud of low dust, and the king auroch is the only one who remains, staring down the hunters.

When he notices the general's lip-licking interest in the augury of the beasts of the valley below, Themistokles looks between Xerxes and Artabanos, noticing how the king of kings watches without seeing, and it makes him wonder how different each person's experience of the world must be.

Before much longer, the beast-theater below has played out and made clear that the old aurochs will not fall tonight, as the lions retreat and regroup, and the king auroch stomps the Earth. Before long the interest of the watchers wanes quickly one after the next.

Artabanos sniffs, leans over to spit on the earth, and says, "Today is not the day I thought it was," then quickly mounts and heels his horse to ride ahead, leaving Xerxes and Themistokles with the rest of the guard.

One Babylonian prince passes the king of kings making a gesture with his hands like someone writing cuneiform with a writing tool as he says sarcastically, "Wild as old Enkidu!"

Γ

Clowns and poets process recent events in the Agora

The games of knucklebones in the Athenian Agora are most rambunctious in the afternoon, when the country folk have finished their errands and gather around to watch the city teen-agers, who are usually the ones actually rolling the bones while older urbanites wrangle whirlwinds of betting. Newcomers from the countryside often lose their first bets and leave unhappy.

"Which came first, the dice or the number? The dice!"

Today the Agora's two most famous clowns - Magnes the animal mimicker and Chionides who mimes human stereotypes - have each taken positions beside the games of knucklebones happening on either end of the ten-man-long Monument of Heroes.

The crowd around one game roars at the results of a roll, coins change hands among the bettors, and the hovering clown Chionides mocks them all as he mimes a country farmer emptying his purse while grappling with a stick-puppet ox, making even those who are losing money laugh.

A gang of rambunctious teen-aged Athenian boys and girls rambles through the Agora laughing at each other's brazen boldnesses. One of the boys stumbles over the sleeping form of a lumpy-faced old man who has curled up in the shadow of a bush to sleep. The boy falls to his knees, scraping them on the stones of the Agora, and starts to cry. His friends mock him playfully as they help him to stand.

"You woke me," the old man grumbles. When he turns to look at the boys, they all shriek at the first sight of his deformed face - for it is the famous insult-poet Hipponax. He leans his hunched back against the ground to prop himself up enough to shout. "Have you wine for my worldly words, or am I to understand that your parents will owe me when I come to call at your home?"

The malformed old man brandishes the sign around his neck:

POEMS FOR WINE

The boys all laugh when they see the hand-carved letters.

"You are already two sips in arrears, loud lion cubs, for this is the second of Hipponax's poems to reach your ears." He loudly clears his throat, then spits bloody phlegm into the grass.

All the boys groan at the sight. The one who tripped, who has now had time to gain back his courage, steps forward.

"We didn't agree to any contract with you, beast," the big boy, Bupalos, barks. "Don't try to confuse these little ones into thinking they owe you something."

"But Bupalos, that's Hipponax," one of the younger boys whispers. "He's famous. I've heard other poets quote his poems."

"O have you, boy?" Hipponax calls loudly, lolling his eyes in a manner that reveals that he might be blind. "Who have you heard quoting me? Tell them where to bring the jug they owe me."

"This guy's blind, look at his eye," Bupalos sniffs. "Why didn't you see me coming, *Tiresias*? Don't the blind have foresight?"

"Not all blind people have magical sight, you mother-shaming moron,"

Hipponax sighs. "Now go and find a wine merchant and tell them whom to pour on."

"Here, wait," an older boy laughs, coming forward with a wineskin, "I want to hear one of this old codger's real poems. Here, poet, have some wine. And give us a real poem. The kind that rhymes and flows." He hands his own hip wineskin to the seated Hipponax.

The deformed old poet sniffs the tip of the wineskin.

"Didn't piss in this, did you? Smells like wine. I'll risk the plunge."

Misshapen Hipponax holds the wineskin above his head and slurps. The boys all chuckle, watching.

When he has finished chugging, Hipponax brushes his wispy hair over his lumpy, malformed head and turns his half-blind eyes to whatever Muse rides the moment's wind.

"I call this 'Look closer'. A mean donkey who smelled like clay walked down the riverside one day, and tripped over a sleeping turtle, falling and skinning his knees. The foolish potter donkey, thinking the turtle an oracle, asked the turtle for a vision from the gods. So the turtle said, 'Look closer, Donkey, see this fist? It's what I will punch you in the asshole with.'"

The boys laugh, surprised and confused.

"Well that was unexpected."

"The turtle made a fist?"

Hipponax gives his labored, deformed version of a grin and says, "Look closer. I would thank the gods you gave me the chance. "

The boys all shirk back as if threatened.

"Or should I cut you deeper with words, instead?"

Bupalos makes a mime of a courageous laugh and says, "Please, poet, I've been cut by worse than words! I doubt there is a thing that you could say that could actually hurt me!"

Hipponax, the famous deformed insult-poet of Ephesos, stands slowly to face the young Athenian of no known fame named Bupalos, and goes through his tirade-poem without ever leaving eye-contact despite his lumpy, malformed eyes.

And now, sweet Muses of Mount Helikon,
whose fame are widely known across Hellas,
help me to find the proper lexicon
to sing of one irrelevant as Bupalos!
For when a man does not deserve a song,

are any words worthy of being used?
Or does this fameless man even belong
preserved within the world of words at all?
Who in this city cares for Bupalos,
besides his dopey friends and mangy dog,
his lousy mother, drinking with her butt,
all of them drinking from the same pail!

"You've given up on rhyming?"

But no one ever fucked his mother, no!
Such an ox-horned beast nobody would!
So baby Bupalos must have been born
by fucking his own mother! Parenthood!

"O!" a friend of Bupalos shouts, laughing, "he got you good! You know we're never going to let you live that down!"

"Leave him alone," another of his friends tells Bupalos, "or his stupid face'll haunt your dreams."

"Tell your friends," Hipponax grunts, shuffling his body down to a more comfortable rest in the grass, "the ugly man sells poems for wine. Better poems for money."

From across the Agora, seeing this, Protagoras shouts from his makeshift kiosk, "Or, you could save your money for something a little more valuable: the wisdom of philosophies from Abdera, from one who studied with the world-famed Leukippos!"

"No one wants more goofy Thrakian gods!" a passing priestess of Athena named Lexo tells Protagoras. "It's quite enough with Dionysos in the city now, thank you very much."

"It isn't some new god I'm selling knowledge of, fine lady," Protagoras says, "but rather wisdom itself."

"Wisdom is granted by the gods," says Lexo, stopping her stride once she realizes that she will not be able to simply walk by without arguing with this foreigner. "How do you propose to 'grant wisdom'? Wisdom about what? Each different area of wisdom is overseen by some different god. You have wisdom of the vine, and of war, and of political expediency? You 'wise men' reveal your impiety by pretending to own wisdom, rather than borrowing it from the gods, which is what really happens."

    Protagoras clears his throat as he considers how to proceed.

    Lexo looks at his kiosk's sign, which reads

WISDOMRY FOR SALE

    "What is 'wisdomry'?" she asks Protagoras.

    "It's like wisdom," Protagoras replies with a smile.

    "So you're a charlatan? Or are you a clown? Is this a joke?" The priestess is not joking with her question.

    "Wisdomry is my new word for wisdomish things. Inherent in the creation of the word is the notion that wisdom itself is perhaps a fleeting, and ephemeral, and elusive thing. But whatever can best approximate wisdom - whatever can most often achieve the results wisdom ought to achieve - this I am calling 'wisdomry'."

    Lexo shakes her head as she continues along her previous path. "People these days," she mutters to herself.

    Protagoras stands in front of his kiosk looking at his sign for a while, until he decides to change the lettering:

YOUR PROBLEMS' SOLUTIONS

    "So what are the solutions to my problems?" someone asks him while he is still finishing the final word.

    "Wisdomry," he answers, and some around who were there for the earlier conversation briefly laugh.

    Meanwhile, passing nearby with a following crowd of laughter, Chionides the street clown mimes the manner of a haughty Oligarch as he shouts. "Sparta, queen of Hellenic cities, deserves our aid! What sort of Hellenes would we be if we did not send our mighty soldiers to fight beside her once again, and save our queen from the servants who now plague her?" Chionides allows a group of young girls to playfully beat at him with long, soft sheaves of wheat.

Δ

The Athenian Council debates aiding Sparta against the Helots

"Wise councilors, Athena knows the mysteries of wisdom in strategy. I beg you to search for her council in your personal prayers. I am sure she will help you to see the truth - that helping Sparta, while it may seem to aid a city who sometimes seems to be an adversary, in fact would help to pacify that adversary in exactly the way that a good dog is trained - not through punishment and pain, but through care, through security and protection. Spartans are not evil, or stupid. They are merely insulated, and too easily forget that the same wisdom that keeps a hoplite formation demands that Hellenes always remain allies."

"But the Helots are also Hellenes," a fisherman on the council says. "They were Hellenes before the Spartans, in fact."

A man beside him seconds the notion, saying, "The Spartans are Dorians, invaders from the north. Just because it happened generations ago doesn't mean it doesn't count anymore."

"Being Hellenic is not just about where your ancestors were born," suggests a well-liked clam-digger, "but whether you live a Hellenic lifestyle, and adopt Hellenic customs and worship the Hellenic gods."

"No," says a professionless rich man's son, "it's about who your grandparents were, and nothing more. At least, legally."

"I seem to recall it is up to *us* what the laws of Athens shall be, henceforth," suggests the fisherman. "Isn't that why we're a democracy? So whatever the law might be today, the law next year will be whatever we today determine is best. So it doesn't matter so much what the law is, as much as what we think the law ought to be. And when I think about what makes someone something - it's because they act like that thing. Good grandparents can have traitorous, anti-Hellenic grandchildren. It ought to be the sentiment toward Athena in someone's mind that makes them Athenian, I say!"

All the Oligarchs start at once to speak against that sort of unabashed Democrat cosmopolitanism. The Caretaker raps the Stones of Order.

The Spartan ambassador Melanthios steps forward. For a long second, he takes an Aischylean silence to stare at the Athenians before speaking. "Sparta is the strong arm of Hellas. Sparta has come to the aid of Hellas too many times for Hellas to fail her today. King Leonidas and his three hundred staying behind to block the Hot Gates. Pausanias leading the cavalry charge at Plataia. As the heroes throughout Hellas all came to the aid of Menelaos in ancient times to sail to Troi..."

"The Persians invaded our lands, twice. Menelaos' wife was kidnapped," sunken-eyed Myronides retorts. "Those were all righteous, even necessary wars to join. Sparta has enslaved the Messenians and other people who live around them for a century. Perhaps this retribution is not a crime, but justice? It is the Sea God who has wounded you! Is that whom we should wage war against, one of the two major patrons of our own city?"

The council roars with disagreement of every sort.

"Who are you to call servitude unjust?" the finely-dressed old Oligarch Alkibiades shouts. "Hear his truth, wise men of the council. His Democrats would make the slaves the Archons, and the stones the birds, and the rivers the clouds, but they cannot function so! If there is anyone we should all band together in keeping down, it is the slave, is it not? Where none are slaves, *all are slaves.*"

"Helots are not captives fated to servitude by war, or sold by debt, but merely by the bad luck of the location and parentage of their birth," Myronides says. "And every year, Sparta declares war on their people anew, to preemptively account for any violence they want to inflict on any person of that Messenian race. It is indiscriminate and unending siege, and if the workers of the lands of Lakedaemonia find it within their power to rise up and vanquish their overlords, should we not be siding with the more heroic and noble of that battle's participants? No baby is rightly born a slave. Were we not ourselves almost slaves in Persian houses?"

Many on the council cheer in agreement at these sentiments, even some among those Oligarchs who remember fighting the Persian Wars. Only a few Oligarchs make an explicit point of failing to cheer, arms folded.

The slaves at the edges of the room eye their masters on the council, curious where this all could lead, reticent to display desires in the face of Fate.

"WHAT WE SEE WHILE AWAKE IS DEATH,
AND WHAT WE SEE WHILE ASLEEP IS A DREAM."
Pythagoras, *Semicircle*

E

Preisias and the Messenians bide their time on Mount Ithome

Up on Mount Ithome the wind whistles as if it is trying to warn of danger. The plain of Messenia appears miniature far below, like a straw bed spread out nearby, embellished with rows of tiny symbols representing the tents of Spartan soldiers.

Timonos, son of Gylippos the farmer, stands guard over his sleeping family while his father and sister rest at the periphery of the patch of yellow grass where all their fellow refugees huddle in groups on the bare ground.

He gently coaxes a wild goat which has wandered nearby, as finally at long last it approaches near enough to reach for. He can feel the movement of air as it sniffs him.

A stirring behind Timonos startles the goat, and it dashes off the direction it came from, kicking rocks.

Preisias emerges from the shadows between the stones, his leather armor creaking softly. The old Theban warrior's face holds a host of anguishes just at bay, but his eyes keep a mask of gentleness as he watches the boy's shoulders slump in disappointment.

"That was good technique," he says quietly. "Patience. Stillness. You almost had it."

"We need the meat," Timonos mutters, still staring after the vanished goat. The morning mist clings to the mountainside below them, over the valleys where Spartan campfires burn. Up here, their small flock dwindles daily, some to feed the hungry refugees, others lost to the cliffs or eagles. Each escaped goat feels like another small defeat.

"The women tell me you are a farmer's son," Preisias says, settling onto a boulder. "Before all this."

Timonos nods stiffly. "Son of Gylippos. The old and weary. We grew barley. And some olives. For the Spartans." The last words come out bitter enough for him to grimace at the taste of them.

"And now you're a goatherd. And a soldier. And a refugee." The old warrior sighs. "Too many roles for such young shoulders."

"I'm old enough to fight," Timonos protests, but his voice cracks slightly on the words.

"You have always been old enough to fight." Preisias' tone is gentle but his words strike like stones.

The morning wind keens between the rocks like a mourning girl's song. Timonos pictures the mountain tearing at its grassy hair like girls do at funerals. Below, the mist begins to thin, revealing more of the Spartan siege lines encircling the mountain's base.

Letting his tears fall, Timonos moans, "Why must it be now? Why can't it be olden days, or far in the future after all of this is forgotten? I hate that it is now. May it never be now again!"

The Theban thinks a while, nodding understanding, and slightly smiling to appreciate the boy's clever paradox.

After some quiet, he says, "Each god is always somewhere, at every time, child. If grandmother Akhlys Goddess of Suffering were not here with us, then she would be somewhere else with others who would feel it just like we do now, whose experience is not insignificant just because we don't know about it. And Aphrodite, Artemis, and the Muses, though not with us now, *are still out there*, giving joy and inspiration to someone much like you, who is enjoying it just like you would. Just because it isn't happening to you doesn't mean it isn't happening. Believe it or not, the cosmos *is* always balanced. I find some solace at least in that, in my darkest times. The Winds don't know our suffering. They find each day anew with enough goodwill to do their job as they are expected to. And they will blow still when we are down in the Underworld with our ancestors. We can at least try our best to have the same sort of diligent wherewithal."

In view of both Timonos and Preisias, a small blue bird flits down from the sky and lands on the stiff branch of a bush nearby.

"The gods are as real as that blue bird," Preisias says. "And just like her, who was elsewhere until now, and came here for you to see her, they are somewhere out there right now, and sometimes, they will be with you."

The wind picks up again, and Preisias smiles, and stands. "See, there's old Eurus the West Wind. Bringing us the warm breezes of your land of Messenia. Can't you smell the sage? That's the smell of the flowers we walked through the other day - you remember, all those violet spears? They are singing in scent to us now, of your homeland."

The Theban warrior raises his voice gradually throughout his words as he notices some other Messenians gathering close.

"The gods bring us reassurances of our righteousness in small ways," says Timonos' old father as he hobbles up behind his son and takes his shoulders in his hands. "We are truly blessed by the gods to have survived this ordeal this long. Here on the mountain, with this spring and these goats, and each other, we will be safe. You will always have my gratitude, Theban."

Preisias asks, "What of the rest of your Helot people below? You all up here are safe, but this is only a fraction of the population enslaved by Sparta. We do not need to get into the possible ways that the Spartans might be reacting to our rebellion with those who are still under their power."

"Preisias," the elder woman among them, Akantha, says hesitantly, "would you please refrain from calling us Helots anymore? If we are to believe in the future world which we fight for, we ought to change the language we use now to help bring forth that future world, to describe it to the gods. And like we once were, we are again and shall always now be *Messenians*. Henceforth I would like to think that there were only Helots in the past."

Preisias nods, swallowing a tear. "I beg your forgiveness, because I understand what you mean and agree. Still, there are many of your people below, remaining under Spartan threat. Captive Messenians."

"There is no direction down but death," curly-silver-haired Akantha says, and kicks her heel against tough Mother Ge. "All below wish us only to press on, to gain whatever ground we can. The gains add up."

Preisias looks around to gauge the group, then nods his acknowledgement.

"So we shall. Tell the priests to organize the appropriate sacrifices. To Ares Wall-Defender, for courage, skill, and patience, and to Hephaestos Wall-Designer, for we will need more weapons and armor, and to reinforce these simple walls. Consider the least amount of the metal which we have which must be kept as bowls or tools, and give whatever else you can to Korybantos to shape into weaponry. Have the children gather stones for walls. We will fortify, and ready for a long siege."

Akantha slowly approaches Preisias with her arms slowly spreading out, and she gives him a soft but long hug which surprises him. The Theban gathers tears, but keeps them in his eyes. He forces a kind smile for the woman as she parts from him.

To the assembled Messenians, the weary Theban warrior says, "Your great King Korax, through his noble vision and courage, has actually led us into the best possible version of our current situation which we could possibly have found ourselves in. I doubted his strategy, of bringing us to Pylos, before returning here to Ithome, but he was right about the power which the inspiration of your old king's palace would give us all, and the extra time which Sparta spent chasing us about these lands allowed more of your people to join us from among the many farms of Lakedaemonia. We are stronger than we would otherwise be, and more of you are safe than could be. And they are weaker, for having fewer of you to do their work. We should all feel grateful before the Fates' loose weave. Know this - however bad this is, however hard this is, you know it can be worse, and I know it would have been worse. This is our best position. From here, we will heal, and yet gain strength."

"Ares' and Aphrodite's blessings to you, Theban," old Akantha calls out, and all present loudly agree.

As the Messenians are spreading back out to their families, Preisias looks around and notices young Timonos staring down at the inauspicious stars below - those fires of the Spartan camps down on the plain. Timonos sees Preisias approach, and hardens up his body.

"I will kill every Spartan I meet for the rest of my life," Timonos says quietly, but loudly enough to be heard.

"Tell me why you want to risk your life so," Preisias demands, sitting carefully in his armor on the edge of a nearby high rock.

Timonos takes a moment to start, and once he does, his face becomes hard, and tears begin to fall from his eyes despite himself. "Almost ten years ago," he says, "I was just a small boy on my father's farm. And I had an older brother ... Nothon. That brute Hippokoön killed him, just to put fear into Father. He did it right in front of me, and my father, and my mother. Because Nothon was strong. I lived that day because I wasn't strong yet. He put his sword into my brother's heart and just walked away. Told us to plow harder. I will never forget it."

The Theban listens, nodding, instantly compassionate for the boy's story and soon weeping with him. At the end of his story, once it is clear he can say no more, Preisias reaches out to grab the boy in a hug, but then remembers his armor, which could hurt the boy's mostly nude body, so he quickly begins to strip it off, and several long seconds later once his body is also bare and won't hurt the boy, he grabs him tightly in a full-body hug. He grasps Timonos' hair in his hands and holds his mouth close to the boy's ear.

"I will avenge your brother Nothon," Preisias says. He holds him tight for a while longer, trying to let that one line linger in the boy's mind, before he adds, "But we need you at the arrow tower, where you can protect your sister. If he were here, we would put you and your brother there together, but now it is just up to you."

He pulls away and looks into the boy's eyes.

"Live. Protect your sister. Build a great mind out of yourself. Enjoy the beauty of the world. Feel this breeze. It is important for you to live. Do not be fooled into death, boy. Live."

As they are emerging from their embrace, Timonos gasps at the sight of a young woman crawling over a rise and into view, her hand all red with blood and curled to protect the damaged fingers, her arms and shoulders all badly abrased with small rocks still stuck to her.

Niome's eyes meet his.

Timonos runs over to help the injured young woman to stand, and quickly the nearby women among the Messenians swarm her to clean and care for her and find out where she's from.

Timonos stays on the periphery of her care, with his little sister beside him. Before long, his little sister Eleni joins the women caring for Niome, and when she does, Timonos does too, deciding simply to pretend that he is one of them. Quick glances between the women confirm that he will be accepted.

Z

The first Krypteia

Under dark of Nyx, in the yellowing meadow of Artemis Willow-bound, beside that Huntress Goddess' now-toppled temple on the north side of ruined Sparta, hundreds of Lakedaemonian women and children stand together, murmuring so quietly that despite their number the soft wind on the trees can still be heard over them. Above, the Moon is a curved stitching needle, barely visible beside her sister's son, the bright twilight star Hesperos.

Mice listen intently to the fearful quiet from their holes.

Black-veiled Queen-Mother Gorgo stands upon a temporary wooden pedestal at the head of the assembled Spartan women.

"It is almost a new Moon, and a new Earth which she will shine upon. We are not the women we were before the world turned upside-down. We are not the women our ancestors were. We are the women of today!"

The Queen-Mother's closest handmaidens walk among the crowd, handing out crude, cheap, recently-made bronze blades wrapped in leather so fresh there is still hair and blood on some of them. They whisper as they hand out knives, "Keep hidden, steal food, kill at least two. Get their blood on you. Come back bloodless and feel the whip of Artemis."

"Poseidon spared our children!" Gorgo shouts across the assembled women and children. "He spared us women! His earthshaking primarily killed men! And it was to show us that Spartan men are not our power! Nor are our houses, nor the temples to our gods! Spartan *children* are our power! Our children are the blades with which we stab into the future!"

Gorgo's new Helot assistant, a fire-eyed old man named Laomedon, stands beside her and holds high above his head two hands each filled with several gleaming knives all splayed out in two fans.

In the front of the crowd of assembled women and children are Pausanias' family - her cousins Sophronia and Nikeia, and hard old Laothoe, with their various female servants, Laothoe holding young Pleistoanax by the shoulders.

Gorgo beckons Pleistoanax to come and join herself and her own son King Pleistarchos, who stands beside her silently, afraid in the presence of this many Spartan women. Pleistoanax hesitates, clinging to his grandmother for a moment, but when she lets go of him Pleistoanax hangs his head and walks up to the front of the crowd, joining Gorgo and his cousin the king.

Gorgo puts a hand on each boys' back and raises her head so high that her black veil falls back.

Loud enough to be heard in the back, Gorgo shouts, "As soon as they can hold a blade, a Spartan is as powerful as they will ever be! Man or woman! For it is Ares' invention of the blade which rules all, and it is a power which he gave to his lover Aphrodite, our warlike mistress, and only a willing mind is required for any mortal to wield one. A blade of any size can kill!"

The meadow of Artemis Willow-bound shifts shadowed with the crowded dark forms of the entire Lakedaemonian valley's population of women and children, all of whom know that if they were the ones who had stayed home, they would have been in danger from both their own Helots and the rest of these Spartan women here now. All know nowhere is safe tonight. The mothers and grandmothers hold their young ones close, while the young ones silently watch and listen, ever learning.

"As we speak, our own household servants of yesterday skulk and plot as rebellious shadows of tomorrow. They have forgotten why we are their masters, and perhaps so have we. Tonight, we prepare to remind them. But tomorrow night, on Hekate's Supper, no Moon will shine. That is the *kairos*, the moment we must act, the moment in between Time. In that darkest night, that is when we will be the hidden things that come out of shadows to kill. We will run among the ghosts of that darkest night and call them our sisters. Tomorrow night will be a new festival of darkest Nyx, when we noble Spartan women and our children will move out into the shadows to kill Helots in secret."

A hushed murmur erupts upon the crowd as all process what they're being told.

"Never again will Spartan women let our slaves forget what they must fear. Blood will feed Hekate this month, and her hounds of Tartaros and the vengeful spirits of our murdered daughters and sons will run with you through the dark night. Tomorrow night you will be the Secret Ones, you will be the Hidden - the *Krypteia*. Tomorrow night, like Echidna of the deepest cave, you will birth a new world's nightmares - demons never to be rechained in Tartaros, to frighten our enemies' grandchildren's grandchildren until aeons yet to come!"

Spartan grandmothers clutch their blades, looking to each other. All wince with fear in one way or another, though most wear angry masks of bravery over their grapples with grief. Their black-veiled Queen-Mother's voice moves this generation easily, for it is one of the only voices they have ever heard quiet everyone in earshot, no matter who.

Queen-Mother Gorgo shouts, "Tonight *we* are the ghosts of our grandmothers! We are the ghosts of ourselves! And the ghosts of our children. For if we do not do this now, tonight, then we are already dead. Our way of life is dead. Sparta, Lakedaemonia, are dead. So rise up, ghosts, and take back life from the living!"

Newly twenty-one year old King Pleistarchos and his cousin Pleistoanax, who is bigger and more muscled than the king though he's only seventeen, do their best to appear strong and confident, standing beside Gorgo on either side, her hands on their backs since both are now too old to put her hands on their heads as she used to. Their fears are eased, at first, by the knowledge that in most of the tough duties of

Spartan children's education the kings are generally exempt, but at the end of her speech Gorgo steps in front of them and turns to address the royal cousins, and they can feel her coldness fall over them like the shadow of a stormcloud.

"You two will go out together to help each other," Gorgo says to King Pleistarchos as she puts a fine, bronze dagger into his hand. "This blade belonged to your grandmother. It is hungry for two lives. So you'd better feed it before you return. Do you get my meaning?"

Both boys look at the knife with fear and nod.

"And if you lose it, it will find you again, even hungrier. You hear me, Pleistarchos? This dagger will drink your blood if you don't feed it. You are a Spartan. Aren't you?"

Young King Pleistarchos and his teen-aged cousin Pleistoanax side-eye each other nervously.

"Now, go, you kings, and kill unseen."

H

Aischylos and his chorus perform his play The Aigyptians

At the Dionysian theater in Athens, the rugged horse-tender Antiphon sneaks into his seat beside Perikles halfway through Aischylos' second play, a little horn full of raisins in one hand. He offers a raisin to Perikles, who waves him away, slightly annoyed.

On the stage, the twelve men of the chorus lie in a row beneath blankets, acting as if asleep, while Aischylos, in the mask of a princess, sneaks among them holding a prop dagger.

The scene is dark, lit only by lamplight, for the Moon is just a sliver.

"What have I missed?" rough-voiced Antiphon asks.

After a long pause in which Perikles wants not to answer, but Antiphon dully glances between him and the raisins as if patiently waiting, finally Perikles whispers, "These are the daughters of King Danaos of Argos. They've been betrothed to the princes of King Aigyptos of Aigypt, but their father has made them all promise to murder their husbands on their wedding night. But this one, Hypermnestra, has fallen in love with her prince. So I suspect the twist is that she is not going to be killing her love."

"Ooh, interesting," Antiphon nods with a smile. "Her father surely won't like that."

Perikles nods, then gestures to the play as if to say "watch it yourself".

Down in the center of the theater, Aischylos raises his dagger high and sings, "We, my sisters, fair maidens all still aglow with the bloom of maidenhood - how torn our hearts now are, between two demands from our noble father! To love or to kill? The unknown man, who could be anyone - the task of the girl is usually to love whomever she is given to. Can we now do the same, but kill?"

In the stands, Antiphon elbows Perikles. "This is racy, no?" he chuckles. Perikles can only nod.

Each of the members of the chorus then break away from each other, their female Aigyptian masks nearly-smiling demurely, and mime, one after another, but in rapid succession, coaxing to sleep and then silently knife-murdering their new husbands, covering their mouths to silence unheard screams. Each of the daughters of Danaos plant their knife into their new bridegrooms, until the last, the youngest, Hypermnestra, cannot bring herself to, and kisses her man instead, waking him.

The crowd gasps and the rude few murmur.

Θ

Spartan women and children deliver terror in the night

On Noumenia the Moonless Night, the stars above Lakedaimonia seem to throb in the misty air like embers in the ash on the floor of a forest fire.

Mouse families everywhere see owl shadows against the stars.

Spartan women and children spread out across the land of Lakedaemonia, slinking toward Helot farms and villages unseen, hiding in the brush, clutching their primitive knives, prepping their souls for terror.

The dark Eurotas River breathes in the darkness, lapping at the reeds. Nine Helot women crouch in the mud, their children pressed against their backs like baby otters. Steam rises from their fear in the cold air.

"I heard their plans," whispers Kydilla, who serves in Gorgo's kitchen. "They spoke of becoming demons. Of teaching their children to hunt in the darkness." Her hand trembles as she draws a long bronze hairpin from her hair, which tumbles beautifully, unseen. "But there are older magics than theirs."

The youngest mother clutches her baby tighter. "Should we run? Find new homes in other lands? I would rather be a slave in Athens than a Helot here one more day."

"No," says old Alphito, her voice rough as bark. "Running is what prey does. We are not that." She takes the hairpin from Kydilla. "We are daughters of the dark ourselves. Come closer, future grandmothers."

One by one, the women press close. Alphito pricks each woman's thumb with the needle, letting the drops fall into a claw bowl she holds. The children watch silent as rabbits. "Blood calls blood," Alphito chants barely louder than the river's whisper. "Hekate Three-Faced, Daughter of Nyx, hear us. We offer freely what they would take by force."

The other women take up the chant, their voices entwining like snakes on a herald's staff.

Hekate Three-Faced, Daughter of Nyx, hear us now!
Dark Mother, Queen of Crossroads, it is we who birth and die,
who bleed with every Moon, who know Night's secrets true,
take this, our offering, our prayer, our fear, and send us strength!

A young boy whimpers. His mother hushes him with a hand.

White-haired Alphito dips her fingers in the bloody mud, then draws ancient symbols on each woman's forehead which gleam in the starlight. "Make their blades bend. Make their eyes slide past. Make their minds clouded with terror of deeper darkness than their own."

Something moves in the reeds downstream. The women freeze.

But it is only a water snake, its wriggling ripples catching starlight as it swims past. The women watch it go, and something shifts in their eyes. They are no longer prey hiding from hunters. They are something else, something older.

"The Spartans think they invented terror," Alphito whispers, marking the last child's forehead. "But terror was born in the dark with us, with every mother who ever had to hide her children. It knows us well. The dark remembers."

The river laps at mud-sunk feet, taking their blood downstream.

Moonless black enshrouds the humble shelters where Helot field workers sleep. They keep no fire tonight. Only the soft sounds of sleeping, breaths, coughs, and the restless turning of the elderly, reveal they remain.

A child's foot finds a dry twig. The snap is quieter than a wing, but to the Spartan women and children encroaching silently upon the Helot farm, it sounds like thunder. All stop, and the handmaiden of Gorgo who is leading the party, Thelia, raises her hand for stillness.

They are ten women and eight children, all gripping the crude bronze blades which they were given. The youngest, a girl of nine, trembles so hard that her mother has to grip her shoulders to hold her still. None of them have ever killed people before.

No alarm is raised. The sounds of distant sleep continue once the heartbeats of the listeners make room.

Tall, long-limbed Thelia, just a teenager but the most courageous here, signals with her hand, and moves forward with the adult women in the group, their black clothes cloaking them as Nyx. They reach the first shelter's doorway, which stinks of blood magic recently painted.

But something, a scent, or sound, or whisper from a god, wakes the old grandmother inside who is sleeping nearest to the door. Her eyes open to darkness, and her shriek at seeing eyes shatters the quiet.

Chaos floods.

The Spartan women surge forward, brandishing their knives, their children copying, but they are not warriors. Once inside the hut, they hesitate. In that hesitation, the Helots all awake.

A Helot man kicks out the door of another nearby shelter with a mattock in his hands. His wife follows immediately with a cooking knife.

"Demons!" a Helot child shouts from his straw bed. "Demons in the night, Mama!"

The children in the hunting party begin to cry. The spell of silence breaks, and shouts, screams, and the meaty sounds of desperate darkness combat take its place. A Spartan woman goes down, struck by a wooden pole, pinning her small boy beneath her.

More Helots emerge, armed with tools. Strong from their work and fighting for their families, they push the women back into the darkness dragging their children with them. One woman trips and is helped up by her daughter. But she has landed on her knife. After just a few fruitless tugs, her daughter runs to join the other women, leaving her immoble mother there.

"Cowards!" Thelia shouts. "Fight!"

But the Helots surround her with their improvised weapons. A stone flies and meets her head, and the Helot with the mattock fells her, then watches the rest of the shadows vanish into the night.

This clutch of families stand guard till Dawn, hugging their tools, watching the night. The children gather in the central shelter, the old grandmother singing soft songs to soothe. No one sleeps.

Beside Helos, a Helot village on the southern coast of the Eurotas valley, the Sea sits Moonless-dark and quiet but for the creak of ships out on their moorings.

The soft sift of chariot wheels on the coastal sand is dampened as Nikaia, daughter of Laothoe and sister of Pausanias, stands with the reins loose in her hands while guiding her horse-drawn car toward the Helot village slowly, five fellow noble girls trailing behind in a line like dancers, knives akimbo. Symbolically, she wears on her shoulders her dead brother's old breastplate which he wore at the Battle of Plataia, which she has always wanted to wear into War.

Just as they are coming into the edge of the little fishing village, Phlogios, black steed of Pausanias when he lived, who is drawing the chariot, snorts and stops. His ears swivel to the cluster of fishermen's huts ahead.

"Calm," Nikaia whispers, trying to control him, but the horse fights the bit.

The women trailing the chariot gather round it when it slows and look to their leader in the car with uncertainty.

From one of the huts comes the subtle sound of children singing a Messenian lullaby to themselves.

Nikaia reins Phlogios forward.

But Phlogios plants his hooves in the sand, and refuses to move into the village from its edge. Nikaia snorts, herself, then gets down from the chariot car to approach her brother's noble old horse from the side, while signaling her companions to each attack different huts in the village.

When her hand touches him, Phlogios rears up tall, nearly kicking Nikaia.

She jumps back.

Phlogios screams loud and steamy, shattering the silence of the night - a war cry which he was known for years ago, when carrying Pausanias into battle.

Before Nikaia can grasp his reins, he lunges forward, breaking free of the chariot's car with terrible strength, shattering it in two. The horse thunders forward toward the huts.

Lamps flare to life inside each home. Families emerge from doorways, adults shouting. But Phlogios has eyes only for the children. He separates and then circles two, screaming challenge at the approaching Spartan girls, his hooves marking out a boundary in the sand as he turns and circles.

The two small boys press against the horses' flanks instinctively. Phlogios lowers his head, eyes rolling to keep the Spartan girls in view, steam rising from his nostrils in the cold night air.

Nikaia wields her blade, but her hand shakes in the presence of such seemingly forceful fate. One of her companions whispers loudly, simply, "Gods."

The horse who carried her brother in War stares at bold Nikaia. She remembers suddenly, with terrible clarity, how Pausanias used to feed him figs, how the horse would lip them gently from his palm. These eyes, though, seem more like Pausanias'.

Adult Helot men and women shout curses at the girls behind Nikaia, who shout back threats, flashing their knives.

Nikaia gestures generally to tell the other girls to attack, and they all spread out with their expensive daggers to do what violence they can. But her eyes remain locked in with the horse's as it nudges the two Helot boys to climb onto its neck and broad back. They cling to Phlogios' thick black mane, trembling, following the gesturing hand of Fate.

With one last challenging snort to Nikaia, Phlogios lifts his strong neck to slide the second boy back onto his back with his brother, turns, and canters into the darkness, away from the village, toward the distant woods, while the aristocratic killers spread innocent blood.

A cave in Mount Menelaion hides a clutch of fearful Helots who feel safe enough, deep in the dark, to tell a story.

"When the Dorians first came down from the north," the old woman whispers, "they did not yet know how to be cruel. That was something they learned, slowly, generation by generation, like farmers learning which crops grow best in which soil."

The cave's small hanging fire catches the tears in her eyes. Around her, children huddle close - not just her grandchildren but all the young ones from the nearby farms, brought here to hide on this moonless night while their parents make preparations elsewhere.

"Tell us again about King Nestor," one small boy asks. "Before the Spartans came."

"A hundred ships he sent to Troi, our King Nestor. A hundred ships full of free men, not slaves. In those days, our grandfathers' grandfathers walked these hills with straight backs. In those days--"

Something moves in the darkness beyond the fire's eye.

The old woman stops mid-word. For a moment, no one breathes.

"Mother!" A teen-aged girl nearest the back of the cavern screams as hands grab her from behind. Other shapes emerge from deeper passages in the rock. The Spartans have found another way in.

The fire pot goes out with a crash. Darkness floods the cave.

Children scream. Metal scrapes on stone. Words are swallowed by chaos.

"Run!" the old woman shouts. "Remember! Run!"

The children flee like startled birds, some toward the cave's mouth, others deeper into the tunnels. Their screams echo, multiplying in the darkness until it seems like the entire mountain is a stifled cry.

A knife finds the old woman's throat as her last thought is of King Nestor's ships, their sails bright against a bronze sky, and the children scatter into the Night like seeds cast by an angry god.

This night, many nightmares which will haunt the living world for generations are first born redly screaming, and none who survive it ever again mistake the darkness for being empty.

"BESIDE THE FATES AND OLD DEATH WAS ACHLYS,
ANCIENT GODDESS OF SUFFERING, CAKED DRY WITH FILTH,
SUNKEN WITH THIRST, KNEES SWOLLEN, NAILS OVER-LONG,
NOSTRILS BLOODY, DUSTY FACE MUDDY WITH TEARS,
JAW CLENCHED, EYES WIDE, EVER-GRINNING."
Hesiod, The Shield of Herakles

I

King Pleistarchos and Pleistoanax feed the knife blood

King Pleistarchos and Pleistoanax hide together just outside a quiet Helot farm, deep in the darkest night.

A heron watches from the reeds, well-fed from fishing, its body white in the blackness like a little moon.

All lights inside the hut have been put out to feign that there is no one home, but in the otherwise utterly black moonless darkness the faint red throb which emanates from the few embers which they have kept alive in their fireplace belies that there are likely Helots huddled inside.

"They hide from us," twenty-year-old King Pleistarchos whispers. "They fear us. If you and I go up to them, that will be exactly what they fear coming true."

Teen-aged Pleistoanax nods, his face streaked with tear tracks through dust, though his heart is now too dry to cry more. Now he just stares, unblinking, thinking.

"You have to help me. You can't make me do this myself," King Pleistarchos pleads to his cousin.

Stone-facedly, Pleistoanax whispers, "I don't want to do this any more than you do, but you know that we have to. It's kill or be killed. That's life. We don't get out of this just because we're royal. Your mother will kill us."

Pleistarchos shakes his head. "Maybe we can devise a clever alternative. Like Odysseos might do."

Pleistoanax chews on his lips, tasting his own blood. "Odysseos didn't hesitate to kill," he whines, fearing that there may be no way out.

"He did sometimes," the young king offers. "Sometimes he did something else instead, some clever ruse, or dressing up as a woman, or something..."

Pleistoanax shakes his head, sucking on the blood from his own lip between sentences. "It all leads to killing. It's all so someone can kill someone. It doesn't matter if it's you or not. If it's me or not. People will die. My father let a slave kill him. I never knew him. But the slave who killed him is a good person. Her name is Niome. She fled with the other Helots. And I hope she's alright, wherever she is."

The young king turns to his cousin with distant eyes, swinging between eye contact with Pleistoanax and the most distant darkness. "Sparta is cursed," distant-eyed King Pleistarchos whispers. "But maybe those who die never really lived. Maybe once life is over, it never happened."

Pleistoanax shakes his head, confused, frightened, haunted by bedtime stories of bloodthirsty phantoms who roam the night and pretend to be loved ones. He genuinely wonders if he's really awake.

"Maybe it's better that some people die." King Pleistarchos rises to his full height and strides toward the farmhouse, loping through darkness and making no effort to hide.

Pleistoanax follows not far behind, only to avoid being left alone in the deep dark. He quietly whimpers as he creeps.

"The blade only needs blood," the Agiad king of Sparta says to the night around him. "She didn't say we have to kill everyone we meet. Just bring some blood out."

Pleistoanax finally finds more tears to cry. Though he keeps his face hard, his voice shakes as he asks, "Whose blood?"

Young-hearted King Pleistarchos sees his cousin's fear and swallows his own. Lifting the blade slowly so as not to frighten Pleistoanax, Pleistarchos slowly drags the sharp blade into the skin of his chest, opening it up, gently whining against the pain and the warm release of wine-dark blood in a river between two ribs.

"No!" Pleistoanax cries out, confused, but also understanding.

Neither of them look, but they hear the Helots inside the building whimper unseen.

"I know," King Pleistarchos grunts, weaving strength and pain in his mind. "I know what I can take. I know how much it takes to feed the dark gods and their attendant spirits. I know what my mother doesn't even know. I know the depths of the great darkness, Pleistoanax." He laps at his own tears around the edges of his mouth as he has seen his mother do. "I know everything, Pleistoanax. I know everything I need to know."

The king cuts himself again, slowly, on the other side of his chest, releasing much more blood down his torso, grimacing. He puts his other hand into the streaming blood, lets some dam up and pour over it, then wipes it warmly on his face, creating a Haidean mask, spitting it off his lips.

Pleistoanax stares through low eyes at the king's red face in the darkness, hunched down into himself like a baby bird trying to vanish. Tears stream from him, but no sound.

The king wipes his blood carefully up and down the blade. "Now, I hope, I beg of all the darkest gods, that this cursed blade is satisfied," Pleistarchos whispers cautiously to Pleistoanax, sitting across the shadows from him, and sets the knife upon a rock between them.

Pleistoanax thinks about what Pleistarchos has said, looking with horror at the knife, then gasps in relief and begins to weep thunderously like a river during a storm.

Inside the house where the Helots huddle, the two royal cousins can hear whispered fearful prayer songs.

King Pleistarchos puts his cloak over his cousin, to quiet him but also to hide the wicked world from him, and because he has seen mother birds do similar. Pleistoanax stares blindly, warmed within his cousin's bloody cloak.

K

Aoide is freed from her cell

Moonlight falls through the high window, making the two old Pythia skeletons glow. Aoide has stopped flinching when she looks at them. After a season or more in this room, they feel almost like companions now, these women who were once vessels for Apollo's voice before they were bones. Aoide has never asked about them, but through context clues has come to understand that they were Pythia centuries ago, and have been revered that long as bones.

"Sappho's early verses were all riddles," young Eromede says, setting down her wine cup. Of the three currently-living Pythia, she's the only one who visits Aoide regularly here where their old servants keep her secret. Aoide is always glad for her company. "But her later ones, they cut like knives straight to the heart."

"Are they riddles, or are they mysteries? Is there a difference?" Aoide asks, thinking of songs she used to sing with Dikasto.

Eromede replies simply by singing.

> *The Moon and Seven-Sister stars have set.*
> *In the middle of the night, time flows,*
> *and I slumber ever-alone.*

Aoide smiles. "I love it when she just experiments with our expectations of rhyme or rhythm. Or makes their usage unexpectable. It feels like such beautiful, realistic chaos!"

"And yet, just words," Eromede says.

Aoide glances at the skeletons. "Some kinds of loneliness are better than others."

"Are you faring alright here in the mountains?" Eromede asks her.

Aoide shrug-smiles. "I know that I'm being protected. But I don't understand from what. But I am grateful. But ... if safety is another chain ... then I may just need to reject safety itself."

Eromede eyes her carefully. "Well, we won't let you flee, child, so don't think about it too hard."

Aoide glances again at one of the old Pythia skeletons. "The old ladies say she used to sing to the sacred snakes, songs no one else could hear. I think," she says carefully, "that maybe mystery and clarity are just different kinds of truth."

"Careful," Eromede smiles. "You're starting to sound like a poet."

"Isn't that what got me locked in here? Speaking dangerously?"

"You're here because you know the difference between a song that pleases and a song that changes things. Between pleasure and power." She nods toward their silent audience. "Just like they did. And the men who think they run our temple always fear the introduction of a new female of potency. But we are working to make room for you back at the temple. It will just take time. Like all things."

The moonlight shifts. For a moment, the skeletons seem to lean forward, eager to hear more. But they keep their secrets, as they have for generations.

"They say Themistoke sang at her own funeral," Eromede says. "No one wrote down the words."

"Why not?"

"Because some songs are too true to survive."

Aoide scoffs. "Or because it didn't really happen."

"I'll tell you something about Themistoke that isn't in the official histories," Eromede says, refilling both their cups, mixing water into the wine.

Interrupting Eromede, the door opens. Opho enters followed by Aigisthenia, and a couple of their attendant elder women. They've brought more wine, and a small hanging brazier that fills the room with sweet smoke.

"We come with Skythian smoke!" Aigisthenia laughs happily.

"Telling tales?" Opho asks, but her smile is warm. She swings the brazier near to the skeletons, casting their shadows hugely onto the wall.

"She should know what kind of company she's keeping," Eromede says, taking Aoide in a little one-armed hug.

"Themistoke could smell lies, they say," Opho says. "Even before she became Pythia. They say that's why Apollo chose her, because she was already doing his work in her own way."

Aoide asks carefully, "Apollo chooses the Pythia? What about old Echidna?"

The Pythia all smile at each other.

"She caught the temple treasurer stealing," Eromede adds. "Just by the way he walked. Said his shoes were carrying too many secrets."

"But it was Aristonike who truly mastered prophecy's art," Aigisthenia says. Her voice drops lower, becoming music. "She spoke in patterns so perfect even the gods had to pause and admire them. Every word a pearl, every sentence a necklace fit for Aphrodite herself. She really knew how to move the minds of men."

The three Pythia exchange glances in the brazier-light. Some message passes between them, quick as lightning. Aoide begins to wonder if she is somehow being tested by these women. She imagines herself as a Pythia, but doesn't want to ask if that is what they are testing her for, because she feels like she ought to either know or not know, but not ask.

"Tell her about the rings," Opho says softly.

"And when Aristonike died," Aigisthenia finishes, "they found her rings had left permanent grooves in her fingers, like the spirals inside shells. And when she died, they found a swarm of bees had made their home in her roof beams. Still there, I believe." She shows some soft, barely-visible grooving on a finger bone.

As Aoide is looking closely at the ancient Pythia's finger bone, the brazier flames suddenly leap higher, startling her, and her little jump startles all the Pythia. All four women gasp and then laugh together, only finally hearing the distinctive rhythm of Kliko's walk, accompanied by another set, lighter, quicker, once they find a break in their laughter.

When the door opens, the rush of fresh air makes the flames dance wildly. The Pythia skeletons' shadows dance against the wall.

Kliko enters first, her face unreadable as stone. But it's Hydna behind her who carries a foggy white robe, folded so carefully it seems to glow in the dim light, white and gold. Hydna's strong hands tremble slightly holding the garment with such delicate care.

"It is time," Kliko says.

Aoide starts to rise, but Hydna steps forward first, holding out the folded cloth.

"The gods have spoken through many voices," Eromede says formally.

Opho adds, "They have tested you, watched you, judged you. Now they have decided."

Aigisthenia whispers with a smile, "It was us, *we* chose you."

Kliko's face betrays nothing. "You are to be freed," the old priestess says. "No longer a servant of the temple, but one of its caretakers. A priestess in your own right. You will work with the Pythia, Aoide. They have chosen."

Hydna carefully unfolds the white cloth she holds - a priestess' robe made of gauze and shedded snake-skin with a single thread of gold at the hem. Aoide stares at it, understanding slowly dawning.

"But first," Opho says quietly, "you must tell us what you see."

Aoide pauses with the priestess' garb before her. She thinks.

"I see that this robe is not a gift but a binding. Another kind of cage, just larger than the last." She meets Kliko's eyes with intentional drama. "But I accept it. Because some cages are also wings."

The three Pythia exchange glances. Hydna's hands tighten on the robe. Kliko's stern face softens slightly.

"Well said," Eromede murmurs.

"Am I safe?" Aoide asks, eyeing the Pythia to remind them what they had just talked about.

Opho just nods. "Kliko and Hydna have made sure the temple is safe for you now. Goryntas has been mollified, and ... let's just say he has moved on." She smiles slyly. "Men have been moved, who remember what happened. And the other men have been reminded where the power here really lies."

Hydna steps forward with the robe and drapes the translucent snakeskin around Aoide's shoulders, and the combination of the weight of the gold thread and the ephemeral barely-there-ness of the shedded snake skin make Aoide feel simultaneously heavy as Mount Parnassos and airy as a cloud, and somehow the combined feeling reminds her of her black vision of the Sun circle, which, when she wants to, she can still see the faintest hint of, burned into her memory if not her actual eyes.

Λ

The Athenian Assembly votes again on aiding Sparta

Athenian men are gathered at the Pnyx hill once again for the Assembly. Roiling marbleized clouds overhead move fast, whirling at their edges, dropping just a haze of soft raindrops. The trees that surround the field of the Pnyx sway and shiver in the damp wind.

"Zeus' hand moves," someone whispers to his friends.

Kimon moves through a sea of assuring backslaps from those who have fought with him as he heads toward the bema.

Perikles and Ephialtes stand with some other men from their neighborhood, Perikles wincing in weather which he would normally bring an umbrella to.

"An army of All-Hellenes marches. All those who consider themselves brothers in civilization, who worship the gods of Hellas, are gathering in fraternity to fight at Sparta's side against those who threaten her very life." Kimon pauses, and squints at the Assembly.

"Enslaved Messenians," someone interjects.

"Helots, the Spartans call them," another man adds with disdain.

Kimon asks, annoyed, "Do Athenians count themselves among that host of modern men? Or is our place at the head of that great and noble table of Hellenic civilization to be given up, to be usurped by Thebans, or Makedonians, or Thrakians?"

The Skythian city-slave archers who flank the bema chuckle to each other at this comment, and seeing that reaction from those captive foreigners particularly stirs any feelings of superiority among the men of Athens spread out across the Pnyx.

"I say Athens is still at the head of the Hellenic table," Kimon continues, projecting confidence, "and of course we ought to join our brothers in protecting our own, as they would do to protect us. Who here truly believes that if Athens were threatened we wouldn't see Spartans coming over the rise?"

"Yeah, because they'd be the threat," someone says, and many laugh.

Kimon glares at the joke, and stutters for a moment over trying to protest, but quickly snorts and decides to ignore it.

"We are the best of men. I know that you will vote to do what is right, and send an army under my command to go and join the rest of the Hellenes in bringing aid to Sparta in their time of need. Do what is right, Athenians."

Kimon steps down from the bema.

The herald holds high his snake-staff. "Will we send an army under Kimon to join the cities of All-Hellas in giving aid to Sparta?"

Morosely, but with a sense of gravity and honor, a slight majority of the Athenian Assembly raises their hands to send Kimon with an army to the Peloponnese, to aid the Spartans. It is difficult to tell just from the raising of hands which side really won, but those deemed the losing side do not challenge the decision.

Those who voted in the minority bemoan that it will be the end of Athens, and while the war party congratulating Kimon are starting a cheer, the anti-war party begins a chant, repeating "Rabbit trap! Rabbit trap!"

M

Ephialtes and Perikles discuss Democratic tactics

The Temple of Herakles Protector-From-Evil has come to serve as a secondary gathering spot for the Democrats, situated as it is just a stone's throw down the street from Themistokles' old Democrats Club House, which is now owned by his first wife and her new husband, who have evaded participating in politics since Themistokles' exile. The common presence of actors at this particular gym has long been enough to keep the Oligarchs away, and that absence of Oligarchs has also helped to encourage the current disproportion of Democrats.

Ephialtes is jumping a loop of rope, in a new fashion which men from Kos have recently introduced as an exercise. Perikles stands beside him, lifting heavy stones over his head in the old way.

Between jumps, Ephialtes windedly says, "You know, friends, maybe this is the time for us to make a big move. Now hear me out."

Perikles puts down his stone, sits on it, and gives Ephialtes his full attention.

"With Kimon away from Athens for at least a month or two, that is when we reveal my proposal! With his leadership absent from the discussion, I'm sure we'll have a -- well, it won't be a sure thing, but it's the best conditions I can think of, for us to succeed." He stops jumping and wipes his oily face with a rag.

"It is a risk, though, as well," Perikles notes. "If Kimon goes out and gathers glory on the battlefield, he could come home even more beloved and empowered than he left. Every battle is a chance to die or be wounded, but it's also a chance to save the lives of others and show the gods your skill. You've fought with Kimon, you should know. Sending him into battle is a guaranteed way to give him even more glory."

"But he'll be out of town. That's what's important. Like they say - out of sight, out of mind. If he gains a little glory in battle, that's fine. It's not like he doesn't already have that. The people's minds won't change about him just because he has a little more of what he already had. But his absence during this debate will completely change the way it would go."

Perikles pauses, thinks, and nods.

Ephialtes says, "I remember my mother told me once that there is a special time for everything, and that the finest things can only be done within their fleeting perfect time - the *kairos*. Like the hole the shuttle must pass through when weaving. It can happen only then, only there. Or the moment the arrow must be fired to hit its target. Last time, we missed the mark, because we fired too late. We took Kimon on when he was here at home. But the loop of opportunity which we must fire through, that is when Kimon is away! This is then. That is now. This is our moment."

"LET A MAN FIRST LEARN TO FIGHT BY DARING MIGHTY DEEDS,
NOT WHERE THE ARROWS MISS, GUARDED BY SHIELDS,
BUT FIGHTING UP CLOSE HAND-TO-HAND, CAUSING WOUNDS,
WITH HIS LONG SPEAR OR HIS SWORD, TAKING ENEMY LIVES."
Tyrtaios, Spartan Poet

N

Kimon leads the Athenian army into the Peloponnese

Kimon marches a contingent of veteran Athenian soldiers all loyal to him past Eleusis, Megara, Isthmia, and Argos on the way into the Peloponnese, toward Lakedaemonia, the land of Sparta. Just past Argos and its great Temple of Hera Argive, the ancient lake at Lerna lies in a swampy lowland between the mountains and the sea.

Kimon's top lieutenant Hagnon explains to a younger man, "Lerna is supposedly one of the few entrances to the Underworld. Local legend says that no man who has tried to reach the lake's bottom has ever returned to the surface. In legendary days it was home to the many-headed dragon *Hydra* whom Herakles defeated with fire, and local merchants often assure travelers that creatures of that sort still haunt the swamp. But don't worry, they don't. Herakles dealt with that long ago, for all of us. Imagine being bold enough to destroy all the monsters for posterity ever-after!"

Armies from Thebes and Lokris are gathered here at Lerna on their way to aid Sparta. Both armies are singing songs about All-Hellas in a spirit of internationalism, but Kimon has his men start singing a distinctly Athenian song by the old poet-statesman Solon as they disperse to gather water at Lerna's famous wells.

> *We sing as heralds of Salamis Island's fame,*
> *Instead of speech we sing this tale in rhyme,*
>   *For it was we who fought to save Ajax's lovely isle,*
> *And put away dishonor for all time*
>   *As we grow old we may learn many words and names*
>   *But the minds of the gods will always hide*

"It was the daughters of King Danaos who discovered these wells," the wellkeeper says, just making small talk, as Kimon leads the Athenian lines into Lerna. "Each is named after a different Danaan princess. So your men can go fill up at the Well of Aktaia, over there near the canal, beside that group of Thebans at the Well of

Bryke."

"I see them," Kimon nods, noting the group of Thebans with their distinctively side-notched Boeotian shields. "Thank you, friend."

As Kimon leads his Athenian soldiers to the well he has been pointed toward, the wellkeeper walks along with him and keeps chatting about what he's been seeing over the past few days as armies from every city across Hellas have been passing through. "Yesterday the Tegeans were here, with the men from Qorinth, and the previous day the Megarans came through."

The leader of the Theban contingent approaches Kimon with a flirtatious swagger. "Epaminondas of Thebes," the man says, introducing himself with a less-than-subtle flex of his pectoral muscles.

"Kimon of Athens," Kimon says with a respectful nod. "I see Thebes sends her best men."

"We are the Sown Men!" Epaminondas declares with a sudden rush of enthusiasm, rattling his armor. He grasps his sword hilt, but only in a ceremonial way. "We're the sons of the men who grew out of the dragon's teeth which Kadmos sowed upon first founding our city."

Kimon nods. "I've heard of your men, of course."

"Dark days in Lakedaemonia," says a passing old man hobbling by on his short cane, interjecting into the two men's conversation. "Death day and night, a cursed land!"

Epaminondas unpuffs himself and nudges Kimon with his shoulder. "Today great Sparta has their day of danger, and it is we who must protect them! Nice of the gods to provide a bit of balance in the world!"

Kimon raises an eyebrow and says, "Perhaps there is a limit to the usefulness of keeping slaves. I find more than a few unwieldy."

Epaminondas chuckles and shrugs. "You ever wonder if we ought to just let their slaves kill them, and then just split their land among the rest of us? I mean, it's not like Gorgo wouldn't do the same to our cities."

"You think an officeless woman is the one running things in Sparta?" Kimon asks with derision in his eyes.

Kimon and the Theban commander both look up as the rising clatter of distant armor heralds the arrival of yet another squadron of Hellenic soldiers - these men from the town of Sikyon, heralded by their shields which bear monstrous, triple-headed eastern chimeras.

"Here comes Eupompos and his Chimeras," Epaminondas comments to Kimon. Then he nudges him and adds, "They're all hiss and no bite. I fought beside them at Plataia. Mostly shepherds' sons."

Kimon gives a soldierly smile and asks the Theban, "Weren't you in the center, Thebes and Sikyon, at Plataia? You in the center saw some of the hardest fighting. I saw that big Persian brute with the giant axe that you all had to take on."

Epaminondas nods, remembering. "In the center, yes, beside the cowardly Sikyonians who think fighting is shouting. And yes, that axe giant, I remember him. An Aithiopian he was, not a Persian."

"Well, they all become Persian, under Persia's yoke. That's the curse of Empire. Your Fate knotted like the Gordion Knot with the will of one power-mad King of Kings, King of Souls."

"Yes, but I mean this man was from Aithiopia. Anyway, two of my Sown Men took that brute down, skewered with a spear from each side. You must have been on the left, then, I suppose, with the Athenians, of course?"

Kimon stares into the distance of the past. "We were on the left, yes."

"I'll never forget that hillside," Epaminondas reminisces, clearly back there in his mind. "I never want to return. Have you been back since?"

"To Plataia?" Kimon asks. "I have. On business."

"O right, you're some kind of big important man with many different sorts of concerns, I suppose," Epaminondas chides. "They clean up the bodies?"

"At Plataia?" Kimon asks. "Yes, of course. You can buy Persian bones from that battlefield in the Agora at Athens today."

Epaminondas shakes his head at that. "Merchants and vultures. No one respects the blood of the soldier, as no one but the soldier knows that no blood is nobler."

Kimon says, "Everyone's blood is the same. Courage and honor are not about giving blood. Sweat and cum are what a living man of vigor must produce. A useful soldier keeps his blood."

Ξ

Phaenarete guides a friend through a challenging childbirth

Early morning, in the dark before Dawn, sweet-eyed Phaenarete crouches in a birthing hut with her younger friend Semele and a leather-skinned old priestess of Artemis Who-Soothes named Krakea.

"You'll be fine," Phaenarete tells her friend Semele. "I've been through this. It will hurt, but Artemis will see you through. Don't be afraid if you see a little blood. It's normal."

Semele smiles weakly, gripping her older friend's hand for comfort.

Wrinkle-eyed Krakea throws down some ritual blankets and then carefully kneels before Semele's open knees.

For many long hours, Phaenarete sits with her friend while the older woman bathes and coaxes the hopeful mother's squirming birth canal, variously cooing and shouting for Semele to try harder. But only blood and water and birth fluids pour out from her.

Phaenarete keeps petting Semele's ever-sweatier hair and letting her clutch and grasp at her hand and dress. The younger woman groans and whimpers, but never shouts or cries, hoping it will lead to stories of how brave she was.

Until finally she gasps and bellows out an uncontrollable cry, at which Krakea rises from her thighs with blood-soaked hands.

Finally Krakea creaks, "The child will not come. I'm sorry, but only one of you will survive. It is time to turn to the old Blade of Artemis."

Phaenarete's heart jumps with fear. She has seen the old antler knife used, but only in the most dire circumstances, and never with positive ends. Seeing it reached for summons visions of blood. Without realizing, her horror starts to escape her through a fearful moan.

The wise old midwife stops Phaenarete with a calming shush, "Sh sh sh, it is Artemis Protector-of-Girls. It is Artemis herself, the goddess as a tool. It is an ancient way. Shhh, girl-child, let the goddess work," as she pulls down from the wall the ancient hewn-antler known as the Blade of Artemis.

Phaenarete keeps her eyes on Semele, and clings to the weeping woman's hand. "I promise, Semele," Phaenarete whispers sweetly, "the pain will not last forever. You are not alone." Sweet-eyed Phaenarete's instincts to soothe overtake her terror just barely.

Golden-haired Semele, just a few years younger than Phaenarete and born in the same neighborhood, clings to her older friend's eye contact like a drowning sailor.

The midwife Krakea pushes Phaenarete back again to give herself space to straddle Semele's hips. The half-lame but keen-eyed and true-handed old woman feels carefully along Semele's stomach, tapping with the antler blade after her touches.

"Please, don't cut me with the antler," Semele begs.

"Artemis Protector-of-Girls is here to help you, girl," Krakea coos. "Trust the Wild Goddess."

Phaenarete shrinks back, transformed into a younger version of herself by the old woman's words and tone. She hovers as if ready to help, but really knows she is frozen.

"Cry out, child," Krakea tells young Semele. "Let the goddess hear your prayer! Cry out to wake your child within! Words are but imperfect crying! Cry, child, cry!"

Carefully, surely, as Semele screams, Krakea pushes the antler into her skin and guides it downward, slicing a long portal into the young woman's belly. Old Krakea reaches in and parts the skin, then uses the blade carefully again to open the womb within.

Phaenarete's mind goes blind with horror. She is looking, but she can hardly process what she sees. She just keeps gripping Semele's hand and petting her hair and cooing, "It's alright," unheard over the curdling screams which fade to whimpers quickly, and then last breaths.

Phaenarete finally realizes that she can hear herself saying "It's alright" softly, and that her friend's head is limp.

Krakea opens young Phaenarete's eyes with her thumbs, and sighs a long sigh.

"You are so kind, child. I am sorry that you had to be here when Hera took your friend and her boy. Artemis does not always win this struggle."

Phaenarete finally lets herself start to weep, and falls against Semele's golden curls.

"Go and hug your baby," Krakea tells Phaenarete, petting her hair.

Phaenarete masks her tears throughout her walk home, but as soon as she is inside her own house with only little Sokrates by her side, her tears burst.

Sokrates throws his little arms around his sobbing mother.

"Mother, what's wrong?" he asks her, already sympathetically crying himself but not knowing why.

"I'm okay," is all she can sniffle between her gasping sobs for a while.

Sokrates trots over to their water basin and scoops up some water for his mother in a little clay cup.

While she is finding her breath and receiving his cup, Sokrates' friend Chaerephon's voice shouts from down the street, "Sokrates! Come play!" His spindly legs carry him crashing into their doorframe moments later.

"O please, Dew-drop," his mother Phaenarete pleads lovingly, "stay inside with me today instead of running off with your friends. Stay inside with me and listen to another story about some animal or other."

"Alright mother," Sokrates says with a kind smile. He apologizes with his eyes to Chaerephon.

Chaerephon does not hide his dismay, and even groans at the ground for a moment, but Phaenarete will not release wriggling Sokrates from her grasp, so his friend eventually squeaks and runs back off among the shadows and their pedestrians.

"Thank you, my sweet baby," Phaenarete says between kisses into her son's hair before finally releasing him to his own volition.

He remains on her lap for a while despite his freedom.

"Chaerephon needs me," Sokrates says. "He doesn't have a sweet and loving mother like I do, so he needs kindness from me like a lost baby goat needs milk from a bucket. I'm like a bucket for him."

"You're right, Dew-drop, I know that," his mother agrees, petting his hair proudly. "It's kind of you to spend time with him and be kind to him. You're a good bucket."

"His mother was driven mad by Dionysos," Sokrates says, repeating what he has heard.

"Yes," his mother simply agrees. "But it isn't kind to tease her about it; she struggles against the god's affliction. It is easy not to see the struggles that women hide." Phaenarete struggles to maintain a stiff face, but her emotion underneath shudders it despite her efforts, and as she keeps trying to smile at Sokrates, nevertheless several tears fall down her cheeks.

"O Mother," Sokrates coos, "what's wrong?"

Phaenarete tries to shake her head to brush it off, but Sokrates crawls up to her bodily and forces her to take him into a hug, which makes her laugh with loving gratitude.

"I am so thankful that the gods gave me such a son," she says to him, and she kisses her hand and touches the little nearby idols of her ancestors that sit at the edge of the hearth.

"You made me what I am," Sokrates says into her armpit.

"I was just the doorway the gods let you into the world through," Phaenarete sighs, wiping her tears with one hand while clinging to the boy in her lap with the other. "You've made yourself this good young man. I'm so glad I got to be your mother, Dew-drop."

"What made you cry, though?" he asks again, looking sweetly up to her eyes.

Phaenarete slows her breathing to keep from crying again, then finds her son's innocent eye contact and says with dispassion, "My friend Semele has been pregnant with a child, you know. But Hera must have been looking away, or angered somehow, or something, because ... Semele died today. The baby just wouldn't come out, and ... Hera wouldn't save her."

Sokrates, only half-joking, whispers, "Maybe the baby just didn't want to be born."

Phaenarete snorts a disgusted sob at that thought, and twists her face in confusion and grief, not knowing how to respond.

"I'm sorry," Sokrates cries, overcome with empathy for what his mother has described and embarrassed about what he just said. His mother tries to cheer herself up at the sight of her son's tears.

"O, no no, I'm sorry that I shared that with you," she says, wiping his tears with a fold of her dress. "It's too hard and sad to share with someone your age. You're still supposed to be living in the world of birds and nymphs and honeybees and flowers, not vultures and demons and wasps and weeds."

"No, it's okay, Mother," Sokrates says. "I want to know. I'm old enough. I want to help you with what's hard. I'm tough. Did the baby live?"

Phaenarete looks at Sokrates and squints, drops one tear, but keeps the other, and shakes her head but says to him, "Yes."

Sokrates, looking into his mother's eyes, sees that she is lying, but tries to smile at the fiction she's presented.

After a few moments of thought, he asks her, "Is it possible to find out what Hera would have wanted that we didn't do?"

Phaenarete sighs and shrugs. But then she shakes her head again and says, "It might be."

She sits looking into the hearthfire for a long time, clearly thinking about that, while Sokrates plays with a lock of her hair, until finally Phaenarete pulls Sokrates close and whispers to him, "Thank you for staying home with me today. Sometimes I think you must be an oracle of some kind, Dew-drop. Because you help me understand my own mind better. Dew-drop, I'm supposed to be teaching you!"

Phaenarete tickles Sokrates, who giggles profusely.

Their husband and father suddenly rises from his bed, where he had been napping. "Ugh," he grunts half-awake yet startled from a now-forgotten dream, "I forget what I was just running from." He looks around and finds the amused faces of his wife and son. "What birds are singing?" he asks, to find the time of day.

Phaenarete sniffles, "Day birds, darling. It is day." She goes over to him and sweetly caresses his hairy back.

"I need a bath," he grunts. "Again I have sweated as I slept."

"Dear husband," Phaenarete sniffs, "first, I want to tell you what your fine son has just inspired in me, when we were talking just now. I've decided that I want to dedicate myself to work just like you do - only to the work of midwifing. I want to learn what can be done better. I want to help women."

"O gods," Sophroniskos groans playfully, grabbing his wife and hugging her tightly again. "This is how you find good love, Sokrates - you look for the most difficult woman in the neighborhood, and that's how you'll know you've found the right one!"

The husband laughs with a big roll of his eyes, then, and kisses the wife, just as a flashback memory starts her crying again.

"O now what is this?" Sophroniskos jokes, unaware of the previous emotional strain. "I was only joking, sweet-one! Women, and their inscrutable emotions. Man will never know peace, Sokrates! Know what I mean?"

Sokrates tries but struggles to smile, thinking, worrying, unsure.

ATHENS

O

The armies of All-Hellas meet to aid Sparta against the Helot army

Hellenic armies have gathered in a valley west of Mount Taygetos, in the land that used to be called the kingdom of Messenia, now thought of as simply the windswept western Peloponnese. Few live in this region anymore, and it is called a cursed land. Here, at the foot of Mount Ithome, armies from every Hellenic city within marching distance have gathered together to support their Spartan allies against Sparta's own enslaved people, called the Helots.

Up on Mount Ithome, the Messenians who used to be called Helots move stones day by day to reinforce the ancient fortifications that were broken down by Spartan hands generations ago. They have a spring up there, and a small flock of goats and sheep, so they will be able to survive for years.

Coming upon the scene from the east, Kimon and his men of Athens see the sea of Hellenic shields and helms diverse in shape and color gathered loosely around the base of the mountain.

"All-Hellenes are here," Kimon's lieutenant Hagnon says. "It's like the Olympics."

Hagnon points when he sees a group of Spartan knights riding up.

Kimon nods. "They send someone to meet us before we arrive. I can't think of good reasons for that. But let's stop here and let them come to us, see what they mean to say before we start our entry song."

The red-caped Spartan messengers at the head of the arriving troop greet Kimon stern-faced beneath their helmets. "The kings of Sparta would have a meeting with you, Athenian."

Kimon just frowns softly, and nudges his horse Arion to follow the messengers, nodding Hagnon to accompany him.

Down in the valley, the army of Sparta is all lined up behind their dual kings Archidamos and Pleistarchos, and that sea of shields marked with lambdas - L for Lakedaemonian - is intimidating even to Kimon. He wishes he knew how to instill such discipline in an entire cohort of men, and once again he is reminded why he admires the presentation he sees of Spartan society, seeing it as an outsider looking in.

"We do not want your aid, Athens," King Archidamos declares, as Kimon and Hagnon approach on horseback. "Go home."

Kimon stares at the Spartan king with confusion. He glances to the other king and asks, "Is this how Sparta treats her friends?"

King Pleistarchos just grimaces to Kimon in a way the Athenian cannot read. Kimon squints, and looks back to Archidamos.

"We have heard from your kings," Kimon says. "What do the Spartan people say?"

King Archidamos raises a finger and nearly smiles. "Your democratic assumptions. We know you have a heart like Herakles, Kimon, like a Spartan. But Herakles didn't ask everyone in the world what to do. He knew. Democracy appeals to the *worst* of men, and empowers them to control the best. We do not need democratic ideas being spoken around those who are fighting slaves against their freedom. We need men who know how to listen. So go home, Athenians. Go home and talk about what has happened here."

Kimon just blinks and shakes his head, not knowing what to say.

Nikomedes, cousin to King Pleistarchos, says from behind King Pleistarchos, "This is a Peloponnesian struggle, between Peloponnesians."

"Aren't we all Hellenes?" Kimon asks. "Don't we all worship the same gods? Think of the Serpent Column at Delphi, dedicated to Nike Victorious by *All-Hellenes*. Sparta did not defeat Persia alone. Let us be brothers not only in external struggles, but also in internal ones like this. Let Athens help you."

"We go to collect wounds," King Archidamos growls. "You go home and sing goat songs. Sparta does not need Athenian help."

"But you do want Theban, and Elian, and Achaean help?" Kimon asks, genuinely confused for a moment.

"Perhaps the cities of the Peloponnese, and those with whom we share ideals of strength and tradition, might form our own league."

Kimon stands like a statue in the face of that information for a moment, his mind racing with strategic reorganization.

"Democracy is an illness of the mind," King Archidamos says to Kimon, looking past him to address his soldiers as well. "We don't want it spreading."

King Archidamos of Sparta turns and walks away from the Athenians, leaving Kimon to slowly redden with embarrassment and anger. He plunges his sword into the earth and sits against his shield, at which signal all his loyal soldiers groan and cry out to voice their leader's unspoken emotion.

That afternoon, just before sunset, the merged Hellenic armies march up the slopes of Mount Ithome to attack the entrenched forces and families on the summit, while Kimon and the Athenians watch from the hills of Mount Menelaion on the east side of the Eurotas Valley.

Kimon and his contingent of Athenians watch the battle from the edge of a woods on the other side of the valley, as the great armored Hellenic soldiers are, wave after wave, held back and kept at bay by the superior position of the Messenians on the mountain.

Halfway through the theater of war, Hagnon leans in to whisper to Kimon, much like he does during Athenian plays in the Theater of Dionysos, but with wartime gravity today. "A small party of men has left to fight in the battle despite commands."

Kimon shakes his head and shrugs, feeling more defeated than he ever has in battle. "A foolish effort," he sighs.

"Perhaps not," Hagnon replies. "They went to fight with the slaves."

"So Archidamos was right," Kimon notes.

Armies of Hellenes put on a good show of harrying those entrenched on the summit, but arrows and stones and makeshift spears are given extra power and precision from their height, and their desperation, and no ground is gained by the armies attempting to ascend. Hour after hour, they are repulsed.

Before the sun has set, the armies of Hellas pull back and leave the families on Ithome to defend with rushing hearts all night against more attacks which never come.

Π

Aoide is summoned to the Pythia

"Let's see who can spot the most auspicious bird from here."

Aoide listens from her spot on the hillside amidst the trees just outside the sanctuary wall, as on the other side of the wall a young priest guides some visitors, a group of strangers from regions both near and far, in appreciation of Apollo's many supposed manifestations, among which are the movement of birds.

"There - a hawk!" one visitor exclaims.

"No," the priest replies gently. "Watch how it glides. That's Apollo's own eagle."

Aoide doesn't need to see the bird to know they're both wrong. It's just a kite riding the afternoon mountain winds. She's learned to hear the difference in their wing-beats, these past months of listening from hidden places, just as she knows the flowers and herbs of the mountain from their scents. Just as she's learned to hear the difference between true inspiration and performance, and between power and pretense.

A temple slave appears at the corner of the sanctuary wall. "They're ready for you."

She follows him through paths she was once forbidden to walk, past columns she once cleaned and repainted. Older priestesses pause in their duties to watch her pass. Their eyes follow like owls.

The inner sanctuary smells of laurel and incense. Three members of the Council of Priests wait with the Pythia, arranged like players in some divine drama. Light falls through high windows in sheets, turning dust motes to gold. Aoide studies the patterns they make in the air, like bird tracks in sand, like letters in some older alphabet. She's learned to use such natural inspirations to guide her mind, though not in the way that those who want to wrangle prophecy-makers think.

"You will be a full priestess. You will work with the Pythia, and the priests, in the administration of the work of Apollo. Are you ready?"

Aoide nods reluctantly, unsure.

"You'll attend to the sacred snakes," old Perialla says, as if describing simple kitchen work. "Change their water. Know which ones hunger. Learn their moods. Our cooks catch mice for them; you'll have to mind them, too"

"Some days the snakes dream of truth," Eromede adds quietly. "Other days they dream of blood. You must learn to tell the difference."

The new high priest clears his throat. "More practically, you'll help prepare the Pythia. The fumes from the sacred spring are ... demanding of the body. Sometimes a Pythia may need steadying. Sometimes they need waking. You'll learn to read their faces like weather."

Aoide looks to the Pythia, trying not to express too much in view of the high priest, though she catches a little secret smile from each of them.

"And the suppliants?" Aoide asks.

"That is for the high priest. He'll screen them first," Opho explains. "Sort desperation from true need. Kings may command audiences, but even kings must be ... managed. Made to understand their place in the order of things. That is men's work. Men listen to men, in daylight." She smiles with feigned demurity.

Aigisthenia says, "But it is true that even for us the real work happens before the prophecy. In the listening, and learning. In the poetic practicing. In knowing when to speak and when to maintain mystery." Her fingers move constantly when she speaks, as if weaving invisible threads. "Sometimes the greatest wisdom is in deciding who should not hear the god's voice at all."

"I will keep record of the words of the Pythia," says Perialla. "Every word must be preserved. But not every word must be preserved accurately." She gives Aoide a mysterious look. "Truth and tradition have their own requirements. I, as the creator of the written words, will have the final voice."

The high priest adds, "The god speaks through all things, not just through fume-dreams and snake-tongues. In many cases, he speaks through women's hands."

"And through silence," Eromede adds. "Sometimes especially through silence."

Aoide looks to each face in turn - the priests with their careful masks of authority, the priestesses with their patient placidity, the Pythia with their knowing eyes. The attendant slaves waiting just outside the doors, enjoying a break from commands. She sees how power moves between them like light through water, how each plays their part in this ancient dance.

"And if I see something they're not meant to see?" she asks carefully. "If the god speaks ... unexpectedly?"

Aigisthenia smiles. "Aoide rhymes when she means something particularly meaningful."

The high priest looks over to the Pythia and back to Aoide, but his face remains neutral.

"That," says Perialla, "is why we chose you. Because you already know the answer to that question. You see, Aoide, the world is only that which is understood. The world *is* more the words which describe it than the thing being described. The words make the world real within the mind. And insomuch, as creators of the words, we are the creators of the world, the translators of the world."

"The Pythia is the singer of the song which becomes the world," Eromede translates.

Opho sings, "With words we weave the world we want."

Aigisthenia nods. "We are words first, and foremost."

One snake raises its head from the bronze bowl and sticks out its tongue with a little hiss, breaking the tension and making all the older folks chuckle. But Aoide and the other Pythia keep sharing a silent smile which is long and meaningful, while Aoide's heart races like a chariot.

"It has no body, no head, no arms,
no back, no feet, no knees, no genitals.
It is one wondrous Mind unfathomably alone
unoccviting the mysterious Kosmos
with its thoughts like light."
Empedokles, *Purifications*

P

The Council debates Ephialtes' proposal

One councilman explains to another, "A group of fishermen from a village just down the coast which has conveniently been gifted a splendid new fig orchard this spring, and who are now acting as pawns of the Oligarchs in exchange for it, have been wasting debate time with nonsense all morning in the Council House, so that the Democrats trying to present a case have been unable to begin until late in the day, after most of the unaffiliated fools' minds have been addled all day by confusing nonsense. It is an intentional trick which Alkibiades' son Kleinias has been bragging about inventing for days."

"You don't know the name of the village?"

"I'm from the hills; I don't know what they call the different docks."

Sweaty-browed Antiphon shushes the two whispering councilmen.

Antiphon, a rough-hewn horse tender who has become one of Ephialtes' more trusted Democrats, is the one representing their ideas on the Council today. He is a man who is more accustomed to shouting at fellow horse-riders than speaking to most other types of men.

"Listen here, hillfolk. Idle time waiting for deer is over. It is time to get down to real business. Too long has the real power of our city been hoarded by the same few families who had all the power generations ago, before Solon tried to fix things. It is up to us to continue the work of Solon, instead of let it collapse back to the old and unfair ways before. It is time for us to create mechanisms in our system which will protect us from future tyrants. We have already seen that it is possible for men who wish to become tyrants to consolidate power, to purchase the support of fishermen and the like..."

The fishermen who had been stalling all day start to shout but Antiphon treats them like rowdy teenagers, grinning and shaking his head at them and simply ignoring and speaking over their protestations.

"...So it is up to us better-minded men to institute laws which will guarantee that only good-faith actions will lead to political power. No longer should the power of the Areopagos hold back our city from its true possible height of glory! Athens is a beacon across the world, shining the light of democracy. We have saved the world once, with the might which democracy can wield in war. Now let us wield the great might of our many minds to better the lives of the many!"

Old Kritias rises with some difficulty, and a bit of help from a kind young Democrat ox-hand beside him, only to shout, "By 'the many', he means our slaves! The ultimate goal of these radicals is to hand knives to our slaves, that they might cut our throats in the night like so many sons of Danaos, so that these fishermen can ultimately occupy our country houses and marry our daughters and tell the sons of the future that we never lived."

Kritias' claims are so egregious that both sides of the debate begin arguing before he has even stopped speaking, and he only finally finishes his thought once he sees that he has become unhearable over the din.

After several seconds of angry debate within the stands, the day's Caretaker stomps his stick to try to wrangle order. The noise gradually dissipates, but before silence is achieved, someone takes advantage of the quieter space and shouts at Antiphon, who still stands holding his scroll.

"So the Areopagos would be entirely stripped of all power! What would be the point of even being on it? Why would anyone put themselves up to be Archon ever again?"

"The Areopagos will retain their authority over matters of murder, and other highest crimes," Antiphon explains. "But they must not be able to veto the will of the people. And maybe without those who desire lasting power, we could start to see people putting themselves up to be Archon who actually just want to administer justice fairly!"

Cynical laughter and jocular jibing joins the argument, starting dogs barking outside.

ATHENS

Σ

The Agiad royal family dines

Ocean-eyed old Laothoe says, "It is good to have family eating together."

The Agiad royal families, Laothoe and hers, and Gorgo and hers, sit together at an outdoor dinner table at Laothoe's farm in the warm twilight. The old sage Simonides sits next to King Pleistarchos but tries his best to get no one's attention. Big-shouldered Nikomedes, brother of the late Pausanias, takes up the space of three people with his careless arms and legs.

Nikomedes asks Simonides, "Who are you again, and why are you here?"

"Simonides," the old man carefully says, looking around nervously. "I'm here to train your young king in my Memory Theater."

"Ignore him," Gorgo sighs. "He knows to keep his mouth shut now. He is here as a favor to Pleistarchos, a pet for the turtle."

King Pleistarchos feeds the turtle in his lap some scraps of leek from his own bowl. Old Simonides is the only one who sees it, and it makes him smile.

"No," Laothoe declares, "please, I would like to hear what our king is learning. Tell me of this Memory Theater. Your use of the 'theater' metaphor makes it sound quite ... let's say Athenian."

"Some prefer to call it a Memory Palace," Simonides says. "Lord Pleistarchos, would you like to explain?"

The young king sighs, annoyed to be called upon, but lifts his head away from his turtle and looks past his family to the darkness beyond the courtyard's torchlight. "It is a method for creating everlasting memories in one's mind. By creating a cast of characters who only exist in your mind, and a theater there which can depict anything, so that all your dreams and memories can reside there."

"This sounds like powerful magic," old Laothoe says with a nod to Simonides. "What words do you use, specifically, to invoke the aid and favor of Mnemosyne, Memory-keeper and Muse-mother?"

Simonides keeps a stoic eye contact with his hostess, and says, "All the work of my method is purely inside the silent mind. That makes it powerful in many ways - including stealth. No one can know when you are making use of the Memory

Theater. Even gods."

Queen-Mother Gorgo asks Simonides, "Do you have mental methods for giving a man courage? Or perceptiveness? Or the respect of his peers? Fortitude? You have become famous for writing poems lauding great men, but can your poems create them?"

King Pleistarchos turns away violently. He looks to his middle-aged uncle Nikomedes for some support, but Nikomedes just gives him a hard look back. He then looks to his cousins Pleistoanax and Kleomenes, who both just stare back wide-eyed. Pleistarchos and Pleistoanax have a moment of eye contact which almost becomes something, but they both look away from it.

Simonides, who can also read the room, shrivels his face with discomfort but replies, "These virtues are passed on from parents, if they are."

Gorgo speaks over his response, saying, "Because your comrade King Archidamos seems to be the only real king of Sparta these days. It is he who other cities look to, who has the voice which men of Sparta hear and believe. When Herakles intended that your two thrones rule equally."

King Pleistarchos touches his turtle for courage and haltingly says, "Maybe, if Sparta were a bit more like other lands, we would have more friends. Maybe, if we weren't seen as a threat to all..."

Nikomedes, without looking up from his food, says, "Sometimes it is better to have *fewer* friends."

His mother Laothoe keeps her eyes on Nikomedes for a long moment, then looks to her grandsons, Pleistoanax and Kleomenes. "Boys, do you understand why it is better to be feared than *liked*?"

Little Kleomenes just nods under his grandmother's gaze. Pleistoanax, however, looks to his older cousin the king across the table. Laothoe notices this, and Gorgo notices her notice.

Gorgo says, to Pleistarchos but with her eyes on Laothoe, "As our Helots now know, and those who we women still have within our sway also know, fear and pain are the whip which drives the chariot of state. Let that be their Memory Theater. Remember the reasons you have to fear - to fear everything in the world. Your neighbors, your slaves, but if not them - then wild beasts of the forests and Sea, the very weather itself. Better to fear the machinations of Man."

"Ultimately, we ought to fear ourself," Pleistarchos spits quietly to himself.

Simonides sighs, pulling the attention his way again. "Noble Spartans, I am a very old man. I have lost most of my fear, knowing that pain, and nearness to death, are no threat to me, for they would bring nothing new or strange to my life. I am already in pain; I already expect death. This is the best peace I have ever known in my life. And it brings me the most courage. But it also brings sadness. Because I have outlived my own sons. I watched the light disappear from their eyes, and I buried their bodies in the ground."

Gorgo and Laothoe both hear this grimly and look to each other with brief flashes of familial compassion.

Nikomedes finishes eating and stands up from his seat. "We have all buried loved ones," he says, "it is not notable enough to be due a poem." He looks to his mother, then his cousin the king, and frowns, and leaves the table.

T

Ephialtes presents his proposal of new laws to the Assembly

Ephialtes ascends the bema. He clasps his hands in front of himself, struggling not to appear nervous as he turns to face that sprawling sea of his countrymen all gathered for Assembly - disrespectful fishermen, patient veterans, impatient merchants, desperate beggars, respectful aristocrats, his own friends, famous athletes, fire-eyed hill men - all waiting in their myriad emotional states to judge his proposal.

"The gods have upheld this democracy. Against all odds, against the mightiest armies of mortal power, our beloved gods have protected this city's institutions. Our homes, our temples, may burn under the Persian torch, but our glorious *ideas* can never be stolen from our minds!"

A few among the assembled men begin to nod and applaud.

Ephialtes smiles, and he sees that when he does so it makes Perikles smile in the crowd, and that gives his smile fullness.

Smiling, Ephialtes continues, "There would seem to perhaps never have been anything in this world that pleases the gods as much as the Hellenic endeavor to enfranchise *all men* with the great dignity of political power."

Democrats in the assembly whistle and nod with pride.

"And yet there are still men in this Assembly who do not have access to the halls of power that the rest of us do. Themistokles himself showed this city that glory has no relation to wealth - that greatness can come even from modest origins. And we all know that it is very possible that *none of us* would be alive now if not for Themistokles' cleverness eighteen years ago. His gambit, and his leadership, saved this city."

Thukydides, proudest and boldest of the Oligarchs of the moment, raises a fist and shouts at Ephialtes, "You risk the outrage of every noble man and all their sons, pot-maker. Be careful what you wish for, as there are many versions of mob-power!"

"You hear this rich man threatening us, like some Peisistratid from the generation of tyrants?" Ephialtes barks at the many Democrats who he knows hate rich men.

Those loyal Democrats roar with derision against the threats of the rich and the old ways.

Ephialtes continues, with ever stronger conviction and confidence. "I propose, we propose, a change in the laws of the Areopagos, whose ability to veto anything at all which our wise Assembly has agreed upon has given those few who become Archons far too much power over their fellow Athenians. Simply holding one office for one year should not give a man the power to block the legislations of his fellows. And we all know, it is no surprise, that the men of the Areopagos are by and large the older men among us, those of the previous generation, and their closedness to change and new ideas from this Assembly simply undermines the very purposes which it was initially created for, by the wisdom of old Solon."

Aristocrats and Oligarchs groan and boo, but it is just a speckling among the louder barks of agreement by the many poor and disenfranchised folks surrounding them.

"Our proposal is to remove the veto power from the Areopagos, and to move all trials to the regular courts, except for those of the highest seriousness, such as murder, treason, or crimes against our gods."

The merchants' groans rise quickly, whipped up by a bellows of weighty Oligarch ogling, until the sons of rich men and their adherents are all barking out their plans to take revenge upon the Agora shops of Democrats.

The herald holds his kerykeion high to regain order, then declares, "Let us vote now, whether to bring this proposal by Ephialtes to the Council!"

The movement of hands makes it instantly clear that the vote will go for the Democrats and their new proposal. Democratic delight arises throughout the poorest in the crowd, and their allies among the intelligentsia.

The Oligarch Thukydides, signaling with his eyes to some other Oligarchs elsewhere in the crowd, lights a conspicuous hand lamp and holds it high above his head, as some of his fellow rich men do similarly.

Down in the Agora, Thukydides' son Oloros and his young friends see the signal their fathers had warned them about up on the Pnyx, and they start kicking the dirt in excitement at their chance to wreak havoc.

"Time to teach the Dems that there's a price of chaos to be paid when the better men aren't given the power we're due. Only leave the luxury stalls standing, boys, knock down the rest!"

Oloros and his excited friends spread out through the Agora in groups of two or three, all kicking and tearing down the poles and skins, crates and jars, transforming the shops of the Agora into a big mess.

Shopkeepers who aren't citizens, women and foreigners, emerge from their nearby homes and go to work protesting the destruction, some actually fighting the Athenian young men, but most refraining to do so for fear of punishment, while still doing their best to shout curses and pleas.

Birds flutter away in flocks. Street dogs and window dogs unite to cheer the show.

Sokrates watches as the chaos of tumbling tents moves steadily toward Simon's shop like a rolling storm. Someone swoops him up from behind and carries him back away from the action, into the crowd of dismayed women and slaves, before the bad boys get there to kick down Simon's stall. Sokrates looks back; it was Simon who grabbed him.

"Careful," is all he says as he watches and holds little Sokrates' shoulders.

"Won't you stop them?" Sokrates asks him worriedly.

Simon just shakes his head no.

The shoemaker watches the approaching wave of destruction with the same calm he uses to evaluate a crooked seam. His hand stays firm on Sokrates' shoulder.

Euripides' mother Kleito appears suddenly from the crowd, her vegetable-stained apron still on, face flushed from running from her own stall. Simon beckons her toward the overhang where he and Sokrates and a few other merchants are watching the chaos from, just behind his stall. "Have you seen Euripides?" she asks, breathlessly, and Simon shakes his head No.

Oloros and his gang swagger down the row. They kick over Simon's tent poles with the same careless entitlement young men use to scatter sleeping dogs. The awning collapses with a sound like wings breaking. Market-mice flee in all directions from beneath the fallen leather, their usual boldness abandoned.

Through the back curtain, Sokrates watches as the young nobles continue their progress. They're drawn forward by the sound of breaking pottery from the next stall, leaving Simon's ruined workspace as casually as wolves leaving a picked carcass.

The sounds of chaos echo off the buildings all around - women crying out, men shouting, commerce shattering. All up and down the street, merchants' chalk marks recording debts and promises fade in a sudden, unseasonable drizzle. From the roof of the Temple of Hephaistos, doves take wing in confusion, circling the market before murmurating over the Acropolis. Even the usually fearless street dogs slink away into shadows. Only the stone herms marking the street corners remain unmoved, their bearded faces wearing their usual serene smiles, dicks ever-hard.

Once the chaos has passed, Simon and Kleito share the effort of searching through his upturned workspace.

Simon, holding up one of the leather straps with quotes etched onto it, remarks, "As you see, the true wealth was not seen, and so not stolen."

Y

Kimon leads the Athenian army home, stopping at Megara

Returning from Lakedaemonia, Kimon's men arrive at the outskirts of the independent city of Megara, halfway between Qorinth and Athens. They are met outside the city by a group of city elders surrounded by men with ceremonial swords and high Megaran helmets.

"Megara greets you Kimon," says the eldest of the elders, "with these provisions and waterings for your animals. We thought to bring prostitutes, but having just come from Qorinth, we assume you have all recently had your fill of that particular honey..."

"Athens thanks you," Kimon says with a suspicious look, "but I wonder why you've met us outside, if not to keep us from entering your city?"

"Megara tires of other cities' armies emptying its cupboards in the aftermath of victories elsewhere. It is a difficulty of our central location near the isthmus."

Kimon nods with a long sigh. "I understand," he says. "Megara has our thanks for all you bring. We won't linger long, and I'll instruct the troops not to enter your walls."

The emissary bows with gratitude as he departs. One of his slave attendants turns around as they are leaving and says to a nearby Athenian, "You know, this tree is a thousand years old! It's where Homeros first sang the Iliad! Have fun!"

The Athenian who was told this smiles to his fellows sitting around him, and together they are all start singing some lines from the Iliad.

The anger of Achilles, sing of it, goddess, through me!
That awful rage which brought so many Hellenes so much grief!

Through the singing Athenians, a man with Persian eye-makeup and hairdo, but wearing a simple Athenian slave's tunic, staggers into the midst of the citizen-soldiers and is guided ultimately toward Kimon.

Winded, the Persian man starts speaking before he can fully form words, and Kimon pats his back with a little laugh to assure him patience.

"Take your time, man," Kimon says. "You've just run from Athens."

"What was that man's name - from Athens?" the Persian slave asks, with a laugh of his own. "Who ran from Marathon, supposedly?"

"Pheidippides?" Kimon asks. "He really made that run."

The Persian man nods. "I feel like him."

"So what is it you've run to tell me?" Kimon asks. "You're one of Kallias' men, yes?"

"Yes! My name is Garshasp."

"Persian?" Kimon asks with sudden distaste for the man.

Garshasp notices Kimon's reaction to his Persian name and stands upright, fearing suddenly for his life. "I did not fight Hellenes, sir," he says. "I was captured, from my town, and sold at Delos."

Kimon nods coldly and awaits the information with less patience than before.

"My master Kallias has sent me running, and I ran the whole way - as often as I could - so that I could tell you before you got to Athens: your political enemies have gained ground. A man named ... I forget."

"Ephialtes and Perikles?"

"Ephialtes, that's it," nods Garshasp. "He has been granted a great victory in your voting system."

Kimon nods. He thinks about the news in silence for a moment. Then he says to the Persian slave, "Tell your master to sell you as soon as he can. He is married to my sister, and I don't want her served by a Persian."

The two men hold eye contact with each other there beneath the apple tree. Finally Garshasp gasps and looks away, swallowing his tears and nodding.

"Go," Kimon orders him. He begins walking back toward Athens. Kimon watches him walk until he is far enough away that he must shout to say, "Run!"

While still in sight of Kimon, Garshasp makes sure to appear to be running.

"I will have that cider after all," Kimon says to the Megaran elder with a sigh, sitting on a box of apples and taking one from the bunch to bite. "I believe we will linger a day or two."

The Megaran elder throws his hands up with annoyance, but nevertheless signals to his men behind him some sign meant to indicate that the Athenians will be staying after all.

Amyntas gives his boss a questioning look.

Kimon explains, "I don't want to arrive too close to Ephialtes' victory. Kallias was wise to inform me. We should let the people forget that euphoria for a few days. Perhaps we'll have some Megaran honey after all."

Φ

Aoide asks after Dikasto

When Aoide first arrived tens years ago, Delphi had seemed like a palatial labyrinth to her, but now it feels like a claustrophobic ship, an edge around every corner. Aoide knows its every shadow better than she ever knew Athens, and better than she wishes she did.

Now, she often dreams of getting to leave with any of the random foreign visitors to explore the fantastical lands she hears them describe - hot India, wintry Keltia, wild Iberia, mysterious Nubia, luxurious Afrika, magical Kolchis, peaceful Hyperborea, exotic Tartessos; the legendary Gardens of the Children of Evening in the distant West.

But she is a priestess now, no longer just a girl made of longings. Aoide understands the complexity of the sanctuary and what it does, what it means to All-Hellas, to all Hellenes. She does not feel anymore like she can simply reject the place and rebel openly. She now feels that she must do so secretively, while maintaining the rituals which keep power in the Pythias' songs.

The sacred spring speaks in riddles all night. Aoide lies awake in her new quarters, listening to water moving beneath the temple floor, remembering how she and Dikasto used to imagine it was carrying messages from the gods. Now she knows better - or thinks she does. Now she knows the gods speak through institutional silences as much as through prophecy.

Morning brings duties. She helps prepare the temple for suppliants, watching how the other priestesses move through sacred space like dancers performing steps learned over generations. Their grace masks something harder. She sees it now in the way they avoid her eyes when she passes, in how conversations stop when she enters a room. Somehow, even among the other priestesses, she is still treated differently. She wonders what they all know, but doesn't ask. Some of them are the girls she used to dorm with, years back when they were all little.

But Dikasto is no longer here, and the silence around that fact makes Aoide feel that there must be some kind of danger attached to the question.

While cleaning the bronze bowls for morning offerings, she finds herself studying her reflection in the polished metal. "I could command them to tell me," she whispers to herself. But the face that looks back is still half-stranger - veiled priestess, powerful and powerless all at once.

A young girl brings flowers for the altar - bright mountain blooms Dikasto loved. Aoide's hands shake as she arranges them. She remembers Dikasto's loose laugh, her courageous explorations, her refusal to pretend. "The gods are just masks we make to hide our fear," she'd said once, here in this very spot. Now Aoide wonders if it's the other way around - if perhaps we're the masks, and the gods wear us fearful of being seen.

The day passes in ritual motions. Incense. Prayer. The endless stream of suppliants from every distant land seeking wisdom. Aoide performs her role dramatically, feeling the weight of her new robes like armor. But beneath each careful gesture and measured word, a question burns: How many priestesses before Dikasto disappeared? How many girls who asked too much or saw too clearly?

At sunset, she finds herself in the treasury, surrounded by offerings from kings and beggars. Gold gleams in the fading light.

As darkness pools over the valley, the night birds begin their songs - the same ones she and Dikasto used to jokingly interpret as omens. She decides to read the songs as an omen, and finds courage building inside her chest.

The suppliants leave the sanctuary for the village surrounding it, or their camp sites nearby. Only the priests and priestesses and their attendants remain through the darkness.

Aoide makes her way to the girls' dormitory building up near the top of the sanctuary. As she passes the tall, twisted old Serpent Column in the square, she sees old Kliko see her, and gets a questioning look, but she ignores it with a mask of confidence, and enters the noisy girls' room.

All the young girls quiet their boisterous conversations when the priestess, Aoide, enters the room. One girl who Aoide remembers from the previous year, skinny Hermippe, grabs Aoide's eye contact and gives her a little look indicating that she's glad to see her, and glad she's alright.

"Priestess," several girls say reverently.

"There was a girl my age," she says carefully, "who used to sleep here. She was my friend."

"Dikasto," Hermippe whispers.

"Where is she?"

"She's gone," Hermippe replies hesitantly in a soft voice.

When no more comes, Aoide snaps, "Where? Where's she gone?"

Hermippe just shakes her head. "We don't know."

"I heard they took her to the city of Larissa up north, to protect her," one of the girls Aoide doesn't know says from across the room.

"You don't know that," the girl beside her says.

"I heard they sent her to her father for being with a man, and he killed her for it," another girl says.

Some newer girls gasp at that suggestion. No one retorts against it. All remain silent. Aoide looks to Hermippe pleadingly but aggressively.

"It's none of those," Hermippe says reluctantly, cringing with her face.

"What happened?" Aoide asks.

Hermippe sighs carefully. "I don't know."

"I'm a high priestess now," Aoide whispers, perhaps too loudly. "You will answer me."

"I can't say! Because I don't know." Hermippe gives Aoide a look of annoyed disappointment, but before she can say anything more, the door to the dormitory opens and the priestess Kliko creaks into the room with a candle and her long whip.

"Who's talking in the dark?" Kliko snaps into the darkness. But then she sees Aoide at the window and bows her head to her. "O, priestess, what can we do for you?"

The older priestess' whip curls around her legs. Aoide looks into her eyes questioningly.

"You overstep," Kliko says. Her voice is mild as milk, which makes it worse. "A priestess you may be now, but some questions remain forbidden."

"Dikasto is my friend."

Kliko's replies are quick and curt. "She was property of the temple."

"She was not property!"

Aoide can feel the younger girls behind her holding their breath.

The whip twitches as Kliko's fingers flex on its handle, but Aoide doesn't move at all. "You sound like her again," Kliko says. "All that dangerous fire. She was not a girl who can be controlled. She had to leave the sanctuary."

"I am not being controlled, either," Aoide defiantly asserts.

Kliko very slightly tilts her head, but says nothing.

"What did you do to her? I demand to know."

"You cannot *demand* to know anything. You find out, or you don't." Kliko makes herself tall, unbending her body. Though she is old, she unfolds like a mantis, all angles and sudden height. "What we did was protect the temple. What we did was maintain order. What we did was exactly what we will do to any girl who forgets her place in the great chain of being. Our sanctuary must always be an oasis of *order* in the desert of this chaotic world."

"I am a priestess now," Aoide says again, but her voice shakes.

"We are but vessels," Kliko snaps. "Pipes for voices greater than our own. That is all any of us are. Even the Pythia themselves. The moment you think yourself more..." The whip rises slowly in its bend like a striking snake.

But Aoide stands her ground. "If you strike me," she says, and her voice has changed, grown deeper, older, "you will answer to more than the Pythia."

A cold wind moves through the dormitory though no window is open. The younger girls press back against their beds, sensing something ancient stirring.

Kliko's eyes narrow. The whip trembles in her hand.

For a long moment they stand there, like figures painted on a temple wall - the old priestess with her thorned whip, the young one with power gathering around her like storm clouds, the watching girls like a trembling chorus.

Finally, Kliko lowers the wrist holding the whip. But her smile stays sharp.

"So," she says softly. "You have learned something after all. Very well. Keep your questions. Keep your power. Keep whatever wings you think you're growing. You have the Pythia's eyes and interest, so you have their *aigis* shield. But if you want knowledge, you will have to find it ... wherever knowledge is to be found."

The door closes behind her. The cold wind dies. The torches steady.

Aoide stands shaking in the center of the room. Around her, the younger girls begin to weep silently from fear and relief. She wants to comfort them, but her body feels distant, changed. Power still hums in her blood like angry bees.

"What happened to Dikasto?" one of the smallest girls whispers to the group, as if to be caught up on the story.

Aoide looks at the closed door, back at the girls in their beds. She looks to the one who is in Dikasto's old bed and says, "You're sleeping in her bed."

In the corner, a spider reverently wraps her new eggs, barely knowing why.

X

Kimon's Contingent returns to Athens

When Kimon arrives back at Athens with his army of loyal soldiers, both the Oligarch and Democrat political leaders are waiting at the Dipylon Gate to greet him, and crowds of those who follow politics are gathered along the grave-lined sides of the road to watch the spectacle of what will be said.

Kimon's army, knowing this, arrives striding confidently in tight formation, their full armor recently cleaned and gleaming in the high sunlight. The soldiers receive a warm cheer from the Athenian citizens, including their own families, and many flower petals are thrown. Once near the gates, Kimon himself emerges from the ranks of the group, his helmet's bright red horsehair crest standing high above his noble face.

Kimon looks right at Ephialtes. He glances over at Perikles briefly, recognizing his part in events, but focuses on Ephialtes and does not acknowledge at all his own Oligarchic comrades Alkibiades and Thukydides, who notice this.

"Welcome home, Athenian soldiers," Ephialtes says past Kimon, to the soldiers.

"We return from a slap in the face by Ares to a slap in the face by our own patron Athena," Kimon says. "The gods would seem to have aligned the stars so as to maximize Athenian disgrace, this month."

"I say let Sparta fight her own internal battles with her own soul," Ephialtes declares past Kimon, to the crowds amassed along the roadside. "You have returned home with all our boys who left, and no Athenian has died needlessly. I say the gods have blessed us today. Come, gentlemen, and get watered, fed, and comforted, and tell us your stories of the Peloponnese! Did anyone have to fight a Hydra at Lerna?"

ATHENS

> "ALONG THE ROAD WITH NO WAY BACK,
> TO THE HOUSE FROM WHICH NO ONE RETURNS,
> WHERE THEY EAT DUST IN DARKNESS,
> THOUGH CLOTHED IN WINGS LIKE BIRDS."
> Ereshkigal, Assyrian Poet

Ψ

Xerxes takes Themistokles to view an ancient ruin

Once they are near the ancient city's secret location, Themistokles' blindfold is removed.

"Nineveh is a secret hidden in the desert now, its location known only to my royal guard," Xerxes explains as they approach the sand-blown hills on horseback.

Xerxes and Artabanos are riding up to a desert hill behind a small royal entourage of six horsemen while Themistokles holds onto Artabanos' back.

Ancient stars silently rise from the black Euphrates River.

"Two hundred years ago Nineveh was the height of civilization. Two hundred years ago man-made river roads brought all the waters of the distant mountains to this spot, for Sennacherib's garden city. There is a reason it must be kept secret. Some of the greatest treasures of mankind are hidden here, beneath the mask of sand."

Xerxes pulls his horse to a stop at the top of a rise, and signals to Artabanos to pause here a moment. Themistokles, looking around Artabanos, sees what Xerxes has stopped for - the ruined city on a broad, low hill ahead, completely dark - not a fire in view but the stars.

"Once, long ago, there would have been hundreds of thousands of people right over there," Artabanos says, pointing at the dark ruin. "So step carefully, and mind your tongue, for there are now that many ghosts."

Xerxes adds, "My grandmother said that water still flowed along

Sennacherib's river road in her childhood. Now it is dust."

"Shall I lead us in?" Artabanos asks Xerxes, who nods curtly. Artabanos then kicks his horse and gallops down toward the silent city. Xerxes follows, with the royal guards not far behind.

The hoofbeats echo eerily off the low wall-ruins as they enter what was once the greatest city in the world. Sand has drifted between the buildings like snow, smoothing the edges of fallen stones, half-burying elaborate carvings of winged bulls and lion-headed eagles. Their horses' hooves sink deep with each step, making them walk nervously.

Themistokles, still holding tight to Artabanos' waist, finds himself gripping harder as they pass beneath a massive arch. Even half-tumbled and worn, it towers above them like a giant's door. Fading starlight catches the remains of blue glaze on the bricks, making them shimmer like fish scales.

"The Ishtar Gate," Xerxes says softly. "Once it was higher than ten men standing on each other's shoulders, and covered in lapis lazuli from the mountains of the east. My grandfather remembered seeing it whole."

They ride in silence through what must have been a broad avenue, though now it is little more than a gap between mountains of rubble. Here and there, Themistokles glimpses hints of the city's former glory - a hand carved from alabaster reaching up from the sand, the head of a brass serpent gleaming dully, fragments of wall paintings showing gardens and hunts and battles between men of varied ancient costumes.

One of the guards behind them mutters a Persian prayer.

"The ghosts here are blind," Artabanos says suddenly, after a quick response to the guards in quiet Persian. "That's what the locals claim. Too much sand in their eyes after all these years. But they can still hear. Still touch." He laughs, as if mocking a fear he's seen in Themistokles, but Themistokles just shrugs annoyedly, not having reacted at all otherwise.

They rein their horses to a stop before the remains of what must have been a palace. Huge stone lions still guard the entrance, their faces worn smooth by centuries of wind. Xerxes dismounts first, then helps Themistokles down from behind Artabanos. The Athenian's legs are shaky from the long ride.

"Leave the horses here," Xerxes commands.

The guards light tall royal torches, though Themistokles notes their hands aren't entirely steady. The flickering light makes the shadows dance between the columns, suggesting movement where there is none.

"Stay close," Artabanos murmurs. "Don't dare touch anything."

Xerxes leads Themistokles into the building, ruined and dark. The walls are lined with mostly-broken shelves, in some of which are stacked old, clay tablets full of ancient cuneiform writing. Xerxes goes to one and brushes away some spiderwork.

"This is what I brought you for," the Persian King of Kings says. "This was the Great Library of Ashurbanipal. Here are stored all the ancient texts of Assyria and Babylon. Look at this one. It's the oldest version we have of our oldest epic. A story of two warriors, one a wild, strong man from a backwater region, like yourself, and the other a wise and cultured king from the city, like me, and how they first battle each other, but then become the greatest of friends."

As he picks up the tablet, the corner he is holding onto breaks, and the rest of it falls back onto the shelf, shattering a bit more when it lands. Xerxes snorts with surprise and brushes off his hands.

Themistokles jokes, "It appears this story, even, now, is dust."

"We have other copies," Xerxes says, moving on. "Most of this is just bureaucratic ledgers and such. It is the business of scribes to keep themselves in business. The salient point is this - my father's Apadana may be magnificent, but this - this horde of knowledge, our history, the voices of our grandfathers, and their grandfathers, gathered into one trove - this was the height of civilization. And it was abandoned. We are on the waning side of civilization, Hellene."

Themistokles looks around himself at the ruined palace's dark dust, and says, "There are no buildings this large and ornate in Athens, and there never have been. And I wonder if perhaps we are lucky never to have known extravagance at this scale. So there is no tradition of it, no expectation or hope that one man could attain so much power."

Xerxes runs his fingers along a shelf of clay tablets, leaving tracks in the dust. A spider scurries away from his touch, vanishing into the darkness. In the torchlight, his face looks suddenly older, more weary. The King of Kings falls silent, staring into the darkness as if seeing something beyond the crumbling walls. When he speaks again, his voice has changed, become almost childlike in its vulnerability.

"Throughout his life, throughout my childhood, my father was a god-like man. But in his final year, he withered into a frail skeleton, and no one knew why. And for all of his great works, and wise things he told me, the words of his which I think most often back to are some which he said to me in his final days. He said, 'Time drains out of the world continuously. We are either climbing against its flow downward into lightless death, or sliding with it. Climb or slide. Living is clambering. Stop fearing death, and it will find you quick.' And I have feared death stronger than ever, ever since."

Themistokles inhales deeply and slowly, full of thought.

"Was your father also a god-like man?" Xerxes asks Themistokles.

Themistokles answers with a sad look, "My father was a mere sailor, with no ambition."

Xerxes doesn't seem to know how to respond to that, and after a moment of silence continues along as he had been.

The final door leads to a wide, dusty courtyard surrounded by high walls.

"This empty, debris-strewn lot was once the famed Hanging Garden of Babylon - called so because it's where they hung the captive Babylonian god Marduk stolen from Babylon, so - a mockery. The first paradise, designed by one man, Sennacherib, for himself. It inspired my grandfather's own interest in gardening. Great Grandfather Kyros. But the man is gone, and his creation has eroded."

Xerxes gives Themistokles a sad look through his darkened eyelids.

"All men vanish, and their wishes with them. Now all is dust."

Themistokles looks upon the ruined garden thoughtfully a while, then says, "The gods are simply elsewhere now."

Ω

Sculptors and artists discuss creating the images of the gods

Particles of dust float through a shaft of light between Phidias and the massive stone block that he needs to carve into a goddess. Somehow it is only the dust that occupies his mind. From within the hot grasp of artistic uncertainty, each mote of dust, which once was part of the possibility of this piece of art, now represents a possibility gone, and as they glow in shafts of sunlight they seem to Phidias like an armada of minuscule mistakes.

"The gods become, with my will," he whispers to himself. "I create the creators retroactively with my imagination."

Across the workshop, Sophroniskos raises an eyebrow and shakes his head, trying to ignore the younger artist's melodramatic internal monologuing. Phidias has not even noticed him all day.

The marble looms before Phidias, perfect in its possibility. Each unsculpted surface contains infinite potential faces of Athena. His tools lie untouched beside the block: the finest bronze chisels from Qorinth, measuring devices from Aegina, tiny ceremonial figures of Daidalos and his mechanical servants from Krete whose ritual purpose the young man has yet to fully grasp.

Late morning shifts into afternoon. The dust motes dance a different dance in each hour's unique angle of light. Phidias has not moved.

Other sculptors come and go from the workshop - Myron overseeing, apprentices working on architectural details, journeymen crafting votive offerings. They give the young master a wide berth. They've learned to recognize this mood, this paralysis of possibility. They keep their eyes from landing too long on him lest they receive one of his wordless outbursts of annoyance. In the corner, Sophroniskos remains steadfast in his work on a simple bannister head.

As the workshop empties toward the end of the day, Phidias finds his wine jar. The first cup is for libation - poured out for Athena herself. The second is for courage. By the third, he's playing knucklebones against himself on the workshop floor, using the sound of the bones against stone to drown out the weight of expectation.

Perikles' silhouette darkens the doorframe of the shop, casting a sunset shadow across Phidias long enough to cause him to finally look up.

"The city pays for your time," Perikles says from the doorway, only half-joking. "And your marble."

Phidias looks back at his game. "Tell me - when you speak in the Assembly, do you just walk up to the bema and open your mouth?"

Perikles thinks for a moment. "That's different. Anyway, I was just being playful. We don't actually pay for your time."

Now Phidias does look up. His eyes are wine-bright but focused. "You prepare your speeches in your mind first. You test different words, different rhythms. You imagine how they'll land."

"Speech is not sculpture."

"Yes it is." Phidias gestures at the untouched marble. "Every chip I take from that stone is permanent. Every cut changes what's possible to continue with."

The knucklebones clatter against the floor. Perikles watches them settle.

Phidias says, "If I did not spend a lot of time doing *this* work," wobbling as he stands slowly, "this thought work, then the physical work of making in the world what I've designed in my mind would only be able to create something lousy. I sculpt in my mind first, so that I don't have to use up all the marble in the world winnowing down my many ideas."

Perikles nods. "Fair enough," he says. He thinks for a few moments, then asks, "Have you had any setbacks in your thought work?"

Phidias looks at him with a smile. "That's a good question," he says. "But no. I've already learned that the most important skill is patience. Patience and diligence, and the courage to experiment. And reverence to the Muse. There are a number of most important things." He smiles to himself.

Perikles nods, understanding and comparing the thought to his own concerns. He begins to pace the room and look at the other sculptures being worked on.

Watching Perikles, Phidias continues, "It seems at first that a million different possibilities could be right. But as you remove the wrong, fewer things are right, until you have found what a thing really *is*. This is how I think the gods tell me what to make. They give me a strong sense of what they *don't* want, so I remove that."

"I am not sure if I'm unable to understand you because you're a genius, or because you're drunk," Perikles laughs.

Phidias smiles. "Even sober, I'm poor with words. Stone speaks slowly. But with precision."

Perikles nods and squints out something like a smile. He tells Phidias, "I will try to be more patient."

"Patient!?" Phidias laughs. The wine has loosened something in him, some dam of thought that usually holds back these floods. "You think it's about patience?" He stumbles to the massive block, puts his hands against its cool surface. "Every morning I come here and look at this stone. And Athena stares at me out from it. Somewhere in there. Yesterday I saw her stern, annoyed with me. Today..." He traces a line in the air. "Today I saw her tender. Athena Counselor. Which face is true? Which mask does the goddess wear?" Phidias leans toward the cool stone and presses his hot forehead against it. "When Homer sang of gray-eyed Athena, he could change the words next time. When Polygnotos paints her, he can paint over mistakes. But this..." His voice cracks. "This will stand forever. Every man who ever prays to Athena will see her through my eyes. Through my hands." He turns to Perikles, swaying slightly, and Perikles sees his delicacy and moves in to catch the artist's crumpling body as he continues to rant, ever more slurringly. "It would be too simplistic to say that I see now that the world is nothing but interwoven masks placed upon a faceless chaos. And it is now my task to carve the mask of the goddess which future men will see her through. How dare I? How dare I? I ask you, functionally, how shall I dare?"

Perikles helps young Phidias down onto his bed of straw.

"You're drunk, man; first ease your mind."

"Do you not see the eyes of future men's gaze upon you, Perikles? As a man of significance, a man surrounded by glory as your name itself implies? I do, and I'm just a boy engorged with hubris!"

But then once his body is supine and laid upon the straw, Phidias falls almost immediately into sleep. Words make small noises in the back of his throat as he continues to think them, but they are kept in his dreamworld now.

Perikles rises from the sleeping artist and only then notices quiet Sophroniskos, Phidias' fellow sculptor, seated across the room in front of his own effort, a dog-faced gutter spout.

Sophroniskos just nods, knowing the important man is not here to see him, so Perikles just nods back, nods to little Sokrates with a smile, then takes his leave. Sophroniskos breathes a long sigh once Perikles has left.

Sokrates watches him from under his father's worktable.

"Do you wish that he had asked *you* to make Athena?" Sokrates asks his father. "Or are you glad you don't have that responsibility?"

Sophroniskos frowns at his son thoughtfully for a long few seconds. "Why would you ask me that?" he asks.

"I'm just curious whether making greater artworks is something you ever think about."

"Greater artworks?" Sophroniskos sniffs, glancing at the dog head he has been forming. "What is so un-great about this hound?"

Sokrates shrugs with a half-smile.

Round-shouldered Sophroniskos slumps in his stool and throws his arms. "You must think your father full of faults. Just lazy-minded and basic, going nowhere slowly. I bet that's what you think, isn't it Sokrates? You look at other men's fathers who are making good money, or younger artists who are getting quick glory, and you wonder, 'Why isn't my father achieving these things?' Well, the answer is that it's not so easy, Sokrates. Sorry for the harsh lesson, but there is no real fairness in this world. The gods do not choose the best. They select randomly, by lot, with knucklebone dice. And many, many men just never land a lucky roll. Okay?"

Sokrates furrows his face, afraid of the wrath of his father at his angriest.

Tired-hearted Sophroniskos sees his sweet ten-year-old boy's reaction and withers a bit more, and groans out his frustration loudly like a bear.

"O Sokrates, you don't know what you're asking," Sophroniskos cries. "Life, art, ambition, are all so much more complicated than you can understand at your age. Honestly, I hope you never know them. I tell you, son - stay ignorant. Don't learn. Don't grow ambition. Ignore the disappointing world and its siren-songs. Be a fool, my son, and stay a fool!" And he starts tickling Sokrates with his firm, fat fingers.

ATHENS

in the 80th Olympiad

7

HERA MAN-PROTECTOR

A

Ephialtes and Perikles discuss politics on the eve of an ostracism

Oxen are led in a long train into the city for their sacrifice during the upcoming Assembly, when the annual vote will be taken on whether or not to ostracize a citizen this year. Sons of Oligarch pottery merchants are gathering shattered shards very visibly in wheeled carts, to make the upcoming vote seem fated to pass, while a group of clever but irritated citizens annoyed by political clashes and hoping to avoid an exile vote try to explain to onlookers that the effort is merely an attempt at psychological manipulation. Ephialtes keeps wincing at the clattering of the shards, having been brought up in a house where breaking bowls and pots - the family's livelihood - was a primary sin, but also because he imagines his own name being written onto each piece. Staring down into the accumulating piles of *ostraka*, his expression grows distant and morose.

"These bowls. These shards. This vote. It feels like the future is a foregone conclusion, has already been decided, and we are now simply parts in a device forced by our surrounding parts to enact our role due to our position, choiceless and inevitable."

"Come on now," Perikles says, trying to redirect his thoughts but not yet having a specific idea how to. "You're playing into their desires."

"We know there will be a vote to ostracize, and that it will come down to myself against Kimon. Like how Phidias described the image of the goddess already existing within the stone, I see my name already written in future form on each of these pot-shards." Ephialtes adds, mysteriously, "I wish I didn't have to have a name. I hate my name. I should have never dared to become a well-known person!"

"All mortal living risks the attention of the gods," Perikles says, "but I assure you - for however much faith one can have in human knowledge and effort, we have electioneered circumstances among the convincible the best we can, and I do not think you have anything to fear. The poor are with us, and in them, the one thing you can trust - *numbers*. See, I agree with you about the inevitability, however my thought is that we are inevitably safe."

"My life comes and goes by the pot," Ephialtes moans. "I first appeared to most Athenians as just some name on a cup, and will disappear as a name on a broken shard of the same."

Perikles gives his friend a reassuring pat on the back. "You are so much more than cups, Ephialtes. You're what fills them."

"It's alright," Ephialtes sighs, holding up one large piece of jar which still shows most of the painting that was on it - one man dressed in Persian animal skins bent over, with the words 'Butt-fucked at Eurymedon', and another man nude but for a cape, clearly a Hellene, holding his hard dick in his hand. "It's my one military victory. Ah, look, there's Mikon!"

"Ephialtes! Perikles!" says the painter Mikon. Walking down the street past them, he leaves the group of younger painters he had been walking with and prances over to where the two friends stand.

Ephialtes explains to Perikles, "Mikon is working on a series of paintings for my father's pots, to go along with the epic painting he's doing for the new Stoa!"

Mikon nods, shrugging. "I need to find more workers to get them all done, but yes, they are coming along. My primary focus, of course, has been my painting for the Stoa, as that will last for posterity, whereas pots, as we all know..." He raises his eyebrow at Ephialtes, strongly indicating pottery shards, and through them ostracism, and through that, the fact that Ephialtes is the known target for Oligarch votes to exile.

Ephialtes frowns. "I get you the most prestigious position to put your painting, and you just mock my family's livelihood." Then he smiles and laughs and slaps Mikon's arm to confirm he's playing around.

Perikles asks Mikon, "What's the subject matter?"

Mikon replies with a nod, "I agree, ultimately the subject doesn't matter at all."

Ephialtes laughs, "No no, he's asking what is the subject of your paintings."

Mikon laughs, "Ah! King Theseos."

"The minotaur's labyrinth," Perikles assumes aloud.

"Actually, I'm doing Theseos versus the Amazons."

"Ah, the War with the Amazons. Imagine if we had lost that war."

"We'd be ruled by women, and we'd be the ones having to birth and breastfeed screaming babies," Mikon muses.

"I'm not quite sure that's how it would work."

A couple of Mikon's young painting students approach the famous painter with their pots. One of them is nineteen-year-old Euripides.

"Master," the other student says with a snide tone, "Euripides is writing on his pots."

"It's context," Euripides explains. "People ask me who the characters are so often, I'm putting it in the image."

Mikon takes the pot from the student's hand and looks at the scene painted there - a man surrounded by women, with text surrounding them indicating that they are the Athenian King Theseos and Amazon Queen Penthesilea and some text describing the action.

Mikon shakes his head. "Euripides, stop. This is unacceptable, what you've done. Look, you've written *all over* your painting. It is normal to include *some* writing, perhaps the names of certain figures, or of the region where the action takes place, that sort of thing, but you do not need to write whole poems in the negative space of your painting. That's not what painting is for. You need to tell your story with the imagery! If your imagery requires a lot of additional explanation in text, then your decision of what to depict has failed. Show me, don't tell me."

"But people all look alike in paintings," Euripides sighs.

"Not when good painters do it," one of the other students retorts.

"I like the look of the imagery with the writing," Euripides says with shy courage. "The writing is its own kind of imagery, just as the imagery tells a sort of story."

"You need to decide whether you want to be a painter or a writer, Euripides. You can't combine both, or you simply fail at both. The arts have been organized into their various formats for a reason. You will make the Muses jealous! Now do you want to make paintings, or do you want to write poetry?"

Euripides, choked by his attempts to swallow down tears, just shakes his head.

"Ugh, go take a walk and calm down, boy," Mikon sighs at him

Young Euripides gets to his feet and trots off into the Agora's crowd, holding his arm over his eyes to hide his crying. Mikon shouts after him, "Come back when you've decided which artform you want to do!"

"The work increases daily," Perikles says, rubbing his temples as they leave Mikon and walk past the painted columns of the new stoa. Groups of citizens cluster around the tables of money-changers, their voices wrestling. "Every new proposal requires more men who can write, record-keepers, chiselers. Democracy has an endless appetite for documentation."

"You could hire citizens instead of slaves," Anaxagoras suggests, pausing to let a line of grain-laden mules pass.

"Citizens add up. They're expensive." Perikles watches a slave boy struggle with a water jug twice his size as he follows his master down the street. "Our treasuries would be emptied within a few years. Though lately I find myself thinking of my old tutor Damasias whenever I visit the slave market. He taught me how to read, when I was just a boy, and he was just a slave. Truth rings true from any tongue."

"My father never owned slaves when we were growing up," Ephialtes says, nodding to a group of supporters near the green-grocers' stalls. "He liked to say 'A poor man's dignity is worth more than a rich man's comfort.' But once our business got rolling, his creditors demanded the efficiency of slave workers. And now here I am, debating how many to buy for the city recordkeeping. Circumstances change us."

"Speaking of change," Anaxagoras gestures toward the line of foreigners waiting to sign up as *metics* so they can work. "There's another possibility. The resident foreigners - free, educated enough for scribal work, but their labor costs less than citizens'."

Perikles nods positively, but sees Ephialtes' smile shrugging reluctantly, and frowns.

"I wish it weren't so," Ephialtes says, "but as welcoming as our city is to foreigners, the non-urbanites on the Assembly, the folks from the coasts and hills who don't know these foreigners, just don't trust them."

Lazy-eyed Lysimachos says, "Well the slaves are there, already enslaved by the War Goddess, Enyo City-sacker. Someone's going to buy them, and benefit from their use. It might as well be someone like me, right? I mean, aren't I giving up an opportunity if I let someone else buy the slave? After all, I know how to actually make use of them with kindness and patience, and give them *good* lives of servitude. If I don't buy them, someone else will, someone who will treat them worse than I would. Doesn't that make sense?"

Perikles nods. "It does, of a sort."

"But what about trying to legislate away the very state of servitude?" Ephialtes asks. "We could make servitude illegal in Athens. Isn't that part of what Solon was attempting to begin, when he set down the first laws of democracy? The end of economic slavery?"

"Well, he outlawed *debt*-slavery," Lysimachos corrects. "I don't think he ever intended *all* slavery to be outlawed. He just didn't want *Athenians* enslaving *each other* for unpaid debts anymore. But if your city falls in War, what else do you expect? Would you rather die?"

Ephialtes raises an eyebrow and shrugs with his face. Lysimachos shakes his head with a sniff.

"You wouldn't rather die," Lysimachos asserts confidently.

"Freedom from slavery is a great idea, but we can't make it illegal elsewhere," Perikles notes. "And the slave market is an international system. Lysimachos is right. Better to make enlightened use of an unethical system, than fail to benefit from it altogether when there is no stopping its use by others. If the gods find it distasteful, they will organize events differently in order to stop it."

Ephialtes suggests, "Perhaps Mankind can be a role model to the gods." He thinks about it another moment, then adds, "As sons can be, sometimes, to their fathers." He looks Perikles in the eye, knowing this will resonate with him personally.

Perikles nods, filled with warmth by the reminder that his friend knows him well, and is such a good man. He joins Ephialtes in his smile, and embraces him quickly but heartily.

Lazy-eyed Lysimachos sees them beaming at each other and laughs, clapping them both on their shoulders and saying, "You boys. No two men were more fit for each other."

Perikles and Ephialtes both smile in thanks. Perikles pats Lysimachos on the back roughly to dispel the sweetness boyishly. "You are a good friend, Lysimachos."

Two passing wives of Oligarchs, huddling together beneath their veils to seem properly demure in public, nevertheless give Ephialtes and Perikles the evil eye as they walk past, whisper in harsh tones to each other, and one lifts her veil to spit on the ground in their direction.

"The people's anger needs a focus," Ephialtes says quietly.

The three men move gradually to a corner of the Agora where the wind covers their words more.

Perikles speaks low. "It's been five years since the last ostracism. We could try to wrangle the vote against it ... or we could put our efforts early toward *whom* we want to ostracize."

"Kimon would be the obvious target," Lysimachos muses, always eager to discuss combative politics. "But he's too popular with the veterans. If we fail..."

"Not Kimon," Ephialtes interrupts. "Alkibiades."

The other two men stare at him.

"Think about it," Ephialtes continues. "Kimon's the spear, but Alkibiades is the purse. He's the one who organizes the Oligarchs, who plans their moves. Kimon is just the likable one they put up front. And he lacks Kimon's military glory to shield him."

"I fear Alkibiades is not known well enough by our own Democrats, though," Perikles suggests in a whisper, looking around at the people in the Agora doing their business and debating their concerns. "And we know that they will be aiming their own votes against us at the same time."

"Against me, you mean." Ephialtes' smile grows grim. "Yes, I expect they will. But better one man at risk than our entire cause. We let it be known we're moving against Kimon. Let the Oligarchs gather their political phalanx around him. Then, when the voting comes..." He mimes a knife fighter's feint and strike.

"Feels like playing knucklebones with the Fates," Perikles says softly.

"This will depend on our discretion and timing. Let's spread the word carefully. Kimon is the threat. Kimon is the target. But we keep our channels open, and in the days right before the ostracism, we spread the real name. And when they're all looking at the lion..."

"We kill the snake," Perikles finishes.

Ephialtes smiles. But then he says, with a little nervous chuckle, "We *subdue*. How about that? Words matter."

On the crowded Pnyx, when the vote comes, hands fly in a fast flock like the scattering of doves in favor of an ostracism, and it becomes clear very quickly from the immediate chatter that the Oligarchs plan to aim for Perikles, not Ephialtes.

"Sea-onion harvest! Sea-onion harvest!" the Oligarchs all chant together as they walk down the hill of the Pnyx and back into the city gates.

B

Athenians gather to watch Aischylos' plays during the Dionysian festival

For the springtime Dionysian city festival, once again all of Athens is bedecked in decorative vines and flowers and dicks. Hundreds of men and women mingle and chatter around the Temple of Dionysos, slowly making their ways to the wooden seating set up on the hillside behind it.

Ten-year-old Sokrates trudges up the steep dirt path between the wooden seating which has been installed in concentric arcs facing down onto the central stage with the big *skene* building behind it, where they drape the curtain on which the background is painted. His father and mother walk ahead of him, but Sokrates has refused to hold either of their hands, as he feels the eyes of other boys his age here in public and doesn't want anyone to know that this is his first time out to the theater. At only ten, he is among the younger audience members. Puppet plays for children are performed elsewhere. Being here makes Sokrates feel extremely mature.

Everyone in town is here, as are many strangers from far away. Sokrates hears four or five different unfamiliar languages being spoken. As he and his parents find their seats high up in the back, he wonders how far away some of the foreigners further down in the stands might be from.

Down on the stage, priests of Dionysos are setting up a large wooden prop meant to represent a loom for the first scene of the tragedy, which has been advertised as being about *Penelope*, the long-suffering wife of Odysseos.

Sokrates asks his father, "Do you think we shall see Odysseos kill Penelope's suitors?"

"Well, they usually don't *show* that sort of thing, but they may talk about it," Sophroniskos replies.

"I hope we get to hear more from Penelope than the suitors or Odysseos, myself," Phaenarete remarks as she seats herself. "But unfortunately men just don't know how to write women well, so they tend to avoid doing so at all."

Sophroniskos continues, "Now when the tragedy commences, Sokrates, remember to stay perfectly quiet. Only rude people interrupt the performance of an artist, and actors are artists just like I am."

"But what do they make?" Sokrates asks. "Words?"

Phaenarete suggests, "Tears and laughter?"

Sophroniskos laughs softly and nods. "Yes, in a way. I was thinking something more like - revelations about the subtle struggles of humanity."

Sokrates nods. "But since we can't see that happening in each other, we have to measure it in things like tears and laughs."

"True enough," Sophroniskos nods.

"Do either of you boys want a horn of honeyed grasshoppers?" Phaenarete asks, leaning across her husband to playfully pinch her son's nose. "I brought three owls - one for each of us to spend."

Sokrates squeals and nods.

Phaenarete stands and walks over to the snack sellers.

Sophroniskos leans down to his son and whispers, "You're not a baby anymore, Dew-drop. Don't squeal like a baby out in public, okay, big Herakles? Try to act like a man in public. Or like older boys at least."

Down near the central stage, Sokrates notices a couple of well-jeweled Oligarchs helping a group of white-haired, dark-skinned Aithiopian dignitaries to their seats. Two ruddy-skinned, red-haired Kelts nearby nod to them politely, and the four men all shake hands.

"Why do those men have such different skin?" Sokrates asks his parents.

"Which men, where?" Sophroniskos asks his little son, not having seen the group in question and looking around the stands. "Hermias has a scar from that boat accident. Is that who you see?"

"No, he means those Aithiopians and Kelts," Phaenarete explains as she is returning with a couple of hollowed boar tusks stuffed with honeyed grasshopper bits. "Those people are from distant lands called Aithiopia, in the south, and Keltia, in the north" she explains to her son. "Remember, I told you about how King Kepheos and Queen Kassiopeia were the two vainest people alive, and that's why they were going to marry their daughter off to the Kraken, for more beauty from the gods. But Perseos saved her, with the help of the gods. They were Aithiopians."

"O I remember the princess and the Kraken! So they're bad people - Aithiopians? They're vain?" Sokrates asks.

"No, no, not those people," Phaenarete replies, "just certain of their ancestors from the story - King Kepheos and Queen Kassiopeia. But we have ancestors who were no better. Think of what King Theseos did. Some good things, but also many bad things. That doesn't make *us* bad. So those men are probably perfectly pleasant people. In fact, they're here because they're important dignitaries!"

Sokrates asks, "So is it because of their vanity? Or is that the beauty they got from the gods?"

Phaenarete corrects, "I told you, they're not necessarily vain people, those people there. But their skin is dark because one day Helios the Sun God agreed to give the reins of his fire chariot to his son Phaethon, who was young, and had little experience with how things can turn out. And he made some mistakes, and flew too close to the Earth, and the Sun-chariot burned the lands to the south, south of the Sea. There the Earth remains scorched, and can't even grow any grass anymore, and so now it's just an expanse of endless scorched sand in Libya and Kyrene, and in Aithiopia, where those men are from. And the people there, their skin was burned by the Sun-chariot, like when we cook things in a fire, which is why we call them *Aithiops* - burnt face."

"Do you think that hurt?" Sokrates asks, touching his own cheek.

"You've been burned before," Phaenarete replies, pinching her son on the thigh and making him squeal. "What do you think?"

"Well," Sophroniskos sniffs with a little smile, "that is the legend, at least. Aithiopia isn't a real place, though, Dew-drop. Those people just look burnt-faced because they live in southern Aigypt or Libya. The further south people are from, the darker their skin tends to be. That's all it is, really. There are actually many different lands with dark-skinned people, and some dark-skinned people from our own land, whose ancestors came here long ago. It's only a fable that they were burned by the Sun God's chariot. It's important not to say something like that to them, for example. They're regular people just like you. Their lands just have different Winds."

"Well," Phaenarete sniffs back, "that's what people *used* to say. It's what I was told by my mother."

"Here you see again, Dew-drop- people long ago were like children compared to people today," Sophroniskos tries to explain. "They didn't have as much experience, and so they made more mistakes. Like Phaethon in the story. But we've learned from them, at least with some things. Like not offering up our children to ancient monster-gods just for a little more beauty. Trust me - if we could, you wouldn't be here and I'd be a lot more handsome!"

Phaenarete slaps her husband's knee and they laugh together. Sokrates smiles.

Sokrates points at the Keltic dignitaries sitting next to the Aithiopians. The ruddy men are making each other laugh boisterously and wearing tight-fitting leather garments that hug each leg.

"What are those men wearing? And why are they so red? Were they burned too?"

"No, just the reverse with them," Phanarete explains. "Those men are from a very cold place, and their skin is white and red from the cold north wind, Boreas, constantly whipping their faces."

"Don't point, Dew-drop" his father tells him. "Those are called pants. Northern barbarians wear them. Don't mention them. There's no telling how men who wear pants will behave. And they get really mad when you question them about them. Steer clear of men who wear pants."

"Where are Aithiopia and Keltia?" Sokrates asks.

"Aithiopia is south of the Sea, like Aigypt," his mother answers. "They have pyramids in Aithiopia too! They like to do that in the south, for some reason - make pyramids of stone. And Keltia is in the north, on the way to Hyperborea."

Someone nearby shushes the family, as the actors down on the stage are beginning to arrange themselves into their chorus line and the musicians on the side are beginning to transform their preparatory cacophony into the harmony of the show's opening sounds.

Down on the stage, behind his beautiful, wisened mask of Penelope carved from pale Aithiopean ivory, Aischylos-as-Penelope, that patient wife of the wanderer Odysseos, begins to weave at his prop loom like his character is playing a huge harp, while an actual harpist fingers real strings softly offstage.

Γ

Anaxagoras shares his new work of writing

"Among the olive rows, just a short walk north from Athens' Dipylon Gate," explains the gentle Athenian tour guide to the well-paying foreign visitors following her, "it has become the custom for thinkers to linger and expound their thoughts while intrigued listeners sit or follow as necessary to remain in earshot of the teacher they wish to hear. On any given day, at least one or two, and sometimes as many as a dozen, supposed wisemen of varying levels of respect and fame will pace the rows and share their thoughts. Those who come here often have been dubbed *followers* by those who would choose to mock them. Not that I am one to indulge in such behavior!" She chuckles and motions for them to follow further, and the foreign visitors smile at the Athenian youths among the olives as they pass, gawking.

Big-bodied Protagoras lately maintains the largest crowd of all, but several other sages have recently begun gathering their own groups of curious followers here, just outside the city walls. Anaxagoras usually gathers a crowd when he deigns to visit the grove, but he does not visit often, so he can also still sometimes arrive inconspicuously.

On this morning, as the Sun plays with a cloud just above the eastern mountains, Anaxagoras arrives with a thick scroll under one arm which he is excited to share, so he is dismayed to find it is one of those days when none of the students following their teachers between the olive trees seem to recognize him.

Protagoras paces, speaking to the group that is gathered around him.

"All wisdom, you see, is like a game," the big Abderan tells his listeners. "You don't need to be 'right' - you need to *win*. The supposedly wise man who has found some nugget of unimpeachable truth, but who has been imprisoned by his fellows so that he can make no good use of it, has obviously achieved nothing with his so-called wisdom. You must speak in the language of those around you, in order to participate in *real* wisdom. You cannot simply go around spouting incomprehensible yet somehow *true* utterances, like some wildman or wizard whom no one can understand. This is how wizards will try to fool you - by saying nonsense, and telling you that it is wisdom. But wisdom is only what works, between men. That is, between people."

One of the two young women in the audience bows her head with a demure smile of gratitude for being noticed. She knows she can do little more than listen quietly, without potentially stirring up the wasp nests within the hearts of traditionally-minded men.

"O look, here's my favorite debate partner, Anaxagoras of Klazomenai! Welcome, Anaxagoras!"

The followers of Protagoras mirror their master's respectful attitude and shower Anaxagoras with a few moments of welcome and praise. The incoming Ionian can't help but smile broadly in reaction.

"What's that you carry, there?"

"Why, it's the first copy of my book!" Anaxagoras replies with carefully minimized pride. "I paid your friend Euathlos to copy it from my original, on the off chance that someone else might want to own a copy. He's said he'll make more copies if there's interest."

All the listeners coo with admiration at the man who has completed an entire book.

"I hope you checked to make sure he copied it correctly," Protagoras chides. "Euathlos is the quintessential idiot."

"He can read and write perfectly well these days," Anaxagoras assures. "It only goes left-to-right. I've confirmed the copy is correct, of course. It must be, for the format of the piece is metered and rhyming, and could easily be mistranslated!"

"Are you a sage or a poet, Anaxagoras?" Protagoras asks with derision, side-eyeing the book. "You should probably choose one or the other. You cannot supplicate yourself simultaneously to truth and meter."

ATHENS

"Solon was a poet as well as a sage," Anaxagoras replies coolly.

"He compares himself to Solon."

"What's its title?" asks Archelaos, who had been listening to Protagoras. He reaches out to receive the scroll to look over it.

Anaxagoras says proudly, "I've called it *The Flows*."

Archelaos opens the top part of the scroll to the first words, grins and nods and says, "*The Flows*! I like that. I'm already intrigued! And look at your artful handwriting!"

"The handwriting is Euathlos'."

"So it's about pissing away your time measuring the same thing once a year?" Protagoras jokes. Some of his students laugh.

"Yes," Anaxagoras confirms. "It is about that, essentially. About what I've learned over many years of taking diligent measurement of the same things at the same times of the year, and what it has taught me about the myriad flows of nature."

"Is it an atheist text?"

All hush to hear his answer. For all he has discussed in Athens over the years, Anaxagoras has become most famous, to the minds of those who don't know him well, as the foreigner who has suggested that the gods might not exist.

Anaxagoras shrugs and says, "It doesn't explicitly contradict the concept of the gods. But it does not *require* the gods to be mentioned, to describe the evident flows of nature. So no, it is not an atheist text, but it does not include stories of gods."

"*The Flows*, eh?" Protagoras muses, glancing at the thickly rolled scroll from across the shoulders of the young men between them. "Is that what wisemen from Ionia are doing now, writing books? I should write one myself. I would call it *The Throws*! For it would contain the best methods for how to idea-wrestle with other men."

Anaxagoras nods and chuckles with the students. "Clever," he acknowledges with genuine friendliness. "I would very much like to read that if you do write it."

Protagoras sniffs, "Well I do not intend to read *The Flows*, my friend. I am not particularly interested in flows. I avoid women during that time of the month."

His more puerile followers laugh at the joke. Anaxagoras wrinkles his face. Some of the men nearest to the few women present make faces at them, and the women look to each other for solace.

"Well, let me just say that I do hope you decide to write a book of your thoughts, Protagoras! I would love to read it. I tend to find that all new ideas are worthwhile, even if just to reveal what other people are thinking, even when they are wrong or follisome!"

Protagoras sniffs at the backhanded compliment. "Wrong? Follisome? Tell me, Anaxagoras, by what measure do you judge an idea wrong? When it disagrees with your own thoughts? Or when it fails to match what you imagine the universe to be?"

"When it contradicts what can be observed," Anaxagoras replies calmly. "When it fails to account for the evidence of nature."

"Ah yes, your beloved nature." Protagoras spreads his wide arms. "And who observes this nature? People do. And what do they observe it with? Their own senses. Their own minds. So really, you're still just measuring ideas against other ideas, which devolves into a chaos of subjectivity without some *contextual lens*."

"The flows of nature remain constant," Anaxagoras says, picking up a stone. "But our understanding of them grows. Each generation builds upon the knowledge of those before. The Seven Sages didn't know about Pythagoras' discoveries of logic. Pythagoras didn't know about what Herakleitos and Anaximander and Parmenides have come up with in our own days."

"So you think yourself wiser than Solon?" Protagoras scoffs.

"Not myself specifically. But consider - we men today know things that the Seven Sages couldn't know, not one of them! Because knowledge silts up further down the river of wisdom over time! This is an example of the flows which nature produces - not by the work of any particular god, but simply because that is how things occur, how they flow."

Protagoras opens his mouth to retort, but the younger men gathered around them begin speaking first, excited to participate.

"He's right," Archelaos says eagerly over some of the other men talking amongst each other. "Think of numbers, proofs, and geometry: each generation has built upon the last. Thales couldn't have understood Pythagoras' proofs, without the context of the thinkers who came between them, and now we go even further..."

Anaxagoras smiles and nods to his young friend

"And in medicine," adds another youth. "The Aigyptian scrolls are useful, yes, but the men of Kos are learning new things about the body every year, and spreading their knowledge around the Seas in tiny little scrolls filled with immense knowledge!"

"That's precisely my point," Anaxagoras nods. "Knowledge doesn't dry up like a stream in summer. It grows like a river joining other rivers."

"Except when wise men die," one youth adds morosely.

Anaxagoras nods with a twisted smile, shrugging. "Or go mad," he adds.

"So if wise men can go mad, then who determines what is good knowledge?" someone asks.

The bold young woman says, "Not the priests - they only keep the old ways. Not the poets - they only sing old songs."

"The teachers," suggests one.

Protagoras suggests, "There are idiot teachers."

"The thinkers," says another.

"Everybody *thinks*," Protagoras chuckles in quick response.

"So what *kind* of teachers?" Archelaos presses. "What kind of thinking? When a man goes to market seeking fish, he looks for a fishmonger. When he needs shoes mended, he seeks a shoe-maker. But when he seeks understanding of nature's flows..."

Protagoras groans, "Stop saying 'flows'!"

"...of numbers' mysteries, of the mind's workings - what kind of man does he seek? People know to avoid cabbageheads and scoundrels who are obviously so. But what makes a person seem wise?"

"People like us, truth-thinkers."

"Truth-thinkers is a stupid word. Nature-knowers is stronger."

Anaxagoras says, "I worry that too much alliteration and fancy wordplay might make people think we focus more on poetical turns of phrase than actual wisdom. Let us call ourselves simply friends-of-wisdom, *philosophers*, how about that? I've heard that was the term which Pythagoras preferred."

Protagoras says, "How about wisdom-doers - *sophists*. I do not just *love* wisdom, I am someone who *does* wisdom. There is a difference between an art-lover and an artist, no?"

Archelaos, with a wry grin, suggests, "Wisdom-doers is weird."

Anaxagoras shakes his head minutely, shrugging with frustration to Protagoras. "I'm curious, friend. We are friends. So why do you feel the need to be so antagonistic toward my ideas?"

Protagoras quietly thinks about his reply for a moment, eyeing the skinnier Anaxagoras up and down calmly. "Wisdom deserves a good grapple."

Anaxagoras shrugs and nods as if that is a sufficient answer.

"A good throw?" one student yelps excitedly.

Protagoras points at the young man while eyeing Anaxagoras.

Protagoras then addresses the gathered listeners and shouts, "Thus, *The Throws*, the perfect name for my upcoming book which will outline these ideas!"

Anaxagoras smiles, and gestures relenting the point.

Protagoras' fans cheer. One shouts, "Hail, Protagoras, great wisdomist!"

Archelaos says, "Friends-of-wisdom, flow over this way to hear about Anaxagoras' *already-extant* book *The Flows*!"

Anaxagoras good-naturedly gestures for him to ease down on the competitive arrogance, while thanking the young man with a smile for his support.

Δ

Themistokles is a witness to Persian royal justice

"Hellene, awake!"

Themistokles is wrenched from peaceful dreams of sailing by an Aithiopian courtier at the door of his bedroom in the courtiers' wing of Xerxes' palace. "Hellene!"

"What is it?" Themistokles asks sleepily, covering his nakedness with nearby furs. "Why have you awoken me?"

Seconds behind the Aithiopian are two Persian guards, their scimitars in their hands. They flank the doorway as the courtier lowers his head and says, "We are summoned to the throne room."

"In the dark of the night?"

"Immediately."

Frowning, Themistokles stands and wraps a tunic around himself.

"May I oil myself first?"

The Aithiopian courtier shakes his head no, gesturing for Themistokles to follow him urgently. The guards emote dissipating patience, and Themistokles has experienced their disrespect for Hellenes, so he decides to waste no more time.

In the throne room of Xerxes, the King of Kings sits upon his golden seat wearing his fullest royal regalia - a sprawling purple robe studded with jewels and embroidered with gold meandering lamassus. A tall Persian crown is on his head, and he sits high in his chair as if the crown weighs nothing, projecting as much power as he can.

At this time of night, the extreme trappings worry the sleepy Athenian expatriate. As soon as Themistokles enters the room he can tell that someone is going to die. Every courtier in the room is afraid; even Xerxes is afraid.

"Hellene," Xerxes barks upon seeing Themistokles, "I'm glad you're here. This is something that everyone needs to see."

As Xerxes is speaking, Themistokles' attention is stolen by the sound of more armor marching down the hall he just came down, at the other end of which now the general Artabanos is being led somberly by six royal guards in full battle-dress. As they approach and Themistokles stands aside to make room, Artabanos avoids eye contact though Themistokles tries hard to achieve it.

When Artabanos becomes visible to Xerxes in the doorway, the courtiers on either side of Xerxes start to hiss and groan out curses.

Artabanos is walked by the guards into the center of the room, facing Xerxes. He, like Xerxes, is dressed in the fullest regalia of his office. Themistokles, near the doorway, can only see Xerxes' face, and the backs of Artabanos and the guards.

Xerxes says angrily, "General Artabanos - my most trusted military advisor for over twenty years - you stand before me now a traitor, murderer of my own son, murderer of the prince who was heir to the throne of the whole world."

Themistokles and several other courtiers gasp at the revelation.

Eye-blacked Xerxes' voice creaks like a ship cresting a high wave. "You have murdered my sweet Prince Dareios. First grandson and namesake of my god-like father, who built this great palace, this great city, who gave you your life. You have killed the heir to the Empire. And so you have forfeited your life, and the lives of all of your followers, and your family, and all the men and women of the village of your birthplace. Your own children will be hung from their feet, drenched in honey, and fed to the desert ants. I will treat your loved ones like the old ways, traitor. You'll see."

Xerxes looks to the guards at either side of Artabanos with a deadly serious nod, but in a flash his expression switches in surprised reaction to some change in theirs, and fear knocks the mask of power off his face.

Just as quickly, the guards move away from Artabanos and toward the throne of Xerxes. All hearts lurch.

The courtiers at either side of the King of Kings shrink away, shrieking, as the back four guards turn their blades to threaten the many sycophants surrounding the room and the front two guards both bring their weapons down upon the King of Kings, shattering at once and with only a few blows rending apart his royal body, purple robe and all.

    Xerxes' surprised screams of agony are brief.

    "Don't worry about the robe," the general Artabanos says dryly, turning around to face the courtiers, including Themistokles. "Burn it."

    Artabanos scans the living, seeing if any more need to be killed. All cower, except Themistokles, who, though afraid, simply watches with wide eyes in horrified stillness.

    "There is a new King of Kings tonight," Artabanos declares, gesturing to the hallway, where two more guards have arrived with the eight-year-old Prince Artaxerxes, a small-framed boy, younger brother to yesterday's heir, just awoken. "All hail Artaxerxes."

    Artaxerxes, new King of Kings, rubs his sleepy eyes with his toy giraffe. He barely sees the gore for what it is.

    Themistokles discreetly hides in moonshadows beside some tall curtains, watching closely while trying to remain insignificant, focused for now only on surviving the night.

    The other courtiers murmur in a cacophonous whisper, "All hail, King of Kings, Artaxerxes," as the wails of women just hearing the news begin to waft down the hall.

    Artaxerxes the child king stares horror-struck into the dying last blinks of his father and predecessor as life leaves Xerxes' bulging eyes.

> "WISDOM HAS BEEN BUT THEATER THROUGHOUT HISTORY.
> THE DEAD ARE INITIATES OF THE ONLY TRUE MYSTERY."
> Hegesipyle, Thrakian Poet

E

King Archidamos of Sparta arrives at Delphi to speak with the Pythian Oracle

A busy cloudy summer day in the Sanctuary of Delphi is the sort of time when the volume of arguments and debates echoing out from inside the crowded little sloping stone city actually drowns out the sweet innocent songs of the shepherd poets out in the hills. Delphi today is a cosmopolitan stone bell, ringing with the internecine concerns of cities all across Ge.

Visitors from the western cities known broadly as Greater Hellas all speak of the eminence of the city of Syrakous, and how its power and wealth eclipse even Athens' League of Delos. Island cities bemoan the preeminence of Athens when others speak of the Delian League, and the debate of independence versus communal power is heated. Eastern cities of Ionia and Asia speak of Persia as a momentarily embarrassed war dog who has been slapped down at Eurymedon, and lost some power for the moment, but gained some in the sense of a need for revenge. Meanwhile those who hail from south of the Sea in Aigypt and Libya all speak of the *kairos*, the moment, when it might be possible to secede from the Empire and become independent again, while the new emperor is young, hearing the cases made by the islands against Athens.

To all this Aoide listens, weaving through crowds and catching the eyes of men while remaining unseen, feeling as if she is exactly where she is meant to be.

King Archidamos of Sparta emerges from the crowd gathered round the Serpent Column in the plaza just outside the Temple of Apollo at Delphi. The Eurypontid Spartan king declares with authority that makes younger men around him shrivel away, "I will be the next in line to speak with the Oracle! Sparta will have a consultation with the Pythia!"

One of the younger priests of Apollo begins to approach with a goat on a line, but King Archidamos shows them the palm of his hand.

"Go fuck your goat. I'll see the Pythia now. Sparta saved Hellas in both Persian Wars. I am her competent king. Now get out of my way, foreigners." He pushes through a group of well-dressed and thoroughly offended Carthaginian men to place himself at the very front of those waiting to be heard by the priests of the

ATHENS

temple.

Dextrimon steps forward, least intimidated among the elder priests. "King Archidamos of Sparta, no longer a boy. You have returned to Delphi. When last you were here, your father had just died..."

"Yes yes," Archidamos interrupts, trying to keep the priest from telling the rest of the story, since he obviously knows it himself.

But the story is for the crowd around them, so the priest finishes, keeping eye contact with Archidamos peering through a mask of respect.

"...your father had just died, and your grandfather Leotychidas brought you to us with his new daughter, sweet Lampito, your baby aunt, to see if it was proper to marry the little girl off to you, the new king. And bless that wedding Apollo did, didn't he? How is your noble young aunt-wife, little Lampito?"

"She is not little anymore," King Archidamos fumes coolly, "much like myself. A strong young son, in fact, we have created together." He turns to address his words to the crowd as well, shouting, "Agis! My son, the next Eurypontid King of Sparta! A long time from now. Anyway, priest, yes, I am back, as you noticed. Now remove yourself from my path."

The King steps past Dextrimon and his entourage of muscular Spartan bodyguards follow behind him close enough that there is nothing that can be done to stop them without starting a fight.

Inside the Temple of Apollo's dark and smoky space, Aoide and the Pythia are sitting together wafting smoke to each other playfully when the King of Sparta and his big armored men walk in, the outside light glinting all around them in halos. The Pythia gives Aoide the looks she gives when they are both admiring a handsome man, and it disarms the slight fear Aoide held. She laughs a little as the men gather, but slinks into the shadows where she knows she is expected to remain for now.

"So this is the great Pythia," King Archidamos sneers spitefully.

"What is your question to Apollo?" the Pythia asks.

As soon as she speaks, he becomes serious again. King Archidamos braces himself against the winds of fate. He speaks slowly and carefully, obviously having crafted his words with precision, knowing the sometimes fickleness with wording which prophets are known for.

"If the army of Sparta were to invade Attika, and make war upon the city of Athens itself, in this coming summer, would Sparta see victory in that endeavor?"

The Pythian chamber fills with sweet smoke as a priestess places a laurel branch into the fire. King Archidamos remains knelt before the tripod, his red cape pooled around him like blood on the temple floor, but he does not look down like most supplicants. He looks right at the Pythia, studying her.

Above him, the Pythia sways slightly, her eyes unfocused.

"Son of Zeuxidamos, who bears War's heavy crown, your fathers' fathers built their house on stolen ground, now Ge the Earth herself rejects your people's weight. She got her grandson the Sea God to shake what cannot stand - stone walls, stone hearts, stone laws which bind the land. The slaves you made will make you slaves in turn unless you learn to bend before you break. Your strength becomes your weakness, pride your fall, until you see that walls don't make a home, that borrowed glory fades like morning frost, and what was never yours was always lost. The choice comes thrice: to yield, to die, to change. Choose wisely, king whose kingdom rests on sand."

Archidamos' hands clench on his thighs. "Speak plainly, oracle. You did not answer my question."

The Pythia's head snaps toward him, her eyes suddenly sharp as knives. "Plain speech is for plain minds. Very well. Your slaves have found their courage while your warriors lose their nerve. The gods tire of Sparta's cruelty. Bend now, or the breaking will destroy you all."

"Sparta does not bend," Archidamos says.

A snake hisses its tongue out through a hole in its basket. Archidamos glances over to it, and the Pythia takes that moment to drastically shift the tone of her expression during his glance, so that he is disarmed to see her again when his eyes return. She is successful, and his eyes widen, his cheeks harden.

"Then Sparta will break," the Pythia says simply, her voice her own again. "I have seen it. The choice is yours, but the consequences belong to all your people."

The sacred snakes rustle in their golden baskets. Through the temple windows, the morning star glows like a watching eye.

Archidamos surges to his feet, his hand going to his sword hilt. His huffing breath snorts through his nose, but he keeps any words in his mind inside. The temple guards shift uneasily, their spears glinting as they move. Behind the tripod, the high priest raises his staff, though his hands tremble slightly.

"Take care, King of Lakedaemonia," he warns. "You stand on Apollo's holy ground. Even Kroisos of Lydia, with all his gold, could not bend divine will to mortal desire."

"Kroisos ruled barbarians," Archidamos snarls. "We are Spartans, sons of Herakles!"

"And was not Herakles himself enslaved?" the Pythia asks softly. "Did not Zeus himself command it, to teach him humility?"

The sacred snakes raise their heads, tongues flicking. Outside, clouds pass before the sun, throwing the temple into sudden shadow.

"You dare compare Sparta to..."

"I dare nothing," the Pythia interrupts. "I merely speak what Apollo shows me. If truth angers you, quarrel with the god, not his voice."

The priests of Apollo form a subtle line between the king and their Pythia. Their faces are calm, but their knuckles are white on their staffs. They have seen kings come in anger before.

"Remember Kleomenes," old Dextrimon murmurs. "Remember how madness took him after he tried to force a prophecy."

Archidamos' face darkens like a storm cloud. For a long moment, the only sound is the crackling of the sacred fire. Finally, the king's hand falls from his sword. "Apollo's wisdom is noted," he growls. "Sparta will find her own meaning from it."

But as he turns to leave, the Pythia calls after him, "Consider quickly, son of Zeuxidamos. The water in your time jar drains fast."

The temple doors boom shut behind him. The priests collectively release their held breath. But the Pythia continues to sway on her tripod, her eyes distant, seeing something that makes her shiver despite the sacred fire's heat.

After the priests have sighed and wiped their brows and chuckled to each other to ease the tension, Aoide takes a quiet moment to ask the Pythia, "How do you know that what you're hearing is truly the inspiration of Apollo?"

The Pythia squints at Aoide's question, but takes it with a nod, and thinks about it for a long time as Aoide brushes her hair with one of the ancient bone combs from the stash of relics which only the Pythia are allowed to use.

Finally, after Aoide has forgotten she asked the question, the Pythia answers, "You know that what you're hearing in your mind is real, not because of any mistake of certainty, or because you are merely pretending to be certain, but because you have actually summoned the spirits with which you intend to commune into your mind. Among us, you alone can know what you have done within your mind, but some gods can also know. Your mind is a space - a space bigger and yet also with shorter distances than this stony space outside of our minds - and you can summon spirits there; including Apollo himself. When you summon some spirit to your mind, just like calling out a name in a field, sometimes a different spirit will answer the call before your intended recipient - but you can always tell, if you know the person you are calling for."

Aoide shudders. She has always been unnerved by the notion of ghosts, and has long tried to dispel the concept from her mind as impossible and contrary to the evidence of nature. And somehow imagining them able to inhabit her mind makes them seem even more disturbing and invasive.

"How do you know you know Apollo?" Aoide asks again.

The Pythia minutely smiles at the chance to consider such a question, looks away a moment as she thinks. "Not all do. Many might simply have glimpsed in their minds some nymph and mistaken him or her, or seen a distant vision of Hyperion in the heavens and thought that star-chained titan was the brilliant, far-flashing boy god we love. Many live mistaken and never know it. But when you do meet Apollo's pure brilliance in your mind, you will know it. He is *Phoibos* - bright-shining - brighter than any other god, and clear."

Aoide quietly says, "Brighter than the sun," remembering that moment that the sun became black to her sight.

The Pythia seems to see that light illuminate Aoide's mind, and smiles. "You have met him," she says. "You do see what I mean."

"He gave me once the pure knowledge of a perfect circle, when I gazed upon the holy sun chariot," Aoide says. "He blinded me for a few days, and all I could see, all I could think about, was this perfect black circle. More perfect even than a sunset. Just black."

The Pythia squints and smiles, intrigued and confused. "I have never heard of anything like that," she says.

Z

Sokrates and friends help Simon rebuild his shoe shop

"Always rebuilding," Simon sighs. "If it isn't barbarians destroying our city, it's our own sons."

The wrecked Agora shops are all in various stages of their rebuilding.

"Why don't we ever see gangs of girls do this sort of thing?" Euripides asks Simon while the tall teenager helps balance a canvas up on its poles.

Simon nods and shows intrigue with his mouth. "That is an excellent question, Euripides. What do the rest of you think?"

"Because they're not allowed to roam around like boys," Krito suggests as a possibility.

Simon says, "That's true. But, somehow, I suspect not the right answer to this question."

"Maybe we should ask some girls," Sokrates realizes aloud as he is lifting a pole into place. "Why can't we hang out with girls?"

Simon laughs a little and sighs and nods. "I suppose it is mainly because their fathers would not be very happy about it. But it's too bad, perhaps, because it would seem you're probably right - the best answer about why girls do or don't do something would be to ask them."

"If only," Euripides jokes with a sigh. The others laugh.

Sokrates balances the pole he has raised while Euripides and Krito grapple together with a heavy oxhide canvass which they are supposed to throw over the high poles, but it is proving difficult to manage, as increasingly is Sokrates' pole. Simon, seated due to a lame leg, points and gestures and reaches out fruitlessly, laughing.

"My feet hurt," Sokrates groans, rubbing one pudgy little foot with the other.

Simon shuffles forward on the ground to inspect Sokrates' sandals and sees that his feet are squished into them. "Sokrates, you need new shoes. How have I not noticed that? You know, it was your feet that first brought you to me!"

Euripides laughs, "It's our feet that bring us everywhere, Simon!"

Simon chuckles and corrects himself, "I mean to say it was his *shoelessness*! Your eye on words is sharp as ever, Euripides!"

As the afternoon progresses, the boys begin working in companionable silence for a while, each finding their rhythm in the task. Sokrates struggles with the heavy poles but refuses help, his face reddening with effort. Krito ties off the corners of the canvas with the efficiency of someone who has helped his father with such work before. Euripides moves with surprising grace for his gangly frame, remembering and acting out scenes from recent theatrical plays in his mind while he works, slightly miming without realizing. Simon watches them all with quiet pride, offering occasional guidance with his pointing fingers and gentle words." Mind that corner there. The wind will catch it if you don't secure it properly. Yes, good."

The shop begins to take shape. What started as scattered poles and canvas gradually transforms back into something that could shelter a craftsman and his work. The boys step back periodically to view their progress, wiping sweat from their brows, sharing satisfied glances.

Simon stands back on his good leg after twisting the final pole into the earth, and assesses their work as a whole, with a hand shading his eyes from the low afternoon sun.

"There, boys, what do you think? Good as new."

Sokrates says, "Except in this case, new isn't good. Because it doesn't have any of the work you put into the old thing, any of the fine details that had accrued, or the memories in the little corners. This place is just like some little bald crying baby of a shoe shop."

Everyone laughs at Sokrates' weird comment, making him grin.

"You remind me of yourself when I first met you, you know," Simon recalls, sitting tailor-style in the street where he was standing. The boys all around join him in sitting, forming a large group which passersby start to flow around. "When you were only this high, you came into my shop and I tried to give you a free pair of shoes. But what did you do? You took them right over to the public fire that they kept in front of the old ruined Temple of Zeus over there and gave them to the Storm God because you felt he needed your help."

The other boys all laugh. The shadows of the afternoon slowly grow. Sokrates smiles at the old man who seems to know him better than he knows himself.

"You have always known the virtues of the bare foot, Sokrates," Simon says. "And this new shop is a..." Simon has to stop talking to cough for a long time, which his young friends wait patiently through. Then he continues, "...This new shop just might be more like a bare foot than a baby. It's just pure, and close to the Earth, and no heavier than it needs to be."

Simon looks over at the new little tent they have set up. "I like to think that it shows how young I still am, and that I can start over anytime."

The boys help Simon arrange his tools on their new hooks. Krito organizes the leather scraps by size while Sokrates sorts the awls and needles. Euripides sits in the corner, scratching away at a piece of leather with a stylus, trying to capture something of Simon's wisdom.

"Be careful with those words," Simon jokes. "Leather remembers everything you write on it. Unlike a wax tablet, or the sand, you can't smooth it over and start again. Skin remembers."

"That's why I like it," Euripides replies without looking up. "Words should have permanence. They should leave marks."

"Are words like thought footprints?" Sokrates asks.

"Thought scars," Euripides mutters.

Simon laughs and shakes his head. "You're so serious, young artist. They aren't scars. They're more like ... neighbors. Like memories that decided to stick around."

Euripides groans again, his eyes moving between his own scratched-out writing and the lines written in leather strips on the high beam opposite him. "Simon," he sighs, "how are you able to make everyone like you, and laugh at everything you say? Nobody likes me, and I don't know how to say things that people like, and so I don't know how to write characters that say things that people will like. How can I be expected to know what great men of experience would think or say?"

"Well, the theater is different than the Agora," Simon notes thoughtfully. "It seems audiences in the theater enjoy the behavior of characters which they would not enjoy seeing in the marketplace for real. Your characters don't have to be likable, necessarily. Look at Sophokles. He wouldn't know how to write a respectable person on pain of torture!" The boys all laugh. "But he can certainly end the day with an ivy crown."

"So, it doesn't matter how terrible I write, because audiences will only ever like ox-shit," Euripides cynically tries to translate what Simon has said.

"Not so much that," Simon says, "but they definitely seem to love characters whom no one would actually want to know if they were real - so we get warriors and royals, with the voices of poets but the behavior of teen-aged rascals. Whatever you do, Euripides, it seems to me that you will have been successful if you've done anything different than anyone else is doing."

Euripides throws his hands in the air. "So all I need to do is what no one else could possibly do! Simple!"

"Simpler than you think," Simon suggests.

H

Milo the Pythagorean spars with Athenians at the White Dog gym

At the White Dog gymnasion on a cool, overcast afternoon, Kritias, Kimon, and Alkibiades lift stone weights with Kallias and a few of his other rich priest friends while their young adult sons pay the famous Olympian victor Milo to wrestle with them.

Surrounded by a circle of his friends, Kleinias son of Alkibiades walks across the sand to Milo's huge form and attempts to strut.

"Look at this monster," Kleinias mocks, "he looks like the images Aigyptians make of Herakles."

Milo says, "That's because Herakles *was* an Aigyptian."

Kleinias scoffs a laugh and looks back at his brother and friends. "Please," he snorts, "Herakles is the ultimate Hellene. He's from Krete. Everyone knows that."

"No, Herakles was from Sikyon," Hipponikos son of Kallias says from the sidelines.

"Who told your mother stories?" mocks Kleinias' older brother Axiochos. "Herakles was born on Mount Ida in Krete, where Zeus was raised as a boy, the true cradle of Hellenic culture."

Giant-shouldered Milo just watches stone-faced as the boys all argue, and by the time they are finished he has very gradually expressed the most minute of grins.

"Herakles was the son of Ammon," Milo says. "He traveled all across the world putting up pillars in honor of his father. And, perhaps, I'll admit, it's possible that he did indeed start this gym here, because I know he traveled all up and down the length of the world. But he was definitely born in Aigypt, and was an Aigyptian, just like me."

One of the younger boys asks, "Who is Ammon? Some Aigyptian king?"

Milo nods to him. "One of our greatest kings. And now you all worship him by the name of Zeus, I believe."

The Hellenic boys all laugh groaning and fall upon each other, looking around wide-eyed to see if any priests overheard that blasphemy.

Hipponikos the priest's son shakes his head. "Herakles was a Hellene," he sighs, hesitant to argue with the giant Olympian. "And Zeus is a god."

"You're free to believe what you like," Milo says calmly. "Or shall we let this contest of strength determine the answer?" Then finally, Milo grins broadly.

Kleinias laughs softly at that and shakes his head. "Let's just grapple. Don't throw me, please, okay?"

"I have learned not to make promises," Milo says, getting into stance to receive a wrestling attack.

Kleinias lunges first, is easily deflected. While Milo shows him his error, the others catch their breath, their fathers' voices drifting from the colonnade where they are quietly discussing politics over wine.

"They talk too much and act too rarely," Kleinias' older brother Axiochos says, wiping oil from his shoulders. "Nothing changes. Ephialtes still speaks in the Assembly, still turns the poor against us."

"Your turn," Milo calls to Hipponikos, who steps forward to attempt a throw.

"Father says democracy is like a plague," Kleinias adds, watching his friend's failed attempt. Hipponikos gives up quickly.

"Again," Milo commands. "Mind your stance."

"Then perhaps it needs stronger medicine than old men can provide," Axiochos suggests carefully, moving to take his own turn against the champion. "They have too much to lose now. Too many reputations to protect. We who are young have the luxury of being able to take bigger risks."

Milo lets strong-legged Axiochos get a grip, then shifts slightly, showing the others how to maintain balance.

"What are you saying?" asks one of the younger boys.

Axiochos grins and winks at his fellows, pressing harder against the wrestler's defense.

Milo moves like lightning. Suddenly Axiochos is airborne, then slammed hard enough against the ground, driving the air out of his lungs. He lies there gasping, tears welling in his eyes despite his attempts to hold them back.

"In Aigypt we have a saying," says Milo. "The crocodile weeps."

"And what does that mean?" Hipponikos asks while Kleinias kneels to help his brother.

Milo just stares at the young man derisively, giving him time to think.

"It's nothing but Aigyptian to me," Kleinias dismisses the phrase as meaningless, while Axiochos swallows his tears breathlessly.

ATHENS

> "IF YOU WANT AN ANIMAL TO DEVELOP
> NOT SIMPLY A FONDNESS BUT AN ABSOLUTE CRAVING
> FOR THE COMPANY OF MAN, YOU MUST PROVIDE THAT
> THE ANIMAL ENCOUNTERS ONLY HUNGER AND THIRST
> AND FLIES IN SOLITUDE, WHILE FOOD AND DRINK AND COMFORT
> COME ONLY FROM THE HELP OF MEN."
>
> Hippodoros, *On Horsemanship*

Θ

Euripides goes on a boy-scout trip

On his nineteenth birthday, Euripides travels up to the northern borderlands of Attika with a cohort of other Athenian boys of his same age, where they have been tasked with patrolling the border hills as scouts. It is a duty which falls on all Athenian boys sometime before they're twenty years old, but Euripides has been secretly believing he would somehow be able to avoid it, and certainly didn't expect to be riding in the back of a cart with nine other sweaty teenage boys, and nobody from his neighborhood, on his birthday.

To soothe himself, Euripides sings little songs from *The Odyssey* just barely audible to himself while the boys around him wrestle and shout.

*"My name is Nobody. Yes it really is Nobody
which my mother, father, foes and friends call me."*

"Quit your noise, boys," the cart-driver bellows at the rowdy teen-agers as they laugh and spit at frogs hopping out of the way of the wheels. "When you're out scouting, that sort of racket'll summon some brigands. They know the careless laughter of boys well, trust me. We may not be at war, but the poor wretches who live in the hills are always at war with sanity. It's not just Thebans you need to be on the lookout for up here, but Pelasgians too, with no sense of humanity or cultivation.

They'll skin you right up, and not worry about your cries. They'd rape a frog!"

"Shut your fly-catcher, cart-driver," replies Kleinias, the Oligarch Alkibiades' son, with an unctuous grin to the other boys. "If you were a scout-master, you wouldn't be driving a cart. We're not stupid, and we're not here to take advice from some lowly donkey-master. Mind the road, donkey-kisser."

The cart driver glares but turns his head away and takes it out on the poor donkey pulling them all.

Euripides continues singing unheard.

"Then, Nobody, my gift is this for you:
I'll eat Nobody last among his crew."

Up ahead, the ancient stone watchtower of Eleutherai appears at the crest of the hill, surrounded by the long scout tents where Euripides realizes he and the rest of the boys will likely be sleeping. The scout master Grylla stands beside the tower's worn steps, a weathered man with a face like old leather and arms thick with the kind of muscle that comes from real work, not gymnasion showing-off.

"Get those packs up here," he barks at the arriving boys. "Then fifty squats, each of you. Need to awaken those muscles after that cart ride!"

The other boys drop their belongings and begin the exercise with varying enthusiasm. Euripides stares up at the stone steps leading to where he'll have to carry his pack, each one looking higher than the last.

"Ugh, my body is so heavy," Euripides moans. "The bigger I get, the more I hate having to lift myself."

"The pull of Ge is the pull of chthonic fate, toward death and dissolution. You better get good at lifting yourself, or start learning Orphic passages to sing to Persephone as she looks down upon your shade."

Grizzled Grylla gathers the boys in a loose circle. The summer dust rises around their feet as they shuffle into place, some confident, others, like Euripides, trying to hide their uncertainty.

"Welcome to the borderlands," growls Grylla, eyeing each youth in turn. "Here's where you stop being your mothers' sons and start becoming Athens' shield-bearers. Every man who's ever stood in the phalanx started right here, just like you, learning what it means to guard our territory."

Grylla paces the circle's edge, his limp barely noticeable. "The Persians came through these hills. The Thebans watch us from these hills. The mountain folk raid down from these hills. Athens needs men who know every path, every cave, every spring. Men who can move silent as wolves and strike like thunderbolts."

His eyes linger on Euripides, seeming to smell his fear. Euripides feels himself be seen, and the other boys' eyes falling onto him, and his body grows hot. Whispers wander, until they are shouted down.

"No whispers now! Some of you have never slept under stars before. Some have never gone hungry, or tracked a boar, or kept silent watch through the dark hours. That will change. By the time you return to your comfy beds, you'll know how to build a fire in the rain, how to read tracks in the dust, how to kill your dinner with a sling or spear. And you'll finally be useful to your city, instead of just hungry loads."

He draws his sword and plants it point-first in the earth. "But first, you need to know your own strength. How to use your body as a weapon, how to take a hit and give one back. The phalanx isn't built of men who flinch. Starting today, you'll wrestle, you'll run, you'll fight with staves until your hands blister and your muscles scream."

Several of the burlier boys grin at this, already eyeing the smaller ones like wolves sizing up lambs. Euripides tries to make himself even less noticeable.

"Get acquainted with your fellow scouts," old Grylla commands. "You'll be trusting each other with your lives soon enough." He yanks his sword from the earth and strides off toward his tent, leaving the boys to size each other up.

The afternoon sun beats down on the practice field as the youths stand to cluster and jostle, old friendships and new rivalries already forming. Those from the same neighborhoods gravitate together, while the larger boys puff themselves up and the smaller ones seek allies. Euripides hangs back, watching the others with the careful eye he usually reserves for studying plays, until suddenly-

Euripides' breath leaves his body as he is tackled from the side by tall, lean Nikias, who lifts him into the air, laughing, and carries him bodily over to the open field, where he collapses with him in the grass. Several other young men, some younger, some older than Euripides, but all much larger, rush over and begin to pile on top of him and Nikias.

Feeling like he can't breathe, and with darkness crushing down upon him as more and more muscular young men join the laughing pile between him and the sky, Euripides suddenly feels he has no choice but to scream. When he feels at first unheard, he gives the scream all of his might.

"Alright, everybody, get off him! Come on, get off the man!"

Nikias' voice is like a hand reaching down into the Underworld, and it is followed quickly by light pouring back in upon Euripides' shut eyes, and hands lifting him up onto his knees.

"It's okay, little one, you're fine. Calm down."

Nikias pats Euripides on the back and says, "Breathe normally, kid. Just breathe normally and you'll be alright."

The words make Euripides realize he has been gasping and shrieking through his sobs. He's able to begin to control himself again, though he can feel little now past the heat of embarrassment.

"Welcome to the mountain!" an older boy named Pythodoros shouts, laughing at Euripides cruelly.

A small and sturdy boy Euripides' age named Philippos, who lives on the other side of the well from Euripides' family, rides up on a horse, pulling its reins to a stop just in front of the other boys, showing off his deft control over the animal.

"Euripides!" Philippos shouts excitedly. "Who dragged Euripides outdoors?"

"My soul dragged my body," Euripides replies, fleetingly attempting good nature. "I'm here of my own choice."

"Well maybe he is to be a worthy citizen after all," Philippos remarks. "Ever been on a horse, Euripides?" He reigns his horse to step forward and back, kicking little bits of earth up around Euripides. "Want a ride behind me?"

"No thanks," Euripides replies, unable to hide his annoyance.

"Ever been on a horse?" he asks again.

"You sure seem to care a lot about horses," Euripides snidely notes.

"If I didn't love horses, why would I be named Philippos?" Philippos shouts with a big laugh. He is the loudest boy Euripides has ever met. "I figure that if I keep riding all the time, then by the time I'm an adult I'll have the best chance I can of being the best Athenian knight on any battlefield!"

"Battles aren't won on the battlefield anymore," Nikias replies, attempting to sound modern and wiser than his sixteen years. "They're won behind walls, in planning rooms, with writing and drawings, and by correctly reading signs from the gods in nature. Horsemen are the same as rowers."

All the rich boys moan derision at that modern, anti-aristocratic notion. One shoves Nikias from behind, but Nikias, taller than that boy, turns and punches him hard in the chest, knocking the boy back onto his butt in the grass, and causing all his friends to laugh.

"Don't shove me, or I'll shove you into the ground," Nikias tells his fellow aristocrat's son.

Pythodoros snidely asks Euripides, "Hey Euripides, have you ever seen a woman naked?"

"No!" Euripides retorts, as if the question was a test of his morality. "How would I? Do I look married to you?"

"Here's what you need to know about women, Euripides. See, now, this is O-mega, the big O. Only girls have that. That's what you want to aim for, that's the *kairos*. But right down below it is the O-micron, the little O. That's the butt-hole, and everybody's got one. You've got one, don't you?"

Euripides shakes his head.

"You don't?"

"I'm shaking my head in dismay, not negation."

Someone else shouts, mocking the airy voice of a girl, "Euripides lacks a butt-hole!"

"Euripides claims he doesn't have a butt-hole. Let's find out!"

Philippos and his friend Pythodoros start grasping at the bottom of Euripides' tunic, forcing him to slap their hands away and flee a few feet back.

"When you're beautiful yourself, sometimes girls will want to impress you so much they'll show you some skin. Pulling aside their dress like this..."

One of the youngest boys, Pyrilampes, just an early teen, mimes being a flirtatious girl, batting his eyelashes and coyly pulling his own tunic down along his muscular shoulder.

Euripides watches, confused, reddening.

"What do you think, Euripides? Would you turn your head if a girl did this?" Pyrilampes pulls down his tunic to reveal his chest, licks his fingers and grabs his nipple, moaning with mock pleasure.

All the other boys laugh again, and Philippos and Pythodoros playfully shove Euripides from behind.

"On the gods, that's what the Alkmaeonid girl Deinomache did to me the other day," Philippos tells the boys beside him. "She shows me her nipples whenever I want. I just peek over their wall and she shows me everything."

Pyrilampes holds out a small drinking cup with images of women cavorting sexually with men, all nude, with penises actually appearing to enter the bodies of the women in various places. It is the first time Euripides has ever seen such imagery, and his face immediately gets hot with embarrassment at the sight of it.

"Does this give you a boner?" Pyrilampes asks Euripides. "I'm willing to sell it. I just found it in the woods; I didn't steal it; I promise."

Under the heat of the midday Sun, his head rushing with overlapping embarrassments, Euripides faints to the grass, unconscious.

Euripides wakes moments later, to the laughter of his peers, as they drench him with water from a big jar. He sputters and flops like a fish on the dock.

"Give him room, give him room," Nikias commands the others as he kneels down toward Euripides and pats him on the chest. "You're alright, Euripides. You just got too hot."

The younger boys laugh, already starting to move away together toward a discus toss being wound up across the field. "Euripides got too hot," they chide, saying it suggestively.

Nikias helps Euripides to his feet and keeps his arm around his shoulder as he walks the wobbly boy over to a large amphora full of water. He says, "Here," as he presses Euripides' back forward to bend him down in front of the water and then splashes some in his face. Euripides sputters, but then drinks some and quickly washes his face. Nikias laughs at the sputter.

"Ignore fools," Nikias says with a confident smile. "Be cool, slow to react, self-assuredly calm. The best wisdom my father ever taught me. There will always be fools and idiots, no different than new children. Just don't react to them. You don't owe them a response, even in body language. It is folly to worry about what they think or say. In modern terms: just ignore everyone uncool. Be cool. That's all you've got to do."

Euripides smiles, appreciating the sentiment. He feels cool with Nikias, and though it is an entirely new concept to him, being *cool* is suddenly all he cares about.

Sitting in the grass with a view down the hillside he just came up, into the plain of Attika below, knowing his home city is there beyond the horizon, active and alive just like himself, just unseen, Euripides thinks about his place in Athens, about being a man, a citizen, and an artist, and remembers being a child, and wonders about being a free and responsible adult.

In his view beneath him, but high above the land below, an eagle floats low on the wind. Euripides marvels at seeing the top side of a flying eagle, and feels like he could imagine the view from the Moon.

I

Periboea meets someone new

Patiently Periboea sits against a low wall on the street, watching her cousin Perikles discuss the building of a house in town with some architect and his assistants. Passing men's judgmental eyes drag across her like oxen furrowing a field one direction and then the next. She does her best to smile politely to those who appear noble like her, and to ignore those who don't.

Her mother and her aunt Agariste arranged this day for Periboea and Perikles to spend some time together, with the obvious intention of preparing them for possible marriage prospects, but he has spent the whole time talking to this builder about possible plans for houses and possible locations, and has ignored her.

So now, twenty-two year old Periboea sits alone, feeling neglected, intermittently listening to the men and watching the clouds transform above the city, wishing that she could be that formless and free. Two hawks dance in the sky, and she imagines them just-married. She wonders how far hawks travel, and if they gossip with the clouds.

Among the other daytime city-goers, the rich priest Kallias and his teen-aged son Hipponikos come down the lane speaking casually with a couple of other men from their neighborhood, followed by several of their well-dressed household slaves, with stolid Elpinike colorfully veiled in the middle of the slaves, eyeing everyone on the street with curious derision. The group slow their gait and all gradually come to a stop when Kallias sees Perikles standing with the architect by the old burned out corner lot.

"Hail, Perikles!" Kallias calls out. "Hipponikos, let us stop here a moment and speak with this fine man. Have you two met?"

Perikles gives Kallias and his son a cordial wave, but also tries to indicate with his lack of response that he is in the middle of a conversation with the architect Hippodamos. Perikles notices Elpinike with the slaves; they make eye contact only briefly, then each look away again.

All of this Periboea watches, without herself being seen.

"Planning on moving closer to the action, finally?" Kallias laughs to Perikles. "Or is it more about getting away from your mother at last?"

Perikles politely smiles and feigns a laugh. "Exactly," he says.

The architect Hippodamos says, "I was just explaining to Perikles all of the possibilities in this lot here. I'd say it's one of the best available within the walls. It faces south, as any good house ought to, and it's on a fine street just a quick walk from the well in the neighborhood square, but not *right on* the square, which, though it may seem exciting to younger men, older wiser men like us know that you don't need that kind of noise in the evenings. You want to be at least a little bit separated from those who wander at night. This lot is the perfect balance of removed and central."

Kallias nods, examining the size of the lot, the surrounding buildings, and the rubble of the old ruin which stood here before the wars. He points to one piece of broken wall at the back of the lot, which happens to have the scorched remnants of a colorful and finely painted wall mural still visible upon it. "Look there," Kallias remarks, "a fine painting was in the last house here. That means that a clever man chose this lot before you."

"Yes, who did live in this house before?" Perikles asks.

"Iakolos," Hippodamos nods morosely, "who fell at Plataia."

The men all grimace reverently in recognition of the man's sacrifice. Kallias, the oldest of those present, nods as he recalls. "Iakolos was a clever man. His family lived here for three generations. Happiness still lingers with the spirits here, I can feel it."

"I too get good vibes from this lot," Hippodamos agrees. "This is a place for happiness."

Perikes explains, "I am still not sure about living solo inside the city wall. I don't want to come off as aloof or as if I hold myself higher than my fellows, but at the same time, living right on an urban street removes a certain buffer that I've enjoyed..."

Kallias tells him, "I know exactly what you mean, Perikles. But I assure you there is more to be gained by living among the people than you gain by living within your own family wall. It is a double edged sword, urbanity - to be close to the action, seen by the people, hear their voices every day. But if you want to get into politics, I think it will be good for you."

Perikles nods, sighs, and thanks Kallias with a smile.

While the adults are talking, ocean-eyed Hipponikos, son of Kallias, smiles at Periboea and saunters over closer to her, nervously pulling at the ropes on his tunic. She can't help but smile playfully at his shy forwardness as he tries to maintain eye contact with her.

"Good morning, beauty-face," Hipponikos coos.

She briefly grimaces at his weird wording, but brushes it off quickly. "Good morning, Hipponikos." She struggles not to smile, to avoid seeming too flirtatious. Men always compliment her smile, and her mother assured her that such compliments are the triggers of romance traps.

"I thought it might be the Muse Kalliope herself at first," he flirtily jokes with a shy little chuckle, looking down at the street.

Periboea fake-laughs sweetly at the sentiment, partially to dismiss it.

"Who's your father?" he asks her. "I know you're an Alkmaeonid but I forget who…"

"Megakles," she answers. "Why do you ask?"

Hipponikos shrugs. "Just trying to determine if he's as rich as me."

Periboea chuckles at that unmasked arrogance. She shakes her head at him as if disappointed, but cannot stop smiling. "We're comfortable," she whispers, unable to speak full volume without laughing.

"Well *we're* the richest family in Athens," Hipponikos says, swaggering closer. "Probably the whole world. So however comfortable you are, imagine being a lot more comfortable. You know what I mean?"

"Are you trying to make me feel bad?"

"No, no," Hipponikos whispers, inching ever closer to Periboea so that she can smell his sweaty body. "No, I would only want to make you feel good. I mean, you're probably the most famous old rich family in Athens! I don't know what old folks say about it, and I don't much care."

Periboea smiles to feign gratitude at his feigned avoidance of the topic of the supposed old curse on her family.

"What does your father do?" Periboea asks him. "I mean how did he make his money? Other priests aren't as rich as he is. I never knew what people mean when they say…"

"'Enriched by the ditch'?" Hipponikos sighs, glancing back at his father. Periboea nods.

"Yes, it's all I heard at the gymnasion when I was a boy. 'Enriched by the ditch'. Well I'll tell you the real story if you want to know."

Periboea shyly says nothing, but keeps her eyes on Hipponikos to listen if he intends to tell the tale.

After a few shy moments, Hipponikos sits down on the low stone wall beside Periboea.

"So, perhaps you've heard it told that my father, at the Battle of Marathon, famously went into battle in his full priestly garb, being the torchbearer of the

Eleusinian Mysteries. And the story is that after the chaos of battle, some Persian mistook his priestly dress for the garb of a king, and showed him the hiding place of some Persian treasure, hidden in a ditch..."

Hipponikos and Periboea both look up and away from their conversation, as it is interrupted by the louder conversation across the street - that conversation between Perikles and Kallias and Elpinike.

Kallias shouts, "Perikles, living on his own, and within the walls! What a great idea! It is an excellent location. And your family has some of the best furniture in Athens for you to choose from, so I'm sure the inside will be as fine as you want it to be once the structure is built. Very fine, Perikles, very impressive."

"Well, impressive isn't what I'm going for," Perikles replies modestly. "I'd prefer just-good-enough. But it's true - for me, just-good-enough needs to be quite fine." The two men laugh, understanding the benefits of luxury.

"You going to use Persian wreckage, or try to make it look pre-war and not include any of that, all old-style?"

"I don't want to look like I'm trying to look ostentatious. But I also don't want to look like I'm trying too hard to appear less wealthy than my family is. So I thought I'd include some Persian beams, to match the mode of the moment, but do something fancy to them like our grandfathers might've. Well, those of us whose grandfathers were ostentatious Oligarchs."

Perikles and Elpinike have a small laugh together, while Kallias just raises his eyebrows.

A passing old man shouts at Elpinike from the group he's with, "Get back to your weaving room! Get your woman where she belongs!"

Kallias, struggling to remain friendly in the face of the insult, shouts back, "She can weave sometimes and walk others, friend!" Then he turns to his wife and whispers, "Ignore them. Apropos - the old ways."

Hipponikos whispers to Periboea, "You know, I have often wondered if my step-mother's eyes might be wandering ships, and now I'm wondering if Perikles might be their port of call."

Periboea frowns at that, eyeing her handsome and well-respected cousin Perikles and watching that previous vision of her future spin like a rolling knucklebone in the dusty Agora, and then turning back to handsome Hipponokos and wondering if the Fates might be more like dancers, open to inspiration, rather than weavers, who follow a plan. The thought fills her with the urge to dance. But she doesn't, not in public. She saves the feeling for later, when she can express it to herself with no leering men around.

ATHENS

K

Artabanos summons Themistokles to the Apadana

The many-columned Apadana is empty of everything but echoes, as Themistokles steps nervously from rug to rug across its sprawling stone floor, past column after column which feel to him like the masts of innumerate ships. Intermittently, he is back at the Battle of Salamis, creaking Persian masts falling all about him. The Persian guardsmen who summoned him from his chamber keep a respectful distance behind him on either side as they cross the sprawling columned room together.

Here and there, huddled around columns, one in each group holding a lamp, clusters of courtiers whisper to each other, silencing upon seeing the Hellene stride lampless through the darkening dusk-lit space, which gets more shadowy the deeper he goes.

At the deep side of the cavern of columns, standing with a foot upon the throne of the King of Kings, is the wisened old general, the late Xerxes' right hand man, Artabanos.

Artabanos looks up as Themistokles gets close.

"Athenian!" he calls out, as he has taken to calling Themistokles for lack of other Athenians in Persepolis these days. "You've already had dinner, I hope."

Themistokles nods, but then realizes the shadowy space might hide his gesture so he also says, "I have, General."

Artabanos' eyes alight at that moniker. "You honor me. You too are a general."

"An admiral," Themistokles corrects. "Our word is *trierarch* - master of ships. In my case, many ships followed my call."

"So I've heard," Artabanos nods. "I wasn't there."

"Weren't you?" Themistokles asks, with a quizzical cock of his head. He steps forward toward his fellow commander, who takes his foot off the throne and turns his full body toward Themistokles. "I thought I remembered hearing your name - that is to say, when I heard it here, I thought I recognized it as having been among the generals who fought with Xerxes in Hellas."

"You're thinking of Artaba*zos*," says Artabanos. "I am Artaba*nos*. We both hear that confusion often. No, Artabazos - who led wild Parthians and Khwarazmians on the march into Hellas - he's now king in Phrygia, living the good life with his beautiful Khwarazmian wife and many children. He earned it, with all his work in that war. That is exactly what I wanted to speak to you about."

"About your friend with the similar name?"

Artabanos laughs.

Smiling, enjoying the laugh, Themistokles tries for one again, asking, "Khwarazmian whores?"

Artabanos puts a hand on Themistokles' shoulder, laughing, but getting serious beneath it. "Stop. You're too funny. About what a man can earn for himself by serving King Artaxerxes with honor. The King of Kings is powerful enough to be able to bestow kingship itself. Haven't you ever imagined yourself as a king? Every boy does."

Beardless Themistokles shrugs. "Owning my own ship was all I ever wanted," he says, thinking back with honesty to his own childhood. "And only in Athens could I have gotten that by simply dedicating myself and working hard. You think an oarsman's son could really rise to a position of power in Persia today? Or in one of these other barbarian lands you all have conquered? In Athens they can."

"You Hellenes call other people barbarians, as if you alone can lay claim to civilization. And yet your people, more than any other, sews the seeds of its own society with the dragon's teeth of lies! Hellenes are born liars!"

Artabanos' largest guard mutters something in Persian, and Artabanos laughs and translates for Themistokles, saying, "In Persian, he just said: 'Why learn Hellenic, the language of lies?'"

Themistokles scoffs, offended, and begins to try to form a rebuttal but Artabanos barks over him, and quickly Themistokles decides to stay silent instead.

"You celebrate those who pretend to be those who they aren't, and worship this behavior! You live a life of illusion and denial, and call it civilization. But everyone else knows that a Hellene is as likely to utter a lie as a truth. And so there is no way for civilized nations to make pacts with Hellas - because you cannot be trusted. There's no way to be certain that your supposed treaty or alliance is not just some farcical mime or tragic play, or trick horse! Yes, you see, *I've* actually read *your* great stories, and I know your Hellenic tricks! You give your tricks away in your own tales!

"Now - *if* you are someone who can be trusted, and this whole submission to Xerxes has not, in fact, been one of those masks from your holy theaters or false gifts filled with curses, then you will have no problem coming to the service of your king now, King Artaxerxes, and use your knowledge of your countrymen to help in our coming fight against them. If you do, I can assure you, you and your family will be treated as well as any other king under the King of Kings."

Themistokles' expression makes Artabanos squint-smile at him, and gently touch his beardless face.

"You shaved your beard," he says.

Themistokles nods slightly, moving his face gently away from the hand. "I did," he says. "It seems to be the fashion here."

"I like it," Artabanos says after a moment. Then he raises his chin again. "How does King Themistokles of Magnesia-on-the-Meander sound?"

Themistokles catches his own reflection in nearby bronze, dark in the shadows of the Apadana. For a moment, he imagines it as being the face of a king. It makes the old Democrat in him want to spit. Nevertheless, he looks back up to the Persian general with a raised eyebrow, as if to show that he is intrigued.

Artabanos steps slowly toward Themistokles as he says, "Now tell me everything you know about the Athenian general called *Kimon*. To be clear, that is K-I-M-O-N."

Λ

Kallias confirms with whom he stands

At the White Dog gymnasion, the middle-aged Oligarchs are gathered to lift weights and debate. Their sycophants linger and listen, while their slaves sit in the shade and wait. The Sun is high and hot, and the nude, oiled men all glimmer in the light.

Hawk-eyed Alkibiades lifts a stone above his head and jokes, "If only Democracy were more like wrestling. A simple throw could end Ephialtes' career all at once." He tosses the heavy stone onto the sand.

Thin-limbed old Kritias, too frail now to lift much weight, simply lifts his arms and bends his knees in the subtlest of exercises. "That young supposed sage from Abdera, Protagoras, has made some fine comparisons between the throws of wrestlers and those of word-wranglers like ourselves. Like in battle, so also in law, it would seem it is what works that matters, not what is abstractly labeled as correct."

Increasingly-round-bodied Kallias stands leaning against one of the columns at the edge of the sand. He says, "If only poor Athenians realized that what's good for rich men would be good for them, if they could only get rich themselves! After all, there is nowhere I know of, nor any time I have heard of, where a smart-minded young man with nothing can make a fortune simply by showing cleverness and courage. Wouldn't you say that's true, Kimon?"

Kimon stops the vigorous military jumps he had been repeating, catches his breath for a moment, and signals to his slave Amyntas for some water. Once the man has brought him a cup and he has drunk from it, Kimon speaks, but during that whole exchange everyone else just waits for his answer.

Finally Kimon says, "It is true. There is nowhere that men have more freedom and opportunity than Athens. However it is also true that nowhere holds more traps and false paths. With the diversity we've invited into this city - by which I mean both foreigners and local hill folk who would otherwise never have felt welcome in this urban space - we have gained untold benefits and untold hazards. The past no longer foretells the future, I fear."

Tall Thukydides tosses a heavy stone to Kallias, who dodges it rather than try to catch. Thukydides grins meanly at him and says, "What we need is to regain hold of the reigns of this city. I'm telling you all - every bit of wisdom anyone needs comes from running a farm. And one must never let their hands slip from the reigns of a horse or ox. And this democracy, it was never intended to transform pathetic hill men into nobles through some kind of virtue-magic! It was intended to *protect* us from their envy and anger by making it appear that they have power, when really we are simply using them like oxen with our hands on the reigns of law, the reigns of coin, the reigns of what we call culture and tradition! Fools from the hills or foreigners from barbarian lands don't know any better than we tell them, so we need to get back to telling them to expect to do our bidding, instead of acting like just because they have *numbers*, they have *power*."

"They have power when they have smart leadership," Alkibiades notes. "Ephialtes is their power. You think anyone else cares as much as he does? No. But with his voice echoing so loudly, everyone has come to think they care. Shut up that voice, though, and you'd see how quiet the Democrats get."

Kimon's eyes get serious, and he looks between all the other men to see how they respond to that comment. No one else appears as concerned as he does, so he says, "I don't like the apparent implication."

Alkibiades just grins for a moment to act like it was a joke, and starts lifting his stone again.

Kallias carefully suggests, "It would seem if their leadership is moving more minds than ours, then their ideas might have more merit. Especially considering the extra resources our own efforts have behind them, with the momentum of our wealth and fame. Our problem is that half of this city thinks their own ignorance is just as reasonable and viable to run things as our erudition and excellence."

"Our problem is that we Hellenes fight among ourselves, leaving us weak to the real enemies - like Persia," Kimon says with frustration. "We should stop coming up with plans that involve struggling against our countrymen, and instead simply find other comrades to *work with*. I have connections inside the halls of power in Lakedaemonia. Yes, Sparta. We make so many concessions to make distant strangers from the farthest lands feel comfortable in our city, and yet we are unwilling to bend in the least for our neighbors with whom we have slight differences! Perhaps with Spartan help, we can influence more Athenians than the Democrats can. And perhaps, though I know it will sound ridiculous to you, perhaps we could even consider working with the Democrats, finding some kind of compromise or mutual goals."

"Spartan influence is the threat of violence - the creation of fear," Kritias says matter-of-factly. "You are suggesting we hire foreigners to inflict terror on our political opponents?"

"Spartan influence is not just through terror," Kimon retorts. "They are models of manliness, of self-reliance. Spartan influence is also as an example, a model. Every Hellene secretly wishes to be like a Spartan man."

"You mean a puppet of the Spartan women?" Alkibiades jokes.

The Athenians all laugh except Kimon, who just narrows his eyes and sighs through his nose.

After their laughter has subsided Kimon says with seriousness, "Frankly, Athenians could learn something from listening to their own women, too."

The men largely look at him as if he's a clown.

M

Aoide disdains the Pythian Games, but meets a famous poet anyway

Colorful flags flutter from the roofs and walls of Apollo's sanctuary at Delphi for the world-famous Pythian Games. Poets' songs fill the valley like butterflies.

Music-makers of every kind cover the grassy slopes of Parnassos in small circles, competing on the air with their songs while dancers appear and disappear around them. All who sing and dance and wordweave throughout the Hellenic world are here.

The Pythian Games are held at Delphi every fourth year, as one of the four quadrennial religious games which draw Hellenes from every corner of the world, two years before and after each Olympic Games. While the Olympic and Isthmian Games focus primarily on competitions of a physical and gymnastic sort, the Pythian Games are more similar to Athens' Panathenaic Games, primarily being competitions of the arts. The Pythian Games are famously seen as the ultimate proving ground for singers, dancers, actors, painters, and other artists moved by Apollo and his Muses. It is the primary setting in which one might become internationally famous as an artist in the Hellenic world. All Hellenic-speaking lands eagerly look forward to the Pythian Games for years beforehand, and insomuch the Games always gather the most devout worshippers of the various gods and spirits of music, primarily bright young Apollo, and all the most famous and beloved artists of the many instruments of music - from the ancient lyre built of horn and tortoise, or drums of literal skin and bone, to the more modern kithar, or aulos double-flutes, and the single and choral voices of song both poetical and simply melodic.

As a priestess explains to a group of tourists and children, "Jealous Hera sent the monstrous serpent Python to chase Apollo's pregnant mother Leto across the world, until Leto finally escaped the serpent on the holy island of Delos and gave birth to Apollo and his twin sister Artemis there, where the League of Delos today is based. Days-old baby Apollo swore vengeance upon the beast that had harassed his pregnant mother, and he chased it all the way to Delphi, where after some grappling he slew it and buried it beneath Mount Parnassos. However, the killing of Python was a crime in the eyes of Zeus, so the Pythian Games were begun by Apollo as penance for that wondrous kill. Now, here, hundreds of years later, Hellenes invent and sing original songs as praise for Apollo's providence. The crowns won in these contests, circlets of bay leaves, are the finest smelling of all the Hellenic crowns of competitive glory - more pleasant than the olive or ivy or laurel."

This is Aoide's second Pythian Games since arriving at Delphi ten years ago. The first time she witnessed all the pomp and glamor, she was four years younger, a teen-ager still, and was still awe-struck by the colorfully costumed dancers, day after day of new songs by the best singers and instrumentalists, nude reenactments of famous feats of Apollo and wrestling matches between the most beautiful of men. But this time, all the same events and ceremonies feel hollow and forced to this jaded twenty-year-old priestess.

She sits atop a wall in the higher level of the tiered sanctuary, with a couple of other girls her age who are still mere acolytes - and so shouldn't be doing this if they weren't with Aoide - watching the opening ceremony in which a naked boy, old enough for muscle but young enough to remain hairless to represent the baby Apollo, grapples theatrically with a large green-painted puppet snake manned by three slightly older priestesses who are old roommates of Aoide's. She and the acolyte girls chew bay leaves, which make the mind rush and the skin shimmer and bring them to cackle laughter when the rituals below evince gasps of awe from the crowd.

One of the elderly priestesses keeps eyeing Aoide with a sneer, disliking the unorthodox place she is seated, but Aoide doesn't care. Aoide feels she knows that the supposed holiness of Delphi is underwritten not by actual mystical secrets but by a long-held performance of known lies, and that those who run this sanctuary are now beholden to her to help keep those lies.

The music throughout the morning has been relatively tranquil and unimpressive, but Aoide's ears are suddenly brought to attention when a singular and unique voice surmounts the others upon the air. Like the most beautiful man in the room, whom all immediately turn to look at, this voice has the immediate reaction of silencing many of the others which had been sharing the wind.

All below Aoide turn their gaze and ears in the same direction, toward the main gate of the sanctuary, where a confident and beautiful young man with long wheat-colored curls but still too young to be much bearded has just entered and begun to sing, a homemade lyre on his arm.

"Bacchylides," the younger girl beside Aoide whispers loudly, and some of her friends coo at the name, as if it bears fame.

"I haven't heard of him," Aoide lies, knowing these younger girls won't remember.

ATHENS

"He's from Keos, but he's been in Phokis for a few years now."

"It's said he came to Mount Parnassos looking for his living muse among women."

"O how unique," Aoide scoffs. "Men all play the same instrument." She mimes a man masturbating, making her friends laugh.

At the last Pythian Games, this young man Bacchylides was a thin teen-ager with the sort of long, scraggly, golden hair that made many mistake him for a girl younger than he was. Aoide barely remembers him from then, now as she studies his beautiful, wise-eyed, twenty-something face.

Now, Bacchylides has aged out of the lankiness of youth and into the full beauty of a young man. Where, before, his eyes held anxious motion focused on those nearby, now they gaze coolly into the distance like a sated lion or a bull that fucks, while his fingers effortlessly flay normalcy against the shimmering strings of his tortoiseshell lyre and the muscles within his shoulders and chest jump and quiver with the intensity which such mastery apparently requires. The melody he delivers to the world is somehow at once surprising and exactly, obviously right, like when a many-angled stone slips easily into its place, while also strange to the ear and definitely thwarting expectations.

"Aoide is entranced," her fellow priestesses chide her, but she ignores it coolly.

Bacchylides continues to play, his fingers drawing sounds from the lyre that seem to hang in the air like visible things. The melody he creates isn't like other music she's heard - it doesn't follow the expected paths, yet each note feels inevitable once struck. Like water finding its way down a mountainside, surprising in its course but perfect in its flow. Aoide notices how the musician's eyes stay distant, focused on something beyond the visible world, while his hands move with apparent precision.

Some in the crowd shift uncomfortably at the strangeness of it, but others stand transfixed. Even the birds seem to pause their songs to listen. Near the edge of the gathering, an old man has begun to weep silently, though his face shows no sadness, only wonder. A young girl clutches her mother's dress, her mouth open in a little O of amazement. A painter, listening to the music, has begun marking with paint upon a long wooden board, moving his brush high on the board with the higher-pitched, shorter strings of the lyre, and lower on the board when the longer, lower-pitched strings are plucked, and moving his hand steadily along the board with the rhythm of song, placing the tip of his brush down to make a mark each time the notes are struck. The watching crowd gradually begins to cheer with wonder as the visual pattern repeated by the rhythms of the music unfurls, forming repeating triangles and swooping loops like fleeting, ephemeral eddies in the river of music caught and made visible.

That day, as the Sun is falling, Aoide slips away from the sanctuary and its buzz of human chatter. She finds a lonely crag just a few minutes' walk away, and a crevasse where two huge cliffs meet and there is a natural space to sit and be hidden from nearly every angle. She crouches there, among some soft green reeds, and gazes out the crevasse at the olive orchards in the valley below.

As time flows her thoughts peacefully, she begins to hum a sweet melody to herself, improvising as she has heard others do.

Hours might pass, or moments. The Sun shifts through the leaves, dancing soon-forgotten patterns across her skin. Her voice rises and falls like water finding its way down stone, no words, just pure sound reaching toward something she can't quite name.

Then, so faint at first she thinks it's part of her own deep well of imagination, the sound of a lyre answering her melody. The strings pick up her tune, echo it back with subtle variations. She continues singing, curious to see where this will lead.

A familiar young man's voice joins the lyre, rich and practiced.

"What spirit haunts these sacred slopes? What nymph of spring or shade? Her song, more sweet than honey-water, her voice like sunlight played." He strums his lyre to indicate that he means played like an instrument. "On morning streams which tumble down from high Parnassos' glades…"

Aoide turns to find the young poet Bacchylides, famous nephew of the more famous old poet Simonides, standing in the dappled leaf-light, his fingers dancing across lyre strings. His eyes sparkle with pretended wonder as he continues.

"Perhaps great Pan has blessed my ears with madness sweet and true, for surely no mere mortal voice could pierce my heart clear through, like Eros' golden arrows when they find their mark anew…"

Star-eyed Aoide finds herself smiling, playing along with his game. Her wordless song weaves around his verses, leading him on a merry chase through key and tempo. The lyre follows, never faltering, and he seems excited for the chase. Their music builds together, growing more intricate, more intimate, and he slowly comes closer among the trees, until finally he sets the lyre aside and begins to sing softly, high-voiced.

"Long-necked swan, you have entranced this poet, as Aphrodite Heavenly steps barefoot across the Sky and takes my hand, useless to fight against, and leads me like a high-horned ox to you."

His voice drops lower, more tender, and like he is trying to mimic a man older than he is, which charms Aoide somehow.

"Sweet is the late fig's hidden heart, and sweet the first-pressed wine, but sweeter still two lips which part like petals when they shine with morning dew, still pure and new, still waiting to entwine…"

Ever closer, their eyes dancing in and out of each other's gentle grasp, they move without meaning to closer to each other's faces. She begins to smell him, and somehow he smells like flowers instead of like boys.

Aoide's melody shifts, becoming something between a question and an invitation.

He moves yet closer, his next words barely above a whisper, audible only to her.

"So let us be like Dawn and Day, who meet in gentle light, when darkness yields to silver-grey, and grey to golden bright. One moment's kiss where mysteries of time and fate unite…"

The last note hangs between them as they each burn alone, inches apart. Aoide realizes, as he continues not to breach that final space, that the decision is up to her. She pictures a kiss in her mind. Aoide finds herself moving toward him as if drawn by the tide. Their lips meet with the delicate inevitability of waves touching shore. She smells past the flowers, smells his skin, his hair, tastes his breath. He takes her head in one of his hands.

But even as the kiss deepens, a different melody rises in her throat.

He pulls away from the kiss with an intrigued smile, to hear her song.

She moves back away from him gently, and sings in answer to his verses, her voice clear but touched with sadness, looking down into the leaf-light on the ground now instead of into his beautiful eyes.

"The stars wheel on their ancient ways. The moon must keep her track. And though two streams might touch and mix, they cannot both flow back. Not yet, not now, the Fates allow our waters to run black…"

"Bold-minded girl," Bacchylides whispers, "how beautiful your courage is. Your mind has been unveiled for many years, that I can tell. Please do not hide your shining spirit from my eyes. I know that other men might like obeisance, but I prefer to ride wild horses, for I know only the wild mind is alive, and only a wild love catches Aphrodite's eye, and I mean to live in the stars with you."

Aoide looks away, into the deepening shadows of Parnassos. When she speaks, her voice carries the distant tone of prophecy which she has been honing recently, even though she feels almost ashamed to use that voice here with this beautiful young man who can write and rhyme and kiss so well.

Aoide sings, "I am only Echo's sister-spirit, a nymph of passing moments. You have caught a ghost in evening light. Tomorrow I will be nothing but memory, a story for your verses." She steps backward, in the direction of the sanctuary, letting the dusk begin to cloak her. "Remember me as mist between the trees, music half-heard. I am Nobody. I am Nobody"

She watches the protest form on his lips, knowing he knows she lies, knowing too that he understands why she must. He returns to his lye and his hands flex briefly on the silent strings, then relax, making an unmusical sound.

Silently, Aoide vanishes, hiding her tears and carefully wrapping her memories in a tight package.

That night, she hears him singing to her from the distant mountainside across the valley, and as she lies awake and listens to his voice she chooses willfully to enjoy it instead of cry.

N

The Athenian Council debates deepening Democracy

"Wasn't it a slave who said 'We whip and chastise petty criminals and elect major ones to public office'?" one Oligarch jokes, to the unselfaware ironic laughter of his fellows on the council.

The Athenian Council House is hot most summer afternoons, so on this one many of the councilors are lingering just outside the open doorway and chatting with friends out on the street while debate goes on indoors. Councilors and the occasional goat are in a constant flow of coming and going even while the careless

Caretaker speaks on the floor.

"It's the gods, as well as men, who show such low judgment," a Democrat points out. "After all, we give the final choice to them. All outcomes of democracy have the hands of the gods in them, as well as each of our own hands. No mortal decides the lots we draw."

Reverent murmuring recognizes the invisible participation of the gods.

The handsome playwright Sophokles, a member of the council this year, sits among the small group of his fellow actors who react to each of his comments with broad facial expressions. Sophokles shouts from his seat, "If the gods are here right now, would one of them please pull whatever is harming me out of my long-pained foot!" as he grasps at his shoeless foot with a grimace.

"What's wrong with your foot, Sophokles?"

"Please," the day's Caretaker declares, banging his staff on the floor, "we have digressed from the debates of the day! Does anyone wish to further debate Ephialtes before he presents his proposal?"

The merchant Nikeratos stands and says, "I'll add what has just come to mind, which is simply this: While we speak of gods and wealth, we should all recognize - it is the Fates who determine which mortal men will be wealthy and which will be poor. As rich fools and destitute heroes can attest to. Aristides the Just, whom no man would speak ill of, died without an owl to his name. And all of history would seem to be evidence that there is no changing the will of the gods! Us giving a few owls to a man whom the gods have deemed will be poor, will not make that man wealthy. The gods find ways to make their will manifest, even if we try to fight them. Like a man trying to hold back a river."

Conservative minds applaud the sentiment, while younger council members grumble about old-fashioned thinking. Sophokles moans melodramatically.

The Caretaker looks around. "No one else? Then Ephialtes, please come describe what you would have us vote on."

Ever-smiling Ephialtes makes his way down to the center of the circular seating and kicks the dust of the ground idly as he speaks, still a bit uncomfortable with the eyes of so many well-dressed men upon him.

"Men of Athens, whom the gods have chosen to represent your fellows - some of you know me, but some of you may not. The older I get, the easier it is for me to forget that there are always new young men entering politics for the first time. So greetings, to those - I am Ephialtes, son of Sophonides the potter..."

"Ephialtes, we all know who you are! Nobody cares more about government than you. Turn a corner in a government building, and there will be

Ephialtes, son and father of democracy, puppeteer and puppet of the people!"

The council largely laughs, some in honor of Ephialtes, some in mockery of him.

Ephialtes smiles. "Allow me to get to my point. This government asks of even its poorest citizens that they work on behalf of all the rest of us, in duties just like our own here. Men like Stakys, who last year died, destitute, here in this very chamber. An officer of this council starved to death here in this very room! While his fellow officers ignored him."

Sophokles groans, gripping his foot in agony and rubbing all around the sore area. Ephialtes looks his direction annoyedly, but tries to ignore him.

"We must make it possible for every man who is called by the gods to serve their city to be able to make that sacrifice to their livelihood. Men have lost entire years' crops, whole seasons' fish stocks, to the service of this city."

"You're the one who wants poor wretches on the council!" shouts Alkibiades. "This is why it is meant to be the work of aristocrats to rule!"

The Democrats on the council all dispute and object like Alkibiades knew they would, and he laughs at them and waves his hand dismissively.

Ephialtes says, "The gods have selected moneyless men to the council. And it is up to us to decide how this council functions. So I say we owe it to the great people of this city to pay them for their work in civic offices! Not only this council, but the generals, and even the archons, must receive a daily wage - enough to survive on!" Already a majority of the councilors are applauding in agreement, but Ephialtes continues, shouting now, "May we never again let an officer of this city starve in office!"

"Haides, mercy!" Sophokles shouts. "Would that *I* could only starve to death!" Many laugh at the comment.

"Sophokles, please!" Ephialtes barks. "Control yourself. This isn't the theater."

"And I am not acting!" Sophokles shrieks, hitting himself in the side of the head with his fist as he stumbles up from his seat and out the door of the council house, past an incoming goat and its guide, intermittently hopping on one foot to grasp his aching toes.

Democrats and Oligarchs join briefly in laughter at the pain of the playwright.

Ephialtes declares over the laughter, "I propose that we make government offices all *paid* positions, of one owl a day. Enough to eat, at least, nothing extravagant."

"Do this, and watch the seats of power *flood* with filth from the hills!" shouts Kritias.

"So, anyway," the Caretaker declares, rewrangling the attention of the council, "shall we vote upon Ephialtes' proposal, that the offices of our government ought to be assigned a daily wage, so that poor wretches can fill those offices without starving to death?"

Some still chuckling at Sophokles' pain, the council votes the proposal down. Ephialtes sighs, still trying to smile, at the sight of the clear majority of hands against.

Ξ

Sokrates finds something missing

"Mother, I'm going out to chat with other boys!" Sokrates shouts into the open front doorway of his home.

Rising from having been crouched right there by the open door where she had been fixing a hinge, Phaenarete cringes against his boyish bellow.

"I can hear you just fine, Dew-drop," she snaps. "Please use your inside voice, even if it is only your head inside."

"What counts as inside?" he retorts playfully, swinging in and out of the doorframe.

"This rectangle, framed by these beams," Phaenarete patiently points out with her hammer.

"What if only my head is outside?" Sokrates jokingly shouts as he hangs on the doorframe with his body inside and his head craned out.

Phaenarete playfully smacks his knee with her wooden hammer. "If any part of it you is in, you are in, and your voice should reflect that. But really, the point is just that you shouldn't shout near people's faces, unless you want people to think you're a rude person!"

"Okay, okay. Anyways, I'm going to the Agora to hang out with some other boys."

"Who are you meeting? Chaerephon?"

"I don't know. Probably Krito at least. Whoever's at Simon's."

Phaenarete waves him off. "Tell Krito to bring home a chicken for me. I'll pay his father."

Little Eridanos just gets smaller and smaller the older Sokrates grows. He runs along its bank close to the reeds, running on a slope, to challenge his ankles' agility.

"Look at Sokrates, skipping like a girl!" some older boys shout, but they are out of sight by the time Sokrates has stopped and glanced around. He lingers at the riverside for a moment, as if he had stopped for other reasons, then continues on to Simon's hyperaware of the way he is walking for a while. But then he turns at the Tyrant-killers and skips again the last few steps to Simon's tent at the corner of the Agora.

Sokrates stops in front of Simon's and stands for a moment with his mouth agape, toddling unsteadily in place.

Inside the stall, everything of Simon's is gone, and an old Aithiopian woman is busy setting up a single flimsy rack, with a pile of long bolts of exotically patterned cloth beside her.

None of Simon's work materials or tools, none of his old scraps in the corners of the tent, and none of the engraved leather strips which had hung for years upon the beam where now the holes from the nails are all that remain, and no Simon.

"Where is Simon?" Sokrates fearfully asks the woman.

The white-haired woman doesn't look up, but just says, "Simon died. We will sell Aithiopian dresses here now."

When Sokrates doesn't immediately leave, she turns to face him and says, "They sell shoes up the way, seven stalls. Men's shoes. Get you set up."

Sokrates slips off his sandals right there, leaving them, and turns to aimlessly wander into the crowd of the Agora.

He is too dazed to know how he feels, just focusing on the feeling of the sand, grass, and pebbles against his feet. Sokrates wanders this way, feeling his neighbors swishing past his tunic, his eyes fixed upon nothing but the stones in the earth, for what feels first like eras, then years, and finally as he is coming out of the trance, it seems only to have been extended hours, but really, to his surprise, the light and shadow of the moment quickly reveals itself to be mere minutes later, and he is still in sight of Simon's tent.

The woman who now owns the space is still staring at him across the many walking legs, her arms akimbo, looking worried about him. Sokrates sits backward onto a rise of grass heavily. Before he knows it, the woman is above him, and he needs to listen to what she is saying.

"Are you alright, boy?"

Sokrates shakes his head. "I knew Simon," he says.

The woman nods. She says, "He owned that shop for a long time, I understand. He must have been well liked, if he could keep selling shoes for that long. He must have made really good shoes."

Sokrates nods, quietly breathing tears. "He was a good man."

"That would be news," she dryly jokes.

All around, people pass, not noticing.

O

Names are scratched on potshards to determine whom will be exiled

The Agora is roped-off with ten lines leading to the ostracism jars.

All the voting men of Athens are gathered in the lines for their particular urban tribes, and the debates within and between the lines are vigorous. There are two primary names being tossed around today as potential exiles - "Alkibiades" and "Ephialtes". Both Kimon and Perikles, as targets, have proved to be strategic feints.

Ephialtes stands with Perikles and a few other high-level Democrats from their tribe on this important day. Ephialtes listens on the wind for his name with worried eyes.

"Be strong," Perikles whispers to his friend. "Like dogs, Hellenes smell fear."

Ephialtes scoffs out a little laugh. "I'm afraid we chose the wrong man. We thought it would be easier to ostracize Alkibiades than Kimon, but perhaps no one dislikes Alkibiades enough. He is not as much a face of the Oligarchs. I know that's why we chose him, but ... O Perikles, I am doubting our gambit."

"The gods have it now," Perikles assures his friend with a hand on the arm. Ephialtes leans his weight into the hand, making Perikles smile.

"We've got you, Ephialtes!" shouts a nearby younger Democrat. Ephialtes smiles and waves. "And with Alkibiades out of the city, there'll be new opportunities for wine merchants!"

"It's not about that, it's about the best government, but thank you!" Ephialtes smiles reluctantly. To Perikles he whispers, "I wish it were easier to count on so many people to do the right thing for the right reasons."

"The right thing is what matters," Perikles playfully suggests, "less than the right reason. The wrong thing achieved for the right reason would be worse than the right thing achieved for the wrong reason."

"I'm not sure reason and result are so extricable," Ephialtes begins to debate.

"They are," Perikles assures him. "Wrong-headed ideas fail to ruin people every day."

Ephialtes laughs and shrugs in agreement.

When they get to the jars, they each sound out each letter as they write it, a tactic they discussed earlier aimed at making sure those around them hear the correct spelling.

ALKIBIADES

"Somebody say my name?" the Oligarch in question says loudly from his own line. "Someone, perhaps, whose name is spelled E-PH-I-A-T-L-E-S?"

Ephialtes just smiles at Perikles.

Gradually the ten lines all file past the voting jars and the counters create several piles, two of which, as expected, are by far the largest.

It becomes clear very quickly which of the two main piles is much larger than the other, and the crowd which lingers around the counters spreads the news just as fast. The name-whispering among younger groups rises into a mocking chant of the letters which make up the exiled name.

ALKIBIADES

Across the Agora from the counting, Alkibiades stands defiantly on a barrel and shouts over the crowd of Democrats booing him.

"I have been wanting to take an extra-long vacation to my erotic hideaway in Ionia *anyway*!"

The exilers laugh, and start to applaud the exiled.

Π

King Archidamos attempts to connect with King Pleistarchos

King Pleistarchos follows a Helot slave past the towering statue of Aphrodite Warlike fully armored and wielding the weapons of her adulterous lover the War God Ares, and up a set of narrow stone stairs hidden in the wall behind Aphrodite which lead up to the second story, where Aphrodite Shapely is worshiped in secret by only those whom the priestesses allow in. There, standing in front of the wood Love Goddess on her stone throne, her face veiled and feet fettered in stone shackles, before her there stands King Archidamos, and beside him stands a beautiful woman dressed similarly to the seated goddess, including fine gold-adorned versions of both the veil and the chains.

"King Pleistarchos," King Archidamos says, "thank you for coming. We need to speak. I've just returned from Megara, and there is much to discuss."

King Pleistarchos stands frozen at the sight of the woman beside the statue of the Love Goddess.

Seeing his discomfort, King Archidamos says, "This is my wife, Queen Lampito."

King Pleistarchos nods politely with a curt smile through his nervous grimace. "I didn't know you had a wife."

"That's because she usually stays at our home where she's safe," King Archidamos replies. "That is how a wife ought to be kept. If other people know what your wife looks like, Pleistarchos, you are keeping her insecurely. She will not be safe. Especially if she is beautiful, like my Lampito."

Queen Lampito steps forward hesitantly, holding out a long-fingered hand and smiling shakily to Pleistarchos. In a soft voice she says, "But that doesn't mean that I am not here, or that I don't participate with Archidamos in our duties of power. I am, after all, the one who must raise our son and heir, who will be the next Eurypontid king."

"King Pleistarchos, you and I are both just men. We are not gods, and we are not demigods. Right? Are you? I'm not." Archidamos smiles at the younger Pleistarchos, who shrugs shyly. "We're not demigods. You're the son of Leonidas, so you're probably the closest man to being a demigod on Earth, but really none of us are immortal. And yet!"

Archidamos lifts his hand away from Pleistarchos to rise and point it into the air dramatically, and he begins to pace between his fellow king and his queen.

"And yet we are yoked with the responsibility that Herakles has given our family lines, hundreds of years ago, when he created our dual thrones. We are chained to the duties of Herakles! You ... and I ... have no choice. We are bound to rule the venomous, shadow-skulking old widows of Lakedaimonia ... who keep all the economic power hidden away in weaving rooms, so that our rule becomes nothing more than slavery to those we rule."

Pleistarchos furrows his brow with confusion.

"I've just come from Megara, where I met with an Athenian from the rabble gang which currently rules their democratic system. He is not a stupid man, just because he lives in a stupid city. And I think that if we work with men like this - men not of 'wisdom' or 'cleverness' but of experience and maturity - men who know how to move other men - I think we can actually *work with* Athens, even as they remain a democracy, in order to help secure *our own* power here in Lakedaemonia against what, otherwise, I fear, might be Sparta's gradual slide into weakness and death as a land of women."

"That is a lot to think about," King Pleistarchos begins to respond.

A little boy runs into the room.

King Archidamos turns to him with a smile and says, "Agis, not right now. We're having an important meeting with my fellow king. Pleistarchos, this is our son Agis, my next in line. Forgive us, he cannot be reigned. Run off, little foal!"

Archidamos shoos the little toddler, who lowers his body into a stance as if about to run back out the door, but instead of leaving, though his body vibrates with the energy of almost running, little Agis remains still and just stares at Pleistarchos.

The Agiad king can't help but smile back. "Hello," Pleistarchos says.

"One day, you will have to marry and have a son, yourself," Archidamos says to Pleistarchos. "Has your mother prepared you for this at all yet?"

Pleistarchos squints at his fellow king. He chooses not to respond.

"To continue the line of Herakles. To maintain the strength of Sparta. Has your mother prepared you at all for what is required of you as king? I have often wondered, but gave your family the benefit of my trust."

The young king's eyes drop to the floor. "I know my duty," he says. "I don't have to do things how you would do things. There are two kings."

"Your father understood this. Leonidas knew what it meant to be king. Every choice, every gesture must show strength."

"You're not my father," Pleistarchos whispers.

Archidamos stops pacing. The silence stretches dangerous and thin.

"What did you say?"

"My father is dead, and I never knew him." Pleistarchos' voice shakes but grows louder. "I don't care what kind of man he was. I'm not him. He died, and I'm what's left."

The first slap is almost gentle, paternal. "No. You are not what's left. You are king. And we need you to be king!" The second slap comes harder, the voice louder. "You are Herakles' blood." The third slap brings tears to Pleistarchos' eyes. "You are Sparta's strength!"

"I'm an actor," Pleistarchos shouts, "playing a role I never wanted!"

Archidamos repeatedly slaps Pleistarchos across the face, until the younger king cowers bodily to the floor.

"We are kings! Commanded by Herakles! We are mere mortal men, Pleistarchos, to flinch and whimper at things like slaps! You are making me look weak by association! Stand up and be a Spartan king!"

Pleistarchos can barely lift his face from the floor, trembling. Behind him, Queen Lampito lets out a small sound, quickly stifled. The little boy Agis presses his face into his mother's skirts.

"What would your father say? Leonidas, who died standing! Get up!"

But Pleistarchos only curls tighter into himself. The silence in the room grows thick as oil.

Archidamos spits and storms from the room, followed by his retinue, leaving young Pleistarchos alone with his shame and the unwatching eyes of the old wood goddess.

Meanwhile, watching through a hole in the wall, Gorgo sits in the dark with Pleistoanax.

"The king is weak," Gorgo says to him.

"Pleistarchos?" Pleistoanax asks with pity in his heart.

"Yes. Your cousin. He is weak, and I do not know why. I fear he is beyond my help. He is the age of a man. But the royal boys don't undergo the *agoge*, that special hard training the rest of the boys go through. You didn't do it either, did you?"

Gorgo's piercing eyes pin Pleistoanax.

He whispers, thinking he is speaking normal-voiced, "I learned to fight. Mother brought in famous warriors to teach me and my little brother."

"But you didn't do the *agoge*. Other boys, who do the *agoge*, have to live for weeks in the wild, fight boars with their bare hands, fight each other and live with each other for years."

Pleistoanax shakes his head to acknowledge that he didn't have to do any of that.

"He'll never be one of the strongest men, like Spartan men are supposed to be. And Archidamos, who is supposed to balance him on the dual thrones, can do no other than dominate him. Nature allows no other, given the circumstances."

"What of the gods?" Pleistoanax asks. "Doesn't this indicate that this is what the gods have chosen to unfold for us?"

Gorgo glares sardonically. "You don't understand the gods, boy. They are not omnipresent, all-knowing beings. The gods battle with each other, they pull the heavens and earth and sea this way and that between them, as you've seen! What one god desires, another might intend to stop."

Pleistoanax nods grimly, recalling the earthquake and wars.

"You've probably heard people talk about fate, but the Fates are three titanic goddesses, ancient beings unlike any human woman, and they and all those like them have long since had their cosmic offices usurped by far less capable, competent, or conscious *men* - gods who rape mere mortals to the point that their very divinity has been gradually diminished through demigods into a world that may one day lack gods at all. Then only men will remain. But the Fates always have surprises in store."

Pleistoanax looks down into his own soul, remembering Niome.

To Pleistoanax, Gorgo then asks, "Have you ever heard about my father - King Kleomenes?"

"Little brother's name is Kleomenes," Pleistoanax replies, beginning to brighten up.

"That's right. Your father named him after my father, who was his uncle. Not very many people talk about King Kleomenes anymore, even though he did many great things. Because he was cruel. Even though many young men revered him, his cruelty keeps the thought of him out of people's mouths today. Not out of their minds, but out of their mouths. But so when my father was killed, and his brother Leonidas took the throne, the new king also took me, the dead king's youngest daughter, his own niece the princess, as his wife, to even more deeply embed his claim on the Agiad throne. After all, the only thing young men respect more than murder is rape."

Gorgo takes a moment to swallow back down her memory of that night. Pleistoanax watches the firelight reflected in her eyes warp like wax.

Haloed in her black veil, Gorgo continues, "The stories are true of him; he was the most lionine of men. But two Olympiads later, the lion died at the Hot Gates with his three hundred true-loves."

Pleistoanax looks down into the dark, imagining violent death. His face twists.

Gorgo grabs his face and pulls it back to hers. "But *I* was born that day. So you see - you can be one person for many years, and then be born again as another. I was not *this* Queen Gorgo, until after my king was gone."

"King Pleistarchos' father was King Leonidas," Pleistoanax says, just voicing his mind's work as it conceives the many royal relationships. "So when Pleistarchos has a son, he'll be the next king." Gorgo watches Pleistoanax's mind work. He continues, "Except your father died without a son."

With a disdainful blink Gorgo dispels the ghost of Pausanias from her mind's eye.

"So the throne went to his brother." Pleistoanax looks up at Gorgo, squinting into the sun. "But you don't have another son. So who would be king if King Pleistarchos died without a son?"

"By Zeus," Gorgo says with a smile, "I believe it would fall to you."

> "WHAT-IS EXISTS; NOTHING DOES NOT.
> KEEP THAT IN MIND.
> FIRST AVOID THIS ROAD:
> THOUGHT OF NOTHINGNESS."
> Parmenides, *How Things Seem*

P

Ephialtes shows Perikles the treasure of Poseidon

The treasury of Poseidon in better times would be housed inside the Temple of Poseidon that once stood at the southernmost tip of Attika at Sounion, where ships from elsewhere first see Attikan land. But since the Persians destroyed that temple, the Sea God's treasure is now instead housed inside a captured Persian trireme from the sea battle at Salamis which has been turned upside-down and repurposed as a treasure-house on the slopes of the hill of the Akropolis, among the olive trees behind the civic buildings of the Agora.

Ephialtes, as the official in charge of Poseidon's treasury for the year, leads his friend Perikles past the Skythian city-slave guards who stand watch over the building, and up to the little hatch which leads inside the upturned ship. He lights a hand-held ceramic oil lamp in the shape of a hydra, with six heads each bearing their own wick. Then he opens the hatch in the side of the old Persian wreck, and leads Perikles inside.

Inside, hidden in the dark, lit only by Ephialtes' fancy lamp and the lines of light that slip between the beams of the rotting hull, is a great pile of gold and silver coins, heaps of jewelry and cups and weapons and helmets inlaid with gems and carved with the finest artistry, model ships recreated with incredible detail and adorned with precious metal in a way that real ships could never withstand, little statues of Poseidon and his fishy children and vassals, and other assorted items of value which have been offered to the temple or collected by Athens in the name of the Sea God.

"Here's Poseidon's treasury," Ephialtes declares, casting his lamp over the horde to reveal its particularly remarkable sparkle.

"It is beautiful all gathered together," Perikles says. "I usually find each coin a dirty little indicator of one man's low value, but this great, gleaming stash reminds one how beautiful and powerful all those ugly, simple coins together can be - just like our democracy!"

Ephialtes nods with a smile. "Yes, how apt! Though I must say, I find some coins quite beautiful, and others quite ugly. But funny ugly, like that deformed insult-poet Hipponax. Not a bad ugly."

Perikles remarks, "Well, however ugly, each coin has the same value."

"Actually," Ephialtes retorts for accuracy, "not quite. I think you might have just revealed how insulated from the concerns of poor folk you are, Perikles, by revealing that perhaps you have never had to trade a handful of coins to a merchant who didn't know and trust you, and who bit and weighed and haggled over the value of each coin you gave him. Each coin is a debate, for poor men, from their weight down to the beauty of the image stamped on their sides. Like Lysimachos talking about his father's shield, and how its image of a lion looked more like some floppy fish after years of taking hits - such a coin, with a distorted sculpture on its face, would no doubt have less value than a newly minted one!"

"That ought not be the case," Perikles retorts.

"But it is," Ephialtes replies matter-of-factly, "at least between two men with few coins. You can only control the actions of men so much."

"Well," Perikles says, "isn't that just what we hope to do with this colossal piece of art about Athena? To move minds in favor of her wise council, to remind men even in distant lands of the primacy of wisdom and careful thought?"

Ephialtes, with a shifting smile, sniffs, "Or just, that Athens has command of Delos' gold? And can afford to show off our great wealth? For what is a great statue of our goddess, except a dozen triremes now unbuilt? It shows to others what we value - fame. And that we feel strong enough already."

"You sound like Themistokles," Perikles says after a moment. "Cataloging ships."

"Someone has to." Ephialtes runs his fingers through a heap of silver coins. "While we build monuments to ourselves, Sparta makes armor for soldiers. While we raise statues to civilization, Persia raises barbarian armies."

"Is that all we are then - just a war chest? Just ships and spears?" Perikles steps closer to his friend. "What's the point of having power if we don't use it to make something beautiful? Something that will outlast us? Isn't life for living?"

"Beautiful things don't defend cities. We're the ones in charge, now. It's different when you're the general commanded to defend."

"Ask the Trojans what power beauty has." Perikles picks up a finely-worked golden cup. "Besides, isn't that what we're really building - not just statues, but symbols? Showing everyone what Athens can achieve when she gives power to all her citizens? What are we doing, if we aren't trying to change things, incrementally, for the better, in a way that will last, like moving stones of law? And like Anaxagoras says of nature, if it is true, that all things flow and accrue in ways that build up, like this treasure here - then doesn't it seem to logically follow that the organizable activities of men might also be able to gradually be made better, and better, bit by bit, building up a mountain of ever-perfected quality of life?"

Ephialtes bemoans, "But just as much as men can move and organize stone day by day, so as well can the gods, or armies, break it back down, day by day, or all at once one day, with the battering of the waters of the Sea, or a single quake of the Earth, or a single stroke of the spear of Ares upon the loving dress of Aphrodite, to turn the happy love of peace into the treacherous misery of war. If there's any wisdom in the notion that precedent reveals what the future might hold, then we would be fools not to expect the order we labor to organize undone by the chaotic whims of gods with desires unfathomable to men."

"I think we've shown, though," Perikles retorts, "that, however little, the force pushing against chaos and in favor of order, and the force pushing against order and in favor of chaos, are not even competitors, and that over time, with the accumulation of silvery wisdom throughout humanity, order and reason win ever-more battles. Isn't the belief in this exactly what drives us to do what we do, as activist Democrats trying to enfranchise ever more of our fellows in a great odyssey in honor of equal justice?"

"I suppose it is," Ephialtes nods, smiling again. "You're right, as always. I see the idea excites you." His eyes glance down with a careful, new kind of smile.

Perikles notices that the hardness of his dick has lifted his tunic to reveal the bulbous head. He inhales slowly, hotness filling his head.

Ephialtes crosses the space between them and takes Perikles' dick gently into his hand, looking down at it instead of into Perikles' eyes. Perikles, however, watches Ephialtes' eyes.

"Let us fantasize for a moment," Ephialtes near-whispers. "Let us imagine what could be."

The sounds of everyday passersby outside the upsidedown Persian warship begin to sound surreal to the young men as their scene evolves.

Perikles lets the fingertips of one hand find his friend's skin. "The League's treasury could be used for more than just ships," Perikles says, another hand moving to untie his belt and further free his dick. "Imagine - public works in every member city, not just Athens. Temples, yes, but also granaries, workshops, theaters..."

"Care for every city's poor," Ephialtes suggests, letting his own clothes loosen. Their bodies draw closer as they warm to the ideas and each other.

"Development of systems of commonwealth. The money that once went to Persian tribute, spread among the people instead?"

"Exactly. And not just money - knowledge. We could send sages and artists throughout the League." Perikles' hand finds Ephialtes as they brace their weights against each other's grasp. "Think how Athens has flourished under democracy. Now imagine that flowering everywhere."

"Even ... even the islands?" Ephialtes gasps as they begin to stroke each other, their rhythms matching their racing thoughts.

"All of them. From Massalia to India. Every person voting."

"Man. Woman. Free. Slave."

"Foreigner."

"Child."

"Madman."

Ephialtes laughs joyously, with abandon. "Why not? We're dreaming, so why not dream large? The treasury could pay citizens for service - not just in Athens, but everywhere. No one too poor to participate. No voice unheard..." Ephialtes' body suddenly tenses, and his face contorts in ecstasy, his words becoming wordless.

Cum rains upon the golden faces of kings.

Perikles keeps tugging, but Ephialtes' grasp weakens as his own excitement wanes, and his hand falls away from Perikles' still bouncing-hard dick.

"It's impossible, though," briefly-frowning Ephialtes mutters, already reaching to tighten his clothes. "The Spartans would never abide it. The Persians would crush it. The rich would buy everyone's votes. The League itself barely holds together now."

Perikles is still caught in the vision, his excitement undiminished. "No, listen - if we start here, show them it works..."

Minutely, but increasingly, Ephialtes starts to shake his head, then he looks to Perikles with disappointment. "It wouldn't work. How would it work? How can democracy work between people who don't share a city, who don't know each other, or have the same concerns? I'm not sure how it would work. Like our own Delian League, which barely holds together."

Perikles nods reluctantly, furrowing his brow and looking into his mind for solutions. "With any goal, you do your best with forethought to determine what the obstacles will be, and prepare yourself to meet them ready. Already we have ambassadors from other cities living in our own, and ours in theirs. Perhaps there could be some way to keep distant cities interconnected."

Ephialtes leans back in the pile of coins and shrugs, gazing off. "At the very least, we know it's not like the world needs something it's never had. You know? If we fail at achieving idealistic goals, the worst that happens is the world remains as unjust as it already is."

Perikles replies, "I don't know, friend. Not to throw my family's position around or anything, but you came into your education late, and I'm not sure you have the best grasp on just how freshly new to the world many of the things we take for granted are - like this democracy itself, most of all. Those who don't know history might not realize that only a few generations ago the world had still never seen a democratic vote, or a theatrical play, or..."

"I get it," Ephialtes snaps, clearly annoyed at having had his family's low economic status called out.

He pushes off the pile of coins he had been sitting against and strides past Perikles toward the little door carved into the upturned Persian trireme they're under.

"I just wanted to show you what all Poseidon's treasure looked like in the afternoon light," he says as he opens the door and then stands in it silhouetted against the very light he is speaking of, "but I guess as his great-great-grandson you've seen all this before."

Perikles shakes his head and says, "Don't be dramatic, please, my friend. This was beautiful, and our debates are beautiful."

He steps into the light and hugs Ephialtes, grasping his neck and looking him in the eyes with a smile.

"Please, Ephialtes, know that our friendship has made me what I am."

Ephialtes smiles, and grasps his friend back. "If I have faith in the natural triumph of goodness, Perikles, it is because of you."

Σ

Kimon hosts a drinking party for friends of Oligarchy

"Truly, I am dying," Sophokles replies, when asked how he fares as he is welcomed into the house of Kimon and his new wife Isodike by their weary-eyed old slave Amyntas. "Thank you for asking."

"I am sorry to hear that," Amyntas replies, taking Sophokles' rain-damp cloak. "Let's get you dry and warm."

"Not because of the weather, alas," Sophokles bemoans in dramatic, archaic language, "but some monster from Tartaros the size of a cow is trying to emerge into our world through the space between my toes!"

"That sounds most unpleasant," Amyntas dryly notes, hanging Sophokles' cloak with a row of others on a bronze hook over the fire.

Sophokles saunters over to the row of cloaks to inspect them. "I see Polyphrasmon is here, as are some painters - Polygnotos, that's his cloak; and Anaxandra the woman; and Mikon the athlete portraitist. A who's-who of sell-outs. Is that what this is - is this the dinner party where artists lose their souls?"

Amyntas simply gestures the way into the next room, through a series of finely embroidered curtains showing stark scenes of rows of boys and girls doing calisthenics and long tables with many quietly eating - both classic Spartan scenes.

Inside the men's room, the partiers are laughing and passing a cup around, each drinking from it until they sputter.

There is Polyphrasmon the playwright, who instantly sees Sophokles and gives him a long, slow nod from his seat in the far corner.

Beside him on another couch are the painters, handsome Polygnotos and strong-armed Hermonax, with their friend the mask sculptor Anaxandra seated between them, she who always brazenly gets into these all-male events with the winking pretense of wearing a men's tunic for the evening. Mikon, a younger painter with less luck with women, sits stewing jealously by himself across the room from them.

ATHENS

Myron the sculptor is standing in the middle of the room, having just been performing some joke which required his whole body, but which he has paused to welcome Sophokles into the room.

"Hail Sophokles!" they all shout together.

"Welcome, friend," Polyphrasmon cloyingly coos, beckoning Sophokles to join him on his couch.

Sophokles frowns and goes akimbo in the doorway, unsure how to proceed.

Myron says, "We were just each answering the party question - whom would you most want to have dinner with, living or dead, mortal or god. I was saying Hephaestos, because of all that I imagine I could learn from him, in skill!"

Mikon jeers the sculptor, shouting, "Simple, boring choice!"

"Make yourself comfortable; sit down," Kimon suggests, touching Sophokles gently but intimately on the thigh for just a fleeting moment as he passes and takes a seat himself. "We have dove skewers just now grilled up! How is your foot?"

"Dreadful! Thank you," Sophokles grunts as he carefully sits.

"Whom would you choose then, young buck?" Mikon asks, sitting down with a thump.

"The choice is very broad, so I must really give the options thought! This is one dinner, after all, and if it were a real thing, this one magical dinner and my choice of whom to bring could maybe set me up for life thereafter in one way or other! Perhaps by saving some poor soul with wealth and awful fate, of old, or better yet by thoroughly impressing gods somehow?"

"This is a young Athenian with strategy in his blood," Kimon jokes.

"One must always be thinking how to set oneself up best," Mikon declares as if it is a maxim. "The future is always better, for smart folks."

Honey-tongued Polygnotos shouts over the other voices, "I would have dinner with Helen, to see if I could woo her without magic or heavenly favors. I bet I could."

"What makes you so sure?"

Looking into the eyes of Anaxandra beside him, the painter Polygnotos says, "Because I know how the light between two pairs of eyes can be the brightest color, unseeable to others."

"Surely whatever god granted your wish would give you Helen *after* everything instead of earlier, since we know the gods hate to give a mortal what he wants!" Polyphrasmon says.

Hermonax turns to Sophokles and says, "So Sophokles, has Kimon convinced you as well to use your art to help defend our city from…"

"Itself?" Sophokles interjects, and stares at Hermonax.

"From Chaos," Kimon says, then adds, thinking Sophokles will appreciate the finesse of the word, "from arrhythmia."

"You know," Polyphrasmon jokes, to be clear, "from Dems."

Everyone laughs.

"You don't want me," Sophokles jokes back, "you want Hipponax."

Everyone laughs even harder, and a jar of wine is passed to Sophokles.

"He would make your enemies kill themselves," Polyphrasmon laughs. "His barbs sink deep and are unforgettable, which as word-thorns means they never heal!"

Kimon corrects carefully, "Our opponent in political matters must never be called our enemy. Enemy means something different. How old are you, Polyphrasmon? You didn't fight Persia, did you? No. Think before you use words of War without realizing their weight. Your father will understand. I remember which ship he was on, which phalanx he went to Plataia with."

A silence hangs after Kimon's barks, which some fill with sips of wine.

Sophokles says, "To answer your question, no I'm not anti-Democratic in my work, Hermonax. I prefer to aim for work which speaks somehow to hidden, hard-to-speak-on truths about this world and human nature, rather than topical gossip of the moment."

"Truths," Hermonax half-laughs. "Art is all parody of truth. Propaganda, inherently. There is no capturing truth. Truth is Zenonic."

"What on Earth does that mean?" Sophokles scoffs.

"Zenonic, as in: nonsensically, ungraspably questionable. Like the ideas of Zeno of Elea."

"He's been drinking," Polygnotos jokingly explains behind his hand.

At the door to the rest of the house, Kimon's weary-faced wife Isodike arrives with a baby in her arms and an expectant look to her husband.

"Sophokles, I don't think you've yet met my wife, Isodike," Kimon says, gesturing out toward the woman carrying the infant. "And with her is one of our fine young twin sons. Like Kastor and Polydeukes they'll be, always fighting together. Which one is this, dear wife?"

"This is Lakedaemonios," careful-eyed Isodike replies, turning the tiny boy in her arms to face Sophokles.

Sophokles smiles cautiously and taps the tip of the little boy's nose. "A most virile name, indeed. You're named after a terribly unpleasant land, son."

"Where's Eleos?" Kimon asks her.

"With the midwife now," Isodike replies, looking back over her shoulder. "I can only carry them one at a time."

Kimon remarks, "I imagine you have two arms and two breasts for exactly a situation like this," perhaps joking but not sounding like it.

"Yes, well, you try holding both your giant sons at the same time for more than a minute, with their teeth latched onto your breast," Isodike groans, and leaves the room with Lakedaemonios.

Kimon turns back to Sophokles with a crooked smile and says, "She has Hera's patience lately. Plenty for the babies but none for her husband."

"As you say, Hera's influence," Sophokles replies with a hand on Kimon's shoulder. "Isodike will come back to you before a year, I promise. I've been through the same thing. If it weren't for Hera's influence on women, no baby would ever survive infanthood, for no one would have the patience for them. You should be glad she does. Some women just give the child to the mountains."

Kimon nods and sighs.

"Your job will be to get those boys running in a few years!" Sophokles says with another slap on Kimon's shoulder. Suddenly, with his step forward, the recurring pain in Sophokles' foot shoots up his leg and he bellows out in pain, gripping Kimon's shoulder for balance as he doubles over to also grasp his toes. "Gods! Have mercy!"

"What ails you so?" Kimon asks, holding Sophokles' arm.

"My foot! No one knows why!" Sophokles groans. "Nothing has ever made me so angry. I am at a total loss, as to what to do."

"Cut off the foot," Hermonax jokes. "You can wear a false silver one like that Boeotian singer who was born without one. What's his name?"

"Silverfoot," Kimon replies.

"His real name, not his nickname."

Kimon shakes his head, not knowing, while Sophokles releases his grip and goes to sit down on a nearby couch. Myron holds out an empty cup for a nearby slave-boy to fill with wine, then hands it to the pained playwright.

Sophokles downs the wine, then gasps at the pain and frustration.

"Perhaps you need to lie down?" Anaxandra suggests annoyedly.

Sophokles sighs loudly, then smiles and bows to Anaxandra, saying, "No, thank you, though. I think I must go and set my foot on fire. Please, have a lovely party without me, and I will just catch you all next time, if I'm still alive."

The party-goers all give Sophokles the requisite smiles at his joking, while also giving the requisite frowns at his discomfort and leaving, then hail him to be well as he gets his cloak and exits the house.

Limping home through city streets, the rain turns to haze, and then sunlight. In the new warmth of the sun, he stops rushing and finds a seat amid the crowds, on a small wooden stool beside a corner herm.

A mime across the street meanly mimics Sophokles' contortions.

T

Euripides, Sokrates, and Krito go camping in the hills

"It would please me if Krito could come out and play!" Sokrates shouts into the open doorway of his friend's house. He specifically avoids phrasing it as a question because the last time Krito's father saw Sokrates he told him that he would answer Sokrates' next question with a fist.

Cranky old Kritoboulos, Krito's father, shouts inside the house, "Krito, wake up! It's Sokrates! Put your shoes on first. Vagrants."

After just two cycles of the nearest bird's song, Krito shows up at the door dancing on one foot to put on his sandals.

"Good morning, Sokrates," Krito says. "What shall we do today?"

"Let's get Euripides to take us into the hills and hunt a boar!" Sokrates suggests.

Krito laughs and shrugs. "With what? We don't have any bows or spears. You want to just hunt a boar with stone-hewn staves like men who slept in caves?"

"Sure," Sokrates agrees. "Show our prowess to the gods, right? Come on, let's see what Euripides thinks! Maybe his father will loan us some weapons to hunt with. He likes manly things."

Again Krito laughs as he follows Sokrates who starts off down the street, past a row of middle-aged mothers chatting and beating their rugs at their doorways in the morning light. Sokrates barely dodges one old man's chamber pot contents tossed out a tiny window, and this starts Krito laughing uproariously such that he is still laughing, and trying to show Sokrates how much he was laughing, as they are arriving at Euripides' father's house past the neighborhood square.

"You almost really got it back there!" Krito laughs.

Sokrates just grins and nods, hands on his knees, winded from jogging uphill.

Having heard them run up to his house, Mnesarchos opens the front door and gives the two familiar boys a long, annoyed look up and down. "What are you two vagrants doing here so early? Don't your mothers have chores for you in the mornings?"

"I did my chores," Sokrates says.

"We did our chores already," Krito agrees, nodding, winded from laughing while running. "We wanted to see, sir, if Euripides might be interested in going out for the day with us."

"Hunting!" Sokrates blurts.

Mnesarchos gives Sokrates the same look he gives idiots. "Hunting what, mice?"

Krito shrugs. "Adventure," he says, mimicking boldness.

Grizzled old Mnesarchos and baby-faced little Sokrates look to each other and both nod, impressed with the creativity of Krito's answer, then both smile at having done the same thing.

Just then Euripides shouts from around the back corner of the house, where he has a wooden spade in his hand.

"Father, where is the old hoe?"

Mnesarchos says playfully, "Euripides, it seems like your friends need you more than the herbs do today. Clean your tools and put them away, and then you can spend the day with these little kids if you want to."

Sokrates, and then Krito in mimicry, both hug tightly onto Mnesarchos' legs, shouting various gratitude. Sokrates looks up and asks, "And could we borrow a bow?"

"No, I'm not giving you kids any weapons."

Just then, rambunctious wild-haired Chaerephon races up to the three and tackles Krito in a running hug as he shouts, "Where are we going? I've got weapons!"

Mnesarchos sighs a slight laugh.

Krito, Euripides, Chaerephon, and Sokrates tramp off into the wilds together, toward the wooded slopes of Mount Kithairon north of the city, where deer and ibex, boar and hare, lion and bear roam their wallless kingdom.

The three are all city boys, having grown up primarily within the walls, amidst the bustle of heavily-populated Athens, so all three of them are relatively new to camping outdoors. They giggle and wonder together over each new discovery along their way up the babbling River Ilissos, into ever more bird-filled forests.

"Listen to the songs!" Euripides shouts. "There must be a thousand choruses of birds, just here!"

"Perhaps it's an Assembly of Birds!" Sokrates jokes.

The birds of the forest sing from every direction, filling a few trees at the edge of one particular meadow to saturation. The three friends sit across the meadow from them for an hour and just watch and listen, before continuing.

Further up the mountain, they see a fox up ahead, its deft red tail dancing as it slowly chases some unseen prey.

All afternoon the boys explore the woodlands and hillsides of Mount Kithairon, watching the Sun set slowly over the Peloponnese and naming the stars which they recognize once they appear.

"That's Hesperos, the evening star."

"Notice how the stars gather slowly to their Assembly," Sokrates jokes, continuing his Assemblies-of-Nature theme of jokes for the day.

"So what are the stars, then, do you think?" Krito asks.

"They're voters," Chaerephon jokes to Sokrates, making him laugh.

"They're gods," Euripides says with a sigh. "Or they're symbols of gods."

"Like letters," Krito nods, as if understanding and agreeing.

"What does that mean, symbols of gods?" Chaerephon asks. "What's the difference between a symbol of a god, and a god?"

"I mean like maybe the stars are like monuments for the gods, but living, fiery, magical monuments, that sometimes move with life like Pygmalion's sculpture." Euripides suggests. "I don't know."

Sokrates repeats, shaking his head, "I don't know either. But they're beautiful."

An owl hoots distantly, but the sound is enough to startle the boys, who all huddle close together and then laugh at their reaction.

But then, above the soft din of crickets and breeze, a noise slowly rises out from within the forest, as it gradually grows closer - first the simple flourishes of a shepherd's pipe, but then the voices of adults, reveling, many voices in laughter and song accompanied by strange, unfamiliar shrieks and groans and shouting. In sharp bursts the laughing voices shout with a passion resembling anger, then return to the laughter of madness.

The boys all huddle together in the dark, hoping to remain hidden from whatever is coming. Euripides notices that Chaerephon seems least shocked by the strange revelry, in fact he has grown sullen at the sound of it and looks away from his friends, and Euripides points this out to Sokrates.

"What is it?" Sokrates asks Chaerephon, who appears to know.

Chaerephon starts to cry quietly and hesitates to speak. He tries to pull away, but Euripides, much bigger than him, holds him back down and softly punches his arm.

"Don't go anywhere," Euripides whispers to the younger boys. "I don't want them to hear us. But who is that?"

"The Maenads," Chaerephon sniffs. "The raving women of Dionysos. They're not dangerous. They're just stupid." Chaerephon grabs a small rock from right beneath himself and throws it in the direction of the distant forest, where the torches of those making all the noise are beginning to glow off the distant trees and scatter tall, black, dancing shadows beyond. "They just drink wine and fool around until they're sick. They do it until they die, some of them. They don't care about anything, because they think Dionysos gives them all they need in wine."

"How do you know so much about them?" Euripides asks.

Sokrates eyes Chaerephon a moment, then explains, "His mother used to go with them."

"Used to!" Chaerephon shouts. "She still does, sometimes! She'll never be rid of them. If she fails to go, they'll show up at the house asking where she was and why she doesn't care about Dionysos anymore. And she always goes back to them eventually. I won't say it while they're near, because he might be near too, but ... I am not a fan of Dionysos and his reckless mirth, let me just put it that way."

Krito suggests, "Let's go home. We shouldn't be seeing this."

"No way," Euripides retorts, fascinating beyond belief.

"We might see Chaerephon's mother," Sokrates realizes aloud, not sure yet what that might mean.

Chaerephon pushes Sokrates bodily against the ground as he gets up and stomps off down the hill, somewhat quietly, but in rush. "Come on, guys, like Krito said, let's go."

Krito follows, but stops and turns when Sokrates doesn't.

Sokrates stays for a moment beside Euripides, who remains hunkered tight against the grass staring through it at the distant revelry illuminated by dancing torchlight. He looks back and forth between his friends.

"Sokrates!" Krito whisper-shouts, and beckons with a twitch of his neck. Eventually Krito sighs loudly and continues on after Chaerephon into the dark, toward town.

"Go on," Euripides whispers, not looking at Sokrates. "This isn't for babies."

Sokrates frowns questioningly at his much older friend, considers some retorts for a moment, then finally slinks off after Krito and Chaerephon, standing to run once he is out of sight of the revelers, as he is frightened by being alone in the darkness.

His heart racing, Euripides remains, silently hidden and watching what he knows he is not supposed to see.

The women, wrapped in garlands of ivy and nothing else, prance and jump about the field together, throwing their bodies into the rhythms of the drumming, laughing and wailing, some weeping, some cumming, while stomping amongst them the tall and muscled man-as-satyr casts his lust spells in the air and against the offered bottoms and begging laughing faces of the cavorting *maenad* women with the long hard bouncing *thyrsos* of his bulbous-headed dick.

"Iacche! Bacche! Coccke!" the women shout and sing, mocking the religious songs of the Mysteries, forming their own profane ritual erotic words, and rebelliously meaning nearly nothing, all at once.

> *If you see us, you must lie!*
> *Fuck or die! Fuck or die!*
> *If we even meet your eye*
> *you must fuck tonight or die!*

They dance, and kiss, and drink, and suck, and puke, and fuck, and wrestle, and cum, the women tearing at the man as if to impress each other in their efforts to force him to keep fucking them, and he howls and sings and laughs at their attempts to defeat his dick for the night with overwhelming sexual demands.

Participating manic dancing women break off occasionally to join the lurking male worshippers at the shadowy edge of the revelry who pleasure themselves on their own or have their own miniature ritual fucks there in mimickry and reverence of the central orgy.

Euripides peers through the shadows as if wearing a Nyx mask. Overwhelmed by confusion, loneliness, and fear, unsure where he is expected to fit into this chaotic sexual cosmos, Euripides sits in the darkness and weeps silently with wonder, engorged, vexed, intrigued, and perplexed by his own mysterious fear and desire.

Two little frogs hop up curious, but remain unseen, croaking warnings against his halting steps out from the audience to become an actor in the play.

Y

Aoide follows an old friend

Aoide is awakened from happy dreams into darkness, and at the foot of her bed a shadowy yet familiar form stands, then quickly leaves the room.

The form slips away, but its presence fills Aoide's suddenly awakened mind with fear.

She sits upright in her bedding with a hand on the pulse in her throat for several long moments in darkness before her mind recognizes the form of whom she saw, and she gets up with a newly excited adrenaline, before her eyes have even quite yet adjusted to the darkness, to chase after her old friend Dikasto.

Out of the dormitory and into the streets of the moonlit sanctuary, Aoide races as silently as she can command her slapping feet and rustling nightdress to go. She keeps having to stop herself from calling out "Dikasto!" as she follows the vague sense of a fleeing shadow from alley to alley and then out past the walls of the sanctuary, into the woods.

On the steep slopes of Mount Parnassos under the scatter of glittering stars and a bright half moon, the form ahead of her becomes clearer, trudging up the mountain's rugged slope and touching each tree the way that they did as children, when they still believed in the *dryad* nymph spirits that supposedly inhabit each one.

She follows the shape of her old friend, certain in her quickened heart that it is a ghost she's following, but needing to find out where it leads. As she remembers believing that they held spirits, each tree she passes seems to contain instead a ghost now, as well.

Aoide follows the phantom up the steep sides of the mountain and down again on the other side, down through some woods to a little river valley between the hills, then up the steepening slope of Mount Parnassos, to an area of big boulders and short dry grass.

At a large stone, the size of a titan's fallen skull, where a man could use one eye hole for a door, Dikasto kneels near a natural alcove in the rock and seems to give minute attention and reverence to something there. Aoide crouches at a distance and waits, unsure yet if her old friend has sensed that she has followed her, or if Dikasto thinks that she is alone now.

Finally, after a few long minutes, Dikasto stands again and heads off through the snow, not back to the sanctuary but back down the mountain to the west. Again Aoide follows her far enough behind to keep from being seen. She is only briefly able to glance at the area where Dikasto knelt as she passes it, for fear of losing her as she moves on, but when she notes there a small jar nestled in the snow and rock, she tells herself that she must return here on her way back to find out what that is.

Aoide follows Dikasto to the Korykian cave, a supposedly haunted old cave high up in the mountains west of Delphi, where according to local legend three dark nymphs called the *Thriae* live deep in the furthest chambers. It's said they will either murder or give oracles to unwary visitors, depending upon their mood, or perhaps the person's fate. As far as Aoide understands from the rumors, no one goes here anymore, and the legends of the nymphs are as hollow and empty as the cave.

However, when she gets to the cliffside where the Korykian Cave opens into darkness like a big black triangle blacker than the rest of the night, and she sees the phantom enter the blackness, Aoide suddenly wonders and worries anew about all the scary stories she's heard about this place.

Soon Aoide realizes she is alone in the dark forest, with only the stars to comfort her. She crouches there, struggling between heading back to Delphi, or heading into the dark cave to see if Dikasto is real or if it was just an apparition or some deadly divine web.

Fear moves Aoide's feet backward, but her body keeps her facing the cave, until she finally overcomes her body's instincts and forces herself to actually step back up toward the Korykian Cave and enter.

The darkness of the cave seems overwhelming, even at the edge of its entrance. Shadows overtake mere feet inside.

But a gentle sound emanates barely audibly from within, as well, which Aoide can only hear once the heartbeat in her ears dies down. It is Dikasto's voice, humming an old tune which she used to sing to the kitten Ailisto, echoing from myriad directions against the stone cave walls.

Aoide feels like she is inside her own mad dream. She presses herself into a shadowed alcove, hardly daring to breathe. The fire's dancing light throws strange shapes across the cave walls, and there, outlined against them, sits Dikasto, utterly still, like a statue of herself, wrapped in dark cloth that seems to silently battle the firelight.

For a long time, Aoide sits in silence and just watches her friend, trying to silence the loudness in her heart, glad just to see her form in the world. She gradually confirms for herself that the motionless black form *is* moving, barely, breathing.

Then comes the scrape of sandals on stone, a caught breath, and a murmured prayer in foreign-accented Hellenic. Dikasto's form's head turns, then returns to stillness slowly. Silence again, heavy as temple incense. Even the fire seems to hold its crackling for a moment.

A woman's shape appears at the cave's mouth, occluding the stars. She takes one step inside, then freezes. The darkness here is different from the darkness outside, thicker, older. She takes a long moment to adjust to it.

The woman clutches her offerings tighter, their rattle betraying her trembling hands. Bones, coins. Three more steps, each slower than the last. The fire throws her shadow huge against the cave wall, but Dikasto's shadow seems unnaturally still, as if painted there.

The woman starts to stumble as she descends the slope toward the fire and the form, catches herself, then looks up, and finally only then sees what waits in the shadows. Her mouth opens soundlessly. There is something impossible about Dikasto's stillness, something that feels mystical.

When the stranger finally finds her voice, it comes out as barely more than a whisper. "Are ... are you ... the Black One?" the woman asks with fear in her throat.

"I am the one they call the Black One," Dikasto whispers creakily, hardly moving, but opening her eyes so that their whites shine from the scant moonlight leaking into the cave.

The woman falls to her knees weeping. "I beg you, Black One, tell me what will become of my child in the Underworld. He had only four summers in the sunlight, before the mountain lions took him. Please tell me if he has found his brother in the house of Haides."

Dikasto sits silently for a while.

The cave echoes only the tinkling sounds of some small bones which Dikasto is shuffling near her feet.

Then Dikasto-as-the-Black-One groans, "The city of Haides Many-Host is a populous place - the biggest city in the cosmos. As they would have done in life, your boys are living separate lives there now. But be assured that they have each found friends."

The stranger's shoulders sag with released tension, and something between a sob and a laugh escapes her. She presses the coins into the earth before the Black One's feet, bows three times as she backs away. At the cave's mouth she turns and flees, her footsteps racing buoyantly into the night.

Dikasto maintains her otherworldly stillness for several long moments after the woman has gone. Then, so gradually Aoide almost doesn't notice at first, she begins to soften. Her shoulders drop slightly. Her hands uncurl. The mask-like emptiness of her face cracks just enough to let through a flicker of exhaustion.

The fire pops, sending sparks dancing. Dikasto reaches out to take the coins, and for just a moment she moves like her old self, like the girl who used to sneak extra honey cakes from the temple kitchen. Then the movement freezes, as if she senses she's being watched. Her hand withdraws back into shadow. She resumes her statue's pose, waiting for the next supplicant, or perhaps just waiting.

Aoide knows she should leave. She has seen more than enough - more than she was meant to see. Yet she lingers, studying her friend's profile in the firelight.

Finally, Aoide forces herself to move. Her legs are stiff from crouching so long in shadow. She grunts despite her best efforts, and darts a glance at the Black One's form. She doesn't move, but somehow Aoide knows she heard her.

She makes her way carefully toward the cave's entrance, stealing one last glance at the dark figure by the fire.

As she's reentering the cool outside world, star-eyed Aoide notices a familiar darting color in the bushes beside the cave's entrance, and she turns just quickly enough to see the slinking tail of little Ailisto, or perhaps a kitten of hers now grown into an adult that looks identical, slipping secretly into the darkness of the cave at the edge near the wall, trying to remain unseen.

Aoide weeps with an immediate heaving gulp at the sight, but tries hard to keep her emotion quiet, as she doesn't want to add any amount of regret or sadness to Dikasto's mind. But seeing the cat, and realizing that she must remain friends with dark Dikasto, and that neither of the two who she had previously thought were lost are in fact alone, that they have each other, fills her heart with so much warmth that all the sadness which had previously filled it all pours out like wine displaced by a stone.

The night still heavily black, she summons silent bravery to start back toward Delphi through the darkness. But halfway, where she had turned to follow Dikasto up the mountain earlier, she pauses, and remembers the reverent moment she had seen her friend have near the boulder higher up.

Though her skin aches from the cold, Aoide makes her way back up the mountainside to the snowy part, and up the steep pebbly slope to the stone where Dikasto knelt.

In a crook of the rock there, hidden in a little womb of Earth, where only one who knew to look would find it, is a little ceramic jar with a rough line-painting of Artemis Huntress scrawled onto one side.

The stars watch, hushing each other.

She sits at the jar, worshiping the unknownness of its contents for a while, frightened at the prospect of what she'll see, until finally, with a rush of courage and curiosity, feeling like Pandora, she opens it.

In the jar are a tiny human skeleton and a few dry flowers.

"THE BEST THING FOR MORTALS IS NEVER TO HAVE BEEN BORN,
NOR EVER TO HAVE LAID EYES ON THE SHINING SUN,
BUT, BEING BORN, A MAN OUGHT TO RUSH THE GATES OF DEATH,
TO REST WITH EARTH ALL PILED UP AROUND HIM."
Theognis, Megaran Poet

Φ

Spartans worship violence at the Temple of Artemis Willow-bound

On the fields of Artemis Willow-bound, the men and women of Sparta are out exercising, practicing old holy war dances, grappling with each other good-naturedly, and going through the motions of their military formations in small groups, the men on one side of the field, shiningly oiled and nude under the sun, and the women on the other, also oiled but covered by short loincloths and breastwraps. This morning, everyone in the city who considers themselves Spartan is here to show their countrymen that they still have strength.

King Archidamos is as nude as any other man, but for the royal golden torc worn around his neck to maintain a clear distant indication of his office.

King Pleistarchos, however, is not participating, and instead sits upon a traveling throne in his full regalia, making a performance of his disinterest whose audience is attempting to appear to ignore it. The games go on without him.

Queen-Mother Gorgo sits near her son the king, quietly chatting with some of her fellow middle-aged Spartan widows in a gaggle of black.

Laothoe nods toward the Agiad king with Gorgo's attention on her, and whispers discretely, "How is the king? He does not participate in the Struggle of Artemis?"

Gorgo says with practiced nonchalance, "He does what he wants. He is the master of his own will. He alone knows what is best for him. I am far too old to be trying to control him like a child, whether he is a man yet or not."

Laothoe smirks coolly.

On the field, all the teen-aged and twenty-something Spartan boys are being gathered by the mothers and mistresses of their lives who would chide them for not being here, softly laughing together at the fact that they are able to be so controlled, joking that it must be magic. In the ruins of the Temple of Artemis Willow-bound, the old stone altar still remains while all which used to surround it has fallen and been cleared away, and on that old stalwart altar the oldest priestess of Artemis places a large hunk of sacred cheese, the size of a man's head. Aged carefully, the cheese crumbles a bit onto the altar and instantly spreads its unique scent.

"Today," the aged priestess shouts onto the wind, for all the boys and men to hear, "you show how much you want this Holy Cheese!" and she unfurls her long, thick, thorny whip.

Around her, six other muscular middle-aged priestesses of Artemis, huntresses from the hills, spread all around the stone altar with its odoriferous ritual treasure, each wielding their own special ritual whip, hand-made uniquely by themselves, one very long and thin, one many-tailed like a hydra, some thorned like the high priestesses', some merely meant to snap.

The seven priestesses all welcome men to come and take some cheese if they can, whipping the air for show and warning.

King Archidamos makes a show, himself, of pushing through the hesitant crowd to be the first to go in past the priestesses and take a hunk of cheese. He takes a lash from each of them, before he makes his way back out through the onrushing secondary brave few to go in.

The Spartan Eurypontid king offers some cheese to other men, but all refuse, not having earned it, and forego the offer to go in and face the whips instead.

Only a few who face the whips get through; most men are lashed away. Many who get through regret success. Long torso scars on Spartan men are usually from this. Blood spatters the altar of Artemis Willow-bound as another boy lunges for the sacred cheese.

Pleistarchos watches from his place of honor, his mother seated beside him in a rare red dress instead of her usual black. She seems buoyant today, as if some weight has been removed from her soul, and in his dark humor he can do nothing but glare at her apparent happiness.

"Even the pain is false," the king mutters, loud enough for only his mother to hear. "We pretend the whips make us stronger, but they only teach us to pretend better." His eyes follow a particular boy who reminds him of himself at that age, watching the child's desperate calculation of pain against glory.

"You sound like a Persian," Gorgo says, her red veil rippling in the wind. "Or worse - an Athenian philosopher."

The crowd cheers as blood arcs through the air. Mothers shout encouragement to their sons, their voices fierce with pride.

"At least they question. We just endure." Pleistarchos gestures at the ritual before them. "Generation after generation, enduring nothing but our own collective madness. Even the priestesses are bored. They've forgotten why they whip; they just know they must." Then he throws his gaze over to his mother in her red dress and asks, "Why have you suddenly stopped wearing black? Do you no longer grieve?"

Gorgo says, "I realized that it had been twenty years since I lost your father. A woman can only grieve for so long. Sometimes, it is time to come back to life again. Perhaps I have over-grieved. Perhaps I have smothered you with my grief. Perhaps it is time for us to…"

Pleistarchos interrupts her by handing her a small scroll, wrapped tight in a black ribbon. "I have written you a poem," he says.

Gorgo squints at her son, shaking her head slowly, and takes the scroll. She unfurls his words slowly, reading as soon as she sees them.

Pleistarchos watches the whipping of the boys. One makes his way through the whips all the way to the sacred cheese of Artemis and grabs a chunk, but falls on his return through the whips, and is surrounded on the ground by priestesses for a long violent moment before they spread out to focus on other boys.

Gorgo finishes reading her son's poem, her throat tightening.

"Do you think you're the first?" Her voice cuts under the crack of whips. "To believe Haides' kingdom might be better than Zeus'? To wish the weight of Herakles' blood could drain from his veins? Why would you give me these words?"

"Not drain," he whispers, watching another boy's blood join the rest on the altar stones. "Turn to poison. Transform us all into what we truly are - monsters wearing the masks of men."

"These are not your thoughts," Gorgo hisses. "These are demon-whispers. Shadow-talk." She hands the scroll to one of her nearby maidservants and barks, "Burn this."

King Pleistarchos growls, "Everything is shadow-talk." A boy screams, then bites it back proudly. "Every Spartan word is just echo and pretense. We call murder 'glory' and torture 'training' and think the gods can't see through our lies."

"Stop this."

"Why? Because it's true? Because you know that every drop of blood we spill just makes the Helots hate us more? Makes All-Hellas hate us more? Because you know that every boy we break just breaks something in Sparta's soul?"

Gorgo growls back, "You will remember who you are. You are the son of Leonidas. You are the Spartan king."

Pleistarchos finally looks at her, his eyes dry of tears. "I know exactly who I am, mother. I am mercury. Beautiful, deadly, and impossible to hold."

Below, the priestesses ready their whips for the next wave of boys.

"You know the graveyard of suicides," Gorgo says casually.

Immediately regretting it afterwards, her son falls for her ruse, and asks, "There is a graveyard of suicides?"

"No," Gorgo snaps, turning around to face him with desperate dismay and derision. "There is no graveyard of suicides. Because suicides are forgotten; their graves are hidden and unmarked. Because nothing offends the gods more."

"The gods don't love anything," Pleistarchos sighs, annoyed. "Even Aphrodite doesn't love. Hera doesn't love. Gods can only *rape* mortals with their power. At best they merely *cause* love, against our will, which is just another curse, another madness! Only that which we feel in the depths of despair, when we have thrown off all of our warming cloaks of hope and desire, only then do we know the truth. Men of this corrupted Age of Bronze call truth madness so that madness can be masked as truth."

"We never should have let that supposed sage Simonides come speak with you, son. I'm sorry we didn't put you through the *agoge*. I'm sorry that your father didn't live long enough to raise you as a man."

"I am a man, mother! Unlike Spartan dogs, I *am* a man! Maybe you have never known a man before, you mere Spartan-maker, but here is one! A man of new metal, beyond iron or gold! A man of mercury."

Gorgo grows cold-eyed. "Mercury is poison."

King Pleistarchos appears briefly proud when he says, "So it would seem I am as well."

The jaunty voice of King Archidamos walking over toward them startles Gorgo and Pleistarchos both out of their quiet, dark conversation. "Well then, what are you two talking about? Grand strategies of the Agiad clan? Let us work together, Pleistarchos, and stop this wrestling match of power. Herakles meant us to work as one."

Gorgo pretends she has been speaking strategy just as Archidamos has assumed, immediately straightening her demeanor. Pleistarchos, however, sees this with immense disdain, and sinks back into his own inner shadow-land.

"We must get Sparta back on her feet," Gorgo says. "All-Hellas is watching us, after this chaos with our Helots, and they can see that we have held our own, but also that we were weakened, and we must show the entire world that Sparta can re-strengthen as fast as we need to. We must put on some show of real force."

Some Overseers see the two kings in conversation and take the opportunity for an impromptu gathering of the leadership, heading over to join in.

King Archidamos says, "Athen is our main competitor now, with their 'Delian League' filling their treasuries with riches from around the Sea."

The eldest Overseer adds, to have his voice be noticed, "Yes, indeed, as in days of old, we have a clash of Hellene cities, so we should find our generation's best heroes to clash against theirs."

The red-veiled Queen-Mother says, "This is not a clash of cities, like in ancient days, when everything was personal. No one cares about such mythological reasoning in modern times. Today everyone understands that this is a clash of ideas! Athens is not Athens, she is a *democracy*! As is Argos, and Miletos, and all the cities of the Delian League. Or if a city with a healthy Oligarchy finds it must make allies with the Democrat cities, make your bets that before long that city will be overtaken by its Democrat faction. Individual cities, and their greatness, dissolve before the crushing wave of democracy. Only Oligarchies made of *stone*, like ours, and stone walls built of many stones, like a league of Oligarchies, can hold back this oncoming tide."

"You see only the wave," Archidamos says, running a finger along the rim of his cup. "I see the currents beneath. Athens isn't one thing - it's nobles pretending to be Democrats, Democrats dreaming they're nobles, unscrupulous merchants playing both sides. Each faction has its own hatreds, its own fears. We need only to amplify them."

"The tide is the tide," Gorgo murmurs tiredly.

King Archidamos leans forward. "Consider how they already tear at each other. The rich fear the poor will vote away their wealth. The poor believe the rich plot to enslave them and take back control. The native-born suspect foreigners. The craftsmen hate the merchants. Every Assembly meeting becomes more bitter than the last. This is the story our ambassadors tell."

"Spartan unity is our strength," the eldest Overseer voices. "Athens' risky openness to diversity gives them access to foreign magic, but ultimately angers the gods of Hellas."

"Their openness is a *kairos* open for attack." Archidamos stands and starts pacing. "We don't need armies. We need rumors. Whispers. We send men to Athens - not as spies, but as … let's call them agents of chaos. They befriend Democrats and tell them the nobles plan to overthrow the democracy. They drink with nobles and warn them of Democrat plots to seize their property."

"You suggest we play their game?" Queen-Mother Gorgo's question drips with scorn.

"I suggest we play *all* their games. Support the Oligarchs when they clash with Democrats. Aid the Democrats when they war with nobles. Fund the most extreme voices on both sides. Let them think their worst fears about each other are true." His eyes gleam. "When Perikles speaks of commonalities, our friends will shout him down. When Kimon's supporters call for moderation, we'll ensure they're branded as traitors. Words will be our weapons. We don't need to break Athens ourselves. We just need to convince each faction that the others are already broken beyond repair. They'll tear down their own walls from the inside."

"This is presently Persia's tactic," Gorgo suggests, "but of All-Hellas. To split us up and pit us against each other."

An Overseer who has been having trouble following along asks, "So like Pausanias before you, you find a role model in the actions of the Persian barbarians? Is All-Hellas a dark idea, cosmopolitan and Persian, or is it patriotic, and anti-Persian?"

Archidamos shakes his head with frustration, focusing on Gorgo. "You avoid learning about combat so that we men may focus our entire life on it. You would be wise to listen to us when it comes to matters of War, rather than think that you know the War God well from your weaving room."

"No one knows the War God better than Aphrodite, his mistress," Gorgo reminds. "Who wears the War God's armor? His woman!" She points to the statue in the temple. "Who whispers with him in the night?"

"We are the Earth," one of the older priestesses of Artemis says, interrupting the conversation with a bloody whip in her hand. "We're the clouds and the Rainbow; we're the rivers and the trees! You Men just live here on us! Women are *where* you live! You can't even imagine how to destroy us, for if you did you would end up back in total chaos. We give you a field to play your bloody game in."

The old woman kicks dust in King Archidamos' direction.

X

Elpinike puts forth a proposal to other rich men's wives

A cooling rain keeps most folks indoors in Athens on this grey afternoon.

The women's room in the house of the richest family of Athens is the largest room in the house, for Elpinike is the one who manages the money and home. She has finely decorated the large room where she spends most of her time, often hosting parties for other noble women with every luxury that she can imagine they might want. Birdcages, whose occupant birds are recycled regularly for variety in their colors, surround the room, high up in ornate nooks built into the tops of each of the four walls. Opulently cushioned curved couches occupy more space than a more economically organized room would allow. Elpinike likes her spaces to seem slightly extreme, even strange.

Among the day's visiting neighbors, Elpinike recognizes Isodike, her sister-in-law, Kimon's wife, whom she has only borne proximity to once before, at her brother's morose wedding years ago. She has otherwise, in the time since, successfully avoided spending any time with her. Isodike, also knowing this, smiles apologetically to her sister-in-law, and waves minutely.

"Welcome, brave and graceful Athenians," Elpinike's gregarious neighbor Eupraxia trumpets excitedly, opening her arms to the arriving group. "Come, find a cushion. Tell a slave what you want. We were just talking about our favorite actors; who's yours?"

"O, Aischylos!" laughs the first entering, an older middle-aged woman with an ornately braided tower of grey hair. "May he never lose those muscles! And that voice - deep and resonant like Triton's horn. I'll be true, he makes me wet as the Sea."

The comment makes some women gasp and others laugh as they all settle in around the room, sitting upon cushions and against the walls. The few slaves in the room offer food and drinks from platters they hold.

"Speaking of wetness," purrs Eupraxia, reclining against an embroidered cushion, "did you see the new statue of Aphrodite they've putting up near the Dipylon Gate? The one carved by that boy sculptor, the one with hardly any hair on his body? Where's he seen a woman like that? I would believe she was frozen in stone by Medusa's severed head. How can someone carve marble to resemble a wet cloth on skin?"

"My father won't let me walk past it, makes me take the Agora road. Says it's indecent."

"Everything's indecent to Megakles," Isodike notes dryly. "Remember how he carried on about the running girls at the Heraia?"

"Well the statue *is* rather shocking," Ianis adds, accepting a cup of wine from a slave girl. "You can see everything through that dress. Though I suppose that's the point."

"Kallias says it's great art," Elpinike remarks with a careful smile. "He knows the boy who did it."

"Oh yes, I'm sure it's the *skill* he admires," Eupraxia laughs. "Men always have such noble reasons for staring at naked women, don't they? I'm sure Kallias hung around while the boy had his model stand for the piece, just to ogle her."

The other women titter at that, and Elpinike tries not to glower.

"The cloth merchant tried to cheat me again," Eupraxia says, accepting a honeyed fig. "Acted like I couldn't tell Milesian wool from common stuff. Then my husband walks up and suddenly the real goods appear."

"They're all like that now," Isodike adds. "Remember old Hermias? His son won't even show me the good oil jars unless I bring a male slave."

Elpinike adjusts herself on her cushion, gesturing for more wine to be brought out. "At least your husband lets you go to market. Mine gets twitchy if I so much as look at the household accounts in front of him. I can only go out by his side or he has a thousand questions about what I did and who saw me and what sort of face they made. Though he loves to show me off."

"It's not just the merchants," adds the young Alkmaeonid girl Deinomache, picking at the embroidery on her sleeve. "Our neighbor caught me teaching his little son some letters last week. You'd think I was feeding the boy poison. Perhaps I was," she adds with a bitter laugh. "Words are dangerous things, aren't they? Especially in a woman's mouth."

"What else can you expect from Pandora's daughters?" The women snicker sarcastically.

"Well, Pandora, mistress of all hardships, *did* release myriad miseries upon the world."

"As if a man wouldn't *also* have looked in the jar," Eupraxia laughs.

All the women variously debate the notion.

Deinomache says, "It is a classically male move to have given the risky act to his woman to do, so that if it fails or goes wrong he can blame it on her. It is exactly like what my Kleinias does. Anything that *could go wrong*, he tells me to do it, and if it goes wrong, he blames me."

"O are you and Kleinias, son of Alkibiades, to be a couple, Deinomache?"

"We'll see. We're friends."

"It's our grandmothers' way to blame Pandora for all the troubles of being a woman," Elpinike says. "Surely we want to be better than those creaky old broads. I already know there is plenty that my mother said which was really just to shut up babies, and said in fear of the reaction of my father. And now that I live on my own - fuck all that."

The women all variously nod a general agreement, but many simply do so due to expectations of cordial agreeableness.

"We women should just take over the Assembly," Elpinike throws out in a burst of courageous thinking. "Walk out there and demand our equal place. Take their homes hostage, and not take No for an answer."

"There isn't room," interrupts Ianis. "It's already too crowded on the Pnyx."

"It's not about room!" Elpinike laugh-scoffs, shooting a quick glare at Ianis. "It's about justice, and whether it is right, and whether it is fair, and if it is strategically viable. If it would work, then it would be right. The question is whether it would work. And I think it could."

All the other aristocratic women go silent.

Boldly, Elpinike continues, "Surely they would not throw every one of their wives in prison, particularly us noblewomen. Really, we could do whatever we want, if we wanted to. We *allow this*."

"You would test the men?" Ianis asks carefully. "When all the laws are on their side?"

"Not our men," Eupraxia adds, "but the male gods. It's they who decide. Hestia, Hera, Demeter, and Athena all know better than to try to revolt against their husbands and brothers. They know, and show us, how to live our own sorts of lives, despite our men. Around and beside them, not against them. Well, only against them sometimes. But only against them in ways that we know we will still end up at home together at the end of the night. We live in a cosmos ruled by a well-known rapist."

"This democracy is not something invented by the gods. It is the work of men. And, of course, men made it to work best for them. It doesn't necessarily work best for the gods, and it *definitely* doesn't work best for *women*. Men created this democracy, so why couldn't women create *our own democracy?*"

Isodike, thinking it a big joke, suggests, "Theirs doesn't include us, so maybe ours shouldn't include them. After all, if it didn't include them, they wouldn't have to even know about it. And if they don't know about it, how could they work against it?"

Elpinike gives a hearty look of camaraderie to her sister-in-law. The gathered noblewomen chuckle at the question, but Elpinike looks around at them each, underscoring it as a question worthy of real thought.

"They would beat us," one older woman suggests. "They have the strength, and the lack of compassion, that makes them the most vicious of all animals. Watch a pack of men bring down some poor wolf, and then tell me which one is wild. Pythagoras the great sage suggests that we shouldn't even be killing animals for food or sacrifice!"

Isodike says, "In Sparta, Kimon tells me, the women have much more power and freedom."

Nods and intrigued eyebrows, as bowls of grapes are handed around which deflect the notion.

"I don't think a democracy of women would be any better than this democracy of men," Deinomache says. "Kleinias has shared about how selfish and guileful the men of the Assembly can be, and honestly it didn't sound much different from the girls I know! A democracy of women would still have the same problems."

"Not all women. And not all men. Just the noblewomen and noblemen. Now that, I imagine, would be an Oligarchy to be beloved by the gods. Rule by the right few, but all of the right few."

"You know, Elpinike, you have the most creative mind!" Eupraxia coos with a clasp of her hands. "Really, this whole hypothetical scenario has been like watching a fantasy on the stage. You know what you absolutely ought to do? You should write up this idea, and give it to some man to put his name on, and actually get it produced! Wouldn't that be a squawk? And we would all secretly know that it had come from the mind of a woman, a male-named Athena from the head of a female Zeus!"

"Do not call me female Zeus," Elpinike sighs, feeling unheard. "And honestly, the last thing I want to imagine is men prancing around in masks miming my envisioned rebellion as a farce to my face."

Some of the women laugh at that comment, at which Elpinike glares around to see who did, suddenly infuriated to be in such company.

Deinomache sees her seriousness and acknowledges, "It is true that the laws are unfair, it really is. But also we have everything we could want. With the power of men comes the danger. In war, we women usually only have to worry about a change of regulations or rituals with some change in leadership; whereas men have to worry about being totally wiped out. Everyone wants a woman around, while no one wants a man around. I say let them play their violence and power game; let them have it. Who of sound mind would want to join that deadly competition? Care and subservience are the most powerful armor. That's why women live to the oldest ages."

Lydia, the oldest of the women at the party, finally speaks up with a point of a grape stem. "Do not say that war is fine. Do not go thinking you would be safe in war because you are a woman. War-madness overtakes men. Reason whimpers under Pan's hoof during war. Being a woman is doing all the work to avoid war at all costs, every day, home by home. Only girls long for freedom. We know there is no freedom from responsibility."

Elpinike sighs and tries to find a face of camaraderie again in her sister-in-law Isodike, but she instead finds Isodike patiently nodding agreement with old Lydia.

Isodike shyly shrugs. "Sister-in-law is perhaps the boldest among us. But the stories I remember most clearly are the stories of horror - the true stories of what really happens to women in war. These stories usually aren't the ones that get told by men. We must be careful what we wish for."

Elpinike sighs and says, "If we don't explore the possibilities, we will never find out what could have been. I don't know if my experience is much different than most women, but I have found men *easy* to manipulate and convince, and I find it easy to imagine a scenario where we could take control of our society not unlike what the women of Sparta have done. If any of you have friends in Lakedaemonia, you might hear the real stories, the ones the men don't tell, about who really holds power there. It is the women. And the strength of their men is a mask, a weapon wielded by the women in power. If we wanted to, if we merely planned and asserted ourselves, steeled ourselves against the initial push-back, I think we could take the reigns of this chariot."

"Yes, but, really ... Let's not," Eupraxia replies with a smile. She gestures to one of her slaves for more wine as she utters, utterly unironically, "We could have it a lot worse."

Ψ

Sophokles visits the temporary altar of a visiting god

"At a temporary temple which he's set up in Piraeus, right off the docks, he practices healing magic. He uses herbs, sticks and stones, breathing exercises. He invokes no gods. But he makes people well. Believe me."

"If he invokes no gods, what is the point of his temple?" Sophokles asks with a doubtful look. "Who does his altar's smoke go to?"

"I call it a temple for lack of a better term. He uses an altar, but he puts *you* on it. But not like Iphigenia or something - he doesn't sacrifice you. He just inspects you there. The only name he invokes is his order's teacher, a man named Asklepios."

"Though I love the gods, I'll try anything at this point. He isn't an *atheist*, is he?"

"No no, he doesn't *disdain* the gods. He just doesn't invoke them."

Sophokles' little son Iophon reaches up to tug at his father's tunic. "Father, when it rains like this you can catch eels, they say!"

The Kos fellow Sophokles has been talking to smiles at little Iophon and says, "You like eels, boy?"

Iophon clams up at the stranger's question.

"Answer the question, Iophon," his father tells him.

"I want to have caught an eel so I can tell the story," Iophon admits.

The stranger looks back to Sophokles. "It's just information. No harm in getting it looked at, right?"

Sophokles shrugs and shakes his head, then grasps his foot again to scratch at the edge of the pain. "It sounds like more rural magic to me, which hasn't worked so far, but I'm willing to try anything new at this point."

Sophokles, carrying a small parasol to block the misting rain from his wincing face, makes his way through the crowded Piraeus alleys with little Iophon chasing behind him, to the corner where the priest of Asklepios of Kos has his little streetside table set up.

It is a long, low table with a straw-filled cushion on top, where an old grey-haired woman is presently lying, while the young priest peers into her open mouth. Many onlookers watch in weirded-out silence.

"Your tooth is dying, I am sorry to say, and it is poisoning your entire jaw. I have seen this before, on Kos. You will definitely need to lose the tooth, and it is still possible that the poison is too strong already."

"Who poisoned me?" the woman asks, as the priest pulls away from her mouth and she sits up.

"Your tooth! When it died, it released a miasma of death which seeped into the bone of your jaw, or so it appears to me. Would you like me to pull the tooth out?"

The old woman clasps a hand to her face and coughs a little half-hearted shriek at the thought, then stands and begins to shuffle away from the scene.

As Sophokles approaches him, the priest is calling out after her, "I will be here until winter, if you want more help!"

Sophokles says to the man, "I have heard you can heal. But I am worried after what I've just seen."

"O hey, you're Sophokles!" The priest gathers his excitement then smiles half-heartedly to Sophokles and says, "Every problem has a different solution. What's troubling you in your body, friend?"

Sophokles lifts his leg and puts his foot up on the table. He gestures to the red and swollen toes. "My foot, you see, has been hurting now for months. Right between my toes, a sore that ebbs and flows."

"O Sophokles, king of words, even in pain!" coos an eavesdropping woman nearby, a fan of the actor. Other listeners titter.

"Well, let me take a look at your problem. You say it is your foot?"

Carefully, the priest gets very close to Sophokles' foot with his face, and begins to press and pull and prod with a long metal pin, noting with nods when Sophokles groans or yelps in reaction.

The healing priest takes a pouch from his belt, fingers through many similar tiny rolls of papyrus inside, then pulls one out and carefully unfurls the tiny tube to the length of his arm. Written all down the length of the long, narrow scroll are the tiniest visible Hellenic letters. This priest seems to know the contents well enough to be able to search it quickly for what he is looking for, holding the little scroll very close to his face and scrolling it quickly up and down past his squinted eye. Finally he stops on one line, draws the tip of a metal pin along it to confirm he is reading the correct line, then laboriously spends the next long moments rerolling the delicate papyrus scroll around the pin as he explains.

"So, my friend, I have just examined your symptoms and these scrolls which I copied personally from the libraries on Kos, and I am fairly certain that I've determined what is ailing you."

Sophokles gasps with grateful relief, grasping at hope.

"My friend, I suspect that what you are suffering from is a *foot worm* - a sort of miniscule serpent known to invade specifically the feet of men who walk about in swampy areas unshod. If you would allow me, I will use my tool upon your foot delicately, in order to test my theory. If I am correct, we should see the head of the tiny beast emerge. Then, with some luck, I may be able to use a second tool to capture the beast."

He sits upon his fold-out stool in front of Sophokles and lifts the playwright's pained foot onto his own knee, holding his little metal instrument and stick at the ready as if he is about to dine upon Sophokles' toes.

"May I?" he asks after Sophokles stares dumbstruck for too long.

Sophokles just inhales slowly and widens his eyes.

The priest takes that as a silent consent and leans in to do his work. Pain is immediate when the priest begins prodding at the area between the playwright's toes, but the priest knows just how to hold a struggling man, and it is only a few forgettable moments of blinding pain before the sudden warm relief that accompanies the sight of a little red worm head squeezed out between the tips of the tools.

"Behold the culprit of this foot crime!"

"Just do what you must," Sophokles mutters, imagining a disastrous battle about to begin.

"Now to get him out." The priest carefully attacks the worm with the tip of his twig.

"Gods, please help this man," Sophokles beg, grappling against pain.

As he works the priest explains patiently, "Asklepios taught his followers a way of thinking, but he doesn't demand worship like other gods. He just wants us to help heal each other. But you're welcome to call out to whatever gods you'd like to. I've heard more names than you can probably imagine. All react to the same treatments the same way. Asklepios, god of healing, favors only knowledge and care and consistency."

"If you say so," Sophokles groans.

"Trust me," the priest says with a bright smile as he carefully wraps the head of the worm around the small stick of wood. "I studied with the healers on Kos, and then sailed to Argolis to learn from the healers at Epidauros as well. Most healers you meet will only have studied at one or the other. But I possess the knowledge of both schools!"

"Impressive," Sophokles grunts, grasping a stranger's hand.

Very carefully, the priest turns the twig with his thumb on the tip of the tiny serpent, and as it rotates the serpent winds round the wood, revealing itself inch after inch to be ever longer than expected, while Sophokles groans in pain like a broken harp of Haides, until finally the little dragon's tail slips out and the priest tugs the entwined serpent and stick away from Sophokles' relieved foot.

"And here," the priest explains calmly, "is your foot worm."

"*Thank you*, friend," Sophokles says to the priest, weeping with relief. "Tell me where to give to your god, or patron hero, or whoever he is. This is a relief I will never forget." He gazes with gratitude at the strange worm coiled around the tiny stick. "I can't believe that thing was in my foot."

"Don't thank me," the priest says, "thank my master Asklepios, and the cosmos for having a consistent physical nature. Where Chaos ebbs, Man can thrive."

Sophokles nods, noting the name with a grateful long sigh. "I will praise Asklepios all my days."

The actor-playwright's son little Iophon runs up and looks over his father's shoulder, asking in too loud a voice, "Does this mean you can take me fishing, finally?"

"Oof," grunts Sophokles, "give my foot until next month, at least."

"I never get what I want!" Iophon instantly starts weeping and runs off back toward their home before his father can grab him.

The priest of Asklepios throws the serpent and stick into a nearby brazier's fire, and says to Sophokles, "I can give you a bigger stick for that ailment."

Sophokles frowns at the priest who just helped him. "I'm surprised at you," he scoffs. "I would think you were more modern-thinking than that. I, friend, am not the sort of father who would beat his son into submission like some goat. I want to raise my son to understand how to have relationships of mutual respect, so that he doesn't become some cruel man like our own fathers were, or worse, think that other men can treat him that way."

The priest of Asklepios shakes his head and says, "Before they're ten, they need the rod, or they'll run all over you."

"I'll listen to you for *foot* problems," Sophokles snorts as he turns away from the man. "I see not all problems require the same experts."

Ω

Sokrates meets a new friend at the festival of Artemis the Bear

Dressed as bears in brown capes which hang behind round-eared fur hoods, the young girls from all the villages of western Attika dance together down the beach at Munychia, for the festival which climaxes the month of the same name. Each little girl carries a little cake made to resemble deer or boars or other creatures of the forest beloved to Artemis, covered with poppy seeds to resemble fur, and stuffed with wax-tipped stick candles. The candles light the little girls' bear masks and false ears in the evening light as they bring their cakes down to their waiting, singing families.

Families with children are gathered on the Munychia sand overlooking the Straits of Salamis in the blue twilight. The western Mount Hymettos is crowned in early stars.

"I'll rip your belly!" little Periktione giggles as she jumps down a little dune of sand, into the light of her family's campfire.

"I'll rend your cake!" her father laughs, grabbing her down into the sand.

"No, don't! It's my baby! It's my bear baby!"

Holding two torches high into the air over her head, the beautiful young priestess of Artemis shouts so everyone on the beach can hear, "Tonight, great Artemis, we imitate the bears of the forest in worship of your wild virginity! Unspoiled by the world of men, you alone understand the heart of the young girl who longs to romp through the meadows and befriend the noble creatures of the wood!"

With august gravity, the high priestess of the temple of Artemis Bear-lover declares, holding up a long roll of cloth, "Tonight, in honor of those mothers lost in childbirth, we dedicate all those fine products of woven cloth which women by no fault of their own having lost their lives in childbirth have abandoned in their homes. Here we gather that lost cloth, that fine work of living hands now gone, intended for lives that never came, and dedicate it to you, Artemis Bear-lover, for your care given to all girls."

Phaenarete delivers her friend Semele's unused infant cloth to the priestesses of Artemis, who reverently thank her and kiss her head.

The girls in their bear masks notice little of the heaviness of the high priestess' words, and she sighs with gladness at that as she smiles away her sense of the serious things.

Eleven-year-old Sokrates stands up onto a flat beach stone and notices his head is higher than his own mother's, points this out to her silently with a little smile. Tired-eyed Phaenarete gives her boy a sweet smile as she wraps her veil around her shoulder against the beach breezes.

The twentyish Oligarch boys Hipponikos and Kleinias sit together at the edge of the surf, making crude jokes about all the girls, though when adults pass by they quieten. A smaller merchant's son closer to Sokrates' age named Kleon tries to sit near them to hang out with them, but they continually move away from him, eventually making a puerile game of it, until Kleon starts flinging sand at them and is chased back to his parents.

Sokrates watches all this with shy, glittering eyes, while his mother watches him.

"Go and play with other children, if you like," Phaenarete suggests. "I know you miss your regular crew, but other children can be friendly too. Go on." She gently pushes Sokrates by the butt with her foot, and he hesitantly continues walking into the flitting forms of other folks.

Sokrates pretends that he is an adult, swaggering unseen among the girls in bear costume and boys seeking their eyes. He imagines that he is like his mother, or father, and knows what he is doing and has confidence. He tries to imagine knowing better than everyone he sees.

Then Sokrates smiles and gasps slightly as he recognizes a pair of eyes beneath a bear mask looking right at him, herself also grinning toothily. He cannot place where he remembers the eyes from, but they are somehow profoundly familiar, and comforting, and he thinks of Simon's shoe shop. She sees him see her, and twining her fingers to put her shyness somewhere else for the moment, she crab-walks over to Sokrates with a side-eye, and in a rare ebb of courage Sokrates doesn't move, and lets her approach.

"What's your name?" the lanky bear girl asks.

Shyly, "Sokrates."

"I'm Diotima," she replies. "Or I usually am, but tonight I'm Yrsyla the Bear Queen! Are you a boy or a bear?"

Sokrates furrows his brow at the question but then answers, "I'm a bear," though he looks at his own arms thinking about how he is not wearing any bear costume.

Diotima grabs Sokrates' hand and prances off down the beach with him stumbling behind her. Excitedly she sings, "Good, then I don't have to eat you! Luckily I don't have to eat him! Now come with me, little bear, and let's find someone else to eat!"

She takes him to a makeshift table on which several little cakes have been set up, each decorated with the images of different animals - deer, boar, auroch, sea serpent, hedgehog - and stuffed with dozens of flickering finger-sized candles.

"Here's one for bears to eat!" Diotima shouts as she picks up a hedgehog cake and carries it off down the beach. With her hands full, Diotima does not take Sokrates' hand this time, leaving him there by the cake table with the decision of whether to follow her or not. Sokrates shyly takes one of the cakes.

After he watches her continue down the beach without him for a while, Sokrates finally scampers back down the beach in the other direction, back to his mother. He shows her the cake in his hands.

"Is that for you? Or is that for the bears? Did someone give you that?"

Sokrates nods. Then, rather than explain, he just points.

Phaenarete squints at him and hugs him.

"Mother, why don't girls and boys play together? Why don't I know any girls? You were a girl once. What's up with them?"

Phaenarete laughs. "Well, that's a big question, Dew-drop. Boys and girls and just different. Not totally different. Mostly they're not that different. But they are a little different, they are. And girls prefer to keep boys out of their goings-on. But then, later in life, once they both grow up, it flips and men prefer to keep women out of *their* goings-on. It's like two gangs, like those boys you so admire in the Agora who kick stalls and shout at each other. It's just a way of separating people, really. It would be better if there were just one gender, and no separation, wouldn't it?"

"I do want to know girls better," Sokrates says, looking off in Diotima's direction.

"It's confusing, when we keep you so separated and don't talk about why, I guess, isn't it?"

Eleven-year-old Sokrates shrugs and puts a finger in his cake.

"Don't do that, dirty boy!" his mother laughs, and takes the cake from him. "If you're going to eat it, eat it civilized, with fork or knife or something. Boys."

Sokrates glances off in the direction of the dancing bear girls. His mother sees the pubescent curiosity behind his eyes amid the reflected firelight. She thinks back for a few moments to her own youthful romanticism.

Phaenarete asks her son, "Has your father talked to you about sex yet? About the love that happens between men and women?"

Sokrates shakes his head with a worried, embarrassed grimace.

"Look, Dew-drop, you're eleven years old so I suppose you might as well learn this now, from me, before you learn it wrong from older boys," Phaenarete says with a little sigh, taking Sokrates by the shoulder of his tunic and guiding him over to a large overturned tree which they can both sit on. "Now you know how you have a little penis and testicles between your legs there, and how I don't have that? Well what I have, and what every girl and woman has, instead of that penis, is a sort of cave, called a vagina, which leads to a place under my belly where new babies can grow."

Sokrates cocks his head with curiosity, looking at his mother's stomach and trying to imagine.

"How does that happen?" he asks her.

"Well," she begins hesitantly, thinking quite how to put it, "so Eros, the son of Aphrodite, has this bow ... and when anyone is hit by one of its arrows, they fall in Love with someone they are looking at. And when men are in Love, often they know it because their penis grows and becomes firm, and when this happens usually they will have an incredible urge to be with a woman. Some men will keep this urge at bay by simply learning to control their urges. But some men are so afflicted that they become wild satyrs, mad with lust and willing to be hurtful in order to fulfill their selfish desires. I don't understand what keeps one man from falling into such behavior and another unable to resist it, but if you have any sensations that feel like turning into a gross, lusty satyr, in your mind, turn around and go the opposite direction. In your mind."

Sokrates thinks about that, a bit confused, and worried about what he apparently could turn into.

"So that's what you want to learn how to do - help women have babies?" he asks with genuine confusion about the whole process.

"To give birth," she explains, "not to have the initial sex, just the birthing part, and caring for the child while carrying it both inside and on the breast."

He stays close to his mother for the last hours of the festival, his body pressed against her side, watching from across the waves of faces as the little girl and her hard-eyed father both glance once or twice in his direction.

He looks to the stars and wonders how old they are, when they each lost their way as humans and fell victim to the sort of adult drama which led to them being made into simple stars.

Later that evening, as Phaenarete and Sokrates are walking back up the beach toward the path back to the city with the rest of the crowd, a foreigner unfamiliar to them, the Phoenikian engineer Melqartshama, approaches Phaenarete with polite hesitance and catches her attention with a gesture and a smile.

"Hello, good Athenian woman, and please forgive the intrusion of a stranger, but my daughter wanted me to give this to your son." Melqartshama hands Phaenarete a small sheaf of driftwood bark.

Drawn in charcoal on the bark is the snarling face of a hedgehog.

"Thank you, friend-stranger, and please thank your daughter on my son's behalf! His name is Sokrates, if she asks. And I'm Phaenarete, wife of Sophroniskos."

"My daughter's name is Diotima, and I am Melqartshama of Phoenikia."

"I like that you gave your daughter a nice Hellenic name," Phaenarete says with a smile to the girl.

"I thought Athenians would like that," the Phoenikian says. He bows his head and leaves their presence again, as Phaenarete looks down to Sokrates to show him the drawing.

"You're blessed by Aphrodite today, Dew-drop," his mother says happily. "Some little girl loves you."

"Mother, please," Sokrates whines quietly so other families won't hear, "don't call me Dew-drop. I'm not a child anymore."

Tired-eyed Phaenarete stops her steps, and Sokrates, continuing, loses her hand for a moment before turning around to find his mother quietly shedding tears and smiling at him.

"O mother, I'm sorry!" he cries sympathetically. "It's not my fault. Time just marches on!"

Phaenarete laughs a short sharp laugh, nods, and takes her son into her arms for a quick tight hug before playfully pushing him away again as they continue to walk back home along the beach surrounded by gentle torches and romping girl-bears.

ATHENS

8

ZEUS ASH-MAKER

A

Perikles gets inspired at the Olympic Games

The scent of simmering bull flesh leaps along the breeze as the Sun God brightly warms the fields of Elis for the Eightieth Olympic Games.

As ever, seemingly All-Hellas has gathered. Glistening muscles stretch and strain under oil and sunlight and the gazes of fellow Hellenes. Throngs of men amble in cliques, enjoying their portion of the holy meal being shared as smoke with the gods. White clouds watch from the horizon like the women in white dresses who likewise are unwelcome but interested enough to peep the proceedings from afar.

Many men stop to marvel at the new marble infrastructure which has been built since the last games four years ago. "These are the first Olympic Games of the future," one young man notes to an older man while beholding the bright new Pelopion.

The ancient ash mound at Olympia called the *Pelopion* is one of the central landmarks of the Olympic Games. The short grey hill is the hardened buildup from many generations of sacrifices made on top of the tomb of the ancient King Pelops, after whom the whole peninsula of southern Hellas, the Peloponnese, was named. By ancient tradition begun by the sons of Pelops themselves, heralding the opening rituals of the Olympic Games and beginning of a new four-year *Olympiad*, the eldest priest of Zeus carefully carves out each step into the high, black ash mound with a religious trowel as he ascends, then an attendant leads a strong, black ram up the steps to have its head pulled back and its throat slit, then to be burned in its entirety as a *holokaust* for Zeus Cloud-Gatherer, King of the Gods, its whole body's ash added to the Pelopion.

This year, however, there is great controversy among attendants, as the ceremony to start the Eightieth Olympiad is put on just a bit differently than ever before. Since the close of the last Olympic Games, the Arkadian architect Libon has been hard at work organizing a whole new look for the entire sanctuary. Hardly an angle lacks some new structure of marvelously sculpted and colorfully painted marble. But it is the new infrastructure at the Pelopion that is the most controversial. Where there had previously only ever been the black ash mound, now there are fine new marble steps, carved and painted with images of Pelops and his children, leading up to a bright bronze platform. It is definitely impressive, but in a modern rather than an ancient way, so it is the younger men who tend to prefer it, and the older men who find it inappropriate.

Aischylos is here to watch the chariot races, hoping to be inspired with images of what the ancient heroes would have looked like and felt when they rode their bronze cars into battle in the old way which the races merely mimic.

Kimon is here to run, and has a car and horses in the chariot race, knowing that King Hieron of Syrakous is to be his primary opponent again this year for gold in that contest.

Milo is here as coach to a couple of competing wrestlers who are both fellow adherents to the Pythagorean Mysteries. They all wear cloth bands around their arms with colorfully embroidered magical triangles, which have already been judged not to be illegal triangle magic after complaints from superstitious opponents.

Perikles, Ephialtes, Lysimachos, Antiphon, and several younger men who have begun to consider themselves Democrats, are all here as a group representing Athens, wandering together between the many events to cheer for Athenians. Among the new Democrats is the young sculptor Phidias, who despite his youth is already close with Perikles and Ephialtes through his work on their projects. It is young Phidias' first time at Olympia, and he is awe-struck by the new architectural infrastructure which has been built in recent years.

Phidias tells Perikles, "I've heard the architect, Libon, used Pythagorean magic in his plans. I've also heard he's here!"

"Of course he's here," Ephialtes replies, "All-Hellas is here. And especially if he has all this to show off - he is surely here!"

"I mean to try to find him and speak to him!" Phidias says excitedly as he heads out into the crowd.

Antiphon and Lysimachos follow young Phidias but veer off to greet the Athenian charioteers, leaving Ephialtes and Perikles alone for a moment amid the busy crowd.

"So the year of your wedding has begun," Ephialtes nonchalantly notes. Perikles kicks his ankle softly. "Hey!"

"At least I still have several months to brace myself," Perikles sighs. "Mother wants the wedding to happen in the month of Gamelion, of course, for auspiciousness, so I get to wait until winter. I'll admit, I've never felt more like Persephone - bound to a marriage for another generation's reasons."

"You don't want to marry Periboea?" Ephialtes scoffs. "Why not? She's beautiful, erudite, rich..."

Perikles just shakes his head. "I know my cousin too well. I mean her no ill; I can't speak ill of my own family. But to feel the arrow of Eros as other men speak of it, I still think I don't know that feeling yet. And marriage before love ... it just feels wrong to me. I don't want to just live my life in that old traditional way. It's not what I had wished for myself. I didn't want to build my life like my parents, but instead courageously as a modern person, ignoring norms as reasons to do anything and living instead for virtue and wisdom. And yet here I am, doing what my mother wants, becoming the sort of man which she would prefer to see her family create. Besides which - I happen to know, from my other cousins' gossip, that Periboea *has* felt the arrow of Eros, and it points her eyes in the direction of someone other than me, a young man her own age."

"O merciless Aphrodite," Ephialtes moans. "Whom does the girl think she loves?"

Perikles sighs. "Of all people, the son of Kallias - Hipponikos."

Ephialtes sniffs out a little laugh. "All young women see are muscles and jewels. She won't maintain that lust and greed for long. She'll grow up, mature, and come to care more about a man of intelligence and kindness and depth, like you, rather than a handsome, exciting, rich boy like that. Especially with you guiding her, as her husband."

"I don't know," Perikles says pessimistically. "I fear Hipponikos is perfect for Periboea. He makes her laugh with ease."

"He makes no one else laugh," Ephialtes sniffs.

Perikles reluctantly offers, "A good sign that the gods meant them for each other."

"She is to be yours," Ephialtes says, looking his friend in the eyes. "Eros is a trickster. But Hera is not. You know what I mean? The Goddess of Marriage is very matter-of-fact, and forthright. Marriage is not about love. Love is a butterfly jumping from this flower to that. Marriage is about producing legally-valid children who are Athenians, and raising them to be good ones. It's more like running a workshop together - a workshop for creating Athenians. Love ... look for love outside of your marriage."

Ever-smiling Ephialtes looks left to his friend. Perikles shrugs, looking away. Softly, sweetly, Ephialtes frowns, unseen.

Walking on, they pass a crowd who are admiring the new marble buildings all over Olympia. Perikles nods to point out those public conversations to Ephialtes, and they both listen as they pass.

Perikles says, "This is what I want for Athens. Look at these stones. This is what the gods want us to build in - this material that won't erode. You can see - clearly they were right to build it, as Zeus has not objected! Indeed, when was the last Olympics that he didn't rain on the races - the Seventy Fourth, twenty four years ago now? When the old temples stood, before the Second Persian War. We need a modern city like this, full of monuments and temples and civic glory. To show both the gods and all the men of Earth that Athens is great."

"Try taking the people's warship money now, I dare you," Ephialtes jokes. "Persia still looms, and the rumor is that Themistokles himself now stands by the young new Persian king's right hand, ready to use his naval brilliance against us. I've heard it suggested that perhaps it was even Themistokles himself who, like Odysseus of the clever plans, somehow organized the death of his old enemy Xerxes and now puppets this new Persian king as the master of the boy-king's mind."

"That can't be true," Perikles says, shaking his head, finding the idea absurd when he pictures it. "That's just Persian propaganda meant to frighten us."

"Well, just be patient with the pace of your plans, Perikles," Ephialtes proposes with careful thought. "We can see here today the mixed reactions to these new buildings and infrastructure - some love the effort put toward worshiping the gods, but others see it as changing the long-held traditional ways. They have become accustomed to these ruins. Some may prefer the Pelopion forever to be little more than an ash mound in the earth. Perhaps men can only be expected to be able to change what they expect from the world so quickly, and rushing them might snap them back upon you like a branch to the face."

Perikles notices the architect Libon standing talking with a small group who are admiring the new Pelopion. Phidias hovers at the edge of the group, seemingly too shy to interject.

"Let us help young Phidias," Perikles suggests, as he guides Ephialtes to follow him over that way.

A Theban city leader named Epaminondas has the architect's ear when Perikles and Ephialtes are approaching. "It is magnificent," he says, "but as a leader of a city myself - Epaminondas of Thebes, by the way, perhaps you've heard of me - I can only wonder what it must have taken to convince the Olympians to change! The Pelopion is one of the most sacred landmarks of Hellas. And the ash mound was such a natural thing! To replace it with such a vision of the future, in modern marble, it seems easy to imagine it never being able to happen. And yet here you have made it happen! How did you convince the Olympians to let you do this?"

Libon says, "I can speak only to the inspiration Zeus provided me. One night, at the end of summer last year, a great storm came through the Peloponnese and lightning lit our whole city from every direction for hours. Several trees were smitten and burned by the Storm God's thunderbolts. So I traveled north to the Oracle of Zeus under the sacred oaks of Dodona, and there, through the rustling of the leaves, Zeus told his priestesses to tell me that those burned trees were Zeus showing me where he wanted new stone dedications. And it struck me, the thought like a thunderbolt, that if he was removing trees for the purpose - I figured what he wanted must be large."

Phidias listens closest, nodding and seeming to imagine phantom artworks himself.

Perikles offers, making all the other noblemen from other cities turn and look him up and down, "It is truly magnificent work you've done. We at Athens would be wise to do similar work in our own city."

"Athens, who is so honored by Hestia?" asks Epaminondas of Thebes with a haughty scoff. "I thought you Athenians had decided to keep your city in the state the Persians left it - ashes."

Perikles sighs through his nose to calm his anger before he responds. "You must not have been to Athens recently, Theban, for if you had, you would see that we've already repaired most of our city. But it's true that we have respected our old temples by not yet rebuilding them. Perhaps in a few more years, our Akropolis will look much different. But one who earns scars in glorious combat does not shy from their display."

Many who are veterans, which is most of the older men here, nod and murmur hushed understanding. A few begin to compare scars and war stories. One eyeless veteran looks at Perikles' scarlessness, making him blush.

Libon nods with a smile, taking young Phidias's shoulders in one arm and pulling the lad close. "You Athenians have indeed been doing great things lately. We all see it. Everywhere across the world they speak of Athens, and what she is becoming. You should be very proud!"

Ephialtes offers, "We are working on even further enfranchising the people of Athens. The more the gods reassure us it is beautiful to do, we will continue down that path. Our work has only begun, though. Recently we tried to make government offices *paid* work, so that even the poorest men can afford to actually do it. But that effort was not successful."

"Not successful *yet*," Perikles asserts optimistically.

Beside him, Thrax visibly shrugs and quietly sighs. All three men notice and look to him quizzically. He shakes his head to be ignored, but Perikles says, "Please, Thrax, you know I like to hear your thinking. What just came into your mind?"

Thrax says carefully, "I just think that it may be a much longer road than you realize, the road to the full enfranchisement of Athenians." When the three men look uncertain in reaction, he continues, "I know that legally I am not one, but *I* would consider myself an Athenian. I have lived in Athens nearly as long as I can remember. I feel like an Athenian, I speak like an Athenian, and people mistake me for an Athenian with as respectfully as you treat me. Athens is my home-town. But I am a Thrakian slave, taken in war, and sold at Delos to your father Xanthippos. I am not free, I cannot participate in your government, and I will never earn an owl for anything."

Perikles gets a dismayed look and says, "O Thrax, if you want some coins to spend here, I'll give you some!"

"That's not the point," Thrax grunts, annoyed. "It would be better if I could *earn* some coins by being my own man. But Athenian law prevents that. Nevermind."

Perikles shifts uncomfortably, looking away. Ephialtes, though, leans forward. "What do you mean, Thrax? How would you earn coins?"

Thrax shakes his head, wishing he hadn't spoken.

"No, please," Perikles insists gently.

Ephialtes adds, "We talk of expanding freedoms, but perhaps we don't understand..."

"It's nothing," Thrax mutters, but Lysimachos has joined in now.

"You've served our families for years, Thrax. Speak freely."

Thrax looks between these powerful men, advocates for democracy who still own human beings. His jaw works silently for a moment before the words come, slow and reluctant.

"Consider that for each man, the only world is *his* small world," Thrax offers hesitantly. "So it seems to me that for most people there is no democracy. Not for me. Nor for any other slave. Nor for Anaxagoras, or any other foreigner. Nor for Periboea, or any other woman. Nor, functionally, even for the poor man who cannot afford to take a year off from the farm to take some office in the city. If the scale weighs us as either an oligarchy, ruled by a lucky few, or truly a democracy, ruled by all folks, then I'd say the only honest measure would show that there is not yet any real democracy in the world - only the *mask* of democracy. But if anything would function as *footsteps* toward that idea, it would be the enfranchisement of ever more people with equal votes, and equal *opportunity* to actually *participate* in that democracy."

Ephialtes and Perikles listen, processing in their minds all that Thrax is saying. Ephialtes begins to nod, while Perikles sighs and shakes his head.

"But we need to aim for things that are actually possible," Perikles retorts. "We all know that there are never going to be slaves holding office."

"What about the Skythian archers who protect us all, and who are the public property of the city itself?" Thrax says.

"That's not so much an office imbued with powers and responsibilities," Perikles begins to say, but Thrax interrupts him. "They're just slaves owned by the city."

"You've never spoken to those men, because you don't speak Skythian, but I do. They have extensive responsibilities, and they are the ones protecting the most important men in the city, and yet they are still treated as slaves."

"Well they *are* slaves," Perikles says coldly. "They have been captured. Should we make all our enemies citizens?"

"Maybe."

The comment from Thrax stops Ephialtes in his steps, and Perikles and Thrax stop walking as well, and turn to him.

"Am I your enemy?" Thrax asks Perikles and Ephialtes in a moment of unguarded exasperation.

Perikles ignores the question. "The gods obviously don't think there is any dishonor in taking enemies captive when you conquer another city, or they would stop the practice. Would you prefer to have been killed when your Thrakian town was conquered?"

Ephialtes, however, is deep in thought on the matter.

Thrax sighs and blinks with frustration, suddenly feeling that he ought to stop sharing his true thoughts.

"Of course you're not my enemy," Perikles says, "but obviously our cities were once at war, and ours was the victor. If there are not captives taken in war, then what would be the point of war? We would fight, determine a victor, and then nothing would change? I don't love war either, Thrax, but it is one of the processes of the world, like rivers flowing, or men shitting."

"It is most like men shitting," Ephialtes agrees, remembering men shitting as they died on the battlefield at the Eurymedon River. The more he remembers the experience, he loses the ability to cast the imagery out of his mind, and it starts to make his breathing grow more and more rapid.

"You alright, Ephialtes?" Perikles asks his friend.

"Speaking of slaves," Libon says crassly, and gestures to an approaching Spartan Helot messenger wearing a small royal torq indicating that he works for one of the kings.

"Pardon me," the Helot messenger apologizes as he approaches the conversing men. "May I speak with your slave?"

Perikles nods perfunctorily, and turns back to his friends as Thrax goes off with the Helot. When he finds Ephialtes' eyes again, his friend is gazing into the distance, as if into the future foresightfully.

"I don't know, Perikles; I think maybe it could happen. Men know what's right, when faced with it. They just fear the overwhelming power of evil. But when leaders stand up for what would really be right ... their countrymen rise up behind them. And I'm beginning to think that, as generations of people roll on like waves on the shore, it is possible for them to keep giving each other boosts of momentum, and perhaps for this next generation of Hellenes to actually make for themselves a world of equal law for all. A truly just and fair society. When I first got into politics, I thought the best a non-nobleman could hope for was to steal some small amount of power for those who were under-represented, but now I'm really beginning to think that maybe we could actually transform our government into whatever would be truly *best*. I can see the path, the mechanism. It is a stuck mechanism, a long path, but it is *not* false, *not* just a fleeting dream."

Perikles nods, feeling like he lives inside his friend's dream, or like the Moon reflecting the bright optimism of his friend the Sun. Ephialtes puts his arm around him and pulls him close.

"We're going to need men like you, Perikles. It used to be all that people respected was gruff, silent warrior-types. But more and more, it's actually erudite, educated, knowledgeable, and patient-minded men whom other men respect. And in that environment, you'll go far."

An Athenian patriotic chant rises from some distant racing field, making the two men smile to each other quietly for a while as they enjoy the vicarious successes of their city as a song on the wind.

It is not long before Thrax returns to the group, with young Phidias by his side.

"Phidias!" Perikles welcomes him. "You found my man! And did Libon show you what you wanted to see?"

Phidias opaquely says, "He showed me some things."

"We were just headed to the disc field," Ephialtes suggests.

"Thrax, what did that Helot want to say to you?"

He waits until they've moved slightly apart from the other festival-goers before speaking.

"The Helot serves King Archidamos," Thrax says quietly. "The king wishes ... conversation. Without the ambassadors. Private conversation."

Ephialtes and Perikles exchange serious, intrigued glances.

"With whom?" Ephialtes asks.

"With those who speak for Athens' Democracy faction, he said." Thrax keeps his voice low. "Which, I assume, since he spoke to me, meant you. He suggests Megara. Neutral ground."

Ephialtes studies the grass for a long moment, then looks to Perikles. "You should go. You're better at this. I don't do well around Spartans. Never have. They make me too nervous. But you..." He produces a confident smile. "You have a way with kings."

"And if it's a trap?"

"Then better me here to raise rancor about it." Ephialtes puts a hand on his friend's shoulder. "Go. Hear what the wolf has to say."

Down on the field, a disc thrower from Greater Hellas lands a throw far beyond all the rest, and the crowd cheers. Perikles and Ephialtes cheer just to join in, not noticing what happened.

Ephialtes continues, "Meanwhile, I will work on our machinations among the men, and their wives, convincing all that Kimon would rather spend ten years in Spartan lands as a guest anyway."

Perikles nods, nervous about the potential of the plan to backfire and get one of them, or one of their friends, exiled instead.

"What are you looking at?" Perikles asks young Phidias, whom he has caught staring past him into the distance, toward the scaffolding around the nearly-finished temple at the center of Olympia.

Phidias says, looking past him, "Zeus."

Perikles tries to see what the artist is seeing, but sees nothing.

B

The Fates' needles pierce the fabric

In the deep shadows of Nyx, a cloaked form arrives at a crossroads high in the hills of northern Attika, digs beside a certain recognizable square stone, and pulls out from a small hole beneath it a sack containing a worn old bronze theater mask carved in the shape of a tongue-bearing gorgon face with serpent hair. Inside the mask are a tiny dagger inscribed with another gorgon face, and several rows of gold and silver coins, each from distant cities - griffins, crabs, pegasi, octopi, mazes, and lyres stamped opposite the faces of famous kings.

After collecting all the items and refilling the hole, the figure then takes out a pouch of their own, filled with a mash of wheat meal and mulberries and crushed falcon feathers, which they spread on their forehead with careful reverence as they whisper, barely audibly, "Hekate Three-faced, cause me now to become my shadow, invisible to those who I do not wish to see me, because I know your secret names and symbols, and who you are at each time of the day, and what your true name is."

The bronze-masked shadow stops at the first crossroads herm, touches their crotch and is about to salute the face at the top, but they stop.

Carefully, looking down both paths and behind themselves as they approach the herm, the masked figure raises up the iron dagger and strikes the face of the herm, marking the nose. Next they swing the dagger in anger at the herm's dick, chipping a corner off a testicle.

The masked shadow looks down all paths again, and sees no gods in any direction. The stranger then heads down into dark Athens.

Lamp lights darken; ghosts hide.

ATHENS

Γ

The new Painting Portico is revealed in the Agora, to some controversy

Doves line up along the inner pediment of the Temple of Hephaistos, always interested to spy for crumbs when crowds gather below.

Athens' new Painting Portico has been covered by scaffolding and skins since its construction began two years ago, but for the past few days, between its recent completion and the festival to celebrate its final reveal, the building has been covered by a stockade of tall palm branches interwoven in a pleasant pattern, so none might peek at the paintings inside before the official reveal. As the paintings arrive from the artists' studios where they were made, crowds have gathered at that north side of the Agora to watch the cloth-draped pieces get carried in and to guess at their contents.

Though the political maneuvering for its completion has been maintained over the many months of the new colonnade's construction by Ephialtes and his Democrat cohorts, it is the painters of the grand artworks within whose fans now fill the excited crowd. Still it is Ephialtes, freshly famous from his recent political machinations, who stands before the people now, ready to introduce the new building and its paintings, while the painters Polygnotos and Mikon are late and nowhere to be found.

Normally competing, today the two most famous clowns in the Agora, Magnes and Chionides, are both wearing similarly-fashioned hats designed to look like big sea onions, though there is hotly debated uncertainty among the men and women of the Agora as to whether this is meant to be in support or mockery of Perikles, whose nickname in recent years has been reappropriated by his Democrat constituents as a term of endearment. Equally unclear, a large potshard sign hung around the neck of a fan of Magnes who lingers drunkenly beside him all day reads:

SEA-ONION-HEAD FOR ATHENS

Hipponikos, the handsome and well-dressed young son of Kallias, twenty-three now but still skinny as a teen-ager, trots up to Ephialtes panting from the run. "I found Mikon. He was out past the walls, collecting colors. But Polygnotos is nowhere to be found. Not even his assistants or his mistress know where he is!"

"Thanks, son," Kallias says with a pat on Hipponikos' back that he quickly regrets with a grimace. He wipes his sweaty hand off on his own tunic. "Now go jump in a fountain or something."

"We can do this without Polygnotos," Ephialtes proposes to the other Democrats around him, but half of the assembled crowd groans with disagreement. "The man has already done his work. The artwork now speaks for itself."

Ephialtes raises a hand to signal his friends at the curtains to be prepared, then says to the assembled crowd, "The great democratic mind of Athens decided to dedicate our city to the creation of a great set of artworks to show the gods and future generations our pride, and our skill, and our wisdom, and the nobility of *all* of our great citizens! So, without going on too long, please enjoy with me this revelation of the beautiful new Stoa of Paintings!" He drops his raised arm, and the curtains covering the new stoa and its contents are pulled away, to the delighted applause of the city.

Ephialtes' smile has never been brighter.

Excited, delighted conversation fills the air as the men and women of Athens move in together to the shady columned portico filled with new and unseen paintings by the most famous painters of Athens and beyond. The two huge centerpiece paintings, sharing equal space on either side of the stoa and facing each other, each as long as several men on end, are Mikon's painting of the Battle of Marathon, and Polygnotos' painting of the Siege of Troi.

Shining-haired Agariste beams her pride upon her son as she guides a group of her most prized noble friends and fellow art lovers to see her speak to the mastermind of this city-beloved project.

"Perikles, son of Xanthippos, my darling," his mother says as she kisses him all over his face hyperbolically to make her friends all laugh.

"O Mother," he protests.

"We are all just so proud."

One of the aristocratic women, Eupraxia, notes, "I love how you chose to make the two large paintings the same size, and facing each other, one east, one west, in perfect divine symmetry. One faces one way, one faces the other way."

Perikles says, "Actually, the symmetry came from not being able to give either of the artists more space than the other, which was a story of haggling with many acts."

The aristocrats all chatter and chuckle at understanding the frustration of dealing with artisans.

"Actually," Ephialtes adds, "I like that they're symmetrically placed, and facing each other, so that they artistically are presented as equivalent, holding the Athenian triumph at Marathon as equivalently glorious as the sacking of the greatest city of the ancient world by the heroes of old."

The Oligarchs among the nobles, that overpowered minority, chatter general agreement with Ephialtes' city pride. A rowdy, likely drunk group of younger Democrats wrangled by the horse-trainer Antiphon rush up to shake the hands of the famous Democrat leaders. Perikles gives his friend a look and a smile, and Ephialtes laughs as they think the same thing.

Perikles and Ephialtes stand together proudly, accepting the congratulations of their compatriot Democrats, as the gasps of the crowd viewing the new paintings for the first time rises to a notable din. It is quickly unignorable, and the Democrats' self-congratulations peter out so they can better hear what is being said in the shocked and titillated crowd.

Perikles turns to inspect the paintings quickly, to see if he can find what has shocked everyone.

It is a scene from the Troian War, as that city is being taken by the Hellenes, so the chaotic scene of pillaging and rape is difficult to take in quickly. But Ephialtes sees it before Perikles, and whispers to him.

"Princess Laodike," he whispers.

Princess Laodike, famously the most beautiful of the Troian King Priam's many royal daughters, is near the center of the painting's battle, in the rapacious grasp of Achilles, who is clasping chains onto her wrists as she gazes into his eyes with what appears to be lust, her body heaving in desirous reaction to his bulging proximity, as the beginnings of a chasm threaten to open beneath her to answer her prayers to be swallowed into the earth rather than taken captive.

Murmurs are quickly spreading that that most beautiful woman of Troi is very clearly painted to resemble long-necked Elpinike, who has often been called the most beautiful woman in Athens, and Achilles, that most skilled and handsome hero on the Hellenic side of that war, has more than a passing resemblance to a slightly more-muscled version of the painter himself, Polygnotos. Or so word travels that others seem to think so.

Though their names are in everyone's mouths, neither Elpinike nor Polygnotos are anywhere to be seen within the crowd. And quickly, Kallias and his son Hipponikos also make themselves absent, to hide from the whispers about their widely-imagined embarrassment.

> "MAY SEAWEED RISE UP FROM THE MUCK TO CHOKE YOU,
> AND LEAVE YOU LYING SPENT UPON THE SHORE,
> FACE-DOWN, GRINDING YOUR TEETH INTO THE SAND,
> DISCARDED LIKE A FORGOTTEN STREET DOG."
> *Hipponax*, Ephesian Poet

Δ

Kratinos searches for his missing friend

"Give me a mask! A smiling mask to hide these tears! A youth mask to hide this slide into senility! A lady mask to hide my wifeless shame!"

Sophokles and his actors all look up from their reading, as drunken Kratinos stumbles into the theater of Dionysos with his whole body quavering except the hand which holds his wine-flask.

"Have you seen my Hipponax?" he asks the darkness.

"The deformed old fish-faced insult-poet, that Hipponax?"

"Yes, that Hipponax! Cruel songbird of the hideous face!"

"He's your friend?" asks Ion of Chios, who has been acting with Sophokles' chorus for a couple of years now. "I wouldn't think that he would be friends with anybody. He's like meanness made man. Pseudo-man."

"It sounds like you've seen him recently," Kratinos begs, focusing on Ion and stumbling over to him. "Has he insulted you recently? I haven't been able to find him for months, and no one I speak to has seen him since before winter. I fear the worst."

"I don't know if death would be the worst thing for a man like Hipponax," Sophokles cruelly jokes, but no one laughs and he immediately regrets it. When the girlfriend of one of his actors gives Sophokles a glare, he says, "What? The man's an insult-poet himself."

Middle-aged Ion, whom Kratinos has zeroed in on, tells him, "I have not seen him since last year, when he was in the Agora mocking the clowns. I'm sorry,

Kratinos. Maybe he left for another city."

"Maybe he went to Delphi to find a new fate," Sophokles suggests half-mockingly.

"This Hipponax sounds interesting," remarks one younger actor.

"He is!" Kratinos shouts, releasing more tears. "You may make jokes about him, but please, Sophokles, do not wish him dead!"

"They say his barbed poetics drove his enemies to suicide!" the actor Ion remembers hesitantly. "Like Bupalos, who displayed that mean sculpture of a lumpy face and said that it was Hipponax's face. Hipponax excoriated him in uproarious jibes in the Agora, and not long afterward the man broke his own neck on a rope! If a murdering knife must be buried to destroy its curse, what must be buried when only words are what cut?"

"The mouth of the man," one young actor suggests jokingly, then covers his face with a mask when all look back to see who said it.

"Come on now," Aischylos says, "the words did not kill Bupalos. He himself killed himself, with the rope. It is the rope, and Bupalos himself, who were cursed in that deed. Not Hipponax's words, nor his mouth nor tongue! Anymore than it is my words which upset those who are upset by a turn of phrase in one of my plays. It is their own hearts which upset an audience. Which is part of why I do not think people should bring children to the theater. They are too easily confused and disturbed!"

Kratinos sing-shouts, "But we are all children, all but the eldest gods! Are we not all indeed confused and disturbed? Is that not the point of our endeavor, as artists, as actors?"

"Confuse and disturb? No," Sophokles replies. "Inspire and intrigue, perhaps."

"I see Kratinos' point," suggests young Euripides shyly. He has been hanging with the actors for the past few months, since falling out with his painting boss Mikon. "I mean, if art is meant to move souls, then those unprepared for it must be allowed to experience it. It shouldn't merely be for those who don't need it, who already know the wisdoms it contains. Right?"

"Indeed," Aischylos agrees, "just as I was telling you earlier, in regard to your own freshness as a writer. You must put yourself into the arena and fail, as must people's souls struggle in the thought-arena of art, and perhaps there are some moments of confusion and disturbance in that grapple. But still, there is some boundary, as obviously the youngest and most foolish are simply not even amenable to the format at all, and there must be some threshold at which a man's mind is ready to process our form of art. Paintings are better for the young and the stupid."

"No one knows what they have not seen! No one understands what they have not heard!" Kratinos shouts with drunken abandon. "If there is no more Hipponax in the world, then I will need to take up his effort! You all smell like the Sea is menstruating!"

The actors squint, frown, and shake their heads. Euripides smells himself.

"Perhaps it is better," Sophokles suggests to Kratinos, "that Hipponax disappear into the unknown, rather than be known to have died. Isn't that more mysterious and dramatic?"

"I want him here!" Kratinos cries. "I want him alive." His drama suddenly gains gravity, as does his body, and he falls to a seated slump on the ground, his limbs heavily flopped upon himself.

Hesitantly, a few of the more empathetic younger actors step over toward Kratinos to physically comfort him, Euripides among them.

"Listen, listen," Kratinos slurs, grabbing Penander's arm for balance. "I've got it - what if ... what if Zeus and an ox had a baby? He thought it was Hera, but it was just some regular ox! No, no - what if Hephaistos and a donkey made love and their child was raised by fishmongers!"

The actors exchange bewildered glances. Sophokles leans forward, frowning. "The point is to explore what the gods *might be*, *could be*, not things which could never be. The gods do not like being mocked as if absurd. There's room in plays for exploration, young men, but not *that much* room."

"Better - better!' Kratinos staggers to his feet, nearly pulling Penander over. "I'll be ... I'll be Dionysathena! Part wine god, part wisdom goddess! I'll dance wise thoughts while drinking from two wineskins at once!"

"You're drunk," one of the actors says flatly.

"Yes! Like my new god-character! Who is also part fish! A swimming, drinking, thinking fish who tells everyone they're stupid!" He attempts to demonstrate all three actions at once and nearly falls, but expertly avoids it in a drunkard's dance. "Hipponax would have understood! He knew that everything is everything else if you look at it right!"

"This isn't theater," Sophokles says, mostly to assure the younger actors. "This is grief."

"Grief! I'll show you grief! I'll grieve the gods! I'll make Herakles mate with a cloud! I'll have Hermes deliver messages to himself and misunderstand them! I'll show Artemis hunting her own reflection!" He spins in place, arms wide. "Hipponax knew - he knew that nothing is what it claims to be! Everything's a mask upon a mask upon a mask!"

He lurches toward the exit, briefly slipping on a mask of an old drunkard in the dew-damp grass. The actors watch him go in uncomfortable silence. Penander starts to follow but Sophokles catches his arm.

"Let him be," the playwright says. "He will sober up. Young men, take note: the theater is for showing life as it is, which sometimes requires invention and creativity, but ... not whatever that was. And I wouldn't walk too close behind a man who is that angry at the gods."

E

Aoide moves minds with her poetry

Seated on her tripod amidst mystical vapors, the Pythia proclaims, "Never."

The dignitary from distant Massalia cocks his head, awaiting more, then looks to the male priests beside the young woman when he does not get what he wants from her. They lower their heads minutely as they return his stare, waiting for him to accept her answer. Finally, after some soft bullish snorts from his nose, the Massalian man turns dismally away and steps back out into the sunlight from the dark shadows of the Temple of Apollo.

"Next," the Pythia commands her priests.

Aoide watches from the wall, processing it all.

Since her recent twenty-third birthday, Aoide has been the Pythia named Opho's sole personal attendant, so she must be near and at the ready all the time, but by now she knows that when she is working the Pythia will never have needs, never break character, never appear to summon Aoide, but nevertheless there are times when Aoide will be needed, and Aoide herself must determine when that is. The priests, the other slaves, even the Pythia - all trust Aoide's judgment about the Pythia's needs.

In the hour before sunset, when the day's suppliants have gone and the evening sacrifices haven't yet begun, Aoide often walks the sanctuary's paths to take in the conversations when pilgrims' guards are down. The shadows of statues stretch like sundial markers across the stone steps. Visitors from distant cities gather in small groups, sharing wine and stories, their various dialects mixing on the evening air.

She passes a cluster of Spartans lounging against the treasure-house of Sikyon. One single elderly Sikyonian man sits nearby, watching them with dismay at their rowdiness near his city's sacred treasures. Their voices carry louder than is customarily considered proper for sacred ground, and their laughter has an edge of mockery. Seeing it from below, they are all gazing up and describing the statue of Apollo which stands before his temple.

"Look at those soft hands," one sneers. "No calluses from a spear shaft there. The sculptor should have given him a lyre made of spider-silk!"

"Delphian Apollo," another spits the name like an insult. "All riddles and meaningless words. Give me Spartan Apollo, who knows how to fight!"

"These Ionians and their slave-boy gods," a third adds. "No wonder the Persians almost conquered them."

"At least the Persians are honest about being warriors," the first agrees. "Not like these temple-soft people with their poetry and their prophecies. If it weren't for the chariot races, I would never come here." He spits on the sacred way.

Aoide feels a familiar heat rise in her throat - the sensation she has come to see as Apollo's anger moving through her, and listen to. She lets her sandals strike the stone more firmly, making her presence known. The Spartans turn, ready to bark at whoever dares interrupt them, but the sight of her temple garments makes them hesitate. She glides closer, arranging her face into the masklike expression of mystery she has learned from the Pythia.

"Twenty-six Olympiads ago, King Kroisos of Lydia sent two messengers to Delphi - old, wisest Solon, Athenian sage whom to his city its first laws of democracy gave; and younger, also wise, but stranger Aisop, ugly slave from Thrake with the lameness and wisdom of Hephaestos."

The Spartans look at each other, listening.

"Both men spoke their wisdoms to the Delphians, but Solon's couched in kindly words and etiquettes familiar, and Aisop's crude, direct, and filled with turns of phrase foreign and confusing. In the end, it was Solon who left Delphi with an oracle for King Kroisos, and who lived a long life, while the insulted Delphians charged Aisop with a false crime of temple theft and threw him from that cliff before he could see another day."

The Spartans frown. One of them turns and looks over the precipice they are standing beside, then back to Aoide.

"Thus democracy, wisdom, and one man - Solon - were saved by simple etiquette and custom, by not being offensive to his hosts. And another, poor Aisop - already world-famous for his tales though he was not yet the age of an elder - met his end too early, where you now stand, just for being rude."

The Spartans shift uncomfortably, their earlier bravado curdling. The one who spat now stares at the very spot with a horrified grimace, as if expecting Aisop's ghost to rise from it.

"We meant no..." the youngest begins, but his voice trails off under Aoide's steady gaze.

"The Far-Shooter's arrows can pierce minds in many ways," she says softly. "Through wisdom, through music, through prophecy. Even the mightiest lion must sometimes bow to a shepherd's pipe. Wise rulers know."

The Spartans murmur appropriate phrases of respect, backing away with careful steps. They leave their wine jug as an impromptu offering, their voices now properly hushed as they disappear among the treasuries.

From his seat on a nearby temple step, where he has witnessed the entire exchange, handsome young Bacchylides lifts his lyre and begins to sing quietly, still startling Aoide at the sound of his voice despite its smoothness.

"See how the priestess tames the wolves! No whip, no spear, no shield, but only wisdom's gentle force is required to make the mighty yield. Like moonlight on the midnight sea, a girl's power half-concealed..."

Aoide breathes slowly through her nose for a few moments, composing silently in her mind, while she tries to stop from smiling at Bacchylides. They have a little dance of eyes.

Poets can see two worlds through different eyes,
granted visions of both what is and what could be.
But Inevitability, poor woman,
knows only ghosts walk this world wild and free.

"Cruel songbird," Bacchylides sings. "You know not what your songs can summon in mens' hearts."

Aoide keeps herself from smiling, though she wants to, when she says, "O I know."

The evening parts them once again, but their minds do not.

Z

Euripides struggles to write

Euripides sits in the sand on Munychia Beach, a roll of cheap Aigyptian paper and a few chunks of charcoal beside him in a rough lambskin bag.

He watches as his friend Nikias, the handsome young nobleman just a couple of years younger than his own twenty, emerges nude from the surf and strides with ease up the beach to join Euripides. He stands for a while there, letting his beautiful body dry in the sunlight, no doubt fully aware of how he looks.

"What are you doing?" Nikias finally asks. As he sits in the sand beside Euripides he sees the scratched-out few words written at the top of the otherwise blank sheet.

"I'm writing," Euripides says morosely, not looking away from his lambskin.

"It looks more like you're just staring silently," Nikias jokes.

Euripides adjusts his tunic and sighs, rubs his own neck. At the sight of that, Nikias crawls behind Euripides and begins to massage his neck and shoulders for him. Euripides shows a shy, confused grimace only to the gods.

"I won't claim to know how to listen to the Muses," Nikias says, kneading Euripides' shoulders roughly, "but from what you describe to me, it sounds like you do, so maybe all you need to do is relax and start writing whatever they're putting into your mind."

"It isn't that simple," Euripides sighs. "I don't think the Muses just write these things for us. They maybe inspire us to imagine certain things, or start us off with some inspiring vision or sound or the like, but when it comes to what actual words to compose your sentences with -- I mean, just think about it! Consider writing a line of poetry. Then imagine all the subtle changes you could make to that line of poetry in order to make it better. And what is better, when it comes to something like poetry? Consider how many different ways there are to say any one idea!"

"Well, it needs to be in meter, so it flows and it's memorable, and it needs to rhyme sometimes, so it's fun to listen to," Nikias says thoughtfully.

"First of all, I'm talking about the substance of the words, but even when it simply comes to the form - no - that's just the tradition!" Euripides shouts, standing up with some difficulty in the loose sand. "Think about Aischylos or Sophokles - two of the most famous playwrights - and they're famous because they *innovated*, because they did things that were not the tradition! And then those things *became* tradition! Think about Aischylos - he *invented* the theatrical scene we think of today, just by adding a second person for the main actor to talk to. For years, that's all plays were, two actors and a chorus. Then Sophokles added a third person, and now *that's* the norm. So maybe ultimately there can be four, or six, or any number of characters in a play at once!"

"I think at least space would limit the number. But you think too hard about these things," Nikias says, standing.

"No, I don't think that I think too hard about them," Euripides spits. "I think that these things require a lot of thought!"

"I think you have yet to be certain about what these things take, as you haven't yet completed anything, nor even begun," Nikias chides with a composite of impatience and friendliness. Then he adds, "You're special, Euripides."

Euripides looks over at his new friend with shy tenderness, and the beginnings of a Euripidean version of a smile.

"I can tell," Nikias adds, looking away, not comfortable yet in such a tender moment and trying to keep it boyishly irreverent. "And I know that I'm not going to be a writer. I just don't have the ideas that people like you have. I don't know; I guess Apollo just didn't choose me. But I want to help those who *are* chosen, because I love the process, and the artform, so much! I just love theater people! I love talking about plays, and songs, and characters."

"Yes, so do I," Euripides smiles. "And when the actors talk about the different stories, and what it takes to inhabit the characters - it's that which interests me most of all! I want to act, but no one writes the kind of roles I want to inhabit."

Nikias nods and kicks some sand. "Like I said, Euripides, you're special."

"My problem is - how do I know what to write? You know, I've heard our stories; I've heard many versions. Somehow when stories are being told around a hearth at night it doesn't feel as important that all of their parts be correct and beautiful and all work together perfectly ... But a play, a piece of theater which will be written down and which actors will perform for the entire city, for the God of Ecstasy himself? It must be great! It can't have mistakes! If it could be better, it should be! Phrynichos was fined for his play about Miletos! How am I supposed to know which version of a certain story is the best one for me to represent?"

"You know," Nikias offers with a shrug and a sigh, "I imagine at some point, when you're writing about some story you've heard elsewhere ... at some point it becomes *your* story, and it doesn't matter anymore whether it matches exactly the truth or the previous version you heard or any of that. It's your version now, and whatever you make it, that's what people will know it as having always been."

Euripides considers that thought for a moment in silence. Then he groans, saying, "Exactly, but what if *my* story is stupid?"

"Impossible." Nikias flashes his friend a beautiful glimmer of the eyes, touches him heavily on the top of the hand, and says sweetly, "Come now, and read me some lines of Euripides."

Euripides smiles, glowing a blush. All budding poetic lines in his mind stop dancing and sit, to watch him in silence.

Like two actors rehearsing, replaying moments they've seen others do, the two boys begin to lean their faces toward each other there amid the hushing quiet of the ocean waves.

The sound of young laughter and feet dashing through the sand towards them turns their attention to Euripides' lambskin with all of his writing implements, which has just been snatched up by wild-eyed Chaerephon, who races now away with it. Euripides decides to pretend not to know the boy. Instead, he just sits heavily and cries as Nikias jumps up and futilely dashes after the thief for a few strides before giving up, weary from swimming.

Chaerephon scurries around the corner of the alley as Sokrates sits crouched against a wall, waiting for him. "Run, man, run! Come on! Move, move, move!" Chaerephon yells, scrambling as he races past Sokrates with a little fat lambskin in his arms and turns another corner, almost slipping onto his side in the process.

"What did you do?" Sokrates asks as he gets up and runs after his friend.

"There was another guy there, and he chased me!" Chaerephon explains as they run together down a few more alleys, mingling into the crowds on the streets and turning a couple of corners just in case there is still a need to lose a pursuer, and then finally coming to rest behind some bushes in a little patch of green between several warehouses near the Piraeus docks. "But I think we're clear now. Here, sit down, check this out."

"What did you do? Did you take that from Euripides?" Sokrates asks as Chaerephon excitedly unfolds the lambskin to reveal the paper and charcoal sticks inside. "I told you not to mess with him. He's our friend."

"Ex-friend. It's a play!" Chaerephon laughs. "I heard them talking about characters. Just think - there's a whole world of characters right in here. Maybe we can sell it to some other playwright."

"But there's nothing on it," Sokrates retorts, unrolling the paper to show that it is entirely blank. "He hasn't written it yet."

"No, look," Chaerephon says, pointing to some scrawled characters near the top of the paper. "There's the play."

"That isn't even a complete sentence. It might just be part of a title, or a note, or something," Sokrates laughs. "Can't you read?"

"No," Chaerephon replies, as if surprised to be asked. "One squiggle of lines looks the same as another to me. You mean you can read this?"

"Yes. It's just a few words, it's not even a complete line. This isn't a play. It's just a fragment, hardly even a sentence! We can't know if this was a line of dialogue, or a description of action, or the title itself!"

"What does it say?" Chaerephon watches Sokrates' face for the answer instead of looking at the figures on the paper.

"It just says '...for the god is now here...'" Sokrates furrows his brow in thought, eyeing the letters with uneven spacing between them, and then adds, "It could say, however, '...for the god is *nowhere*...' There is no way to be certain. Because it isn't clear where the letters of one word end and another begin."

"Maybe we can sell it for half price."

"But perhaps that ambiguity was intentional, and both meanings are intended to balance or clash with each other. What a sophisticated piece!"

"Then maybe we can sell it for double the price!"

"It's not..." Sokrates starts to try to explain, but doesn't know where to begin. "I really don't think this is something anyone would buy." Then he has an idea and excitedly suggests, "But we could write our own play on the blank spaces! Or draw animals."

"That sounds like work. We're thieves so that we don't have to do our own work. You don't get it at all, Sokrates. You've got a lot to learn."

"You're the thief," Sokrates retorts. "I told you I didn't want to be thieves with you. Especially stealing from boys we used to be friends with."

"We're all thieves from each other, every animal on earth," says a filth-covered stranger lying on the street not far away. "I once had my last scrap of food stolen from me by an angry butterfly!" The man vomits wine, startling the boys into fleeing in fits of disgusted laughter.

H

Athenian leaders discuss the expansion of their city wall

The way from Athens to Piraeus is lined with food stalls and artists of every sort peddling their crafts along a straight path westward out from Athens toward the harbor. For most of its length, one could easily not realize they had even left either place on the way to the other, so busy are the crowds on this path most days.

Now this year's ten elected Generals are walking from Athens to Piraeus with the city Archons and the current leadership of the Council, both Oligarch and Democrat, and discussing with a visiting architect the idea of extending Themistokles' city wall out to surround the Pnyx and its neighboring hills, which are presently just outside the western gate.

"As you see, there is already a wall of wretches," one of the Oligarch councilors jokes to the visiting architect, who laughs, nodding.

Kimon, most respected among the Generals, leads his peers and the gaggle of politicians as the others trail like ducklings. Perikles, there as an assistant to Ephialtes, stays close by his friend and listens carefully when Kimon interacts with the visiting Miletian architect, Hippodamos, whose eagerness to advocate for the project has made Kimon instinctively distrustful.

"It won't be as difficult as you think," Hippodamos explains. "If you just plan everything ahead of time wisely, we will be able to build this wall as a straight line directly from your western gate, and the more we let my geometers confirm everything is straight and perfect, the cheaper and faster it will be. The city councilors of Miletos found our work so much beyond even their expectations that they gave us this fine bronze lion, which is a symbol of their city."

Hippodamos hands one of the grumbling Oligarchs a hand-sized bronze sculpture of a lion with a wide, roaring mouth, and gestures to pass it around the group so all can see its excellent craftsmanship. Some of the artisans whose stalls they are passing ask them to pause so they too can briefly view the beautiful Ionian artifact.

"The answer is not walls," Kimon suggests. "Strength does not come from armor, but agility. The mightiest Hellenes, the Spartans, consider their warriors to be their own city wall, and their men spend their time building up *themselves* instead of expensive walls. Strong societies need no walls. We should put the same money instead into strengthening our people. We should build gyms, not walls."

"Look, we do need some walls," Thukydides retorts with an impatient glance at his fellow Oligarch, "but we may not need the longest wall that has ever been built. Where will it end? All we need to do is to extend Themistokles' wall to enclose the hill of the Pnyx. He should have built it that far out to begin with."

"Our power is the Sea, so our wall should extend to the Sea," Perikles retorts, surprising the rest around such that they all turn toward him at the same time. He fights through the awkwardness of that moment to continue, "Athens' special strength is her navy. Sparta doesn't want Athens to have a powerful wall - not because walls don't work, but because they *do* work, and they fear Persia coming back into Hellas again and taking that walled fortification for themselves. But what Sparta still doesn't understand is that Athens can stop Persia no matter how big its army is, if we keep our great wooden wall of ships strong! And with just a slightly longer wall than we were already planning to build anyway, we could connect our city to our harbor at Piraeus, and always have access to the entire ocean, even under siege. We would be unstoppable."

To his surprise, several of the other politicians, their aides, and even the visiting architect Hippodamos of Miletos, all applaud the idea. Some of the Oligarchs present scoff at the applause and fold their arms in annoyance, though even a few of them, Thukydides included, must shruggingly acknowledge the wisdom of the concept. A couple of old councilmen near him slap Perikles on the back in positive affirmation. It knocks the wind out of him with surprise.

Hawk-eyed Kimon sighs, looking away. "You Democrats love spending rich people's money."

One of the less-famous Democrats says, "We've seen the strength of a people working with one mind, one heart, one goal, like at the Battle of the Straits. Democracy beats Despotism, and it will every time."

Everyone feels obliged to harrumph agreement.

The group continues walking toward the docks, as Perikles tries to continue outlining his idea.

"Access to the ocean means both that we can project military might outward with our navy, but also that we can continue to accept trade from our colonies, which as you know is where we get enough grain to feed everyone in this city these days."

As soon as he takes a breath the Oligarch Kritias taps Perikles on the elbow with the amethyst on the end of his cane. "Keep it short, especially at first. We have agreed. Let us move on. If your idea ever bears fruit, it will not be while men my age still live."

    The oldest men chuckle silently or in coughs.

Θ

Aoide is given a new task

A massive golden throne is being carried with exceptional care by a team of burly Qorinthian men into the Sanctuary of Apollo at Delphi, to be set up in the Qorinthian treasure house. It is hailed by a Qorinthian herald surrounded by a chorus of heavily made-up Qorinthian women as supposedly being the ancient throne from which King Midas of Phrygia ruled in ancient times, and the muscled men who are carrying it on a litter through the main gate are putting on quite a show of how heavy it is.

    "King Midas' throne!" the herald keeps shouting. "Midas of the golden touch!"

    "They're trying to act like it's solid gold," the priest says to Aoide as they watch the work together from one of the higher stone terraces that loom above the action. "As if to imply that it was some throne of stone or wood which was turned to gold by Midas' magic."

    "The man was magic?" Aoide asks with a wry grin.

    "Cursed, allegedly," the priest says. "Cursed to turn anything he touched into gold."

    "O, what a terrible curse!" Aoide replies with unmasked sarcasm.

    "Well, he too thought it to be a blessing at first. Until he kissed his daughters goodnight and they all turned to solid gold."

    Aoide shrugs. "Could be worse."

    "Yes, well, anyway, it is just a story. And I'm not sure what the Qorinthians think it has to do with *their* city, for Midas was a Phrygian king who never would've set foot in Qorinth. No doubt they have some story for how it came into their possession through some legendary adventure."

The priest starts to walk back toward the towering Temple of Apollo, and Aoide follows. A passing group of younger priestesses - the sort of girls she used to be, with their baskets of flowers - eye her as they pass, but Aoide has no time to think about them.

"It is, of course, just a chair covered with molten gold. Not an insignificant amount of gold, for sure, but certainly not solid gold. And do you know how I can tell, Aoide?"

He doesn't give her time to answer, as she is still catching up with his longer-legged strides.

"Because if it were really solid gold, those men would be trying hard to show how *easily* they carried it, not how difficult it was. Instead, they pretend that it is heavier in order to make others think that it must be solid gold."

They watch together as the Qorinthian men finally set their burden down, making an even greater show of their relief than they had of their strain. The gathered crowd murmurs with reverence.

"Even holy offerings become performances. The gods may know the truth, but men ... men need spectacle. They need to believe they're seeing something extraordinary."

He turns to face her directly, his expression shifting from wry observation to grave intent.

"Listen to me, Aoide," the priest says with utmost seriousness. He waits an overly long moment, just looking into her eyes. Then he says, "You will be the next new Pythia. The other Pythia have selected you."

Aoide's throat closes with shock, briefly causing her to choke on saliva and cough. For a few long moments, Aoide is suddenly richly aware of her sensory surroundings - the warm sunlight and cool breeze, the smell of a sacrifice cooking somewhere, the lightly dancing curl of white hair on the neck of the priest watching her silence. She curls up a smile at him, but he reacts as if she is Medusa.

"What?" she asks.

"Your face," is all he says in response.

She does not change her face. "Who decided?" she asks.

The priest stares at her for a long time before finally saying, "Apollo decided long ago, apparently. It's why he's graced you with his inspiration."

"Why me? Why would the Pythia choose me for such an important position?"

"Well, as I said, Apollo chose to groom you for it from birth, all evidence would seem to reveal." The priest just shakes his head slowly. "Why, only Brilliant Apollo can know. You shouldn't question his inspirations. You should deliver them unprocessed, unfiltered."

"I know."

The priest nods, and smiles. "We know you know." He thinks another few moments, then adds, "Consider it this way - he did not so much choose you for who you are, as he chose you to be the one he would shape into who he needed."

Aoide squints at the man, wondering if she should let the mask of her ignorance slip at all, wondering how far that can be pushed before the whole theater of it all begins to collapse. She keeps the mask on here.

The priest goes to place a circle of twisted laurel onto Aoide's head, but in a sudden realization, she pulls away.

"Wait," she says.

The priest looks confused, though keeps smiling.

"The story of Apollo and Daphne. Daphne didn't love Apollo, though he loved her, so she fled his advances until a river god agreed to make her into the laurel to escape Apollo, right?"

"The river god Peneos," the priest nods, "right."

"So this is Daphne. This laurel. The laurel which Apollo himself is said to wear like clothing. Has he no respect for the wishes of this girl, who transformed herself in order to avoid his touch?"

The priest shrugs, no longer smiling. He reaches out again with the laurel wreath. "He's a god," he says.

"O poor Daphne," Aoide coos, caressing the laurel crown.

The priest chuckles lightly, coughing at the end. "Aoide, at best it is the transformed Daphne's great-great-grand-daughter plant, not the actual victim of Apollo's lust herself. Time has diluted all majesty like rainwater when you leave out wine cups overnight. And though crimes and curses *do* pass down through semen between parents and child forever, it also forever dilutes, such that the oldest crimes exist within us all in merely miniscule amounts, so we can still taste them sometimes, but their poisonous effects dissipate or become bearable."

Aoide asks, "Do I have a choice?"

The priest sighs and looks into her eyes for a moment, lowering the laurel crown. "Yes, of course you do. You could leave this place right now, if you want. Become a regular girl out in the world. Or you could become the Pythia of Delphi."

Aoide gazes into her memories, and realizes that she has no idea what it would be like to be a regular girl.

ATHENS

That night, a special meeting is organized by the elder priests in the plaza outside the front of the Temple of Apollo, for Aoide to meet and speak with all three of the current Pythia. Others are cleared from the area, and it is the first time Aoide has ever seen the square before the temple so empty. Just the stars above and the fire steadily burning atop the tall spiral Serpent Column.

The three Pythia walk out from the Temple's entrance one after the other, making a show of the way they move like ghosts and stare with certainty.

Feeling hidden, Aoide watches silently, processing.

"We have chosen you, Aoide, to be the next Pythia, because we know that you understand us already. You speak our language. And our non-language. We do not need to explain ourselves to you. You already understand." Opho's voice is barely above a whisper. "How as three women who create one voice, we must share a mind. The oracle's voice must remain constant, even as the woman behind it changes, and so we three must remain interwoven with each other, like the serpents of the Serpent Column, so that any one visitor might not recognize whose voice he had heard - other than that it was the Pythia."

She moves closer to a low brazier's fire, holding out a hand to its warmth. "When I was younger, I thought our role was simply to relay Apollo's words."

The other Pythia chuckle, making Aoide smile curiously. "How old are you?" she asks Opho.

"She's twenty-six," Eromede sniffs.

"Years as Pythia are seven-fold," Aigisthenia suggests, to which the other two Pythia nod.

Opho's eyes meet Aoide's across the flames, and in Aoide's mind it feels like a bronze mirror, seeing herself as another woman. "The three of us must maintain one voice, though we speak it in turns. Not identical, perhaps - Apollo's truth has subtle shades which each of us will see separately - but recognizable as from the same source. When I give way to Aigisthenia, and she to Eromede, the suppliants must feel they still consult the same oracle. We three Pythia play the mortal role of the needles of the Fates. The Fates - Klotho, Lachesis, and Atropos."

Aigisthenia says, "You, Aoide, will be the new Atropos, which has been Opho's role."

Aoide asks delicately, thinking of Dikasto, "Why this change? What is happening to Opho?"

Opho says, "I leave this summer for Larissa. Other wisdoms call to me."

"You *choose* to quit being Pythia?" Aoide asks.

Opho looks to the others for a moment, then back to Aoide. "It's your time now," she says.

"What wisdom is there is Larissa that Apollo can't give you here?"

"There is wisdom older than Apollo. Women of Ge. Mysteries too important to even be known beyond the secret few. The ultimate oligarchy of feminine wisdom. I have read Sappho, and yet I ... I *do* expect, or hope, at least, to touch, or know, the Sky."

Aoide looks around at the priests lining the edges of the square, watching the four young women from a distance.

"So I will be able to leave whenever I want, like Opho?"

Aigisthenia and Eromede look to each other, then to Opho, who answers, "If you are able to replace yourself properly, one day, yes."

Aoide looks up at the few stars visible through holes in the clouds, but they keep quiet.

Until the first hazy droplets of a soft rain begin to cool Aoide's face, which makes her smile.

I

The wedding of Periboea and Perikles

The bride's tears rhyme with the raindrops hazily falling on the cloudy morning of Periboea's wedding to her city-esteemed cousin Perikles.

Alkmaeonid weddings are famous in Athens for being glamorous and expensive, and the wedding of Periboea and Perikles has been expected to be the most ostentatious yet. The bride and groom's sister-mothers have been working on confirming this for years now. Myriad sculptors and florists and musicians and mimes have long been planning for this possible future event, and are prepared now with elaborate plans and arrangements ready to unfold.

Periboea, for her part, has been fantasizing about this day ever since grandmother Koesyra started telling her the stories of the weddings of the gods, and her ancestors, who were themselves descendents of gods.

Now, with her wedding day's morning foretold to be rain, her personal body slave, the date-eyed Berber woman Imilke, paints swirls on her arms as she reassures Periboea that rain is always a blessing, however much it might inconvenience the party's plan.

"He doesn't love me, though," Periboea sniffles. "Not like a lover loves."

"Just you wait," Imilke whispers. "The real love comes *after* the wedding. Everything after you are married is totally unlike life before."

"Were you married, in Berberia?" Periboea asks Imilke, who she knows is older than she appears.

Imilke gives a melancholy half-smile and glances into her memory, then says, "I was married for three long and wonderful years. Before we were captured and sold apart."

"What war were you captured during?"

"Not war, just piracy. May the gods curse Qarthago, city of family-snatchers."

Periboea squint-frowns at the thought of surviving violence, being a captive, separated from your love, and sold in a foreign land as a slave; all she can think to do is try to indicate with her face that she is as empathetic as she can be. "And did he love you well?" Periboea then asks.

Imilke nods, her memories mixing, the bitter with the sweet.

Suddenly the sound of children's laughter precedes Periboea's two youngest cousins, Klarelia's little toddlers Terpsichora and Landos, wearing garlands of wildflowers and shout-singing, "Hymen, Hymen, king of weddings! Hymen, come and party with us! Hymen, Hymen, god of weddings! Ready these young folks for love!"

"You two, go back outside and leave us alone!" Imilke snaps at the two little ones, who run back out the way they came just as fast as they burst in. Imilke returns to adjusting Periboea's veil, her practiced fingers working swiftly but gently.

"They mean well," Periboea says softly. "Everyone means well today, I know."

"Hush now," Imilke replies, but her voice has softened. She steps back to survey her work, then reaches to adjust one last fold. "There. You look like Hera herself on her wedding day." She hesitates, then adds, "Though perhaps with a kinder smile. Let Hera be Hera. You are Periboea!"

Periboea struggles to maintain her smile as she rises. The weight of her wedding clothes feels suddenly overwhelming - all the gold thread, all the expensive dye, all the expectations woven into every fiber. She has fantasized about and role-played with her sisters this very day many times in the past, but the real moment ahead fills her with dread. Through the window, she can hear the gathering crowd in the courtyard, their voices rising and falling like waves.

"I should go down," she says, though her feet seem unwilling to move.

"Take a moment first," Imilke suggests. "Walk in the back garden. Let the morning air clear your head." She adjusts one last curl of Periboea's hair. "The whole day doesn't have to be ceremony."

"They're waiting."

Imilke smiles playfully. "It is the wife's prerogative to make them wait. Use your powers. Get comfortable in them."

Periboea nods gratefully with a little sniff of a laugh, and makes her way down the familiar steps to the garden, Imilke following and holding her skirts carefully. A minute of sun through the clouds has burned away the dew, but the air still carries the scent of wet earth and flowers.

Old Grandmother Koesyra sits in her garden chair, weaving crowns of flowers. "Hello, dear girl," she says. "Almost a woman."

"Hello, Grandmother."

She passes her sweet family dog, Lykokroke, lying with her head on her paws in the grass, lazily eager-eyed for pets. On her head someone has placed a garland of colorful flowers, and on the flowers a few little butterflies have momentarily lighted, softly opening and closing their wings.

"O look, dear," Imilke coos, pointing out the butterflies to Periboea. "Surely that will show you that the gods have blessed your day. Look at the magical crown they've given Lykokroke!"

Periboea smiles and carefully crouches next to her dog, petting her rump to avoid disturbing the butterflies.

"You may be right," she says. "Thank you for your patience."

Imilke glows. "There should be nothing but happiness for you today."

"Help me be brave. Tell me a story of a happy marriage."

Imilke slowly paces the garden while Periboea pets her dog. "They say when Zeus first saw Hera, she had taken the form of a trembling dove seeking shelter from a storm. He transformed himself into another dove to comfort her. Only after they had flown together did they reveal their true forms. Their wedding feast lasted three hundred years."

"And Persephone?" Periboea prompts, though she knows all these tales by heart.

"You know Persephone fought her marriage at first. Fought it hard. But now she rules two kingdoms. Even the Lord of the Dead bows to her will for half the year." Imilke reaches forward and adjusts a fold of the dress across Periboea's shoulder. "Sometimes the marriages we fear become our greatest source of power."

"What about mortal girls? Tell me about Helen."

"Which time?" Imilke laughs softly. "Her first wedding, all the young men of Greece drew lots for her hand. Or her wedding to Paris, which launched a thousand ships. Or when she returned to Menelaos, and they say her beauty made him forget nine years of war." She pauses. "Though perhaps Helen isn't the best example. Why don't you tell her about *your* wedding, Grandmother?"

Koesyra looks up from her circle of stems.

"Every flower in Attika bloomed that day, even though it was winter," the old woman says. "And when we walked to the altar, my feet never touched the ground. Aphrodite herself lifted my steps!"

Imilke laughs and says, "Come now, Grandmother, don't give her mythical impressions of what will never be!"

"I am speaking figuratively. You will have a lovely time, Periboea."

Periboea takes a deep breath, stands. The butterflies flit away at her movement. Over the courtyard wall she can hear the chatter of her friends and family and myriad Athenians she doesn't know. All of Athens waiting to see an Alkmaeonid bride.

"Ready?" Imilke asks softly.

Periboea nods, and steps toward the courtyard arch from the garden.

The gathered Athenians all cheer at the sight of the bride.

When Periboea steps out into view, her bright purple dress and saffron veil bring to Perikles' mind every other wedding he has seen as a boy, he sees the communal joy in the eyes of all his friends and family and compatriots cheering, and suddenly he is filled with the wonder of being part of the ancient traditions of Hellenic men and women, and he feels a warmth that makes him enjoy all that he had been dreading in the months leading up to this moment. His mother's pride warms his face.

"All the gods and goddesses have been given their gifts today," Periboea's mother Agrinoe says, as her sister, Perikles' mother Agariste, stands beside her smiling proudly and clasping her hands together tight. "The astronomers have told us that the stars can provide no more auspicious day than this one, for our two children, Perikles, and Periboea, to be joined in god-beloved marriage, like Zeus and Hera, like Kronos and Rhea before them, and like the Earth and the Sky first of all."

The attending crowd, including the many Alkmaeonid family members of the bride and groom - myriad aunts, brothers, cousins, sisters, uncles, all rich, all called cursed - all applaud and cheer. Usually-smiling Ephialtes squints out a tear of mixed solution.

His family and friends begin crowding past Perikles and Periboea to say their respectful words and tell each one how beautiful they look.

Perikles notices then, sitting beside his cousin Deinomache is Kleinias, son of Alkibiades the recently exiled aristocratic merchant. Beside Kleinias on his other side sits his older brother Axiochos, who is already looking at Perikles with a mischievous sneer.

Resignedly Perikles makes his way over to them and stands over the seated young folks. He makes eye contact with Deinomache first, who smiles smarmily and then gets shy and looks away from her cousin's gaze, into the grass. She summons Lykokroke with a kiss, to come and lick her hand, as distraction.

Perikles turns his judgmental gaze to Kleinias, whom he remembers being among the first who mocked him as "Sea-Onion-headed" years ago. He makes Kleinias speak first.

"Perikles, congratulations!" the young Oligarch's son shouts. "Your wedding day! What glory you find yourself around! And just think, one day we may be relatives, if I decide to make Deinomache my wife after all, as we've been discussing."

Perikles blinks extra-long, keeping his eyes shut just long enough to show his distaste tastefully. He smiles and nods. "You would be lucky to win the heart of such a clever and noble young lady," he says.

Deinomache smiles to him demurely without looking away from the dog.

Perikles turns to Axiochos, who laughs for no reason beside his younger brother, and asks him, "Axiochos, by the Winds, why are you here? Who invited you? Or are you just a leech stuck to your little brother?"

Axiochos glares and huffs, but doesn't answer because he has no answer. Perikles looks away from him, giving him only that briefest moment's attention.

"Deinomache," he says in parting, "why don't you bring Kleinias to meet Periboea. I don't believe he's congratulated her yet."

Axiochos silently fumes until the others leave him alone, and then vanishes from the party silently in embarrassment once he is out from under eyes.

As the platitudes and gratitudes are paraded and graduated around the happily mingling crowd, a sudden rush of wind interrupts all conversations with a wet heavy haze for a moment, and all turn to discussing it. Everyone shivers, some cuddling close to their loved ones, as the crisp wind rushes over their shoulders. A giggle spreads through the men and women of the crowd, as all remark about how the presence of Boreas the North Wind during a wedding is traditionally quite auspicious.

The bride and groom lead the procession out from the Alkmaeonid family compound and down the cobblestone streets, under the slow rain of tossed flower petals from the roof decks of their festive neighbors, to the Temple of Aphrodite Heavenly, where a priestess is waiting for them at the entrance wrapped in a gold-embroidered dress and wearing the same goddess-loved flowers as the bride has in her hair.

Aphrodite's beautiful priestess smiles at the two as they approach.

"Athena, Artemis, and all the virgin goddesses smile down upon you today, Periboea. And Hera Ox-eyed, hostess of all weddings. Welcome. Come and join me at the altar of Aphrodite. Hestia Hearth-keeper has warmed the fire for you to take to your new home."

At that, again, Periboea begins to cry, covering her eyes with her arm.

Perikles holds her close, doing his best just to seem securing. "We'll be alright," he says quietly to his cousin.

Periboea nods nervously beneath her saffron veil.

Perikles' mother Agariste steps forward with the ritual bath water, gathered at dawn from the Kallirhoe Spring. She pours it over their joined hands while humming the melody of an ancient hymn to Hera Ox-eyed.

"Let all bonds be loved by the gods," the priestess of Aphrodite intones, "Let all unions be fruitful."

An older priestess of Hera joins her and sings the words to the song which Agariste was just humming.

O gold-throned Hera, sister-wife of Zeus,
queen of immortals, greatest of beauties,
you who temper the mighty thunder-bolt,
find love in your heart for this mortal joy!

Animal squeals resound, startling the bride, as a ritual knife is put into a young pig for the goddess, its blood caught in a silver bowl, and the celebrating crowd cheers. The priestess marks both their foreheads with crimson, and Perikles and Periboea cannot help but grimace to each other, and laugh a little, at the old ritual.

As he is expected to, although it feels absurd since they have lived close-by since they were small, Perikles says, "I receive you into my father's house. To share my fire and water, my bread and wine."

"I come to your hearth," Periboea responds, "to tend your fire and bear your children."

The wedding torch is lit from the sacred flame of Hestia Hearth-keeper, to more applause. Agrinoe places Periboea's hand into Perikles', then leads the procession with Agariste back to their homes at the Alkmaeonid compound, and around the courtyard three times, the guests following and showering them with dried figs and dates while singing.

Hymen, Hymen, king of parties,
Hymen, come and party with us!
Hymen, Hymen, god of weddings,
ready these young folks for love!

Hired musicians strike up flutes and lyres as the final circuit ends. The bride's mother steps forward to remove the saffron veil, revealing Periboea painted with tear-streaked white lead and rouge. Agrinoe laughs a little, and puts the veil back over her.

"Let's eat!"

Slaves bring out roasted meats, honeyed wines, flat breads, and olive salads. The guests recline on couches brought outdoors, while professional dancers perform, but all eyes keep returning to the new couple. Periboea barely touches her food. Perikles drinks more than usual.

"Mind your drinking, Perikles," Lysimachos says from the next couch. "You need to be able to use your dick tonight!"

"Lysimachos, please..."

Next to Lysimachos, Ephialtes laughs. "Perikles will have no problems, I imagine. He is the descendent of gods!"

Upright Agariste steps in to interrupt her son's conversation with his friends. A Persian slave girl holding up her veil for her, Agariste says, "Do forgive my interruption, please, my son, and fine Ephialtes - I almost called you noble! So noble-like is your soul - but I have great news to share, on this magical day, and I am happy to share it with you both. You know, Ephialtes, I wondered about you at first, when you first showed up in this courtyard to study with the noble boys, but now I would consider you welcome in this courtyard anytime. Truly."

Ephialtes smiles and does a slight bow in archaic deference.

"What's the news?" Perikles asks his mother, annoyed by her unpleasantries.

"Your cousin Aoide, in Delphi," Agariste replies, putting a hand on Perikles' shoulder. "You know, when you were younger I wondered if she might end up being the mother of your children - so close were you two all the time..."

"We were good friends when she was little," Perikles agrees. "How is she?"

"Honored, blessed," Agariste replies, smiling with pride. "We've arranged things at Delphi so that our Aoide will be the next new Pythia." She beams as she watches Perikles process the news.

Perikles gasps. He looks over to Ephialtes, both running through their minds all that this might mean. The influence of the Pythian Oracle's words move minds everywhere that Hellenes are aware of, but most of all where men speak Hellenic words.

Agariste whispers, "Our family now has a direct line into the voice of Apollo, heard by all of Hellas. We can now command the world. The powers we will gain from this positioning will echo, and build. Echo, as we used to call her. You will make use of her, Ephialtes, with Perikles' help; I will inform her of your wishes for the voice of Apollo." Her whisper's volume rises with her excitement.

"Mother," Perikles shushes, at which she instantly closes her mouth and straightens up. But her grin quickly returns as she eyes the young men.

"I can hardly believe it," Ephialtes says.

"Hubris will bring down more than one man; hubris is the kind of thing that can bring down a family," Perikles says carefully. "I don't want this family to be destroyed by hubris. And I worry about letting the Pythian Oracle be affected by our influence. It may be beneficial to us that Aoide is Pythia - but that is up to Apollo, not to me. We must not attempt to corrupt his oracle."

Agariste frowns, but instantly begins to hide it. She makes a face at her sister, who glares briefly at Perikles.

Agrinoe whispers, "You should know better than to ever foretell ill luck. The gods, like dogs, smell uncertainty. Know better."

"Power exerts itself despite your desire," Agariste says quietly. "Perikles, you either yoke an ox or it will tear up your farm. Aoide will be Pythia. I do not even think it would be possible for you to avoid using that fact for your own benefit, in one way or another. The Fates wrangle reigns like Amazon horsewomen, not webs like Arachnid spiders. They do not pretend Men lack wills."

Periboea approaches behind Perikles and takes his arm, looking to all as she only catches the last few lines of the conversation on entering. "Must the Fates remove a breast to better weave, do you think?"

Agariste, like an aunt, briefly grabs Periboea's breast, then her face, as she gives Perikles a long dominating glance, and slowly turns to leave, singing, "Hymen! Hymen! Party with us!" in the creaky accent of the ladies of her generation.

As night falls, the bawdier songs begin. Young men make increasingly ribald jokes about the wedding night to come. Perikles and Periboea pretend to ignore their friends' and neighbors' crude humor, increasingly finding each others' gaze for comfort.

Finally, long after twilight has faded to night, it's time for the procession to their new home - Perikles' new house which he has been preparing in the city for their arrival. The wedding party spills into the streets, bearing torches, dancing in a line and singing, while children run ahead throwing nuts and flowers. Neighbors lean from windows to watch the spectacle.

From one window in the neighborhood of Perikles' new house, the Oligarch Thukydides leans out with his son Oloros and shouts, "Welcome to the neighborhood, newlyweds!"

At their doorway, Perikles holds Periboea's hand as she steps across the threshold for the first time, so that she won't stumble, which would be inauspicious.

Inside, the marriage bed waits, strewn with rose petals and fertility charms and surrounded by dick-shaped candles which someone else has set up for them.

Periboea looks to Perikles with a shy smile.

Perikles grimaces and explains, "I didn't do that. That must have been our mothers."

Periboea sighs slightly, wishing it had been him.

Boreas the North Wind closes the door.

K

Aoide visits the Korykian Cave for advice

Everyone else is asleep down in Delphi, as Aoide creeps quietly beneath the bright, gibbous moon up and down the hills behind Mount Parnassos to the Korykian Cave, where her friend Dikasto keeps watch as a nymph called the Black One.

Tonight is the evening before Apollo's birthday on the Sixth of the month. In her mind, Aoide asks Apollo and Artemis to watch after her and keep the dangers of the night away. Still, marching through the crunching grass and branches in the darkness, unknown-anythings mere inches of shadow away, she is only able to keep fear at bay with a psychic spear held out firm and swiveled into every heavy shadow.

Low-eyed Aoide arrives from out of the dark to find the Korykian Cave's entrance flickering with the faintly rising and falling long shadows of a fire deep within.

She waits at the entrance and listens for a while, hoping her cat-friend Ailisto might happen to slink by, but when she hears nothing after a while she eventually steps inside. She doesn't hide her footsteps.

Within, Dikasto is sitting beside her small fire, cuddled with Ailisto on a small bed of dried grass. Ailisto jumps down and hides in the shadows when Aoide becomes visible.

Dikasto looks at her with her own eyes first, then quickly puts on her cold-eyed mask of the Black One. The Black One stares at Aoide.

For a moment, Aoide questions herself and considers leaving before saying anything, but finally she summons the courage to speak.

"Black One," Aoide says, "please forgive me. But I needed your wisdom, and could not wait."

"The Athenian girl is about to become the Delphic oracle," the Black One says. "The Fates' tapestry's threads are being pulled together after much complex wefting. The Alkmaeonids' plan has blossomed fruit after years of cultivation."

"It's not that," Aoide squeaks, choking on a rising tear.

Firelit from below but otherwise a mask of shadow, the Black One cocks her head at an angle, surprised by Aoide's emotion.

"I need to beg for your forgiveness," Aoide cries. "I've gotten everything and have deserved none of it. You've gotten only traumas, and have deserved none of them. O Dikasto, what can I do? How can I create fairness out of the echoes of madness?"

The Black One grabs a handful of dirt and pebbles from the floor of the cave and throws it at Aoide. Aoide closes her eyes and feels the dirt speckle her face; she takes one small pebble to the closed eyelid, which hurts, but the pain of which she silently bears.

"Never say that name again," the Black One whines. "This is the Black One, nymph of the Korykian Cave, and that person whose name you used is gone from the cosmos. This is the time after that person."

"My friend, my sweet old friend," Aoide whimpers into the cave's darkness. "What happened while I was away?"

The Black One leans forward looking into Aoide's eyes, her skin stained with ash and wild herbs, her hair tangled with owl feathers.

Aoide takes this chance to read the story of her old friend's eyes for a while. Dikasto stares for a long time, composing. Then she speaks in a dark voice.

"Dikasto walked in sunlight once," the Black One says, her voice rough as the cave walls. "She danced with a boy who sang to goats. His music made flowers grow in winter." She traces patterns in the ash with blackened fingers. "When her belly swelled like the Moon, they cast her from Apollo's light. So she took shelter in shadows. Made friends with bats and blind things. Learned their songs. Like--"

The Black One shrieks, loud and sonorous, right in Aoide's face.

Then she screams, less musically.

"And," she says, almost comically, and then makes her most horrifying howl yet.

Aoide bursts into tears, feeling abused by the volume, but not wanting to run.

The Black One's little groan that follows sounds like stones falling.

"The baby came too early. Too small for this cold world. The earth was hungry that day." Her fingers stop moving in the dust. "After, Dikasto fed herself to the darkness. Let it eat her name, her memories, her girl-self. The Black One was a story she had heard. And once folks learned that the Black One held court here in this earth palace, they started coming. Asking questions she can't answer. So she rolls the bones, and they interpret her screams. When there are no words to come."

Aoide reaches toward her friend's ash-stained face, but the Black One slaps her hand back, and shrieks.

ATHENS

A scramble of stones by the mouth of the cave startles both young women, and they look to see the form of a man standing silhouetted against the stars. Aoide shrinks back, but the Black One faces the man and takes on her disarming monstrous manner as he approaches with utmost hesitation.

"Forgive me please, mountain nymph!" the man shouts over the wind and distance. "I've come to beg for an oracle, if it's true that one can be had here. Are you one of the nymphs of the Korykian Cave?"

The Black One answers creakily, without moving, "I am."

A wind from the west picks up, enters the cavern briefly and whips all hair.

The old man kneels carefully and lowers his head. "O please, great nymph, friend of the gods, I have nothing more to give than these two coins, which I'd been keeping for the Final Ferryman."

"I will give you a cheap oracle then," Dikasto growls. "Leave me the coins, and I will answer your question, for Haides is not ready for you."

The man hobbles down the steep slope toward her the rest of the way, sending rocks tumbling back behind his steps, and shakily places two Athenian owls into the Black One's little hand. Up close, he smells strongly of wine.

"What are you known as, among men?" she asks him.

"Kratinos, son of--"

"I don't care who your father was," the Black One interrupts.

Kratinos looks confused, then happily intrigued by that response. He starts to inspect the young woman's dirty face more closely now that they are near to each other, but she has become expert at projecting an aura of otherworldliness.

"What do you wish to know?"

Kratinos shakes his head, gazing off into the space between them. Tears begin to fall from his eyes, and his face shudders, and he is for a few seconds unable to create understandable sounds through his blubbering, though he is clearly trying to speak. Eventually, he becomes understandable despite his heaving sobs.

"...My good friend ... Hipponax ... the funniest poet ... the gods took him ... he is gone, and he was old, and deformed, and I'm sure he's dead ... and I just don't know how to communicate to anyone else the sort of conversations that we had together."

"His ghost has visited us," the Black One groan-whispers. "I have given him a ride in my belly."

Kratinos looks up with brightness. "Is that true? Does he live again, anew?"

The Black One says, "It was just a ride, a respite in a womb. He did not live, outside."

Kratinos peers compassionately into the eyes of the young woman. "I can imagine your pain. How did you know him?"

She looks up at Kratinos. "By his face." Then, shocking all who see it, she says, "It looked like ... this!" and she pulls a face at once comical and horrifying, holding it for long enough to embed the fear of that face into all who saw it. Aoide shrieks, and Kratinos screams and hides his own face, then peers through his hands to see the last moments of her mask and groan with sad, amused confusion.

The Black One quickly returns to her sulking norm, as if the moment never happened. Aoide's and Kratinos' hearts still race.

"Hipponax visited the Earth to create, with me, a new spirit, called Comedy, which it is now your task, Kratinos of Athens, to guide like a new child into the world."

Kratinos scrunches his face in confusion, then starts softly laughing.

"Whatever you are," Kratinos says to Aoide across the space between them, barely audibly, "you will have my everlasting gratitude, and every time I drink, I'll drink a bit for you."

Kratinos scrambles hand-over-foot back to the mouth of the cave and back out into the surface world.

Aoide sits with her old friend for a long silence, not wanting to leave, but not knowing what to say, and for a long time the Black One sits without speaking again.

Until, out of nowhere, she begins speaking in Dikasto's voice, though the longer she speaks, she gradually takes on the voice of the Black One again.

"I hated him when he was in my belly. But once I saw him breathe, I couldn't hate him. But I couldn't love him, either. Not enough. The gods didn't mean for him to see more than one day. But he did see that day."

Dikasto's face is still again by the time Aoide raises her eyes. But then her old friend also looks up, and sits with Aoide in eye contact, while Aoide's face shudders but the Black One's remains utterly motionless, though they both weep streams of tears.

"This isn't fair," Aoide says, suddenly in doing so feeling like she and Dikasto are back to being the girls they were when they met, and the context of their lives more like they were back then. Aoide makes the kind of playfully cynical face that she would have made as a young girl, and she sees beneath Dikasto's forlorn mask her friend notice the look and recognize it.

For a fleeting *kairos*, the Black One smiles just like Dikasto used to.

The Black One smiles minutely then, more like she does now, on the rare sunny day when she forgets her cloak of pain.

"You hear the gods, Aoide. If you ignore that, may Python's skeletal revenant who lives beneath this mountain swallow you down to Tartaros," she says, meaning it.

A poem already forming in her mind, Aoide reluctantly nods.

"Now go," the Black One says, looking down. "We must not speak again."

Aoide breathes her tears back in and sighs, then nods, wanting to respect her friend. She stands and slowly turns to leave.

"...Often," Dikasto adds. When Aoide looks back, she is giving her an old funny face. Aoide bursts into tears again, at which the Black One brings her mask back up. Aoide slowly nods, weeping, wipes her face, and leaves the cave.

Silently, Aoide trudges slowly back down the mountain, watching her steps upon the stones, while composing a poem only for Apollo, intending to forget it once she's done.

Λ

Oligarchs clash at a drinking party

The house of Isodike and Kimon is warmly crowded with wine-softened Oligarchs and their slaves and hangers-on on this cool, purple-skied Spring evening. A band of musicians pluck out occasional flourishes of music, while at the corner of the patio the artist Anaxandra paints onto a board a portrait of the living scene. The painting ends up being a portrait of a bunch of drunk Oligarchs sitting staring at the painter.

"These sheep and their shepherds are going to sink our grand old Thesean ship of state, if we don't figure out a way to do something about it."

Careful-eyed Thukydides scoffs, "Solon's experiment of democracy!"

"Democracy is no more the problem," Kimon says, "than the problem of a trireme is its many rowers. You simply need to understand how to command these new, modern methods. Democracy and the trireme are the same. Neither goes anywhere without organized leadership. I say, specifically, *organized* leadership, because *disorganized* leadership can be worse than chaos. And that is exactly our problem. Regardless of our disagreements in the process of decision-making, we *must* be able to work together with the Democrats to actually man this grand old ship of state, and trust that when our leadership is good, it will lead to the ship going our way."

Kallias and Elpinike sit drinking from the same wine cup.

"Kallias," Thukydides shouts, "why are you here? Don't you vote with Themistokles' Democrats these days? One would think your noble wife's better breeding might rub off on you, but obviously this is just further evidence that good-nature only exists among those from good families. In fact, friends, have we considered the notion that Kallias here might be a spy, a double-agent here to listen to our political planning and deliver that intelligence straight to his preferred comrades?"

"I am here for the company, not the politics," Kallias offers. "And Themistokles is long gone. Yet he still haunts you like a ghost. Why?"

Kleinias, twenty-something son of Alkibiades, says, "He's here because he's rich, just like the rest of us. He's here because he doesn't want to drink with poor folks."

Kallias counters, "No, son, I enjoy drinking with poor folks as well. Not just any poor folks, but some certainly."

"Why don't you take better control over your husband, Elpinike?" Thukydides boorishly jokes, causing young Kleinias to start laughing uproariously at the outrageousness. "Seriously, though," Thukydides doubles-down after seeing that reaction. "You should just tell him you won't suck his dick anymore unless he starts voting with the Oligarchs again."

The men all laugh at the thought.

Elpinike stares at Thukydides cold-eyed, trying to hide her smile. She also tries to avoid the few young female prostitutes who have stopped sucking or touching the dicks of their companions for the moment, while all are laughing. The young whores all eye Elpinike, and avoiding giving them encouraging glances back takes all her effort.

"That is not a bad idea," she says as the laughter dies down. Then, to bring back the laughter she adds, "If only I sucked his dick to begin with."

The men abide expectedly with ejoculations of laughter.

"I think we men will be retiring now into the men's room, to do and speak of manly things."

The few wives who were present roll their eyes, kiss their husbands, and take their leave.

In the mens' room at Oligarch parties, everybody has their dick out. Those who deign to keep theirs hidden are assumed to have some unsightly excuse, and will usually be mocked into revealing their reason for not at the very least masturbating. Only slaves who aren't involved in the sex are expected to refrain entirely. Even the passionless old men will at least go through the flaccid motions for show, to keep from making anyone else uncomfortable.

"Think of what old Peisistratos did when he returned from exile a hundred years ago."

Kleinias shakes his head, unsure. "What did he do?" he asks.

"You need to learn your own city's history, man," Kimon scoffs.

Before he tells the story, lion-eyed Kimon snaps in the air to summon the attention of his slaves, then gestures to them to break open a new jar of wine and start bringing more cups around.

"Peisistratos was a tyrant of our grandfathers' generation - an Oligarch, in the old way. As such, he was exiled by his political enemies not once but twice! Which says something; he was exiled, returned afterward, and was exiled again! And this - when he returned to the city the first time, he did so in a chariot with an unknown, beautiful woman dressed all in armor right by his side in that chariot. 'Athena!' the people thought, of course! Of course it was just a girl, an impostor, an actor playing the role of the goddess for him. But that didn't matter to the people, who were fooled just long enough to vote him back into power again, letting him rule as tyrant for another six years before he was exiled the second time."

As Kimon tells the story, two middle-aged Libyan women bring around a couple of trays full of fresh cups of wine for everyone.

"You forget the important part of Peisistratos' story," Kritias croaks. "Before he was a tyrant, when he was still simply an elected official in office for the first time. How did he consolidate power as a tyrant to begin with? Because keep in mind, young Kleinias son of Alkibiades, this was all long ago, but still *after* Solon invented the democracy. In some ways, the democracy has two phases - before and after Peisistratos."

Kimon lowers his head, knowing, but letting Kritias tell the story.

Kritias continues, "Once he became Archon, Peisistratos took his own sword and secretly wounded himself and several of his poor mules, as a ruse to convince the people that he had been attacked by his political enemies and needed to be given a team of bodyguards at public cost. Then, with those strong men under his command, and the support of the poorest hill people whom he had enfranchised into the government, he was able to take the Akropolis by force and seize control of the old buildings of government. The ones from before, before the Persians burned them all. You see, it is force, and threats, that always provide political leverage. Clever gambits can only gain you tools to gain the ability to use force, but they are not such force themselves. Using force always takes courage, and few men have that. And sometimes it is *only* courage that's required, and nothing else."

"As shown by the tyrant-killers, Harmodios and Aristogeiton."

All the old Oligarchs turn to Kallias, who said it.

He smiles, too rich to worry. "All they needed was a blade hidden in their hair, and the courage of lions, to kill the tyrant Hippias son of Peisistratos. And take back the democracy for the people, from the tyrants, forever."

Kleinias looks around at the delicacy with which all the older men look at each other as they consider how to respond. Young and drunk enough for ignorant courage, he looks to his older brother Axiochos as he says, "I think Kallias is trying to say the answer is a knife for the tyrant ... Perikles."

The whole room lowly hisses and murmurs at the utterance.

"They thought you were going to say a different name, I think," Axiochos laughs. "Not your future cousin-in-law."

Kleinias says, "Perikles is the real Democrat danger, not his clown of a friend. Perikles is actually a nobleman, and other nobles listen to him. He sounds like someone erudite, regardless of the vulgarity of his meaning. Ephialtes just sounds like some agora bum trying to annoy you with pleas to womanly virtues."

"No," Kimon says with a sudden frown, after thinking about it for just a moment, his thoughts taking a bit longer with someone's mouth on his penis.

Polyphrasmon removes Kimon's dick from his mouth for a moment and looks up with salivating surprise.

With a snort Kimon looks down and says, "Not you, son. You're fine." He takes the playwright by the hair to guide him back down, but looks up with a glare at Thukydides and points to underscore, "I was talking to *you*. You cannot do this. You must stop them."

"Wheels are already in motion," Thukydides retorts, shrugging and beginning to turn away. "I'll let you finish."

"Don't turn away from me," Kimon snaps. "If you make me remove this beauty's mouth, I swear to Aphrodite I will never help you again. You turn around right now and come back here and answer to me, Thukydides. I don't care how much sway you think you have. I know you need me. And I will not allow any irreligious, underhanded, illegal framing of our political enemies for crimes that they have not committed. That includes entrapment into some crime they would not have committed without your devices. Ephialtes is a fool, but he is not corrupt, and I will not have you set up any sort of contrivance to the contrary. I have been falsely tried myself, by that two-faced rat Perikles, but we will not lower ourselves to their standard. That is why we are better than they are. So stop your wheels, even if you have to sacrifice a foot to them. Do you understand me?"

Thukydides watches back and forth between Kimon's serious expression and the man at his crotch slurping ever more vigorously. When Kimon asks his question, Thukydides doesn't hear it, focused instead on the dick being sucked, so Kimon in frustration pulls himself away from Polyphrasmon's mouth and shoves him to the side with a frustrated grunt.

The loquacious dick-sucker barks in protest. "Hey! I'm no whore, here. I thought you were the kind of men who own horses. But even a horse wouldn't stay with you."

"Gods damn it," Kimon groans, "I'm never going to finish in this room now." He stands, his full phallus in his hand, and heads for the door and the bright sunlight outside it, muttering, "Now I'm going to have to go find some satyr."

"I thought you Oligarchs would act like high class people do in stories," the other young escort scoffs to Thukydides.

"Surprise is the spice of life," Thukydides mutters back as he tosses a handful of owls onto Kimon's empty chair.

M

Perikles meets in secret with a potential rival

Dressed as a merchant, Perikles makes his way into the east gates of the city of Megara, just past Eleusis on the road from Athens to the Peloponnese.

He follows a path between the city wall and a stream whose name he does not know to the famous Wax Herm drinking house, which has been closed down for the day as a favor to him and the person he is here to meet. At the back of the ivy-covered house he meets the proprietress, a sturdy and confident widow named Melora who lets him in the back door.

Inside the Wax Herm, which appears particularly spacious now with nobody else in it, only one of the tables is set, and across it from Perikles sits the Spartan Eurypontid King Archidamos, also disguised as a merchant.

As soon as they see each other's costumes, the two men both laugh.

King Archidamos stands from his seat and meets Perikles in a soldierly arm-shake, then a big, surprising hug.

"Welcome," the Spartan king says, and gestures to the table. He shouts to Melora, "One bowl! Fuck two cups. Let's drink together and then write our names on the cup like our fathers used to, eh Perikles?"

Perikles nods and laughs loudly, playing along with the manly behavior, though it is not his usual style. He flops down onto the little wooly couch beside the table. Archidamos lies down across from him and grabs an apple slice from the spread of finger food already laid out.

Melora returns to the kitchen to put the final touches on the cheese plate she is about to bring out for the two city leaders.

"Good of you to invite me, my new friend," Perikles remarks. "What should I call you?"

"King Archidamos," King Archidamos replies. Then he laughs, letting Perikles laugh. "What do I call you, my friend? Simply Perikles? Son of Xanthippos? Now there was some kind of man. I saw him fight once, your father. How old are you? Which one of us is older?"

"I'm thirty-five." Perikles grabs a sprig of grapes.

ATHENS

"O you're the older one," Archidamos nods, crunching on a big bite of apple. "I'm thirty-one. I was a boy when I saw him fight."

The two men both nod, maintaining friendly but competitive eye contact. Perikles sniffs out a little laugh, and Archidamos squints at it.

"What's that?"

Perikles hesitates, then admits, "I never saw my father fight. Where did you see him?"

"The Battle of Plataia," King Archidamos replies, "when the tide turned. He was leading some Athenian phalanx that kept their spears tighter together than I've ever seen. Like a flock of birds moving as one. All to the rhythm of his voice. I can still hear it. I was just a small boy that day, but I remember it. Some of my earliest memories are those battles."

"That's late for earliest memories," Perikles notes.

"Nothing mattered until then," Archidamos muses.

"What would you have been, about ten or eleven years old? I was fourteen, almost fifteen. Just barely too young to fight."

"That must have been hard."

Perikles shrugs. "I will admit, though hesitantly to a Spartan - I have never really wanted to fight. I prefer collaboration to fighting. And not only do I prefer it personally, but it tends to produce better results."

Archidamos thinks a moment, then gestures broadly. "Nobody really likes fighting. We just know we'll sometimes have to. And how other men will look at us if we don't."

"Anyway," Perikles says carefully, trying to retain control of the conversation. "I remember my earliest memory - and it was much younger than that. Ten years before, in fact - during the First Persian War."

Archidamos raises his eyebrows and sits back a bit, ready for a story.

"I was on the roof of my babysitter's house which overlooked the Agora in Athens, the way it looked before Xerxes burned it, and I was playing with a toy chariot, when Pheidippides ran up to the old Fountain House."

Archidamos sits up respectfully, recognizing the name, knowing this story.

"I could see the fear in everyone's eyes. I couldn't hear what he was saying - he was barely able to speak. But folks who were helping to give him water just kept listening to his whispered words and then running off into the crowd, wailing. I couldn't understand it. Until later that day my father came to pick me up from the babysitter, when usually it would have been my mother. And he told me, 'Perikles, barbarians from the east have invaded Attika, but we have fought them back at

Marathon.' I didn't find out until years later that the man died just later that night, of exhaustion."

"Well I should imagine so!" Archidamos laughs. "How far is it from Marathon to Athens? Farther than I'd want to run. And that after running to Sparta and back, before the battle, right? That feat gets forgotten."

"I've heard various versions of the story." Perikles smiles. "It depends who sings the song. I only saw the man being given water."

"I was born only just the year before that," the Spartan king says.

Picturing the scene from a youngster's point of view, Perikles says, "I was five. The Wars entirely color my youth. That's why I hope to help Peace to rule while I'm an adult."

Melora the tavern keeper comes out from her kitchen with a tray of cheeses, a couple of knives, and a single wide drinking vessel of the old shape - the kind old men drink out of these days - filled with sea-dark wine.

"So tell me, King Archidamos," Perikles says as the tray is set out before them. "What led you to want to speak to the Democrats of Athens?"

King Archidamos says, "Let us each drink first. I've heard it said that the Assyrians prefer to consider any important problem both sober *and* drunk, and that wisdom would always seem right in both states."

Perikles nods at the common anecdote. "Indeed," he says. "With enough cheese, I should be able to keep pace with you, I think."

"So, despite what might appear to be the case," Archidamos says carefully considering his words, "Sparta is not actually run in secret by Leonidas' widow Gorgo. That woman's influence is on the wane. And my own power, as the Eurypontid King of Sparta, of the line laid down by Herakles, is back on the rise. Too long has the Agiad throne of Sparta played the primary role in her politics. But our situation with the Helots in recent years made perfectly clear to the real men of Sparta that putting their security in the hands of a snake-haired woman like Gorgo will only lead to doom."

Perikles nods, intrigued, unfamiliar with much of Sparta's internal politics, trying to glean as much as he can from what he's hearing.

King Archidamos says, "Her line is cursed. They are a whole cursed family. Dead-eyed, iron-hearted lions, with taste only for death to sate their own bloodthirst. No sense of the interests of men. Their kind must not continue to sway Spartans."

Perikles bites his lip and tries to avoid grimacing at the mention of a family line being cursed. He wonders if the Spartan king knows of his own family's old supposed curse, and looks up at the man with a mask meant to hide his discomfort and uncertainty.

King Archidamos shifts himself in his chair a bit, eyeing Perikles' reactions, then changes topics.

"Under my leadership, recently Sparta has made close allies with Qorinth, where we drove out their tyrants, and Elis, whose control over the sacred Games of Olympos was won with Spartan aid in days of old."

Perikles nods, rubbing his beard and sitting back.

"With the leaders of the Oligarchs of those two cities, I have reorganized our own Peloponnesian League, like the one of old which existed before All-Hellas came together in the Persian Wars. I will tell you straight - it is intended to be a direct counter to your own watery Delian League. But our League's feet are on solid ground instead of some wavering deck-boards."

King Archidamos watches Perikles for his reaction, and Perikles keeps his face clear as he thinks about how he ought to respond, until he finally creates a confident smile and nods.

"I think this is good," Perikles says. "This will be healthy for all of Hellas. Two great leagues, rising together, equally aided by and threatened by each other, unwilling to go to war due to the power of the other. Like two athletes competing for the same goals."

Archidamos asks, "All-Hellas, huh? Do we have the same goals?"

"As Hellenes," Perikles nods, "I think with enough conversation, just like this, we can only eventually come to a mutually agreed conclusion of what is right. I will tell you this, this I have truly come to believe - where there is disagreement, I have found, it is nearly always about what is the *truth*, not the conclusion which any truth implies. But there is always only one truth, and with enough careful time spent together in seeking the same truth, I find men can always be made to come to agreement about what is right."

Archidamos folds his arms and nods, listening. "You have a high estimation of the spirit of the common man, don't you, Perikles?"

Perikles chuckles to himself and scratches his head. "I would not exactly say that, but I do have a high estimation of the spirit of the *masses*. There will be fools, and wretches, and even evil men who take advantage of shadows or ignorance, but when there are also enough good men and civic-minded people doing good-faith work on behalf of all, and helping others to better understand what they do not have the perspective yet to grasp well, it would seem, history would seem to show, that the winds of Mankind can sweep along the wretched and the fools and the evil men within the moving cloud of good works, and we all, despite them, move forward into finer territory, into a land of better behavior - the future."

"You Athenians talk too much." Archidamos laughs heartily and downs a few big swallows of wine from their cup.

Perikles watches, hiding a grimace, and takes a long sip from the cup after Archidamos.

Archidamos says gruffly, to lean into it being a joke, "So tell me about this curse of the Alkmaeonids!"

Perikles smiles tightly as he carefully puts down the wide cup and then simply says, "No," in a way that makes Archidamos laugh hard.

"Perikles, I think this should be the beginning of a prosperous friendship, which can only benefit both our cities."

They each drink from their cup, watching each other from behind smile-shields.

"Let's say 'lands'," Perikles jokes, then winks at Archidamos when he explains, "I'd hardly call Sparta a *city*."

Archidamos stands fast out of his chair as if he is about to angrily pounce on Perikles, but he just as quickly starts to laugh and sits back down, at which they both laugh heartily and drink again.

N

Ephialtes takes in the evening

Under the moon shadow of the Tyrant-Killer statues, where the long street of Potter's Alley meets the Dipylon plaza by the gate, Ephialtes emerges from his father's pottery shop and wipes sweat from his face, the heat of the evening unavoidable even outdoors.

As he looks up at the stars in the clear sky, Ephialtes is reminded that such evenings, when he can picture everyone in Athens sleeping on their roofs, always make him feel cozy with the knowledge that they are all under the same starry sky.

"The gods shine bright tonight," his father says as he joins him on the street, wiping his hands on his apron.

"Do you think they're the gods, the stars themselves?" Ephialtes asks idly as he gazes upward. "Not just, like, signifiers of the gods or whatever?"

Doggish old Sophonides shrugs with a short laugh. "I can't keep track of what people are saying about such things nowadays. When I was a boy they said they were the gods visible. That one there is Ares, the red one - that's what they said at least back when I was young. I guess because it looks like he's got blood on him. I always figured it was like looking down from a hill onto a broad city, when you can see everyone's little lamp and torch lights flickering below. Only these are the gods' lamps, and they're extremely far away, and they're up instead of down. But I don't know what modern philosophers are saying about them."

"That makes sense," Ephialtes agrees. "Say, father - speaking of the gods..."

Sophonides gives his son a warm look and a smile.

"Why did you name me after the giant of nightmares, Ephialtes?"

Grizzled Sophonides chuckles to himself and thinks about it for a moment. "Your mother didn't like the name. But I thought it would make you fearsome. See, I was often chided as a boy for being a pushover, for being too willing to please others. So that's what I thought a man ought to be, back then, when I was young - fearsome. It's what I thought I wasn't able to be. So when I was young and you were new, it's what I thought I wanted for you. But you turned out so far from a giant of nightmares - you're a man of kindness. My friend, my son. I hope your name hasn't given you trouble."

Ephialtes half smiles, shrugging.

The evening has cooled pleasantly after a hot day. Sophonides lingers in the doorway of the pottery shop, watching his son gather his things to leave. The old potter's hands are still caked with clay, so he tries again to wipe them on his apron.

"Sure you won't stay for dinner?" Sophonides asks. "The new kitchen slave brings exciting new lentil recipes from the east."

Ephialtes gives his father the smile that he only gives to him. His father has been burning lentils the same way for twenty years. "No, I think I'll just walk a while."

"Politics weighing on you again?" Sophonides keeps his voice carefully neutral.

"Always." Ephialtes adjusts his belt, checks that his sandal straps are tight, like his father always used to remind him to. "But sometimes I like to pretend I'm just a potter's son out for an evening stroll." He laughs a little to make his father smile.

Smile he does, and nods, understanding. Sophonides reaches out to brush some imaginary dust from his son's shoulder. "Well then, just be a potter's son. The poor folks' troubles will still be there tomorrow."

"Always, unfortunately. Goodnight, father."

"Goodnight, my boy."

Ephialtes watches his father retreat back into the shop, then turns to start his walk. After a few steps, he finds himself humming a tune from the recent Dionysia. He's never felt he had much of a voice, but it makes him happy to do when no one is around to complain.

A whistle stops Ephialtes' stride.

"Forgive my song," Ephialtes says, "I thought I was alone."

He turns around to see a hooded person in a short cloak, standing low on muscular legs. The hood shadows the face, but it is clearly beardless.

"So Athens builds statues to honor assassins?" the strange voice asks as its swooping nearness reveals that the face is a bronze mask, ever-frowning, eyes squinting a hideous frozen glower.

"So tyrants might fear," Ephialtes says with fear and courage swirling in his heart. As Ephialtes is saying these last words, the cloaked stranger grabs him by the belt and lunges into him with a hidden blade.

"A vote, then, against tyrants," says the voice behind the mask as it maneuvers its blade back and forth inside Ephialtes' ribcage.

The mocking mask moves close to Ephialtes' face as they struggle, Ephialtes' hands trying to pry the masked figure's small fingers away from the dagger in his ribs. As their fight for the knife moves its blade around inside poor Ephialtes' torso, the Bronze Mask hisses, "Haides' welcome," then releases the blade and dashes away.

Ephialtes falls backwards at the killer's release from the struggle, and upon hitting the ground the breath is dashed from his body. Blood soon wells unceasing from Ephialtes' open mouth.

By the time his friends have been summoned and Perikles kneels beside his dying comrade amidst a crowd of weeping onlookers, poor murdered Ephialtes' movements are minimal.

"Nothing can be done," is said, and repeated, as if to comfort, amidst the wailing of the terrified. The repeating of those words builds fury in Perikles' heart as he clutches his friend's limp hand. "Nothing can be done; nothing can be done."

Through his blood, Ephialtes gurgles to Perikles, trying to speak but unable to form words. Perikles leans in close to listen, weeping.

It is only moments before poor Ephialtes is choking on blood, and his father, old Sophonides, desperately wipes it away from his mouth and neck like he's bailing a boat. Perikles stands away from him, unsure what is best for someone in such a state.

Soon after Perikles stands away from him, Ephialtes relents to the draw of Death, and he sinks heavily against the Earth. Sophonides keeps cleaning his motionless son.

Fear whirls Perikles. Every person in the weeping crowd suddenly might hide a blade, in his mind.

Wails build into a storm.

Standing, staggering, Perikles fumbles his way home, through the whispering and shouting crowds, fearful as if he were pushing through an enemy army, until at the gates of their home he finally falls into the arms of his worried mother Agariste, who has already heard the news, and grasps him tight now fearing for his life, shouting at her slaves to shut and bar the doors.

Ξ

Themistokles arrives at his new kingdom in Magnesia

The great Meander River divides the city of Magnesia on its snakelike way west to the Sea, the two sides of the city linked by the ancient stone bridge called Bellerophon. The mountain river glitters under the sinking Sun as the royal train of Themistokles winds its westward way down from the highlands to the little city in the river valley below.

"Excellent cucumbers here," says young Oxanes, in a bald attempt to raise Themistokles' cloudy spirit. "You haven't tried them yet, but you'll love them. And the figs are as healthy as anywhere, and will make you a very nice profit every year, I guarantee."

"Figs," Themistokles repeats morosely without really meaning anything.

"You'll love the cucumbers," Oxanes says again.

"I don't want a single cucumber, nor do I want this whole rich region's wealth of figs. All fruit is ash in the mouth of a man whose only future is fighting his countrymen. All wealth is dust when it must be used for war against one's own city."

"Magnesia-on-the-Meander is your city now," Oxanes retorts cautiously. "Your wife wouldn't want you calling her by your previous wife's name, would she?"

Themistokles cracks a smile at that comment, and nods to Oxanes. "Your point is taken, Oxanes. But I wouldn't call this a city. Overstuffed village, more like. Have you ever been to Hellas - I mean the mainland, west of the Aegean Sea and all its islands? Attika or the Peloponnese?"

Oxanes shakes his head. "I've been to Sardis once. But I haven't gotten to travel much. Sardis is a real city, though. It's much older than any of those Hellenic mainland cities. Except maybe Mykenai or Tiryns. But Sardis is still a thriving city, unlike those ruins."

"I've been to Sardis," Themistokles sniffs. "It is definitely a city. A small one, but old, and beautiful, for sure. But Athens - now there is a true city. Even after the Persian torches. Though you should have seen it before them, in its old glory. But I know it's not the structures that make a city; it's the people. We saved Athens; we started to rebuild that very same month. I won't go on about it, but you should see Athens someday, Oxanes. It's the real jewel of the world."

Oxanes says, "We have wonders here in the old world too, my king. Perhaps you've heard of Magnesian iron."

He hands Themistokles an iron amulet on a thick cord. As soon as he has it in his hand, he feels it pull oddly toward the sword at his side.

"I have, but I didn't think it would be quite this real!" Themistokles gives Oxanes a look of disbelief, and plays with the subtle attraction between the amulet and his iron weapon.

"There's a wiseman in Magnesia who owns a magic stone that he uses to pull the power out of such pieces, so the attraction is strengthened. He has two pieces that he has strengthened so much that they cannot be pulled apart from each other."

"Incredible," Themistokles muses, playing with the edges of the attraction between the amulet and his sword. "It seems to begin to pull strongly toward my sword at about a finger's width away, but I can feel the pull from all the way up here."

"Old Thermopos has stones that have been activated so strongly that they can pull iron up off the floor from high above."

"You'll find I'm hard to convince when it comes to stories of magic, boy,"

Themistokles says good naturedly with a sigh. "I have seen too much of reality to be fooled by what could never be. In truth, I wish real wisdom upon no man, for it brings only misery. So-called wisemen are fools, but they're wise to be. Fools have it best in this world."

Oxanes nods with a shy look, but then adds, "There's magic stones ahead, you'll see."

Themistokles sighs and looks to the horizon. "I fear there isn't enough magic in the world to pull the cursed future out of my bones, Oxanes. The Fates have already woven my path. I ride west to prepare a war against my own people."

Themistokles stands in the entryway of the fine palace at Magnesia, with his whole family and their own families all assembled before him on the magnificent mosaic which adorns the square before the palace, depicting Artemis and her maidens hunting myriad mountain beasts. The great number of his children, their husbands and wives, and grandchildren, all gathered here now at sunset, brings great heaving tears to Themistokles' breast before he is finally able to speak. Dutifully and sweetly, his children all wait through their father's tears.

"Children," new-bearded Themistokles says, gesturing to them all and holding his heart, "grandchildren, those whom my children love: it warms and breaks my heart to see you all gathered here together in Magnesia, in the kingdom of your father, the once-great defender of democracy."

"Hail," says Themistokles' son Archeptolis, who is first in line to inherit, "King Themistokles of Magnesia-on-the-Meander."

Themistokles shakes his head and waves away the comment with a hand, a familiar gesture to those who know the man, and know that it means he has more to say, and that what is to come next will be interesting.

"This kingdom, this monarchy, my son, is not what it seems. Not in my hands. If you know me and do not think that I have other plans than to be king of some Asian mountain, then you have not understood me."

Archtepolis raises his hand and says, "If I may." Themistokles gives him a long pause before finally nodding and gesturing to speak. "Father, we are so close to Hellas. We are practically in Ionia. Miletos is less than a day's ride away. We must not give up hope."

"Hope for what?" Themistokles barks with a swallow of sadness in his voice. "I am a king. But I am also the servant of a king. A king of kings, of all things! Apparently, in life, it's kings all the way up. We all live under the weight of the control of an infinite series of masters, all the way back to Ouranos, to Ge herself! We are slaves of the Earth, Queen of Fate. We cannot just do what we want, my son. We may live right next door to such apparent freedom, but we are not free."

Archtepolis sighs loudly, then shouts, as if with honor, "Then we should fight for freedom!"

Themistokles looks into his oldest son's idealistic eyes. "You don't know what that means," he groans. "Come with me. You deserve to know this."

Themistokles leads his son away from the rest of the family and into the king's personal chamber, where maps and plans of an invasion of mainland Hellas are scattered on the tables. Themistokles sighs, and says to eager Archtepolis, "You see, we are all going to need to learn to get used to a new sort of way of life, my son."

Archtepolis, still misunderstanding his father's meaning, nods and smiles, enjoying the texture of exotic fruit in his fingertips and gazing about the fine, eastern-patterned room.

O

Aoide becomes one of the Pythia

The youngest girls of Delphi are bathing in the Kastalian spring, and Aoide is with the teenage girls called *Amazons* who are armed with spears and put on watch in case any satyr-of-a-man tries his luck at stealing into the secret moment when so many are so vulnerable. Aoide leans on her spear, but keeps her eyes on the younger acolyte Amazons behind her, making sure that they are more on-guard than she is, since she is the supervisor today. Aware of her eyes on them, the Amazons watch vigilantly.

In the sacred pool, one of the younger girls starts splashing the others and laughing. A teenage Amazon caretaker raps the lizard-killer end of her spear on the stone floor and shoots a glare at the frolicking girls, but she is startled to be chided herself by Aoide, who barks, "Ease off! Joy is righteous. It's what we're here to protect." The Amazon sniffs and shrugs and turns away, unwilling to test Aoide's authority.

Audible before she appears, old Kliko approaches in her long robe which drags leaves in autumn.

"Aoide," Kliko says in her gravelly voice, raising her neck up with seriousness once she emerges from the woods. "You are to come with me."

Instantly Aoide feels the chill of her cell again, and the fear of that place comes back to her like the memory of a dream, but she reassures herself that the priestess' demeanor would be more careful if this was bad news, and that her more natural iciness is actually a good indicator that nothing is wrong. Aoide hands her spear to one of the other girls near her, crosses the wet stones and follows Kliko back up toward the sanctuary gate.

"Do not ask what this is about," Kliko tells her early in the walk, leaving Aoide free to think in silence as they pass through dappled sunlight on their way up the slope.

At the main gate, Aoide notices what at first she thinks is a memory - her parents standing to the right of the gate with a few other Athenian adults, no doubt relatives of hers she's forgotten. It is moments into seeing them before she realizes they're really there. But the priestess' silence about them, and their happy-eyed silence as she approaches the gate, just watching her quietly and motionlessly, tell Aoide not to call out to them. Still she does force a smile to match theirs. Aoide's parents both glow with pride.

The switchback road up past the treasuries to the Temple of Apollo is lined with onlookers who seem to know something Aoide doesn't. She begins to worry again, that there might be some kind of ritual she's yet unaware of, for girls her age, which might be about to endanger her. Everyone's seriousness is palpable. From corners of the sanctuary horns blow three long notes each deeper than the last, echoing so they seem to come from everywhere at once. The gathered crowd parts reverently to the sides of the streets. Aoide feels every eye upon her as she takes her first steps in the purple robes of office, their weight still strange against her skin.

"Remember to breathe," whispers sweet-eyed Phaeneris, adjusting the golden-threaded veil one last time before stepping back.

The elder priests surround her, their faces unreadable. None of those who were here when she first arrived still work here now. Behind them come the younger priestesses and the new temple girls, their baskets heavy with fresh flowers and herbs. As they walk, they scatter bay leaves over the hot coals in the bronze braziers that line the sacred way, releasing Aoide's favorite scent in great volume.

At the first of the nine steps leading to Apollo's temple, the high priest raises his staff. "Who approaches the house of Apollo Far-shooter?"

"Aoide, the Pythia," Aoide responds, her voice steadier than she feels.

"What brings you to his threshold?"

"The fate that brings all things to their proper place."

With each step, the questions grow more complex, the required responses longer. Ancient formulae that Aoide has spent months memorizing now flow from her lips as naturally as long-learned epic poems. The crowd's murmuring grows when a pair of eagles appears, circling the temple's peak, while Aoide is conferring with the priests.

"The god's messengers approve," someone shouts. The high priest allows himself to share a small smile with Aoide.

Inside the first chamber, before the eternal flame, Aoide finally sees the other two Pythia, barely keeping their proud smiles at bay beneath masks of serious ritual.

"As it was in the beginning," intones Kliko, now the eldest priestess, "when first the Earth-Snake guarded wisdom here, before Shining Apollo's coming; as it has been through all the years of prophecy since; as it shall be until the last mortal tongue falls silent - the voice of truth requires three to speak it."

The high priest pulls back Aoide's heavy veil. Another priest approaches holding a basin of water from the Kastalian Spring. The new veil they place upon her head is heavily wet, divine water running cool down her neck and spine.

"Through you, Apollo's light shall shine," the priests chant together like a chorus. "Through you, his words shall flow."

Then the big bronze doors to the inner temple groan open, revealing the inner sanctum, only ever glimpsed until now. Now she passes through them, into mysteries she has only imagined. The air grows thick and strange. Invisible vapors rise from cracks in the ancient stone, making the torchlight dance.

"Here," says the high priest, pausing before a rough black stone the size of a melon seated reverently upon an altar, "is what Rhea gave Kronos to swallow in place of Zeus." In the torchlight, its surface seems to writhe with shadow. "See there the stain of the Titan's spittle?"

Aoide secretly makes a grossed-out expression.

Next they show her the polished golden eagle heads that they say once adorned Apollo's bow. Beside that, the first oracle bone, its surface carved with words in a script totally unfamiliar. Aoide nods, at once intrigued and nonplussed, wondering about the true mysteries behind how long each object has been here and when its legend was begun.

"And now," the high priest says, his voice dropping to a whisper, "the heart of all our mysteries."

They guide her through a final doorway, into a chamber that feels older than stone itself. Kliko raises her ornate hand-lamp. "Behold the *Omphalos*."

What Aoide sees in the pulsating illumination of lamplight is a huge stone egg, as high as a tall man, and carved with a single spiral shape coiling round the course of it from top to bottom. At first sight, this strange, ancient carved stone called the Omphalos is beautiful and bizarre, and Aoide feels like she is seeing a god, even despite her better wisdom.

But Aoide continues to look at the giant carved stone as she is spoken to, and she gradually uses her doubt upon it, and with each continued moment of sustained doubt she feels she draws energy out from the supposedly magical work of divine art and into herself, who, she considers, through being able to know better, transcends even this world-famous artifact with her own mundane human power of reasoning.

"If at the beginning of his reign over the cosmos, Zeus set two eagles at either edge of the world and instructed them to fly simultaneously and at the same speed away from their edges, what would they find when they meet?"

Aoide has heard this story before, but she answers as if she has just figured it out through logic, "The center of the world." She plays her part in the theater of the moment.

"This place is where they met, and it was here that Zeus Cloud Gatherer placed this marker stone, to signify the very navel of the Earth. And like the navel marks the spot where the child used to be connected to the mother its precursor, so this Omphalos marks the spot where the Earth was once connected to the Sky. And like the navel connects child to mother, so this stone marks where Sky and Earth were one," the new old high priest intones. "But there are other connections, other navels, hidden from mortal sight."

Emerging into the lamplight, all three Pythia surround Aoide, as behind them on the walls, their shadows writhe massive.

"To be Pythia is to become such a connection," Eromede whispers. "A living umbilicus between divine and mortal minds."

"Your voice must become a vessel," Opho continues. "Empty of self, ready to be filled with god's breath."

Aoide wonders if these are ritual words, or the women's own original, and as she considers it she realizes that her uncertainty is their poetic success, and her senses of mystery and knowledge further intercoil.

"But first," Aigisthenia says, "you must learn to see."

They bind Aoide's eyes with dark-blue cloth which smells of laurel and honey. She is briefly reminded of the cloak which put her to sleep when she was secreted out from the temple, and wonders if some new sort of sleep or dream is in store for her today.

Strong hands guide her to kneel before the sacred tripod.

"Breathe the vapors," they command in unison. "Let your thoughts dissolve and mix with the gods'."

Sweet smoke fills her lungs. Her mind returns to when she was just a girl and first arrived at Delphi, first caught the scent of these vapors outside the temple. The darkness behind her eyelids begins to move, to pattern itself into shapes she almost recognizes. She feels her consciousness stretching, thinning, reaching toward something vast and distant.

"The human mind is a closed room," Eromede's voice seems to come from very far away. "None can see inside another's thoughts. That is why we must speak, to share the contents of our minds with each other. Most men think that they can see inside their own minds. But even the wisest of us only see what comes to the surface of that deep pool. We can pray into our minds and see what comes back to us from the depths, like supplicants of ourselves, burning the sacrifice of our intention with the hope that the gods of our secret interior might deign to grant our wish. But here, at this ancient crevasse where Apollo slew the serpent Python, here the universal god of wisdom, brilliant Apollo, shares his gift of clear sight, and foresight, with those whose minds can handle it. It is said that only Apollo can see into men's minds. But Apollo does sometimes give that gift to others, and this is a place where he does so. Can you, Aoide, see the difference in your mind between your own and Apollo's voice?"

Though kneeling, Aoide keeps her back as tall and strong as she can, trying to emanate grace. "I can," she says and, even though blind-masked, attempts to project cool confidence.

"Then I am no longer Pythia," says Opho, "and you are the new Pythia, voice of Shining Apollo."

Bright in the firelight, here where she is revered, Aoide stands, and starts to sing.

Π

The funeral of Ephialtes

The body of Ephialtes lies upon a tall pyre, dressed in his simple potter's tunic. Two silver Athenian owls have been placed in his mouth for the Ferryman.

The funeral for Ephialtes, despite Perikles' request to his friends that it not be made a political affair, has been planned with such an eye to modesty and reflecting Ephialtes' lack of interest in luxury that there is grumbling throughout the crowd from the beginning that it is all a big Democrat show. But really, to Perikles' eye, that just speaks to how closely Ephialtes' true character matched the civic virtues held up by the Democrats - modesty, compassion, duty.

The trappings around him are an overt demonstration of modesty, of thrift and brevity. The stools and tripods are cheap and minimal. The sacrifice to Haides is just one pig, with only enough meat for each mourner to have a token shred of the cooked flesh. Only Ephialtes' father Sophonides, a round old man now, though still livelier than most his age, stands nearest to the pyre, where the family traditionally stands; they have no other living family. Shy before masses, he has offered the honors of speaking *good words* about the man - a tradition called *eulogy* - to his son's best friend Perikles.

Perikles stands now before what feels like all of Athens, even larger than the Assembly - men, women, children; slaves, foreigners, citizens; rich, poor, destitute. Yet with all the young and old female faces facing him among the male ones softened by sadness, it feels more like he is giving a heartfelt speech to his extended family rather than the businesslike sort he has gotten used to giving only to men at the Pnyx. Athens, at this moment, feels to him like it is one huge Alkmaeonid family gathering.

"I had hoped to never have to speak at a funeral. I never felt like I would be able to meet the necessity of the moment, in eloquence, in beauty of words. This was true when I failed to meet the challenge, as a younger man, of speaking at my own father's funeral. This is more true than ever of my great friend, and undoubtedly one of Athens' finest sons - Ephialtes. But I will try."

Perikles lowers his head and begins to weep, despite himself. He covers his face with his hand, and heaves tears into it.

He struggles to raise his head again to face his countrymen, and can barely hold it aloft at first, but as he speaks he regains the strength of his neck and ends his speech as upright as he has ever been.

"I loved Ephialtes," Perikles at first weeps. "As much as I love my own brother Ariphron, and my mother Agariste, I loved Ephialtes the same. So I feel for his father, fine Sophonides, and welcome him into my family in any way that he wishes to consider himself so welcome, henceforth. My love for your wonderful son, my friend, passes on to you."

Sophonides silently weeps, beaming his smile to Perikles as if desperate to be seen as grateful. Perikles smiles back, sheds some tears, and reaches out toward Sophonides symbolically, then wipes his own face with the shoulder of his tunic.

"Ever-smiling, Ephialtes rose above the day-to-day frays of Athenian petty disagreements, and had a view of the larger picture, of our people's long but ever-progressing march toward self-government, toward equal power - *isocracy*. Every month, with every conversation, with every new mind illuminated by better understanding, we drag ourselves away from the swamp of the hydra of Oligarchy, and toward the high Akropolis of our best possible selves by the light of the Lamp of Democracy."

Oligarchs in the audience begin to grumble, but know they can't do so too loudly without being deemed irreverent. Nevertheless, a few in the back begin simply to leave in silence.

Perikles acknowledges, "I know that it will be thought controversial by some, that I spoke of politics at the funeral of this fine and modest man. But I know that such sentiments - of the enfranchisement of the poor, of the essential equal dignity due all men who have done no offense to the gods - such sentiments being shared between men keeps Ephialtes' spirit alive. We all know that when we continue to speak of such matters in the way that he would have, it makes Ephialtes smile wherever he might be now."

A murmur of discomfort ripples through the remaining Oligarchs at this political turn. One of the priests steps forward slightly, catching Perikles' eye with a subtle shake of his head. But Perikles just pictures the little smile he knows Ephialtes would've given him, seeing him see all this.

Perikles continues, his voice growing stronger. "And what did our friend smile most about? What lit his face with that famous grin? It was when he saw Athens take another step toward true democracy. When he saw poor men finally able to serve as archons, as councilors, as magistrates. Though the last vote failed, his efforts are maintained by his friends, and will succeed! That every citizen might be paid for their service to the city, that poverty should not bar any worthy man from helping to guide Athens."

Several of the wealthier citizens in the back begin making their way toward the edges of the crowd. Perikles' voice rises after them. "We see today that Ephialtes' vision lives beyond his life! We see citizens debase themselves to make political points, rather than give honorable respect to the dead. When one man does good, it is a lamp which shines on all others, revealing how good we all could be, and casting shadows on how good we're not."

Some of the departing Oligarchs pause, caught between pride and shame. A few slowly return to their places, eyes downcast. Their fellows who continue leaving seem to shrink as they go, marked now not just by their public absence but by the weakness of their conviction compared to those who stayed.

"Yes, return," Perikles calls. "Even those who opposed him in life can honor him in death. And goodness can always be returned to. For what Ephialtes wanted was not to tear down the rich, but to lift up the poor. Not to destroy tradition, but to fulfill its promise that any Athenian might serve his city. Democracy is now our tradition! He died for believing that a poor man's wisdom might be match to a rich man's folly. Shall we prove him right or wrong by our behavior here today?"

The crowd stirs uneasily, but no one else leaves. Even those who opposed him fiercest in life seem to understand that walking out now would only prove his points about who truly loves Athens and who loves only power.

"I loved Ephialtes," Perikles finishes with a sniff of tears, "and I will always love him. And the love he had for our city is what will inspire me as we move into the future together, Athenians."

Once he is stepping back down into the crowd, he is met with only love and adulation, and those who were offended clump together in the back, hiding their whispers.

One after another, Athenians come up to thank and congratulate Perikles, to share memories of his friend, and assure him that they are with him now. The first to approach is an elderly potter, a friend of Ephialtes' father, his hands rough with clay-scars. He takes Perikles' arm in a workman's grip. "My son serves on the Council now," he says, voice holding back tears. He just nods, as the rest is understood - Ephialtes made that possible. Others follow - a fishmonger, a carpenter, a rope-maker. Each shares some small story of how Ephialtes touched their lives, how he listened to common men as if their words carried weight. Even a few of the Oligarchs who stayed come forward, some grudgingly, others with genuine respect.

"He was wrong about many things," old Oligarch Thukydides offers back-handedly, "but never dishonest, never cruel."

    The line of mourners continues until finally Lysimachos approaches. Unlike the others, his face bears a look of grave concern beneath his grief. He makes sure to get and hold Perikles' eye contact once he is in view. He carries something wrapped in fine cloth. Once with Perikles, he reveals what is beneath, a finely-carved recreation of the Shield of Achilles, referencing the death of Patroklos.

    Lysimachos says, "Listen, Perikles. This is, of course, a symbol meant to connect your friendship with Ephialtes to Achilles' love for Patroklos, obviously. But it's also not a metaphor. It's also a real shield. Meant to remind you to protect yourself for real."

    He puts the shield in Perikles' hands. The weight of it surprises Perikles, and forces him to use his legs.

    "Use it," Lysimachos tells him. "Protect yourself. Physically."

    Perikles gravely, minutely nods. He hands the shield off to Thrax.

    Before his whole city, then, Perikles solemnly receives the priest's torch and alights the pyre beneath his friend.

    Everybody drinks from cups provided to the public long ago by Ephialtes, his name already nearly worn away from frequent use.

    A light rain begins to sprinkle as the fire consumes once-smiling Ephialtes.

    "Zeus hates to see such a fine man burn!" someone shouts.

    "He weeps for Ephialtes the Kind!"

    That starts Perikles weeping, to hear how his city loved his friend.

    Eteobouta, that wisened and white-curled high priestess of Athena calls out, pointing at the haze above the fire, "Iris! Goddess of the rainbow! She is here to take Ephialtes by the hand!" And at that, a great storm of weeping grief rises in a many-voiced chorus.

ATHENS

P

A next generation of Athenians get their names

Pomegranates inexorably ripen, until Persephone's return from the Underworld begins to reawaken the life in every plant and person while Helios gradually shifts his course back northward.

The long-ruined Temple of Athena on the Athenian Akropolis is crowded now with the family, friends, and financiers of the city's Oligarchs, as two new babies from wealthy families are being named on the same day.

The Sun and spirits are high.

Modestly-jeweled women wearing expensive textiles and all-morning hairdos murmur pleasantries and share tales of when gods and heroes were tiny babies. Bright white clouds lazily wander the lagoon-blue sky. While anyone from the city is technically allowed, teen-agers hired by the Oligarchs dissuade poorer people from ascending the ramp to the Akropolis, so they mostly watch the festivities from below. Only the bravest young spies sneak up to watch up-close, including wandering teen-aged Sokrates and Krito who were initially only trying to get past the other teen boys, unaware what was beyond.

The wizened old priestess of Athena, Eteobouta, unable to stand since a recent fall, sits upon the litter she was carried in on. Eagle-eyed Eteobouta raises her hands to gather the attention of those nearby.

As silence quickly gathers out of respect, Eteobouta creaks, "Today we confirm, with great child-bearing Hera, that even while spirits of vengeance skulk among us and seek to take to the kingdom of death beneath the Earth those who have wronged the gods with hubris, still nevertheless new life continues, and new men are named after old ones. So, dear mother Hera, please do not let this day be one of curses, but let your mighty wrath agents keep their work elsewhere. O gods, please do not hate these babies for the crimes of mankind."

Perikles winces and lowers his head when the priestess indirectly accuses his friend of hubris, but he keeps his mouth closed. Murmurs slip through the crowd like fishes.

The priestess reaches out her wrinkled hands, beckoning the nearest of the two new mothers to hand her child over. Eteobouta asks her, "And what is the name of his beautiful mother?"

"I'm Melissa," she says with a blush and a glance to her husband.

"Thank you, Melissa - he looks beautiful and healthy. And what shall be the name of this child, now that he has lived long enough to show that the gods do want him in the world? I did not hear you the first time."

"We will name him Kritias, after his grandfather, who was the grand nephew of Solon." Melissa tries to hide her prideful smile and retreats back into the crowd to rejoin her husband, pulling his arms in to wrap her. He holds the crooked old cane of his recently deceased father, old Kritias.

Very old Eteobouta says, "Each generation destroys and rebuilds civilization," as she holds the baby in her hands and raises him high above the sacred flame. "This child, great gods, we name Kritias. May he build and nourish only what you gods love, and destroy and hinder only what you hate."

Carefully, with aid from her young assistants, Eteobouta hands the baby back, then gestures for the next one. Oloros steps forward with his wriggling infant.

"And you, young man?" the priestess asks Oloros, who becomes instantly shy in the presence of his child. "What will your son be named?"

Oloros looks back at his wife, Hegesipyle, daughter of Thukydides, who is the one all the other Oligarchs are looking to now with Alkibiades exiled. "We name him Thukydides," Oloros says, "after his noblest grandfather." He nods to his father-in-law, picturing the farm he bought for the young couple and all that he himself owes that now-top Oligarch.

New-grandfather Thukydides coolly stares from a distance at his tiny namesake. "You take a big risk naming someone after me," he says. "Better raise him well, or I'll have to destroy him."

Oloros grimaces out a smile to act like the comment was a joke. Hegesipyle puts a comforting hand on her husband's shoulder from behind.

"Welcome to the city of Athena, young Thukydides." Eteobouta looks at the baby for a moment, tickles his nose, then holds him up above her head to show the crowd. "May you live long," the priestess says, "and live to tell our story when we ourselves are shades below."

Baby Thukydides starts to piss while held aloft, sending a tiny stream down onto his father, who sputters with disgust and turns and runs through the crowd toward the nearest fountain. Eteobouta lowers the baby again quickly and hands him off to Hegesipyle as the assembled loved ones all laugh.

"You may leave certain parts of the story out of the telling," Eteobouta says to baby Thukydides as a joke to those around her, while all laugh again.

Krito, watching from the sidelines with Sokrates, turns to his younger friend with a kind smile. "This reminds me of when you were named."

Sokrates smiles in return.

Krito hugs his friend from behind, remembering when they both were littler. "They handed you to me," Krito says. "And I remember looking into your eyes and you were already this person, just like anyone else."

Sokrates chuckles at the thought of himself as a tiny baby, like the ones being passed around the adults at the sacred fire. He wiggles out from Krito's grasp.

"You haven't changed much," Krito jokes.

Sokrates laughs loudly and slaps his leg. Krito is surprised, and eventually embarrassed, by how funny Sokrates finds it, as older folks squint at them across the sunshine.

He explains, "They told me to watch after you that day. And I've been making sure you were okay ever since. Even when you didn't necessarily really want me around. I keep my eye on you, Sokrates."

Sokrates takes his older friend in a one-armed hug.

The priestess notices the friendly warmth. "Boys?" Eteobouta asks, approaching Krito and Sokrates with the baby in her arms. She holds little Kritias out to them, asking if either would like to hold him.

"It's your turn," Krito says to his young friend with a smile wiser than his years. He gestures to the priestess to hand Kritias to Sokrates.

Sokrates takes the little baby in his arms, but tiny Kritias is already screaming before the handoff begins. Sokrates tries to pet his soft head, but baby Kritias keeps jerking away from him, crying and lurching. Sokrates comically grimaces around at the adults.

"It will be up to you boys to make sure little Kritias and Thukydides know how to be good when they grow up," Athena's old priestess tells the boys. "You and all your friends."

New-grandfather Oligarchs Kritias and Thukydides side-eye Sokrates and Krito with suspicion and derision as they sniff off the notion of their grandson-namesakes being influenced by such nobodies.

Σ

The funeral of King Pleistarchos

"O Haides Many-Host! Welcome our King Pleistarchos to your bloodless realm of death! Eighteenth mighty king of the Agiad throne! Bestowed with power by old Herakles, the hero Leonidas' only son is dead!"

Pleistarchos' body burns atop a pyre piled up on the cobblestone between the temples in the center of the wallless city of Sparta.

The herald raises his staff of coiled snakes high above his head as he shouts, "O Zeus of the Thunderbolt, King of Gods and God of Kings, please grant a long and powerful reign to the new nineteenth Agiad king of Sparta, King Pleistoanax!"

Gorgo stands black-veiled beside the fire, closer than anyone else to the heat of the flames, her black veils sucking in the pyrelight, just a form of living shade haloed in flame.

The men of Sparta, gathered all around and watching stoically, all hail the new king in loose unison, while their wives and daughters make a show of wailing and pulling at their hair, as is the tradition at funerals.

"Hail, King Pleistoanax, son of Pausanias, new king of the Agiad throne of Sparta!"

Pleistoanax receives the crown handed to him from the leader of the Overseers. He glances at black-veiled Gorgo, then at his fellow king Archidamos, then the sea of Spartan faces spread out before him, and he places the woven metal crown upon his head. King Pleistoanax squints against the cheer of his people, as against the wind.

"Hail King Pleistoanax of Sparta!"

The priest of Haides begins to carve the cooked flesh of the funerary sacrifice, a giant boar brought in by the Eurypontid king's best Helot hunter.

While Gorgo stares into the flames, the Overseers begin a dramatic effort at ignoring her drama. Both are performing, filled with meaning.

The rich scent of roasted boar mingles with incense as the priest's knife works. The gathered Spartans eat in tense silence, many eyeing the Helot hunter who brought down such impressive prey. He stands apart, head bowed, pretending not to notice their stares.

"Look at that one," mutters the youngest Overseer, nodding toward the hunter. "Skilled with a spear, loyal enough to be trusted in the woods alone. That's what we need more of. I love him and fear him!"

"And how do we get more like him?" asks another, tearing meat from bone. "Every lash we give makes the rest dream harder of that mountain."

The eldest overseer wipes his mouth. "The stick and the sweet fig, that's what's needed. When they see a Helot like him, well-fed, trusted with weapons for the hunt, perhaps even given a better plot of land to work..."

"You'd reward them further?"

"I'd make the distance greater," the elder corrects sharply. "Between the loyal and the rebellious. Let them see what good behavior brings. Then when we break the backs of troublemakers, their fellow Helots will think twice about following that path."

"The trusted ones can help us watch the others," adds another, warming to the idea. "They'll work harder to keep their privileges."

"And we must work them harder still," the lead Overseer says, his eyes cold. "Those who serve well earn their rewards through double labor. Those who resist..." He lets the thought hang like a whip in the air.

Heads nod around the circle.

"And what about those rebels on the mountain? How much longer can we allow them to light their fires up there like a lighthouse of freedom?"

"We cannot simply give more soldiers to their arrows. Their ground gives them advantage."

"What would Odysseos do?"

"The detente has grown stale," the elder Overseer says. "We cannot storm the mountain; they're too well defended. And we can stop their runners bringing provisions, but we cannot stop them catching birds, and young ones find their way through in the night. We cannot stop their reprovisioning, at least enough to feed the few of them that they need to survive. They will stay on Mount Ithome until Zeus or some other god decides they must descend. They are a beacon of potential freedom to all our working Helots. We must consider new and modern methods to besiege!"

Gorgo listens patiently, but with cold, unreceiving eyes. When the Overseer finishes speaking, she queries with her eyebrows to confirm he is done, then says, "The Helots on the mountain still have courage. They will feel like heroes for the rest of their lives. We must not give up the lives of our most powerful young boys into the bottomless grave of that endeavor. The Helots on Mount Ithome are no longer a threat to us. But if we try to make some example of them, and send our forces against their fortified summit, they will only get stronger, and so will the courage of those Helots who still work for us. No, foolish old man, you must put away your silly remnant of an erection and actually consider what you want, and the results of your actions. Assaulting Mount Ithome would not get us what we want."

The Overseers all look to each other for a few long moments of silence, as if testing whether they will acknowledge her at all or not. But her long-held glare, even through her widow's black veil, penetrates their collective psyche enough to bring one man to answer.

"They can't stay there, harrying our forces, a beacon to our own Helots that freedom is possible!"

Gorgo nods. "That's true. So we give them what they want. We tell them that they have won, and we let them leave."

"We give up Messenia back to the Helots?" the Overseer bellows. "We would never keep another slave, then, if there was a land of freedom just a quick evening's stagger away. Go back to your well-earned grief, dear widow. You have borne too much death in your life for any person to bear."

"We do not give them Messenia, of course," Gorgo sighs. "We do something international, we get some other Hellenic land, like the Athenians, to escort them to some neutral spit of land far from the Peloponnese where they can set up their own little city, far enough from here that our own Helots will never hear of or think of them again."

"Sparta does not lose wars!"

"Sparta does what is in her best interest," Gorgo replies. "Lose, win, what are these? Children's games. Words are nothing! Sparta will not be dissolved from inside by her own pride. No, you will approve this, or you know exactly what sort of horrors I will visit upon you each. You will even make this appear to be your own idea."

The Overseers all glare silently. They don't dare even glance at each other; they all gaze steady at black-veiled Gorgo.

King Archidamos saunters up and says, "The Queen-Aunt is right, of course. Wisdom weighs the same on any tongue. The Helots on Mount Ithome cannot continue to be our focus, but they cannot stay there in the middle of our lands like a lighthouse of freedom, as you say. And there is no one better to fool into taking them under their own wing than the Athenians. And it just so happens that there is also no greater *competitor* in the children's game of worldwide-power than Athens, right now. We must find ways to weigh them down, and giving them the problem of Ithome is just the way. They will think it a chance to prove their 'goodness', as a show to gain allies. And once they have their hands full, with armies all across the sea, that will be the time to take out their feet, by invading the old way - land."

Gorgo says, "Athens is already wounded, and by her own hand. But it is not an obvious wound. It's an old wound, a self-inflicted one, and though it is small enough to seem insignificant, it is one of those wounds that festers and spreads the fever of Ares throughout the body slowly. Athens' wound is called *democracy*, and so long as she is so wounded, we do not need to rush in and try to finish her off. Invasion is a foolish man's dream. We simply need to let Athens fester, go mad, and die."

"Foolish woman!" King Archidamos spits with derision, standing from his throne to show the full height of his tall, muscular Spartan body. "Now you mask your cowardice as wisdom. You see, men, this is why it is important to think critically! Lest you be bamboozled by a clever, weak person. Athens grows stronger every year, despite the chaos that their democracy instills. It is their location - the luck of their land - not any decisions made by their men, who are no wiser or braver than any other group of Hellenes. Wisdom is not an Athenian invention. But because of where they sit, on that peninsula of Attika, with its advantageous position for use of the Sea, and all the silver beneath Sounion, they grow like Memnon into a colossus on the world battlefield. But if we were to invade before they knew what we were doing, the Spartan army could crush the Athenian army *on land*, and just as our grandfathers added Messenia to Spartan control, we could add Attika as a Spartan treasury and defensive head-land, and give Attikans a new name, like Helots."

"You fall for the same trap of ambition, set by the gods, as Athens does," Gorgo retorts. "They spread their power thin because they think they are more capable than they are. But anyone who understands a phalanx knows that most of the time the strongest position is to stand your ground, to stay where you are, to stay tight."

Archidamos shakes his head and glares coolly at Gorgo, trying to appear above her insults. "Unlike your Agiad boys, I practice regularly with the ranks of soldiers. I am not unaware of the function of a phalanx, woman. And I will not hear your disparagements again. I am not a child like I used to be. And I have *never* been *your* child. And now you have no child at all. You have become irrelevant, and I expect you to disappear as you ought to."

Gorgo hardens her face so as not to reveal any affect. She lets her black veil shift down over her eyes.

"We have a new Agiad king today," Gorgo says, "and it will be up to King

Pleistoanax whom he chooses to take wisdom from. You will not see me shy from his side just because you might wish me out of the picture."

One of the Overseers is bold enough to ask, "What were the poor young king's last words?" His fellows give him awkward glances wishing he hadn't asked, since most have heard gossip about the truth.

Gorgo glares at him with silence which chills all those around.

She says, "I would not have his final words spread. They are dangerous, madness too powerful to be released into the world. If it were known he wrote them, they would do more than Hekate and her hell-hounds can toward summoning lost souls down to Haides too soon. His words, like him, must burn. A twisted, cursed oracle was he."

King Archidamos hardens his face. "I must know, woman. How did he die? What miasma befell my fellow king?"

Gorgo sighs, and stares into silence. Tears begin to fill her eyes.

Without speaking, she shows Archidamos a piece of old goatskin on which many bits of dark old poetry have been written in dark old blood, but most recently, on top of all the other letters in black, modern squid ink, are the large words

EXCESSIVE VOID
UNCERTAINTY DESTROYED
NO MORE SELF

Old Triops says, "Young Pleistarchos was always cursed. In the end, he did not even have the power to defeat himself. He was above and below himself. The poet in him waged war against his own throne, and could only lose. The king has killed himself. Long live the king."

ATHENS

T

A great leader of Athens is exiled

The day has come for Athenian men to get into ten lines by urban tribe and vote for whom to ostracize from the city. But first, the final speeches are given in the Agora.

Meanwhile, an enmity between two window dogs who can see each other down the street has all the dogs in the city howling without knowing why.

"The end of democracy! If Perikles is ostracized, it will be the end of democracy! Not just here, but everywhere!" As Athenian men from the city and countryside mingle in the streets surrounding the Agora, an eager young Democrat woman dressed in a theatrical mimicry of the armor of Athena First-in-Battle stands repeating this sentiment from the open doorway to her home. "The end of Democracy if Perikles is ostracized!"

As he passes her, Perikles approaches the young lady and whispers to her, "Listen, friend - think of changing the focus of your statement. I don't want people thinking of my name, but rather of Kimon's. Instead of saying 'Don't vote to exile Perikles', perhaps say '*Do* vote to exile Kimon!' Some men might get confused, hear my name, and write it down."

The woman listens eagerly to the famous man but seems confused by his words. Nevertheless she shrugs and begins using the new language. "The end of democracy if we don't vote to ostracize Kimon! Keep Perikles, exile Kimon! Do vote to avoid the end of democracy!"

The Agora is roped off to guide the city's ten urban tribes to their particular voting jars, later in the day, after the cases are made. The Skythian city-slave archers are busy organizing the pot shards to be written upon.

Each sound of pottery reminds Perikles of his friend Ephialtes. He feels certain that the man's ghost lingers on the warm breeze today.

Whenever he thinks of Ephialtes, Perikles fears for his own life. He imagines phantom bronze masks on every unfamiliar face, before they resolve back to reality. Nevertheless, Perikles does his best to put on a brave public face while waiting in his line. Some of his neighbors commiserate politely with him, as to how difficult it must be after his friend's murder. He wears the mask of a strong-willed but inexpressive grief which quickly turns into a truly necessary helmet against the real grief all the talk of it summons in him.

"We will continue to search for Ephialtes' murderer, but the gods and spirits of vengeance will make sure that justice finds him either way, whether he is tried in Athenian courts, or the wild natural courts of the Erinyes - those taloned soldiers of Nemesis Revenge-bringer."

Since the murder of his friend, people in public have mostly left Perikles alone, save for occasional soft polite glances and pleasantries of empathy. Outside of his one-on-one meetings with fellow Democrats, in public he primarily only hears whispers from a distance.

While he waits quietly and eavesdrops, Perikles strategizes in his mind. The ostracism could go one of three ways, as he sees it. Even if his side wins, and Kimon is ostracized today, then suddenly he will be the primary political actor in the city, and will be as vulnerable as any man. Or, he could be ostracized today, and forced to leave the only city he's ever known before his political career has even had a chance to blossom. Both fill him with fear. Worst of all, ever since Ephialtes was murdered it has been clear to Perikles that he would be next in line for the same fate if the murderers mean to continue their evil work.

Wearing his helmet forward and covering his now-famous face, Perikles has made sure that his beard is cut in a distinctively sharp fashion, so that he can be recognized by helmet and beard alone. Still, the visor is too narrow for him to see like he would prefer, and it is challenging to breathe in the heat of the metal, so once he has stood upon the bema and has faced the Assembly crowd before him on the Pnyx for what feels like long enough, he pushes the helmet back onto his head to reveal his face, and to breathe.

To his surprise, the reveal of Perikles' face to the crowd is met with a sudden and roaring applause, and the feeling of joy hits Perikles bodily like diving into warm water, forcing a grin upon him.

"Onion head!" a young voice shouts, but there is nothing but love in its tone, and though it makes Perikles wince for a moment, he cannot help but continue to grin as the epithet is used along with others such as "Hero!", "Olympian!", "People's King!", "Golden Beard!", and "Zeus!", some sarcastically but some in actual loving adoration. The few Oligarchs and their friends in the Assembly who do not cheer him say nothing instead, and watch negligibly with folded arms.

"Men of Athens," swift-eyed Perikles begins, trying to quiet the applause, but those words raise the level of the cheer for a few moments. Perikles grins and tries to gesture again for quiet. Finally he is able to continue over a diminishing grumble from the Oligarchs who had been drowned out by the applause until it faded.

"Men of Athens, I am here to give my perspective on the challenging question before us all - who among us should be exiled for ten years? And, as we have all come to understand by now, the political dynamics of our population have winnowed the viable votes to two candidates - myself, Perikles, son and friend of Athens, and noble Kimon, son of Athens, but friend to Sparta."

Those who disdain Spartans grumble and hiss. Kimon's loyal contingent of veterans make their stalwart silence loud.

"Perhaps, like me, you can already smell the thunder of coming change." Perikles thinks of Aischylos, and the way he holds a long pause on the stage, the power that builds up. He holds such a silence, facing down the listening crowd; his blood rushes with the courage necessary. "Ours is a city which has taken a bold and virtuous risk, in taking the reigns of power from the few, and giving it to *all* the people, and the gods. And though those without faith in the common man would warn you that this weakens us, we all here know that those are lies, as history has shown over the past hundred years that democracy only brings Athens wealth, power, and glory! Because the gods can see what is right and good, just as clearly as we can!"

The crowd cheers democracy.

"The leader of the voices which have struggled these past years to take us backward, to return us to an oligarchy where you have no power, no say, no sway, the leader of those voices is well known to us all, is it not?"

"Kimon!" the crowd responds. Perikles nods, tightening his face to keep a smile off it when he sees Kimon glaring from the middle of the people.

Perikles says resolutely, "Today you have the chance to solidify the gains of democracy by removing her greatest obstacle. If exile we must, then exile's target is clear. Let us write down one name, K-I-M-O-N!"

Athenians roar with debate, and the roar hardly ceases through the voting and counting of the votes. Rumbling conversations compete for the air, until a hush falls with the rise of the herald's snake staff.

"Who else would speak?" the herald shouts.

All look to Kimon, who stands with arms folded, as if the ultimate laconic response of nothing is all that is necessary. His veteran comrades murmur an angry whispered song.

"Let us go now, and write our votes on potshards."

The crowded mass of Athenian men moves gradually down to the Agora, where their ten jars are arranged by urban tribe, for potshards on which names will be written.

As Ephialtes and Perikles wait in their line with Lysimachos and some other fellow Democrats, they overhear several young men in the neighboring tribal line asking each other how to write Ephialtes' name. Perikles confidently shakes his head at the others, to not worry, and not appear worried.

The shadows have barely shifted before the voting has already been made clear to those counting - the vote is for Kimon. Word spreads through the tight crowd nearly instantly.

"Kimon," says the herald, after the potshards have been counted and the majority is more than clear. "You have been exiled by your fellow citizens. Your property will not be confiscated, but you may not return to Athens until ten years have passed." He holds aloft his *kerykeion* staff, so that his words are known to be official, and he himself, as messenger, only a mask.

Kimon exits silently through the voting crowd toward his home, ignoring the cheers and jeers the best he can, his sycophants and slaves forming a protective phalanx around him until he pushes though and ahead of them to walk alone.

The crowded Agora does not focus on Kimon's disgrace for long, however, and in a wave across the group of thousands very suddenly everyone turns to face Perikles, and several cheers start at once and merge into a resounding roar.

"Zeus!"

"Perikles! Zeus!"

"Onion-lympian!"

"Long live the democracy, and the freedom of all men! Keep the power with the villages! It is the end of the power of rich Oligarchs, and a new day for the common man!"

"O Prometheos, now give power to all of the people!" shouts a female voice among the men, mostly unnoticed.

"Hail, Perikles, earthly Zeus, and Athens born anew and motherless directly from his brain!"

"Democratic colored capes, for sale today only from Kleanetos!"

"Zeus, king of the gods, who has made all men kings!"

"Hail Democracy, king of governments!"

Lysimachos smiles with his friend, standing where Ephialtes would have been, and then takes Perikles' hand and hold it high with his own, and the Athenian Democrats all cheer. Women leaning out their windows begin to sing an old song by Solon, the inventor of their government.

O Athens will not perish, by the will of mighty Zeus!
For his great mind-child Athena is our sweet caretaker,
she who makes smooth that which was rough, and soothes foolish outrage,
and withers springing weeds of ruin, and mollifies the mad!

Y

Youth gangs of the Agora mix it up

The agitation of the crowd after the ostracism vote stirs the birds in the Agora. Bird-watchers among the women and foreigners argue over the potential for omens within the minor peculiarities of the swooping of the flocks, as they do with every flight of birds. Some teen-aged boys just too young for Assembly jokingly debate what omens might exist within the squawking and gesticulating of the bird-watchers.

Patient, distant-eyed Phaenarete is at the Fountain House again, carrying a big water jar with twelve-year old Sokrates at her side. She grimaces at the tone change up on the Pnyx. Many other women nearby worry aloud to each other openly, comfortable doing so with most of the men away together on the hill.

"Glory be to Hera and her patience, for all I hear in Zeus' chanted name is the praise of a cheater."

"We're a joke in other cities' eyes now. It's an upside-down world. The noblest men are exiled and the crudest men are given monuments. The gods will flood this world again if we're not careful."

"And who are the good men, and who the bad, cousin?"

"My husband can do just as well running this city as any nobleman! Frankly I'm proud of our men taking the reins from those cruel, rich old donkeys after all this time. We need more power, to more people!"

"All your husbands listen more to my whores than to you. And my whores listen to owls clinking together."

A group of young men not yet of age to vote at Assembly but old enough to cause trouble begin to gather near the Monument of Heroes, taunting each other and passersby, and kicking the stakes of market tents. Two of the gangs, competing groups each composed of the sons of Oligarchs, a few scattered others with the sons of Democrats and the apolitical, none mature enough to know why, gather quickly in corners of the Agora, and begin projecting threats across the crowd against each other and the city itself.

"Here we go again," someone bemoans.

Protagoras and Anaxagoras stand with Archelaos amidst a cluster of men from Abdera who all arrived recently on the same ship, and who have brought news of Protagoras' old friend Demokritos, and his imminent arrival on the next boat.

Anaxagoras says, "In both war and in peace, the real threat is the same - teen-age and twenty-something young men and their foolish sense of immortality and misguided righteousness."

Protagoras nods while drinking carefully from a broad cup, trying to indicate that he would have laughed were his mouth not occupied.

Elderly Eteobouta, high priestess of Athena, happens to be seated nearby on a stone bench, just as two laughing teen-aged boys race past to catch up with their friends, and she moans, "Even these visiting foreigners can see the clear truth: the youth of Athens simply are not what they used to be!"

Phaenarete pulls Sokrates close into her arms, but at twelve years old he is just old enough to feel the need to shrink away. She whispers next to his ear, "Don't be like those boys, Dew-drop."

"Mother, please, don't call me Dew-drop in public," Sokrates grumbles. "I'm not a baby."

"Well, I worry about you becoming a man," she admits. "Be something new, won't you? Don't be like those young men, or those old men. Just be Sokrates, okay?"

"Fine," Sokrates sighs, before racing off just to get distance from his mother.

Soon he finds wild-eyed Chaerephon among the clusters of agitated citizens in the Agora.

"Sokrates!" Chaerephon welcomes his friend with a big hug. "The teen-aged boys are about to wreck some shops. Let's get ready to grab some scraps they miss! Shopkeepers will ignore us," and then he interrupts himself with a growling noise that he can't control and fights against, then continues, stuttering, "while, while they're, while they're going after the big boys. Sorry, there's a lion cub in my mouth. Yesterday mother said it's there to scare the birds. Let's go, come on!"

Among the first of the crowd of Athenian men returning from the Pnyx, Euathlos strides with his usual friends past the restaurant where Protagoras and the other Abderan men are seated, drinking, and as he passes he chides, "I may not be a wiseman, Protagoras, but I can still become a member of the city council!"

Euathlos' friends all laugh and slap his shoulders in congratulation. Protagoras scowls silently as he watches them pass.

"Who was that?" Archelaos asks.

Protagoras thinks about it for a moment, then takes a bite of his apple and says, while chewing, "I think that I shall not recall his name."

Phaenarete laughs at that.

Meanwhile, the oldest of the Athenian men returning from the Pnyx finally arrive into the Agora and begin to shout and brandish sticks at the over-rowdy Athenian teen-agers who have been upsetting tents and stalls while the women and foreigners simply huddle, flee, or watch.

Once the old men begin barking against the behavior, finally then the twenty-somethings start to take charge of wrangling the teen-agers, by kicking and sticking and whipping them with anything at hand, once they feel they are allowed.

Kimon strides through the Agora followed closely by his slave Amyntas, and Oligarch boys follow soon behind shouting assertions of vengeance against the Democrats.

Sokrates and Chaerephon watch the older boys stalk through the Agora upsetting everyone they pass, threatening and scoffing and disdaining. As they're watching the chaos flow, suddenly they notice another teen-aged boy not far away looking at them.

"What's happening?" one of the younger neighborhood boys asks Chaerephon.

"The bad boys are storming the city," Chaerephon says. "They do this whenever the good guys win. Just because they're mad. But the good guys always clean up afterward. It's okay."

Out from the fray, a nearby whistle turns the boys' attention to another boy across the Agora. It is Antisthenes, a boy about Sokrates' age of thirteen. He's from the Edge neighborhood southeast of the Akropolis, across the city from their own neighborhood, so Sokrates, Krito, and Chaerephon have only interacted with him a handful of brief times. He gestures minutely for them to follow him.

Reticently, Sokrates breaks from his group and follows Antisthenes to the mouth of a narrow alley, only realizing once he's getting there that Chaerephon has hesitated to follow him, and waits watching across the Agora from him.

Suddenly about a dozen teen-aged boys swarm around Sokrates like a cloud of wasps, hovering too close with short sticks held out as stingers in a way that seems harmless to passing adults but sends the intended threatening message to the smaller boys without dilution.

The leader of this pack is the youngest boy, only Sokrates' age and not a finger taller or shorter than he is, but with the swagger of a teen many years older. It is Kleon, son of the leather merchant Kleanetos.

Chaerephon races up to Sokrates' side as soon as he has seen him surrounded by other teen-agers. He takes Sokrates' hand. Slowly the other boys from their neighborhood trickle over to watch.

Kleon wears new-smelling child-sized leather armor riveted all over with little bronze lion heads. He stands with his hands and hips akimbo, scanning Sokrates and Chaerephon.

"Who is this pack of raggedy rabbits?" Kleon mocks, unsure which dirty-faced boy to address as this gang's leader.

"I'm Sokrates," Sokrates offers with a touch of sudden shyness.

"I'm the Wolf of the Night!" Chaerephon shouts strangely, making even Sokrates side-eye him with confusion.

Kleon and Antisthenes give mocking glances back to their friends, who all laugh at Chaerephon. "Listen to these weird little barbarians."

Antisthenes explains, "Well listen: we're gathering little urchins like you guys, to be part of our gang. If you're with us, then you'll be safe from the Chaos Boys. But if you're not with us, then we can't protect you. But it costs an owl to join. Think you can find an owl?"

"Who are the Chaos Boys?"

"Another gang. Mean guys. They're over there kicking down that tent. You could be next."

Little twitching Chaerephon steps forward with shuddering courage. "We're Athenians!" he shouts. "Just like you. None of us is above the other!" Chaerephon squeaks deep in his throat, then covers his mouth with embarrassment.

Antisthenes and the other boys standing beside Kleon - Hagnon, Lykos, and the rest - all laugh, but Kleon himself just smiles through a crooked half-grimace. The rest of the boys holding the threatening sticks, dirty-faced city orphans with little to lose, silently watch Kleon for cues.

Kleon snaps, "You sound more like a roost of bats." He squeaks back at Chaerephon. All the boys behind him join in like a chorus at the theater, all squeaking high-pitched squeals at Sokrates and Chaerephon.

The few other neighborhood boys who sometimes follow Chaerephon slink away into the crowd, no longer wanting to associate with the two boys being mocked. Sokrates and Chaerephon soon stand alone.

"Look, your friends are leaving you, little bat!" Kleon mocks.

"You smell like piss," Sokrates comments to Kleon, wrinkling his nose.

Kleon turns his well-honed sneer to Sokrates and examines his face. "This is new leather, idiot," Kleon snaps.

To help his friend, Antisthenes snidely mocks, "Have you never smelled new leather before?"

Sokrates just shakes his head, honestly acknowledging that he hasn't. Then he asks, "So did someone have to piss on you?"

"Leather needs urine to - look, you're gonna get it, kid," Kleon sputters angrily.

"His father *collects* urine," Antisthenes adds, but Kleon smacks him to stop.

Haughty Kleon spits, "It's part of the process. Now shut up about my leather. You don't even know what you're talking about. You'll have to forgive my friend Antisthenes, street rats - he's hardly better than you; his mother is from some family of Phrygian goatherds. But then you bums probably don't even have fathers, do you, street bums?"

"No," Sokrates says, not wanting Chaerephon to answer before him. "We don't. What of it?"

"I thought so. Whores' sons, right? Or did your fathers just die in the gutters of the city after crawling here from some cave when they were too old to hunt and gather anymore? Well look here, whores' sons - just because no one in this city is going to beat you like a slave doesn't mean that anyone in this city is going to treat you with goodwill either. But maybe, if you do what you're told, you might be able to stomp with us. *If* you do what you're told."

"And if you each get us *one owl* as dues for club membership," Antisthenes adds, and not-so-subtly winks at Kleon, who shrugs begrudging agreement.

"You think you two can each find an owl?" Kleon asks Sokrates.

Chaerephon chirps.

"Wrong bird," Kleon jokes, and his friends behind him all laugh. He slaps the knees of those who aren't laughing, so that they laugh at least a little for him. "We were talking about owls, and he made the sound of some other bird; that's why it was funny," he explains gruffly to his friends who weren't laughing immediately. "I bet these rabbits have never even held a coin of their own."

"Let's leave these urchins alone," Antisthenes protests, pulling his friend back. "I don't want to get in trouble, and there's nothing that messing with them can get us."

Kleon goes up and makes a mark on Chaerephon's face with dark ash from one of his leather pockets. Chaerephon, not understanding, at first thinks he has been honored, and smiles, but the mean laughter of Kleon's friends quickly recolors his understanding. Kleon glower-grins.

Sokrates grabs Kleon's hand to get some of the same ash in his own fingers, and marks his own face with the ash in the same way that Chaerephon's is marked.

Kleon gives Sokrates a confused expression, but also sees that the move has somehow totally stopped all the derisive laughter and Kleon's friends all stand disarmed as well, unsure how to react. Kleon turns, then, and pushes back into the crowd to head back to the neighborhoods he's more familiar with, signaling to his friends to follow. All Kleon's friends trail behind like ducklings, quacking. Antisthenes lingers longest, trying to figure Sokrates out, before moving on with the rest.

Chaerephon and Sokrates look at each other, ash-masked.

"This is our gang's look," Sokrates says.

Chaerephon squeaks. He grimaces, but then beams at Sokrates.

"Let's go find Krito."

Sokrates and Chaerephon skip like they are younger than they are through the alleys of Athens until they are in front of the house of Krito's father Kritoboulos.

There, sitting beside the little goose hut attached to the edge of their house, sits Krito, cross-legged like Simon used to sit. In his lap is a big goose egg, partially cracked, with the tip of the nose of a nearly-born little gosling sticking out of a large crack.

"I'm to mind this new baby goose, who's taking forever to come out of his egg," Krito explains. "Mother was worried the bigger boys might smash it, so I've been put on permanent watch all day."

"Just crack it open and let him out," Chaerephon squeaks, kneeling down to peer inside the hole at the face of the hesitant little baby inside. The goose baby's nose peers out and sniffs at Chaerephon.

Krito shakes his head. "If I help him, he won't be strong enough. Mother says he has to get out on his own, and if he doesn't then he just wasn't meant to grow old. But I hope he makes it. I've become friends with him already, even though I've only seen the tip of his beak and the glimmer of his eye."

Chaerephon and Sokrates sit down beside Krito and fawn over the sniffing egg for a few moments.

After a while Krito asks, "What are you two up to?"

"We just started a gang. This is our mark."

Krito asks, "Can I be part of the gang? Can I wear ash like that, too?"

Sokrates says, "Of course!", and marks Krito on the face with his still darkened fingers. "There you go. Ash Gang for life."

Krito asks, "What's our gang about?"

Sokrates says dryly, "Ash."

"Revenge," Chaerephon growls, partly joking.

Krito and Sokrates laugh, but Sokrates quickly says, "No, no, that wouldn't be good. We just need to be better than them, and we'll beat them that way."

After another inadvertent grunt and squeak, Chaerephon asks Sokrates, "But don't you think Athens would be better off without mean people like Kleon and Antisthenes? Especially when they have money, so other people treat their behavior like it's good whether it is or not. It makes people think that's how you ought to behave. He's awful. He's an evil monster. He's like our version of the kind of monster a hero has to fight, don't you think?"

Sokrates shrugs and says, "I'll be honest; I think we're just not meaning the same thing by certain words, and we're talking around each other, and if we dutifully and carefully spent the time with each other to confirm what each other actually means by what we say, we would all find that we are less at-odds with each other than we had thought, and we would probably agree about a lot more than we do. Certainly, at least, that which is self-evident, right?"

Chaerephon looks into his thoughts, considering the notion. Krito watches them both, then starts nodding.

Krito says, "I think Sokrates is right. Misunderstandings are the heart of every problem."

Chaerephon thinks about it. "But think about this," he then chirps suddenly. "No one intends to misunderstand something. Right? Why would anyone do so? And if they did - then what they intended to think was to misunderstand. Right? And so, if no one ever intends to misunderstand, then who causes misunderstandings?" Chaerephon blinks rapidly, excited at the feeling of having articulated an apparently original thought.

Sokrates and Krito look at each other and think hard about Chaerephon's query, while the wild-eyed Chaerephon dances in place with excitement about the thought.

"Hermes, I guess?" Krito says. "That's why we salute his herms."

Sokrates suggests, at the same time, "Eris, the Goddess of Discord? Or maybe Hermes, Hermes when he's mad for some reason."

"So we should placate Hermes, or Eris, then," Chaerephon suggests. "Maybe our gang is called Hermeris, a combo of the two gods!"

"You can't just create new gods' names," Krito says.

"Isn't Hermaphrodite a combined god like that?" Chaerephon asks.

"Yes but Hermaphrodite was born; they are a real god. You can't just *invent* gods with your own mind."

"What's the difference between inventing something with your mind, and finding something with your mind's eye which already existed in the world of thought?" Sokrates asks the group.

"What world of thought?"

"The invisible world of unthought thoughts," Sokrates suggests. "Ideas awaiting thinking-of."

Chaerephon shakes his head. "That doesn't make any sense. There aren't any unthought thoughts. That's like saying 'unwet water'."

"But any thought I have is a thought anyone else might have had just as easily. It's not like I'm inventing something that never existed before. It's more like I've found something, seeing something in my logic-eye, a thought, which already existed as possible to be found, somewhere in some kind of hypothetical, or metalogical, realm of thoughts."

Krito raises his eyebrows at his friend and tries to decipher what he meant, his mind spinning.

Chaerephon shakes his head, ignoring Sokrates mostly by now. "You sure are weird," he tells his friend, which is what he always says once Sokrates has gotten so abstract that he can't follow the thought process anymore. "You're lucky we're patient with you, man. But I love you, Sokrates. I love you, Krito. We're going to get some other guys, and we'll be the best gang in the Agora. You'll see."

"Okay, we'll be the best gang in Athens," Sokrates agrees. "Now we just need to figure out - what exactly do we mean by *best*?"

The little egg with the goose beak darts a tiny lick of its tongue out to tickle Krito's hand, making him laugh, which sets all the boys laughing.

"TO BE THOUGHT, AND TO BE, ARE THE SAME."
Parmenides, *How Things Seem*

Φ

Aoide gives her first oracle as Pythia

A wild lion growls from the moonless dark somewhere high above the Delphic sanctuary on Mount Parnassos, on Hekate's Moonless Night Noumenia between the months of Spring.

In her bed, Aoide barely hears it, but the wildcat's growl infuses her imagination. In her mind, the kitten Ailisto has grown into a full-sized lion, and roars to the wandering ghosts on this unguarded Moonless Night, singing to the shades about wild, worldly, wordless thoughts.

Star-eyed Aoide lies in bed, unable to sleep on this night before her first day acting as the Pythia. She keeps imagining the giant monstrous serpent Python, or its ghost, living inside Mount Parnassos, waiting beneath her to reap revenge on her for ever being disingenuous about her inspiration. Or Apollo Far-Shooter, watching her for sure from whatever great distance, ready surely to blind her mind for hubris or lies. Or the Black One, sitting silently disappointed in her shadows.

Yet still, she is Pythia. Of all people in the world, the Fates have arranged that it be she whose words are heard as true. As false as all words are.

She is startled to find pre-dawn blue light already slipping through her windows when her young assistant Phaeneris arrives at her bedroom door to summon her for ablutions. She realizes then that she must have been sleeping after all, or have entered into some kind of trance that made time pass without her noticing, despite having just been dwelling within those eternal mid-night hours when one wonders if the sleepless night will ever end.

As she stands unclothed in the Kastalian Spring and lets Phaeneris wash her body, Aoide stares out across the great expanse of air that hangs above the valley, wondering about the relationship between dreaming and time. She thinks about Kronos - that ancient titan of time, the grandfather of Apollo and many other gods - and wonders if he experiences time himself, or merely manipulates it somehow from outside.

Quietly, Aoide composes a little arrhythmic song while she bathes, and once she has settled on its form she sings it faintly, to herself, heard only by young Phaeneris and the morning birds.

How I feel is not my true condition,
for all which appears is but an apparition.
From the Earth and the Great Mother's dreams I arise,
an echo freed to reveal my own mind.

"Time to go, priestess," Phaeneris says meekly, waiting on her whisper-singing mistress.

Again, Aoide is surprised by the passage of time. She steps out of the water and lets Phaeneris wrap and pin her dress and then drape her in the Pythia's gauzy purple veil edged with heavy golden threads, while singers and flutists perform wordless mystical maximical melodies in honor of her imminent parade through the sanctuary.

Bright airy music introduces Dawn on this day when the Pythia will prophecize.

Aoide sits on the Pythia's tripod, amidst the invisible vapors of Apollo, her feet curled comfortably beneath her thighs, fingering the golden threads in her purple veil.

The temple snakes stir within their bowl.

She allows her eyes to close and open as the vapors prefer, trying to keep her mind distant from the desires of those around her. She understands the lonely mental watch she must maintain in order to best hear the gods' voices within her, the true desires of the cosmos weavers.

Out from the doorway to the daylight world, into the dark interior visibility within the shadows, steps an older man with ink-darkened eyes, dressed in a finer set of clothing and jewelry than Aoide has ever seen on a single man. The man walks past the priests and up to Aoide herself, avoiding looking her in the eyes. Reverently he kneels before her.

"Inaros, Prince of Libya, son of King Psammetichos of Aigypt," says the high priest, each word intimidating Aoide more than the last with the significance they resonate. This is a famous, important, and controversial person. She has heard Hellenes debate about his politics and plans. The priest continues, "Is it your own fate, or your country's, that you wish to know?"

Prince Inaros says, "My own."

Aoide dwells briefly within a long moment in which she knows only fear and uncertainty, and can imagine the possibility of her complete collapse here and now. Centuries of mystical theater could be undone, she imagines.

But something within or without her summons another fate from her body, and she begins to speak words she has not already thought about.

"The King of Kings owns many things, but does not own your heart, Prince of Aigypt. And one Aigyptian heart, as Lord Anubis knows, can weigh enough to leverage the entire cosmos."

Then, as she hears the words which form immediately, she thinks about what she might prefer to say, she pictures Athens, leading the Delian League, helping Aigypt to weaken Persia and bringing new glories to democracy, to fairness and good. She sees century-long fast-whirling eddies within slow generational tides in a flash of wording.

Aoide adds, "Listen to Boreas, the Northern Wind, for allies' names."

Prince Inaros squints at Aoide, Pythia of Delphi, and his expression goes through many shapes of inner turmoil before landing on a dramatic mask of resilience and resolve. At first he seems confused, but as he gradually finds the confidence in the Pythia's gaze he is able to discern now with confidence and clarity the thoughts he has been harboring in his own heart, which has been given a simple but powerful ossification by the steadfastness of Aoide's eyes and the silence she maintains as punctuation.

Prince Inaros turns and faces his advisors with confidence. "The Hellenes. To our north. As I told you, the Hellenes will help us."

The prince's much-older advisor eyes Aoide dartingly and whispers to his prince, "I suggest we work over those words for a while before we feel sure we understand their meaning. This is Delphi, Inaros. This really does *mean* something, but the meaning is never what seems *obvious*..."

The two young Aigyptians leave the sanctuary with their entourage, and the echoing of their voices fades. The priests look to Aoide, who narrows her eyes back at them.

"Rebellion in Aigypt, against Persia," the oldest priest says aloud, seemingly just to process the thought, but also to start the conversation. "It would not succeed. Aigypt would only serve to distract the great dragon of the Empire."

"Apollo's thoughts go to his mother, to his birthplace," Aoide suggests.

"Delos," one of the younger priestesses says, putting it together in her own mind and voicing everyone's thought. "The Delian League." The young priestess gives Aoide a look of wonder.

"A setting sun of power in Persia, a reseparation of the many nations now yoked within that one mechanism, would be the rising sun of Hellas. Apollo also knows how to slay dragons, doesn't he? It seems he loves the League of Delos. Perhaps Apollo loves a worldwide democracy, instead of kings on kings on kings."

The debate continues, between the priests but quickly spilling out onto the streets of Delphi where it is taken up and evolved by poets and concerned citizens of every ilk and origin.

Aoide breathes slightly through her nose and pictures old Ouranos the Sky being exhaled out from Ge the Earth right here at the *omphalos* in the earliest times. Briefly she imagines her own location as the actual center of the cosmos, and her own mind as its sole acting consciousness. She feels her dreams like eagles see the look on every face on every shore across the Sea.

X

Themistokles prepares his family for what's to come

Inside the throne room of the simple old Magnesian palace, new King Themistokles watches as his steward Oxanes demonstrates the properties of a macehead made from the local lodestone, famed for cohering with iron. Themistokles marvels as the loadstone mace pulls softly toward Oxanes' iron helmet, and clings when they meet.

Oxanes says, "They say it's the old bones of Hephaestos' mechanical slaves. Even destroyed, their work with iron lingers in their bones, and you can see how their bones grasp for it." The Magnesian mace pulls toward the iron helm when pulled away.

"Fascinating," Themistokles muses with wonder, pulling the mace head away from Oxanes' helmet, which is tipped off his head by the pull of it. Oxanes laughs and catches the helmet as it falls. Themistokles shakes his head and says, "The gods truly are real. How else could such magic be imbued into stone?" He touches Oxanes' face tenderly. "Be sure to put my two finest coins in my mouth for the Ferryman. The old Aigyptian coins from Buto. In case the ferryman is Aigyptian. Some say he is."

Oxanes nods with a grim smile. He adds, knowing his master likes a joke, "And if he's Greek, then he won't care where the money's from."

Themistokles smiles a little at that. "Keep my work alive in my bones," he says to his new friend with an immediate return to solemnity.

Another slave arrives at the doorway to the Magnesian throne room, and Oxanes relays that man's nod to Themistokles. "Your family has arrived."

Themistokles tries not to frown. "Bring them in," he says with a nod. "Tell sweet Mnesimone to bring them all, even the youngest ones."

Oxanes leaves the room for a few minutes to gather the king's family.

Themistokles stands the whole time in thought, struggling not to falter in his intent. He faces away from the doorway as his family files in, so he can only hear them, not see them, as his eyes and throat grapple against each other in an effort to maintain composure.

Finally, when the noise of entrance has faded, King Themistokles of Magnesia-on-the-Meander turns and breathes, takes his large family in all at once. They are many, upright, and beautiful, and the vision breaks his wall against tears. But he pretends the warmth on his face is just sunlight.

His oldest son Archtepolis tells Themistokles, "Father, King of Magnesia, savior of Athens, you do not have to do this."

Themistokles cannot form a smile, though his face shows that he tried. "Peace requires this action," Themistokles says. "They will not use you as they would have used me. You will be able to make peace with your Asian neighbors here, and avoid the war with Hellas. I would not have."

The old man-shepherd Themistokles stands and beholds his whole family gathered: his young wife Mnesimone, holding their new baby girl named Asia close to her neck, patting her; their older daughters clinging to her knees, still small; and all of his grown daughters and sons from his first marriage to sweet old Archippe, except those who predeceased him whom he imagines awaiting him now in the Underworld with their mother.

"I have won, here in Persian lands, a kingdom for my family," Themistokles says to them. "I have gained the goodwill of not only my one-time enemy, Xerxes, and now also his son Artaxerxes, but also his subcommanders, including the general who now puppets the new king. You will not be under threat here. I do think I am leaving you safe."

Oxanes begins preparing a drinking horn.

"Make a good home here in Asia, my children," Themistokles says to them all. Indicating his wife, he says, "Remember my love for this fine woman, and give her as much love as I would have. And each other - visit each other; do not disperse and forget that you're all one close family. I know that the Ionians will treat you well if you treat their land as if it were your own. For it is yours now. It is my wish that the sons of Themistokles will be wise rulers in Asia, with their sisters married to neighboring kings in peaceful alliance. But if you must ever go to war ... win."

"We love you, father," his daughter Mnesiptolema whispers.

"I do this for Athens," Themistokles declares to his family, all gathered together on the other side of the room, watching him. "To protect Athena from the threat of my strategic mind."

Archtepolis, step-brother and husband of Mnesiptolema, and the one who will inherit the kingdom, shakes his head downward ever faster with confusion and frustration, until he must catch his head with his hands. His step-mother-in-law Mnesimone reaches out to comfort him, but Archtepolis pulls away from her hand and trudges hurriedly out of the room, his young step-sister wife following soon behind.

Themistokles watches them leave with dismay, but does nothing. He wrinkles his face at his remaining family in a final attempt at a smile. Doe-eyed Mnesimone gives him a mask of a smile, but cannot stop herself from shaking her head minutely.

"There's a joke I'm eager to tell King Xerxes," Themistokles says, mostly to himself, with a strange, soft frown.

Mnesimone turns away from him and begins touching her small children gently and gesturing for them to look away as well. Themistokles' older children see this and all look to each other about keeping their eyes on their father in some kind of semblance of honor.

That big-bearded man-shepherd is silent as he slowly but unceasingly swallows down the deadly contents of the horn until it is empty. His face shrivels in disgust as soon as he lowers the horn from his lips.

Dutifully Oxanes wipes the bull's blood from his king's chin with a rag, and then helps the man-shepherd hobble over to the ancient, golden Lydian couch that he will die upon, while his two families quietly watch with grief and horror, or weep and hold each other.

ATHENS

"ALL THAT OCCURS ARE THOUGHT AND THE INEXORABLE."
Leukippos, *Big World Theory*

Ψ

Philosophers gather to celebrate the life of Oenopides

"Things alike cohere!" wide-grinning Demokritos shouts to his old friend Protagoras as he sees him approaching.

Protagoras holds out his arms to receive the smaller and younger Demokritos in a big hug. "Thinkers find each other," he agrees.

Anaxagoras, Protagoras, Archaelaos, and Demokritos have gathered after dusk here just outside the city walls, at this place where old Oenopides used to like to lie and watch the stars, as here is where he requested that they should spread his ashes which now shift their weight within a deerskin bag in Archelaos' arms as he shifts his own weight with nervous angst. Archelaos' other arm is used to help a very old man to stand - another old friend of Oenopides even older than he was, named Metroniskos.

"My friends," Demokritos says, minimizing his smile, "I come bearing sad news. Protagoras, you in particular will be sad to learn - our wise old friend from Thrake, Leukippos, has passed into the Earth."

All present lower their heads respectfully and groan sad sounds softly.

"He was very old," Protagoras explains to the younger ones.

"As was our friend Oenopides," says Archelaos, "who also, here, has died."

The very old man Metroniskos stutters, "It is the Age of Death, these years! All things which were are passing to dust, and nothing new will replace them. The Earth will all be gone before too long."

Anaxagoras smiles softly and says, "Well, I'm not too worried about that, actually. All things have finite shape, in both form and in time - Fates' string's width, as it were - and just as other things went on before we came, so other things will happen surely long after we die."

Metroniskos makes an old-man sound deep in his chest.

"What's this mysterious circle?" Demokritos then asks the group, to bring things back to life, tapping with his walking stick at the barely-visible circle of stones upon the earth which the assembled few men have gathered within.

"A question for nearly any context!" Some chuckle.

Archelaos explains, "This was where Oenopides told us we would see a confluence of stars this night."

"It says 'Unknown god' in very old letters, over here," says Anaxagoras, tracing out the letters etched into one central stone with his own stick, "so I assume it's the ruin of some ancient temple or altar to a god unknown to the discoverer of the ruin. And so, rather than get it wrong in describing to whom this stone was dedicated originally, they indicated their own uncertainty."

"Or, perhaps, the dedication *was* known, and it was simply a dedication *to* 'the Unknown God'. The god of the unknown."

"Is there such a god?"

"I don't know."

The two middle-aged men chuckle together.

The dark stars twinkle briefly bright then vanish behind passing invisible clouds.

"You know who might soon be about to find out?" Protagoras irreverently jokes, and deerskin bag containing their old friend Oenopides from young Archelaos. "Old Oenopides."

"You know what strikes me?" Archelaos suggests with a quiet, sad voice. "Since he is no longer alive in an old body in the world, he is no longer *old* Oenopides any more than he is *young* Oenopides. He is, frankly, now, let's say *the late* Oenopides, but perhaps most inherently he is now simply *Oenopides* as he was and always hereafter shall be - Oenopides *entire*."

"Listen to this wise young man," Anaxagoras remarks to the others, nodding with a proud smile. "A noble thought, Archelaos."

"You've found a clever-minded follower, Anaxagoras," Demokritos admires aloud. "My own pupil ever disappoints." He eyes bulky-bodied Protagoras, to indicate him, but grins to indicate he is trying to be funny.

"I disappoint only if your expectations were for a loss," Protagoras retorts. "I've got more followers than this. I just have them well-trained to leave me alone except during certain hours, because I like my free time."

Demokritos, laughing playfully, asks, "Are any of them clever like this kid?" When Protagoras goes through a series of equivocating expressions in considering his response, Demokritos just laughs again and gestures broadly.

Archelaos says, "Anyway, this is a funeral. Oenopides never did like pointless prattle. He would have preferred this many wisemen talk about something interesting."

The older philosophers all laugh and groan at the implicit diss.

Protagoras agrees, "Oenopides-entire was a measurer, not a wonderer. He wanted answers, not questions. Let us get this on with."

"Here we bury the ashes of Oenopides," says his oldest friend Metroniskos, with tears in his throat. "We have put you in a bag instead of an urn, so that, if you are still there in these ashes, you have a way to get out and merge your new form with the soil around you, and, perhaps, become the bed for some flower or tree of some unknowable tomorrow."

"Gods hear this man's prayer," Demokritos says with a nod. "I give my own voice only to second what he has just said."

"Hear, hear," Anaxagoras agrees, patting old Metroniskos on the back as he unsteadily stands.

"I have, at least, my own good son Meton, who has shown an interest in keeping up Oenopides' star-watch," Metroniskos says.

"Thank the gods for the next generation's ability to take our dropped batons," Protagoras notes morosely. "For there is not enough time in one lifetime to do much good. Half a good, at best, can be sought for."

"Come now," Demokritos comforts his older friend. "At least we are blessed with one virtue by the gods - we do not really know what's going on."

Protagoras shrugs and half-laughs to Demokritos.

"To the unknown!"

"To the Unknown God." They all wordlessly grunt agreement.

"Consider: this ancient ruin is from an era that seems both archaic to us but also very familiar. Men in those days must have lived mostly much like we do now. They didn't have the bureaucracy that we have to deal with..."

"They didn't even have some of the letters we have! Look at how they spelled 'unknown'!"

"...But they woke in the morning to the Dawn and ate when they were hungry, if they had the food. They just might not have eaten such an international sandwich made from Bosporan wheat and Sikilian fish, and a little Nabataean spice, like we might today. A sandwich is practically as complex as a trireme! Theirs would just have been whatever local berries and birds they might have collected that month."

"What a small world Ge has become."

"Old women do tend to shrink," doddering old Metroniskos notes with a chuckle. Demokritos bursts out with laughter which lasts some time.

"And yet in many ways, also, we have regressed since Homeros' days," Anaxagoras says. "Consider the plight of the woman, who by all evidence from the words of poetry from those days was a freer person than she is today in modern Athens."

Protagoras says, "And consider the Unknown God - clearly, the unknown gods. We have come to know some new ones since the old days, and so still there surely remain more yet unknown. Seems to show that Mankind's knowledge will always be insufficient. As long as there might yet be new gods born into the world."

"And yet also ever greater, like a never-filling pot into which water keeps pouring. Does the pot grow as it is filled, like a bladder? Or is there just a hole in Mankind's mind-pot, like in a time-jar, perhaps designed to keep him only-so-wise?"

"If I were a primordial titan creating something like Mankind, I might make him just too dumb or blind in ways he can't fathom to be able to see or harm me."

Elderly Metroniskos coughs. "You young men these days. I'll never understand where you come up with these ideas. Most of it sounds like nonsense to me. I'd say you need to get organized. You're probably confusing this poor younger fellow."

Archelaos says to the old man on his arm, "I actually find it very useful, as a young man, to have all these different wise fellows to hear differing perspectives from."

"I strongly suspect that our fate depends upon how we influence the young, and what they learn from us," Protagoras says. "Perhaps a school with many voices is not a bad idea."

"He makes a good point, though. Order, organization, is a virtue. Consider it this way - who would want to go to the cacophonous school which contradicts itself?" Anaxagoras retorts. "At some point Mankind must choose what is correct, and what is good, or return to the Chaos which originated this world. Surely there are best practices in professions, and clearest truths in wisdom, even *proofs* Pythagoras would say, and it is those which should be taught. What's useful about education is each generation not having to do all the work of relearning how to do everything itself, but instead learning the lessons of one's grandfathers and building on that wisdom - right?"

"And yet one man's wisdom does not always work for another man," Demokritos notes.

Protagoras protests, "Wasn't it you who was just saying that many minds triangulating wisdom together can measure more than one single mind? Like men with two eyes can see better than men with one? So, many voices..."

Demokritos says, "We just keep losing knowledge. In such men as Oenopides, who go and die. And old Leukippos, who taught me. All they alone knew is lost, or taken from Earth to Haides' kingdom, at least. Were it not for words. Words! Hail, Words! Many go on and on about how wonderful the gift of fire was, but it was the gift of words that was even more valuable! I say what is real about the world ... is composed of words!"

"...He says while warming himself at a fire," Protagoras notes wryly.

"Fire is also important," Demokritos laughs. "But words are, perhaps, more so. By the way, I brought several copies of Leukippos' book to sell."

"One needs to live, to survive Winter, before it is useful for anyone to speak or write a single word," Metroniskos says.

"I fear civilization has gotten too old," Protagoras muses dryly. "Perhaps like a man, one day it will die, and leave this world again to the beasts."

"Or perhaps when the last man dies the gods will roll up the earth like a rug and shake all the animals and plants and all their filth out of it, then spread back out a land of just gems and metal," Demokritos muses surreally.

"Hey you kids and wisemen!" the old woman shouts from her high window. "Get out of the weeds there and be quiet or you'll wake ghosts for everyone! How dare you old men corrupt our city's youth with your night hijinks! Teaching how to recite the alphabet while sucking a cock, I bet! Well save your cock for Asklepios, God of Healing, who will no doubt need to burst your pustules there for you!"

Hidden together, Sokrates and Krito can't help but snicker loudly at that. The older men hear it and start to scan the area idly with their eyes.

"Mercy, you dirty old woman," Protagoras shouts back finally. "We'll agree to be quiet if you don't say another filthy word yourself! Now good night, please, fair decrepit maid!" The younger boys snicker at this final line, despite his agreement that their group would be quiet.

"By the gods, that little one probably hasn't even got any hair besides on his head," the old woman continues, making all the men and boys down in the weedy temple ruins groan again.

"Good night, handmaid of Hestia," Demokritos calls out with a sarcastic nobleman's accent.

The old woman slams a shutter and mutters her way back to her bed.

"Come on, all, let us each make our ways back home while there's still some pinch of dusklight left," Anaxagoras says, already starting off himself toward Perikles' house. "The city is a bit too narrow-pathed to navigate by stars alone, and it doesn't look like anyone here has a lamp."

Then Archelaos sees the younger boys and says, "Hey, who's that hiding in the shadows? We've got a couple of young followers listening it, it appears."

"I thought I heard girls snickering," Demokritos chides.

"We're boys!" Krito declares as he climbs out of the bush shadows, pulling Sokrates with him.

Archelaos recognizes them both and groans. "You two! Krito, this guy is a bad influence on you. Every time I see you on your own, you're acting perfectly respectably. Every time I see you with Sokrates, it's some goofy situation."

"We told Oenopides that we would..." irreverent thirteen-year-old Sokrates starts to explain.

More careful than usual in front of so many respected sages, seventeen-year-old Krito interrupts his friend. "We told Oenopides that we would come pay our respects to his monument."

"Well," Protagoras says, "it appears his monument is actually just an ancient unknown ruin. And if he told you about some confluence of stars, like he did us - the joke is on us, as we suspect the stars are, also, us."

They all stand beneath the stars, watching them in silence for a long moment. The sounds of the distant city begin to seem to be coming from the sky.

Looking down from the stars, teen-aged Sokrates asks thirty-year-old Demokritos, "What do you think light is?"

Demokritos smiles, and looks into little Sokrates' eyes, watching the reflection of the light of a public fire behind himself. "Well, it seems to me that it comes primarily from the Sun, and fire."

"And stars," Anaxagoras notes. "Which would seem to indicate that the Sun and stars might just be distant sky-fires. Speaking of the stars, of course, in classic Oenopides fashion, he ended his days with a new mystery for us," Anaxagoras says with a sigh.

"Do tell," says Demokritos, sitting down, intrigued.

"Well, the last words he said to me were these - 'Tell them the answer is twenty-four.' But I didn't know who he meant by 'them', and he was unable to utter more before his end."

"Twenty-four," Protagoras repeats, considering the unknowns in the problem. "And 'them'."

"He surely meant *something*," Archelaos sniffles, quietly crying as he imagines Oenopides' final concerns. "So he must have had some kind of understanding with someone, which included Oenopides finding an answer - a number - and he found it! We should ask those older folks who knew him best if it has meaning to them."

Old Metroniskos proactively shrugs and shakes his head, staring in space.

Anaxagoras sighs and says, pacing, "Seems to me it's a smart man's duty to do these things - ascertain the truth by means of either personal discovery, by witnessing it, or by logic, by reasoning it out, or by seeking instruction where possible; or if these things aren't possible for one reason or another, to select the most reasonable of all posited positions which human intelligence has supplied so far, and using that as your sail to catch the wind of your thought and move you toward wisdom."

"You know what would be a lot easier, though," jokes Demokritos, "is if the gods would just write a book."

The men all laugh.

"I do not think this world is *about* something other than itself. It is not representative of something greater." Anaxagoras smiles, and touches the rainbow-stone on his amulet. "It is both a simple place in which all things act the same, and a complex place where no two things are alike. Each version of the telling is true. Each new mind adds a whole new universe. Perhaps that is, or at least comes close to, what Anaximander meant by the *unlimited*."

"Is that a gathering of friends of Oenopides?" a voice calls out as it approaches along the path from the city wall.

"Look who I found," says another more familiar voice, the Phoenikian engineer Melqartshama, arm in arm with a handsome young fellow by his side.

Demokritos' eyes grow wide when he sees the man, and he calls out, "By Hermes Pathfinder, is that Zeno of Elea of all people?"

"It is I," the confidently walking silhouette confirms.

The gathered friends all look to each other with intrigued expressions, confusing the teen-aged boys.

"Who's that?" asks young Archelaos.

The older men laugh.

As the man approaches, Demokritos explains, "It is Zeno - the young, handsome, and already widely-respected philosopher from the West, whose star of fame rose as a boy when he was just the clever young lover of his more famous teacher Parmenides."

Handsome twenty-something Zeno squints and snorts a tiny laugh at the introduction, then confirms concisely, "I am Zeno, of Elea." He smiles just enough for it to be seen.

Demokritos bows slightly and steps forward. "I am Demokritos, of Earth. These are my friends Sokrates, Krito, Anaxagoras, Archelaos, what was your name? Metroniskos. Protagoras ... in no particular order. We welcome you to this city of our current residence, Zeno."

"I, for one, am from here," Archelaos laughs, stepping forward and offering Zeno his hand, "so I can welcome you as an Athenian, to Athens."

Zeno shakes the young man's hand and smiles to all.

"What brings you to this fine city, Zeno?" Protagoras asks.

Melqartshama explains, "We were speaking about devices for the theater. He mentioned a confluence of stars, and I knew it must be the same that you all spoke of."

Zeno says, "I heard of the illness of your friend Oenopides, whom I understand you all tonight are here to say goodbye to. I am sorry for your loss, by the way. He told me of a confluence of stars which would only be visible from Athens, on the final nights of this month. I had hoped to arrive earlier, before the good old man was gone. But the ship I was on had to do some erratic maneuvering to avoid pirates."

All nod understandingly. "He told us all of the great confluence to be seen tonight; we have yet to see it in the Sky."

"Whether he can ever know or not, I'm sure Oenopides would be honored by your coming," Archelaos says. "I didn't realize that he was so well known."

Zeno nods, "His study of the stars was of use to us all."

With a wry smile, and knowing the truism which Zeno is already famous for among thinkers, Anaxagoras asks the famous young man, "Have you traveled far to be here?"

All the philosophers present laugh at the implicit joke. Archelaos shows that he's confused.

Zeno smiles and replies with little affect, "I am here now."

"What's so funny?" Sokrates asks.

"I have proposed a truth of nature, based on logic," Zeno explains, "which runs contrary to how nature *appears* to us."

"He has suggested that there cannot be any change in the world."

Archelaos considers the notion, squinting.

Zeno slowly blinks, coolly motionless.

"However far a thing might want to travel, there will always be at least half of that distance left to travel - no matter the distance. So in that way, all distances are infinite."

"Unless..." Demokritos suggests, holding one finger in the air as he thinks a little longer about what he is about to say. "Unless ... unless there is a finite *size* of space, or of things - an *indivisible unit of size*. Let's call it *indivisible*, an *atom*. That would account for the reality we see - which is that things can actually cross spaces, and do in fact change their state."

Zeno squints uncertainly, but then thinks about it.

"It would have to be much smaller than we can see," Anaxagoras notes. "I would say from experience that you can keep making smaller and smaller sections, in reality. I don't suspect there is such an indivisible level."

"It would have to be smaller than the eye can see, that's certainly true," Demokritos shrugs. "But perhaps its logic is enough for our minds to see it."

Archelaos suggests, half-joking, "Perhaps we are colossal titans compared to that most elemental scale of nature."

Anaxagoras notes, with a glint of intrigue in his eyes, "And perhaps the gods are actually incredibly tiny!" He laughs, enjoying the thought.

Metroniskos frowns at the blasphemy, and Melqartshama shakes his head to agree with that silent sentiment.

"Consider water," Protagoras proposes, holding out his hand with nothing but imagination in it. He pokes around in his empty as he says, "If I had a droplet of water here, and a sharp pin, I might be able to separate it into two smaller droplets. But imagine if I tried to keep doing that to each smaller droplet, continually halving them into smaller and smaller sections of water."

"There might eventually be a droplet so small that you would not be able to separate it?" Archelaos asks.

"And would that not, then, be the ultimate *atom* of water, its smallest possible amount - one unit of water!?" Demokritos laughs. "We would have found the true shape of water, the size of its single unit rather than its plural form. I bet it would be a sphere!"

"In spray, and mist, and dew," Anaxagoras adds, "I have seen droplets far tinier than you would be able to separate with a pin. And yet for each one, I would bet you an owl, you could always find a smaller one."

"Forever, you think?" Demokritos asks Anaxagoras. "Do you not think there would be a smallest possible droplet of water?"

Anaxagoras thinks about it for a moment, then shakes his head with a smile. "I would bet an owl that smallness can continue into infinity just as hugeness can. Unfortunately I would guess that certain sizes simply reach the horizon of our ability to perceive them - both the small and the large! Consider the size of the Earth, which those of us who can do Geometry understand is a sphere and must be immensely huge!"

"Two men triangulating and communicating can perceive what one alone cannot," Demokritos adds. "And with writing we can triangulate together across generations of time! And what if there could be some similar method for triangulating what is *smaller* than one can perceive!?" He laughs again at the apparent absurdity of the thought.

"I can't imagine what that would be, but it is interesting to consider," Anaxagoras muses.

"It is fun to consider," Demokritos sighs, sitting and putting an arm around Sokrates' back. "Isn't it fun to whip ideas like horses and just see where they run? I tell you, I would rather understand one original cause, one natural elemental truth, than be King of Kings of the whole Earth, regardless of whether it helped me make money or friends. Just to understand, and to be sure! Better yet, to be able to explain it! To understand the fundamental mechanisms of the cosmos ... there could be nothing more inherently valuable to me than that."

"That's only because you're already rich," Protagoras says dryly.

Demokritos laughs, but then shrugs and nods in acknowledgment.

"Consider this, though," Demokritos then says, crouching beside Sokrates in the darkening dusklight at the edge of the ancient ruined temple. "Wisdom also requires something like light. It requires information - words, like these I speak. I shine some on you, you shine others back at me. The world reflects its many colors brighter for our better understanding."

Sokrates muses, "It feels like the more I understand, the more questions I have."

Demokritos nods, smiling. "It's not because you understand less - but merely because you are aware of more of the things that you don't yet understand;

but certainly you didn't understand any of those things before; you just didn't even see them with your mind yet as ideas awaiting understanding!"

"Ideas awaiting understanding, right," Sokrates nods, thinking hard, looking back and forth between the city around him and the stars above. "It's like when I climb a tree and see more of what had been around me."

"Very good, boy," Demokritos grins. "You are climbing the tree of knowledge!"

"And yet," Sokrates wonders, "from high in the tree I can only see the tops of the heads of others, not look them in their eyes. You know, metaphorically."

"Yes, well," Demokritos agrees hesitantly, "metaphors are sometimes useful lenses from one angle but not every angle."

"No, I think the metaphor does still work," Sokrates disagrees, and stops walking, making Demokritos stop as well. "When I stay down among my fellows and friends, I can still see their souls in their eyes, and they can see mine. No, I don't think I want to float above my fellows, or understand the world like a bird could, if it means giving up seeing the eyes of my friends evenly. In rising high, one only gains a certain viewpoint by trading another."

"How old are you?" Protagoras asks the boy.

"Thirteen," Sokrates replies shyly.

Demokritos looks into his memory a moment and says with a smile, "A wise Aithiopian woman I met once told me this ancient bit of wisdom - to travel fast, go alone, but to travel far, go together."

Usually-grinning Demokritos then crouches beside Sokrates and squints hard at him with a bittersweet, crooked half-smile.

"Listen, child, and remember: Mental fires may forever burn, but Mankind still might never learn."

Sokrates frowns at that.

Demokritos chuckles and keeps his eyes on the boy. "You doubt?" he asks.

"I think that Man will learn. Men and women, Mankind."

"What makes you say that?"

Tween-aged Sokrates wrinkles his face, considering how best to concise the idea, until finally he nods to the voice in his head, and gives his answer like it's a question.

"Because, as things alike ... all truths cohere?"

Demokritos says, "May wisdom stream and pool across the desert of innocence! And bloom ... what, young man, what is the flower of wisdom?"

Sokrates dances slightly as he answers, "Song!"

Demokritos laughs and laughs.

"ALL THOSE AWAKE BEHOLD ONE WORLD,
WHILE EACH WHO SLEEPS PERCEIVES THEIR OWN."
Herakleitos, *On Nature*

Ω

Writers clash over what is good writing

Late at night by lamplight, Aischylos' actors are working together to deconstruct the backdrop tent at the theater of Dionysos, while Aischylos and Sophokles sit upon the hillside where the wooden seating has just been taken down, overseeing the process from there. One new young actor has been tasked with organizing the many expensive and beautiful masks on their hooks on the back wall of the skene, and is taking great, nervous care at the work.

"Whatever you do, be careful with those masks," Sophokles calls out, at which the man slows his work.

Aischylos' toddler Euphorion follows Sophokles' older son Iophon like a lamb, and though it annoys little Iophon, the two fathers smile down at them while they chat, so Iophon bears Euphorion's irritations and lets the littler one remain within a toddler's arm's reach.

Euripides, wanting to be close to the action of the playwrights, has agreed to watch the toddlers, but sits near the playwrights. Watching the little ones from the theater seats, Euripides recalls being that small, how Krito used to follow him around that same way. Remembering his old friend starts a sadness in his throat which he swallows. Sullen-eyed Euripides, recently past the festivities of his twentieth birthday, is here to babysit the two children, but has decided to take this opportunity to speak to the famous playwrights about the challenges of art.

"I worry that I'll wrestle with the Muses and my mind only to write a piece of work which means a lot to me but no one else even knows exists. And why tell any story?" Euripides asks. "Just because the Muses sing them to me? They might as well be ghosts." He sighs and mumbles, barely audible, "Why not keep them to myself? Why does it not suffice just to imagine it?"

Old Aischylos says, gesturing to the altar of Dionysos, "Because no one, man or god, can hear your unspoken thoughts. And Dionysos will drive mad the man who refuses to share what the Muses sing to him alone."

Sophokles adds, "And we need each other's ideas. We would be lost without each other's dreams. We only really know what to do by listening to each other."

Aischylos sits down with Euripides as the younger fellow dries his tears, sitting hunched on the steps of the Dionysian theater. Dark clouds hide the stars above. Aischylos' beard is long and white, now, while Euripides' first patches of black chin curls are less than a year old, though the chin is twenty.

"Whenever you tell a story, you inherently make it your own. But it also becomes your listener's. Because each time the story is told anew, it has a new opportunity to evolve. And so you don't need to worry about getting the characters right or wrong, if you are following the voice of the Muse you hear in your mind, for ultimately all of the characters will really be versions of *you*. And the story will be inherently *yours*, from having been sieved through your voice. You cannot get art wrong. And you cannot write a story wrong. Like the river which cannot be stepped in twice. The wiseman Herakleitos noted that a flowing river is never the same each time you step in it."

Euripides sighs.

Aischylos says, looking for a star between the clouds, "Each time you tell any story, you recreate the whole cosmos. For that story."

"Well, thankfully Chaos has already created the actual world," young Euripides scoffs. "To serve at least as myriad inspirations for the better worlds of our artwork. I just find whenever I try to materialize my imagination, it fails, and what I have produced becomes mundane shit."

"I know you're having a hard time, Euripides," Aischylos comforts the boy with a hand on his back, "but trust me - the first twenty years of your life are *utterly unlike* the following years. Adulthood is better than childhood, and childhood is nothing like it! So, while you have spent this whole time learning, you have learned nothing useful about being an adult. With what you've learned, you should now begin learning completely anew."

Euripides smiles and sniffs a little laugh at that.

"What had you achieved by the time you were my age?" Euripides asks the older playwright.

Aischylos explains, "Well, I grew up around the first playwrights, watching their rehearsals near Eleusis as a very young boy, so I was extraordinarily encouraged from my earliest days by those around me. It just wouldn't be fair to compare yourself to me, Euripides."

"You grew up around the theater in Eleusis?"

Aischylos nods, sipping from a bowl of warm milk. "When I was a boy I saw Thespis himself reenact the moment years earlier when he first stepped out from the chorus and invented the tradition of acting out dramatic tragedies. Before that it was just songs, of course - just a chorus singing their *dithyramb*."

Sophokles adds, "You know, boy, these plays haven't always had lots of different characters all speaking to each other..."

"I know," Euripides nods. "I've been seeing plays since I was little. I remember when Aischylos introduced the second character, and when you, Sophokles, introduced a third."

"You remember that, eh?" Aischylos groans self-effacingly. Aischylos ends his chuckle on a sigh, nodding. "Not everyone your age remembers those earlier plays. It's strange to see the past disappear over the horizon, and to speak to new actors who haven't even heard of events that occurred only a few short years ago."

"Dareios invaded *thirty years ago*," Sophokles says with emphasis on the length of time, and all the others groan at the mention of it.

Aischylos thinks about it with a furrowed brow, then coughs, "It cannot have been that long."

"Dareios, not Xerxes," Sophokles clarifies.

"Right," Aischylos nods. "Xerxes returned ten years later. But then even that..."

Sophokles finishes Aischylos' sentence, nodding, "...Is now *twenty years ago*. It was that year that I first sang in a chorus, still just a short boy. How have we gotten so old?"

Aischylos shakes his head, flashing back to his grim memories of war. "Thirty years now without my brave brother. We have gotten old, Sophokles, only by dodging death."

Sophokles sees his fellow playwright's change of demeanor and quiets his voice to a graceful calm. He suggests tenderly, "Tell Euripides of Kynegeiros."

Euripides reverently turns to old Aischylos to give him his full, respectful attention.

Aischylos swallows his sadness. "My oldest brother. I am my mother's middle one, and Ameinias, who made himself a great hero at the Sea Battle of Salamis, is our family's baby. But he was too young when Dareios came, so it was just Kynegeiros and I who put on armor to defend our home against the Empire, at Marathon, in the First Persian War."

Some of their actors, most of whom are new and young, stop their work and gather around, sitting on the theater stands or the grassy ground, to listen quietly. Sophokles puts a hand kindly on Aischylos' back.

Penander whispers, "I hear you calling both your brothers heroes, Aischylos, and yet it is *you* who fought in *both* wars."

Aischylos blinks and squints with discomfort at the visions in his memory. "We all expected to die. So we had that much courage - the courage to use up the last of your Fate's string. And when we finally turned the battle's tide, and that enormous Persian host began to actually flee back to their ships and try to get back to the safety of the water, Kynegeiros was among a few brave men who ran into the water and grabbed onto the sterns of the ships to hold them and keep them from sailing."

"Athena First-in-Battle by his side," one young actor adds.

Aischylos continues, "Glory-minded Kynegeiros ran into the water, killing two Persian soldiers as they were boarding, then saw the ship pulling back onto the waves, so he grabbed the stern to hold them there. But a Persian ax came down upon his wrist, chopping off his hand with one hit."

The listeners show their sad masks.

"But Kynegeiros had the spirit of Ares in his heart, because without missing a beat he simply grabbed onto the ship with his other hand!"

Some of Aischylos' actors grunt with delight at that, but quickly avoid laughing with narrative pleasure, remembering that the story is true, and that the character is Aischylos' real dead brother.

Aischylos hangs his head to say, "They chopped that one off just as swiftly as the first."

All listeners' groans are swallowed swiftly into silence.

"It was I who dragged him up the beach. But there was nothing I could do."

At that, Aischylos suddenly begins to weep, utterly unperformed. He catches his face in his hands, himself seemingly surprised by the suddenness of his emotion. Sophokles and other nearby actors touch him compassionately.

Twenty-year-old Euripides watches the old actor's genuine emotion with intrigue and awe. He begins to shake his head and gaze off into a haze of dismay.

"I'll never be great. I was born too late for legend. The times of heroism were before me, and now the world is bland and boring. I'll never be able to be as great as you all. I'll never know better than someone like you how to write profound words. What's the point?"

"Stop it, Euripides," says Aischylos, swallowing his grief, "it wouldn't be fair to compare your writing to my own. And no one would ever think to. Of course I am much older and more experienced and actually knew those who knew Thespis! Whereas you are this young man new to the world, and a different world than the one I have lived in. Surely whatever you write will be very different than what I have written, and that is a good thing!"

Euripides listens, shrugging and nodding along as if it all makes sense and he understands.

"You're right, it wouldn't be fair," Sophokles adds with a playful grin, "but in exactly the opposite way you refer to, Aischylos. Euripides will have the opportunity to be even greater than both of us, Aischylos, for he was born much later, and therefore will have the previous efforts of ours and those of all our contemporaries to educate himself from, and to learn the mistakes from. Euripides, if he takes the path now, surely has the opportunity to be the best writer among us!"

"Except me!" shouts Aischylos' little son Euphorion, throwing his arms in the air like a victorious sprinter. "For I am the youngest one here!"

The actors hail the toddler with a jolly cheer.

"I think, young man, you simply need to stop trying so hard to be *correct*, and start thinking about what *could be*. What could have been! The audience wants to hear a story which speaks to them, and which shows them what they could be. No one really knows how anything *really* went. Your aim in telling a story is not to be *correct*. No telling of a story is *correct*. Only the moment itself was the *correct* telling of the story. Everything else thereafter is a *myth*, and it is not your goal to be as correct as possible, but instead to be *entertaining*, to become *popular*. You need to create stories that people will want to hear! Or they will not be retold. In fact people will be annoyed to have heard it. Even if it was what you would call *correct*."

"But what people like varies, doesn't it?" Euripides suggests. "And what even one person likes changes day by day."

"Yes, well..." Aischylos begins, as he is interrupted by the following commotion.

The clop-clopping of a donkey's hooves turns everyone's eyes to see wine-weary Kratinos with a mask of the ghost-of-Dareios from *The Persians* on the top of his head, riding on the slow-walking back of a donkey as if it is a royal palanquin.

Slurringly the actor sings, "The god of laughter creeps into his sanctuary under dark of night, to find lost phantoms playing in the moonlight! An audience to witness this greatest modern event - the birth, the introduction, of the newest artform to the stage of Man's poor tragedy. The ghosts all laugh! The gods all laugh! Bring comedy, bring comedy, they tell me! Bring that old style of Hipponax to the highest summit of creation, the stage, they all command." He sloughs off the edge of the donkey to a staggering standing position and takes a slug from his shoulder-slung wineskin. "I am the laughter's slave."

The actors laugh.

Sophokles says, "You know you're funnier *without* that mask on, Kratinos. Let us see your absurd face, come on - take off the mask."

Aischylos says with just a touch of warmth, "Kratinos, you are still grieving. Give it time. In that wide-ranging and heavily populated realm of ghosts, surely Hipponax is doing exactly as he did up here, and giving a few shades a chuckle by aggravating many others. But mind how much you drink without water, or Dionysos himself will guide you down there to meet him."

Kratinos melodramatically reaches up toward his quivering mask very slowly and pulls it down over his face as he says, "Like Aischylos, I linger on the silent moment, unspeaking, allowing silence to reign over all like Nyx does between the days, distinguishing them from each other and making them countable, so my silence..."

"What silence?" Sophokles blurts. Aischylos glares at him for vocalizing the obvious hanging-threads of the joke.

Kratinos interrupts their awkward moment by aggressively pulling the ghost mask off his face, to reveal yet another mask held tight against his real face beneath it. This second mask is a woman's face, displaying a frozen look of the male fantasy of prim beauty.

Most of the male chorus members laugh.

"After all," Kratinos continues as the laughter abates, "is not silence that highest virtue pursued by all women who fear men the right amount, as men fear gods?"

A passing couple of women on a walk together in the street not far away, surprising all the actors by proving to be within earshot, loudly boo the sarcastic misogyny.

A few of the actors laugh again, but fewer now, as others within the chorus take that moment to quietly consider what it might be like to be any of the women they know.

"I know just how she feels," remarks one young singer in the chorus named Ajax. "I've always felt this man-skin of mine was just a mask over the real me. I always felt more like Arachne than Ajax."

"Ajachne," another suggests for a new name.

All the others around them react with positive shouts at the merged name, and the newly-named Ajachne smiles broadly, while also shyly shrugging at the rare attention.

"And so am I then Dionysalexandros!" shouts Kratinos, awkwardly trying to slip back into the actors' favor, and referencing both Dionysos, God of Ecstasy, and Paris Alexandros, the Troian prince whose abduction of the Spartan Queen Helen led to the infamous ten-year Troian War.

"Why Alexandros?" Aischylos hesitantly asks.

Kratinos-as-Dionysalexandros looks behind himself quickly, scanning the skene for props from recent plays, and then grabs a soldier's helmet and places it high up on his head in the manner that Perikles does.

The actors all laugh, recognizing it as Perikles immediately.

"I, Dionysalexandros, have chosen from among the goddesses which one is best, on behalf of my city, and I have chosen - Athena, Virgin Goddess and Wise Counselor! She born of no fuck at all, but straight from a man's mind! Athena Fuckless! Depiction of woman born with the help of no woman at all! And all other gods can go fuck each other elsewhere, frankly. And for my wife, I choose - myself! I mean, my sister. No, wait, my cousin. Certainly no commoner! But strong be the power of the commoners, of those whom I trod upon! Come, now, gods, and show us what reckoning this world is due! I presume it could only be good!"

His rant builds with the increasingly positive reactions of his audience, the half-drunken actors taking a break from their work, but by the time he is done he is slurring heavily and slinging splashes of red from oversized gestures with his wineskin.

Sophokles says, "Seriously, though, what is this supposed to be, Kratinos?"

"I've been tasked by the gods," Kratinos slurs, trying hard to stare into Sophokles' eyes through the eye holes in his own mask. "There will be a new form on the stage unlike anything that has come before!"

"Nothing is unlike anything that has come before," Aischylos scoffs with a dismissive hand wave. "Everything is like something, everything comes from a predecessor that is like it. Perhaps, like us, you have some small innovation in mind, but I doubt that anyone can imagine a truly new form."

Euripides scoffs, "You were *just* telling me how the first twenty years of life are unlike the rest. It seems things are more often *unalike* than alike, that the texture of the cosmos is more about difference than similarity."

Kratinos speaks over the young artist, shaking his head, addressing the older playwright. "Then I am you, and it is *you* saying these things, Aischylos! No, I say I am *not* you, but only *me*, and the thing that you will see coming out of *me* will be unlike anything before it..."

"I do not ever want to see anything coming out of you," Sophokles jokes, "but if I do, I would bet money that it will be composed of the same stuff you put in. Which tonight I suspect has only been wine."

"Bright lord Apollo, original author of every poem, sing to us now, through me! And yes, I am inspired! Aischylos, the lord of poetry has given me the piece title first - and it shall be called, as I look in your eyes, *Ode to Your Mother...*"

Aischylos laughs, then frowns, then eyes Kratinos carefully as he continues his rambling.

"Here we go," Sophokles sighs.

"...O Muses, who dance upon the flower-strewn slopes of Mount Helikon, sing now of just how much like a centaur's butt must the face of a woman be to have a son so comically-faced as Aischylos, alleged master of the Athenian stage?"

"Wow," Aischylos replies, shaking his head, trying not to uplift the lines by laughing at them. His chorus, behind him, are not as able to control themselves, and get angry quickly after being tricked into laughter.

Kratinos continues slurringly, "How dim-wicked must be the lamp-mind of such a dick-head capable of being fooled by man or god to spill his boy-seed inside such a woman?..."

"Cheap, raunchy, tiresome barbs," Sophokles says.

Aischylos stands and approaches Kratinos slowly with a careful hand out to steady the man in case he falls in his direction. "Kratinos, in all seriousness, you are a great actor. Take these ideas to where they will be welcome. Not the City Dionysia, but maybe at the village festivals in the wintertime, like the rural, irreverent Lenaia festival. They put on little plays in the villages then. Rural communities will be much more receptive to this silliness. But the City Dionysia is for a certain kind of ... higher class material..."

"...Reveal, Muses, from through the obscuring veils of lies and time, which goat too horridly malformed to sacrifice found its way into the bed chamber of that ugliest and stupidest of women on the moonlit night of her amory when she was expecting her husband, and why when that unmanned husband came upon his bedmate with the goat, he chose not to intrude, but instead..."

When the drunkard leans too close to him and almost has to grab him for support, Aischylos can hear no more, and shoves Kratinos away, and off his feet. "Go home, Kratinos!" he shouts. "Dream away your grief."

From the muddy ground, Kratinos waves a fist and shouts, "I am the very god Dionysos whom you shame, Aischylos! Never come crying to me again when you shame some *other* god or goddess, like you did to my fine sister Demeter..."

"This isn't funny," Sophokles chuckles, standing to support Aischylos.

Aischylos playfully glares at Sophokles for laughing.

"Where are our children?" Sophokles suddenly asks, looking about.

Aischylos laughs once nervously. "Yes, that was our young friend's task, wasn't it? And here we have distracted him. Where are our boys? Euphorion? Iophon?"

"Euripides, this is your fault," Sophokles half-jokes with a mask of real anger which quickly summons real tears onto the face of the delicate young Euripides.

"Playwrights of the theater, ear-hungry voices, we know how to sing many mythological things, but we also sometimes, by Fates' mistake, depict reality." Standing from the mud, Kratinos throws back his head and shouts to the stars, "Now tell us, gods - is it more artistically glorious to you that a story to be sad ... or funny?"

Out from the shadows, little Euphorion appears, with a big old-man mask over his whole upper body, his mouth visible through an eye hole and one of his pudgy little arms reaching out through the open mouth. Echoing from within the mask, his high little voice shouts, "Or horrifying?"

As if in answer Kratinos shrieks and jumps with fright, which startles Yellow the donkey who kicks the air, frightening Aischylos who lurches back into Sophokles who bumps Kratinos into Euripides, and the four's group tumble causes some among the chorus watching them to burst out with laughter, while causing others to react sympathetically as if the same has just happened to them, one of whom cannot stop from stumbling all the way back through the open doorway and into the shadows of the inner skene.

The chorus cries cacophonous as myriad masks of queens, clowns, and soldiers, sages, goddesses, and fools all shatter beneath a tumbling cascade of old softwood dicks from the shelving above, transforming in one loud instant a few archaic ceramic caricatures into twenty times as many shards on which now one day real Athenians' names will be written.

This has been

ATHENS
or, The Athenians

The novel will continue its essentially true story in

Book Two - *The Age of Silver*

Book Three - *The Age of Gold*

Book Four - *The Age of Heroes*

Book Five - *The Age of Iron*

Major Characters, Book One

Aischylos - Famous playwright veteran
Alkibiades - Wealthy aristocrat merchant
Agariste - Alkmaeonid, Perikles' mother
Anaxagoras - Curious Ionian visitor
Aoide - Alkmaeonid priestess-spy
Archidamos - Spartan Eurypontid king
Aristides - Called "the Just"
Artabanos - Top Persian general
Chaerephon - Sokrates' excitable friend
Dikasto - Rebellious Delphian priestess
Ephialtes - Optimistic Democrat leader
Euripides - Young aspiring artist
Gorgo - Sparta's Queen-Mother
Hipponax - Famous insult-poet
Kallias - Rich holy torchbearer
Kimon - Traditional military hero
Korax - Messenian rebel leader
Kratinos - Wild drunken actor
Krito - Sokrates' lifelong friend
Niome - Enslaved Byzantian princess
Perikles - Alkmaeonid aristocratic Democrat
Periboea - Cousin to Perikles
Phaenarete - Sokrates' young mother
Phidias - Young wunderkind sculptor
Pleistarchos - Spartan Agiad king
Protagoras - Visiting Thrakian thinker
Simon - Kindly shoemaker
Sokrates - Curious, questioning boy
Sophokles - Actor turned director
Sophroniskos - Sculptor, Sokrates' father
Themistokles - Hero of Salamis
Thrax - Perikles' closest slave
Xerxes - Persian King of Kings

George Dalphin is an artist in many media
Some of his previous work, as of this writing:

Novels

Bob Wacszowski, Necromancer 2011
Thirsty & Drowning 2007

Short Movies

Last Night on Marius-β 2024
Wolf Peach (with Brianna Fern) 2023
Stygian Blues (with Derek Kimball) 2023
Your Universe Is Weird (series, with Joe Foster) 2023
Space: 1974 (with Joe Foster) 2016   Pale Earthlight (with Joe Foster) 2022
The Star Side (with Joe Foster) 2014   Neurophreak (with Joe Foster) 2015
The NPC (series, with Joe Foster) 2014
Upload 2012   Krampus 2012   Bardo 2012
The Rejection 2011   Manifest Destiny 2011
Doubting Thomas 2010   "Payment" 2010
Don't Be 2009   I Was Jesus and Dracula 2009

Albums, as Headphoneboy

Emit 2018
You're Dead 2007
Acts (I, II, III) 2005
Listener 2004
The Great Masturbator 2003

www.manlikemachines.com

Made in United States
North Haven, CT
23 July 2025